Enemy of My

The Executive Office

Tal Bauer

A Tal Bauer Publication

www.talbauerwrites.com

This is a work of fiction. All characters, places, and events are from the author's imagination and should not be confused with fact. Any resemblance to persons, living or dead, events or places is purely coincidental.

All rights reserved. No part of this publication may be reproduced in any material form, whether by printing, photocopying, scanning or otherwise without the written permission of the publisher, Tal Bauer.

ISBN: 9781549682438
Second Edition
10 9 8 7 6 5 4 3 2
Copyright © 2016 – 2017 Tal Bauer
Cover Art by Natasha Snow © Copyright 2017
Edited by Rita Roberts
First Published in 2016
Second Edition Published in 2017
Second Edition Published by Tal Bauer in the United States of America

Warning
This book contains sexually explicit content which is only suitable for mature readers.

Dedication

Dedicated to my husband, who will always be my Jack.

To Rita, my editor & very dear friend.

And to Christina & Parvathy, two wonderful people who helped make this all happen.

The Executive Office Cast

White House

Jack Spiers: President of the United States
Ethan Reichenbach: First Gentleman and former head of Presidential Secret Service Detail
Scott Collard: Ethan's lifelong best friend, and new Presidential Secret Service Detail Lead
Levi Daniels: Close friend of Ethan and Scott; also on the Presidential Secret Service Detail
Elizabeth Wall: Secretary of State, and Jack's closest advisor in his Cabinet
Lawrence Irwin: Former Director, CIA; promoted to Chief of Staff after attempted coup
Pete Reyes: Press Secretary
Kate Triplett: Director, Secret Service
Todd Campbell: Director, FBI
Richard Rees: Director, CIA
Olivia Mori: Deputy Director, CIA
Meredith Peterson: National Security Advisor
Diana Ramirez: White House Counsel
Lewis Parr: Secretary of Defense
Sarah Carter: Attorney General
Julian Aviles: Secretary of Homeland Security
General Bradford: Chairman of the Joint Chiefs
Admiral McDonald: Director of Naval Operations
Gus Miramontes: Special assistant to the President
Jason Brandt: First Gentleman Press Secretary
Barbara Whitley: White House Social Secretary
Jennifer Prince: White House Floral Designer

Russia

Sergey Puchkov: Russian President
Sasha Andreyev: Former Air Force officer
Ilya Ivchenko: Director FSB (Russian State Security Services)
Dr. Leo Voronov: Presidential Physician
General Moroshkin: Russian General, Western Military Headquarters

Marine Corps Special Operations Team

Lieutenant Adam Cooper
Staff Sergeant Wright
Staff Sergeant Coleman
Lance Corporal Park
Corporal Kobayashi
Lance Corporal Ruiz
Corporal "Doc" Camacho
Corporal Fitz

Madigan's Faction

Former General Porter Madigan: Traitor to the United States
Former Captain Ryan Cook: Former Army Captain convicted of war crimes

Saudi Arabia

Prince Faisal al-Saud: Royal head of the Saudi Intel. Dir. Former SID agent
Prince Abdul al-Saud: Governor of Riyadh

Other

Captain Leslie Spiers: US Army, Deceased – wife of Jack Spiers, killed in action in the Iraq War
Jeff Gottschalk: Traitor, former Chief of Staff; killed in attempted coup by Black Fox
Colonel Song: Central Military Commission, People's Republic of China

Prologue

United States Disciplinary Barracks
Leavenworth, Kansas
Maximum Security Z Unit

Boots struck the metal grate, forty-two footfalls each minute.

A young military policeman—no more than a kid—strode along the catwalk overhanging Z Unit, the strictest supermax cellblock within the maximum security military prison at Leavenworth.

One half circuit completed.

In one of the cells beneath the catwalk, former Captain Ryan Cook sat in total darkness, listening to the fading *clang, clang, clang* of the MP's steps.

Z Unit's prisoners were housed in total isolation and complete darkness. No outside privileges. No windows. No lights. Just a four-by-twelve concrete cell and an endless, impenetrable black.

Clang. Clang. Clang.

Another half circuit completed. Cook started counting again, starting over at one.

Three more minutes—one hundred and twenty-six footsteps.

Stripped out of his orange prisoner's jumpsuit, Cook squatted in the center of his cell, his eyes fixed to the ceiling. Fabric torn from his uniform stretched over his eyes, tied tight behind his head. He kept a silent count as his fingers spread along the cool concrete floor.

Once, he'd been a decorated Army captain. Once, he'd led men in the crucible of combat, and then after the invasion, when he was supposed to lead them in rebuilding a country ripped to shreds with nothing more than bullets and baling wire, he'd found a new purpose instead.

His men had loved him. Iraqis had feared him. No, not just feared him. Were in terrible awe of him. Cowered from him. The Butcher, they'd said, muttering in Arabic just barely out of earshot. *Iblis Shaytan*. The Devil himself.

Clang. Clang. Clang. Forty-two footsteps more. One half circuit. The MP would be on the far side of the catwalk, just past the single entry to Z Unit, an electrified sliding steel door over a foot thick.

Cook inhaled. Closed his eyes.

Forty. Forty-One. Forty-Two.

A whisper of sound, the slide of metal against metal as the locks disengaged on his cell door. Above Cook's head, a circular cover of solid steel slid aside, the door to his cell not on the wall, but above him. Like a cage.

Light filtered through, halogens overhead meant to blind the prisoners when the cell holes opened for feedings or for hose showers. Through his blindfold, all Cook saw was a wash of orange and shadow.

Clang. Clang. Clang.

Cook leaped, grasping the edge of the cell's opening before pulling himself up and out. Muscles rippled along his back as he moved silently and landed in a crouch.

No alarms and no wailing klaxon for this. No alert to the slow-striding guard, pacing away from Cook.

Clang. Clang.

Cook sprinted toward the sound, following the pattern of footfalls he'd memorized in his sleep, heard day in and day out for years, an endless drone of rubber on metal, clang after clang.

The kid saw him at the last second—a blur of muscles and rage, naked and scowling, teeth bared like the feral creature they thought they'd caged. Spit flew from his lips as he snarled and leaped, throwing his full body weight onto the soldier.

"What the fu—" The guard reached for his weapon and his radio at the same time, grabbing neither. Cook grasped his neck, squeezing tight, and took him to the ground, focusing all of his impact, and all of his weight, onto the kid's throat.

They hit the catwalk with a crash, the guard's flak vest, rifle, and helmet clattering against metal. Beneath them, prisoners in the other Z Unit cell holes started to grunt, animal growls and shouts into the darkness. Then pounding, as they banged on their concrete walls and stomped on their steel toilets. A cacophony of rage, of violent men contained in blackness.

The guard's hands grasped at Cook's, fingernails digging into his knuckles. His legs pinwheeled, unable to throw him off. Cook perched like a gargoyle on the guard's chest, a vulture of death. His other hand rose, grasping the kid's scrabbling hands.

He squeezed. Bones crunched, ground together.

Sputtering, the kid wheezed. "Please…" he grunted. "Please…"

Cook grinned, more a baring of teeth than anything else. He leaned forward, until he could feel the kid's panicked pants against his cheek, and closed his fist tighter around his throat. "Shhh."

A gurgle, as the kid struggled to breathe.

There. There it was.

With a bellow, Cook clenched his fist, crunching through cartilage and hyoid bone as his fingers closed around the bony extensions of the kid's spinal cord. Blood burst from the kid's mouth in a shocked cough, an explosion of agony that coated Cook's face and hands. He squeezed again and yanked, feeling the satisfying crack and splinter of bones, decapitating his skull from his spine within his neck.

Cook let go and dropped the lifeless body to the catwalk, leaving him as a limp sack of blood and broken bones.

"Captain."

He turned toward the voice, coming from the direction of the single door to Z Unit. Blood dripped down his cheek, catching on the scraggly hairs of a beard he'd never been allowed to trim.

"Captain. Phone call for you."

Through the orange cloth, Cook could just make out the dark outline of a man in full battle rattle holding a sat phone. His eyes were adjusting to the sudden light after so long in the black. He walked forward, measured steps until he reached the phone.

Beneath him, the prisoners of Z Unit were howling, banging on their cells, throwing themselves against the walls. Some banged their heads against their toilets, even after their skulls split open. Intense solitary broke even the most hardened of men.

But not Cook.

"*Captain Cook*," a voice on the sat phone said. "*I promised I would come for you.*"

Cook slid his blindfold back, dropping the bloodied strip of fabric on the catwalk. He blinked and met the eyes of the soldier who had handed him the phone. Six foot four, a bruiser easily over two hundred and sixty pounds, and kitted out in full battle rattle, the near giant of a man averted his eyes from Cook, looking down with a blink.

"General Madigan," Cook said, his voice catching on the syllables. How long had it been since he'd spoken? "I never lost faith."

"*Saddle up, Captain*," Madigan said over the phone. "*We have a lot of work to do.*"

3

Shockwaves Grip Nation as President Moves Gay Lover into White House

Shockwaves gripped the nation as the announcement that Ethan Reichenbach, former United States Secret Service Agent and gay lover to President Jack Spiers, has moved into the White House, taking the role of first gentleman of the United States following his resignation from the Secret Service. The stunning announcement came late Friday afternoon, with the White House appearing to minimize the impact, and Press Secretary Pete Reyes refusing to comment further.

The move comes on the heels of a tumultuous six months at the White House. From the attempted coup in autumn to the revelation of the president's clandestine gay love affair, President Spiers has been continuously rocked through autumn and winter.

Leadership from the Republican Party rushed to distance themselves from the president and Reichenbach. Polls indicate President Spiers's popularity surged briefly following the attempted coup and again after the United States and Russia led a joint UN force against the Caliphate-held lands in the Middle East, but plummeted shortly after.

One possible source of the plummeting poll numbers might be the increasingly negative attacks coming from the Republican Party, led by Senator Stephen Allen. Allen has repeatedly blasted the president as a betrayer of the party's platform, a liar to the American people, and an opportunist who is putting his own interests before the nation. "When will we do something about this president?" Senator Allen said recently in an interview with TNN's Full Court Press. "And when will the president listen to the people saying 'Enough is enough. We don't want this kind of person leading us.'?"

1

White House

It was a well-known rule of politics: if you wanted to release controversial news, you did so on a Friday afternoon after three thirty. Hopefully, it would be buried in the market's closing bell at four and the public's general lack of care for political news that bled over into their weekends. Everyone would be distracted, the assumption went.

Pete Reyes, President Jack Spiers's press secretary, released a one-sentence statement on a Friday afternoon following Ethan Reichenbach's move back from Iowa, two days after Ethan stood in the Oval Office and told Jack he was coming back for good. To stay as his partner and to live in the White House with him.

It was unprecedented in American politics. There were no guidelines for this, for an unmarried couple sharing the White House Residence, much less two unwed men. Men who were lovers.

Pete exhaled as he posted the press release on the White House website and leaned back in his chair, biting his lip.

The White House welcomes Ethan Reichenbach as the president's partner and first gentleman of the United States.

Thirty seconds later, his office phone rang. And rang. And rang.

Monday morning dawned cold and overcast in Washington DC. A heavy snowstorm, unusual for early spring, threatened to descend over the capital, and ice clung to the edges of the White House windowpanes, crystalizing in fragile patterns across the glass.

Inside the White House Residence's master bedroom, a banked fire smoldered, the last few coals still glowing from a late night blaze. Curled up in the president's bed, buried beneath a heavy down comforter, Ethan pulled Jack close, nuzzling the sleeping president's forehead with a slow kiss as he stroked his hands up and down Jack's bare arms. One of Jack's legs tangled through Ethan's, their naked bodies warm and pressed together.

"Good morning, love," Jack breathed, stretching into Ethan's arms. He pressed a soft kiss to Ethan's jaw before relaxing back, boneless, his eyes closed and a small smile on his lips. "Waking up in your arms will never get old."

"Shhh," Ethan whispered. "Stay asleep. Let's ignore the world today." He squeezed Jack's shoulder, bringing him close. Ethan's next breath caught in his throat.

If only they could ignore the world. Or the world could ignore them. Had he made the right decision? Had coming here been the right thing to do?

"Stop that." Jack pushed up to his elbows, leaning over Ethan as the comforter slid down his shoulder. "Stop worrying. I can feel you working yourself up." He leaned down, pressing a kiss to Ethan's forehead. "Everything will be fine."

Uncertainty flooded Ethan. "Your vice president resigned because of this. Because of me."

Vice President Glen Green had submitted his resignation—publicly, in a huge press conference called on Saturday afternoon at the steps of the Naval Observatory, the vice president's residence—and announced that he could no longer continue to serve in the Spiers administration. In an administration that so blatantly and openly trampled on the values of the Republican Party. Unspoken was the statement that he couldn't—wouldn't—serve with a president in love and living with another man.

Tensions between Jack and his party had simmered just below boiling ever since his public announcement that he and Ethan were lovers. When Ethan had lived in exile in Iowa, and tried to stay out of sight and out of mind, the grumbles of discontent had stayed—mostly—contained.

But with one sentence on Friday and Ethan's new role in Jack's life, *everything* changed.

The roar of the press, the outcry from the loudest and most vitriolic in the Republican Party, and the reaction from overseas leaders nearly deafened the White House. Their first weekend together in the Residence had been fraught with cascading reports of bad and worse news.

Green's resignation was one of several handed in over the weekend. There were spaces in the administration to fill.

"It wasn't because of you. It was because of us." A moment, and then Jack shrugged. One corner of his mouth quirked up, a wry grin. "I never liked him much anyway. He helped win the fringes of the Republican

Party." He wagged his eyebrows. "Don't think I need to worry about placating them anymore."

Ethan tried to smile. His hands stroked up Jack's arms, over warm skin and sinewy muscles. He wanted to pull Jack to him, kiss him senseless, make slow love to him for hours, and search for reassurance and safety in the wrap of his arms and the slide of their bodies. "I don't want to do anything to hurt you. I don't ever want to hurt your presidency. You do too much good. The world needs you."

Smiling again, Jack shrugged and sat up. The blanket slid all the way down, pooling at his hips. A star-shaped scar puckered the skin over his left shoulder, the lingering remnants of a bullet fired by Ethan to save Jack's life. "I'm okay with one term. Just a few years until we're free. Then we can be us. Not have to worry about all this." His hands found Ethan's and squeezed.

"You're worth more than one term."

Leaning in, Jack smiled as he hovered over Ethan's face. "And you are worth more to me than this job." A quick kiss to Ethan's lips and Jack bounced back, stretching, before turning and sliding out of bed. "Shower with me?"

After they had showered and traded flirty grins at their sinks while shaving, and after Ethan had scrambled eggs for both of them, they padded toward the double glass doors at the landing above the main staircase, taking them down from the Residence to the public spaces of the White House.

As they passed the Yellow Room, Ethan slowed, glaring out over the Truman Balcony.

The doors to the Yellow Room had been left open, an attempt to grab and pull as much of the gloomy late winter light as possible into the Residence. Through them, Ethan could hear the distant chants of the protestors held back at the perimeter fence of the South Lawn.

Jack wandered inside, shoving his hands into his suit pants pockets. The cries of the protestors grew louder, and from the windows, they could both make out the distinctive coloring of the hate-filled signs and banners. Some stated that God hated both Jack and Ethan. Several called for God to kill them, and others cried out that this was God's punishment on America. More proclaimed Jack the antichrist.

"Even this snow won't keep them away, huh?" Jack called over his shoulder. "They must really love shouting at nothing."

When Ethan stayed silent, Jack made his way back to his side.

Ethan looked down, avoiding his gaze.

"Hey." Jack ducked, finally making eye contact. "Those nuts are meaningless."

"I never wanted you to experience this." Ethan looked away again, over Jack's shoulder, glaring through the windows toward the protestors. His lips pursed as he sucked on his teeth, and his chest tightened, hard enough that he had to suck in air through his clenched jaw. "I never wanted you to have to face this kind of crap. The press, the political attacks. Protests." Ethan closed his eyes and thunked his head back against the doorframe.

This was everything he had wanted to shield Jack from. Screaming mobs filled with hate, political rivals jockeying for who could draw the most blood, and an intrusive media slinging accusation after accusation.

All because of him.

"What's the alternative? We stay in hiding and sneak around? You stay my dirty little secret?" Jack shook his head. "We tried that. It didn't work. This, us together? This is what's right."

Ethan's eyes flicked back to Jack. Swinging from the Secret Service and a life dedicated to silent, steady protection to the oh-so-public life under the microscope as Jack's—as the *president's*—boyfriend was still a struggle. He'd made a career out of stability and steadfast surety.

A life of careful footing, of not taking any unnecessary risks, and following the rules… and then he'd met Jack. And he'd thrown his entire life rulebook out the window. Jack was a force of nature, a blue-eyed tornado that had sucked all the air out of his world. His smile had slammed into Ethan, throwing him off balance, but it had been his beautiful soul that had pulled him headfirst into the fall. And fall he had, so deeply in love with Jack.

Jack was right, at least partly. He—*Jack*—was worth it.

"I need to take my own advice, huh?" Ethan tried to crack a tiny smile. He'd welcomed three different presidents to the White House, each time briefing them on just how much their life was about to change and how public it was about to become. How much of a fishbowl the White House truly was.

"You told me to ignore ninety percent of the garbage that was thrown at me and play hardball with the final ten percent. Hurl some surprise curveballs back at 'em."

"I think you managed to surprise everyone." Ethan grabbed Jack's hand. "No one saw this coming."

"Not even me." Jack smiled and led them away.

Ethan took a deep breath.

It was his first day as first gentleman of the United States.

Enemy Of My Enemy

Jack squeezed his hand as they headed down the stairs, never letting go.

At the bottom, Secret Service Agent Levi Daniels smiled at them, waving good morning and holding out two paper cups of coffee from the White House mess, still steaming. "Two sugars for you, Mr. President, and black and burned for Ethan."

Chuckling, Jack accepted the coffee and then turned back to Ethan. He pressed a kiss to his lips. "Knock 'em dead," he whispered.

He headed off as Ethan smiled, blushing. Jack looked back before the Secret Service agent striding in front of him pushed open the door to the West Colonnade and he disappeared toward the West Wing.

Daniels stayed behind, sipping his coffee and standing with Ethan in the silent Cross Hall.

"Not going with the president?" Ethan frowned at his friend. Daniels was Agent Scott Collard's second-in-command of the Presidential Protective Detail surrounding Jack. Ethan had once been the lead, but Scott took over after Ethan's forced transfer to Iowa six months prior.

"Nah." Daniels's eyes twinkled. "My best buddy is going to his first day at his new job. I gotta support that." Daniels gestured down the Cross Hall toward the East Wing and the domains of the—traditionally—first lady. Furious carpentry work over the weekend had changed all the signs in the East Wing to read "First Gentleman."

Inhaling deeply, Ethan nodded and set off, Daniels falling into step beside him. One of Daniels's hands rose, gripping Ethan's shoulder and squeezing for a long moment, but dropped before they turned and headed into the public hustle and bustle of the East Wing.

Eyes slid sideways, the staff from the East Wing of the White House all seemingly hovering in the lobby, waiting to catch a glimpse of Ethan as he entered.

Ethan pushed through, nodding and giving his best tight smile to the crowd.

"Relax," Daniels breathed at his shoulder. "You've got your constipated agent face on."

Ethan threw a glare Daniels's way.

"These are your people now." Daniels's eyebrows arched high as he nodded to the mass of humanity.

His people. Jesus. The Office of the First Gentleman, all his. Swallowing, Ethan tried to smile again, though he couldn't fight the nerves clutching at the back of his throat.

Daniels stayed by his side as he escaped up the stairway to the second floor of the East Wing. On the quieter second floor, the Office of the First Gentleman made its home. Oil paintings of former first ladies hung on the walls, and at the end of the hallway, a corner office overlooking the Kennedy Garden, opposite the Oval Office, sported a shiny brass doorplate, reading, "First Gentleman, Ethan Reichenbach."

"Fuck me," Ethan breathed. Just last Monday he'd been moody and grumpy with Jack on their nightly Skype call, bemoaning his exile in Iowa. He'd been frustrated, missing Jack and Levi and Scott and everything about DC, and Jack had offered him the impossible: be his first gentleman.

He'd dismissed it out of hand. He didn't want to be a freeloader. The first gentleman earned no income. It was a ceremonial position only. He'd be an anchor on Jack's neck. An albatross. They were trying to stay out of the public's eye, not catapult into it. There had never been an unwed first gentleman before, certainly not a gay first gentleman. The whole idea was a disaster. He'd already done too much damage to Jack's presidency.

On Wednesday, he'd flown to DC, stood in the Oval Office, and told Jack he'd take it. He'd resign from the Secret Service and move back to DC, ending his exile. He'd move in with Jack. They'd build a life together. No looking back.

That new life had started immediately. They'd danced the night away at the White House Correspondents' Dinner, and Ethan had torn up his return ticket to Iowa. Thursday he'd faxed in his resignation. Friday he and Jack took an early day, spending the weekend ensconced in the Residence as Pete released the announcement to the world.

And now, this.

It was too much. Ethan turned away, breathing hard as Daniels gripped his shoulder again.

"This is history, man." Daniels smiled, warm and bright, and Ethan's nerves screamed. "I'm so damn proud of you."

Damn him. Damn Daniels. Ethan closed his eyes, took a deep breath, and opened them to glare at Daniels. "This is insane. I don't deserve this. I'm not this guy. I shouldn't be here."

"That's exactly why he fell in love with you, and why you *are* here." Daniels gave him a gentle shove, pushing him down the empty hallway to the office that bore his name. "Get going. Your staff is waiting inside."

His staff. Jesus.

The heavy white door whispered over plush carpet as he entered his office. Inside, one man and four women rose together from two pale blue couches facing each other before a large desk. They smiled and waited, silent.

He froze until Daniels jabbed him in his kidney. Ethan strode behind the couches to the wooden chair waiting, obviously, for him. He nodded to his staff and tried to smile. "Good morning. I'm Agent—"

Clearing his throat, Ethan quirked his eyebrows at his staff as Daniels grinned from the back of the room. "Sorry," he said. "I've got to get used to dropping my old title. I'm Ethan. Ethan Reichenbach."

The smiles from his staff were indulgent, grins and nods that told him that yes, dummy, they knew exactly who he was.

"Please, sit." He fumbled a bit, waiting for his staff to sit, and then he remembered that they were waiting for him. Embarrassment burned his cheeks as he tried to clear his throat again and bear it.

Daniels covered his grin with the palm of his hand and looked away.

"Can you all tell me a little bit about yourselves?" Ethan nodded as he unbuttoned his suit jacket and tried to sit comfortably in the ornate—but heinous—chair.

"Mr. First Gentleman," said an older woman with short red hair curled into fluffy rolls that perched around her face like a football helmet. "Let me be the first to greet you with your new title." She smiled warmly at Ethan, her hands clasped in her lap and ankles crossed just so. Her immaculate red suit was pressed and starched, and a string of pearls hung at the hollow of her neck, just below a fold of aging skin starting to sag.

Mr. First Gentleman. He flushed from head to toe and squirmed.

"Please, Mr. Reichenbach will do just fine."

"Mr. First Gentleman," she gently corrected him with an incline of her head. She would have been a socialite contemporary of Nancy Reagan and carried herself with a class that proved it. "My name is Barbara Whitley, and I am the White House social secretary. I serve at the pleasure of the first gentleman." Another warm smile, and Barbara's head tilted. "And please let me say that I am absolutely delighted to be working for you, Mr. First Gentleman."

The gentleness radiating from Barbara calmed Ethan, just a touch. "Forgive me, Ms. Whitley. I may have protected the president, but I'm not up to speed on the full breadth of your duties."

"I am responsible for the planning of all social events at the White House, in coordination with you, of course. From something as simple as an afternoon tea all the way to a full state dinner."

That was a big job. Ethan blinked. "I have to admit," he said, shifting in his seat again, "I'm not really one for afternoon tea."

"I do look forward to expanding this Office's social calendar to include your unique tastes, Mr. First Gentleman." With that, Barbara sat back and proverbially passed the baton by turning to a thin man in his early thirties who peered through wire-rimmed glasses and tried to surreptitiously scroll through his smartphone at the same time.

"Hi there. Jason Brandt, press secretary to the first lady, I mean, first gentleman." Brandt corrected himself, smiling and shrugging apologetically at the same time. "I would like to get some time on the calendar one-on-one with you to plan our communications strategy and media messaging. I've received some guidance from Pete over in the West Wing, but I'd like to craft a uniquely first gentleman message as well—"

"We'll discuss that," Ethan interrupted. "As a matter of principle, we'll take all of our press and media cues from the West Wing." He fixed Brandt with a stare. "We will work in perfect sync with them."

Brandt nodded once and waved his cell phone. "And I have about ten thousand interview requests. Want me to filter through and put together a shortlist of quality candidates? We've got our choice of any network or journalist—"

Another squirm. The chair back was digging into his spine no matter where he shifted. "No interviews."

Brandt blinked. "Mr. First Gentleman—"

"No interviews. The president and I have agreed. We're continuing to keep our personal lives private."

Silence. Brandt's eyes darted around to the rest of the staff, who all looked away. "Mr. First Gentleman. You and the president are trailblazers. This is unprecedented in American history. The public has a right to know—"

"We have a right to live our lives in peace."

"With all due respect, Mr. First Gentleman." Brandt frowned and swallowed. "If you don't set the tone of your own media, it will be set for you. Comedians. Late night talk shows. Spin doctors at the news networks. Columnists. Politicians. Everyone who is anyone has an opinion on you and the president. You're not doing yourself any favors by staying silent."

Somewhere down the hall, a phone rang in an office, muffled through the heavy door. Ethan's eyes rose, and he found Daniels's quiet gaze fixed on him. Daniels gave him a tight smile and an almost imperceptible nod.

"I'll bring it to the president." Swallowing, Ethan turned to the next of his staffers and tried to smile.

Enemy Of My Enemy

"Jennifer Prince, chief floral designer." She grinned, her short blonde bob swinging at her shoulders. "I take care of all floral arrangements in the White House. Have you enjoyed the bouquets up in the Residence?"

Ethan froze. He knew there were flowers in the Residence, and he'd swiped a rose once or twice to present to Jack, but he would be hard-pressed to describe anything that was actually up there.

He fixed a bright smile to his face, so wide his cheeks hurt. "They're great!"

"I really hoped that you and the president would like them." She clapped her hands together and smiled, scrunching up her shoulders. "I'll make sure to keep them coming."

"Thanks." He kept his smile bright and big, and across from Jennifer, Barbara made a soft cooing noise, obviously taken by his cultured appreciation of beauty and class.

At the back of the office, Daniels coughed, but the crinkles at his eyes and the shaking of his shoulders gave his silent laughter away.

Two more women introduced themselves, his director of policy and projects and his chief of staff. Ethan blanched when they asked him what sorts of political activism he wanted to pursue as first gentleman.

He hadn't once thought about the political activism he was supposed to engage in. Did not sinking Jack's career count? Could he mount an anti-anti-Jack campaign? Would that be too obvious?

They settled on starting with veterans' and servicemembers' support and advocacy. He and Jack shared a special passion for veterans, and for making their lives better.

His chief of staff spoke last. "You should probably know that historically the office of the first lady has been staffed predominantly by women. We all served under the former administration, and we remained on, filling in as needed for certain events. We certainly hoped that we'd have a first lady to serve, but we were satisfied with our limited roles." She smiled. "You didn't pick us yourself, Mr. First Gentleman, but we're all happy to be here. And we're at your service."

"Thanks." Ethan surveyed his staff. Floral designers, social secretaries, and political activism. It was a far cry from intelligence briefs, counterterrorism investigations, weapons training, and the protective detail. But this was his life now. He'd chosen this. He'd chosen Jack and everything that came with him. And he didn't regret that, not for a moment.

"Thank you, everyone. I have to admit, I'm a bit shell-shocked at how fast this all has happened."

Barbara huffed a light laugh and nodded as Brandt's eyes went comically wide and his head bobbed from side to side.

"This is a culture shock for me. I'm more used to weapons quals and chasing terrorists. But with your help, I'm ready to learn. I'd love it if each of you stayed on and helped me."

The looks from his staff softened. Barbara hummed as she fingered the pearls around her neck.

"This isn't going to be easy," he continued. "Mr. Brandt, I'm going to apologize right now. Jack and I..." Ethan trailed off. "It really would have been easier for everyone if we had stayed in hiding."

"No, Mr. First Gentleman," Jennifer said as Barbara shook her head. "This is better. And we're all here because we want to be here. The people who chose to leave vacated their offices over the weekend. This is *your* staff, Mr. First Gentleman. We're here for you."

Damn it. He shouldn't get choked up over a staff of socialites and floral designers, but Ethan's throat clenched. "Thank you."

His chief of staff stood, glancing at her cell phone. "It's nine twenty, Mr. First Gentleman, and your first appointment is here."

"My first appointment?"

Smiling, she nodded but said no more. At the doorway, Ethan's departing staff made muffled greetings to someone waiting outside. When Barbara finally slipped out, with a wave and a smile back over her shoulder, his first visitor stepped into his office.

"Mr. First Gentleman." Director Kate Triplett of the United States Secret Service smiled warmly at Ethan as she crossed the office, holding out her hand.

"Director." Ethan took her hand and shook. "Please, Ethan is fine."

Director Triplett's eyebrows arched high. "Mr. First Gentleman, you of *all* people should know that we have pretty strict rules about formality around here."

Both Daniels and Ethan chuckled and looked down as Director Triplett *mmhmmed*. "Please, sit down, Director. It's great to see you again."

"It's good to see you too, Mr. First Gentleman." Director Triplett sat delicately, crossing one leg over the other. "I was sad to receive your resignation last week. We lost a truly great agent."

Ethan smiled but said nothing. The verbal praise was a balm to the scathing letter of reprimand that had appeared in his file when he was transferred to Iowa. It had to be done, but it still stung.

"Since you are no longer employed by the Secret Service, Mr. First Gentleman, we need to discuss your security procedures and your protective detail."

Protective detail? Wait, that was only for politicians, cabinet members, officers of the state, important diplomats. Not for him. He wasn't— No, there had to be some mistake. Shaking his head, Ethan tried to speak.

"You are the first gentleman of the United States," Director Triplett smoothly interrupted. "You are required to have a full protective detail of Secret Service agents."

"What about before?" Ethan frowned. "In Iowa?"

"You were still in our employ then, and our attorneys decided that your special expertise and the community of agents around you would offer you a similar level of protection without putting an undue strain on your personal life. We also implemented a few special programs, which we never informed you of. Suffice it to say, you were protected in Iowa and on every one of your flights back and forth from Des Moines to DC, Mr. First Gentleman, even before you had an official status." Director Triplett leaned forward, smiling. "But now, you are a private citizen, out of our employ, and an expressed member of the first family. Your protection is one of our number one priorities."

Ethan's stomach plummeted. "A full detail?"

"A full detail that will be based here in the East Wing where you office. Your condo will be secured and monitored twenty-four-seven, even while you are living at the White House. Your personal vehicle will be locked up at our secure site. Anytime you need to be transported, the Secret Service will escort you to and from your location. You will have a team of close protection agents and a supporting protective detail working for you around the clock. Your detail will provide you with individualized security and threat assessments on a daily basis and provide you with personal security at all times."

It was the same speech Ethan had given to three presidents. A cage of protection settling down around the protectee. He'd watched their gazes harden as he'd outlined their restrictions in freedom of movement, but he'd never thought that those protections would ever turn around and cage him.

"Director..." Ethan swallowed. "I'm familiar with the speech."

"Good. Then you also know there's no arguing with the protective detail or with the agents assigned to your protection." Director Triplett raised one eyebrow.

"Yes, ma'am." Ethan slumped backward. He frowned. "Who will be on my detail? I know all the senior agents in DC." Were they rotating agents from the field back to Washington? Setting him up with strangers? Maybe other agents who weren't so keen on Ethan's choices and behaviors, like what he'd just escaped in Iowa?

Director Triplett tried to smother her grin as she looked sidelong at Daniels. "In light of recent events, I've decided to issue a verbal order of understanding. Agents who have a prior relationship with you or with the president will not be barred from continued service with either of you two."

Ethan sat up straight. "Director?"

"Please meet the head of your protective detail, Mr. First Gentleman. A true gem in the Secret Service, First Gentleman Detail Lead, Agent Levi Daniels."

Daniels beamed, wide and toothy, and held out his arms when Ethan jumped to his feet. Ethan wrapped him up in a huge bear hug as Daniels slapped at his shoulder, laughing.

"Levi! You're second in command in the West Wing! Why would you transfer over here?" Historically, the detail protecting the first lady had less standing than the agents protecting the president. The presidential detail was where it was at. Everyone who was anyone in the Secret Service wanted to be there. "Why would you come down here?"

"Because it's *you*, man." Daniels pulled back but kept one hand on Ethan's shoulder. He beamed. "Because it's you, and I can't let anything happen to you. I'm so damn proud of you. You and your man both."

Jack had repeatedly asked Daniels to call him by his first name, and while Daniels hadn't relented in Jack's presence, he had taken to calling Jack 'your man' while he and Ethan were alone.

"Some of the other guys wanted to come over, too. Few guys from the swing shift. Beech. Caldwell. Hanier. They didn't want to leave you. We were all so pissed when you got sent to Iowa—"

Director Triplett cleared her throat as she stood and smoothed her skirt.

Daniels kept going, covering his slip. "And it was easy to fill your detail. All volunteers. Every single one."

For the second time, Ethan had to fight against his throat clenching, against a swell of emotion that threatened to swallow him whole. Loyalty, devotion, comradery, and his brothers in the agency. He'd spent twelve years with most of the agents Daniels had mentioned. One of the biggest gut-punches of being transferred to Iowa, after losing such close contact with Jack, was the disconnection from his colleagues and his friends.

"Levi…" He didn't know what to say.

Daniels let him off the hook. "Mr. First Gentleman," he said, dipping his head toward Ethan. "I'm going to set up your detail headquarters office right next door. We're working on connecting the feed from Horsepower so we'll have the same real-time intel in both locations. Scott and I plan on sharing the morning briefs."

"Sounds good, Lead Agent Daniels." Ethan returned the honorific.

"I've got to get going." Director Triplett held out her hand for Ethan. "I wanted to personally congratulate you, though, Mr. First Gentleman."

He didn't know what to say. He smiled as he took her hand and tried not to look constipated.

"We'll leave you to get settled in your new digs."

Daniels and the director headed out. The heavy door slid shut, and then Ethan was alone in his new office for the first time.

He exhaled. "First gentleman of the United States." His gaze darted around his office, taking it all in. Across the Kennedy Garden and the Rose Garden, he could just make out the white columns of the Oval Office. He'd never, not once, imagined that this would be his life.

In his pants pocket, his cell vibrated. Pulling it out, Ethan swiped through the screensaver—a picture of him and Jack dancing at the Correspondents' Dinner some press photog had snapped—and found a message from Jack.

Thinking of you. Hope your first day is going great, love!

2

White House West Wing

"We've got a packed morning, Mr. President."

Lawrence Irwin, Jack's chief of staff and former director of the CIA, bustled into the Oval Office, over a dozen of Jack's staff trailing behind him.

Noticeably absent was Glen Green, as of Saturday, the former vice president.

Jack waved good morning and gestured to the couches, waiting for his team to settle in and get comfortable. Most had already been working for hours, though it was still early. As a rule, Jack had three carafes of coffee waiting for his staff each morning.

Pete Reyes was the first to grab a cup before he leaned back with a heavy sigh. His shirt was rumpled, partially untucked in the back, and his tie was loose.

"Long night, Pete?" Jack tried to smile as he leaned back against his desk. Pete had to deal with the immediate reaction and outcry from his and Ethan's actions every time. White House press secretary wasn't an easy job by any stretch, but Jack and Ethan had made Pete's job infinitely harder. Some days, Jack wondered when Pete would throw in the towel.

"Long weekend, Mr. President."

"Do you think we've seen the worst of it so far?" Irwin, sitting across from Pete, leaned forward with his padfolio balanced on his knees and peered over his glasses at Pete.

"God, no," Pete scoffed. "They're just getting going."

"Who?" Irwin frowned.

"Everybody. The press. Congress. The governors. State legislatures. Foreign press. Private blogs. Your grandma." Pete closed his eyes and let his head fall back, sinking into the couch cushions as he spoke to the ceiling. "This is going to be an epic bloodbath."

Irwin's gaze pinched.

Jack busied himself in the heavy silence that followed, wheeling his desk chair around to sit with those clustered around the couches and chairs in the center of the Oval Office. Lewis Parr, secretary of defense, held out one of the carafes to Jack with a question.

He shook his head with a smile. "Good morning," Jack said again, nodding as he sat. "Let's have it. Hit me."

Irwin went first, summarizing Congress's reaction to Glen Green's resignation. "Congressional leadership is already making noise about replacing Green. They want a name by the end of the week. Confirmation hearings within the month."

"Let's beat them. I want a shortlist of candidates by the afternoon. I've got a few people in mind, but I want to see what you put together."

Pete spoke next, rising like a broken marionette from his slump on the couch to hunch over his coffee cup as he poured a refill. "Media reports are still in a state of shock. We're seeing a sixty-forty split of negative to positive press. The loudest commentators right now are calling this an illegal move. Saying that he doesn't qualify as a member of the first family and doesn't belong in the White House, or as the first gentleman."

Diana Ramirez, his White House counsel, jumped in, "We reviewed the law extensively before the announcement. Public law 95-70, Section 105, subsection E. 'If the president does not have a spouse, such assistance and services—such as those provided by the office of the first lady, or the first gentleman—may be provided for such purposes by a member of the president's family whom the president designates.'"

"It's the word 'family'," Pete said, squinting. He held up his fingers as if he could grab the word between his index and thumb. "They don't believe that Mr. Reichenbach qualifies as a member of the president's family."

"Federal law has historically been overinclusive when defining 'family.'" Ramirez nodded to Jack. "There's more than enough precedent in current statute to take this to court. A same-sex partner in a committed, long-term relationship qualifies as a member of the family, according to numerous federal agencies and regulations."

"Long-term?" Pete frowned again. "Do we have a definition of long-term? Because, Mr. President, that's probably the second most asked question I get. How long have you two been together? Do we meet the definition of long-term?"

"It's open to interpretation." Ramirez spoke before Jack could. "There's more flexibility when it's not defined."

"Could also come back to bite us in the—"

"All right," Jack said over Pete. "All right, thank you both. Pete, you know my policy. No comment on my personal life, and that includes how long Ethan and I have been together."

A heavy sigh as Pete looked down at the carpet. "Yes, Mr. President." He squinted back at Ramirez. "Can I quote you on that? Give that statute to the press?"

Ramirez looked first to Jack, who answered for her. "Yes, please do, Pete. But keep it low-key. You know my limits."

Pete nodded and leaned back, resting one arm over the back of the couch and rubbing his eyes with his free hand as Director Campbell, FBI, and Director Triplett talked together, briefing Jack on the spike in threats against him and Ethan.

"We believe most of the chatter is people getting excited and running their mouths. We don't have any credible threat information at present. Seems to be an explosion of anger and verbal diarrhea, but we'll be running down every lead."

"Do we need to change our security procedures?" Jack frowned at Director Triplett.

"No, Mr. President. We're confident that our current procedures are effective. We can keep you safe here. The first gentleman has just been briefed on his new security detail as well."

Jack tried to smile, but Director Triplett's words struck a hollow nerve. His chest tightened, and he tried to swallow past the sudden lump that rose in his throat. He blinked, and in the darkness behind his eyelids, the Oval Office flashed, changing from the taupe, beige, and blue pattern he'd picked out to a bloodstained, destroyed wreck, littered with shot bodies. Blood and brains dripped down the walls, and in the center, Ethan stood, firing shot after shot. The sound, the clap of the bullets, seemed to echo behind Jack's heart, heavy bangs he could practically feel vibrating through his bones.

We can keep you safe here.

Jack opened his eyes and plastered a smile over his face. "Thank you, Directors. I appreciate your diligence."

Meredith Peterson, Jack's new national security advisor, went next. "Mr. President, we are picking up dramatically increased chatter overseas. Your announcement has given our enemies plenty to scream about. Leaders from Al Qaeda, the Caliphate, Al-Shabaab, Boko Haram, and AQIM have all called for renewed strikes against 'The Great Satan.' They're using this past weekend to drive some pretty strong hatred."

"Have we picked up anything moving to the operational stages, or is this still just chatter?"

Julian Aviles, secretary of homeland security, spoke. "None of our operatives or our intercepts are pointing to a direct threat yet, Mr.

Enemy Of My Enemy

President, but I think we need to be on guard against some kind of attempt, perhaps a lone wolf attack trying to capitalize on the situation."

The situation. Jack frowned. *The situation. This past weekend.* They were talking around him and Ethan.

"Keep searching. Push our collections and our analysts to be certain. We can't let anything slip through."

The two nodded and sat back as Lewis Parr took his turn. "Mr. President, results have come back from testing the human remains our joint Russian-American Special Forces patrol found in the Iraqi desert outside of Mosul. Positive ID on Al-Karim. We believe the time of death was about a month ago, maybe six weeks, based on the condition of the remains. We weren't able to find the cause of death, sir. His condition was too badly deteriorated."

Al-Karim, the terrorist leader of the Islamic Caliphate, a man who had been receiving orders from General Madigan, former vice chairman of the joint chiefs of staff, leader of a failed coup, and a fugitive traitor to his country. Finding Karim's desiccated body in the Iraqi desert was a victory, though not as strong as if they'd captured Madigan himself.

Soon. They'd get Madigan soon. Jack's teeth ground together whenever he heard Madigan's name and a blazing fire lay banked in his soul, rage fanning the flames of vengeance. They'd get him. They would. Irwin devoted half of his energy to tracking down the rogue general. Madigan had to come up for air sometime.

He pushed past his thirst for revenge. "Excellent, Lewis. That's a major victory. Our combat operations against the Caliphate are making a major dent. I'll get on the phone with President Puchkov later today and we'll draft a joint statement for simultaneous release."

Parr nodded. "Joint operations with the Russians are going well, sir. Commanders on the ground report that sharing the bases in Northern Iraq has been mostly smooth sailing. A few scuffles between the ranks, but at the operational level, it seems to be working."

"Russians and Americans working together." This time, Jack beamed. "We did something right."

Chuckles around the room before Elizabeth Wall, secretary of state, began to speak. Her words tempered everyone's momentary lightness. "Mr. President, we have a list of six countries who have released statements stating that you and the first gentleman are no longer welcome within their borders. In each of these countries, homosexual behavior is punishable by death."

A heavy silence fell over the Oval Office. Jack did his best not to fidget as the eyes of his staff all slid to him, staring.

"What countries?" He cleared his throat, a slight hitch to his voice.

"Iran, Mauritania, Sudan, Somalia, Yemen, and Nigeria."

Exhaling, Jack closed his eyes. "Pillars of our foreign policy, to be sure." He tried to smile.

"Nigeria's president spoke on a national talk show this weekend and specifically called you 'a disgusting animal.' Uganda's president issued a statement calling homosexuals 'worse than diseased dogs and pigs.'"

Silence.

Jack held Elizabeth's stare as the room stilled, everyone freezing. A slow exhale sounded, and someone set down their coffee cup, the porcelain clinking against the table in the oppressive quiet.

"We never liked them anyway," Pete chimed in, breaking the silence with a petulant snap.

Elizabeth's eyes flicked to Pete. "They're not our favorites in the world, but Uganda is host to African Command and several clandestine military bases. And," she said, turning back to Jack, "their statements don't bode well for LGBT citizens in their countries. Pro-LGBT protests broke out in both countries but were shut down by the police with some heavy repression. We should react."

Slowly, Jack nodded. He cleared his throat, a rough sound in the heavy office. "We need to do so delicately. Uganda is a strategic partner for our military and we don't want more of Africa pivoting to China. We've lost a large foothold in the continent in the last two decades." Leaning forward, Jack rested his elbows on his knees and rubbed his palms together as he stared at the carpet. "But not at the expense of human rights."

Elizabeth nodded. "We also may have a problem with Saudi Arabia. Saudi imams are calling for a reaction from the royal family, who so far haven't commented at all. Homosexual behavior is outlawed and punishable by death there, too. We think that the royal family, to save face, will have to issue a strongly worded statement condemning this weekend."

"Condemning *me*," Jack corrected. "We can call it what it is. Me and Ethan together."

Elizabeth looked down at her notes. "We're preparing for every possibility, Mr. President. Including a statement denying you entry to the Kingdom. We're also preparing to recall our ambassadors from Saudi and the other countries. I believe we should recall them before any expulsion order is given. We don't want to look reactive."

Jack braced his elbows on his knees and clapped his hands in front of his face. His index finger bounced off his pursed lips.

"Should we be talking about cutting off these guys' foreign aid?" Pete sat up again, glaring. "Why *not* threaten to pull out our bases from

Uganda? Forget them! And, Mauritania is one of the world's biggest shitholes. Good riddance. Somalia sucks. Iran still hates us. Why *not* cut off our aid? Most of those countries get something. Some of them quite a lot."

"Yemen has been getting military assistance against Al Qaeda for years," Meredith Peterson said quietly.

"And about twenty million dollars from us." Pete slapped his knee, his face twisted into a frustrated grimace.

"Seventy-five other nations also outlaw homosexual behavior, Mr. President." Elizabeth pulled out a sheet of paper from her padfolio. "Their governments haven't said much so far, but we're expecting statements." She glanced at Pete. "If we're cutting off aid to one nation, do we cut it off to everyone? You're talking about changing our entire foreign policy. We need to keep the moral high ground. America does not waver in the face of other countries' invective—"

"Why not cut it *all* off?" Pete spread his arms wide. "These countries want to be dicks—"

"That's enough." Jack sat back, but he gave Pete a smile. "Thank you for your support, Pete. It means a lot. But, we can't go changing the global order because backwater dictators are trying to spit in my face. If we pull out of Uganda, the rebels there would mount a counterstrike and we could lose the stability in East Africa that we *do* have. Elizabeth—" He turned to her. "I agree with you. We've got to play this carefully. Reach out to the ambassadors in-country, in those six, and in Uganda and Nigeria. Ask them for their take. If there's even a hint of insecurity or turmoil, recall the whole staff and shut down the embassy, but be sure to say that this is a temporary measure for the safety and security of our personnel. And, I think we'll be okay in Saudi."

Elizabeth raised her eyebrows but said nothing. "And what about the condemnation of you and the first gentleman, Mr. President?"

Jack turned to Pete. "Pete, I need you to craft a statement shaming these countries with kindness while keeping our diplomatic and strategic position unchanged."

Pete sighed heavily and scrubbed at his eyes with his fists. His shoulders bounced back and forth as he thought, humming. "How about... 'The United States wishes the people of blah blah country well and stands for equal human rights for all LGBT citizens everywhere. We... invite the government to join the world on the right side of history?'"

"Something like that, yes." Jack nodded to Pete and Elizabeth. "Get together and craft a joint statement. Right now, I'm not ready to cut off any aid or draw down any military missions. And I don't want to sink to their level. I'm not going to compromise America's moral standing in the world to hurl insults at a bunch of narrow-minded dictators."

"Pretty sure they think you're already morally compromised." Pete spoke quickly, but ducked his head as Irwin shot him a death glare that promised a private reprimand away from the Oval Office.

"We've got to prove them wrong. Elizabeth, get your people working on a project to fund LGBT rights groups in those countries. Let's take an affirmative stand for equality everywhere. And put our money where our mouths are." Jack stood and buttoned his suit jacket. His hands trembled, but he hid them in his pockets quickly. "Thank you, everyone. Have a good morning. I've got to make a call to President Puchkov."

International Reactions Mixed to President's Announcement;
Embassies Evacuated Due to Security Concerns

International reactions have been mixed to President Jack Spiers's announcement that he was moving his homosexual lover into the White House. Six nations immediately banned the president from their borders, and others took to their national media to loudly denounce the president and Mr. Reichenbach.

Riots broke out in several countries across Africa and the Middle East. Embassies in Sudan, Yemen, Nigeria, Mauritania, and Zimbabwe were temporarily closed, and all staff were flown out of the country. Secretary of State Elizabeth Wall said that the closures were done out of an "abundance of caution" for their staff, as the United States evaluates her continued and ongoing diplomatic relations in light of the negative statements from some world leaders.

Not all world leaders were negative, however. The United Kingdom's Prime Minister offered her congratulations, as did the President of the EU and the Chancellor of Germany. Canada's Prime Minister issued a statement to their media, congratulating President Spiers and Ethan Reichenbach. And, in a surprising move, Russian President Sergey Puchkov took time at the end of his briefing at the Kremlin to offer his personal congratulations and best wishes to the president and his partner.

3

White House West Wing

"*Mr. President!*" The booming voice of President Sergey Puchkov, erupting through the Oval Office's telephone with such glee, never failed to put a smile on Jack's face.

"Mr. President," Jack greeted the Russian president warmly. Somehow, he and Puchkov had grown to be almost friends as the United States and Russia had partnered closely to combat the Caliphate in Iraq and Syria. Once, Sergey had called him a *pidor* president—a faggot president—and had shut Jack out. He'd called back with a very Russian non-apology after Ethan had saved the world, and ever since, Sergey had repeatedly invited Jack and Ethan to visit Russia together. He asked about Ethan on every call. He stood with Jack at the UN, and he'd rescinded Russia's infamous homosexual propaganda law. Whatever had happened in the past, Sergey was making a real effort with Jack.

It was a bright spot amid an ocean of negativity.

"*There is still time for you and Mr. Ethan to come to Russia for Russian winter.*" Sergey's voice held a faint hint of teasing. "*I promise you. You will never have a winter like Russian winter. Is good for you. Good for the soul!*"

Jack laughed. "Sergey, that's very kind of you. We had to promise the Secret Service that we'd stay put for a while, though."

"*Ah, yes, yes. What with your big announcement.*" Even over the phone line, Jack could hear Sergey's grin. "*Congratulations are in order for you and the first gentleman, Mr. President. Za Lyubov!*"

Jack did his best to translate Puchkov's Russian into the language translator on his laptop. He'd learned, over the course of their talks, to have the program open and running during their conversations. Sergey liked to keep him on his toes.

Za Lyubov. Russian toast, meaning "To Love."

Even with their political relationship growing closer, Sergey had never openly expressed such warm sentiments to Jack before. His brand of affection was more of the harsh, teasing variety. Jack fought for words. "Sergey... Thank you." He exhaled. "This hasn't been easy—"

"*Nothing truly worthwhile ever is.*"

Was that exhaustion staining Sergey's voice? Jack frowned. "Sounds like you know from experience."

Sergey sighed. "*I rose up through Russia under President Putin's reign, Mr. President. One day, we will talk. I will tell you that story.*"

Former Russian President Putin. A man who had almost driven the world to war and polarized Russia and the United States. He'd finally vacated the presidency under murky circumstances, and his first successor had died two months into his tenure. Sergey had been elected next, after the government had been dissolved, and so far, eighteen months into his six-year term, he'd survived. Russia was teetering, though. Their economy kept declining, and corruption kept skyrocketing. Discontent had grown within Sergey's country.

It couldn't be easy being president over there.

And yet, he had befriended Jack and was kind when he didn't have to be. Jack smiled. "You're the only head of state to offer personal congratulations so far."

"*I beat the British? And Europe?*" A slapping sound, like Sergey had clapped his hand on his desktop. "*Ha!*"

There had been statements issued by the offices of the other leaders and received by the State Department. Europe, as progressive as they were, and the United Kingdom, with their special relationship with the United States, wouldn't misstep so far as to remain silent on the matter. But Sergey was the only one to speak to Jack and personally offer his congratulations.

"*I would have phoned you sooner, Mr. President,*" Sergey said, sobering slightly. "*Matters here stole my time today. And, I wanted to let you and your first gentleman relax before the storm descended upon you.*"

"Descend it has." Jack sighed and pinched the bridge of his nose. Snatches of his staff meeting, his daily briefing, tugged at him. "I have good news for you, though. Something good from this morning, anyway." Sergey made a grunting noise on the phone, and over the speaker, leather creaked, like he was leaning back in his chair. "We got a positive ID on the remains our joint team found. It's Al-Karim."

"*Zeabis,*" Sergey breathed.

Jack typed away. His translator beeped back. *Russian Slang. Zeabis: Fucking awesome.* He grinned. "Yes, Sergey. '*Zeabis*'."

"*Ha! You speak Russian terribly, Mr. President. But, Al-Karim dead is a good thing. A very good thing. Your general cannot use him in the Caliphate anymore.*"

"Parts of our intelligence community believe that Al-Karim was executed by members of the Caliphate. A retaliation against his collusion with Madigan." Again, the fires within Jack roared, a thirst for vengeance and blood.

"*Very possible. We can hope the ties between your general and the Caliphate have been severed.*"

"He's not my general, Sergey." He balled one hand into a fist, and two of his knuckles cracked.

"*Apologies. This terrorist, this madman. Madman Madigan.*"

"Sounds fitting." Jack smiled down at his desktop. "We should issue a joint statement. Pete, my press secretary, is swamped with damage control. Think you and I can bang something together?"

"*Two intelligent men such as ourselves? I, of course, being the more intelligent.*" Sergey laughed. "*Yes, I think we can manage.*" The sounds of Sergey sliding his laptop closer and pounding on his keyboard echoed over the line. "*My day is winding down, so I can give you this time now. And, I can make a statement in two hours, Mr. President. At seven o'clock in Moscow.*"

A quick glance at the dual clocks Jack kept on the sideboard behind his desk. One showed local time, the other, Moscow time. Two hours. Noon in DC. "Sounds good. Let's get busy, Mr. President."

Ethan watched Jack's short press conference from his office, smiling as he listened to Jack describe the joint US-Russian Special Forces mission that had recovered Al-Karim's remains. Jack praised the Russians for their assistance, and in an inset video, a translator repeated President Puchkov's praise for the United States and for their joint mission against the Caliphate.

He left his door open after that, and in the afternoon Barbara poked her head in, smiling as she knocked in a cute pattern against the heavy wood.

"Come in, Barbara." He stood, holding out his hand for her. She took it with a gentle, delicate grasp, and Ethan tried not to crush her palm in his. "How can I help you?"

Barbara had a bin in one arm, overflowing with folded papers and cards. "Mr. First Gentleman, I thought you might want to see these." She took one card off the top of the stack and passed it over.

"*Congratulations!*" Screamed from the top in bright rainbow colors. Inside, the card was signed simply, "*We believe in you. Sincerely, the Lombardi family.*"

"Cards from supporters came in today, Mr. First Gentleman. I have eight more bins, just like this one."

"From who?"

"People who support you and the president. Not everyone is full of hate."

Sometimes it was hard to remember that when the loudest voices were the ones most hurtful. "Eight other bins?"

"Eight other bins *today*. We'll get more tomorrow. And the day after."

"Can you bring them all in here?"

Barbara nodded. "Would you like me to draft a reply for your review? A letter of thanks from you and the president on your official letterhead? We only receive mail that includes a return address, so we can send replies to every single one."

The next card was an anniversary card, but the wording was appropriate. "*To the both of you and your loving relationship.* Signed, *Jim & Evan Gameros.*"

Ethan had to swallow, but still, his voice was hoarse. "Yeah, Barbara. That's a good idea."

She slipped out with a smile, and Ethan reached for the next card.

Ethan's phone buzzed an hour later.

You free? Irwin wants you to head over to the Oval.

He frowned. *[Everything okay?]*

Remember his offer?

Lawrence Irwin, former director of the CIA, before Jack fired him for—ostensibly—getting Ethan killed, and then rehired as chief of staff after Jeff Gottschalk's complete betrayal. He'd texted Ethan last week after his resignation. *I'm not affiliated with the CIA anymore—officially—but I know the agency could use a man like you. Would you be interested in one of the more special programs? Continue to serve your country?*

Only in conjunction with Jack, he'd said. And only if it didn't jeopardize Jack. Or them together.

[It's my first day!]

Guess we'll find out together what he's up to.

Jack was behind his desk checking his laptop as Ethan plopped down on one of the couches and waited for Irwin. A few minutes later, Irwin ducked into the Oval Office, clutching his padfolio, phone, and a stack of red folders marked "Top Secret." He was alone, and he sat across from Ethan with a smile and a nod to Jack. "Mr. President."

"Special meeting today, Lawrence?" Jack settled beside Ethan and offered his chief of staff a cup of coffee.

Irwin traded one of the folders for the coffee. "I have information on Madigan, Mr. President. Some disturbing new actions to report." His gaze shifted to Ethan. "And a plan."

In the folder, photos stamped with *"Fort Leavenworth—Maximum Security Z Unit"* were stapled to heavy sheets of cardstock. Below the photos were layouts and diagrams of the prison detailing ingress and egress points from an infiltration team. More photos followed of an open cell and a prison guard's body covered with a tarp. Blood on the walls, on the floors. Bloody footprints. Behind the photo boards, an analysis of the prison break.

"What is this?" Jack's eyes lingered on the last photo board and a bloody M drawn inside a circle. "What are we looking at?"

"Friday night, Fort Leavenworth's maximum security Z Unit experienced a break-in. We don't have full details on how this occurred, but at least three of the guards are unaccounted for and one is dead. We suspect the missing guards may have aided an infiltration team on the ground."

"Who escaped?" Ethan flipped through the photo boards, squinting at the isolated drop cells and the heightened security evident from the photos. "This doesn't look like a normal prison block."

"Z Unit is where we dump the worst of the worst. Our darkest criminals from the military. People we don't want to ever see or hear from again. We just want them to disappear."

"No capital punishment? No death penalty?"

"Too public. Z Unit really is a black hole." Irwin passed over another folder, flipping it open to a full-page color photo of an Army captain in his dress uniform, glaring hard at the camera. Across from the photo, a decorated service record listed oblique references to major actions in the Special Forces. At the bottom of the service record, an entry listed the captain's demotion to private and sentence to Fort Leavenworth following closed proceedings. The charges weren't shown. "Former Captain Ryan Cook is the only prisoner who is missing. The Butcher of Iraq. He led a Special Forces team there for five tours. And he served alongside Jeff Gottschalk and then-Major Madigan."

Something slithered down Ethan's spine, a memory just out of reach. Something mixed in with the sand and sun and bombs blasting all around. He squinted at Cook's face. There was something about him, something familiar.

Jack frowned. "When? What time frame?"

Looking up, Ethan's stomach clenched when Irwin answered. He knew Jack's history almost as well as his own. He'd been in the middle of his army career, and though he'd been in the Special Forces, he'd never crossed paths with Madigan.

And at the same time, Leslie Spiers, Jack's deceased wife, had been serving her country in Iraq. Had paid the ultimate price.

It was how Jack oriented himself to the war. Before Leslie's death and after Leslie's death. Ethan had learned that slowly, and he never commented on it.

"Do we know where Cook escaped to?"

"Nothing definite, Mr. President." Irwin shook his head. "He seems to have vanished, just like Madigan. No sightings within a thousand miles of the prison. We searched the airports in all the states surrounding, both major and municipal. Nothing."

"Damn it."

"Something else." Irwin passed over the last red folder. "A possible lead. Yesterday, a prison in northwest Colombia was attacked and overrun. All prisoners escaped in the mayhem. No one knows who the attackers were."

Ethan spoke as Jack flipped through the photo boards. "Are you thinking Madigan? Even in Colombia?"

"Absolutely," Jack growled and passed a photo board to Ethan, a snapshot of the overrun prison. Blood pooled on the ground, stained the walls, and puddled in the dirt around the destroyed prison's grounds. Ethan's gaze caught on a very specific bloodstain. Captions on the top photo oriented the camera: *northwest cellblock; close-up of the cellblock's walls.*

An M written in blood and closed in a dripping red circle.

"The same symbol from the Leavenworth breakout. And here."

"So you think Madigan managed to get to Colombia? Could Cook be there as well?" Jack's voice had dropped, a harsher, hunter's tone.

Ethan glanced sidelong at his lover. This side of Jack was new.

"We don't know. We just have two symbols connecting two prison breaks within days. One we know has a direct affiliation with Madigan. Could he have gone to Colombia? Could Cook? It's possible. But to what end?" Irwin pursed his lips and shook his head. "I promised I would bring you everything, Mr. President. Every possibility, every hint of something, no matter how small. We haven't connected the dots on this one just yet. It's still evolving. But Cook's escape is a dangerous signal, Mr. President. If Cook was assisted by elements within the prison, then that means Madigan still has access to people loyal to him. People we don't even know about."

Ethan's chest filled with lead, tightening until he couldn't breathe. Madigan was still out there. His reach, as Director Campbell once said, was very, very long.

Dark fury roiled within Jack's eyes. "Thank you, Lawrence. I do want to know everything, no matter how small. I want to run him into the ground and then bury his coffin where no one will ever find him."

"We all do, Mr. President." He threw a quick glance at Ethan. "Which is why I asked both of you to be here. I have an idea, and I'd like to bring Mr. Reichenbach on board."

"Me? How can I help with this?"

"I want to stand up an off-the-books covert strike team. Dedicated one hundred percent to tracking down Madigan and, ultimately, taking him out. A black team. A kill squad. Completely clandestine. Run it through the CIA's black budget and pull from the CIA's collected intelligence feed, including the raw intel we get from the NSA and FBI. And, they'd get their orders straight from the president."

"I don't have the experience to run a strike team, Lawrence. I can't order them around in good conscience."

"The team will be answerable to only you. I would provide strategic direction and political cover through the CIA. And, I'd like Mr. Reichenbach to run the operation."

Ethan frowned. Maybe once, he'd been the man who could do this, but that wasn't him anymore. "Sir, I'm flattered, but—"

"You served in the Army for thirteen years. Assigned to the Fifth Special Forces group, you served three tours in Iraq and one in Afghanistan. In Afghanistan, your team took over the villages controlling the highway on the Taliban's resupply route, starving them out of hiding in the pass. In Iraq, your team captured an insurgent airfield and successfully guided in badly needed resupply missions for the Peshmerga forces. You captured fifteen high-value targets in two years. In the Secret Service, you rose through the ranks quickly, joining the presidential detail after only three years and commanding the detail in twelve. You have been responsible for the safety and security of the most important men on the planet."

"Didn't do so well in Ethiopia."

"On the contrary. You got the president out alive. You took a hellish situation and you made it a win for the president."

Jack's hand settled on the small of Ethan's back, his thumb stroking soft arcs across his suit jacket. "You do have the experience, Ethan."

He glared down at the carpet, Jack's choice of beige and cream redone after the Oval Office had been destroyed. By him. He pushed that aside. "I want to see Madigan caught and killed. I do." He fixed Irwin with a pinched glare. "But I can't be running around the world chasing shadows and ghosts. Not anymore." He'd left that life behind. Now he was a different man with a different life. With Jack. Hunting shadows and chasing monsters made from the darkness of men's souls turned even the best people toward a darkness they didn't want to face. Made hard choices a constant living thing, an itch that couldn't ever be scratched. He'd fought back from that life once. Not again.

"You would run operational command from here. No field work. We'd have to find a tactical commander who can lead a strike team anywhere in the world and who can report back to you for command direction. But, for you, we'd want to keep your involvement out of the public eye. Your main duties would remain here in DC as the first gentleman. This would be something extra. And not to put too fine a point on it, but the whole operation should involve as few people as possible. Just the members of this room, in fact." Irwin fixed a pointed look at Jack and Ethan, and the emptiness of the Oval Office.

"Authority would be granted through secret National Security Presidential Directive?" Jack sat up, though one hand stayed on Ethan's back.

Irwin nodded. "Yes. That way it's totally off the books. No one would know. And we'd need an eyes-only directive to the head of Special Operations Command with orders to task a team to exclusive presidential direction. If we had such a team now, they could be on the ground in Colombia giving us the answers we need."

"I like it so far." Jack turned to Ethan. "What do you think?"

He'd have distance from the dirty business, but not much. And a nimble, aggressive strike force dedicated to hunting down Madigan. Fast, agile, and unencumbered by the bureaucratic tape holding others back. An immense amount of responsibility, and a huge weight of power. Unfiltered intelligence. Worldwide purview. The authority to act anywhere, do almost anything. "Do you trust me to lead this for you? This is huge."

Jack smiled. "I trust you with everything."

Irwin continued. "We'd need to select the right special operations team for this. Someone we can trust completely. Someone who can take this mission and lead his men—"

"I know who." Ethan interrupted Irwin. "I already know who can do it."

Irwin's eyebrows rose.

"And so do you. He's one of the only men I trusted when the world went to hell. We still don't really know who all is connected to Madigan's Black Fox unit, but I *do* know that when I needed to trust him, this man came through."

He'd fought through the White House with Ethan, fought to get Ethan back to Jack's side from half a world away. Had rescued him from the wastes of Africa and hauled him to safety in a bolt-hole in Saudi Arabia. Hell, he'd even been targeted for death by Madigan. That had to be some kind of seal of approval. "Lieutenant Cooper and his Marines."

"I remember him. He could be good." Irwin nodded and turned his attention back to Jack. "Mr. President? Your thoughts?"

"Give me a day to think it over. I do need to run it by counsel. I'll let you know."

Irwin stacked the Top Secret folders and then pulled out a sheet from his notebook. "I also have a short list of vice presidential candidates for you to review, Mr. President."

"I have a suggestion, too. Elizabeth Wall."

"Secretary of state Wall?" For the first time in a while, Irwin looked surprised.

Ethan watched Jack as he leaned back on the couch. Secretary Wall was a strong secretary of state, and she'd been a pillar of Jack's Cabinet through his first year. He listened to her counsel more than others, at least, from what Ethan had seen when he'd been in the White House.

"She's a go-getter. And yet, she gets the balance that we have to strive for right now, especially with everything I've done. I like how she views the world and how she approaches her decisions and her foreign policy."

"All excellent reasons for keeping her secretary of state, Mr. President."

"And I also know that she wants to make a run for the White House. Her political star is rising. I'd like to help her along. She'd be a great choice to pass the baton to for the next term."

"Jack…"

"I don't want two terms, Ethan. I really don't." Jack's hand moved to Ethan's, covering the back of his before Ethan snaked their fingers together.

Enemy Of My Enemy

"And thoughts of a replacement secretary of state? If she accepts?"

"I'd like to ask her. I think she'll have good insight. I'll reach out, make the ask, and let you know when I hear back from her."

Jack stood, and Irwin and Ethan followed. "I'll work on getting you more information from Colombia, Mr. President. And I'll be waiting for your decision."

Ethan stayed with Jack through the afternoon, sitting beside the Resolute desk and talking through the ramifications of Irwin's strike team proposal. It was almost like old times, the two of them in private, discussing the political problems Jack faced. Almost. This was bigger, larger, and more surreal than anything before.

Diana Ramirez joined them, picking through the finer legal points of a strike team dedicated to the tracking and execution of an American citizen. A traitor, to be sure, but an American citizen. Legal precedent from a decade prior granted Jack's predecessors the authority to conduct extrajudicial executions of anyone who was an imminent threat to the United States and whose arrest was impractical, including American citizens. Still, Ramirez was exacting in her work, in protecting Jack from potentially catastrophic decisions.

Ethan sat back, and though he tried to listen, his mind was elsewhere. Back in the sands of Iraq and the mountains of Afghanistan. Before he'd been an agent, he'd been a soldier, and accepting this mission would bring him right back to those days. To the days when he hunted bad men doing evil things.

Squinting, he gazed out the windows of the Oval Office. *That* was the kind of reductionism he'd used for years. What he was truly about to do was open up a part of himself he'd buried. Reach back and touch a piece of his soul that had gone dark, twisted from death and war.

There was a part of him, buried deep, that wasn't a good man. Jack didn't see that side of him. He kept it hidden, buried under years of pushed-aside memories and an iron-clad grip on his heart.

Or, at least, he'd *had* an iron-clad grip on his heart. His eyes traveled over Jack's profile, over the lean, accented features, the Roman nose. His kiss-soft lips.

Ethan's world, his life, and even he himself had changed. Was continuing to change every day.

But, no matter what, there would always be that part of him, that pitch-black, oil-slick place buried in his soul that held all the things he never wanted to remember. He could feel it slide, slippery, like a snake against the base of his spine. The last time he'd touched his darkness, he'd been facing Jeff Gottschalk, a man who had a gun to Jack's head. His hatred had roared and he'd delighted in Jeff's murder. Crawling back from the edge of that had been soothed by Jack's love and he'd poured himself into what they had together. It had been a balm against his demons, a soothing caress that tamed his darker underbelly. Did he want to go near that again?

The opportunity to take down Madigan, the man who had almost taken Jack from him, called out to him, though. That shadowy corner of his soul yearned, begging for the chance to retaliate. To destroy.

His hands clenched into fists and his palms itched, desperate for action. He could practically taste the sand on his tongue, the grit of gunpowder and the sun-scorched heat of the desert.

He took a breath, closing his eyes as he dragged in a steady inhale. Things were different now. He was a different man, perhaps even a better man. He was with Jack. He was Jack's first gentleman.

Though, this wasn't what he'd thought being the first gentleman would be. From florists to state dinners to clandestine kill missions.

When would the whiplash set in?

Ramirez and Jack were still talking. "The Constitution defines treason as levying war against the US, adhering to our enemies, and giving them aid and comfort. No individual can be convicted of treason unless on the testimony of two witnesses or on confession in open court."

"I, Lawrence Irwin, Special Agent Collard, and Ethan all gave testimony in closed proceedings as direct witnesses to Madigan's actions. Director Campbell presented his findings from their investigation. Attorney General Carter issued a sealed indictment *in absentia* against Madigan and charged him with treason against the United States. She briefed the National Security Council, and you were present in that briefing." Jack and Ramirez went step-by-step, formulating their case and ensuring all legalities were followed.

Ramirez nodded and finally smiled. "I feel confident due process has been followed in the issuance of the indictment. Former General Madigan remains an imminent threat to the United States. Based on the facts at hand, I believe a National Security Presidential Directive authorizing lethal force against Madigan is legal. I'll have a memo for you in an hour."

"Thank you." Jack shook her hand. "You've done so much for me. Thank you, for everything."

Ramirez smiled, and her gaze bounced over to Ethan for a moment. "Happy to do my job, Mr. President."

Ethan waited for her to slip out before he spoke. "So we are going to do this? A black strike kill mission?"

"If he's making moves again, I want to shut him down before any of his schemes even has a prayer. Intel has been sketchy, but maybe this is where we'll get him. I don't want to quibble. I don't want to waste time. I just want him dead." Jack's eyes were hard.

"Jack..." He swallowed. "I'm with you all the way, always. But you need to know, a mission like this... There will be costs. There will be hard choices to make. There will be tactics needed that might be difficult for you. Men like Madigan don't have limits. They push and push and push until you're past your own borders. Doing things you thought you never, ever would."

Jack was silent.

"I come from that world. I have some history here, and I know the kinds of things we're going to have to do. Going to have to accept. There will be hard choices," he repeated.

"I have complete confidence in you, Ethan," Jack said softly. "I trust you completely in this, and in everything."

Snorting, Ethan looked down. "You know," he said, a mirthless chuckle falling from his lips, "I'm not that great a guy."

"You are to me."

Silence.

"You are." Reaching out, Jack tugged on Ethan's navy tie, gently pulling him close. Jack let his lips hover just in front of Ethan, for a moment, as Ethan stared him down with a quirked eyebrow and a shy smile.

And this was what he loved about Jack. Strength wrapped in an effusive optimism, a soul that promised the world would be a better place if you only just held on and never let go. A solid core of unflappability, the center of him rooted in gentle happiness. Jack radiated joy to Ethan's soul, and he basked in Jack's grins, his playful personality, like a tree turning its leaves to the sun. His whole life was reoriented toward Jack. Who would have thought his world would be remade by this man with a goofy smile and stunning blue eyes?

Leaning forward, Ethan dropped a quick kiss to the tip of Jack's nose and pulled back, grinning at Jack's surprised laugh.

Not missing a beat, Jack closed the fractional distance between them and captured Ethan's lips. His hands fell to Ethan's hips, and Ethan cupped Jack's face, his fingers sliding through the dark blond strands of Jack's hair. The kiss deepened, and Jack's hips started rolling into Ethan's.

Jack pulled Ethan flush against him and turned them both, steering Ethan toward one of the couches as he pushed Ethan's jacket down his arms. Ethan's fingers flew to Jack's tie, tugging on the red silk, loosening it and pulling it free. The tie sailed through the air, draping over the back of the second couch.

Jack's hands dropped to Ethan's belt buckle as his tongue dueled with Ethan's.

"Mr. President—" The door opened and Mrs. Martin, Jack's secretary, walked in.

Whirling away, Jack broke the kiss and turned his back to the door as Ethan collapsed to the couch, sitting and hunching over his lap. He shrugged back into his jacket.

Jack kept his back to the door as he reached out and swiped his tie from the other couch, rolling it around his hand as if he could hide it. "What's up, Mrs. Martin?" Ethan could hear the edge of hilarity in his voice, the forced lightness that trembled on the edges.

"Your photo op is here, Mr. President." She paused, the air thick like cotton. "Should I tell them to expect you in the Roosevelt Room in five minutes?"

Turning, Ethan caught Mrs. Martin's smirk. She was the proverbial White House grandmother, a little old lady who kept the president's schedule in perfect synchronicity and peered over the tips of her bifocals at you if you tracked mud on her office carpet.

"Yes, please, Mrs. Martin. Roosevelt Room in five. Got it." Jack sent a little wave over his shoulder. He didn't turn around.

Ethan didn't relax until the door clicked shut behind Mrs. Martin. He buried his face in his hands and groaned.

Jack doubled over and braced his hands on his knees. A half second later, he snorted, and then a torrent of giggles escaped.

Pulling the tips of his fingers down below his eyes, Ethan glanced across to his lover. He found a red-faced, giggling Jack bent over and trying to palm down his boner tenting his suit pants, his hair sticking up every which way thanks to Ethan's hands.

"Photo op?" Ethan's voice was still husky, and he shifted, trying to will his own erection down.

If possible, Jack's cheeks reddened further. "The Episcopal Diocese of Washington. Bishop Collins. I didn't realize the time." Exhaling again, Jack straightened and adjusted himself. There was still a bulge in the front of his pants.

Ethan helped Jack finger-comb his wild, interrupted-sex hair and then tied his tie for him, gently sliding the knot into place at Jack's neck. Jack cleared his throat, shook his right leg, and blushed again. Ethan dropped a kiss to Jack's pink cheek. "Knock 'em dead, gorgeous."

Ethan headed to the East Wing and his office after that, walking alongside a grinning Daniels. Ethan side-glared at him through the West Wing until Daniels spilled in the Colonnade. "Mrs. Martin told us all."

"Us all" was the team of agents on hand waiting to pick up Jack and Ethan as they made their way around the White House. Scott, Daniels, Welby, Hanier, and others. All had been trying to smother grins when Ethan slipped out of the Oval Office after Jack.

"I'll be sure to walk through mud for her."

Daniels winked and tugged open the door to the East Wing for Ethan. "Your funeral. But the blue balls will get you before she will, I'm sure."

Knocking just before five broke Ethan's concentration. He was back at the bins, looking through the cards they'd received. Dozens stuck up at odd angles. He'd show those to Jack.

"Permission to enter the first gentleman's office?" At the doorway, Scott Collard, Ethan's near-lifelong best friend and lead agent on Jack's Secret Service detail, grinned.

"Scott." Ethan rose and the two met in the middle, wrapping each other up in a giant bear hug, complete with back slaps and squeezes on the shoulder as they pulled apart. "You free? Where's Jack?"

"He's on the phone with Congressional leadership behind closed doors. I left Welby there to pick him up after, along with a bottle of aspirin."

Jack's conversations with the leadership had turned frigid and acerbic, going from awful—after their outing—to cataclysmic after the weekend. Ethan tried to shove the guilt away. "How are you doing?"

"Doing good. Tickled pink that I get to stay here in DC for my daughter's spring break." Scott tipped his head toward Ethan. "Thank you and the president for that."

"We were strongly encouraged to stay put." Ethan headed for his desk, and he and Scott ended up leaning side by side against Ethan's huge desk, hips bumping. "Not like this is going to be a good spring break." Ethan jerked his chin to the snow falling outside the window.

Soft flakes were descending over the city, blanketing the White House grounds. "Oh it's not so bad. It's a great view, Mr. First Gentleman. A step up from Horsepower."

Ethan snorted. Horsepower, the Secret Service command center for the White House, had no view. A basement beneath the president's Oval Office, Horsepower was as much a bunker as anything else. "This can't all be real. I keep thinking I'm going to wake up back in Iowa clutching a bottle of tequila and all of this..." He gestured around his office and then to himself. "It's all just some deranged drunk fantasy I've built."

Scott's eyes softened. "It's real, Ethan. You made this happen. *You*. Despite what everyone told you, even *me*. You made this work with him."

With him. With Jack. With the president of the United States. It still stopped him in his tracks, sometimes, that Jack had decided to take a chance on finding love with him.

It had almost ended too soon.

"All of this would be gone if it weren't for you, Scott."

"And don't you forget it." Scott's tone turned teasing, but the gentleness was still there. "Hauling your big butt across half of Africa and Saudi Arabia. You know my back still isn't right from carrying you, you big ol' baby?"

Ethan leaned his shoulder against his friend. "You saved my life."

"And you saved the world." Scott wrapped one arm around Ethan's shoulders. "Enjoy your life. Stop trying to worry yourself out of this." Ethan snorted, and Scott squeezed his shoulder again, shaking him slightly. "I know you."

Ethan's smile faded, and he looked down at the carpet.

"How are you? Really?"

"I'm... all right. Overwhelmed." He gestured to the bins of cards and thought of Irwin and the strike mission they'd signed up for. "Definitely way over my head and certain that this will all end up a disaster somehow, but..." He chuckled. "But I'm pretty damn happy."

Scott shook his head.

"It feels weird not to be armed." Ethan frowned and mimed reaching for the weapon that used to sit on his hip every single day. He'd had to surrender all of his weapons, even his personal handguns, to Scott after resigning from the Secret Service, as long as he was living in the Residence. "I feel naked."

"Sorry I'm late!" Daniels bustled in. He shed his wool coat and unwrapped a red scarf from around his neck, tossing the snow-covered clothes on the back of Ethan's couch, holding out a six-pack of Ethan's favorite beer. "They just started plowing while I was making the run."

"What the hell?" Ethan looked askance between his two friends, both grinning wildly and popping the tops of their beer bottles.

Daniels passed an open bottle to him. "First day celebration. C'mon, take it. You didn't think we were going to let this pass without some kind of toast, did you?"

Was there a better word, a bigger word, than thanks? How could he convey to his friends, to these two best friends of his, just what their unwavering support meant to him? From hell and back, from the brink of the end of the world to his uncertain steps as Jack's partner, they had never faltered, even when he'd been an utter idiot. "Guys—"

Scott grabbed his shoulder again and raised his beer bottle. "To the first gentleman of the United States. Ethan Reichenbach."

Bottles clinked. Daniels whooped, and the three men drank. "Also," Ethan said after he swallowed, "to Levi Daniels, the new head of my detail."

More cheering, another clink of their bottles, and another deep drag from their beers.

"Harry said to say hi." Daniels smiled, but it was tight. Their friend, Harry Inada, had transferred to headquarters and the intel teams. Getting shot by his boss in the Oval Office had made Inada reevaluate his priorities, especially with twin daughters waiting for him at home. He'd almost quit, but instead, made the transfer to I Street.

"Did you tell our new first gentleman his code name?" Scott spoke to Daniels but winked at Ethan.

"Oh no." Ethan groaned.

"Not yet." Swirling his beer, Daniels slowly smirked. "I can't take full credit for it, though—"

"Under the bus!" Scott shook his head and took a swig. "Traitor."

"This was all Scott's idea."

Knowing Scott, Ethan was up shit creek. "I'm scared to ask."

"We always gotta match the first letter of the code names for the first family. The president is 'Vigilant.' So we had to pick a V name for you." Daniels winked.

Ethan glared at Scott. "Victory, Valiant, Venture, hell, even Vegetable."

"Ohh, Vegetable, I like that. But your code name has already been chosen. It's deployed in the system."

"Goddamn it."

"First gentleman of the United States, code name...*Vigor*."

"Vigor? Jesus Christ!"

"It's accurate." Scott shrugged and downed another drag of beer.

"Daniels here," Daniels pretended to speak into his cuff, pantomiming a scene from the detail. "I've got BOTUS Vigor inbound for Vigilant. Make sure Vigilant is armed and ready."

Ethan's cheeks blazed, heat coursing through him from head to toe. "*Jesus...*"

Scott and Daniels laughed.

"BOTUS?" Ethan finally said, once he straightened and took another long drag from his beer. POTUS was the abbreviation commonly used for the president. FLOTUS was the designation for the first lady. Ethan had expected to see FGOTUS, though he cringed at the possible mutilations of the acronym that were sure to occur.

"Boyfriend of the United States. We thought about FGOTUS, but Director Triplett nixed it. Too much room for abuse." Daniels tipped his beer bottle toward Ethan, an almost salute. "I'm just waiting to change it to HOTUS."

Scott chuckled.

"Husband of the United States." Winking, Daniels managed to grin and drain his beer in the same move, despite Ethan glaring.

"Knock knock." A familiar voice called from the doorway, and Ethan snorted as Scott and Daniels snapped to attention, their Secret Service training ingrained in their bones. Both men tried to hide the beer bottles against their thighs.

Ethan smiled and raised his beer to Jack. "Come on in."

Hands in his pockets, Jack crossed Ethan's office and came to a stop just inside his spread legs as Ethan leaned back against his desk. One of Ethan's hands landed on Jack's hip, his thumb stroking along the seam in his suit jacket.

Jack leaned in for a quick kiss. "Hey, love."

Scott and Daniels grinned.

"Relax, please." Jack waved toward Daniels and Scott. "We're off the clock. The day is done. Time to chill."

"No such thing, Mr. President." Scott, at least, stopped trying to hide his beer.

"Please, it's Jack." Jack smiled as Daniels passed him a bottle.

"You'll never get them to bend on calling you Jack." Ethan drained the last of his beer and set it on the desk behind him. He held back from wrapping his arms around Jack, but just barely.

"I got you to call me Jack."

Scott had to swallow back a bark of laughter as Ethan deadpanned, "And look where we ended up."

"It's a dangerous slippery slope." Daniels's hands balanced in the air, weighing the two sins. "First name… First gentleman of the United States."

"Yeah, yeah. Hey, do you guys want to come on up for dinner? If you're free?" Jack quickly took a drink from his beer.

Ethan stared at Scott and Daniels, frozen in front of Jack. Daniels, at least, had eaten with them before, but not since the aftermath of the almost end of the world, when everything was still up in the air and each day felt like a movie on fast-forward. Reality had been untethered then, and the weight of Daniels staying for dinner in the president's study, just off the Oval Office, was different from having the two senior detail leads up in the Residence on a social visit.

Daniels's gaze darted to Scott. "Sure." He shrugged. "I've got no plans."

"My wife and daughter are at church tonight." Scott shot a questioning glance to Ethan, one last check. "I was on my own for dinner. Was going to hit a drive-through on the way home."

"No, no, no." Jack waved Scott's dinner plans away. "C'mon. Let's go. Prime rib tonight. And there's a bottle of wine the French prime minister gave me as a gift that's ready to open." He stood, grabbed Ethan's hand, and motioned for the door. "After you guys."

Shadows of a Former General Turned Fugitive Terrorist Haunt United States

Not since the days of General Benedict Arnold has the United States experienced so devastating a betrayal at the hands of a man sworn to defend her. Former General Porter Madigan fled the United States following the exposure of his plot to overthrow the US government in a false flag operation to detonate nuclear weapons in Washington DC and in the Middle East under the guise of a Caliphate attack. Madigan has seemingly since vanished, though he remains a serious concern for the US.

Some sources report that he has risen to become the CIA's number one target. "Every incident overseas is looked at through a new lens," an unnamed source said. "Is this what it appears on the surface? Or is there something more? Madigan led US special operations for decades. He knows infinitely more than we do, and we're just playing catch up."

4

South America
Altiplano Plateau

"To freedom."

Madigan passed Cook a tin cup filled with rotgut whiskey. It was too warm, and amber liquid sloshed over the rim. Madigan shrugged his apologies as Cook sucked the alcohol off his fingers.

Above, the Milky Way stretched across the midnight sky, from horizon to horizon, and below, in the valley they were making camp in, freed prisoners mingled with Madigan's handpicked men, the first officers of his new army. Rolled cigarettes and glass pipes were passed around, along with bottles of pesco and tequila. Bonfires crackled, and here and there, guitars strummed softly.

"I'm sorry it took so long. You were rotting in that cell for too many years."

Cook sipped his whiskey. Even though it was terrible by any standard, he didn't flinch. "I always knew you'd come. I never lost faith."

Madigan raised his own tin cup in a silent toast.

"I'm sorry about Gottschalk. He was a good man. A good operative."

"I think that kid could have done anything." Madigan stared down into the amber whorls of his whiskey, remembering Gottschalk's sullen frown and his dark eyes. "He was always up for the hardest project. Always ready for a challenge."

"Chief of staff in the White House." Cook whistled low. "I still remember the young kid we recruited in Iraq."

"He grew up. He did everything perfect. Everything. He deserved more than what he got."

Cook stared at him over the rim of his cup. "He didn't die for nothing. We'll do this, General. Our new world is coming."

"I remember when we started down this path. You, me, and him. Do you?"

"How could I ever forget?"

"We were perfect. We had the world in our hands. So much power. We could have remade the whole world, and then—" Madigan shook his head, scowling.

Everything had changed in the Iraq War. Everything. In the beginning, he'd been a warrior unchained, alive for the first time in his life. They had chased their enemies across the planet, hounded them again and again until they were begging in the dust. Cities rose and fell in the palms of their hands. They owned the whole world with bullets and bombs.

Men were made and defined in the war, their souls cut and hardened in fire and fury. It was the only way to be alive, to feel like you were worth something. To fight, to hunt, to destroy, to bleed. Strength was finally valued, true strength, and he and men like him had a place in the world.

And then, everything changed.

America changed. The presidency. The politics. The people.

They didn't want men like Madigan anymore.

They'd given up on the warrior's dream: the world remade into an iron crucible, all for America's future. America had given up on them. Given up on the missions. Given up on a future of power. America had turned its back on the generation of men they'd forged out of sand and rage and combat.

The forgotten warriors worked hard to figure out how to live again, figure out how to bury that dark part of themselves, shove it deep down into the bottom of their soul and desperately try to forget what they could be, if only. Some took to the bottle. Others grabbed their guns, swallowed steel bullets while screaming in rage.

And Madigan picked up so many more, gathering them close and promising retribution. So many wounded hearts and bruised souls. He'd said, "America turned their backs on us, but we won't forget. We won't ever forget. We will rise again. Forge a new world out of the ashes of their broken promises."

America had decided to change. So, Madigan decided to change, too. He worked instead toward a different future, one for him and the men he'd bled for, ached for, killed for, for the length of his whole life.

He'd give the whole world to them. Let them run free, their hearts blazing.

"How many do we have now?" Cook nodded to the valley and the band of freed men grouped together under the watchful gaze of Madigan's new officers.

"Four thousand after today. We'll get more tomorrow. And more after that. Not counting the others I still have in play around the world, undercover and wholly devoted to our cause."

"I'm impressed. Four thousand hardened criminals? I would expect them to be slitting throats down there by now." He toasted Madigan. "You haven't lost your touch, General. You could recruit the wolves to our cause."

"It's the same way I recruited you. I gave those men a dream and a promise. You were quite a wolf yourself when I found you. The Butcher. I knew I needed you."

Cook's smile vanished. "You swore to me there was a world coming where I would be free. I wouldn't ever suffer again, and I would live all the rest of my days in joy. I could drink the blood of my enemies and bathe in their bones and laugh in the face of anyone who cowered in fear. I wouldn't ever have to hide again." His eyes blazed, gleaming unnaturally in the still South American midnight.

"I'm giving that world to you," Madigan swore. "A new dawn is coming for us, Captain. A new sky awaits us all. We're close. So close."

"What do you need me to do?"

"What you do best. Build up bodies. Harden souls." He nodded to the valley. "These men need inspiration. You can be that for them. And, I have something else for you. Something only you can do."

Cook's head tilted, just so.

"We need to break men as well. Our enemies are not the same as they once were. They have new faces, now." President Jack Spiers and his lover, Ethan Reichenbach, flashed before his mind. How unbelievable that a scandalous affair could bring down his life's work. Only once. Never again. "New alliances. The Russians and the Americans are getting closer."

Cook threw back the last of his whiskey, swallowing it down in two gulps.

"They're going to come after us. Hit us with everything they can. I wrote the playbook they're drawing from, but each man who challenges us brings his own heart and soul into the game. We take that. We take everything they are and we turn it against them. All of them, from the president and his lover down to the men they send to hunt us. That's how we win, Captain."

Madigan leaned forward, gripping Cook's shoulder. "We must turn this world inside out. Tear still-beating hearts from chests. Dig the knife in deepest, where it hurts the absolute most. Break apart our enemies. Not just their minds. Their souls as well."

Cook nodded. "Where do I begin?"

5

White House Residence

Jack refilled Scott's wine glass and sat back, relaxing after dinner. They had all scooted away from the dining table, balancing full wine glasses on their knees as they shared stories. Ethan's eyes were bright, glittering with joy, and the laugh lines on his face pulled at Jack's heart.

He wanted to give Ethan this, this normalcy, this happiness. He'd seen Ethan collapse into himself in Iowa, shuttered and stoic as the world caged them in, but the anchor of Ethan's friends seemed to ease his wary fear.

He'd taken Ethan from his normal life, from the safe anonymity of his existence, and brought him to the world's biggest microscope. Ethan, a man devout in his privacy, had endured an existential crisis before he bent enough to befriend him.

And from friendship to *this*. In many ways, it had to be Ethan's worst nightmare to be so exposed. He'd spent his lifetime living in the shadows, watching and protecting. The spotlight, and the gilded cage of the White House, was going to hurt.

But right now, he could give Ethan this. A night with his friends. Laughter. Normalcy.

And men who were quickly becoming Jack's friends as well. Daniels was impossible to dislike, and Scott and Ethan were practically brothers the way they bickered and played off one another. He and Scott hadn't directly interacted much, other than in an official capacity, since he'd ordered Scott to rescue Ethan in Ethiopia. A mission that had seemingly sent Scott to his death. After his and Ethan's triumphant return, Scott had turned his attentions to his family, and when he'd been promoted to Ethan's position, there was an extra air of officiousness that had settled over the Secret Service.

Not that he could blame them. He'd caused the agency's largest scandal in its history. Starting a relationship with an agent in secret.

Sometimes, late at night, he remembered his and Ethan's first text conversation and the confession Ethan had shared about the power imbalance wielded between a president and everyone else. The darkness chewed on his worries. Had he pressured Ethan into this? Was this, *truly*, what Ethan wanted? He'd been the one to propose they start something, that they "figure this out," this thing that had risen between them. Affection and attraction and so much more, so unexpectedly. Had he pushed Ethan too much? That day, and every day after?

Enough. Ethan was smiling and that was what mattered. Jack tried to focus in on the conversation, Ethan and Scott trading stories about being pranked by the FBI during an interagency operation in their first years before Daniels had joined. Scott was laughing so hard he was wiping at the corners of his eyes and Ethan had one of the brightest smiles Jack had ever seen.

Daniels sat back with Jack, watching the two laugh like children.

"I am not going to miss those FBI dorks." Ethan was still laughing as he twirled his wine glass. "God, they were a pain in the ass."

"I think that's what they said about you." Scott sent a pointed look across the table to Ethan.

"On the topic of Ethan's most embarrassing moments," Daniels said, quirking his eyebrows with a wry grin. "I remember one of my first assignments with you both. The West Point Classic."

Ethan groaned and dropped his head, letting it hang between his shoulders. Scott almost snorted wine through his nose. "With Wilson? Jesus Christ, you couldn't keep him contained!"

"Wilson? President Wilson?" Jack sat forward, his elbows balanced on the edge of the table. Ethan rarely spoke about Jack's predecessors, except to say that, on the whole, they weren't the friendliest people.

"He wasn't a bad guy," Ethan demurred. "Certainly not the biggest asshole we've dealt with. But he must have had ADHD or something. You couldn't keep him still, not for anything."

Scott was laughing into his wine glass. "Say that again."

Jack watched Ethan, waiting for the story with a grin on his face. Ethan gave him a long-suffering sigh but launched in with gusto. He seemed to speak just to Jack, and deep within his chest, Jack's heart beat faster.

Ethan was beautiful, just like this. He hung on the sound of Ethan's voice, the rich timbre and the rise.

"The West Point Classic football game is a pretty big deal. You didn't go this year because the secretary of defense went. But Wilson always wanted to go, and it's a nightmare to coordinate security. The FBI runs the game as part of their Special Events squad, and they don't play well with others, so we end up having to pull rank and force our security plans on top of their infrastructure." Ethan shook his head, groaning. "Anyway. I was younger then," he said slowly, grinning, "and it was one of my first assignments where I was charged with securing POTUS for a segment of the event. It was the worst segment, but I was proud."

Scott and Daniels were grinning, and Scott leaned back, balancing an ornately carved Jefferson dining chair on two of its cherrywood legs.

"So Wilson, who can't be contained for five seconds, follows me down into the basement of the football field. The plan was to stage the president in the visiting team locker rooms until the game started and then bring him up securely. Everything nice and controlled."

"I do know how you like to keep things secure." Jack winked.

Ethan pressed on, his eyes bright. "Those locker rooms were disgusting. I don't know if that's some kind of football thing, where you shit on the team visiting your stadium, but they were rank. I had just walked him in and I was doing my final checks around the room. Well," Ethan rolled his eyes, "dummy me, expecting him to follow the plan. I turned my back on him. Wilson walked in, took one sniff, and said, 'I'm outta here.'" Ethan slapped his palms together, one hand flying forward, mimicking flight. "He took the fuck off, racing out of the tunnel toward the field. The football stadium with twenty thousand people in it, including all of my bosses."

"Oh no…" He didn't mean to laugh at Ethan, but he could just picture his lover, panicked and losing his mind over his protectee pulling an escape attempt. "You chased him down, right?"

"Oh, of course, I chased him down. I was going to bring him back to the locker room and explain to him the importance of listening to the Secret Service." His fist hit the table, and the dishes jumped.

Jack snorted.

"Wilson was a very fast man. I was running all out, but so was he."

"He had a taste of freedom!"

"Yes! And he was taking it! He ran down that tunnel and burst onto the field, right into the directors of the Secret Service and the FBI, a whole bunch of generals, and about all of the senior agents." His arms swung at his sides as he pretended to run. "And then there was me, chasing him out of the tunnel, losing my shit."

Loud laughter filled the room at Ethan's tale of woe. Ethan shook his head, chuckling, and held Jack's gaze.

Jack reached out and laced his fingers through Ethan's on the tabletop.

"We were up in the stands, watching the crowds. We had to listen to this one—" Scott jerked his chin toward Ethan. "—talk, talk, talk about how he was 'securing POTUS.'"

Jack couldn't suppress the snort or the giggles that came after, even as Ethan glared good-naturedly at Scott. "I can see it all perfectly," he said, leaning over and pressing a kiss to Ethan's knuckles.

Scott pulled out his phone and checked the time. "This has been fun, but I've got to head out. My wife and daughter will be home soon." He stood, and so did Daniels.

"We'll have to do this again, and soon. Please don't be strangers." Jack rose with Ethan, keeping their fingers linked. "Drive safe out there."

"They're already plowing. And yes, Mr. President, we should do this again. Gotta keep your first gentleman in line."

"Leave the embarrassing stories behind next time." Ethan pretended to grouse as Scott and Daniels laughed themselves out of the dining room and down the hall toward the main staircase.

"Why don't you walk them out?"

"No, I'll take care of this." Ethan started stacking plates, but Jack stilled him.

"Go. They're your best friends. I'll clean up."

Leaning close, Ethan pressed a kiss beneath Jack's ear. "Be right back."

Jack shuttled plates and silverware and four wine glasses to the Residence's kitchen and started loading the dishwasher. His thoughts wandered, circling back, always, to Ethan. His smile. The sound of his laughter. Jack's heart seemed to swell. He was going to make love to Ethan tonight, slow and sweet. He wanted to feel Ethan in his arms. Taste his kisses. Press their bodies close together.

Footsteps pounded down the hallway, someone running at a fast pace.

Jack froze, the wine glass in his hand slipping free and crashing to the floor. Shards of crystal scattered and the stem rolled away, a long, slithering warble of glass on marble.

Footsteps pounding, running through the West Wing. Gunshots blazing, popping in every direction. Plaster walls exploding. Shouts, guttural cursing. Jeff's face, sneering. Pushing him to his knees with his hands laced behind his head, the world moving in slow motion, each heavy breath seemingly a lifetime—

Pete appeared in the doorway to the kitchen, leaning against the doorframe as he heaved in breath after breath. He was in the same shirt from that morning, now completely untucked, and he'd lost his tie. His pants had a ketchup stain on the knee. "Mr. President." Pete pulled out his cell phone.

Shaking off the clawing memories, Jack stepped over the shattered glass. What would bring Pete running up to the Residence at nine at night? Dread settled heavy in his chest. "What is it? What's wrong?"

Pete swiped on his screen and passed the phone over. "I just got this from the editor of the Washington Eagle. It's their headline tomorrow morning. Their lead story."

On screen, a picture of the Washington Eagle's morning headline leaped out at him, screaming in bold capital letters: "The President's Lover's Lovers". A sub-headline drove the nail deeper into Jack's heart, a heavy swing of the journalistic hammer. "The Fifty in DC Who Told All and the Dozens Still Keeping Their Secrets."

For a moment, he couldn't breathe. The air wouldn't come and his lungs seemed to stutter. His mind went blank. His lips moved, but no sounds, no words fell out.

"Mr. President?" Pete stepped closer, a worried frown on his face. "Sir?"

"What's wrong?"

Jumping, Jack looked up, right into Ethan's worried gaze. He tried to hide the phone, tried to darken the screen before Ethan saw, but it was too late. He moved to Jack's side and gently took it from him, powering it on.

All the while, Pete was talking, a fast torrent of words, but Jack heard nothing.

This is going to kill Ethan.

Color drained from Ethan's face as he read the headline. His jaw dropped as if suddenly broken, unhinged, and his eyes bulged, shock mixing with terror on the edges of his gaze. He stumbled backward, dropping the phone as his back hit the kitchen island.

Pete swore and barely managed to catch his cell before it clattered to the marble tile.

Jack exhaled, able to finally breathe again for the first time since Pete had entered. Sounds came thundering back, Pete's low cursing, the hum of the refrigerator. Colors sharpened, the blue of Ethan's suit pants and the crisp white of his dress shirt contrasting with the light flooring and dark wood cabinets. The paleness of his face.

"Sir, we have *got* to get on this. I've read the whole thing, and... *damn.*" Pete sighed. "We need to come up with a response."

"Can they be convinced not to publish?"

"No, sir. The Eagle is a conservative rag. This is a dream for them. There's all kinds of stuff about traditional values and the corruption of the American way in here. And they take some pretty big hits at you. They don't pull their punches."

Ethan pitched forward, burying his face in his hands.

Jack started for him.

"Sir, the web version hits the wires at midnight. We have three hours to address this. We have to say *something*. Prepare *something*, Mr. President."

Ethan. He had to get to Ethan. He hadn't said a word since he'd read the headline. What was Ethan thinking? Ethan's pain, his bare mortification, loomed larger in Jack's mind than the fallout to his presidency Pete was so concerned with. "I'll meet you in the Oval Office in ten, Pete."

"Sir?" Pete frowned, squaring his shoulders and gripping his phone. "Sir, we *don't* have a moment to waste—"

"Ten minutes." Jack glared at Pete. "I will see you there. Go."

Pete went, his shoulders sagging as he turned and headed out.

Jack stood in front of Ethan, reaching for him. "Say something. Ethan. Say something."

Ethan pulled away from Jack and the sound of his voice. "All I do is hurt you. Hurt your presidency. God, I should never have—"

"Shhh. We'll get through this, Ethan. Like everything else. Together."

"I'm supposed to keep you safe. And all I'm doing is hurting you. And your career. Over and over again."

"Ethan…" Jack fumbled for something, anything to say.

"They're using me to attack you." A surge of anger seemed to flash through Ethan. His hands clenched into fists as he pulled free from Jack's hold. "Go," he growled. "You need to go take care of this."

"I need to be with you."

Ethan shook his head and closed his eyes. "No one needs to be with me right now."

Five hours later, Jack finally stumbled back up to the Residence, to his and Ethan's bedroom.

Ethan's laptop was open on the bed, the Washington Eagle article up and live on the website. Sweat-soaked workout clothes lay in a heap on the floor, and in the bathroom, the shower was running.

Jack plopped down at the foot of the bed. His eyes traveled over the article, picking out the worst of the worst.

Ethan, according to the article, was a man void of morals, a wanton gay manslut with an insatiable sexual appetite. After conquering nearly all of Washington DC, he'd seduced Jack. Salacious detail was paid to Ethan's preferred sex acts, given to the reporter by former lovers, all eager for their moment in the spotlight. One was certain that Jack loved to be pounded through the mattress, since that was, apparently, Ethan's specialty, along with amazing rimjobs. That Jack must give great blowjobs since Ethan loved a good suck. Or how Jack must love to bottom, to satisfy Ethan's inexhaustible appetite.

And Jack was the vapid, empty-headed president who had been taken by Ethan's malicious, scandalous ways. Seduced and led astray. Under the influence of a sex-crazed homosexual. A president who spent more of his days getting bent over the Resolute desk than actually governing. Who let himself be led by the sexual perversions of his lead detail agent, and who also let Ethan participate in governing. A complete failure of a president and of a man, Jack apparently loved every minute of Ethan's heady seduction, so much so that he moved this degenerate into the White House.

Questions raged from the article. Who was Ethan? Who had access to the president? What kind of moral depravity had descended over the White House? How could the American people trust their leader?

The shower stopped. A glass door creaked open and then slammed shut. The sound of Ethan toweling off came from the shut door.

Jack waited.

Ethan froze when he padded back into the bedroom, towel wrapped tight around his waist and beads of water dripping from the ends of his hair. A scar crossed over his abdomen, just to the left of his belly button.

Jack watched Ethan's chest tighten, watched him inhale and hold his breath.

"Did you read it?"

Ethan nodded.

"The White House does not comment on the first family's personal lives or on malicious tabloid trash. Or pieces of salacious fantasy fiction." Jack recited the line he and Pete had hammered out, arguing back and forth for hours. Jack refused to discuss their relationship. Pete refused to let the article pass without a response. Back and forth, for hours.

Ethan looked down, but not before Jack caught a waver of uncertainty in his steely gaze. "Jack—"

Silent, Jack waited. Ethan could take his time thinking through the right way to say something sometimes, and Jack had learned to be patient rather than push him too hard.

A deep swallow, and then Ethan finally spoke. "I'm sorry," he breathed. "Jack, I'm sorry. For everything. For… fucking up your presidency. For all of that." He waved toward his laptop and the article. "I never thought about how everything I've done could hurt you. Fuck… What they say about you. I'm so fucking sorry."

"Ethan, you have nothing to apologize for. Nothing."

"I'm fucking everyth—"

"I don't care about the media." Jack interrupted Ethan's continued litany of his perceived sins. "I don't care, Ethan. I don't care about the papers, about the news channels. I don't care about the columnists. I've spent my whole political career getting ripped apart by the press for one thing or the other. I'm *used* to it. I. Don't. Care." Sighing, Jack's shoulders slumped, and he held out one hand toward Ethan. "I love you. And whatever garbage they want to print has no impact what I think or how I feel. If this was an attempt to make me doubt you, or shake my confidence in you, they failed."

At that, Ethan looked up, finally meeting Jack's gaze with something other than wariness.

Those were brave words. Jack's belly button clenched. "But *you're not* used to this. *I* should be the one apologizing. You never asked for this mess. You never asked for any of this." He gestured around the room, trying to encompass the White House and the political circus their lives had become. "You had a life, a normal, happy, full life. And then I barged in, and I pushed and I pushed, and—" Jack broke off with a quiet exhale.

He looked down. Swallowed.

Their bed had been remade, the Navy stewards bustling through and remaking their world each day, making everything around them look picture-perfect. A snapshot of pristine peace, as if their rooms could somehow imbue that tranquility into their lives. Jack's eyes caught on a loose thread, ivory cotton sticking out awry. Reaching out, he tried to smooth the thread back. It popped up.

All day, he'd tried to smooth everything over, from the moment they'd awoken. Trying to make things perfect. And now, in the dead of night, just one day into their new lives—

Snippets of the article replayed in his mind, sentences that wouldn't let go of his worries. "Are you—" His throat clenched. He tried again, this time looking up and finding Ethan's dark gaze. "Is this what you want? Us? Here?"

Ethan padded across their bedroom to Jack's side. He reached for Jack. Jack pressed a lingering kiss to Ethan's knuckles and then laid his cheek across the back of his hand.

"Jack—" Ethan's voice broke off. His other hand rose, fingers sliding through Jack's hair. "I love you so fucking much. It gets hard to breathe sometimes when I think about you."

Jack stood, and Ethan's hand dragged across his cheek, cupping his face when they were facing each other. Jack mirrored Ethan, holding his face with one hand as their breaths mingled.

"I'm sorry," Ethan breathed. "I'm so sorry—"

"Shhh." Jack nosed at Ethan's chin, his stubble whispering over him. "*I'm* sorry, Ethan. Sorry for all of this."

"Most days I think I'm dreaming. I can't believe this is really happening. I never thought, ever, that I'd love someone this much. Or that you could love me back when I fell for you." As Ethan whispered, Jack's lips found his, and he pressed slow kisses against his words. "I just don't want you to be hurt because of me."

Jack's lips closed over Ethan's. His hands slipped through Ethan's wet hair and slid down his neck, down his back, and into the towel wrapped around his waist. A gentle tug, and the towel dropped to the floor.

Ethan's arms wrapped around Jack, cradling him as Jack pulled their bodies close, until Ethan's warm, naked body was pressed tight to his. *God, I can never get enough of this. You're perfect, Ethan. Perfect.*

He turned Ethan, pressing the backs of his legs against their bed. Ethan collapsed to their mattress, his burning gaze fixed on Jack.

Jack tugged his tie free and started down the line of buttons on his shirt. His cock pressed against his suit pants, against his zipper, already hot and hard at just the sight of Ethan laid out.

"The president must like intense lovers. I've never had a lover more intense or more adventurous than Ethan. It was two days, a whirlwind weekend, but I can still remember it like it was last week."

Stilling, Jack's eyes shuttered closed as his breath faltered. Shirt open, his hands froze as he worked over the buttons at his cuffs. Another quote from the article slammed into him.

"Ethan's a total top. 100%. He gave me the ride of my life, and I loved every minute of it. The president must love it, too. I mean, who wouldn't love being topped by him? He's so talented."

"Jack?" Ethan's voice, an edge of worry cutting through the husky depths.

That damn article. Ethan's lovers, his past, reared in Jack's mind. Brave words he'd spoken before, about the article having no impact on him. Five hours of dissecting each statement, seeing the words on repeat. Ethan's past, his love life before Jack laid bare.

Was Jack really what Ethan wanted? Jack, a complete novice to Ethan's world? He could hardly be described as adventurous in bed. He still didn't know what he was doing, more times than not. His fumbles had to be so far from Ethan's experiences, so incredibly far.

He wanted to be better. Wanted to give Ethan better. Wanted to be everything for Ethan. Wanted Ethan to be so damn happy with him.

Tearing the shirt free, Jack balled it up and threw it behind him. He hurried out of his pants and then crawled onto the bed, locking gazes with Ethan.

For every inch he moved up Ethan's body, he dropped a kiss. A hot lick. A kiss bruise left on Ethan's inner thigh. The bone of his hip. The muscle below his belly button. Gentle nibbles on each nipple. Fingers scratching down his ribs. Kisses rained down on his collarbone, up to his jaw, and behind his ear.

Shivering and shaking, Ethan was a mess of overwrought nerves and panting breaths when Jack finally pressed their bodies together, face-to-face. Ethan grabbed his waist and his thighs wrapped around Jack's hips. "Jack, God, Jack..."

His words ignited a fire within Jack, an inferno of desire that burst from his heart. *Please, yes, God, please, be mine. I want to make it so good for you, Ethan. So good for you.* Never separating, Jack thrust against Ethan, their bodies sliding together. Ethan's fingers dug into Jack's waist and then his back, fingernails scratching over Jack's skin on either side of his spine. Jack rocked faster, harder, driving his body into Ethan's, groaning as he pressed open-mouthed kisses to Ethan's neck and jaw.

"Love you," Jack breathed. "Love you so much. I'll make it so good for you. I'll be good for you, I swear."

Ethan moaned, and his fingers dug into Jack's back. His hands slid down, curving over Jack's ass, gripping tight.

Jack felt his orgasm building. A coil of heat, of tension. Curling around Ethan, his cock slid hard and fast against Ethan's, hips grinding as he gasped into Ethan's shoulder. His teeth closed around Ethan's collarbone as his come swept through him and heat flooded between their bodies.

Beneath him, Ethan stiffened and his head arched back, the long line of his throat exposed as his Adam's apple bobbed. Another flood of heat, sticky and wet on their bellies, as Ethan shuddered and his hands clenched on Jack's ass.

Jack collapsed on top of Ethan as Ethan's thighs splayed wide, his feet falling to the mattress. Heavy breaths filled their bedroom, exhausted pants as Jack rested his cheek on Ethan's shoulder.

The words from Ethan's past lovers kept repeating in his mind, clinging to his memory. Uncertainty hovered on the edge of his post-orgasmic lassitude, a tension that kept him conflicted.

Ethan's hands slid up and down Jack's back. "Jack... You already are good for me. You're perfect for me."

Jack pushed up to his elbows, hovering over Ethan. His chest clenched, his heart hammered, and his lungs seemed to stutter to a stop. Gazing up at him, Ethan's eyes held what felt like the whole universe's weight in love, a look so tender, so full of adoration and devotion, and all for him.

Not one of Ethan's past lovers had ever said anything about Ethan's eyes. Or said that when he looked their way, it seemed like the sun was shining in the sky just for them. Or spoke about how their heart seemed to stop and start with the brilliance of Ethan's smiles. No one could describe just how perfect his laugh lines were, or how the memory of his kiss could stop them in their tracks.

No one else had ever felt that. Ever experienced that.

No one else had ever loved Ethan. Not like Jack loved him.

And Ethan… The way he talked about Jack. Was it possible? Out of everyone from Ethan's past, was it possible that Jack was the man who had managed to capture Ethan's heart? Capture his love?

How could he be that lucky?

"I am with you all the way," Jack whispered as he pressed his forehead to Ethan's cheek, his throat clenched tight. "All the way."

They would make this work, damn it.

6

Moscow

Mono Bar, Moscow's premier gay bar on Pokrovskiy Boulevard, was packed. Mono Bar was one gay bar that had opened under Putin and endured throughout the years. And for months, since President Puchkov's public political friendship with President Spiers had unfolded and President Puchkov had rescinded the worst of the laws against gay Russians, they all were enjoying a tiny modicum of freedom.

Senior Lieutenant Sasha Andreyev, of the Russian Army Air Force, slid his hands down the bare chest of the stranger he was grinding behind. The stranger's ass was pert, his body slender, angular, and Sasha had been grinding against him for several songs. His hands roamed up and down the man's front, stroking skin, pinching nipples, and rubbing his hardening cock through his thin, skintight pants.

His dance partner leaned back, resting his head on Sasha's shoulder. "Are you going to fuck me or not?"

Growling, Sasha's hands gripped tight on his partner's hips. He leaned in, capturing his lips in a searing kiss. His partner bit down on his bottom lip.

"My car is on the street."

"Take me there. Now."

On the way out of the bar, Sasha shoved him up against the wall and sucked on his nipples. His partner leaped into his arms, wrapping his legs around Sasha's waist. Sasha ground against him until a bouncer forcefully separated their sloppy kiss. Laughing, Sasha's partner finally dragged him out the front door and then waited, shirtless, in the cold night, his chest heaving. Moscow's snow had melted from the sidewalk, but drifts clung to the rooftops above and coated the park across the street.

Sasha dragged him close and wrapped his arms around him. Sasha was larger, more muscular, and his arms swallowed his partner. "This way," he said, sucking on his ear.

A block down, Sasha unlocked the passenger door of his rickety GAZ and slid in, pulling his dance partner with him and onto his lap. Kissing turned to unzipping their flies, messy handjobs, and in minutes, the windows were completely fogged. Sasha peeled his partner's pants down and sucked him deep, moaning while he fingered his partner's asshole open. He fumbled blindly in the glove compartment, searching for the lotion and condoms he'd thrown in there earlier.

The lotion was cold, and his partner hissed as Sasha worked it into his ass. A kiss to his cock was his apology, and then Sasha rolled the condom over his own cock and guided his partner down.

In minutes, they were rocking his beater car hard on the streets of Moscow as Sasha grabbed his partner's hips and thrust, driving in and out as deep and hard as he could. His partner moaned, eyes rolling back in his head, and he grasped Sasha's shoulders.

Too soon, he felt the curl in his abdomen, the warmth beginning to spread as his balls tightened. He reached for his partner's hard cock, jerking him fast and rough.

His partner came first, trembling and curling over Sasha with a shout, and his come dribbled all over Sasha's hand and down to his lap. Gripping his hips again, Sasha cursed and drove into him, once, twice, and then released, emptying his load into the condom.

Grinning, his partner nuzzled his face for a moment and whispered in his ear, "Thanks." He slid off Sasha's cock and shimmied back into his pants. "I'm going back. You?"

Sasha panted as his cock softened and the come cooled on his bare lap. "Maybe." He shrugged. Or maybe not. He had a long drive back to the base in Andreapol. Maybe he'd just smoke a cigarette, grab a coffee, and head back.

"See you around." With a wink, his partner pushed open the fogged-up car door and slid off his lap, stepping back into the snow-strewn Moscow street. Sweat glistened down his skin, and goose bumps erupted in the freezing air. He shivered, grinned back at Sasha, and shut the car door behind him.

Sasha heard the crunch of the man's shoes on the wet pavement and watched him head back to the club. He sighed as he slipped the condom off and shoved it in an old paper coffee cup on his dash. He tried to wipe away the come as best he could with some napkins he'd swiped from the coffee shop before he slid his pants back up.

If he grabbed some coffee, ate, and then hit the road, he could be back at the base by five in the morning, before his preflight. Before he went up in his MiG and touched the sky.

Rubbing his hands over his face, Sasha slid across to his driver's seat and grabbed his keys from where he'd thrown them on the dash. The high of his orgasm was fading, replaced by the ever-present pool of dark shame buried in his gut. Why he needed this, he didn't know. Why had the universe made him this way?

Over thirty years of questioning, but he'd never found an answer. He just learned to deal with it, slaking his lust when he needed and then burying his desires as deep as he could.

Sighing, Sasha turned the key in his ignition. The engine sputtered, once, twice, and then turned over.

He'd gotten the need out of his system for now. Time to head home.

Senator Stephen Allen Rips into President and First Gentleman Following Exposé

Republican Senator Stephen Allen tore into President Spiers following a scathing exposé of Ethan Reichenbach's personal life prior to becoming the first gentleman. "This is outrageous," Allen said, speaking to commentators and reporters throughout the day. "Just who is this man, this Ethan Reichenbach? What kind of person is now living in the White House? What sort of influence does he carry over the president? The American people should be extremely concerned about this relationship and the supposed values it represents. Look at what's happened in just a few days. Our international standing has plummeted." Allen went on to say, later, that the president and his partner were "not the kind of men the American people want to have leading them."

7

White House

Day two of Ethan's tenure as first gentleman dawned with snow still falling over DC. The White House was blanketed, and most of DC shivered to a halt, the storm seeming to slow the world down for a moment.

Even the protestors thinned out across the South Lawn.

Ethan woke Jack by slipping under the covers and swallowing him deep before sliding together, body to body. After, Jack wanted to go back to sleep, but Ethan badgered him into the shower. They washed each other slowly, trading kisses under the spray until the White House's old water pipes groaned and the water started to go tepid.

Daniels and Scott met them both at the base of the stairs, along with Secret Service agents dotted at the doors and hallways. A beefed-up presence in the White House had been a staple of life since the attempted coup.

Ethan could feel the hot stares of his former fellow agents. No one said a word about the Washington Eagle article scorching the front pages of DC, but they didn't have to. Their wide, sympathetic eyes said enough.

In the Oval Office, Daniels and Scott crowded close, holding Daniels's phone up for them to see.

"Mr. First Gentleman, your press secretary was on the early morning news shows talking about the article." A video stream froze with Brandt's face and the Office of the First Gentleman's seal emblazoned behind him, side by side with a morning anchor from TNN.

"Shit." A dull throb started at the base of Ethan's skull. "Let's see it."

Scott and Jack hovered as the video restarted. Brandt, nerdy Brandt in his wire-rimmed glasses, talked fast, frowning with a thin crease furrowed between his eyebrows.

"Neither the White House nor the Office of the First Gentleman, comment on tabloid trash or salacious pieces of fantasy media," Brandt said, speaking over the anchor's fast questions.

At least he'd stayed with Pete and Jack's statement so far.

"Do you want to shout about it or do you want to have a conversation?" Brandt glared and the anchor sat back, her lips pursed. "I have a few things to say in response to this article."

"He's not supposed to do this," Ethan groaned as Brandt began to speak again.

"The first gentleman took over his Office yesterday and I had the privilege of meeting him then. This morning, we woke up to a piece of predatory media masquerading as journalism. Please let me remind you that the article you refer to speaks erroneously and egregiously about an American hero. The first gentleman of the United States is a decorated Army veteran and has served with distinction in the Secret Service for over ten years. He is responsible for saving the life of the president, all those living in the greater Washington DC metro area, and countless more overseas. While his accomplishments do not fully describe his character, they provide a remarkable representation."

Ethan stopped breathing.

The anchor tried to speak again, starting with "But—"

"I'm not finished. In meeting the first gentleman of the United States, I found him to be an extraordinary, humble, and reserved man, completely at odds with the salacious story printed today. Every American needs to make up their own mind about the first gentleman, taking into account responsible, factual reporting. As for me, I am a fan of the man, and I'm proud to work for the first gentleman. It's up to the American people now. But I, and everyone here, urge the American people to listen responsibly to their media and to take the measure of the man in full. Don't just listen to garbage."

The camera feed that Daniels was tuned into froze.

Silence filled the Oval Office. Daniels and Scott watched Ethan carefully.

"Well," Jack said, after a moment. "He and Pete are going to be great friends."

Irwin texted just before lunch, asking to see Jack and Ethan behind closed doors as soon as possible. Ethan headed over to the West Wing and ran into Irwin, who was scrolling through his cell phone with another stack of Top Secret folders under his arms.

"Lawrence." Jack gave his chief of staff a tired smile as they both entered the Oval Office. "Don't take this the wrong way, but sometimes I dread seeing you."

"More intel, Mr. President." He looked to Ethan. "I think it's time for us to mobilize."

Irwin opened the folders on Jack's desk and pointed to three different photos of destroyed and smoldering prisons. Mangled cell bars and collapsed, scorched brick stared up from the photos, along with black smoke rising through the air and splatters of blood.

"Madigan?"

"We believe so. The same symbol was found at every site." Irwin passed a photo to Ethan, a series of photo crops showing the bloody M circled on the destroyed prison walls.

"Why does he leave this? Why does he tell us what he's doing?" Ethan frowned.

"He's nuts," Jack said before Irwin.

"Madigan believes he's smarter, better than everyone else. He thinks he can play games with people. Taunt them. He thinks he's playing with us."

"Us?"

"The United States government. You. Me. He knows he's enemy number one and he loves it." Irwin shook his head. "I always thought he was a prick when we shared the Situation Room."

Jack's eyes twinkled. "To be honest, so did I."

Irwin chuckled and then turned back to the intel and the photos. "Three maximum security prisons were taken out in Peru and Bolivia. It looks like he's moving south from Colombia and heading overland. We've got some rough projections on where he might go from here." Irwin pointed to a prison in central Bolivia on a map of South America and to several colored tracks showing possible routes Madigan might take.

"He could stay in Bolivia for a while." Irwin flipped to a new sheet and a dossier on the Bolivian president. "President Angelo Gamez. Your basic South American military pseudo-dictator."

"Haven't most of those guys been thrown out by the people down there?"

"Most have. But he's been reelected in sham elections for twenty years. Rose to power through the Bolivian military. His career really took off, though, after he graduated from the Western Hemisphere Institute for Security Cooperation." Irwin's eyebrows rose. "Guess who his instructor was?"

"Shit." Jack pinched the bridge of his nose.

The Western Hemisphere Institute for Security Cooperation was the controversial school for foreign military and police officers to learn counterterrorism, counterinsurgency, and Special Forces tactics and techniques. Many of the graduates had returned to their countries and instigated bloody civil wars or perpetrated massacres. It was a sore point of international politics for the United States and a dark corner of their military history.

Of course Madigan would have taught there.

"And Peru's head of intelligence services is also a graduate, again, attending while Madigan was an instructor." Irwin slid the dossier for Peru's chief intelligence officer out, setting it beside the Bolivian president's.

"So he's couch surfing with his friends, is that it?" Jack shook his head. "Going from country to country where he can be protected?"

"And possibly building an army." Ethan sighed. "Where have the prisoners all gone?"

"Unknown. There are a few reports of rearrests made, but they've all been mentally unstable prisoners captured out in the open. Standing naked in the street or masturbating in a chicken coop."

Jack's eyebrows shot straight up.

"He's collecting criminals. Breaking them out and getting them to join him." Ethan ran a hand over his mouth. "To what end?"

"We've got to figure that out." Irwin started to stack the photos and folders. He paused. "Do you know how *bad* you have to be to get put in a maximum security prison in South America? These are not good men."

"What's our counter?" Jack leaned back against his desk when Irwin had cleared it and crossed his arms. "What's our move here?"

"We send our strike team." Irwin looked to Ethan. "You ready to take command?"

Ethan nodded.

"I need to draft orders for the SOCOM commander." Jack spun his laptop on the desktop and pulled up the secured document creator. Word, but on classified steroids.

"General Bell might be difficult to work with. He's territorial of his men. We tasked a few units to the CIA in Afghanistan, and it was always a challenge."

"I should fly down there and speak to him. Deliver the orders. Give it a personal touch." Ethan arched his eyebrows to Jack, questioning.

Jack nodded, and the printer in his private study down the hall spooled to life, spitting out the orders on *Top Secret Eyes Only* letterhead from the Oval Office.

"General Bell is in his office at MacDill Air Force Base. I also checked on Lieutenant Cooper and his men. He's assigned to MacDill and SOCOM, and he and his men are not currently deployed."

"I want our strike team down there ASAP." Jack smiled at Ethan. "Feel like a trip down to Tampa today?"

Ethan had a stop to make in the East Wing before heading to Tampa. Daniels went with him, ducking into his office to get ready for their trip as Ethan made his way to Brandt's open door. Four televisions mounted to the wall were all on, replaying at low volume Brandt's interview from that morning and news commentary on the Washington Eagle tell-all article. Brandt had his back to the door and was fixated on the dual monitors arrayed on his desk. Five paper cups of coffee littered his desktop.

"Hey." Ethan shouldered the doorjamb and crossed his arms.

Brandt spun in his office chair, wide-eyed and chewing on the end of an unfolded paperclip. "Mr. First Gentleman." He jumped to his feet.

"I saw your interview this morning."

Brandt waited. He held Ethan's stare and didn't fidget.

"I thought I told you to stay in step with the West Wing."

Nodding, Brandt picked up a printout from his printer. "I did." He passed the papers over, smothering a yawn.

Statements from Pete peppered the papers, similar in sentiment to Brandt's words from that morning but scattered over six different news agencies. Quotes for the media to pick up and play, over and over, defending Jack's character, his morality, and his record of public service. Ethan's gaze flicked back to Brandt.

"You guys don't want to comment on your personal lives. Okay. We—Pete and I—don't like it, but we respect your decision. But that doesn't mean *we* can't say something, as us. The statements weren't from you, and they weren't from the president. They were from me and Pete." Brandt's eyebrows rose, a kind of silent shrug, and he flicked the end of a pen against his palm. "We're looking at a fifty-five to forty-five split of positive reaction to negative, and that's growing larger by the hour. More people are saying the article is garbage and are defending you and the president."

"Your statement is getting a lot of airplay. Pete's too."

Brandt nodded.

Ethan passed back the papers as a smile unfurled over his face. "Thank you. What you said meant a lot. And it was a good strategy. Thanks."

Brandt nodded again, his shoulders straightening as he stood tall. "Mr. First Gentleman, it was a pleasure."

Ethan held out his hand for Brandt. "Get out of here. Take an early day. You were working all night with Pete, right?"

Brandt shook Ethan's hand before grabbing his suit jacket off the back of his desk chair. "We were texting all night. He was so frustrated with the president." He blushed as he swiped his cell phone off the desk. "Sorry. That wasn't appropriate."

"It's all right. We are frustrating." Ethan helped Brandt shut down his TVs and then waved the younger man out of the office. He went down the line, checking in with each of his staffers. Barbara appeared, showing him another ten bins of cards she'd lined up in his office along the wall.

"Is there a way we can display these?" They were up to eighteen bins. "I don't want to just throw them away."

"Leave that to me, Mr. First Gentleman." Barbara's eyes twinkled. "I'll take care of it. Do you need anything for your trip this afternoon?"

"Should be good. I'll be back late this evening."

Ethan grabbed his padfolio and laptop and collected Daniels, who was challenging Agent Beech to a peanut catching contest. Daniels was up by two, and Ethan plucked the next peanut he was about to catch from the air and popped it into his own mouth.

"Rude, man. Rude." Daniels feigned indignation as he and Ethan headed down to the parking garage, where Daniels made a show of opening the rear door of one of the presidential SUVs for him.

Ethan rolled his eyes at Daniels and pulled out his cell phone. He texted Jack as he and Daniels drove away from the White House.

[Heading to Andrews AFB now.]

Travel safe. I'll wait up for you tonight. Now that you're living here, I don't want to go to sleep without you.

[:) I'll be back as soon as I'm done. Should be flying home by evening.]

Your first trip as first gentleman. You're getting an upgrade on your travels. No more commercial flights for you.

[LOL]

Firstest class. First gentleman class. ;)

[I don't care about the plane. It's the guy who comes with the job I'm excited about. :)]

I'm pretty excited about you too.

I've got to get back to the Cabinet, though. I'm getting weird looks from the sec interior. Should I shout "High score!"

[Or I could send you something to make the meeting a lot more interesting...]

I do that to myself quite enough, thank you very much! Thoughts of you are VERY distracting. :) XOXO, see you tonight!

Ethan grinned and stared out the window of the SUV.

One of the perks of being a member of the first family was the immediate access to any of the governmental planes housed with the 89th Airlift Command at Andrews Air Force base. The planes were kept in continuous rotation, fueled and ready to go, with pilots on standby at all times.

"So what's up with this sudden trip?" Daniels waited to ask until they were almost at Andrews, flicking a quick glance to Ethan in the rearview mirror. "If I can ask."

If he could ask. A month ago, Ethan could have told Daniels anything. They had the same security clearance in the Secret Service and they were on the same team, doing the same mission. Now, even though they were still friends, a gulf of protocol and governmental procedure, and a whole new level of clearances, had opened between them.

But Daniels had leaped in front of a bullet for Ethan—and for Jack—and fought and bled for them both when the world was on the line. If he couldn't trust Daniels, he couldn't trust anyone.

"We're forming a black strike team to take out Madigan. I'm going to run operational command."

Daniels's eyes blew wide, shock dropping his jaw open. "Dude…"

"I'm going to soften the orders to General Bell at SOCOM. We need one of his units attached to us."

"Attached to the White House."

"Well, the CIA on paper. But yeah."

"Damn, man." Daniels whistled as he showed his creds to the gate guard at Andrews and sped toward the airfield and the 89th's hangars. "Though, that's a better fit than managing the White House flowers." Daniels winked in the rearview mirror.

Ethan snorted as they squealed to a stop at the main hangar. A colonel strode toward their SUV. Daniels hopped out, but Ethan beat him to the door, and Daniels glared at him over the rim of his sunglasses. "I'm supposed to get your door, Mr. First Gentleman."

The colonel offered Ethan one of the massive C-40 heavy transports, opulent and almost regal, but Ethan shook his head and pointed instead to a much smaller and sleeker C-38.

"Not bringing your staff?" The gruff colonel eyeballed Ethan up and down, his heavy mustache twitching.

"No, sir." Ethan tried to smile, the tight, polite stretch of lips he used with people who irritated him. "We're keeping this under the radar. Small footprint. It's just me."

"And me. His Secret Service protection."

The colonel grumbled but called for the C-38 to be brought out to the flight line and for the pilots to get ready for their briefing. Ethan filed his official request for a flight to MacDill and waited with Daniels, drinking coffee in the hangar's lounge—reserved for executive members of the government—while the pilots were briefed on their last-minute trip.

Then they were in the air, call sign Executive One Foxtrot, soaring down from DC and heading for Florida. Daniels conked out when he saw Ethan burying himself in intel reports and maps of South America. By the time they were getting ready to land, Ethan had covered the windows around him with sticky notes and had the outline of an operation ready for Cooper to review.

They landed directly at MacDill, and a platoon of Air Force security services personnel met them in ten Humvees. Daniels made a point to hold the Humvee door for Ethan. Within minutes, they were parked outside the offices of the US Special Operations Command.

Ethan's trip stalled there.

General Bell, despite receiving a call from Jack personally informing him of his orders and of Ethan's imminent arrival, left Ethan and Daniels in his waiting room for twenty-one minutes.

Daniels rolled his neck, cracking his joints. "This is bullshit."

It *was* bullshit. The general was making them wait. As Irwin had said, he wouldn't be easy to work with. "I know."

A few minutes later, the general's secretary waved them in. "The general will see you now, Mr. First Gentleman."

Finally. Daniels went first into the general's office, making a show of checking the general's domain over before letting Ethan enter.

The pissing competition had begun.

General Bell utterly ignored Daniels taking up his post along the wall. He plastered a fake smile on his face. "Mr. First Gentleman," he said, through slightly clenched teeth. "It's a privilege to have you here."

Daniels's chin lifted, just a fraction.

Bell gestured for Ethan to take a seat as he punched the intercom for his secretary. "I'll be meeting with the first gentleman for about half an hour. Come get me if we go long." He stared at Ethan. "I'm a busy man."

Another slap of disrespect. Ethan's lips tightened. "As am I, General."

"Yes." The general leaned back in his chair, the leather creaking as the ribbons and insignia on his chest rose with a heavy inhale. "Settling into the White House. What is it that the first gentleman does again? Social events? Planting a White House garden? And delivery boy, apparently."

Across the room, Ethan heard Daniels's knuckles crack in the silence that followed the general's words.

"These orders come from the president of the United States, General."

"I don't see the president here."

Ethan's jaw clenched. "You have already received detailed orders regarding the formation of a clandestine strike team tasked to the command authority of the president. And, as part of those orders, you've received explicit instructions as to my position within this new force's chain of command." He pulled out a copy of Bell's orders, hand-signed by Jack, and slid it across the general's desk. "In case you've forgotten any of the details."

The general didn't move. He didn't reach for the orders. He kept staring at Ethan, holding his gaze.

"I'm not convinced of the legality of this tasking. Or of your part in all this. Your character is questionable." Bell's eyes flicked to the folded newspaper sitting on the table next to Ethan's chair.

It was the Washington Eagle. And, right across the top, the article that ripped him and Jack to shreds.

So it was personal. A fuse lit deep within his belly, rage burning slowly as his teeth ground together.

Another thought blindsided him. Was it *just* personal? Madigan had been a part of SOCOM for years. General Bell had been quietly investigated, as had every commander in SOCOM... but what if?

Ethan leaned back, leveling his gaze as his expression hardened. "In conjunction with the attorney general and congressional leadership's directive to take out this imminent threat, and working within the legal framework established delineating executive powers, a judicial review will find that we are on excellent legal ground." A pause. "Which is more than you can say right now, General."

Silence.

"As the representative of the president of the United States, and as the director of this operation, I will ask you once—are you prepared to execute your orders, General? Or should I call the president, your commander in chief, and have him relieve you of your command? I can wait for your replacement to carry out these orders."

General Bell's nostrils flared and his face turned purple. His fingers clenched down on his chair arms. Leather squeaked under pressure.

"We could also discuss the transfer of a team of operators to my command with orders and authorization for them to train and act solely at the discretion of the president of the United States."

The silence in the general's office was oppressive, weighted down with unshed rage and the boxed-in general. *What will it be, General?* Ethan held his glare, watching as the older man's hands trembled where they clenched his chair.

"I came here to work *with* you." Ethan softened his tone.

General Bell's eyes narrowed as he leaned forward. Snarling, Bell snatched up the orders Ethan had slid over his desk. He read through them, twice, and then glared over the top of the sheet at Ethan.

Ethan spoke first. "I have a specific team in mind. Lieutenant Adam Cooper and his Raiders."

A snort burst from the general. He laughed out loud as he shook his head. "*Cooper*? He's a train wreck. I'll be chaptering him out of the Corps by the end of the week. You want him for *this*?" Bell waved toward the sheet, lying on his desk again.

"I've worked with him personally." Ethan frowned. The Lieutenant Cooper he'd known had been a man of competence and quiet confidence, a man who had built a breach plan with him for the White House, no questions asked. A man of conviction and loyalty.

General Bell smirked. "Tell you what." He grabbed the orders in one hand. "You'll get what you want. Lieutenant Cooper and his team tasked to you." Standing, the general crumpled Jack's orders, balling the paper up before chucking it into his garbage. "Two less problems I have to deal with."

Ethan stood and stared.

Bell shook his head, glared at Ethan up and down, dismissing everything about him, and walked out.

Daniels was a ball of frustrated, shaking fury as they exited the office, but he kept his mouth shut as they clambered back into their Humvee.

"I have orders to take you to Lieutenant Cooper, Mr. First Gentleman." The driver, a sergeant, turned in his seat, questioning.

"Please." Ethan stayed quiet, holding a silent conversation with Daniels through shakes of the head as they drove across the base.

Finally, the driver pulled the Humvee up to a large brick building and stopped. Ethan looked out the window and blinked when he saw the building's signage. *MacDill Stockade.* The base's equivalent of a jail.

"What are we doing here, Sergeant?"

"Lieutenant Cooper is in there, sir." The sergeant glanced back. "We will wait here, sir."

Enemy Of My Enemy

Daniels and Ethan shared a long look. They were on their own. General Bell was being especially unhelpful with executing his orders. Did he not realize that Ethan would tell Jack everything?

The stockade was quiet, save for the hum and rattle of the window air conditioner cooling the bullpen where two Air Force security specialists sat in front of computers. One rose. "Can I help you, gentlemen?" He paled when he recognized Ethan and straightened even further before slapping his partner's shoulder as inconspicuously as he could.

"We're here for Lieutenant Cooper. May we see him?"

A slight hesitation as the young airman debated his options. If he chose to confirm the orders with General Bell, they could be there a while.

"Right this way, sir."

Finally, a break. Ethan and Daniels followed the airman through a controlled access point, badging through three sets of locked doors before they came to a line of cells. "Last one on the left." The airman waited at the end of the hall, standing at parade rest as Ethan and Daniels headed for Cooper's cell.

Their footsteps echoed, leather and rubber on old linoleum. Other prisoners were racked out, sleeping on the narrow cots affixed to the walls. There were only three others in the cells. Most were empty, including all the cells around Lieutenant Cooper.

Ethan's eyes narrowed as he approached Cooper's cell. Inside, Cooper sat on the edge of his cot, slumped over, his elbows on his knees and his hands in his hair. His hair was too long, far too long for a Marine, and he had a few days' growth of beard darkening his face. Dried blood splatter stained the front of his green USMC undershirt.

This was not the same man who had helped Ethan survive Madigan's assassination attempt or retake the White House.

"Lieutenant?"

Daniels waited just out of sight while Ethan strode to the center point of the bars stretched across Cooper's cell.

Cooper froze. Slowly, he looked up. His eyes locked with Ethan's. Snorting, he shook his head and dropped his gaze.

What was that? What had put so much defeat and rage into Cooper's eyes?

"What happened?"

Cooper stayed silent.

"How'd you end up in here?"

"I punched out Captain Oliver. One of General Bell's attachés."

Ethan's eyebrow quirked up. "Did he deserve it?"

Finally, some life in Cooper's eyes. He nodded. "And more."

"I'd say well done, but I'm supposed to be politic now."

Cooper shook his head but pushed to his feet. "What are you doing here?"

"Asking for your help. I just delivered orders to General Bell seconding you and your men to a new mission we're setting up. Let's take a walk while I fill you in."

The airman hesitated for a longer moment when Ethan asked him to release Cooper, but eventually opened the cell doors. Cooper, his eyes narrowed as he peered at Ethan, followed him down the hallway and out to the stockade's side yard, where they stood under a palm tree, out of sight from the building and anyone else as Daniels stood guard. Not the most ideal place for a briefing, but it was better than one of the interview rooms inside, where anyone and everyone could listen in.

Cooper listened as Ethan spoke, nodding along, and when Ethan walked through the bones of his insertion mission, sending Cooper and his team to South America, he adjusted a few areas and added details specific to his men and their abilities.

"So, are you onboard? Should I go tell that nervous airman that you won't be checking back in?"

Cooper stared into the sun for a moment, squinting. That look of pinched anger was back, but overlaid with a weariness that was new. When had the weight of the world ended up on Cooper's shoulders?

"Yeah, I'm in." Cooper held out his hand, and Ethan shook it. "When are we wheels up?"

"The CIA is handling all your logistics. Not to put too fine a point on it, but we don't trust General Bell to be as efficient as we'd like. A plane should have landed by now with your equipment. Get your men. Get them briefed. You're wheels up by zero two hundred."

Cooper nodded. "I've got Marines to collect. I'll be in touch." He headed out, walking away from the stockade and the Humvees waiting out front. Whatever had happened, whatever had caused the fight, it was over now, and Cooper was no longer General Bell's man. He was Ethan's, and if Bell wanted to cause a ruckus over that, he'd bring it right back.

But there was something there, some deep-seated tension running through Cooper, and Bell had run into the tripwire for whatever it was.

He'd have to keep an eye on Cooper. Make sure he leveled out.

The airman didn't quite know how to handle Lieutenant Cooper's release, especially since his incarceration had come with General Bell's explicit orders to "let him rot," but Ethan offered to sign for him, and the airman gratefully accepted.

After, he and Daniels hopped into their Humvee and were driven back to the airfield and their waiting jet. Ethan confirmed that the plane Irwin had sent had actually landed and was waiting in a hangar downfield for Cooper, and then they took off, just as the sun was setting over the Gulf of Mexico.

Daniels watched as Ethan gazed out the window. The weight of his stare was heavy.

Ethan finally turned to his friend, eyebrows raised. "Something on your mind?"

Daniels couldn't meet Ethan's gaze. "That general was an asshole," he finally grunted. "Took everything I had not to lay him out." He shook his head and glared, eyes pinched and lips pursed. "I don't understand why people hate you and the president."

"It's not just me and Jack being together." Ethan swallowed, and he frowned down at his hands in his lap as he tried to find the right words. "That's a big part of it, but it's not new. I've been dealing with this my whole life." He looked up. "This... complete dismissal of me as a person. As a *man*. To them, since I'm gay, and especially since I'm out about it, I'm not worth the same as a straight man. My masculinity. It's always suspect. I'm always looked at as half of a real man. And, my sexuality? It's a constant battle. Being promoted to the Lead Detail? That was higher than I ever thought I'd get. There was so much against me, for so many years." He shook his head, staring out the window. "I just never wanted Jack to have to deal with this bullshit."

Daniels stayed quiet. Ethan settled back in his seat and watched the clouds and the sky darken as day turned to night.

Finally, Daniels spoke. His voice was choked, but he looked Ethan dead in the eyes. "I've never met a better man than you, Ethan. Swear to fucking God."

8

Russia
Andreapol Air Base

Sasha pulled into Andreapol Air Base, four hours north of Moscow, just after five in the morning. He'd grabbed another cup of coffee on the drive, keeping awake for his all-night trek home. He'd slept through the day before, readying himself for his bolt down to Moscow to relieve the itch he'd had in his blood and for his next day's overflight of the capital.

As one of the pilots assigned to the 773rd Guards Fighter Regiment, he was one of the best of the best MiG fighter pilots in the Russian Army Air Force. A top gun, a god amongst mortals. He and his wingmen owned the skies. On some flights, they climbed high enough to break the edge of space, seeing nothing but blackness above and the curvature of the earth below. His pencil had floated through the cockpit once, weightless. On the roll and dive back down to Earth, they'd broken the sound barrier, reaching Mach 2.5 before leveling out over Murmansk and the Barents Sea.

There was nothing, not a thing, that could beat that.

He parked in the pilots' lot and hopped out, grabbing his flight bag from his squeaky trunk. A few other cars dotted the parking lot, squadron mates he recognized.

There was a spring in his step as he headed into their hangar. He'd gotten his need out of his system, for the next six months at least. After a shower, he'd change into his flight suit and hang out in the ready room until the morning brief. No one would ever know where he was the night before, or what he'd done.

The halls were empty inside the hangar. No chatter of pilots or loud guffaws as someone called bullshit on another's wild story. Sasha peered into the ready room but kept on toward the showers. Maybe they were all out at a flight line check.

He found everyone in the locker room.

Nine guys, his fellow pilots, his wing leader, and the regiment commander all leaned up against the lockers, out of uniform and in old, ratty sweats. Everyone wore leather gloves and some were flexing their fingers, squeezing their hands into fists over and over. The group was talking quietly, trying, it seemed, to not be noticed. The hum of the fluorescent lights above droned over their soft words.

Sasha slowed when he saw the hockey sticks in the hands of four of his fellow pilots.

Guys he'd called friends.

When the group turned and saw him, he realized he didn't have a single friend in the room.

"*Poluchit' gryaz'*," his wing commander growled. *Get that piece of filth.*

Sasha tried to run, but they cut him off at the door, trapping him in the locker room. Sticks banged on the lockers, harder, faster, a heavy clang that rattled the walls and shook the lights above. He bared his teeth and threw up his fists.

Not without a fight. Not without a fight, damn it.

"*Grebanyy pedik!*" *Fucking Faggot!*

Hockey sticks slammed on the ground, the lockers, as the circle of his wingmates and his commander pressed closer.

"*Goluboi!*" *Faggot.*

"*Huisos!*" *Cocksucker.*

"*Pidor!*" *Butt-fucker.*

With the last shouted curse, the nine men he thought were friends ran at him, hockey sticks swinging wildly. He ducked and tried to punch his way through the descending madness, but a stick cracked him on the back and another knocked the breath from his lungs with a jab to the ribs. He fell to his knees as blows rained down on his kidneys, on his shoulders, and then on the backs of his thighs. Fists flew at his face. His nose crunched. Pain flared across the bridge of his nose, his cheekbones. Blood sprayed through the air, staining the sweats his wingmates were wearing.

Ahh. Now he understood.

Kicks to his knees and arms made him fall face-first to the ground. He covered his head just before a boot flew at his face and hit his elbow instead. His body was on fire, burning where the sticks and boots hit.

He howled, rage and anguish and fury at the betrayal burning from him. These were his wingmates. His commander. He'd never once told anyone about his problem, never once let it slip that he was gay. Things were getting better, he'd thought, what with President Puchkov and the American president becoming friends. But still, he'd never risk revealing his deepest secret. His shame.

A stick slammed between his legs, deep into his crotch. He cried out, rolling to his side as he curled into a ball.

"*Prival!*" *Stop!* His commander, shouting over the din of furious curses, swinging sticks, and wet thumps from his bruised and bloody body.

Footsteps took the men back, and Sasha lay in a heap on the floor under the droning fluorescent light, bloody, beaten, and wheezing. Broken ribs, for sure. A dull throb in his abdomen and his back.

His commander knelt in front of him. He grabbed Sasha's chin, yanking him up off the ground. Squeezing, he ground the broken bones on Sasha's cheek together.

Sasha felt the first hot tear roll down his cheek.

"*Otvratitel'nyy...*" his commander growled before he spat in Sasha's face. A hot glob of spit landed on his broken cheek and bruised face.

Disgusting.

His commander reared back, his free hand forming a fist.

There was nothing left. Sasha shouted, bellowing a wordless cry of rage as he stared his commander down and waited for his fist to fall.

He woke facedown in a snow bank on the two-lane M9 highway, stripped of his flight suit and his uniform and all of his gear. Blood-covered, and in just his undershirt and his boxer briefs, he stumbled out of the snow and toward the deserted highway.

Overhead, the stars shone beside a half-full moon, the first night without snow in over a week. Still, the air was frigid, below freezing, and he trembled. Pain shot through him, his shivers and stumbles upsetting his badly injured body.

A sign in the distance, on the edge of the highway, showed the kilometers to Moscow. Just over two hours, at highway speeds.

He was fucked. Dumped in the middle of nowhere to freeze to death and then be eaten by animals.

It was a tidy murder. They'd planned it well. He'd be classified as a runaway, for sure. And no one would ever find his body. Maybe a bone or two, and he'd be another mysterious partial skeleton found in the Russian wilderness.

Stumbling forward, he limped down the highway, heading for Moscow. He'd get as far as he could, even if it was only a few hundred meters. He wouldn't give up. Not ever.

Ten minutes later, he fell to his knees and couldn't stand again.

Sasha tilted his head back and stared at the stars. He'd flown almost between them, once. He'd touched space. He'd flown so high, and he'd been happy. When he died, he wanted to be staring up at their brilliance one last time.

The darkness grew brighter, suddenly, and then there was a blaring wail and the crunch of tires on concrete. A car horn screaming as headlights shone on Sasha. Raising an arm, he shielded his eyes and curled over himself, trying to avoid the worst of the pain.

Instead of hitting him, the driver squealed the car to a stop. Hinges squeaked in the cold, and the faint sounds of Russian talk radio fell from the open door, mixed with the static that always bled into the airwaves in northern Russia.

"What happened to you?" The driver, a middle-aged man in an old, thick fur coat and woolen cap, rushed to Sasha's side and crouched in front of him. "My God," he breathed. "Who beat you?"

Sasha swallowed. There was no way, no way at all, that he could ever tell the truth. Not to this man. Maybe not to anyone.

Except…

A tiny rush of air escaped his quivering lips. There was one place he could go, maybe. One impossible place, and maybe, possibly, he could get someone to help. Or at least witness what had happened

He shook his head and reached for the older man. "I need to get to Moscow. Please." His chest rattled as he choked out his words, and he coughed, cringing as pain tore through him.

"Are you *Bratva*?" The man steadied Sasha but didn't help him.

Bratva. The Brotherhood. The Mafia. He shook his head. "No. Not at all." His skin was free of tattoos, the marks of the Brotherhood.

The man's eyes narrowed, but he took off his fur coat and draped it around Sasha's shivering shoulders as he helped him to stand. Sasha leaned on him as he stumbled back to his car. He let the man lay him down on the back seat. Another blanket was on the floorboards, and the man draped it over Sasha, bunching the extra around his head until he was cocooned.

When the driver slid back into the front seat, he turned the heater up to full blast, and with one last lingering look at Sasha, put the car into gear and started down the highway.

Sasha stared out the window at the stars until his eyelids dropped and unconsciousness pulled him under.

9

White House Residence

Jack had waited up for Ethan as he said he would, reading through the endless stack of reports and briefs that cluttered the tables and desks in his study. Ethan leaned against the doorjamb, watching his lover at work.

Jack had his reading glasses on and was dressed down in jeans and Ethan's favorite Secret Service sweatshirt from his academy days. It was too big for him, swallowing Jack whole, and Jack had shoved the sleeves up his arms, bunching the fabric. Across the back and over the left side of the chest, REICHENBACH was still boldly stenciled in blue on the gray fabric, even after twelve years. A few silver strands scattered through Jack's dark blond hair shone in the low light.

He was gorgeous. Ethan's heart ached. God, he loved this man. Why Jack? Why this man? Why now, when Jack was president? Who knew, but God, did he love him.

"Hey."

Jack looked up over his readers and broke into a smile when he saw Ethan. The binder from NATO he was reading closed with a snap. "And I'm done," Jack said, standing. "Welcome home."

Home. The White House. His home with Jack. It still blew his mind. "Glad to be back. How was your day?"

"Busy. Elizabeth accepted. She's up for the VP nomination. And congressional leadership accepted her accept. They'll start the confirmation hearings as soon as they're back from recess." Jack set down his glasses and padded around the desk. "How'd it go?"

"Well, I don't think General Bell will make his next star."

Jack sighed. "You showed him the error of his ways?"

A slow grin. "It's like you know me or something."

"Just a bit." Jack winked and pressed a kiss to the corner of Ethan's mouth.

"I briefed Cooper. He agreed, too. He's getting ready for their mission and he's wheels up in four hours."

Jack looped his arms around Ethan's neck. "Mmm, your ability to get things done is so sexy."

Ethan barked out a surprised chuckle. His hands fell to Jack's waist. Jack jumped, wrapping his legs around Ethan's hips. Shocked, Ethan's laughter turned into a soft gasp as his hands cupped Jack's ass.

Jack grinned and leaned in, sucking on Ethan's earlobe. "Take me to bed, lover." He pulled back just enough to meet Ethan's gaze.

Ethan kissed him as he carried him down the hallway to their bedroom.

10

Moscow

Boris, the driver who had picked up Sasha in the middle of the night on the isolated M9, dropped him off at GUM, the brilliantly lit, three-story shopping mall in the Red Square across the street from the Kremlin. Boris left his old fur coat with Sasha, but grumbled about leaving him in the mall's parking garage. Sasha didn't even have shoes, he'd said.

But, Sasha shooed him away, thanking him and insisting he'd be okay while clinging to the fur coat and hunching over because it hurt too much to stand.

"No hospital," he'd insisted. "No hospital."

Boris drove off, and Sasha saw him watching in his rearview mirror until he rose out of the garage.

When he left, Sasha sank to the ground, gasping for breath as he tried not to cry. He'd been holding the worst of the pain just at bay, struggling to not show Boris how badly injured he was. His abdomen was tender and turning black and blue. Internal bleeding. Something was *very* wrong with him. Sweat beaded his forehead, even though it was still below freezing.

Boris had dropped him off before dawn in Moscow. The mall was closed. But across the street were the red walls of the Kremlin, and within, President Puchkov.

If he could just get there. The president wouldn't stand for this, this blatant hatred and attack. Not with his friendship with the American president. Sasha would stand at the gates of the Kremlin and shout, demand that something be done. He'd die, most likely, but something would change. It had to. President Puchkov was going to make the country better. He believed that to his bones.

Sasha pulled himself to his unsteady feet and tried to shake away the dizziness that stole over him. He blinked hard, but the scattered cars swam in front of him, duplicate vehicles spinning in the air. One hand braced against the concrete wall as he stumbled for the ramp, the fur coat still wrapped tight around his shoulders.

He made it across the street, but not to the gates of the Kremlin. He collapsed against the red brick walls, meters away from a dark service entrance, private and closed off from the public. Sasha stared up at the stars, so dim and faint over Moscow, as the darkness closed in around him.

He was still unconscious an hour later when Dr. Leo Voronov pulled up to the darkened private entrance for Kremlin employees. Frowning, Dr. Voronov put his car in park and headed for a lump of middle-class fur coat and messy blond hair lying slumped in the snow.

11

South Brazilian Airspace

"So we're CIA now, huh L-T?" Doc threw himself down next to Adam, landing half-reclined on his bulky pack as he watched the treetops of the Brazilian forest loom through the open cargo doors on the side of their transport plane.

"We're on a CIA mission. But we're working for the president now." Adam checked the map he had in his waterproof sleeve.

"Damn. That sounds extra special. Think we could get out of paying taxes for this? Like in that movie?"

Adam signaled to the pilots in the cockpit and got an affirmative response back. "We're still paying taxes. We're still Marines." He grinned, standing. "And you're still a Navy squid."

Doc flipped him off as Adam spoke over the team's radio, getting his men ready for their landing. They'd flown from MacDill to South America, landing at the Marine base in Sao Paolo before boarding their final transport and flying deep into South Brazil just north of their target, across the border in Paraguay.

Now it was time to land.

The plane descended, skimming over the treetops. Birds screeched and monkeys screamed as the plane buzzed overhead. They'd flown low to avoid radar, but now, coming in for their landing, it seemed as if they could just step out and walk on the canopy.

A break in the trees revealed their landing zone: a glistening, sunrise-drenched stretch of river, calm and gentle, nestled between two forest-covered banks.

"Oh, you fucker," Doc cursed, just close enough that Adam could hear.

Grinning, Adam clapped Doc on the shoulder and grabbed the plane's handholds. Doc was their team's corpsman from the Navy. He was the only naval man Adam had ever met who had a pure, burning hatred of all things wet and watery. Lake, river, or ocean, Doc hated it and was always violently seasick.

Doc grumbled as he grabbed hold next to Adam as the plane's giant pontoons scraped the surface of the river and carved channels in the water. The engines throttled back, jerking the team back and forth in the cargo hold. In moments, they were bobbing on the river as the stabilizer took over, tut-tut-tutting them toward the riverbank.

Adam winked at Doc. "Oo-rah!"

He leaped from the cargo entrance and crossed his arms and legs before plunging into the river. His team followed, splashing in one after the other, and then swam for the shore. Last to jump was Doc, cursing a blue streak as Adam clambered up onto the riverbank and started unpacking his gear from his watertight pack.

Adam chuckled and unfolded the map for his men. It felt good to be operational again, to be in his element. Infiltration, observation, combat. This was his life, a constant pulsation of action and adrenaline. He could stay focused, one hundred percent, on the task at hand. It was all about the mission and his men, and he didn't have time to think about—

Nope, he wasn't going to go there. He'd *promised* himself. Over was *over*. Never mind their mistake, the frantic relief of survival and uncertainty and too much adrenaline combining to create his One Big Fuckup.

Well, his second biggest fuckup. The first was ever believing he could have had—

Nope. Not going there. Never again. He wouldn't even think it.

Gathering his men, Adam pointed out their route through the Brazilian forest and where they'd cross the border to Paraguay. It was a section of the forest used by drug runners that had been taken down by the Brazilians, and the rest of the smugglers were convinced it was being monitored by the authorities and refused to go near. In reality, it was an empty stretch of nothing, and only monkeys, deer, and the jungle birds traversed the border.

Their mission had changed *en route*, and Adam had received new orders from Director Reichenbach when they switched planes in Sao Paolo. A clandestine base in north Paraguay, home to a special operations detachment, had gone dark. SOCOM couldn't raise the base and they couldn't send in a drone to check it out. Adam's orders were to head straight there and see what was going on.

He laid out the plan for his team. At a good pace, they'd get to the base in five hours.

Time to move.

Northern Paraguay

Pennants fluttered in the wind, staked at the end of the hard-packed dirt runway the SOCOM soldiers used to fly in and out of their clandestine base. One had fallen down and rolled across the dirt.

A door banged, blown open and then falling closed.

One of the base guards lay facedown on the ground with a bullet through the back of his head. Sticky blood dried in the dirt beneath his face.

Silently, Adam and his men moved through the base's entrance, ducking from point to point and slipping into the scattered buildings within the small compound. A central facility, a listening post, a drone operation, and a large runway. The base housed two drones and two heavy transports. About twenty-five SOCOM soldiers were stationed there at any given time.

Five bodies were in the kitchen, all shot dead. Another three in the communications room. Four scattered on the tarmac. And, in the base commander's office, the colonel in charge sat at his desk, sprawled back in his chair, a single bullet hole above his closed eyes.

Drawn on his desk, smeared in the colonel's own blood, was a circled M.

Madigan's calling card.

The armory had been cleaned out. All weapons, all ammunition. The Humvees and jeeps parked in the motor pool were gone. Computers had been smashed, communications equipment destroyed, and all radar and tracking systems had been shot to pieces.

Eleven SOCOM soldiers were missing, including the base's executive officer.

So were the drones and the heavy transports.

Adam ordered his men to sweep the base again, making sure they hadn't missed a thing while Doc and Sergeant Shawn Wright gathered the bodies together in the mess.

He called back to DC on the satellite phone the CIA had sent down. A direct line to Director Reichenbach had already been programmed in.

The phone clicked on the second ring. *"Reichenbach."*

"We made it to the target. It's a slaughterhouse. Fourteen confirmed dead, including the commander. And we've got Madigan's calling card."

"Fuck. And the other eleven?"

"No trace. All transports are gone, along with all weapon systems."

Across the sat phone, Director Reichenbach cursed again. *"Hang tight. We'll pull up the satellite imagery overhead and try to find those planes. Is the runway intact? Can you use them?"*

"Yes, sir. The base is ours. They must have used the planes to fly out, so they needed those runways. But some may have left overland in the Humvees."

"We'll search for those too. Stay near the phone. I'll call back as soon as I have something."

"As soon as Reichenbach had something" turned out to be hours later, after the White House had ordered the CIA and NRO to deliver all satellite recon imagery of the base for the past forty-eight hours. They found what they were looking for on the satellite feeds from twelve hours prior: planes taking off from the base, two in a row, hours before the base failed to check in with SOCOM.

Adam reviewed the images on his secured laptop as he talked with Reichenbach on the sat phone. The sun was setting and howler monkeys skittered in the trees, screeching at the top of their lungs. The cries were like nails scratching down Adam's bones.

"We have to follow them." Reichenbach sent another file over their secured sat link, and a new picture appeared on Cooper's laptop. *"Turns out the NRO doesn't monitor the empty South Atlantic all that well. We only have spotty intel on where they may have gone. Analysts have been checking our overflights of all airfields and airports Madigan may have gone to. Countries that hate us, or where he's got some kind of potential connection."*

Adam could only imagine the shitshow of analysis that had descended on the NSA and CIA that afternoon. A real-world immediate action and an urgent request from the White House. People would have been running around like they were on fire.

"One analyst spotted a plane landing in the Jilf al Kabir plateau inside Libya, about 200 miles south of Al-Jawf, near the border of Egypt and Sudan."

"In the Sahara?" Fuck. Of course, it would be there. One of the worst places on the planet.

"Looks like it touched down in one of the wadis. One of the dry riverbe—"

"I know what a wadi is."

Reichenbach waited a moment, but kept going when Adam stayed silent. *"Later satellite overflights don't show the plane anymore, but they also don't show any marks that indicate it took off from the area."*

"So they camouflaged it."

"It'd be difficult to build a base there, but not impossible. They could be setting up shop, or could be moving into Sudan. Both Libya and Sudan are lawless enough that he could hide out under the radar. Unfortunately, the location is out of range of any of our drone bases."

Out of the whole planet, going back to the Middle East was the last place Adam wanted to go. He squeezed his eyes shut. "What about the other plane? You only found one?" Maybe he could send part of his team after the Libyan plane. He could track the second plane.

"We're still searching for it."

Of course. Fuck.

Cooper hung his head, listening. *"We need to send you and your team over there."* Reichenbach hesitated. *"You spent some time in the region. You know North Africa and the Middle East pretty well. Do you have any insight into an insertion point?"*

He should never have fucking accepted this mission. Adam groaned under his breath and tried to block the memories that clamored for his attention. Late nights, sweat-slick bodies, and conspiring together. *Conspiracy,* his conscience whispered. *You'd be thrown in jail if anyone ever found out. Stripped of your command. Of your commission.*

Enough.

"Yeah. We should insert at the Kharga Oasis in southern Egypt. There's a track running through there. The *Darb el-Arba*. The old forty-day road. It's a trading caravan that's still used by Bedouins. It will go right through that part of Libya." He kicked at a bullet casing on the concrete floor in the destroyed communication room. "We'll need trucks. And camels. And we'll have to go in clean. No uniforms, nothing that can tie us back to the US." That part of the desert was deadly, and not just because of the heat or the utter desolation of the place.

And it held way too many memories.

Another long pause over the line. *"I'm impressed, Lieutenant,"* Reichenbach finally said. *"And I agree. We can't have your men tied back to the US government. We're sending a team down with sanitized equipment for desert operations. And cash. They'll fuel up in Sao Paolo and then pick you up and take you to Egypt. Another team will stay behind and deal with the base in Paraguay."*

Goddamn it. "Yes, sir."

"I'll send you all the intel we have on the area, and anything that comes through. And... try to get some rest. The plane will be there just before dawn."

"Yes, sir." Adam pushed himself up from the slump he'd fallen into, hunching over a destroyed comms console and his laptop. "I'll have my operational plan to you before we take off."

"Good luck."

The sat phone clicked as Reichenbach cut the line. Exhaling, Adam leaned forward, resting his forehead on the receiver.

Back to Africa. Back to the Middle East. Back to the Kharga Oasis and the *Darb el-Arba*, even. His life was a cosmic joke. Someone, somewhere, must love to torture him. He squeezed his eyes shut as the memories tried to rise again.

Why couldn't he get *his* smile out of his mind? Why was it always *him*, every moment of every day?

Enough. He had to focus. He had a mission to plan, men to brief, and memories to forget.

12

White House

When Saturday arrived, Ethan felt like he'd been run down by a train and beaten into the tracks. One week as first gentleman and he was ready to hibernate until spring truly began. He'd thought being detail lead had been tough. Politics had nothing on that. How did Jack do it all?

They slept in, Ethan staying nearly comatose well into the morning. Their day started slow and sensual, rocking together, rolling in the covers and trading long kisses interspersed with sloppy blowjobs and stroking each other's bodies. It was almost ten when they finally got out of bed and shuffled to the kitchen for coffee, shared out of one cup while they traded kisses and sat in the West Sitting Hall, watching another light snowstorm descend over DC. Jack perched on Ethan's lap, their hair sticking up every which way and kiss bruises staining their collarbones.

Jack's parents called, and Ethan traded stiff hellos with his mother and father from suburban Texas. Jack's parents had learned about Ethan at the same time the rest of the nation had, and it was still a sore spot for Jack's mother. Ethan hadn't met them yet, but had spoken to them once over Christmas. On the phone, Jack's mother sounded sweet, and she kept asking them to come visit as soon as they could.

At noon, they headed downstairs to the Rose Garden and the snow-covered lawn. Jack challenged Ethan to a snowman building contest, laughing in ankle-deep drifts as flakes dusted his hair and his cheeks turned cherry-red. Secret Service agents watched, most of them younger agents Ethan had supervised before his career had fallen apart. They grinned and called out tips for Jack and heckled Ethan.

Welby sidled up to Ethan, his hands in the pockets of his wool coat.

"Mr. First Gentleman." Over his scarf, the ragged end of a knife scar curled around his throat.

Blushing, Ethan nodded his hellos as he packed the snow around his snowman's middle. He couldn't meet Welby's eyes. Months ago, Jack had asked Welby to buy him and Ethan their first sex supplies. Welby had done it, and Ethan hadn't been able to look at him since.

"I've been meaning to ask you. How are you two doing with your condoms and lube? Do you need me to buy more?"

"Oh my God." Ethan turned away. Heat smothered him, the burn of embarrassment coursing through his body. "Jesus Christ, Welby." Apparently, Welby had learned to loosen up.

Welby scooted closer. He'd been the Secret Service boor, a man utterly devoid of humor or personality. But now, a hint of hilarious mischief danced in his eyes. "I know what brand the president asked for. It would be no problem."

Fucking ground never opened up and swallowed a person whole when they damn well needed it. Ethan turned away again, trying to put the snowman between him and Welby. Jack was laughing as another agent unwound his scarf and tossed it to Jack for the snowman. He would be no help in staging a rescue.

He glared at Welby, the bastard, who was fighting back his laughter.

"I see you've picked up a sense of humor somewhere. Jackass."

Welby slapped Ethan on the shoulder. In his other hand, he pulled out a long carrot and two dark grapes. "Anything for you and the president, Mr. First Gentleman."

"Thank you, so much," Ethan deadpanned. "We've got it taken care of." Mortification burned, but he took the offerings for his snowman's face.

Welby winked and headed back for the West Wing.

Ethan glared after him.

It was Scott who brought Ethan an unmarked brown bag containing lube and condoms every other week. He'd adjusted the type and brand that Jack had bought—the good stuff didn't come from the grocery store—and when he first asked Scott to accept the online deliveries and be his sex supplies mule, Scott, to his credit, had only blinked twice before agreeing.

Jack had no idea.

They took pictures with their snowmen, and the agents all voted Jack's snowman as better than Ethan's. Jack laughed, his eyes glittering, and he kissed Ethan out in the open as the snow continued to fall.

Welby came back a half hour later, standing in the background, nodding to them both.

They made their excuses and slid out, grabbing coats and scarves from Welby's arms on the way down to the parking garage. Ethan turned back and grabbed as many of Jennifer's flower arrangements as he could carry and met Jack and Welby in an unmarked SUV.

Jack stared at him, bemused, a smile on his face.

"One of my staffers is the chief floral designer for the White House," Ethan said, loading the flowers into the cargo area of the SUV, around weapons lockers, mounted shotguns, a med kit, and bulletproof vests. "She was really excited about the arrangements. I thought it would be a nice touch. She'd like it."

"Your staff includes the chief floral designer?" Jack's eyebrows shot straight up, and he fought to hold back a grin.

"She's absolutely delighted that you love her flowers." Ethan pressed a kiss to Jack's lips as he slid into the SUV.

"I most certainly do." Jack winked back at Ethan.

Welby was almost grinning up front, watching them in the rearview, and he waited until their seatbelts were fastened before driving off. They kept the red and blues off and slid out of the underground parking garage like they were any normal White House staffer.

Welby took them through city streets, north via Wisconsin Ave and past the now empty vice presidential residence at the Naval Observatory. Snow fell softly until Welby pulled into the secured entrance at Walter Reed Army Medical Center.

The director of the hospital and a platoon of military police met them at the door. Ethan grabbed the best arrangements and carried them up as Welby glued himself to his and Jack's sides. The hospital director led them, flanked by the soldiers, until they reached the recovery wing for American and Russian soldiers wounded in the ground fight against the Islamic Caliphate.

Jack had opened Walter Reed to any Russian soldiers who needed advanced medical interventions or surgeries as a result of their combined combat operations in Syria and Iraq. Most of the injuries were due to IEDs, but others were there because of sniper fire or missile attacks. Walter Reed and other advanced bio labs were regenerating soldiers' lost limbs, growing clones of destroyed or amputated body parts from the soldiers' DNA and stem cells.

At Walter Reed, some were healing after their replacement limbs had been grafted. Others were waiting for their limbs to finish growing. Many of the Americans and Russians had served in the same area and were wounded together. Now, they recovered together, and in the finest military tradition, were teaching each other the foulest curse words in their languages. The Americans also teased the Russians mercilessly, saying theirs would come to them star-spangled in the red, white, and blue.

The soldiers had been told that morning that the president and first gentleman would be coming by to spend time with anyone who wanted. Ambulatory patients walked or rolled to the lounge on the recovery floor, and patients still confined to their beds with injuries too severe to move left notes with the nurses.

There was no press for this. No media. Just them on their day off, trying to do something good in the world for the people who were risking it all.

Jack was in his element, diving in and listening to everyone's stories. Stories about their deployments and their victories. Their time downrange. Friends still deployed. American soldiers recuperating with their Russian partners introduced each other to Jack, and Jack practiced his horrible Russian, learned from President Puchkov, with the Russian soldiers.

Ethan heard a lot of *Zeabis* shouted from across the room and raucous laughter. He smiled as Jack ducked down and took selfies with everyone, making crazy faces together. Jack signed casts and bandages, and for one Russian, signed his right pectoral.

Ethan moved with the quieter guys, the ones in the back and on the periphery. Jack could make friends with a tree, and in a room full of gregarious military personnel, he was in heaven. There were those, though, who stayed back, and Ethan sat with them, talking quietly about their injuries and their mission and about their lives and future plans.

He thought of Cooper and his men, flying over the Atlantic Ocean and chasing down Madigan's vapor trail. His stomach tied itself in knots. He did not want to be visiting Adam, or any of his Marines, in the hospital. Or worse, at Arlington National Cemetery. Not because of his orders. Not because of Madigan and his fucked-up schemes.

What was Madigan up to now? They were following him, but where were they all headed? Where would Madigan's crazed mind take them?

Visiting the soldiers in their rooms was sobering. Some couldn't speak. Some couldn't move. Jack sat with everyone, talking when he could, holding their hand when he could not. Ethan stayed by his side, and they left flowers in each room.

The drive back was quiet. Ethan held Jack close, arms wrapped around each other as Jack laid his head on Ethan's shoulder. Ethan was lost in his memories, the times when he'd been in combat and when he'd thought he wouldn't make it through the next five minutes. Jack had that look in his eyes whenever he was back in the past, remembering his marriage to Leslie, his wife killed in the war.

What was he thinking? Was he wondering about what could have happened if Leslie had been treated and cared for like those soldiers? If she could have been saved?

Ethan rubbed his hand up and down Jack's arm and kissed his temple. Breathed in the scent of his hair. "You all right?"

Jack smiled and turned in for a gentle kiss on the lips.

"This was a good day." Jack rested his forehead against Ethan's cheek. "With you."

Ethan kissed Jack's temple again. "I love you."

13

Kharga Oasis, Egypt

Kharga Oasis was just like every other desert city Adam had ever seen. Minarets, mosque domes, and satellite dishes dotted flat mud roofs, and scattered, bedraggled palm trees sucked up what little water there was between baking stretches of concrete and squat tan buildings. Morning calls to prayer wailed over Kharga, shaking the already-sun-scorched air. Palms dotted the oasis and the open air market on the edge of town.

Dates and coconuts were for sale, along with limp vegetables and bruised oranges. Water-filled troughs hung on the market's perimeter. Cows and camels shared space, drinking their fill. Dusty carpets and prayer beads hung from every other stall.

Dark eyes watched Adam and Doc as they wandered through, dressed in floor-length thobes and loose keffiyehs over their heads.

The rest of their team were hunkered down outside of Kharga in desert jeeps—and a horse trailer—flown down to them from DC and then across the Atlantic. They'd landed at one of the rendition sites in middle Egypt before dawn and driven into the desert in Egyptian-marked jeeps.

Adam and Doc needed to buy camels. The team would take the jeeps with the camels in the trailer as far southeast as the hard-packed sands of the *Darb el-Arba* allowed, and when the sands shifted, they'd turn to camels. It was hundreds of miles to the region where Madigan's plane had been spotted, and that was a lot of empty desert to cover surreptitiously. Which meant no helicopters, and no Egyptian military aid.

"You sure know your way around here." Doc juggled an orange in one hand, seemingly careless. "Didn't know you knew so much about the Arabs."

He'd helped Doc into the thobe and the others into their Bedouin attire, and then had shown them how to wrap their keffiyehs and ghutras. Raiders they were, but before Djibouti, most of his men had served in the Far East and the Philippines.

Adam scowled. He didn't want to talk about this. Not at all. Across the market, he spotted the universal sign of the camel merchant: angry camels, heavy carpets being beaten out to get rid of the fleas, and a mountain of stinking shit. "Over there."

"Did you work in Iraq before Djibouti? Or somewhere in the Gulf? You're fluent in Gulf Arabic, too." Doc wouldn't let up. "You know, you never said much about where you were before you came to us."

As they drew near the camel dealer, and the milling mass of stinking animals on the edge of the market, one of the camels spat, lobbing a hot, rancid glob of phlegm right at Adam's face. He barely ducked in time. Experience, though, had taught him the warning signs.

Doc, naturally, thought it was hilarious.

The dealer wanted to wheel and deal, and Adam just wanted to get the fuck out of there. He paid too much for ten camels and didn't care when the dealer made a pretentious show of how he'd just suckered the Gulf Arabic–speaking foreigners out of too many of their Saudi riyals. Doc stayed quiet, blessedly, and picked out the camels, following Adam's orders to check the hooves and the bellies for any infestations or bleeding.

As they led their camels out of the market and up the main road of Kharga to the edge of town, one of them spat again, landing a glob on the top of Adam's keffiyeh-covered head.

"I fucking hate camels."

In the old days, when men and camels moved slower, the *Darb el-Arba* took forty days to traverse, from the mouth of the Nile to the edges of the interior in Chad and Niger.

With jeeps and camels, they could make their part of the journey in just a day.

The jeeps took them to the border of Egypt, where they ditched the rusty vehicles and the empty fuel cans and took to the camels through the shifting, sinking sands of the deep Sahara. They rode the camels hard, but the animals were rested and watered, and they traveled the last segment after the hottest part of the day had passed. As the sun lowered in the sky, Adam's GPS pinged.

They had reached the area around Madigan's landing zone.

He spread his men out, leaving the camels and their gear and taking only their weapons as they encircled the coordinates. The plane had landed in a wide wadi, a dried, ancient river bed, but it had been a rough landing. Rubber tire pieces lay scattered, and the plane had driven to its final resting place on just steel rims. The pilot, whoever he'd been, had balls of steel.

Huge swatches of desert camo netting covered the transport, and scrub kicked up from the landing had been thrown on the wings. He and his men circled above, peering down into the wadi and the covered plane. Next to Adam, Doc snapped pictures for the director.

Sergeant Coleman radioed back, saying he'd found tracks leading away from the landing zone. Lots of them. A caravan of camels, perhaps, had met the plane. They'd tried to cover their trail, but missed the edges.

Adam ordered his men down into the wadi. They held around the plane, and then his men moved in, taking up breach positions on either side of the open cargo ramp.

He counted down silently, using hand gestures, his men's eyes fixed on him.

They stormed the cargo hold, sweeping right and left and clearing the shadows.

Nothing moved. Not even a breeze rustled the camo netting. Only their boots scuffing over metal grates and the heavy breathing of his men made any sound at all as they shuffled through the dark cargo hold, scanning the shadows.

Bullets zinged, pinging off the plane's frame. One punctured the metal skin of the fuselage. Sunlight sliced through the darkness and Adam ducked as he dove for cover. His men whirled, covering low or leaping out of the cargo hold as bullets zipped around their heads.

"The fuck is shooting at us?" Coleman bellowed as he took up position next to Adam, trying to find the source of the gunfire.

"It's coming from the cockpit!"

Adam's eyes finally found the shadowy silhouette hiding in the dim reaches of the plane's forward cabin. The sunlight barely reached the cockpit, and whoever was up there had hidden in the shadows. "Cover me."

Coleman laid down a burst of gunfire as Adam snaked up the side of the plane's cargo hold, hugging the metal hull until he slipped into the shadows as well. Ducking, he waited until his eyes adjusted to the near-darkness.

There. Just ahead. A man shuffling into position. Heavy mouth breathing. Whispers, just under the man's breath that sounded like frantic prayers or pleas.

Adam raised his rifle, a compact M4, and slipped closer.

When the shooter rose to take a pot shot at Adam's men down at the end of the cargo ramp, his body crossed the open door of the cockpit, and a perfect silhouette appeared. Adam let loose a burst of fire. Three bullets slammed into the shooter's chest.

Grunting, the shadow fell to the side, losing his grip on his rifle. His weapon clattered to the deck.

Adam ran to him, kicking the rifle down the fuselage to Coleman and training his weapon on the downed shooter. He'd landed on his front, facedown, and Adam used his boot to kick the man over.

When he did, Adam's eyes blew open. Strapped to the man's chest was a vest packed with explosives, and duct-taped around that, what looked the junk drawer of a machinist's shops. Nails, razor blades, screws, and shattered glass.

The shooter looked Adam dead in the eye and raised his hand to his chest. "*Almawt li'amrika.*"

Death to America.

"Go!" Adam hollered, turning and running for the cargo ramp. He waved to his men, waiting and watching for his all clear. "Go! Get the fuck down! Now!"

As he ran, he heard the first burst of the explosives igniting and felt the shake and tremble of the plane. He dove feet first as he wrapped his hands around his head and slid the last ten feet down the plane's belly and over the open cargo ramp, where the rest of his team had ducked down in the sand.

Behind him, the top of the plane blew off, the metal hull shattering like confetti. Nails and screws tore through the plane's body, leaving holes and dots of sunshine streaking through the interior like sunlit strings. Zings sounded, razor blades and nails embedding in the fuselage. All around, fragments of steel, copper, and scorched wiring, the innards of the transport, fell like rain on Adam and his men, dotting the sand with thumps and small craters.

The acrid taste of C4 hung heavy in the air and on the back of Adam's tongue.

"What the fuck was that?" Doc was the first one up. "Everyone all right?"

The team sounded off, all clear, but Doc went one by one, visually inspecting everyone. When he got to Adam, peering into the ruined plane, he grabbed Adam's hands.

Bits of glass and razor blades had shredded through his gloves, and blood was seeping from his knuckles and dripping into to the sand. "I'm fine." He tried to shake Doc off.

"I'll let you know if you're fine or not. That's a lot of blood." Doc nodded to Coleman, who jogged over, took one look at Adam's hands, and arched his eyebrow at Adam.

Outmaneuvered by his own men. Damn it. "Go check out what's still standing in there." He pulled his gloves off by his teeth and managed to smear blood all over his chin as Coleman took two guys and headed back into the destroyed plane.

His hands looked worse than they were. He wasn't in danger of losing a finger or five. While Doc cleaned him up, he kept an eagle eye on his men.

When Coleman shouted for him to come to the remains of the cockpit, he gave Doc a harried look and then jogged inside when Doc let him go.

Inside, his guys were leaning over a mangled laptop that somehow still worked. Wires connected it to the plane's electronics, and it had been in a corner of the cockpit that had been shielded from the suicide bomber. On screen, four video feeds showed in four boxes, live images of what looked like the mangled plane and their team. He saw, outside, Doc repacking his medic bag, and three of his guys watching the perimeter.

And he saw himself, staring at the laptop, his fierce glower filling the screen.

Suddenly, the screen went dark. The feeds cut out.

A cursor appeared on screen, blinking.

Hello, Lieutenant typed out, letter by letter.

"What the fuck..." Coleman cursed.

Catch me if you can. We'll be waiting.

14

Moscow
The Kremlin

Sasha woke with a gasp, bolting upright as he shouted, a wordless bellow. Nightmares clung to his skin, the image of his commander's sneer and the fall of his fist, the clang of hockey sticks on the metal lockers and the concrete floor.

"Easy." An old man's rough voice broke through the haze of his fear. He whipped around and spotted an older man in a doctor's coat next to his bed.

He stared, breathing hard, and then his gaze darted every which way. He was in what looked like a private hospital room, dimly lit, and through the window, the sky was dark. Machines beeped beside his bed. Sensors were fixed to his chest beneath his thin hospital robe. An IV line was taped to his arm, stuck in his vein at his elbow. Dull pain pulsed in his abdomen, and he fumbled through the robe until he felt a line of stitches just over his belly button.

"You were very badly injured," The older man said, waiting for Sasha to finish checking over his body. "You were in surgery for several hours."

"Surgery?"

"Ruptured spleen. We removed it. You would have died if we had not."

The old man's words rang in Sasha's ear, echoing over and over.

"You are bruised and ugly for now, but you will live." Sighing, the old man sat on the edge of Sasha's bed. "I do not know who you are or how you ended up on the doorstep of the Kremlin so injured." He held up a long chain, Sasha's Air Force dog tags dangling. "This man was reported missing and presumed dead yesterday."

Sasha stilled. "I do not know who you are either. Or where I am." He raised his chin, defiant.

"A fair question. I will answer if will you do the same." His eyebrows quirked up, and Sasha nodded once. "I am Doctor Leo Voronov, personal physician to President Puchkov, and you are inside the private hospital for the president in the Grand Palace of the Kremlin." His eyebrows stayed raised. "And you?"

Sasha froze. Ice flushed through him, racing from his head to his toes and then settling in his belly, a hard knot of panic. He'd had a delirious plan, a stupid plan, and he'd headed for Moscow, but to actually *be* in the Kremlin—

"The Kremlin?" His voice shook, and he swallowed, trying to steady himself. "President Puchkov?"

Dr. Voronov nodded. "It is your turn now," he said gently.

Sasha held Dr. Voronov's stare for a long moment before he started to speak in halting, shaking words.

15

Saharan Desert

Madigan's caravan tracks traveled through the wadi, south out of the Libyan Desert toward the border of Sudan and into the northern Darfur region.

Adam had his men rest before they set out, getting a few hours of sleep before hopping back onto their camels and following the trail, this time by the light of the moon, hanging heavy and low over the empty desert. Adam watched their progress on his GPS, and he cursed when he realized they were about to cross into Darfur.

"Hold up," he sent over his radio. The mic at his throat picked up the vibrations as he spoke. All he had to do was whisper. "We're coming up on the border. We need to check it out." He sent four men forward, Sergeant Wright and his partner on camels, and Fitz and Kobayashi on foot, to scope out the border.

They came back after an hour. "Nothing there, sir. Empty desert. No checkpoints. No military. No rebels." Wright whispered into his throat mic, but his voice was clear as a bell in Adam's ear.

Much more important was the lack of rebels. The Sudanese Army wasn't a joke, but the rebels were fucking insane. He'd rather they not have any indication they were poking around in Darfur.

"Keep your eyes open." Adam nudged his camel forward and wrapped his keffiyeh around his face again, covering all but his eyes. He, like his men, wore layers of loose cotton robes, muted shades of desert sand and mud brick tan, interspersed with pops of blue and black. Beneath all of their robes, their black combat uniforms had been sterilized. No rank, no country insignia, and no names. The only identification any of the men carried was a strip of duct tape with their blood type written in marker and wrapped around the radio receiver strapped to their chests.

They saw—and heard—their destination an hour later, glowing over the midnight sand dunes. Bonfires and trash fires sent sparks into the air, and bursts of gunfire spat toward the moon as raucous laughter mixed with shouts and wild boasts. Beat-up trucks with their cabins shorn off shared space with dozens of camels and four Humvees. Ratty tents made from leaning tree sticks and bent metal poles covered with torn fabric and empty UN food program sacks clustered around an oasis of scrub trees. US Army-issue green canvas tents sat primly some feet away, at perfect right angles to each other.

A sprawling market, filled with open-air stalls covered in rifles, machetes, grenades, rocket launchers, and belt-fed ammunition, surrounded a square of sand the size of several football fields. Inside, thousands of men relaxed together, laughing and shouting, some drinking and throwing their empty glass bottles into the trash fires before them. Others shot into the sky, wild gesticulations punctuating the stories they told.

The sheer number of weapons and men puckered Adam's belly button. His guts slid against themselves as every muscle in his body clenched. Rebels and Madigan's forces, mixing together? Madigan's growing army joining another?

Whatever it was, a bad situation had just gotten worse.

Adam hopped off his camel and dropped to his belly, crawling with his binoculars through the rough sand to the top of the sand dune. Doc and Coleman crawled with him, and Doc passed over the camera plugin for his binos as he zoomed in on the crowd.

"I've got positive ID on target Baker." Captain Cook, the Z Unit prisoner Madigan had gone to lengths to break out, was laughing and squeezing the shoulder of a rebel while other disreputable-looking men watched. He snapped a pic through the binos.

"Target Alpha?" Doc flipped through their who's who list of known targets broken out of the South American prisons, and an updated list of missing SOCOM soldiers from Paraguay on a mini tactical tablet mounted on his forearm in a sleeve. "Madigan?"

Adam scanned the crowd again, zooming in on groups of men. He found three of the missing SOCOM soldiers, including the Executive Officer, and one of the high-value jihadist prisoners from Peru, but not Madigan. "Negative. Damn it."

"Maybe he's jerking off."

Adam snorted. "Let's set up a recon point. When it settles down in there, we can send a team in." Once the wildness calmed down, maybe they could poke around in the market undercover.

His men took up position on the dunes, hiding in the shifting sands. They hid the camels a quarter mile back under a rocky overhang. One of the camels spat in its Marine's face as a thank-you.

The dead hours of the night bled on, and the wild gathering never lessened. More men piled out of the shanty tents, adjusting their pants, and others headed in, unbuckling their belts on the way. The gunfire continued, bursts spitting into the night. Cook stayed up, moving from group to group, laughing with some, helping sight the targets on another group's rifles. Some of the South American prisoners got into all-out fistfights, wailing on each other until they were down in the sand and blood wept from broken noses and shattered jaws. No one stopped the brawls.

As the sun peeked over the edge of the Sahara, more rusted-out trucks arrived, and the men in the wadi swelled. More market stalls opened, selling every type of military tech imaginable. Radios, rockets, machetes, binos, NVGs. Purchasers test-fired weapons into the air as men met and chatted, exchanging intel and battle plans. Payments were made between warlords: guns, ammunition, food, and captured women and men. The shanty tents under the limp scrub trees opened their flaps, and dozens of weary, bedraggled women shuffled out. Most were bruised, and some clutched obviously broken arms.

"Jesus Christ." Adam exhaled slowly as he and his men watched the anarchy unfold, this meeting of rebels, warlords, and weapons.

"Can we just call in an air strike?" Doc mumbled. "Wipe all of this off the planet?"

Adam snorted. In the complicated mess of international politics, an unsanctioned air strike undertaken by the controversial president of the United States against a rebel camp in a disputed region of a terrorist state would ignite a powder keg of rage and furious instability around the world. But maybe it'd be worth it.

More trucks and men on camels were arriving by the minute. Adam squinted.

"All right. We need to go check it out. We can blend in. Let's see if we can make heads or tails of what's going on down there." His binos zoomed in on Cook, still standing in the square and chatting to a new warlord. "And get close to Cook."

"So *you're* going down there?" Adam saw Doc's lips move, but his whispers were too low to hear without the mic amplifying his voice. "'Cause you speak fluent Arabic, and that's most of what I'm hearing from down in that mess."

"Yeah. And you're coming too."

"Me?" Doc squawked.

"You're annoying enough to fit in." In reality, Doc had a sharp pair of eyes, and he was one of the better spotters on Adam's team. "Get ready.

Bring your weapon under your robes. Keep your face covered and wear your shades."

Doc cursed but slid down the dune and rolled to his back, getting his gear in order. Next to Adam, Coleman called for a water check as the sun continued to climb.

He followed Doc down the hill and fixed his robes, hiding his M4 under the folds across his chest. They headed back for their camels and grabbed two. No matter which one Adam reached for, they all spat at him. There was some mutual hatred between him and camels, some kind of ever-present disgust.

They circled the wadi and crossed over to the hard-packed sands several miles down from the rebel camp, and then doubled back and approached from the south, heading toward their men on the ridge. Coleman radioed in that he had them in his gun sights, and the rest of the team were covering on the dune.

And then they arrived at the camp, pulling their camels to a stop and tying them up under a scrub tree.

The stench was almost overpowering. Sweat-soaked bodies and sunbaked canvas turned the air sour, along with the acrid stench of burning diesel and rancid trash. Camel-shit fumes wafted over the mass of humanity, the only hint of a breeze carrying the offal. Radios blared, spitting out Arabic beats and angry diatribes from local broadcasts run by rebels. Fast Arabic and local dialects shouted from every direction, and the gunfire *ratta-tatted* in fast bursts. The reverberations shook their bones, and Doc and Adam shared a long look before heading into the ramshackle market.

Adam made a show of checking the edge of a machete at a stall that sold them in messy stacks, the merchant bragging that they were made from strong Chinese steel and cost a fraction of any other machete being sold. Across the stall, stocky rebels hefted rocket launchers and practiced sighting in on the camels.

Three stalls over, Cook was moving, slipping through the crowd of rebel shoppers. He had his shades on and a handkerchief tied around his neck, and his sweat-stained shirt clung to his wiry muscles.

Adam nudged Doc, and the two moved down the line of raucous stalls, ignoring the barkers shouting at them to check their wares as pounding Arabic dance music blared.

They were getting closer. Cook was only two stalls away, his back to them. Adam reached for his M4, holding the grip beneath his robes.

The dance music cut off and furious Arabic bellowed from the tinny radio speakers surrounding them. Vendors paused, reaching for the radios and tuning out the static, trying to hear better.

Adam's gaze fixed on Cook. Their target had stopped.

His palm squeezed on his rifle's grip, fingers curling around the trigger.

"L-T," Doc hissed. "What the fuck is that radio saying?" He stepped close to Adam, crowding him and covering his reach for his own M4. "They're all fucking looking at us!"

One of the vendors turned the radio dial up. Heads turned their way, eyes narrowing.

"L-T!" Doc hissed again. "The fuck is going on?"

Blinking, Adam glanced right and left, and finally listened to the bellowing Arabic belting from the radio. In between the static, he heard one of the rebel DJs shouting about infiltrators, American spies in the region sent there to destabilize the rebels and kill them all. *"We have this information straight from the top, my fellow fighters! Look to your brothers and root out these American spies, these Western pigs sent from their pig president!"*

Fuck. Adam's eyes flicked up and down the market stalls, searching for an exit as the rebels surrounding them closed ranks and started pointing their way. Curses flew as rifles chambered rounds.

His gaze caught on Cook, now facing him, staring at him, and watching the rebels in the market circling their prey.

Cook smirked.

"Fuck!" Adam pressed his mic and radioed his men. "Evac! Our cover is blown! Get out now!"

"We're coming for you, L-T," Coleman barked back immediately.

"Negative!" Adam whipped out his M4 as Doc did the same. They turned back to back, trying to fend off the swarming rebels. "Get the fuck out of here!"

He spotted the machete dealer again and the piles and piles of blades stacked almost four feet high. Beyond the machete dealer's stall, a tarp of limp vegetables lay on the ground, the vegetables withered in the heat. Beyond that, a stretch of sand before the cluster of camels munching on scrub vegetation. A desperate plan formed in his mind.

"Get the camels and circle to the south. Ride hard for Al-Fashir."

"We're not leaving you, L-T."

"We'll be riding south. Take out the bastards chasing us."

"What's the plan, L-T?" Doc's voice had lost his sarcastic teasing, his ever-present cockiness. "What do we do?"

Adam spun them around, still back to back, and shot rounds into the sand at the encroaching rebels' feet, trying to force them back. Most leaped away but brandished their own weapons and bellowed in Arabic, calling them American pigs and promising a painful, slow death.

"Run at the machete dealer. Shoot him and use the blades to leap the stall. Grab one and clear a path to the camels. Cut them all free. Get one and go. Ride south, hard and fast."

"And you?"

"I'll cover you."

Adam exhaled, and his sweat-slick hands gripped his M4. There was no way he'd get out of there, but he could cover Doc.

This was it. He'd be dead in moments. *His* damn smile flashed through Adam's mind once again, but he let it stay, hovering there behind his eyes. *If only.*

"Fuck that." Doc reached over Adam's head and grabbed his vest through his robes, jerking hard and spinning him around. He fired, spraying the crowd of rebels with gunfire. Men screamed, falling to the ground as bullets tore through them. Chaos erupted.

Through the chaos, Cook whipped out a handgun and aimed at Adam and Doc.

Doc fired wildly toward Cook and took off, dragging Adam with him toward the machete dealer's stall. Two bullets to the machete dealer had him dropping to the sand, lifeless. They clambered up the sliding piles of blades, unsteady on their feet, but managed to leap onto the tarp of vegetables as Cook opened fire again.

Three bullets whizzed by Adam's face, one burning through the cartilage of his ear. Blood poured down his cheek and soaked his keffiyeh.

Adam sprayed a wild burst toward Cook, peppering the market. Dealers ducked, and some of the rebels dove for cover while others fired back at Adam and Doc. Stalls collapsed, and ratty tarps swung from broken boards. Weapons and bodies lay in the blood-soaked sand. Destroyed vegetables lay scattered, limp lettuce, squished tomatoes, and scattered potatoes rolling every which way.

He took a moment to breathe, exhaling hard as he ducked behind a narrow scrub tree and sought out Cook. Doc cut loose the camels and shouted at them, smacking their asses to get them moving.

Through the shot-up market, Cook leveled his handgun at Adam and smirked again. His finger squeezed down on the trigger.

Adam exhaled, pressed his rifle to his shoulder, and fired first.

Cook ducked, but Adam fired low, and one of his bullets slammed into Cook's shoulder. Cook dropped, crouching behind a damaged stall and grabbed at his shoulder, his shirt rapidly staining red with blood.

"L-T!" Doc was up on his camel, and he had the reins of another in his hand. "Time to go!"

Adam leaped onto his cranky camel and kicked it hard in the ribs. Snorting, the camel took off, racing south as the rebels in the market tried to chase them. Some ran for the scattered camels as others ran for the trucks, piling in and taking off into the desert on their heels.

The hard-packed sands continued for miles. The trucks would have an easy time chasing them. Desert grit sprayed behind the trucks' tires, and though some fishtailed wildly, they caught up to Adam and Doc.

Bullets flew past their heads. The camels screamed in protest, stamping the sand, trying to go faster.

Adam grit his teeth and tried to lay low on his camel. Next to him, Doc did the same and sent Adam a frantic, sidelong look.

This is it. Shot in the back on camels. Fucking camels. He prayed it would be quick.

"We're coming in from the northeast. Got you in our sights. Ride straight, we'll take out the trash."

Coleman's voice broke over the radio, followed by gunfire cracking the air behind him. Gunfire from his team. He barked out a surprised laugh, relief dizzying his head. Doc grinned.

Coleman and his team ran at his and Doc's pursuers on their camels, flanking the convoy and sniping the drivers and shooters out of the open cabins. Swerving, three trucks crashed into each other and one flipped. The last slammed on its brakes, throwing sand, and the rebels scattered, some trying to return fire and others running to the crashed vehicles.

Coleman's team swept by, finishing off the rebels before swinging up behind Adam and Doc. Hooves pounded and grit sprayed behind the team as they drove their camels as fast as they could in a sprint for the south.

"Good timing, Sergeant."

Coleman stayed quiet while their team rode hard in a wide line, heading for Al-Fashir.

"What now, L-T?" Doc still had a worried look in his eyes and a deep frown creased his forehead. His keffiyeh flopped in the wind behind him, unwrapped from his face as they rode.

He knew what he had to do. He knew who he had to call. He'd known, somehow, that this would be how it would eventually turn out. He couldn't escape, not at all, from the universe's cruel forces.

He almost dropped the sat phone when he tugged it from his vest.

"DC? Thought you said they would disavow us if we caused an international incident?" Doc and Coleman shared a long look.

"Not DC." Sighing, Adam punched in the number he knew by heart.

As always, *he* answered, and the sound of his voice went straight through Adam's chest. His lungs clenched, and he fought to breathe.

"*As-salamu alaykum.*"

Faisal, my God. Even after all this time. I still melt when I hear your voice.

"Faisal," he managed to choke out. "I need your help. Again."

Tough Fight Ahead for Secretary of State Elizabeth Wall in Vice Presidential Confirmation Hearings

Secretary of State Elizabeth Wall headed for Capitol Hill today for the first of her confirmation hearings after being nominated for the vice president vacancy. The House Judiciary Committee opened the proceedings, focusing on Secretary Wall's history of public service and her accomplishments.

However, when Secretary Wall headed to the Senate, Senator Stephen Allen took much of the committee's time, questioning Secretary Wall on her allegiance and support for President Spiers. "Seeing as there has never been a president more threatened than President Spiers, it's reasonable to imagine that you may, in fact, inherit the presidency, having never received a single vote," Allen said. "The American people have a right to know what your beliefs are. Do you support President Spiers's lifestyle?"

In response, Secretary Wall stated that President Spiers and his partner were both personal and professional heroes of hers, especially in light of their actions against the rogue General Madigan, but she refused to discuss President Spiers's personal life.

Multiple senators ceded their time to Senator Allen's line of inquiry, which included questioning how Secretary Wall, if confirmed, would push the president to repair the US's standing in the world and reintroduce family values to the White House.

16

White House Residence

"Mr. President? Mr. First Gentleman?" The low voice of the overnight Navy steward woke Jack and Ethan at four in the morning.

Blinking at the light spilling in from the hallway, Jack's stomach clenched, and one of his hands sought Ethan's. Ethan groggily woke and rolled toward him.

They'd been woken in the middle of the night once before, and it had been terrible news.

What was happening now?

"What's up?"

Shaking his head, Jack tried to focus on the steward's words as Ethan buried his face in Jack's hip. "Mr. President, we're getting reports that a dump of Top Secret intelligence cables has been posted online. Mr. Irwin and Mr. Rees are in the Situation Room now."

"Fuck." Jack leaped from the bed, and Ethan's face hit the mattress. The steward politely ducked out of their bedroom while Jack scrambled for his boxers and pulled a pair of jeans from the back of the couch beneath their window. He tripped over their crumpled clean-up towel, what once had been a beautiful deep navy from the White House now stained with their combined release. He nudged it under the bed as his cheeks burned.

"What's going on?" Ethan grunted as he pushed himself up. His hair stood on end and sleep clung to him, squishing his face and squinting his eyes.

Jack took a moment to kiss his lover's forehead. "Bad news. Top Secret intel has been released online. I'm heading down to the Situation Room. Irwin and Rees are already there." Rees was Irwin's successor at the CIA, the new director, and Jack had a sneaking suspicion that the two men worked very closely together. Close enough that he didn't want to actually know.

Ethan groaned and face-planted back to the bed. Jack heard a muffled curse breathed into the mattress, and then Ethan was moving, sliding out and grabbing his own boxers and pants.

When Jack pulled on Ethan's Secret Service sweatshirt before Ethan could grab it, Ethan tried to glare, but his tender smile spoiled it. He grabbed a plain pullover instead, and in under a minute, they were heading down, running through the White House together, again, in the dead of night.

The night shift Secret Service agents picked them up at the stairs and escorted them to the White House ground floor before taking up silent positions in the back of the Situation Room.

Irwin was already reading through the dumped intel cables on the main screen while Rees was juggling his cell phone and making furious notes on three different notepads.

"I'm here. Hit me." Jack stood behind his chair, Ethan at his side.

"Fifty gigs of Top Secret intel cables, dated this week to two months ago. Reports from the CIA and DIA, mostly describing our clandestine operations in the Middle East and Africa." Irwin spoke while Rees shouted into his cell phone, something about needing to "wake him the fuck up, now".

"Does it identify assets on the ground? Are our people in danger?"

"Yes, sir." Irwin's glower turned dark. "We've found fifteen names so far. We're combing for more."

"Have we reached out to them? Got them to safety?"

"As many as we can. Some are buried pretty deep. One is inside Iran. Others are just as buried, and pretty scattered. Some are in our diplomatic programs."

"Work harder. We need to get everyone into our embassies and out of those countries."

Irwin and Rees nodded, Rees already dialing another number on his cell phone as Jack shared a long look with Ethan.

"Who do I need to start calling?" Pulling out his chair, Jack sat and dragged the secure phone at the conference table close to him. "What leaders do I need to reach out to?"

"It's a long list, sir. Sixteen countries so far. None of them will be happy about our operations on their soil."

"Do I need to ask who did this?"

Irwin leveled his gaze at Jack. "You already know. Madigan."

"How did he get access to this intel? He hasn't had clearance in months."

"But the officers at the SOCOM base in Paraguay did." Ethan slid into the seat beside Jack and pulled a tablet close, reading through the cables. "They could have gotten this for him."

"Our own military, turning against us? Joining Madigan?" Jack's chest burned, and his heart squeezed as he breathed the possibility.

"Eleven of them have." Ethan's eyes were a mixture of agony and rage, a painful hatred that echoed in Jack's soul.

"We've got to stop this. He's sending people to their deaths." Jack grabbed the phone again. "Lawrence, give me someone to call. I'm not going to abandon our people out there."

Northern Russia
St. Petersburg
Western Region Military Headquarters

"Do you have the news on?"

General Moroshkin frowned. The call on his cell phone had come through from an unlisted number and he almost hadn't answered. But he'd opened negotiations with a certain rogue general, and he accepted the call on the last ring.

"Not yet. What is happening?"

"I suggest you get on the Internet. Turn on your news. Your GRU boys will be beating down your door in just a moment, too." Over the phone line, General Madigan chuckled.

Moroshkin's eyes narrowed. His fingers pounded on the keyboard as his mustache bunched together above pursed lips.

America's leaked intelligence cables splashed across the front page of the Internet. A tsunami of outcry lay in the cables' wake, even after only a short time. He grinned, scrolling through the first published cable.

"So, General." Madigan kept talking in his ear. *"This is the second gift I have graciously offered to you. Top Secret intelligence. Names of undercover operatives. Details of operations. America's intelligence community will be seriously shattered after this."*

Moroshkin leaned back in his desk chair. "Yes, you have," he mused. "I have to ask myself, General. Why do you do this? Are you searching for a new home? Do you hope to buy your way into Russia? I am not sure the current Russian president would accept you. He is close to your president."

"Jack Spiers is no president of mine," Madigan said smoothly, his voice dropping to a slick growl. *"And I don't want to start singing the Russian hymn. That's not what I'm after."*

"What is? What is it you want with me?"

Silence, for a moment. "*If you could remake the world exactly how you want, General, how would you make it?*"

Moroshkin stilled. His eyes glanced once to his office door, closed and locked.

How did Madigan know? How had he figured out that Moroshkin had aspirations for more? Had cultivated a culture within his ranks, within his men, that yearned for the days of yesterday when Putin had stretched them around the globe and everyone knew Russia was a force to be reckoned with. What had happened to their country, after Putin?

Slowly, he tapped his finger on his wood desk. "There is much that I would change."

"*As would I.*" He could almost hear Madigan's smile, the slow slide of consonants and vowels rolling around in victory. "*And together, we can bring about that change. You and I. It's time for a new world, is it not, General?*"

Did he take this next step? Start down a path he'd dreamed of, had bellowed for, beaten into the heads and hearts of so many thousands of his own men. He'd said the words, but actually making a move—actually working toward a revolution—was something else entirely.

His eyes wandered to the computer monitor, and the American intelligence cables. Madigan, a man on the run, hunted by the United States, and yet he'd managed to penetrate their deepest secrets. With power like that, what could they not do together?

"It *is* time for a new world, General," he answered, his bushy mustache twitching. "You and I do see eye to eye."

White House

"Mr. President, twenty-one of our assets were named in the cables." Irwin called out across the conference table as Jack slammed the phone down on the Pakistani president. "Thirteen have made it to our embassies."

"And the other eight?" Ethan asked, watching Jack. Jack's rage simmered just beneath his skin. Ethan's worried eyes were heavy on him. Beneath the Situation Room's conference table, Ethan's hand landed on Jack's knee, squeezing.

They'd been calling who they could, desperately pleading for help in rounding up their assets. Some refused to take their call. Others told Jack he was a criminal himself, and his people deserved the punishment that was coming.

"*You've been caught, Mr. President,*" the president of Pakistan had crowed. "*You can't break every law of the planet, of international law, and of God's will, and expect not to reap your consequences. Your sins were bound to catch up to you. This is the price you have to pay for your sexual indiscretions—*"

Jack had slammed down the phone. Fuck international diplomacy.

The Situation Room had filled up, most of his national security staff and joint chiefs in the room. Everyone had their cell phones out, and at least two conversations going on text, email, and cell each.

Director Rees rubbed his forehead. "We don't have any status on the missing eight." He swallowed, his throat rising and falling as Jack stared him down.

Jack had inherited the United States' intelligence apparatus, just like every American president, but when it went off the rails or came crashing down, he was the one holding the cards when the game ended. These lives were on him.

On how he hadn't caught Madigan yet.

His rage, his raw fury, roared, the image of eight Americans dying because of Madigan's games. His plots and his machinations.

He'd always been a peaceful man, but the thought of Madigan dead brought him true pleasure. The thought of him obliterated, wiped off the planet, made his heart beat faster and gave him a thrill of satisfaction so strong he could practically taste it.

Elizabeth, still secretary of state until her confirmation hearing went through, hung up her phone. "Britain has condemned the release of the cables, but they're also being careful to distance themselves from us. They are quietly working on trying to track down where the release came from."

Jack shook his head and braced his forearms against the table. It would be useless. Madigan would have covered his tracks better than that. He'd been two steps ahead of them so far, exploding out of the shadows in a matter of days and sowing death and destruction across half the world.

The phone before Jack buzzed. "*Mr. President, call from President Puchkov.*"

Sergey. Maybe his friend could give him a little smile. Jack grabbed the phone and nodded to Ethan to pick up his receiver as well. Most of the time he spoke to world leaders privately and he didn't have the rest of his Situation Room listening in. But now, he needed Ethan there by his side. He needed his presence. Ethan was a balm to his soul, a soothing refuge in a sea of insanity.

"Sergey."

"*Jack.*" Sergey sounded drained on the other end of the line, like how Jack expected he sounded to Sergey. "*Bad day over there for you.*"

"It's only just begun." Jack pinched the bridge of his nose and closed his eyes. They'd been at it for hours, combing through the cables, trying to keep a lid on the worst of the damage. The priority was getting their people to safety. Everything else could wait.

"*I got my people on this as soon as we heard about the release of your cables. I am sorry, but we were only able to pick up five of your operatives.*"

Jack's head whipped around, staring at Ethan as his jaw dropped. Ethan froze, wide-eyed. "Sergey, you what?" Sitting forward, Jack motioned for Director Rees and Irwin to pick up receivers down the table. They scrambled for the phones, muting their handhelds before answering.

"*Ilya Ivchenko is the head of the FSB, and my close friend. We started in the FSB together. He called his people in Iran, Pakistan, and Libya. We managed to get five of your operatives before the authorities picked them up.*"

Director Rees's mouth dropped open, and he mouthed to Irwin, "Holy fucking shit," as he rifled through his notepads.

Jack spun his own notes closer. The names of all twenty-one operatives were written down, and he'd checked off next to the ones that were safe. "Can you tell me who you picked up?"

Sergey grunted and then started reading the names and countries. "*They are all safe in our embassies, and we are arranging transport to Moscow and then to Washington ASAP.*" He chuckled, once. "*We are not questioning your people, either. And they are being treated very well. Hot showers and food, even.*" It was a lame joke, but it was a tired attempt at humor from Sergey, and for the moment, Jack appreciated it.

Exhaling, he leaned back in his chair and closed his eyes. Gratitude flooded through him. "Sergey…" He didn't know what to say. "You saved their lives. And we're only missing three now. Observers in Congo and Bangladesh."

Beneath the table, Ethan's hand found his, lacing together.

"*I am sorry we could not do more, Jack. We did not have access to those operatives. Our people on the ground are limited in both of those countries.*"

Director Rees scribbled furious notes, making disbelieving gestures to Irwin across the table as the rest of the Situation Room stared, slack-jawed.

"You've done more than anyone else." He swallowed and pressed his lips together. "Thank you, Sergey."

A pause. "*Let us talk, Jack. One on one. When you are not swamped with this.*" Sergey sighed, and the exhale crackled over the phone line. "*I hope you find your missing men. Truly. Please call if there is anything I can do.*"

17

Moscow
The Kremlin

Sergey wandered through the halls of the Kremlin Palace, his hands stuffed in his suit pants, jacket long forgotten, tie left behind at his desk. He'd had Ilya working for hours, trying to find the last three American operatives. They'd even reached out to a few of the rebel groups President Putin had once kept delicate contact with in Congo, but that had been a dead end.

And, a short time ago, the news had broken. All three were dead. Murdered, no doubt. In Congo, the bodies had been put on public display, a warning to all foreigners and spies. Dubious circumstances shouted from the news reports, along with a worldwide blanket condemnation of the United States. Even from her closest allies, as if the United Kingdom didn't have spies circling the globe as well.

It had been a long, long day, and a tragic one. Still, the events had kept his mind off what he had to do tomorrow, and that had been a relief. Now that the day was done, and night had crept through the Kremlin, Sergey's thoughts turned once more to his task at hand.

He paced, restless.

Eventually, his feet took him to the far wing and he found himself wandering past the offices his doctor had taken over. He'd learned, through the years, to only trust his personal physician. He wouldn't be assassinated by a strange doctor's hand.

What was it Dr. Voronov had said the day before? He'd found a man outside the Kremlin, half-dead and frozen, and had brought him in. Well, Voronov had a soft touch. He'd been a kind man when he was young, and age had only made him kinder. He was completely at odds with Sergey's world, and that was one of the reasons he kept the old man around.

Voronov had sent an email about the man, and before everything had broken with the American intelligence cables, he'd meant to read it. Voronov had personally asked him to, coming to see him with a fresh cup of coffee and earnest, worried eyes.

Leaning up against the wall, Sergey fished out his cell phone and pulled up the email. A lengthy military record was attached at the end, a career's worth of overachievement and high honors.

His blood began to boil as he read, and by the time he finished, he nearly threw his cell down the red-carpeted hallway. Instead, he paced, his hands clenching into fists, nearly crushing his phone in his grasp. At the end of the hall, he slouched against a golden column, leaning forward and hanging his head between his shoulders.

Dare he speak out? He was already going to unmake the Russian world tomorrow. Could he demand equality as well?

He was up against so much. His country's remarriage to orthodoxy after the fall of the Soviet Union. A hatred of anything non-Russian, and a firm belief that gays were sent from elsewhere to poison the soul of Russia. They weren't Russian. They were invaders.

Bullshit.

He'd served for years with men like Ethan and Jack, and they'd always hid, layer upon layer of lies and subterfuge. He'd always looked the other way, but had also sat silently while other men did not.

What did that make him?

Sergey closed his eyes.

He was a president marked for death anyway.

If he died for speaking out about this, so be it.

Sergey turned back around, heading for the doors to Voronov's office. He entered quietly and padded through the few rooms Voronov had outfitted for Sergey. X-ray, examination, even surgery. And, on the right, a private recovery room. He'd never used it, but it was better to be safe than sorry.

The door was open, and Sergey realized his mistake as soon as he poked his head through the door.

Sasha Andreyev was awake. His head popped up from the newspaper he'd been reading by the light of the single desk lamp when he heard Sergey's shoes squeak.

They stared at each other, frozen, for a long moment.

Sasha moved first, throwing back the covers and trying to jump to his feet. "Mr. President." He tried to salute, but doubled over, falling sideways back to the bed. Cringing, Sasha bowed his head. "Mr. President, I apologize."

Sergey moved, going to steady Sasha, but aborted, coming up short. He stood awkwardly at the foot of Sasha's bed and his hands gripped the metal frame. "Do not apologize. And do not stand. Do not salute. You need to recover your strength. Rest."

Sasha winced. "Yes, sir." He still didn't move, just stayed with his head bowed, breathing hard.

"Are… you feeling better?" He had no idea what to say.

"I am no longer dying."

"Spoken like a true Russian." Sergey grinned. It faded, replaced by stilted silence. *Do something.*

Sergey crossed to the lone chair next to the bed. He sat stiffly, long arms clasped between his knees. Sasha followed his movements but still kept his head down.

"Please, get comfortable. Do not suffer." Sergey waited, and when Sasha didn't move, he grabbed his pillow and started fluffing it. He was awkward, but Sasha twisted around, shocked, and Sergey grinned again. "So you are not a statue."

Sasha slid carefully back on the bed, leaning against the pillow. "No. Former Senior Lieutenant Sasha Andreyev. MiG pilot." He looked down at his hands. "But not anymore."

"Dr. Voronov told me what you said happened to you."

Sasha swallowed, and a dark glower settled on his face.

"There was… no other reason for this attack?" Sergey fumbled for the right thing to say. He was doing it all wrong. "Nothing else that could have angered your fellow pilots?"

"No." Sasha looked up, and Sergey's breath shorted. Fire filled Sasha's ice-blue eyes, a pure rage focused squarely on Sergey. Dark bruises and the swollen right half of Sasha's face twitched. "I thought they were my friends. I was a good officer. I worked hard. I had to be perfect. I wanted to be a cosmonaut one day." He shook his head, blinking fast, and looked away. "The only reason there was for this was because I am *goluboi*." His chin dropped. "*Pidor.*"

"Do not say that," he said firmly and reached out, grabbing hold of Sasha's shoulder. "Do not call yourself that. I read your military record. You are a great Russian. An officer in our Air Force. Be *proud* of who you are."

Wide eyes shone with held-back tears. Sasha's chin trembled.

Sergey squeezed his shoulder again.

"I hate that I am—" Sasha choked out. He shook his head. "I tried to fix it. I tried to change." He gasped. "I did what I had to, to survive. I put up with this… this *uncontrollable need*. Tried to keep it contained. Only sought release… rarely. I never told *anyone*." His eyes burned and his breaths came fast. "Everything about this, about what I am, I *hate*." He pitched forward, burying his face in his palms as he howled. Beneath

Sergey's hand, Sasha's shoulder shook. He sobbed, rivers of grief, a lifetime of self-hate, flowing through this fingers.

What could he do in the face of so much pain? He felt so small, so inadequate, confronted with Sasha's anguish. Jack's face, his voice, floated through Sergey's mind. Had his friend ever felt this way? Had Jack ever hated himself? Had he ever struggled with who he was and his own worth?

What would Jack do if he were here?

Sergey slid onto the bed, sitting beside Sasha and pulled him close. "Why are you saying these things? A great Russian like you should not be hating himself. No, no, it is not right."

Sasha's tears rained down on Sergey's white shirt, but he stroked his hand up and down Sasha's arm. Sasha's head fell to Sergey's shoulder, tears still falling as he breathed shallowly through his mouth and squeezed his eyes shut.

Sergey rolled his head back, resting it on the top of the metal headboard.

He would dare tomorrow. He would speak. If it was the last thing he did.

Russian President Vehemently Denounces Leaked American Intelligence Cables; Pledges Public Support for American President in the Hunt for Madigan

Russian President Sergey Puchkov delivered a scathing rebuke to the masterminds behind the release of thousands of classified American intelligence cables, which revealed details of intelligence collections and the personal identities of undercover intelligence operators, leading to the deaths of three Americans. The release of the cables is widely thought to be the work of former General Porter Madigan, traitor turned international terrorist who has evaded capture from the United States for almost half a year.

"The world cannot give in to the whims and machinations of a madman," Puchkov said in a press briefing from Moscow. "This madman, Madman Madigan, thinks that he can make some kind of impact on the world with these games of his. No. He is mistaken. He means nothing. He's insignificant, and soon, he will be gone. We remain committed, with our partners in the United States, to combating terrorism around the world, whether that is the Islamic Caliphate or this madman."

China Distances from United States in Wake of Cables' Release

Following the release of classified intelligence online, Chinese officials rushed to distance themselves from the United States. Speaking from Beijing, Chinese President Bai Jiankai announced a moratorium on discussions with the United States regarding Taiwan's status and said that they would be reviewing all further engagements with President Spiers and the US.

While the cables released did not discuss United States intelligence operations in China, President Bai stated that he was ordering a full review of the government, searching for any potential opportunities that "foreign governments may hope to exploit."

China has grown increasingly wary as the United States and President Spiers continue to build a close friendship with the Russian Federation and President Sergey Puchkov. Relations between China and the Russian Federation have cooled considerably as Russia has pivoted to the West.

18

Taif, Saudi Arabia
Summer Palace of Prince Faisal

Adam stood on the rooftop balcony of Faisal's summer palace, gazing at the mountains rising in the distance. Fruit groves stretched away, unending lines of peaches and pomegranates growing sweet and lush. A dull buzz, the hum of insects, droned as the sun started its descent, a tawny orange glow scattering gold over the valley. His mind swam, the heady scents of Taif sliding against memories he could no longer push back, no longer repress.

Six months. It had been six months since Ethiopia, since he'd ran for the safety of Faisal's arms again, and, in a fit of relief, regret, and desperate adrenaline, had kissed Faisal breathlessly and followed him into his palatial bedroom.

What had he thought? That all their problems would disappear just because he'd lived through the attack in Ethiopia? That, somehow, the illegality of their affair would magically vanish? That all of the struggles, everything against them, all of the day in, day out slog they had endured for two years would be different?

Of course it wouldn't. He had known as soon as he'd woken up in Faisal's arms, with his men sleeping below in the sunroom and Reichenbach recovering after surgery. It had been a mistake to kiss him again.

There was a reason he'd ended it with Faisal.

He'd be jailed. He'd be court-martialed. Stripped of his command and thrown from the Marine Corps. Investigated for years. And if the government found out what he and Faisal did together—

Once, he was awarded for superior intelligence operations in the Middle East. He had been like a seer, his commanders had said. Like a soothsayer. He could predict the future with uncanny accuracy.

He'd secretly been working hand in hand with Faisal.

At least, until Faisal's uncle found out about them. Then Faisal was moved, brought back to the capital. He was ordered to stay away from predators trying to woo him into sin.

Nothing could stop their love, Adam had thought. Not even the Saudi royal family. They kept on, meeting in Dammam, Dubai, and Kuwait City, in Amman and Cairo. And here, at Faisal's summer palace.

Nothing could stop their love, except for Adam himself.

Faisal was different then. He wore jeans and long-sleeve shirts and he moved with his people on the ground. When he was plucked back to Riyadh, his uncle, the Governor of Riyadh, put him in loose robes and the keffiyeh, but he and Adam had loved to peel the layers away, together.

Adam dropped his head, letting it hang between his shoulders. Peach and honey tickled his nose and then the endless bloom of roses, thick like a dream. He'd thought he was drunk, the first time they'd come to Taif, when the rose gardens had been in full bloom and the honey was in harvest, and Faisal smiled at him over candlelight and took his hand—

Enough. There'd never been a future for them. He should have ended their arrangement long ago, when he'd had the chance to walk away. He couldn't ever be Faisal's anything. Why had he spent years pretending he could?

He sensed Faisal before he heard him. He'd always been able to. That shiver to the air, the tang of spices, and a punch to his gut that he'd felt from the first night, the first moment he'd laid eyes on Faisal. He heard Faisal crossing the roof to his side. They were the same height, and Faisal stared at his profile as if he'd never seen him before, taking in the tanned lines and his stubble, and the ragged tear in his ear from Cook's gunshot.

Adam had stripped down, taking off his filthy robes, his vest, and his uniform top. He was just in his black fatigue pants and a plain tank.

Faisal stroked his arm. "*Habibi—*"

"We can't." Adam intercepted Faisal's hand and plucked it from his skin. He forced himself not to thread their fingers together. "You know we can't."

Faisal closed his eyes. "I thought, after Ethiopia—"

"Ethiopia didn't change anything." Looking down, Adam gripped the balcony railing hard enough to turn his knuckles white. "It was a mistake. What happened then—it was a mistake."

Silence. The taste of peaches lingered on the air, and he remembered kissing Faisal, tasting peach nectar, and hearing his warm voice whisper Arabic against his shoulder.

"Loving you will never be a mistake to me," Faisal finally said. "If you believe our love is a mistake, then that is your burden to bear." His voice, as always, was soft and gently accented thanks to his private English tutors in Riyadh and his Oxford education. It tore at Adam's heart, always. The tenderness containing a core of ferocity, a hidden fire that rivaled the sun.

Adam squeezed his eyes shut. After Ethiopia, after Adam had gone to storm the White House with Reichenbach, Faisal had tried to reach out to him. He'd called, he'd texted, he'd emailed. He'd tried, he really had, to get close to Adam again.

It had driven Adam to the brink. Always ignoring the calls. Reading the texts and never being able to respond. Leaving emails unread. Deleting them.

Faisal stepped back, away from Adam. "I am monitoring for anything that could be your Madigan. Searching for news reports and police filings. There may be something in the Sudan. Saudi intelligence hacked their central government a long time ago. An email was sent this past hour. A report about a jail being attacked and all the prisoners freed."

"Yeah, that would be Madigan." Time to get back to work. Time to get away from here, and from Faisal. "Can I see the report?"

"Of course."

Adam hesitated. "I— I'm sorry. You know, for calling you. Asking for your help, *again*. I know this can't be easy—" Fuck, it was brutal for him, and he was the one who had ended it.

A sad smile tried to turn up the corners of Faisal's lips. "I've prayed… endlessly for the opportunity to see you again. Allah has delivered. *Al-hamdu lillah*. Seeing you always brings joy to my heart. And, I would rather you call me for help, even now, every time you need it, than worry about you in danger. I am here for you, always." He nodded to the floor, to his men below who were lounging after Faisal had fed them a feast following their rescue. "You, and your men. You care for them so deeply."

Fuck, what could he say to that? Nothing. There was nothing he could say. "Let's go," he grumbled. "We've got to stop Madigan." He took off, heading for the double glass doors beneath the airy arbor off Faisal's bedroom.

"Do you remember last year? Last spring? Almost exactly a year ago?"

Adam stopped. He looked down.

"I would give everything, every riyal in the Kingdom, every single thing I have, to go back to that night and try to change your mind."

"I cannot get your entire team in."

Faisal had invited Adam and his men to his private office where he showed Adam the email scrapped from the Sudanese government's servers and the attached pictures: the prison burned to the ground, guards shot dead, and prisoners escaped. None of the photos showed a bloody encircled M, but the Sudanese agent taking the blurry shots hadn't known to look for one. Adam had started talking about getting his men on the ground and going through the remains when Faisal spoke.

"What do you mean? My team and I have to check it out. This is an important lead."

"I said I couldn't get your entire team in. I can get *one* of you in with me."

Doc frowned and was about to open his mouth when Adam interrupted. "Why would you go over there?"

"The Saudi royal family takes regional Gulf security very seriously. If hundreds of Sudanese prisoners have been released, especially from *that* prison, then the event would warrant a private, personal visit from a Saudi official." He spread his hands briefly before clasping them. "Who better than the head of the Intelligence Directorate?"

"What did you mean by *that* prison?" Doc blurted out before Adam could shut him down.

Faisal shared a long, silent look with Adam.

"What? What's going on?" Doc glared between the two, and even Coleman started to frown. "*You two* are keeping secrets from *us*?" Incredulity drowned his words.

"It was a rendition site." Adam crossed his arms and spread his legs. "The Saudis and the US government shared it. Black bag kind of shit. Enhanced interrogations. The US turned it over to the Sudanese after that kind of thing became politically unpopular." Adam cracked his jaw and clenched his teeth together, hard.

Doc whistled. "That how you two jokers met? Became besties?"

Silence. Adam and Faisal stared at Doc, not blinking.

"Jesus Christ, sorry!" Doc threw up his hands. Faisal frowned at the expletive.

Adam glared at Doc until Doc shuffled back, his hands up at his chest, a silent apology. He turned back to Faisal. "How would we get in?"

"I will demand entry. My position brings some weight. And some fear." Faisal lifted his chin, just a bit.

Adam licked his lips. Yes, there would be fear there.

Coleman frowned. "And why would you know about this breakout? It just was reported to their government. You might have read the email before they did."

Faisal smiled. "I prefer to keep the mystery strong. They will know that I know, and that's that."

Coleman's eyebrows rose, but he didn't argue. He turned to Adam. "You're going with him?"

Of course it would be him. He was the most fluent in Arabic and he had the better grasp on the culture. Pun not intended. "Yeah," Adam said with a sigh. "You all will have to chill here while I do the dirty work." He tried to turn it into a joke, with a lame little smile at the end.

A few of his guys laughed. Faisal's palace had three pools, a basketball court, a gym better than the one on their base, and a media room that was practically a theater. They'd be fine.

At the rear of the office, Doc's eyes lingered on Adam. He felt Doc's stare on the back of his neck, but he refused to answer the questions buried in his gaze.

The flight to Port Sudan took only two hours, but being locked in Faisal's executive jet, alone with him, was torturous. Faisal made himself busy, reading through something on his tablet, and he ignored Adam, save for his endless politeness.

Adam tried to focus on typing up everything that had happened for Reichenbach, from landing in Egypt to flying in Faisal's jet to Port Sudan. He hadn't heard from him in a day, but with the news blaring about America's leaked intel cables and the deaths of three clandestine operatives, Adam let that go. Reichenbach was most likely busy with the president, trying to keep a lid on that situation.

Though, the timing of the release was intriguing. The same day he and his men had been fingered in Darfur, set up by Madigan to hopefully be killed and exposed to the world as American spies and assassins. It had to be connected.

Faisal had brought his own vehicle and driver to Port Sudan, and Adam waited with him on the tarmac as the bulletproof Land Rover was unloaded. He plucked at his suit and tried to forget the heated, questioning stares Doc had sent his way when he and Faisal had left. Why did Faisal have a designer suit in Adam's size in his closet?

He actually had five. They'd been gifts, once.

Adam had thought Faisal would have gotten rid of all his things by now, but when he hesitantly followed him into his closet, there his clothes were, still hanging on his side, like he'd never left.

He'd dressed quickly and grunted when his team tried to talk to him on the way out the door. There and back, and then he could ditch the suit and the memories and work on their next plan of attack.

When the Land Rover was ready, they piled inside and set off, heading for the prison in the desolate reaches of the northern desert. They didn't call ahead, and when their vehicle pulled up, the Sudanese military securing the site scrambled, producing a general and the head of Sudanese intelligence before Adam had rebuttoned his suit jacket.

Faisal stood tall and demanded access to the prison. He talked quietly but managed to convey so much disappointment, as if the full weight of the Saudi royal family were glaring down at Sudan. Once, he'd confessed to Adam that his confidence had wavered after being sent back to Riyadh. He thought he'd been set up to fail.

Seeing him in action again made Adam's heart clench, and he fought back the swelling pride and sorrow that threatened to consume him. Faisal had helped save the world six months ago. He'd been the very first to uncover the connection between the Caliphate and General Madigan. The world owed him everything.

He was a better man than Adam was. Better than Adam ever could be.

In minutes, Faisal and Adam were led around the prison's ruins by the general himself while another soldier went to find the prison manifest. Just who had been in there when Madigan had hit it?

Adam backed Faisal up with fierce glares from behind his shades and beneath his keffiyeh, acting like the intimidating bruiser he was supposed to play. Faisal played his part excellently, distracting the general enough that Adam had free rein to investigate the ruins and take pictures. He found the bloody M on one of the half-collapsed, barely standing walls, and a dead and burned prison guard slumped beneath had a slit neck. He took two pictures and then pushed the destroyed wall the rest of the way down, obliterating Madigan's sign.

After that, they left quickly, speeding back to Port Sudan and their jet before someone from Khartoum could ask questions. Adam didn't relax until they were in the air, soaring over the Red Sea, and on the way home.

On the way back to Faisal's home. Not his. Not anymore.

Adam lay back on the plane's couch and tried to block everything out. He closed his eyes, feigning sleep when he felt Faisal's eyes on him.

When Faisal laid a blanket across him halfway through the flight, he nearly lost it all. Instead, he clutched the fleece as if he could hold on to Faisal and counted the minutes until they landed.

19

Moscow
The Kremlin

"It's time."

In Sergey's presidential office, cameras were set up and television lights washed out all the shadows, illuminating his office for his presidential address. He'd called the news outlets only a half hour before. It would be a surprise to his country, and to the world.

Past Russian presidents had changed the entire world from his office. Now, it was Sergey's time to make history.

Breathing deep, Sergey nodded to Ilya and strode into his office. The film crews stood respectfully, clapping, and waited for him to sit at his desk before they went back to their final details.

And then, the television producer was counting down, signaling *three, two, one*. The lights behind the cameras dimmed and the teleprompter beneath the lens winked on.

For a moment, Sergey stayed silent. His broadcast was going to every single Russian, all around the country. On the television, over the radio, and streaming live online. There was no going back.

He folded his hands on top of his desk and stared into the camera. "My friends, tonight is a very special night. Together, we are about to step into the future with a renewed strength." He hesitated and licked his lips. "We have much we need to improve as a country."

Somewhere in his office, a film crew member hissed.

Sergey kept on. "We have to bring our country back from where we have gotten lost."

Silence, as he breathed. No one in his office moved.

No Russian president had ever said their country wasn't the absolute best in the world.

"Eighteen months ago, I became your president. And I made a promise that day that I would strengthen Russia's prosperity and her character. On that day, I, and my senior leaders, began a systemic investigation of the corruption that has infested our motherland. We tracked all bribes offered

Enemy Of My Enemy

to the Kremlin and to my office. We followed all the money and all political favors through charity organizations, false bank accounts, and fraudulent corporations until we found the roots of this corrupt evil. Our state prosecutor has collected evidence all this time, and is tonight executing warrants against those who have crippled our country. Come tomorrow morning, a new Russia will awaken. Stronger."

All around the nation, doors were being kicked in and FSB agents were dragging out members of the Duma, the federal legislature, senior businessmen, oligarchs who had overreached, military officials too cozy with the *Bratva*, and members of his own government. Thousands of arrests. A national purge.

Somewhere in his office, one of the film crew gasped, and the television producer who had counted him down had her hands over her mouth.

"Every ruble that has been paid in corruption money and bribery to the Kremlin has been funneled into a special account for the state prosecutor's review. As of today, that total stands at just over eight hundred million. But this barely touches the twenty-five percent of our GDP that is lost to corruption annually.

"It is time to put a stop to this acceptance of corruption as a way of life. Beginning immediately, all forms of bribery and corruption will be met with the full force of Russian justice.

"This is not the Russian way. This is not what a strong Russia is made out of. We will fight this evil, just as we have fought every invading force that threatens to destroy Russia. With determination and commitment.

"We will bring about a free and prosperous Russia. Prosperity does not come from corruption, and it does not come from nothing. We will all perform hard work to create our future, together."

Sergey hesitated again. He could end it there. That was enough of a bombshell. His nation would be in shock, the markets rocked, and his economy would stutter while it tried to find its feet again.

No, he must do more.

"And, my friends, we must unite as *one* people. One great nation. All Russians, everywhere, are part of this country. Our GLBT Russian brothers and sisters must be respected. They are equal Russian citizens. All laws of this nation protect *all* of our peoples. Today, I am calling for the creation of the Moscow GLBT Advocacy Center, which will monitor and bring to justice all crimes perpetrated on our GLBT citizens. I will not stand by and watch while senseless violence is perpetrated on my Russian people."

One of the film crew was crying. Streaks of tears rolled down his cheeks, glinting in the reflections of the floodlights.

Another looked ready to puke.

Sergey took a deep breath. "Our future is made together. Your future creates Russia's future. We are responsible for making our motherland great. Thank you, my friends."

The camera winked off.

Silence filled his office.

Sergey stood, buttoned his jacket, and walked out.

White House

Ethan turned to Jack, his eyes wide, mouth hanging open.

Jack watched the dumbfounded news anchors react to Sergey's presidential address.

"Well... They won't be talking about us for a while."

"Should you call him?"

"Tomorrow. I'm sure he's busy right now." Jack stretched, letting his head fall back on the couch in his study. They'd escaped upstairs after chasing their staff out, insisting that they try to get some rest. The news from the day before had been awful, but they had to reset and move on, and they couldn't do that while exhausted. "I can't believe he's been doing this his entire presidency."

"I can see why he likes you." Ethan nudged Jack with his knee. "Why you guys are friends."

Jack rolled his head toward Ethan. "I guess we are both political rebels, huh?"

"Idealists was what I thought." Ethan leaned back, and his face ended up next to Jack's, their lips almost touching. "And good men."

Jack's smile grew slowly as he gazed into Ethan's eyes. All the calamity in the world, all the dark and shadowy parts of governing, and all the moments when he felt like he was never enough, could be smoothed over by Ethan's unwavering confidence in him. Who was this man Ethan knew, this rock star, this good man? He seemed like someone Jack would want to know.

Jack's smiled faded. "Hasn't been a good few days," he whispered. Madigan's resurgence. Their lost operatives. Almost losing Cooper and his team.

"Some days are tougher than others. But you never give up. You always want to make the world better."

"It's like you know me or something." Jack repeated Ethan's words.

"A bit." Ethan winked and leaned forward, pressing his lips to Jack's. Jack's hand rose, sliding up Ethan's neck and through his hair. Tugging, he pulled Ethan onto his lap until Ethan was straddling him and Jack was sliding Ethan's shirt up and over his head.

His lips found Ethan's skin, the fur of Ethan's chest hair tickling him as he pressed lazy kisses across his muscles. Ethan shuddered when his tongue circled a nipple, and Jack's arms wrapped around Ethan's waist, dragging him closer as he kissed down Ethan's stomach. He sucked a hickey onto each hip as he undid Ethan's belt and unzipped his khakis. Slowly, he pushed down Ethan's pants and boxers as Ethan kneeled over Jack's lap.

Jack locked gazes with Ethan, looking up into his endless brown eyes as he licked his cock, slowly, from root to tip. Ethan cursed, and Jack lapped at the head, hollowing his cheeks as he sucked. His fingers traced circles on Ethan's hips and then dragged over his ass, gentle strokes that made Ethan shiver and shake. Goose bumps erupted over Ethan's thighs. Jack grinned up at him, Ethan's cock resting on Jack's tongue.

Gently, Jack's fingers dipped between Ethan's ass cheeks. He looked up again, questioning.

Ethan nodded, short jerks of his head.

He always asked, always. Making love to Ethan was a gift, one he was hyperaware of, and Jack would rather cut off his own hand than make Ethan uncomfortable or push him in any way. Ethan had been self-conscious at first about how he prepared himself for Jack, and Jack had let him have his space. Now, more often than not, Jack helped him in the shower.

Sometimes he reached for Ethan and Ethan wasn't ready. Sometimes, like now, he was.

Jack's blood seemed to sear, his veins burning as lust throttled through him. He wanted Ethan so badly, all the time. Wanted to be in his arms, wanted to hold his body close. Wanted to wrap their sweat-slick bodies up and forget the world, and just make love over and over again. His lust for Ethan had grown exponentially in conjunction with his love, and now, it seemed like making love to Ethan was another way he could say the words, could tell Ethan he loved him. That he loved him so much he would gladly unmake his whole world, his entire career, for the two of them to have a future together.

Ethan stumbled back and shimmied out of his pants. He tripped over his shoes as he toed them off. Jack pulled his shirt over his head and slipped out of his own suit pants, dumping them on the floor. Ethan clambered back into his lap and captured his lips, kissing him senseless while running his hands up and down over Jack's hard cock. He spat in his palm then ran his slick hand over Jack again.

Shivering, Jack grabbed Ethan's ass and squeezed, trying to drag him closer.

Ethan held back. "Do we have any condoms in here?"

Goddamn it. Exhaling, Jack slumped against the couch. "I didn't bring any." They kept their supplies by their bed—lube, condoms, and towels.

"Let's get back to our bedroom then."

"Wait."

Ethan froze. He stared down at Jack. Jack's hands clenched on his hips.

He opened his mouth. Hesitated. Damn it, why was this so hard to say? He tried again, inhaling before he spoke. "Can we get tested?" Jack breathed out, speaking fast.

Ethan's jaw dropped. He stared down at Jack, shock and horror warring across his features, and said nothing.

"I'm sorry." He tried to smile but failed, and his hands flew from Ethan's hips. "I'm sorry, I didn't mean to offend you. I—"

"Is this about the article?" Ethan's voice was fragile, barely a whisper. "Is this about what you read?"

"No!" Jack's hands closed over Ethan's biceps, tense and hard beneath his fingers. "No, God, no. I just—" He pressed his lips together. Held Ethan's worried gaze. "I want to make love to you with nothing between us. I want to ditch the condoms. Both of us getting tested… Isn't that the next step?"

If Ethan had looked surprised before, that was nothing next to the stunned speechlessness that stole over his face. He paled, and his jaw dropped even farther.

God, he was an idiot. Dread slid down his spine. *Great going, Jack. You really managed to dig for that nerve. You should never have said anything. Home run there.*

"I'm sorry. Ethan, I'm sorry. I didn't know it was something that bothered you. We can keep the condoms. It's fine."

Ethan shook his head, still dazed. "I didn't think you wanted that."

"Why wouldn't I want to be as close to you as possible?"

Ethan pressed his lips together and shook his head, but said nothing.

Jack's hands slid down Ethan's shoulders, down his back. Was this more of Ethan's insecurity, his fear that Jack wasn't all in this relationship?

"I want everything with you. Everything. You are *it* for me." He leaned forward and kissed Ethan's stomach, holding his gaze. "You're the one I want to be with. In every way. I want to commit to you. This is one way to do that, right?"

Ethan's jaw clenched so hard Jack could see the bulging muscles pulsing from his neck. He stared down at Jack, and Jack watched him blink fast. "Okay," Ethan whispered. "Okay. We'll get tested."

Jack's cheeks hurt, he smiled so hard, so fiercely. "You want that, too?" Jack stroked his hands down Ethan's back. "You sure?"

"I've never had that kind of relationship. Never wanted it before." Ethan laced their fingers together. "But you are it for me, too. So yes. Let's do this. Together."

Jack pressed a kiss to Ethan's knuckles. "I'll reach out to the doctor." There was a Navy physician on hand for the president at all times, and everything was held in the strictest confidence.

He rolled Ethan's hand, found his palm, and pressed a kiss to the center. "Now, let's get to the bedroom. I still want to make love to you tonight."

Ethan slipped off Jack's lap and helped him stand. Naked, save for their socks, and with cocks half-hard, Ethan led Jack across the hall and back to their bedroom, giggling as they tried to jog. When they hit the bedroom, Ethan slithered onto the bed with a smile. He waited for Jack, stroking himself back to full hardness as Jack grabbed the lube and a condom and then joined him, sliding over his body and wrapping him up in his arms. Their lips met, and then their cocks, and Jack shivered against Ethan's kiss.

Oh yes. Ethan was it for him.

Moscow
The Kremlin

After hours with Ilya, monitoring the arrests of thousands of Russians charged with corruption, racketeering, money laundering, and even murder, Sergey called it a night. The Kremlin Palace was hushed and exhausted. His staff had stayed late, watching him with wide eyes. Harsh whispers carried in the still corridors, his people wondering at the sudden change that was catapulting through Russia.

He thought about turning in, about trying to sleep, but knew he'd get nowhere. There would be no sleep tonight. And none tomorrow, either.

Instead, Sergey headed for the far wing and Sasha's recovery room. His recovery was going well, according to Dr. Voronov, and he'd rested more comfortably during the day.

Of course, he wasn't resting when Sergey got there. He was wide awake, again, and watching the television on the wall, the volume turned down low. His bright eyes fixed to Sergey when Sergey slouched against the doorjamb with a sigh.

Sergey felt like a slob. He'd left his jacket behind and had rolled up his shirt sleeves. His tie was long gone.

Muttering Russian from the television made its way to his ears. His speech. News commentators dissecting his words. Live feeds of FSB arrests around the nation.

Sasha seemed to search for something to say, pressing his lips together and then taking a breath before hesitating and looking down.

Instead of speaking, Sergey moved to Sasha's bedside chair and collapsed. He crossed his arms and his ankles and gave Sasha a small, tired smile.

Slowly, Sasha smiled back.

Russian Economy in Freefall; Anti-corruption Sweep Blamed

The Russian economy endured another day of freefall as their stock market plunged yet again, following Russian President Sergey Puchkov's dramatic announcement of an eighteen-month sting operation aimed at rooting out corruption within the Russian Federation. Immediately following his announcement, thousands were arrested across the country, including many in the government, military, and private sectors. Bitter opposition to President Puchkov's sweeping change has come from many politicians, oligarchs, and high-ranking military personnel, all of whom reportedly benefited from extensive bribery practices.

Many of the Russian businessmen arrested had their assets seized, including ownership of dozens of Russia's corporations. Now state-owned, workers have, for days, wondered whether their jobs would remain. Other companies simply folded overnight, and Russians heading into work found themselves unemployed. Banks have closed and civil unrest has descended on Moscow and St. Petersburg as violent riots broke out when some stores were forced to ration their sales of food and fuel. Fourteen people were injured in St. Petersburg and fifty in Moscow in three separate riots.

The Russian government cannot sustain the amount of business it has acquired nor afford to pay the salaries of so many workers. Russian President Puchkov has not yet outlined his plan for righting the sinking Russian economy, which is quickly pulling down the global economy.

20

White House

"We have to do something for your people, Sergey."

Jack sat with Ethan, Irwin, and Elizabeth in the Oval Office, speaking on a conference call with Sergey and his closest advisors.

"*So many businesses closed their doors in protest, Mr. President. They are the problem. They are driving this country into the ground.*" Sergey cursed in Russian, a long, growling string of words that Jack didn't try to translate. "*Corrupt oligarchs that want nothing but money! They act like Tzars! I could force their reopening. Demand they return to work.*"

Industry had ground to a halt. Aluminum and auto manufacturing, drilling, refining, and mining. Services, from engineering to technology. So much of the economy had frozen.

"We might have a solution, Sergey. It's unusual." Jack dipped his head. "But I think you and I thrive on unusual situations."

Sergey barked out a laugh. "*Let us hear it, Mr. President.*"

"The Russian Federation has taken over these businesses, much like after the Soviet Union collapsed. Your government cannot support all of these industries. By our models, you're going to run out of capital in about two months. Inflation is already on the rise."

"*Sooner.*" Sergey didn't sound pleased.

"We need to inject life into your economy. Get business going again." Jack took a deep breath. "I have a list of American investors and companies that would be interested in partnering with you to get your economy back on its feet."

Sergey was quiet. "*Meaning?*"

"Five-year leases of forty-five percent of these corporations to American investors. The Russian Federation would keep a fifty-five percent controlling share, and profits would be split down the same lines. In that time, our investors would work on restructuring with your people. We'd reduce trade tariffs with you and request our NATO allies do the same."

"*Hmmm.*" Over the phone line, hushed Russian flew in the background, Sergey's advisors talking back and forth. "*Many Americans would be unhappy with this, would they not, Mr. President?*"

"It keeps your industries open, Sergey. Gets your people back to work. Injects immediate capital into your markets. Stabilizes the global economy. Everyone is hurting right now. This is a way to strengthen everyone."

"*And make your American investors wealthy.*"

"You would keep a majority share. Most of the wealth would remain in Russia. But these companies do need to be compensated for their investment. They'll be putting out significant capital in advance of any revenue."

More Russian flying on the other end of the line. Sergey snapped at someone and then coughed. "*My apologies, Mr. President. I like the idea. But fifty-five percent is too low of a controlling share. We want to keep more.*"

Irwin nodded across the desk at Jack, as did Elizabeth. They had expected this.

"How does a sixty-five thirty-five split sound?" Jack went straight to the lowest acceptable percentage from his list of investors. He didn't want to waste Sergey's time. And, his friend had a point.

"*Much more agreeable.*" Fast Russian barked back and forth beneath Sergey, from his advisors. "*I like it. We will discuss it here. I will let you know.*"

"Sounds good, Sergey." Straightening, Jack rolled his neck and prepared to end the call. "We'll be—"

"*Do you have a moment to speak in private, Jack?*"

Jack froze. "Sure, Sergey. Let me clear the room." He nodded to Irwin and Elizabeth, dismissing them.

On the other end of the line, he heard Sergey doing the same, the sounds of doors closing as he bid his farewells.

Ethan stayed, but he sent a questioning look Jack's way. Jack nodded.

"It's just me and Ethan, Sergey. What's up?"

"*Hello, Ethan. Glad you are here as well.*"

"Mr. President." Ethan sat back, still not used to chatting casually with other world leaders, and one whom he had considered a threat the year before.

Sergey sighed. "*I like your proposal, Jack. I think it is very good. My advisors are split, but I know it will happen. So thank you.*"

"Sure thing. We just want the economy moving again."

"*Your people will not like this.*"

"I'll deal with my people. They'll be even less happy if the economy tanks further."

Sergey murmured his agreement and then went quiet.

"What else can I do, Sergey?" Sergey had saved American lives when the cables were released, stood by his side on the world stage, and risked everything on a massive gamble to clean up his country. And he'd taken a stand for equality, supporting Jack when others had vanished. Made changes in Russia for his people. Helping him was the least he could do.

"*You have already done much, Jack. This offer... It is very generous. I thought...*" Sergey began and hesitated. "*I would be doing this alone. Your predecessor was not a man I wanted anything to do with. After you were elected, I did not know if you were a man to be trusted.*" He cleared his throat. "*I tested you, in Prague. Pushed you. But you pushed back. You held your line. And you have been always an honorable man, Jack.*"

"You called me a Russian faggot once, Sergey."

Sergey cleared his throat again, discomfort and regret leaching over the phone line. "*That wasn't about you. Or Ethan. I thought, before, that we could end up here. Where we are now. Political partners, working together. Equals. When you came out about your relationship...*" He sighed. "*I thought your country would not be able to handle it. I thought you were on your way out. That I would be on my own when I had hoped for more with you.*"

"Jury is still out on America 'handling it.'"

"*I was wrong. I was angry, and I was wrong,*" Sergey rumbled. "*And I am glad I was wrong. Our partnership is important to me.*"

His words touched Jack, and he shared a warm look with Ethan. "To me as well, Sergey. More than I can say." Jack frowned. "You sound exhausted. I know what this job it like. Are you taking care of yourself?"

"*Dodging assassins is exhausting work.*"

Jack sat up, his spine straightening, as Ethan's eyes went wide. "Sergey. They're trying to kill you?"

"*Do not act so surprised, Jack. I knew this would come. Three attempts in the past week. Going after the money and trying to clean up decades of corruption is asking for trouble.*" Sergey chuckled. "*We have a saying here. You are only as strong as your* krysha. *Your roof. Your protection. Political, personal, financial, or military. What someone can do is defined by your* krysha. *I just obliterated* kryshas *throughout Russia. What should I expect after, hmm? Well, I am the president! I am supposed to have the best* krysha *of all!*" He sighed, rueful, over the line. "*I have good Security Service agents and my FSB training. Once an FSB agent, always an FSB agent. But I am finding out I do not have much else.*"

"Well, you have us."

Sergey snorted.

"I'm serious." What else could he do? What could he give to his friend that could possibly help? "Look, how about a little breather? Come to the White House. I can promise an assassin-free environment. We'll hammer out the details of this business lease and announce it to the world together."

Sergey laughed. "*People already say we are too close, Jack. That would only make them more eager for scandal.*" A pause. "*But... I will think about it.*"

"Please do. I haven't had a state dinner yet. I'd love to host you, Sergey."

Ethan stared wide-eyed at Jack.

"*I will think about it. I will call you when my advisors are done arguing about your proposal. Until then, Jack!* Do svidaniya." Sergey cut the line.

Jack shared a long look with Ethan before sitting back in his chair. He crossed his arms behind his head and his ankles beneath the Resolute desk. "I don't envy him right now."

"I don't envy his security."

Jack snorted. Ethan looked away. One of his feet bounced up and down, over and over, and he gnawed on the corner of his lip.

Frowning, Jack tried to catch Ethan's gaze again. His lover had been distracted all day, ever since they'd left the White House medical suite after getting tested early that morning. He was fidgeting.

Jack could count on one hand the times Ethan had fidgeted.

"When does your team land?" Maybe it was Cooper's return.

"This evening. They land at Andrews just after nineteen hundred."

"Anything?" Jack's voice was full of hope.

Ethan shook his head. "Not a peep from Madigan. Not since he disappeared into Somalia a week ago."

Jack's head thunked back against his chair as he scrubbed his hands over his face. Madigan had raided the prison in Sudan and then moved south. Ethiopian scouts tracked a large caravan crossing through their highlands, heading straight for the destroyed failed state of Somalia. Since then, no one had heard anything. No prison breaks. No intelligence dumped to the Internet. Nothing at all.

Cooper had stayed in the region, hunkered down at Prince Faisal's palace for a week, trying to find something, any sign at all of Madigan, Cook, the eleven SOCOM soldiers who had joined him, or the thousands of hardened criminals he'd busted out of prison.

Nothing. Not even Prince Faisal had been able to find anything. Somalia was, even to the Saudis, a lost cause and a nearly impenetrable lawless frontier.

So Cooper and his team were headed home.

"On to the next world crises?" Jack grinned at Ethan, trying to get a smile out of his lover.

"I'll let you get back to work. I've got to make some calls." Ethan headed for the door.

"I'll see you tonight."

Ethan nodded, avoided Jack's gaze, and headed out of the Oval Office.

21

Somewhere in Somalia

"The bastard is running Russia into the ground!" Moroshkin slammed his fist on his desk, the sound echoing over the phone line. *"President Puchkov is a puppet of the Americans! He is no Russian man!"*

Madigan stayed silent, letting Moroshkin bellow.

"We have lost billions," Moroshkin growled. *"Our economy, ruined. But worse, far worse than that,"* he seethed, *"is the way this man, no, this traitor, has turned against his own motherland. Puchkov! He is no Russian man! He is nothing but an American flunky! He is too close to President Spiers! They must have something going on together."*

Madigan said nothing. Moroshkin's fury was still building, the general still working up to something.

"He has been turned. He must have been. He has been turned by the Americans, by their CIA. He has been planted inside Russia, to tear us apart from within. This project of his. His love of homosexuals." Moroshkin sneered. *"Does he truly believe that Russians will ever accept these foreign corruptions? No true Russian could ever be a homosexual! It is a corruption of the West! Sent to destroy us!"* Moroshkin's harsh breaths flooded the phone line. *"Perhaps I will get lucky,"* he said slowly. *"Some assassin, some Bratva hitman, will take him out for me. I can take the country after."*

"Some Russians call him a hero." Finally, Madigan spoke, poking the proverbial bear. "They say he's a visionary. Guiding Russia out of the dark ages into an era of modern equality. He's bringing Russia into the first world. A true post-Putin leader."

"Bah!" Moroshkin cursed in Russian, pounding his desk with his fist, over and over. *"He is no hero! He is a disgrace! He is ruining Russia! He must be destroyed!"*

"What will you do about it?" A little push and Moroshkin would go far. Inertia would take over, Puchkov's actions and Moroshkin's hatred coming together in perfect synchronicity.

Moroshkin breathed deeply, grumbling in Russian again. *"I have moved my most trusted officers into key commands,"* he growled. *"We are in control of a majority of the Russian military forces. President Puchkov has some friends. But, they will not be a hindrance."*

"We can use them, actually." Madigan played it smoothly, laying it all out for Moroshkin, and Moroshkin was walking down his path. Walking into his web. "We can use his allies and his friends against him."

"*How?*"

"The best way to utterly break a man, General, is to take him to his absolute limits and then wrench him beyond them. Brutally. Rip away everything a man holds dear, one by one. Strip him of his security. His safety. His sanity." Madigan smiled. "And then he's yours to destroy."

"*In Russia, we are more direct.*"

Madigan chuckled. "Yes, but I promise you. We do things my way, and you'll be in charge of that country in no time. And then moving on to bigger and better conquests."

"*Once, Russia was respected. We were the greatest military on the planet.*"

Madigan stayed silent.

"*We will be again,*" Moroshkin promised, fire and fury in his voice. "*I,*" he said, shaking, "*will see to that.*"

"Only with my help."

"*And what is it that you want after this, General? When I am in charge of Russia, what is it you desire?*"

"The same as you. Conquest. Victory. Looking your enemy in the eye as the life goes out of them, and they know, without a doubt, you have beaten them."

"*You want to destroy America? Your home?*" For the first time, Moroshkin sounded uneasy, unsure.

"It's not destruction, General. It's a resurrection. And not just America, but the world. A new dawn, and a new beginning. With us at the helm," he said brightly at the end. "Are you in?"

Moroshkin kept quiet, humming under his breath. "*Tell me what it is we have to do,*" he finally rumbled.

"Sow the seeds of terror, my friend. Grow dread in the hearts of your enemies, until they choke on the rise of their own bile. Until they cannot stand to live with themselves and the whole world has turned against them."

Moroshkin said nothing.

"Watch the news, General. You will see my work. I'll be in touch for our next step. Soon."

22

Washington DC

Heavy rubber wheels on Cooper's return flight bounced and skidded down the runway. The plane roared over the tarmac, engines whining, flaps and elevators at full extension. It slowed to a crawl and made the turn, driving back toward a hangar on the far side of the airfield.

Ethan waited outside his SUV, leaning back against the hood with his arms crossed. Daniels stood by the open driver's door, glaring at Ethan.

Daniels was done with Ethan's bullshit for the day, and he'd said so as soon as they had left the White House.

Ethan was a mess of frenzied nerves and restless anxiety, and he'd skipped out of the White House to meet Cooper before seeing the Navy doctor for his test results. Jack had texted on the drive, saying that the doctor who had done their testing wanted to speak to both of them, and he'd wait for Ethan's return.

As the plane finally pulled to a stop, chocks were thrown down and the ramp lowered. Ethan pushed himself up and waited for his team. It was important to him to meet Cooper and his Marines, to personally welcome them back and look into the eyes of the men who were risking it all, chasing Madigan around the world to stop his machinations.

He'd come close to losing them already.

A weary group of Marines clambered down the ramp, some still shaking sleep from their eyes. Cooper was in the lead, and a fierce scowl hardened his face. He tried to smile when he saw Ethan and came forward with his hand outstretched.

Ethan shook it. "Welcome back. I've made arrangements for you and your men to bunk down at the base tonight. There's a plane waiting to take your men back to MacDill in the morning."

"Thank you, Director— Mr. First Gentleman. Thank you for meeting us. I know you're busy."

Cooper fumbled, trying to be polite, but his eyes were pinched and exhaustion clung to him. Exhaustion, and something else. Something deeper. Something that ached in his eyes.

"Never too busy for you and your men. Get some rest. You all deserve it." He pointed to the waiting transport at the doors of the hangar. "That's your ride. It will take you to the BOQ and back to this hangar in the morning."

"Thank you, sir." He hefted his pack onto his shoulders and signaled to his men. Ethan smiled and held out his hand for every member of the team, clasping tight and welcoming them home with a personal thanks for their hard work. The team headed across the lot, some shoving each other until their sergeant barked at them to stow it. In minutes, they were on the transport and driving to base lodging.

Ethan watched them fade away. He stared up at the night sky.

"Ethan? You met them when they landed. They're gone now. It's time to go. You know, back home? Where you're supposed to be." Daniels tapped the roof of the SUV with his fingers. "C'mon."

Goddamn it, he did not want to face this.

He'd been careful all his life.

Well, except for once—twice—when the condom had broken, and he hadn't known until he'd pulled out after he and his one-night stand had finished.

And the extremely sketchy blow jobs he had occasionally gotten overseas, back when he was in the Army. He was younger then. Dumber.

And—

Damn it.

Daniels got him back to the White House in record time. Any other day, he would have congratulated his friend for an Indy 500 qualifying round, but now, he felt more like a toddler being led to a time-out chair.

The steps to the Residence seemed too tall. The lights were too bright. Dread knotted his stomach. His hands slicked with sweat.

Jack was waiting in the hall, smiling at him and wearing his Secret Service sweatshirt. Ethan's heart pulled toward Jack. He pushed down the lump in his throat.

"Hey. Glad you got back quickly." Jack pressed a kiss to Ethan's cheek.

"You talk to the doc yet?"

Jack nodded. "Everything's good. He says I'm healthy." Another smile. "He's waiting for you in the kitchen."

The doctor, a Navy Captain, had set up his laptop on their kitchen table and was typing fast and furious when Ethan trudged in. "Mr. First Gentleman." He stood, smiling, and held out his hand. Starched khakis from his naval uniform crinkled as he moved and his ribbons glittered in the kitchen's light.

Just get it over with. "What's the verdict, doc?" He tried not to smear sweat all over the doctor's hand as he gripped it.

"Well, there was something I wanted to discuss with you."

Fuck.

Ethan's ears swam, an underwater dissonance as soon as the doctor began speaking. "Your blood tests showed extremely elevated levels of cortisol, way outside the normal range."

But, with the doctor's last words, reality snapped back into place. "Cortisol?"

"Yes. I reached out to your physician and they faxed me your records. I don't see any indications of a possible adrenal complication—"

"Doctor— Captain—" he fumbled. "What are the results of the *other* check?"

"Hmm? Oh. You're perfectly healthy. Everything checked out there." The captain smiled but went right back to his first speech as Ethan desperately held himself back from heaving all over the kitchen floor.

He was healthy. So was Jack. The last lover he'd ever have. He'd never thought, ever, that he'd commit to someone like this, promising that they would be each other's only. As for his own heart, he already knew and had committed wholly to Jack since the moment they kissed on Air Force One.

Jack was it for him.

Slowly, a smile formed on his face until he was beaming, and the doctor was staring at him like he was about to have a seizure.

"Mr. First Gentleman? Did you hear my question?"

"Come again?"

"Significantly elevated cortisol levels in the blood, like yours, are usually a sign of severe stress, much more than what's usual for someone. Have you been under what you would consider above average or undue stress recently?"

His eyebrows shot up as his laughter exploded, a loud, gut-clenching guffaw, right in the doctor's face.

After he'd apologized and assured the bemused Navy doctor he'd work on getting his stress and his cortisol levels under control, Ethan walked out of the kitchen and found Jack waiting for him, trying to not look like he was waiting, and failing miserably.

Jack's eyes asked the question.

To answer, Ethan drew him close and cupped Jack's cheeks. Jack's arms wrapped around Ethan's waist as Ethan nuzzled his forehead, and they traded soft kisses while the rest of the world faded away.

23

Somalia

Derras was a forgotten town in a forgotten country, a wash of decrepit square concrete buildings, long-faded paint, and splintering asphalt. Sand blew over the roadway, and wild goats munched on desperate desert grass that shot up through the broken stretch of desolate highway. Here and there, a ragged Acacia tree stood, gnarled and bone dry, desiccated in Somalia's decades-long drought.

It was utterly forgettable.

Colonel Song glared through his sunglasses. His plane had landed five miles away in the desert, where he'd been picked up by a Humvee and driven into Derras. His driver, a silent, stoic man with short hair and a handkerchief around his neck, never said a word. But he watched Song like a hawk when he climbed out of the Humvee and looked left and right at a giant landscape of nothingness.

Another Humvee appeared down the road, slowly pulling to a stop. The driver stayed inside, but the back doors opened and General Madigan exited. He had on snug black combat fatigues and a black cap, and his eyes were covered with mirrored sunglasses. His face was shaven, and his boots shined.

He was a man very comfortably on the run from the most powerful nation on the planet. Unfazed at being public enemy number one of the United States.

Colonel Song squared his shoulders and clasped his hands before him. "General. You asked for me to meet you, and I said I wanted to see your potential." He gestured to the desolation surrounding them on the cracked Somalian highway. "This is hardly potential."

"I can't bring you to my main operation. I don't trust you." Madigan grinned as Song's eyebrows rose. "I've got thousands of men in these hills, all training for my army."

"Thousands of men is nothing compared to the might of your enemies."

"Thousands of men with conviction and purpose have brought down enemies ten times their size. It's about the drive, Colonel. What men are willing to fight for. To die for. And my men are willing to go to the ends of the earth for me. For this. For their freedom to *be*, and the promise of a new world."

"And yet, you rot in this wasted country."

"This is a wasted country *your* country has dumped millions into. Why is that?" Madigan put his hands on his hips but kept grinning.

Song stayed silent.

"I'll tell you why. Because there's a beautiful oil field right there, right off the Horn, but these Somali fucks have been too busy killing each other to go drill it. And the pirates make any commercial investment problematic. So, you're betting on both ends. Either the country stabilizes, and you're the good guy, or the country falls apart completely, and you swoop in for the fresh kill." He cocked his head. "Sound about right?"

"I'm not here to discuss China's foreign policy. You wanted me. And yet you waste my time."

"You want to know about my potential, and I'm here with an offer for you, one I won't make again." Madigan pulled his sunglasses off, and he stared into Song's eyes. "Change is on the horizon. When I am done, the world as you know it will have fallen into a wasteland worse than this shithole of a lost country. There will be a new order in charge. You have an opportunity. You can join the side of the winners. Or you can be destroyed, along with everyone else."

Song's eyes narrowed. "What is it you are planning to do?"

Madigan smiled, a madman's smile, and slid his shades back on. He stepped back and kicked the cracked asphalt beneath their feet. "Did you know that this road used to connect Soviet military installations in Somalia, back in the seventies?" He looked into the distance, into the emptiness, and whistled. "Not a damn thing left. Not a damn single thing."

Three steps took him to Song, and he pressed close, speaking in a hushed hiss to Song's face. "Because I destroyed it. I destroyed it all. I have built this world, exactly my way, for decades. And I will continue to make this world, and unmake this world, in the way I will it." He stepped back. "I'm standing on the ruins of the Soviets. And, mark my words, I will stand on the ruins of her successor."

"You would destroy the Russian Federation?"

"I will destroy everything that President Spiers holds dear. Everything. Starting with his dear, precious Russia. His lover. His sanity. And finally, when he's left with nothing, I will end his miserable life."

Silence.

"Now, you and your countrymen can inherit this shithole, and all of its oil, when I am done. I'll even throw in Iran for you. You can have Iran. And all of Iran's oil, too."

The winds of Somalia gusted over the road, kicking up a swirl of scorched sand from the hard-packed grit beside them. Brittle branches from the gnarled Acacia tree swayed, rubbing together like an old lady's bones, groaning and hollow.

Desert wind brushed over Song's polished shoes, whispering like ancient ghosts.

He stepped forward. "To destroy a thing, one must lead that thing to its extremes. You know what you must do?" Slowly, he held out his hand for Madigan to shake.

Madigan grinned, slid his hand into Song's and pumped, once. "We have an understanding, you and me."

"The darkest night always leads to a glorious new dawn." Song buttoned his suit jacket. Their conversation was over. "You may build your infrastructure here. We will not interfere. And, we will be in touch."

24

White House

In the morning, Sergey called back, saying that he would be delighted to visit Jack and Ethan and he looked forward to a full state dinner. And that he liked Veal *Orlov* and *Medovukha*. He'd be there in ten days, provided he wasn't shot, poisoned, or stabbed first.

Jack started to fret when the call ended. Ethan, Irwin, and Elizabeth surrounded the Resolute desk, Irwin and Elizabeth furiously typing out messages on their cell phones to their staff.

"I have no idea what to do now." Jack's gaze bounced from Irwin to Elizabeth. "This is my first state dinner. How do I even get this started?"

Ethan smiled. "Actually, this is my job." He thought of Barbara and Jennifer. "This is all my job."

Barbara gripped her pearls in one hand and the polished wooden arm of Ethan's blue couch in the other when he called his staff together and told them Sergey would be arriving in ten days for Jack's first state dinner.

"Mr. First Gentleman, state dinners take *months* to prepare. So many things have to be done in sequence. The Calligraphy Office needs to be informed. Guest lists need to be drafted. The china must be selected, and the linens. Entertainment for the evening. I have *never* heard of a state dinner happening in less than four months." Her shocked eyes flitted to Jennifer.

"I need to order flowers. I need to figure out what kind of décor we even want, Mr. First Gentleman. For the Russians..." Jennifer bit her lip. "I need time to figure out the right atmosphere for the evening."

"Is this even wise?" Brandt had a deep frown on his forehead. "Russia is a serious hot button right now."

"But President Puchkov has taken a major step forward in working toward equality, and yes, that's something to celebrate." His chief of staff gestured as she spoke.

His staff looked terrified. "President Puchkov's stance on LGBT Russians should be applauded, yes. But in addition to that, he needs to get out of Russia for a bit. He's facing assassination attempts daily, and Jack wants to help however he can." Hissed inhales sounded around his office. "That doesn't leave this room." Nods, from everyone. "We're also making a major announcement at the end of the visit. A partnership between our two countries. Brandt, you can leak that right before the dinner."

Intrigue brightened Brandt's gaze.

"I know this is going to be difficult. But we've got to do it. Barbara, how can we make this manageable?"

"Make it small. A usual state dinner will host three to five hundred. Keep this one around a hundred." She heaved a sigh. "We'll have to be very picky with the invitations. Only the most critical to the president, and to President Puchkov. There will be a lot of hurt feelings after this."

"What else is new?" Ethan tried to smile and lighten the mood.

Barbara didn't look amused.

"Mr. First Gentleman, these state dinners are this Office's Super Bowl. This is what we're here for. And you're asking for a Super Bowl in ten days?" She picked up her notepad. "We will need to figure out what we can do now, *and* get the chief usher in here today." She fingered her pearls, rolling the strand between her thumb and forefinger. "Are you and the president thinking black tie or white tie?"

"Black tie," his chief of staff interrupted. "For this soon, you have to go black tie. No one can get white tie in ten days."

Ethan snapped his fingers and pointed her way. "Yes. Black tie."

Jennifer chimed in. "I have to do an inventory of the flowers on hand and what we can reasonably expect to order for the event. What kind of décor and theme are we thinking?"

Ethan looked to Barbara. He was rapidly getting in over his head.

"Something simple, something that symbolizes the unity between our two countries..." Barbara's eyebrows rose as she looked to Ethan for guidance.

He nodded back. Sounded good so far.

Her eyes closed. Jennifer winced. Barbara pressed on, though. "How about... a simple cream and gold table linen—"

"We still have the Yves Delorme silks on loan," Jennifer interjected.

"Perfect. And... a centerpiece of short red roses, surrounded by white and then blue flowers?"

"I can box everything and keep it low. An ultramodern look and feel? Maybe surround the centerpiece with white candles? I can throw some iron pieces in, try to get that hardy Russian feel?" Jennifer shrugged.

Everyone nodded, making wordless noises of agreement as Barbara smiled.

"Hyacinths would be too tall, but what about if I looked for cornflower or crocuses?" Jennifer turned to Ethan. "They should be available right now..." She trailed off.

Ethan stared back at her.

"Crocuses would look lovely." Barbara reached across the couch and patted Jennifer on the knee. "Oh shoot." She sent Ethan a pained look. "Your state china won't be ready in time. Does the president have any thoughts on what service he'd like to use?"

It was Ethan's turn to look pained and out of his depth.

"What about a retrospective?" Brandt leaned over the back of the couch in between Barbara and Jennifer. "We can pull china from past presidents and set them up at different tables. Pull some information about each setting and president at the tables."

"Oh, I like that." Barbara patted Brandt's arm and beamed. "So, black tie, the Yves Delorme silk linens, red, blue, and white floral centerpieces, white candles, and a guest list around a hundred." She made quick notes on her notepad. "I need to contact the chief usher, the chief of protocol, the chief calligrapher, and the White House chef. We have to set the menu, oh, and pick the entertainment..." Barbara chuckled, a helpless laugh. "If we pull this off, Mr. First Gentleman, I want this on my headstone."

Ethan grinned. "If there is anyone who can do this, it's you guys."

The next ten days passed in a blur of flowers, linens, and blind panic.

Word got out that the White House was planning a state dinner for President Puchkov. Pete and Brandt spent most of their time beating back the press and trying to fend off the worst of the malicious media, hungry for a cheap attack on Jack. The invitation list was a closely guarded secret until members of Congress started leaking their invitations days before the event.

They kept the list small. Congressional leaders, justices, governors, and statesmen who had come out in support of Jack and Ethan. Sergey's Russian embassy in Washington DC and his ambassador to the UN. America's ambassador. Jack's Cabinet, including Elizabeth, who was seated at Jack, Ethan, and Sergey's table.

When Barbara and the chief of protocol fretted about filling out the guest list but worried over inviting the right people, Ethan joined them in the hallway, listening to them argue back and forth about the merits of inviting contentious and oppositional figures as a potential olive branch, or whether that was legitimizing their hate.

Ethan smiled at the display lining the walls. Barbara had taken his suggestion to showcase the supportive cards he and Jack had received to heart and had arrayed hundreds of them along the wall, tacked up at angles so that they could be flicked open and their messages of love and support read.

"Barbara," he interrupted when she huffed out her annoyance at the chief of protocol. "What about inviting some of these people?"

She beamed.

He was in a conference call with Cooper, analyzing satellite imagery over Somalia and discussing Madigan's seemingly complete disappearance when Barbara and Jennifer barged in with a décor emergency. Cooper heard, but wisely said nothing, when Barbara and Jennifer asked him for his final decision on the napkins—medium Persian blue was closer to the Russian Federation's flag color but clashed with the crocuses, while Liberty Blue was a safer choice and went well with the cream table linen and gold accent chairs. Would President Puchkov be all right with that? No one wanted a repeat of the disastrous insult paid to the French president all those years ago when the colors hadn't matched.

Ethan gave his approval and thanked them very seriously for their foresight.

He and Jack skipped hosting an official tasting event and instead spent an afternoon in the White House kitchens with Ethan's staff, sampling round after round of options prepared for the dinner. Russian cuisine was featured for the main course, but the hors d'oeuvres were all-American, with gourmet sliders, crab cakes, guacamole bites, Caesar salad spears, deviled eggs, and even Buffalo wings. Laughter flowed, along with the wine for Barbara and her team, and Jack loved every minute of getting to know Ethan's staff. He thanked Jennifer for her flowers, which sent her over the moon and had Barbara clucking and clutching her pearls again.

Ethan rubbed his hand down Jack's back, the beers he and Jack were sharing making him just bold enough to sneak a squeeze of Jack's ass.

Jennifer and Barbara practically moved into the East Wing days before the event. They checked into the InterContinental hotel across the street, collapsing for a few hours of rest before they headed back to set up the State Dining Room and oversee preparations to the North Entrance and the Cross Hall, where the receiving line would take place.

Ethan gave the hotel his credit card and told them to give the women anything they wanted. He set up a champagne breakfast for the two the morning after the state dinner.

Ceremonial Marine Corps honor guards practiced their movements in the morning and the evening when Jack and Ethan would depart and enter the Residence. They watched their precise maneuvers together, sitting on the Grand Staircase and sharing a beer.

He *ooh*ed and *ahh*ed appropriately with Brandt when Jennifer and Barbara showed off pictures of their gowns and drank beers with Scott and Daniels, who bitched up a storm about the massive security headache that came with all state dinners. He sat in meetings with Irwin, reviewing—ultimately useless—interrogations of the few recaptured prisoners they had managed to grab from Madigan's jailbreaks. He and Cooper pored over drone footage shot over Somalia, but the detail was poor and grainy since they had to overfly at such a high altitude thanks to the anti-aircraft weaponry Somalian rebels had acquired.

And at night, he and Jack fell into each other's arms, sometimes too tired to do anything more than nuzzle a bit before snoring. Other nights he took Jack to the brink, fingers deep within Jack while he sucked Jack's cock, or he dove into Jack's ass, rimming him until Jack's trembling body arched and he shouted, gripping their headboard as his knuckles went white and his arms shook. Ethan licked Jack's release off his chest as Jack groaned, his dick valiantly trying to rise again.

"If that feels that good, the rest of you will probably kill me." Jack ran his hands through Ethan's hair as Ethan lay next to him, bodies pressed tight.

"There's no rush," he said softly. "Whenever you want. Or never, if that's what you decide. It's not for everyone. And we're doing just fine."

"It's not never." Jack shook his head. "I want to. I want to feel you inside me. I'm working up to it."

"Take all the time you need. I'm happy no matter what." He kissed Jack, nice and slow until Jack's eyes drooped and he rolled his head against Ethan's on the pillow.

"Mr. President, President Puchkov will be leaving the Russian embassy shortly. He'll arrive at the White House in one hour." Irwin, almost despite himself, smiled.

They had managed to pull it off. Wing a state dinner in ten days. Jack, decked out in his best tux and a crisp black bow tie, led a toast in the Oval Office, his staff and Ethan's gathered around. He'd passed out the champagne flutes personally when everyone entered. "To the best staff the White House has ever seen."

Everyone applauded. Jack singled out Pete and Brandt for their unflinching stand with the press, and Ethan singled out Barbara and Jennifer for their superhero-esque execution of preparations. Jack toasted the chief usher and the executive chef, and they all posed for an official picture, and a much less official selfie with Jennifer's selfie stick. Jack demanded a silly faces picture, and the office devolved into giggles while they finished their champagne.

Thirty minutes until Sergey's arrival. Jack clapped his hands together. "Let's get this dinner started!"

A state dinner didn't begin with the evening dinner. The official beginning was the motorcade of the visiting head of state arriving at the North Entrance and the formal ceremony greeting his arrival. The Marine Band played and the press snapped photos as Jack and Sergey warmly embraced, grasping hands and then pulling each other in for a backslapping hug. Ethan was formally introduced to Sergey after that as the First Gentleman and Jack's partner. He'd never actually met the man, just eyeball-fucked him in Prague when he'd thought Sergey was a threat to Jack and then listened to his voice on the phone for months after. He stiffly held out his hand with a tight smile.

Sergey pulled him in for a hug, too.

A Marine Corps color guard greeted Sergey outside the White House, holding both the American and Russian flags while "The President's Own" Marine Band played a zippy Russian classic. Sergey grinned and mimed conducting the band while Jack laughed. The almost-frigid spring weather was unseasonably gloomy; the dreary gray light made the North Lawn seem sodden, almost desolate. Patches of snow had melted away and winter-dormant limp grass poked through in patches. Bare tree branches scratched over the grounds, almost skeletally frail. It was not the stunning backdrop to a state dinner that would glisten from the magazine spread.

Jack led Sergey and his small entourage up to the Residence and to the Yellow Room overlooking the Truman Balcony. Hors d'oeuvres and champagne flowed, and a select group of Jack's invitees mingled with the Russian delegation.

Slipping out of the Yellow Room and to the hallway of the Residence, Jack huddled with Sergey in private, Ethan at his side. "We had your luggage brought up through the basement. You're sleeping in the Lincoln bedroom." Jack winked.

World leaders never stayed in the Residence anymore. Not for over a hundred years. They stayed down the street at Blair House. Scott had had a mild heart attack when Jack told him his intentions to have Sergey stay with them in the Residence. He'd turned to Ethan, slack-jawed, as if Ethan could talk sense into his lover.

Ethan had shrugged and grinned.

Sergey, who on a good day was lean and pale, seemed to have aged since Ethan had seen him in Prague the year before. His skin was almost sallow, his cheeks hollowed out, and dark bags seemed permanently etched beneath his eyes. But he smiled at Jack's words and his whole face lit up.

"Excellent, Jack. Thank you. This will be fun, no? We will drink vodka all night long. I have three bottles in my suitcase."

Jack's eyes went wide.

Sergey laughed. "I joke, I joke. But I have a question for you. Might I ask you to arrange a second bedroom? I have my senior aide with me, and I would like for him to stay close." Sergey gestured to a young thirty-something man with blond hair and ice-blue eyes who had followed him from the Yellow Room and stayed at a polite distance, but who was obviously watching them. He stood tall with a military bearing, and his dark suit fit him like a second skin. "Please, meet Sasha Andreyev. My new senior aide."

Sasha seemed incredibly uncomfortable shaking Jack and Ethan's hands, almost painfully shy in the face of the president of the United States. He stepped back, shadowing Sergey's shoulder as soon as his introduction was complete.

Ethan shared a look with Scott, hovering over Jack's shoulder, and Daniels, over his own. Sasha moved like a bodyguard, like a man dedicated to Sergey, and not like an officious aide. Scott's pulse leaped at his throat. Ethan could practically see his stomach curdle. Another potential—though admittedly unlikely—threat to observe.

He smothered his grin with a sip of his wine. Some days, he was glad he wasn't in the Secret Service any longer.

"Of course we can set up a second room. The Queen's Room is right across the hall. Does that work for you both?"

Sergey snapped a joke to Sasha in fast, low Russian, and Sasha finally managed to chuckle. He ducked his head and nodded. "*Da.* Yes. Thank you, Mr. President."

Sergey squeezed his shoulder once and smiled at the younger man.

Ethan shared a long look with Jack and took another sip of his wine.

Jack got the signal that everything was ready downstairs. He officially, and with his characteristic fanfare, asked Sergey to join him for dinner. The guests upstairs headed down a separate way while Jack, Ethan, and Sergey waited at the top of the Grand Staircase. Jack took Ethan's hand

and laced their fingers together, squeezing once before he looped his arm through Ethan's.

They both heard Sergey's deep "Aww" as his phone snapped a picture behind them.

When "Hail to the Chief" played, Ethan kissed Jack on the lips before they took their first steps together down the stairs, arm in arm. Sergey followed behind, single—he'd left both his ex-wives back in Russia, he said.

Thunderous applause nearly drowned out the music. At the base, all three stopped and listened while both the American and Russian national anthems played. Jack and Ethan placed their hands over their hearts for the national anthem, and when Jack took a deep, steadying breath in the middle of the song, Ethan rested his hand on the small of Jack's back.

The last time the national anthem had been played live for Jack was at Ethan's funeral in Arlington.

Sergey looked proud, and yet sad, when the Russian anthem played.

The receiving line, as always, took forever, and Scott, Daniels, and their details were like cats on steroids, obsessively watching and checking everyone who approached Jack, Ethan, and Sergey.

"Relax," Ethan breathed into Scott's ear. "You've got your constipated face on."

Scott sent him a murderous scowl and coughed into his fist, trying to smother his laughter. "Fuck you," he whispered back.

Every guest got a photo with the trio, and at the end, Sergey stepped between Jack and Ethan and wrapped his arms around their shoulders and beamed into the camera. Jack laughed, Ethan's jaw dropped, and the photographer instantly said he had the front-page picture for the morning news.

The actual dinner was elegant and understated. Sergey got a kick out of reading about each of the different sets of china at the tables, and Ethan sent Barbara and Brandt a double thumbs-up.

Sergey made small talk with Elizabeth, wit and verbal repartee bouncing back and forth between them like they were flirting, everything from pop culture to international politics being pilloried. Ethan and Jack shared bites from each other's plates and traded sips of wine. Sasha sat silently across from Sergey and watched his president like a hawk.

Halfway through the dinner, Ethan nudged Jack to his feet. They circled the room, personally greeting and thanking thirty of the guests they had invited from their cards of support and congratulations. They posed for pictures and for selfies and came back to find Sergey recording their antics with a smile.

Barbara had hired a small swing and blues band, and after dinner, everyone moved to the East Room for dancing and more wine and champagne. Jack's hands lingered on Ethan. His smile was a little broader, his eyes a little brighter. Warmth raced under Ethan's skin, a gentle blurring of the world at the edges.

He and Jack led the first dance, swaying together and laughing as the cameras flashed.

"You did amazing," Jack said, beaming as Ethan pulled him close after a spin. "This is perfect."

He shrugged. "All part of my job." He couldn't hold in his grin as Jack threw his head back and laughed out loud. "Not too bad, though, huh?" He spun Jack again, pulling him close for a kiss after. Surrounding them, the guests were smiling, clapping, and radiant joy hung in the air. For the first time, being out and public with Jack felt *good*. Really good. Like he wasn't screwing everything up for Jack, and the world really was on their side.

Jack pressed his palm to Ethan's cheek. "Not bad at all, love."

They took a break after. Ethan snagged two flutes of champagne for them both. Jack made eyes at him as he sipped his, smoldering looks that went straight to Ethan's cock.

They had a few hours left in the evening, but no one would miss them if they sneaked out for a quickie, would they?

Scott would no doubt shit a gold-plated brick, emblazoned with the Presidential Seal.

It would be worth it.

He was just about to grab Jack's hand and whisk him away when Sergey appeared, slapping both of their backs and pulling them into another big hug.

"My friends!"

Ethan bobbled his champagne, but Jack was much smoother. He grabbed Sergey back with a smile. "Are you having fun?"

"This is too much fun," Sergey said, pointing at Jack. "Too much fun for Americans like you. Only Russians can have this much fun!"

Jack rolled his eyes as Ethan spotted Sasha hanging behind Sergey. He smiled at the younger Russian.

Sasha looked like he was ready to bolt, cataloging exits and escape paths through the crowd.

"Mr. President." Sergey made a show of straightening and adjusting his bow tie. He held out one hand. "May I have this dance?" He winked at Jack.

Jack's jaw dropped. "Do you have any idea what the press will do with that?"

"It will be fantastic." Sergey beckoned Jack again. Around them, people had started to notice. "We can take turns leading," he said, trying to encourage Jack.

Jack looked at Ethan. Ethan looked back at him. "Go for it," he said. "Give them something to really talk about."

Sergey beamed at Ethan as Jack took his hand. "I don't trust you, Sergey," Jack chuckled.

"What? Me?" Sergey feigned shocked outrage, leading Jack to the dance floor. "We are allies! Partners! What is not to trust?" He stopped dead center on the dance floor and took Jack politely into his arms, one hand on Jack's hip and the other gently holding his hand aloft.

Everyone stopped. Everyone stared. Sergey stepped off first, leading Jack on a fun, easy swing dance while the band played. Cameras flashed, and cell phones streamed the dance live to the Internet.

Ethan slid over to Sasha, standing stock still with his arms locked behind his back, his eyes tracking Sergey's every movement. Even though he was Russian, and they were a stoic, hard people, Ethan had never actually seen someone look quite so dour.

He glanced back at Sergey and Jack. Sergey had stopped and changed position, letting Jack take the lead. Jack's hand was on Sergey's hip and he steered Sergey back across the dance floor, laughing at something he'd said.

"I know what it's like," he said, under his breath.

Sasha slowly turned, staring Ethan down.

Ethan nodded to Jack and Sergey. "I can tell by how you look at him. It's how I used to look at Jack. Before."

Sasha whipped away, scowling.

Ethan tried again. "I don't remember you from the delegation last year. Sergey said you were new? How did you join his team?"

Silence.

Ethan flagged down a waiter and grabbed another two flutes of champagne as Jack and Sergey continued to dance. Sergey spun Jack and bulbs flashed.

Sasha's jaw clenched.

Ethan passed him a glass.

Sasha played with the stem, rolling the crystal between his fingers before draining half the flute in a large swallow. "I was fighter pilot," he grunted. "President Puchkov…" Sasha's eyes narrowed. "He saved my life."

There was more to that story, like all Russian stories. Ethan waited.

"This," Sasha said, waving one hand around the room, "is very different from what I used to do. I am... uncertain what to do for him." He glanced sidelong at Ethan. "How to make him proud."

"I think you're well on your way," Ethan said carefully. "Fighter pilot, now a senior aide. One he wants to keep close."

Sasha's scowl deepened.

The song ended. Ethan spotted Sergey and Jack searching them out in the crowd. Sergey spotted Sasha first, and Ethan watched his face brighten and a smile break out over his narrow, hawk-like features. "He already sees you. That's something." He didn't want to give Sasha false hope, though. How many weeks had he agonized over Jack, trying to decipher smiles and secret looks and their growing friendship? "I know how it feels. It sucks, it really does. I... really didn't think this would ever happen to me."

And then Sergey and Jack were back, both beaming, and Sergey nodded once to Sasha before turning to Jack, replaying the dance they'd just shared and laughing at the shocked and befuddled gazes from the crowd. Ethan watched Sasha's eyes linger on Sergey, his fingers restlessly playing with his half-full champagne flute, for the rest of the night.

The guests left close to midnight, and Jack, Ethan, Sergey, and Sasha made their good-byes to their staff and guests and trudged up the stairs to the Residence.

"Vodka?" Sergey appeared from the Lincoln Bedroom with an unmarked bottle sealed with wax and a smile on his face. He'd undone his bowtie, and the loose ends dangled down the front of his shirt.

Jack collapsed on one of the couches in the East Sitting Hall outside Sergey's bedroom. "Bring it on," he said, tugging at his own bowtie.

Sasha joined them, sitting silently at the end of the couch while Sergey poured four hefty shots of vodka into crystal tumblers. "To friends," Sergey said simply, raising his glass in a toast.

Jack and Sergey talked and laughed while Ethan wrapped his arm around Jack's waist and leaned back on the couch. As Jack and Sergey wandered into discussing the business lease and investment deal again, soft snores floated up from Ethan. His head rolled until his cheek was resting on Jack's shoulder, eyes closed, sound asleep.

Sergey grinned, halfway through comparing the Russian and American auto industries. "Like a little baby."

"Yours is out, too." Jack nodded to Sasha, asleep and slumped against the end of the couch, still buttoned up in his dark suit.

"Good." Sergey leaned back with a sigh and gazed at Sasha. "He needs the rest. He is still recovering. I was not sure about bringing him along, but leaving him behind was no option either. I am protective of him." Sergey chuckled. "And he insisted on not leaving my side, with the threats and all."

"I can see that. He's protective of you as well. Watched you nonstop during dinner." Jack smiled at Sergey's scoffing dismissal. "Who is he?"

"For that, we need more vodka." Sergey poured another round for him and Jack, larger than the first. Slowly, he managed to tell Jack Sasha's story, about his beating at the base and his desperate gambit coming to Moscow, broken, bleeding, and feverish. About Dr. Voronov collecting him, half-dead, and bringing him back to health. About meeting him in the middle of the night and listening to him sob.

Jack stayed silent.

"I do not know what to do for him. His unit listed him as a runaway and presumed dead before he even arrived in Moscow. Even sending the FSB to the base got nowhere. They are not budging from their make-believe story, and Sasha does not want to pursue charges."

"The betrayal cut him deeply." Jack swirled his vodka and glared out the Sitting Hall's window. He remembered the taste of betrayal, the color. The sound. Betrayal had come in the form of his closest aide, Jeff Gottschalk. A man he'd called a friend. A man he'd known for years, a man his wife had been friends with. "It's hard to recover from that." He shook his head, turning back to Sergey. "How'd he end up as your aide?"

Sergey looked a little helpless as he answered. "I want to help him. He is a good officer. A good Russian. If I had done more, sooner, perhaps…" He trailed off. "He has been very good so far. Learning a lot. I know he's stiff here, but…" Sergey smiled. "I think he will be okay."

Jack held his glass out for another toast. Crystal chimed, and a warm, gentle rightness settled over Jack's mind. The touch of liquor and the edge of inebriation. "Thank you. For what you did in Russia. What you said about your people."

Wordlessly, Sergey held his glass out again, a final toast. "I told you to watch the newspapers, did I not?" He grinned and knocked back the last of his vodka. "Jack, you have my support, and you have my friendship. Always."

Mixed Reactions on Both Sides of Atlantic to President Spiers's Russian Investment Plan

President Spiers and President Puchkov's joint announcement of a US-led investment plan to help the struggling Russian economy was met with mixed reactions from both nations. Some were quick to praise the two world leaders for working together and finding a solution that promises immediate results for both the Russian worker and the global economy. Others slammed President Spiers, saying that his friendship with the Russian president has gone too far.

"President Spiers has really shown his true colors here," Senator Stephen Allen said in an interview with TNN. "He's in bed with the Russians, and I say that figuratively, but maybe literally too. Who knows with this president? President Puchkov is certainly his political boyfriend. It's the biggest case of a Manchurian Candidate I have ever seen. He's pouring American interests into Russia, in exchange for nothing."

Russian media was more favorable, with most Russians eager for stability in their economy. However, a large contingent of anti-Puchkov demonstrators continue to gain support from all areas of the Russian public. General Moroshkin, Commander of the Russian Armed Forces, loudly objected to the investment plan, stating that Russian problems could not be solved by American interference, but only through Russian innovation and determination. His comments garnered immense support among the Russian military and the hardline political establishments.

And, at the state dinner for President Puchkov hosted by the White House, President Spiers and President Puchkov made history by being the first same-sex world leaders to dance together.

25

White House

"Mr. President, we need you to come with us."

He and Sergey were several hours into the strategy meeting with the investing business leaders and their CEOs when Irwin smoothly interrupted, crossing into the room and speaking privately in Jack's ear. Looking up, Jack spotted Ethan at the door, looking grim.

He rose, making his excuses with a smile. Sergey didn't buy it and cut off from his humorous retelling of a bear hunt in Siberia mid-word as he stared at Jack.

Ethan pulled him aside as he stepped out of the Roosevelt Room.

"What's going on?"

"Rogue Islamic extremists have fired on two tankers in the Persian Gulf. They boarded one and took the crew hostage. The other is on fire. The attackers evaded capture and dumped mines into the water at the Strait of Hormuz."

Jack closed his eyes as he propped his hands on his hips. In the list of terrible things that could happen to a president, anything affecting the Strait of Hormuz, the chokepoint for the Gulf in between Iran and Oman, was up near the top. Forty percent of the world's oil transited the strait each day.

"Everyone is gathering in the Situation Room. Elizabeth is getting inundated with frantic calls from the Gulf countries. These terrorists are holding every nation there hostage."

"Son of a bitch." He glanced back inside the Roosevelt Room and met Sergey's fierce stare. The meeting had ground to a halt with his departure, and Sergey wasn't doing a damn thing to keep it going. "Damn it. I'm bringing Sergey down, too. The Russians are operating in the Gulf with us. He'll have something to say about this."

Ethan's eyebrows rose. "People downstairs are going to shit."

Jack chuffed out a tiny laugh. "Yeah, I'm good at getting that reaction out of people." He waved to Sergey, drawing him out of the Roosevelt Room. As Sergey stood, Jack poked his head back in and apologized for having to cut the meeting short. Already, one of Jack's aides was sweeping

Enemy Of My Enemy

in, smoothly asking the CEOs if they'd like a private tour before a cocktail in one of the reception rooms. A soothing balm to being ditched by two presidents.

Sergey didn't ask questions; he followed behind Jack and Ethan through the West Wing and down to the lower levels. Ethan waved off the Secret Service agents who stared at them with wide eyes and made moves to their microphones. Scott stood outside the Situation Room, and he looked Sergey up and down before stepping aside and holding the door open.

All conversation within the Situation Room stuttered to a stop when Jack entered with Sergey on his heels. He moved to the head of the table and stood behind his chair, gripping the headrest. Ethan took up his customary position on his right, sitting in the seat normally used by the vice president. Sergey stood on his left, and he whistled as he surveyed the room, taking in the array of flat-screens showing real-time satellite footage, live feeds from naval vessels in the Persian Gulf, news streams from all corners of the globe, and tracking updates of forces deployed around the world.

General Bradford, chairman of the joint chiefs, made the kill signal to the watch officers in the back, and the screen showing worldwide forces went dark.

Jack fixed General Bradford with a pointed glare. "Everyone, please welcome President Puchkov to the Situation Room. I've invited him down here since his forces are operating in tandem with ours in the Gulf. So, let's hear it. Hit me."

Eyeballs bounced around the room, the silence stretching on for a long, uncomfortable moment. Irwin finally broke the deadlock, clearing his throat first. "This statement was read aloud by the captain of the captured freighter a few minutes ago: 'The Russian Federation and the United States have committed countless sins and must be punished. America's disgusting president is a disgrace in the eyes of Allah. The unholy union between the Russian Federation and the United States of America must be stopped, and both nations must be destroyed. Their nations run on the blood of our lands, our precious oil. We will no longer allow any of our resources to service The Great Satan and her unholy partner, the Russian Federation. Any attempt to stop us will be met with deadly retribution.'"

Sergey dramatically rolled his eyes to the ceiling as Jack took over, steepling his fingers and leaning his forearms on the back of his chair. "Is this the Caliphate? Reprisal for our forces in the region?"

Bradford shook his head. "If they're doing this in the Caliphate's name, they haven't said so yet. We broke their naval capabilities months ago and the Caliphate doesn't have any good access to the Gulf at the moment."

"So who are these guys?" Jack frowned.

"Still working on that, Mr. President. Our best guess at this time is rogue agents."

"Or someone who wants us to *believe* this is the work of the Caliphate." Ethan's eyes caught Jack's.

"Tell me about the captured freighter."

"Nineteen crewmembers, running under a Malaysian flag. The captain is an American, retired Merchant Marine. We've heard the captain's voice but don't have proof of life for any other crewmembers."

"Their cargo?" Ethan leaned forward, frowning.

"One hundred thousand tons of crude oil freshly pumped from the Iranians." Bradford scowled. "Our ships in the water report three large speedboats loaded with explosives dumped mines across the strait and disappeared." He glanced briefly to Sergey but then tapped out a few commands on his tablet and called up the surveillance images taken from the deck of a naval carrier.

"Any idea how many mines were dumped?"

"Spotters estimate at least a hundred. All commercial ship traffic has halted. It's a cluster out there. One of the oil tankers is on fire. Bahrain has sent out their coast guard to assist. At least twelve super haulers were due to transit the strait today, and they're stranded on either side. The freighters outside the strait are sitting ducks. Inside, we've got sixteen thousand sailors and Marines held hostage."

"We're getting panicked calls from every Gulf nation." Elizabeth sounded harried and harassed, and her normally perfect hair was pulled back in a loose clip. Dark strands hung around her face.

"What carrier strike group is currently over there?" Jack pulled out his chair and sat down, gesturing for Sergey to grab one of the spare chairs on the wall and drag it to his side. He scooted over, making room for Sergey at the head of the table. "Sergey, you have three destroyers in the Gulf, yes?"

Wide-eyed looks shot around the room as Sergey nodded.

"We have the *Dwight D. Eisenhower* docked in Bahrain, Mr. President." Admiral McDonald, chief of naval operations and one of the joint chiefs, said. "But they're in port for repairs. The carrier was battered pretty hard by a monsoon on her transit through the Arabian Sea. Blue water over the flight deck. Last estimates for repairs put them at best at seventy-two hours. Which means they're a sitting duck right now."

"Damn it." Jack sighed. "What about the rest of the strike group?"

"We sent two cruisers and three destroyers with the *Eisenhower*. All five are stationed near Kuwait, too far away for immediate action."

"Sir!" One of the attachés to the chief of naval operations leaned in, passing his tablet directly to Admiral McDonald.

Admiral McDonald's expression turned fierce. "Mr. President, spotters have picked up one of the speedboats. It's come out from behind the hijacked tanker and is currently aiming dead on for the *Eisenhower*. It has weapons trained on the carrier and can close the distance to her in four minutes. With the explosives on board, that speedboat could blow a hole in the side of our carrier. And if they detonate into the tanker, the whole thing will go up and devastate the Gulf."

Jack looked to Ethan, for a moment, and then back to McDonald. "What are our options?"

"We destroy them. Now. Before they make their move."

"Can we be certain we can take them out without blowing the tanker, Admiral? Can we act without doing their job for them?"

"Sir, it's a risk we might have to take. In moments, we could be pulling dead Americans from the water."

"If I may." Sergey interrupted, leaning forward and tapping at the polished wood of the conference table. "Is there a phone that I can use? I'd like to call my Commodore in the Persian Gulf, just off Bahrain."

Silence.

In the scramble that followed, one of the watch officers managed to get in radio contact with the fleet admiral on the Russian lead destroyer. Sergey spoke in Russian, and General Bradford snapped for a translator in the room as Irwin and Rees collectively looked like they were chewing nails.

"He's... ordering his destroyer to go between the *Eisenhower* and the hijacked tanker... and the speedboat." The translator, another watch officer, frowned. "He's ordering them to hold their position and shield the *Eisenhower*. No matter what."

The Situation Room, again, stared at Sergey as the line cut out, but this time, with something a little less hostile.

Between a conference call with the Kremlin, radio patches with the Russian destroyers, and video calls with the Carrier Strike Group Commander, they hammered out a quick plan.

With the time and shielding the Russians provided, they were able to put Russian and American fast attack boats into the water, teams of Marines and Russian *Spetznaz* forces onboard. They headed for the speedboat, snipers opening fire when the jihadis refused to yield. At the same time, divers slipped underwater to the hijacked tanker, boarding silently and creeping through the ship. They rescued the crew but slew the hijackers when they charged like raging berserkers.

"*They don't appear to be Middle Eastern,*" one of the Marines radioed back to the *Eisenhower*. "*Maybe North African. Possibly Sudanese.*"

Ethan and Jack shared a long look.

The American destroyer farthest south, the *Forest Sherman*, waited for the Russian destroyer *Bezboyaznennyy* to come down from Kuwait. Together, they headed for the mines.

Creeping out from where they'd hid in Iranian waters were the other two terrorist speedboats that had helped with the hijacking and the attack, each laden high with explosives, enough to rip a hole in both ships and sink them in minutes.

"They know we have to clear these mines." Jack frowned at his staff. "They know we're going to stop them."

"They are wanting us to engage," Sergey growled. "They want to play at war, but they will run when the real shooting starts."

Jack reached for Ethan's hand under the conference table as the two ships, American and Russian, closed in on the mines.

The speedboats started toward both.

There was a live feed of the American and Russian destroyers' bridges piped to the Situation Room. The orders given to each ship had been clear: get rid of the mines; capture or kill the terrorists who placed them.

Alarms sounded on both vessels. Russian cursing flew through over the comms channel. The *Forest Sherman* commander's cool voice rose through the cacophony. "*Ops, status.*"

"*Two ships coming right for us, Captain.*"

Sergey's Russian captain was decidedly less politic with his reaction. He swore in Russian, and the automatic translator typed out on the bottom "*go fuck yourselves.*"

The *Forest Sherman* transmitted over the radio, addressing the Islamic fighters. "*Enemy vessels. Disengage from your course immediately or we will open fire.*"

Jack breathed in deep, and Ethan gripped his hand beneath the table. They both leaned forward, their hands beneath the tabletop. Instead of watching the monitors, Ethan watched Jack.

The *Forest Sherman's* commander spoke again. "*Ops. Maintain course and heading, bow-on to target.*"

Jack's eyes pinched, but Sergey leaned into his side and whispered, "Bow-on presents the smallest possible target."

On-screen, the Russian ship stayed abreast of the *Forest Sherman*, also bow-on to the speedboats.

Fighters on the speedboats squaring off with the two Navy destroyers hefted heavy RPGs on their shoulders.

The *Forest Sherman* commander barked out her orders, lightning fast. *"Light them up. Get me radar on that ship and prepare to fire."*

Jack turned his hand and laced his fingers through Ethan's. His eyes flicked away from the screens, and he held Ethan's gaze. The air seemed to suck from the room, a great vacuum of anticipation and held breaths.

"Both vessels have fired, Captain! Three RPGs coming in hot. Damage control teams to port side!"

More cursing in Russian and shouted orders from the *Bezboyaznennyy*.

Forest Sherman's commander broke over everything. *"Fire with guns. Destroy them."*

The Americans fired first, a long series of rattling bullets that chewed through the speedboats. The Russians joined in, and in moments, both boats were smoking hulks sinking beneath the surface.

"Cease fire." The *Forest Sherman's* order was repeated in Russian on the *Bezboyaznennyy*. *"Resume course to clear mines."*

Jack stared at Ethan as the Situation Room broke into clapping and muted cheers. He kept their hands laced beneath the table as his eyes slowly closed.

Soft Russian floated down the hall in the Residence, Sergey's rolling voice mixed with Sasha's deep timbre. Jack and Ethan had left the two close to midnight sitting on the couches in the East Sitting Hall between their bedrooms.

"Did we stop something or start something today?" Jack was half in and half out of his suit, hesitating as he unbuttoned his shirt. "Was that the Caliphate? Rogue terrorists? Or Madigan?"

Naked and lying on top of the bedsheets, Ethan shook his head. "I don't know."

Jack slumped on the edge of the bed. "I wanted," he finally began, "to make the world a safer place. To make America, and the world, *better*. Work toward... unity." He exhaled as he tipped his head back. "I think I've failed on just about every one of my goals."

"I'm sorry. I know I—"

"No, it's not you. It's me." Sighing, Jack ripped his shirt off and balled it up, chucking it to the floor like a basketball. "All of this madness would have happened whether or not we got together." He crawled into the bed, still in his suit pants, and straddled Ethan's lap.

Ethan rested his hands on Jack's thighs. When Ethan looked up, the naked pain, the uncertainty in his gaze, speared Jack through the heart.

He leaned forward, his palms on Ethan's chest. Ethan's heart thudded against his touch. "Madigan would still have been after me. He still would have tried to take the government. Destroy the Middle East. Would he have succeeded if we hadn't been together? Would you have fought back from the grave as ferociously as you did if we hadn't taken a chance on each other?"

Jack watched Ethan's eyes darken, and his open expression turn to a frown. "I know you may not think much of my professionalism, considering what happened between us, but I have always been one hundred percent dedicated to my job. It wouldn't matter to me if we were together or not. I would have defended your life to the end of mine because you are the president. Not just because you are my lover."

Shit. "No, no, no. That's not what I meant." Groaning, Jack tipped forward. "I think the world of you, Ethan. I think you're a true professional."

Ethan snorted.

"I do. I've never doubted you. Not once. Not with anything." He tried to find Ethan's gaze, but Ethan's eyes slid away. "Hey. I mean it. I've always admired you, Ethan. Your dedication. Your intelligence. Everything about you. I still do."

Ethan's gaze flicked back to Jack. He swallowed. "Sometimes," he began, his voice rough. "I think I should have taken the moral high ground. Decided to walk away from you and what you were offering."

Jack frowned.

"On Air Force One. You asked me if we could give this a try. I should have been a bigger man. Should have said no. Or, not yet. Not until you were out of office. I was worried that this would happen. That it would all come out and everything would fall apart. The world *needs* you, and I've just complicated everything."

"God, I'm glad you didn't do that." Jack's fingers curled through Ethan's chest hair, as if he could grip on to Ethan and never let him go. "You ground me. Seeing you every day and waking up in your arms is what gives me the strength to keep doing this. You are my rock, Ethan." A tiny smile quirked up the corner of his lips. "I'd probably have run for the hills if it weren't for you by my side."

Ethan smiled, and one of his hands rose, cupping Jack's cheek.

"Sometimes, like today, I still want to run away." Jack's voice was soft. "What if those fanatics had managed to sink one of our ships? Thousands of sailors and Marines killed. It's… difficult for me to put our people in harm's way."

"I know." Ethan's other hand rose, and his thumbs stroked over Jack's cheekbones. "I know it's hard. Your wife—" He stopped and pressed his lips together.

"I think of Leslie, yes. But not just her. I think of you, too." Jack peered down at Ethan, trying to pour all of the love he felt into how he gazed at Ethan. Could he ever find the right words, the right actions, to explain to Ethan how deeply he loved him, how much Ethan made him feel alive? "I think of you in Ethiopia," Jack breathed. He grasped Ethan's wrists, holding Ethan's hands to his face.

Memories flew through his mind, like a film reel spinning out of control, colors and sounds and emotions bleeding out every which way. Ethan, a rifle to his forehead as he lay broken and bloody in the dirt road. Jack's screams, seemingly soundless against the helicopter rotors and the shouts of the British soldiers. The cold, almost silent wardroom, and the crackling video showing Ethan, blood-covered and swaying on his knees, a machete to his throat. The white noise and the electric smear when the rockets had blown away Ethan's team on the drone's video feed.

Jeff at his side. Jeff holding him as he sobbed, wailing Ethan's name to the bulkhead as he lost it all for the second time in his life.

Jeff forcing him to his knees and fitting a nuclear weapon to his chest.

"I'm here. I'm here, Jack." Ethan's thumbs stroked over Jack's cheeks as his hands cupped his face. Slowly, Ethan pulled Jack down, until Jack was lying across Ethan's chest, his ear pressed tightly to the warm skin over his heartbeat. "I'm here with you," Ethan whispered.

"Don't leave," Jack breathed. "Please don't ever leave." *I need you, Ethan. So much.*

"Never."

Ethan stroked Jack's back for hours. Jack stayed curled up on top of Ethan, half-dressed, as he listened to the steady thrum of his heart beating until he finally fell asleep.

On the last day of Sergey's visit to the United States, a video was released online and a body was dumped in Moscow's Red Square, beheaded.

On the video, a man kneeled against a white wall as tear tracks stained his cheeks. He was naked, and a rainbow flag had been carved on his chest, paint crudely thrown over the cut outlines. Behind him, a man dressed in black, from head to toe, shouted in Arabic at the camera. Only his eyes were visible.

In his hand, he held a knife.

The man's name was Evgeni Konnikov. The man in black boasted of how he'd set up to meet with Evgeni through the most popular gay hookup app in the world. How he'd tricked him into walking into his own capture and torture. He shouted at length of the evils of homosexuality and how Russia would pay for her crimes. *"Everything you hold dear will be taken from you, President Puchkov,"* the masked man said. *"Including your precious homosexuals. Including your American puppet president."*

Most news agencies censored what happened next, but the agonized screams could still be heard all the way around the world, including deep in the Situation Room, where Jack, Ethan, and Sergey watched in silent horror.

Jack grasped Ethan's hand above the table and squeezed tight as Ethan closed his eyes and dropped his head, letting it hang between his shoulders. Their knuckles went white where they grasped each other.

Sergey sank into what had become his chair, both hands over his mouth, and muttered a prayer in Russian.

He had Ilya secure the body in the Kremlin within the hour and then personally attend to the autopsy while the CIA, NSA, and FBI analyzed the video recording. Jack and Sergey issued a joint statement, condemning the brutal murder.

When Jack's voice choked off in the middle of his statement, Sergey grasped his shoulder until Jack was able to speak again.

"We will never retreat. We will never cower. We will never run. We will never turn back in the face of terror." Swallowing, Jack stared up into the briefing room's lights, letting halos of color dazzle his vision. "The combined forces of the United States, and her ally, Russia, are coming for you. This is a promise."

He and Sergey arrived back in the Situation Room after their statement and found Ethan waiting in the hallway. He glowered at the floor, his jaw clenched with his hands shoved in his suit pockets.

Jack reached for his elbow. "What is it?"

Ethan couldn't look up. "Madigan," he growled. "This is all Madigan's doing. All of it."

"Show me," Jack whispered.

Inside, the national security advisor, Meredith Peterson, and Director Todd Campbell, walked Jack through the evidence. The man in black spoke Arabic with a Sudanese dialect and a North African accent. The camera was a knockoff brand made in Turkey and widely available at street vendors in the Middle East, and especially on routes taken by human smugglers moving from Africa and the Middle East overland to Europe and to Russia. Forensics from Evgeni's phone showed that the murderer used broken English to communicate with Evgeni in a pattern most closely linked with individuals who learned English as an adult and came from an Afro-Arabian background. Evgeni, who also spoke broken English, probably hadn't noticed anything was amiss.

From the Persian Gulf to Moscow, Madigan's prisoners were on the move.

"I must return to Russia immediately." Sergey bid his farewells to Jack in the Oval Office as his aides buzzed behind him, speaking in fast Russian into their cell phones.

Sasha stayed glued to Sergey's side, watching everything and everyone with narrowed eyes. Scott glared back at Sasha, as if having a Russian bodyguard in the White House and so close to Jack was a personal affront to his existence.

"Is there anything we can do?" Jack shook Sergey's hand. "Anything at all?"

"Find this Madman Madigan," Sergey growled. "And make him suffer."

"Done." They hadn't managed to capture him so far. But they would. They would. Ethan seemed to be taking the revelation that Madigan had been behind the murder as a personal censure. He hadn't come up to the Oval Office with them. He'd stayed behind in the Situation Room, not able to look Jack in the eye since he'd met them in the hallway. Ethan's absence from his side was a physical ache. "We'll get the bastard."

"And, would you consider coming to the memorial? I will be giving Mr. Konnikov a state funeral. He is a victim of a terrorist attack, and we honor our fallen heroes in Russia. It would mean much if you would attend."

For a moment, everything seemed to freeze in the Oval Office. Cell phones stopped buzzing, the chattering of Russian by the glass doors ceased, and even the air Jack breathed seemed to shiver to a halt. It was just him and Sergey, and his request.

And then, time resumed. Scott whipped his head around, staring at Jack. Sasha turned wide, over-bright eyes to Sergey. Irwin and Elizabeth, holding court by the couches and typing on their phones, froze.

Where was Ethan when he needed him? "I would be honored to pay my respects, Sergey. I'll be there."

Scott let out a faint wheeze behind Jack, like a popping balloon.

"*Blagodarju vas*, Mr. President. Thank you. I will see you again soon."

"You can't go to Russia with the president."

Ethan stared at Scott and Daniels, his friends facing him down on the other side of his desk in the East Wing. Daniels had asked for a minute of his time, and when Scott walked in, his stomach had curled, souring. "What?"

"You *can't* go with the president." Scott stepped forward, his arms crossed. His expression was hard, a stern glare fixed on Ethan. "There's too much risk right now. Everything is getting crazier by the minute. We have over a hundred real-world threats right here that we have to run down, have to protect you both from, and that was before this attack. And now the president wants to go to the funeral, in *Russia*?"

"The Secret Service's job is to keep the president safe—"

"I *know* what the damn job is, Ethan! And I *know* you think you could do this better, but Goddamn it, do you know how difficult you've made everything?" Scott blew, shouting at Ethan before turning and running his hands through his hair. "I've been running my people into the *ground*. We're operating two hundred percent over capacity. I've got agents sleeping in Horsepower, and they haven't been home in days. We're pulling fourteen- to sixteen-hour shifts. It's fucking nonstop." He glared at Ethan again. "And the fucked-up thing is, even with all of that, I still don't feel that you both are fully protected! Not with every fucking crazy thing that is out there right now!"

Silence.

Daniels stared at the carpet, his hands clasped behind his back.

"You're asking me," Ethan began slowly, "to *not* be at Jack's side while he is at the state funeral for a murdered gay man?"

"I'm not asking. I'm *telling*." Scott held Ethan's cold stare. "I'm sorry. But we have to put our foot down on this. We're nearing the breaking point, and if something were to happen to you, or to the president—" Scott's jaw snapped shut. He shook his head. "Ethan, please," he said through clenched teeth. "You know what it's like on this side."

He did know. Years of battling with presidents and first families, of doing everything he could to ensure their safety and security, even when the first family was determined to be as unsafe as possible. The headaches, the heartburn that came with dealing with recalcitrant, stubborn politicians who thought of the Secret Service as little more than window dressings or accessories. Not being listened to and having to scramble on the back end to cover the security exposures.

He closed his eyes and bowed his head. "I don't like this," he breathed. "I don't like this at all."

"Do you trust me?"

Ethan's head snapped up. Scott was more than just his best friend. He was his brother, someone he had become a man beside. Scott knew everything there was to know about him, had even known about Jack and him from almost the first moment it began. He'd carried his broken body to safety, had helped him retake the White House and save Jack, save the world, and for God's sake, he ran lube for him and Jack. Trust wasn't a big enough word for how deeply he believed in Scott.

"You know I do. With everything."

"Even with him? With J-Jack?" Scott stuttered over Jack's name.

Ethan hesitated. He frowned. Took a deep breath as he searched his soul. "Yes, I do."

"Then *trust me* on this. Trust me to do my job and to protect the president. Trust that I know what I'm doing."

Slowly, Ethan nodded. "I'll let him know."

Jack took the news better than Ethan had.

"If our friends are asking for this, then we should give it to them. They need our help." Jack crossed his arms with a heavy sigh. "Is there something else we can do to help? Somehow relieve the burden?"

"Never leave the White House, ever? Not host any outside personnel? No more state dinners?"

"I'll be crawling the walls if we can't ever leave."

"When the president travels is always the worst." Ethan sank into one of the chairs in the Residence's kitchen. He and Jack were cooking, a dinner of rice and pan-seared strips of steak. A spinach salad, tossed in vinaigrette, and a bottle of red wine waited on the table. "In order to really secure this funeral trip, the advance team should have been on the ground a week before Evgeni Konnikov died."

"Is the security that you guys strive for really possible?"

"It has to be." Ethan's hand came down on the table, a heavy slap. "It has to be, always. It's your life."

Jack looked down. He'd shucked his suit and his shoes after leaving the West Wing, and he wore jeans and Ethan's sweatshirt and walked around barefoot. "It's not just my life. It's your life too, now. And if keeping you safe means you stay here, then that's what we do."

Ethan still wanted to puke at the thought of Jack going without him. Of not being at his side. "Will you be all right?"

"Will you?"

He shook his head. "No. To be honest, no. I'll be out of my mind until you're back." His foot jiggled, an endless bounce against the table leg. One hand dragged over his face. "I've been thinking about Ethiopia all day," he groaned. "How we planned for that."

"This is different."

"Flying into a foreign nation with limited prep time in an area where known terrorist attacks occur? Yeah, totally. Completely unique." Ethan watched Jack's eyes slide closed. "The only difference is, this time, there's been an actual threat against your life. Madigan is still out there."

"He won't ever get near me."

Ethan scrubbed his hands over his face again, trying to block out the memories of Ethiopia, of their careful and meticulous security plan falling apart in tatters around them. Him, Scott, and Daniels all just struggling to survive and get Jack to safety as bullets flew.

Where was Madigan? How could he insert himself so easily back into the world? How far had he spread? How deep did he go? He was an ever-present nightmare, a golem hiding in the shadows of the world.

"Hey," Jack whispered softly, much closer than he'd been before. Ethan opened his eyes. Jack was right in front of him, looking down with a soft smile. He stroked his fingers through Ethan's hair. "Scott's great at his job. I trust him. He was trained by you, and he's almost as good an agent as you." Jack winked.

Ethan snorted. "I'm really not the poster boy for a perfect Secret Service agent."

"You're my poster boy for a hero, and you're the man I love." Jack dropped a kiss to the top of Ethan's head. "And everything will be fine. I'll be back before you know it." He stepped back as the timer went off for the rice. "I'll get the steak. Can you pour the wine?"

He filled their glasses as Jack warmed up the pan. He stood behind him, wrapping one arm around Jack's waist and resting his chin on his shoulder as Jack started searing the steak. "Still going to miss you."

Jack kissed his cheek. "I'd miss me, too." He grinned when Ethan snorted, and then he sobered. "You really are my hero. And you always will be."

What could he say to that? Ethan buried his face in the curve of Jack's neck and breathed in his soft, woodsy scent. The hint of pine that came from his aftershave, the tang of his shampoo. The scent of his skin. "And you're mine. Always."

Fury over State Funeral: General Moroshkin and Hardline Russian Political Party Boycott Proceedings

General Moroshkin delivered another scathing invective against President Puchkov and his plans to honor terrorist victim Evgeni Konnikov with a state funeral in Moscow. "President Puchkov insists on pushing his Western agenda on the motherland. This is unacceptable, and Russians will not stand for this kind of continuing behavior." General Moroshkin and other military commanders scheduled a series of military drills in the Murmansk and Siberian regions at the time of the funeral, seriously limiting the number of military units President Puchkov could call upon to bolster security for the funeral. Hardline political elements within Russia applauded Moroshkin's position and seemed to rally behind the general as an opposition leader to President Puchkov.

Elizabeth Wall Confirmed as Vice President

The House and Senate confirmed Elizabeth Wall as President Spiers's vice presidential appointee, despite bitter confirmation hearings that centered around how Wall would react should she become president. Wall refused to engage in the discussions, repeatedly stating that she stood with President Spiers and that discussions such as those only invited the worst kind of possibility.

26

Moscow

The streets of Moscow were filled with riot police, over half wearing sour expressions, as Jack's motorcade sped him through the capital and toward the Kremlin. "The funeral begins at the House of Unions in two hours, Mr. President." Scott twisted around in the front seat of the armored SUV. "We're wheels up and back to the US in eight hours. We'll be staging in the Grand Palace at the Kremlin before and after the funeral, at President Puchkov's request."

Traffic had been halted on all surface streets, and the infamous Garden Ring circling Moscow, a veritable traffic jam at all hours of the day and night, was empty. Scott's driver floored the accelerator, and their motorcade zoomed down the highway.

"We're mixing up the different modes of transportation, Mr. President. Motorcade to the Kremlin, chopper back to the airport."

A huge section of Moscow's airport had been closed, all air traffic diverted, for Jack's use. Air Force One was parked and surrounded by a combined force of Secret Service and military guards.

"We'll be on you at all times, Mr. President. The Russian FSB has deployed agents in the crowd, and the Russian Presidential Security Services are securing overwatch. Snipers are in place in all exposed areas of the funeral procession. Their security looks similar to what we do for inaugurations."

Jack smiled at Scott. "I trust you, Agent Collard, and so does Ethan. We have every confidence in you." He jiggled his cell phone. "And Ethan says to tell you hello."

"Hey, Ethan." Scott waved back at Jack. "Backseat Agent," he quipped, before turning back around and speaking into his radio.

Over Jack's cell phone, Ethan chuckled in Jack's ear. *"How's it look so far?"*

"Fast." Trees sped by, next to the highway.

"The people? We always try to get a read on the crowd. See what kind of atmosphere we're dealing with."

"They're Russian, Ethan. Not a lot of smiles here on a good day, and things are pretty tense right now."

"You have a point."

Jack changed the subject, picking lint from his pants. "What time is it there? Must be early."

"Sun hasn't risen yet." Ethan yawned. *"But I don't care. I'm talking to you."*

Jack smiled. "When does Lieutenant Cooper arrive?"

"His flight lands in about an hour. Daniels and I are getting ready to head to Andrews."

"You'll find something. I know you guys will." Jack smiled, even though Ethan couldn't see him. Ethan and Lieutenant Cooper were getting together for a review of the intelligence on Madigan, trying to plan their next move. Neither Jack nor Ethan was willing to send Cooper and his men into Somalia blind, not with Madigan's reach or his capabilities unknown. They wouldn't send them on a one-way mission, despite Cooper's repeated requests to saddle his men up and let loose.

"Mr. President, we'll be arriving at the Kremlin in three minutes."

"Gotta go, love. Talk to you soon."

"Good luck."

Jack cut the line as his limo approached the massive red walls of the Kremlin. Guards manning the gates saluted as Jack's motorcade drove through. Ivan the Great's massive Bell Tower, sparkling with brilliant ivory and gold-gilt onion domes, reflected the sunlight. Beyond the Bell Tower, the tips of St. Basil's Cathedral edged over the Kremlin Walls, the array of dazzlingly colorful minarets like a rainbow bonfire straining for the sky.

Jack watched the glittering spires until his gaze was drawn to his left, to the massive Grand Kremlin Palace. Columns marched in line with ornately sculpted windows, a seemingly never-ending façade of strength and power wrapped in white marble and gold.

The motorcade pulled to a stop in front of the entrance, and a team of Russian military and FSB stood posted at intervals, watching the motorcade warily. As much as Jack and Sergey were becoming friends, the security services still had a ways to go toward trusting each other. Jack heard Scott mutter under his breath before climbing out of the car and opening Jack's door.

He smiled at the assembled guards and thanked Scott as he buttoned his suit coat. Squinting, he tried to find Sergey, but his lanky friend wasn't on the steps.

Instead, Sasha walked forward, holding his hand out. "Mr. President. We are honored that you are here with us."

"The honor is mine."

"Please, let me escort you inside."

Scott shadowed Jack's every footstep as he fell into step with Sasha and entered the Grand Palace. Few American presidents had ever been inside, and he resisted the urge to spin around and take in the ornate marble covering the walls, the golden sculptures, the mosaics covering the ceiling, the chandeliers twinkling above. Amber light permeated the palace, and a plush red carpet directed everyone down the main hall.

Sasha took him up a wide, curving staircase to another equally ornate hall, twice as tall as the ground floor. What had seemed like three stories was actually two, and a double layer of windows let spears of sunshine through heavy velvet drapes. Prisms exploded from the thousands of crystals hanging in the chandeliers. An arched ceiling inlaid with marble reliefs stared down at Jack and Scott as they walked, their footfalls cushioned almost to silence. More statues, and more gold-gilt reliefs stared at Jack as he followed Sasha to a double paneled door.

"President Puchkov would be honored if you would wait a moment for him in his residence. He has been delayed."

To enter the home of the Russian president. Another first. Jack smiled and dipped his head. "Of course."

Sergey's home, the official Russian president's residence within the Grand Palace of the Kremlin, was just as ornate as the rest of the building. Sasha led him through the foyer to the sitting room, and Jack found himself seated on a velvet and silk sofa next to a marble table boasting a golden bust of an unknown Russian.

"Aleksandr Pokryshkin," Sasha said. "Three-time hero of Soviet Union. He may be responsible for winning World War II. He is father of modern Soviet Air Force."

Jack whistled. "I didn't know Sergey was a military history buff."

"He had it brought here recently. It was just sitting in dark warehouse."

A slow smile spread out over Jack's face as he watched Sasha. "That was very kind of him," he said, dipping his head to the young Russian.

Sasha looked away.

"The others? They're here, right?" Jack wasn't the only world leader attending the funeral. Britain's prime minister and Germany's chancellor had arrived, as had the ambassador to Russia from Saudi Arabia. Prince Abdul, governor of the Riyadh region in Saudi Arabia, had issued a statement from the Kingdom condemning the murder and the desecration of Islam by the murderer. He was the first, but not the last Islamic country to speak out against the terrorist.

"They are here. They are in Georgievsky Hall, with refreshments."

So he was in the VIP lounge. Jack shared a quick look with Scott.

Scott looked like the world's tensest wind-up doll, just two turns away from blowing out his springs. He was woefully out of place in the midst of Sergey's sitting room, a black suit in a sea of red curtains, diamond chandeliers, and gold-framed oil paintings.

The door opened and Sergey's booming voice bounced over the marble walls. "Jack! I am sorry I was held up. There are a thousand and one complications and only one of me." He stopped at the sitting room door and clapped his hands together, smiling at Sasha and Jack talking to one another. "Let us share a drink before we go down, Mr. President."

Sasha moved, standing shoulder to shoulder with Scott. Scott glared sidelong and shuffled away a half step.

Sergey brought over two tumblers of vodka and sat beside Jack. "I spoke with the family. They are certain that they want you to do this."

Jack swirled the vodka in his glass, staring at the eddies. "Sergey—"

"He was a blogger, and he wrote articles about how much he admired you. How he wished Russia had such a visionary president." Sergey shrugged. "He would be honored. His memory will be honored."

His eyes slid closed. Could he do this? He wasn't quite sure. Even after everything, every single thing that had happened to him from the moment he'd kissed Ethan back, he still wasn't totally certain about his sexuality. What did he call himself? He'd shied away from labels, other than "Ethan's lover and partner." He'd been happy to live in that nether region, the vagueness sheltered by his refusal to speak of his personal life and his dictatorial rule to Pete regarding the media. Now, with the funeral and with Sergey's ask, the world was thrusting him into a role he wasn't certain he deserved. He wasn't a figurehead or a symbol. He didn't deserve that.

He was just a man.

But this wasn't about him.

Slowly, Jack nodded. "All right. I'll do it. I'll be a pallbearer." Standing next to Sergey at the front of Evgeni's Konnikov's coffin, carrying him from his repose in the Hall of the Unions to a gun carriage, and then walking with Sergey and the funeral parade to the Red Square.

It was Scott's—and Ethan's—nightmare.

But he would do it. For Evgeni Konnikov, and for everyone.

The Hall of the Unions had been decked out for Evgeni's state funeral. Huge Russian flags draped the far end of the hall, along with heavy black curtains. Black gauze had been wrapped around the glittering chandeliers above, casting a somber glow throughout the dim room. Mourners had come to pay their respects for five days, and a flood of flowers lay on top of and around his flag-draped casket. Candles littered the floor amidst the blooms, soft flames flickering with the hushed footfalls of visitors. Cards were scattered around the perimeter, tucked into flowers, and lying beneath candles.

An explosion of rainbow had enveloped the dour scene, an overpowering statement in the midst of darkness. Rainbow flags stuck out of bouquets, and rainbow posters and wreaths and necklaces and bracelets bracketed the entire tableau. *"Pride"* and *"Never Forget"* shouted from placards, alongside *"Never Silent."* A framed picture of Evgeni Konnikov sat on a stand beside it all, resting on an unfurled rainbow flag.

Jack's heart lodged in his throat, seizing up as his stomach tightened. A chill swam down his spine as he laid the bouquet Jennifer had arranged and given to him beneath the portrait and on the corner of the rainbow flag. His hands clenched, and when he went back to Sergey's side, he reached out to his right, seeking Ethan.

His hand hung in the empty air.

He took a steadying breath, slowly, and tried to keep it together.

Sergey wrapped his arms around his shoulders. He rested his head on Sergey's shoulder and let the tears roll down his cheeks. Cameras flashed, but Jack didn't care.

This was on him. This was entirely on him.

Rage rose, stealing his breath away. Madigan would *pay* for this. He would pay for all of this. Jack would see to that personally. He felt walls crumbling within him, limits he'd had once before tumbling down. Madigan would pay if it was the last thing Jack did.

Sergey delivered his address, promising retribution against Evgeni Konnikov's murderer. He told of meeting his family and how he'd come to admire the young man for living his life proudly with no regrets and no excuses. How he exemplified everything that made a Russian man great.

He'd hesitated for a moment, stuttering as he stared at the crowd. Jack's eyes followed his stare until he found Sasha seated at the end of their row, pale-faced and looking like he was about to puke.

The family declined to speak publicly, and after Sergey's statement, it was time to escort the coffin to the gun carriage, waiting outside the Hall of the Unions. Sergey rested his hand on Jack's back as they walked to the dais and to the coffin.

His mind went to a strange place as he carried the coffin, a numb, silent place. The crowd faded away, the thousands who had gathered to watch, and he felt the weight of Evgeni Konnikov on his shoulder like a weight upon his soul, a conviction of his failure to catch Madigan. A conviction of his presidency. A conviction of who he was as a man.

Who was he to put himself outside the margins? Who was he to hold himself apart, and different? He loved a man, just as Evgeni Konnikov had. Whatever he chose to label that within himself, for himself, the world had already chosen to label him. And the criticism of the world would still come, no matter what he said to mollify the fears that tried to keep him up at night.

Why did he fear, though? What fear could change his love for Ethan? Why did he keep himself at arm's length?

He was no different from Evgeni Konnikov, and he didn't want to be anymore. It was time to stand up. Be seen, and be known. The decision settled into his soul, hammered down by the coffin weighing upon him.

The gun carriage appeared before them. He followed Sergey's soft instructions as they slid the coffin onto the platform. Ahead, horses brayed and the Sergeant at Arms called for a moment of silence. The color guard, in front of the horses, dipped the Russian flag and stepped off, leading the procession to the Red Square.

Jack walked behind the gun carriage, flanked by Sergey on his right and the family on his left. He took Mrs. Konnikov's hand.

Sasha and Scott shadowed their steps, and more Secret Service agents and Presidential Security Service agents walked on the outskirts of the procession.

Behind them were a scattered few Russian politicians who supported Sergey, but no other world leaders. Just him and Sergey, and then the marchers. Hundreds joined in carrying pride flags and pictures of Evgeni Konnikov. Men and women had draped themselves in full-length rainbow flags and painted their faces.

Along the parade route, Russians stood on the sidewalk, watching with solemn faces. Some waved pride flags. Not enough, though. Others watched, scowling, or turned away when they passed.

The sun was falling from high in the sky, the brilliance of the sunlight warming through the Russian cold, and St. Basil's Cathedral burned like an aurora as they entered the Red Square. Jack raised his face and closed his eyes.

Thunderous booms quaked the air. The pavement beneath Jack's feet rumbled. Silence, as Jack opened his eyes for a moment, and then he saw the column of smoke rising. People running.

Shrieking tore through the Square.

Loud pops broke the perfect afternoon, bangs that Jack had heard before and still heard in his nightmares.

Beyond the parade, another boom echoed, somewhere deep in Moscow.

Sergey whirled, meeting Jack's gaze. Shock lined his wide eyes, and his pale face was slack, his jaw hanging open.

"Mr. President!" Scott crashed into him from behind, throwing his body over Jack's as he ducked them both down, finding cover behind the gun carriage. Sasha leaped on Sergey, dragging him beside Jack as the Presidential Security Service and Secret Service agents arrayed themselves, weapons drawn. Screams echoed from the marchers, scattering away as Jack and Sergey's presidential SUVs pulled in along the parade route, screeching to a halt behind the carriage.

In seconds, Jack was hauled into the SUV, still bent over with Scott draped over his back, bodily shielding him as best he could from every direction. Across the parade route, Sergey was thrown into his own SUV, covered by Sasha. Both vehicles roared away, heading together for the red walls of the Kremlin, opposite the Red Square.

"What the hell is going on?" Jack tried to sit up, but Scott and another agent pushed him down, lying him flat on the seat as they flanked him, weapons still drawn inside the SUV.

"A bomb has gone off at the Red Square, Mr. President. Looks like a suicide bomber. We're getting reports of more going off around Moscow. We're taking you back to the Kremlin and then evacuating to Air Force One."

They zoomed through the Kremlin gates behind Sergey, getting air as they roared over the cobblestones. Sergey's car wound past the Kremlin Palace and took them deeper within to the Senate building and the heart of the Kremlin, completely secluded from everyone else.

Scott and his men set up a perimeter before letting Jack out of the SUV. Ahead, Sergey had pushed his way free, but Sasha still stuck to his side with a gun in his hand.

"Jack!" Sergey jogged back to him, his suit disheveled, hair awry. "Jack, are you all right?"

"I'm okay." His hands shook. Sergey grabbed his forearms, steadying him. "What's happening?"

Sergey cursed in gutter Russian, growling. "The murderer. Madigan's man. He had a dynamite vest under his jacket." He cursed again, and Jack caught General Moroshkin's name in the long string of Russian.

"How many are hurt?"

Sergey's hands ran through his hair. He laced his fingers behind his head as he started to pace. "I don't know. First reports said dozens. The square was full."

Sasha had a cell phone to his ear and a scowl stretched over his face. "Mr. President, there have been five more suicide bombers in Moscow. Casualties are high."

Jack slumped backward, leaning against the side of his SUV. Scott gripped his shoulder. Jack could feel Scott's hand trembling through his touch. "What about Evgeni Konnikov's family?"

Sergey ran his hand over his mouth. "Ilya is personally escorting the family now. They got out of there."

Jack nodded. In his pocket, his cell phone rang.

He pulled it out. *Ethan.*

"I'm all right. Ethan, I'm all right."

"I saw the news." Tension thrummed through Ethan's voice. Jack could picture him pacing back and forth, his lips pursed and one hand fisted over his mouth.

"Bombs are going off all over Moscow. The first was by the murderer. Madigan's man. He had a suicide vest on."

Ethan cursed, and a dull thump echoed over the line.

"I'm all right. Scott got me out." He swallowed, and the coffin on the back of the gun carriage flashed before his eyes. "Ethan—" His voice broke, and he closed his eyes.

"I want you back here. Now. Safe."

Scott was on the radio beside him, calling in their chopper to the Kremlin. Sergey was surrounded, Sasha on his right and another advisor on his left. Frowning, Sergey nodded as he listened to their fast Russian. One of Sergey's hands gripped Sasha's arm, as if he needed the steadying presence.

"I'm on my way. Scott's getting us out right now." Above, his chopper roared, the rotors whooshing over the Kremlin as it came down. Jack turned away, cupping his hand over the speaker. "Ethan… I *need* you." He needed Ethan, badly. He needed to be with Ethan, feel his body, his presence. Feel the clench of muscles in Ethan's arms as they wrapped around him. See the light ignite in Ethan's eyes, a brilliance that came just before his smile, a smile that was Jack's alone. Run his hands down Ethan's back, and run his fingers through Ethan's chest hair. Watch him sleep, and feel him reach for Jack's body. Feel his own heart clench, the force of his love for Ethan so overwhelming, so blindsiding that it scared him at times.

He needed to bury himself in their love. Let go of the world for a moment, and just be a man who had fallen in love with another man. In love with Ethan.

"I'm here, Jack. Always. Come home to me."

White House

Ethan ended the call and braced himself against the window in his office, leaning heavily on his forearm over his head. Eyes closed, he tried to block out the breaking news, the reporter's voice saying Jack and Sergey had been whisked away from the funeral. The bombs going off. Numbers of casualties. Anchors arguing back and forth about Sergey's decision to hold the funeral—and make himself and Jack targets—and the Russian military's absence, their maneuvers outside of Moscow.

"Do you want to take a break, sir?"

Cooper sat at one of Ethan's couches, frozen in place with a folder open on his lap. Three laptops were spread over the table and folders littered the floor. Maps were taped up over the fireplace and satellite imagery lay in a grid on the floor, an aerial view of Somalia and the greater Middle East.

"No." Ethan pushed back and cleared his throat. "No, I want this asshole dead and gone. Let's keep going."

Cooper nodded and went back to comparing the list of Sudanese prisoners within the folder to one of the intel dumps the NSA had acquired: a scrape of the databanks of people moving across Europe and through the regions between Somalia and Russia. The murderer—now suicide bomber—had gotten to Russia somehow. He hadn't flown. The sea route had become difficult, what with the international flotilla monitoring the Mediterranean. That left overland, and for as many checkpoints as there were, there were also holes in borders. Tracking one man across so many wild frontiers was exhausting.

Speaking of exhaustion. Ethan's gaze tracked over Cooper, taking in the deep-set eyes and the hollow cheeks, the scruff of beard, just too long to be called a five-o'clock shadow. Cooper seemed to have traded sleeping for nonstop work. Ethan received emails and confidential reports from him at all hours; intel analysis from the Gulf, potential action plans for entering Somalia, and his own analysis on top of the CIA's analysis of happenings in the Middle East. He passed on information sent from Prince Faisal, again with his own interpretation on top of the prince's.

Every time, Cooper and the prince agreed.

He hadn't sent Cooper's team out in weeks. Since they'd returned, Madigan seemed to lay low, and his disappearance was like an itch beneath Ethan's skin that he couldn't satisfy. Just out of reach, but still there.

"Whoa. Hold up." Cooper frowned at the laptop in front of him and tossed the folder of Sudanese prisoners aside. "This can't be right." Furious typing, as he pounded on the keys.

"What's up?" Ethan waited, watching Cooper's frown turn to a glower.

"This name on the Israeli border checkpoints list. I know this name."

Frowning, Ethan stepped over the pile of folders and sat beside Cooper. "How?"

"He was my high school hero. The hometown quarterback. Everyone wanted to be him. I was a kid, but I thought he was the shit. He joined the Army. I joined the Marines. We kept in touch for a while after. Sergeant Noah Williams."

"What's so unusual about that? There a reason he shouldn't be crossing the border in Israel?" It was a legal crossing at a checkpoint, and his passport had cleared.

"Yeah, there's a fucking reason," Cooper snapped. He typed again, pulling up the security camera footage, showing his former friend's face clearly, and then his passport with a smiling photo of Noah. Last, he pulled up a news report from Google. "He's fucking dead. He died in the Iraq War. In Fallujah."

The news report listed the names of the dead soldiers from the Battle of Fallujah—over a decade ago—from Noah and Adam's hometown, along with their pictures.

A younger Noah stared back at Ethan and Cooper from the news article. The older Noah Williams in the passport had the beginnings of laugh lines around his eyes and had filled out a bit.

"Track his passport. Where has he been?"

Cooper scowled and slammed his fingers on the keyboard. A moment, as the State Department servers searched through their records, and then a list of his border crossings popped up on screen.

Israel. Turkey. Ukraine. Russia.

Ethan pulled another laptop close and called up Noah's Army service record from the DOD servers, silently thanking Irwin for clearing total access for them. In moments, Noah's record popped up on the screen, the DD-214 displaying all of his assignments and his dates of service, all the way up to his supposed date of death.

"Fuck." A sliver of dread had formed when Cooper spoke, but it seemed too phenomenal, so fantastical, that it couldn't be true. Still, he had to check, and he pointed to Noah's last assignment and commanding officer, his stomach turning itself inside out as his heart hammered against his ribs.

Cooper leaned in, reading the screen. "*Last duty assignment: Special Operations, commanded by Major Madigan.*"

Ethan was on the phone with Irwin when Jack made it back to the White House late that evening. Televisions droned softly in the background, an endless loop of the bombs in Moscow playing behind talking heads denouncing Sergey, Jack, and the Russian military. Blame was being tossed in every direction.

Ethan and Cooper had combed through the data dumps and had brought in Irwin's dedicated analysis team at the CIA. In addition to Noah Williams, three other long-dead former members of Madigan's units had appeared at border checkpoints on transit routes to Russia.

He rubbed his hand over his eyes, sighing. "How long has he been secreting loyal soldiers away? Where have they been for almost two decades?" Jack came up for a kiss, and Ethan hugged him close and kissed his forehead as Irwin answered.

"*I can't even begin to speculate.*"

Jack broke away, exhaustion clinging to him. He headed for their bedroom, carrying his small duffel over his shoulder, his only luggage for the trip.

Ethan watched him walk away.

During the day, the FSB had autopsied the blown-apart remains of the murderer. When suicide bombers blew, their heads were usually found intact, separated from the body. Ilya's FSB had found it, and they were finally able to identify the murderer: an escapee from the Sudan prison break sentenced there for his repeated attacks against the Americans and Russians in Iraq, working with the Caliphate. His name was Asim Walif.

"So are we thinking that these ghosts Madigan has kept around smuggled Walif into Russia? Traded cars and personnel to cross different borders? They have clean passports. They can move around. As long as they're not in the States, the fact that they're legally dead won't be an issue."

"*Very probable. We can put out a bulletin for these guys, flag their passports, but there are a thousand different ratlines in Eastern Europe. A thousand different ways to sneak across the borders.*"

"Fuck." Exhaling, Ethan closed his eyes and groaned. "So now we have Madigan's personal ghost army running terrorists across Europe and into Russia. What now—"

"Ethan!" Jack's shout broke through the Residence, shock and horror and terror laced through Ethan's name.

He dropped his cell and bolted for their bedroom. He threw himself inside, his back bouncing off the door as he cleared the corners on instinct, his hands desperate for his old weapon and useless in front of him, clenching air.

Jack stood at the foot of the bed, frozen in front of his duffel, his face white, jaw hanging open, eyes wide as saucers.

In his hands, photos trembled. One tumbled loose and skittered across the floor.

Ethan snatched it up, racing to Jack's side. He grabbed Jack, wrapping his arm around his waist and checking him over before he took the photos from Jack's shaking hands.

"What are these?"

Jack shook his head, mute.

In the photos, Jack sat on an ornate couch beside a gold bust, smiling at Sasha. Scott was facing the camera, but his eyes were locked on Jack. In the next, Sergey walked in, his hands clasped together. Scott was still in the frame, this time looking around the room. Then Jack and Sergey walking through the Kremlin Palace together. At the Hall of the Unions. Jack's head resting on Sergey's shoulder.

Jack carrying Evgeni Konnikov's casket and walking behind the coffin.

The photos were taken *close*. Too close.

And, on top of each image, a red M had been drawn, closed in a circle.

27

White House Residence

Ethan threw down the photos taken in Moscow on the Residence's kitchen island. They scattered, spreading out across the dark marble countertop, brazenly displayed for Scott and Daniels.

Scott's jaw clenched as he stared at the images.

Daniels cursed.

Jack hung back in the kitchen corner, watching as Ethan squared off with his two friends. Daniels hadn't been on the trip, but Scott had, and those photos would have to feel like Scott had been skinned alive, with the perverse closeness the photographer had gotten.

Jack was exhausted from the travel and from the emotional sledgehammer of the day, but Ethan had called Scott and Daniels and growled for the both of them to come up to the Residence immediately.

"How the *fuck* did this happen?" Ethan growled, his voice trembling. Jack watched him, taking in his white knuckles clenching the marble countertop and the strain across his shoulders.

It felt like Madigan was saturating everything, had infiltrated all corners of the planet. Was in the air Jack breathed, in the shadows moving behind him. Hell, he had been in the White House. His phantom still haunted Jack, more than he wanted to admit.

Scott flipped through each of the photos. "Some of these could have been taken by anyone in the crowd. Others…" His eyes flicked up, meeting Ethan's dark and dangerous gaze. "Others were taken when it was just the three, or four, of us."

"It wasn't just the fucking four of you!" Ethan exploded, bellowing at Scott as his face turned purple. Whirling, Ethan's hands rose to his head, fingers lacing behind him as he paced in the space between the refrigerator and the island. "Someone was fucking *there*," he hissed. "With you. With *Jack*!"

"Ethan, there was no one fucking there! I know how to do my job—"

"Do you?"

Fury raged in Scott's eyes. "We can't all be perfect Iceman Reichenbach, can we? If you had been there, the only difference would be you sitting next to Jack in these photos!"

"I'd *never* let him be put in danger!" Ethan hollered. "*Never*! Once was fucking enough!"

"Hey!" Daniels jumped forward, putting his hands on Scott's chest as Scott seemed ready to leap over the island and throttle Ethan. "Hey! This is *not* helping!"

Ethan cursed again and spun toward the refrigerator. He braced himself against the steel doors, hands over his head.

Scott glared at his back.

Jack exhaled slowly and crossed his arms.

"We have two problems," Daniels said when no one spoke. "Who took these pictures and how did they get in the president's duffel?" He looked up, his eyes finding Jack across the kitchen.

Ethan spun. "Yeah, who the *fuck* got close enough to Jack to slide these into his bag?" He was back to bellowing at Scott, his face still purple. "*Huh?*"

"A hundred different people could have been close enough and you know that, Ethan. All of the agents. The crew of Air Force One. The soldiers guarding the plane while we were in Moscow."

"Do we think this is someone on the inside?" Jack stepped forward and reached for Ethan. His lover was barely containing his rage.

Ethan turned to Jack, his dark eyes filled with anguish and rage.

"More traitors?" Daniels frowned. "You think people are still joining Madigan, even after everything he's done?"

"Or people who have been with him all along. We still don't know his reach." Ethan leaned into Jack's touch. "We don't know who we can really trust."

Scott shook his head.

"What do we do?" Jack held on to Ethan's waist, his thumb hooked through the belt loop of his khakis. Ethan's warmth leached into Jack, grounding him back to reality. Ethan was here. He wasn't lost, and he wasn't about to disintegrate into one of Jack's nightmares, full of blood and sand, white noise and Jeff's sneer. "What's our reaction?"

Scott and Ethan shared a long look. As fast as they had been bellowing at each other, they were back on the same page. "Whoever took these wants us to be rattled. Wants us off our game."

"So it's a mindfuck."

Ethan glared. "We still need to close ranks. Make sure everyone who is close in on the detail is someone we can trust, and I mean *really* fucking trust." Ethan gripped Jack's shoulder, holding him tight. "We can't take any chances."

"Every agent has been checked and vetted. I'm not sure it's one of ours. How could they have gotten into President Puchkov's private residence in the Kremlin without moving with me and the president?" Scott sighed. "We might have to look to the Russians for this one."

Jack shook his head. "It still could be one of ours. It's dangerous to pretend this couldn't be done by one of our people." How well he knew. Betrayal colored his every thought, his every worry, after Jeff. "Everything so far has been far worse than we could have imagined. Why not this too?"

No one met Jack's gaze. Scott looked down as Daniels closed his eyes, and Ethan's hand dropped to Jack's hip.

"Russians took the photos, and one of our own slipped it into his duffel?" Daniels squinted at Ethan.

"Possible. We probably won't be able to find the Russian now. But we need to turn everything over on Air Force One. Who on our team helped? Who is working for Madigan?" Ethan's voice shook with rage.

"I didn't have a big delegation. Mostly Secret Service. Press pool, the media guys. Pete and some of his guys. A few others…"

"We have to check every one of them. Every single one. It will take a while. And until then, we close ranks, move only the most trusted agents to the president." Scott stared Ethan down. "And we have to have stronger containment at the White House."

"We're going to be caged in for a while," Ethan said softly to Jack.

"And." Scott closed his eyes. He reached for his weapon at his hip. He withdrew it, and clasping the barrel, turned and offered the grip to Ethan. "Be fucking smart," he growled. Ethan held Scott's hard stare as he grasped Scott's weapon. Scott held on another moment and then let go, exhaling at the same time.

Ethan set the weapon down on the kitchen island.

Scott cursed. "I can't believe I just did that."

"Thank you. I fucking hate being helpless."

"Yeah, you're a real asshole when you get this way, too." Scott glared at his friend.

"Could you get us some range time at Rowley? Private. No one else there. I want to teach Jack how to shoot. Pistols, rifles, everything. I want him prepared, just in case."

Rowley was the James J. Rowley Training Center, where Secret Service recruits finalized their training before becoming Special Agents. Jack knew of it but had never been out there.

Scott and Daniels shared long-suffering looks. "Yeah, I can get you private range time," he said. "Any other impossible requests I can grant?"

"Go home," Jack interrupted. "Get some rest. You did great today. This—" He waved his hand over the pictures on the counter. "This is psychological warfare. It's supposed to shake our confidence in each other. Let's not let it." He nodded to Scott and then to Ethan. "You'll find who did this. I know you will."

"Yes, Mr. President." Scott offered his hand to Ethan, who took it, pumping once. "We'll get started right away." Scott walked out, side by side with Daniels.

Ethan turned the moment they were gone, wrapping his arms around Jack and burying his face in Jack's neck. "I should have been there."

"Hey." Jack stroked his hands over Ethan's trembling shoulders. "Hey, you're shaking."

"I feel like I'm about to jump off a cliff."

Jack pulled Ethan's face up, holding his cheeks in his hands, and stared into his eyes. That haunted, dark look was back, as was the gut-punch from before: failure haunted Ethan's gaze.

It felt like a mirror of Jack's own failure, the wrenching, anguished failure that had yawned wide beneath him at Evgeni Konnikov's funeral. The failure of his duty as a president to keep people safe, and the failure of himself as a man to own up to his reality. To stop sitting on the sidelines.

"I need you right now," Jack whispered. "After today, I need you, Ethan. I need my rock."

Arms wrapped around him, holding tight, and Jack rested his head on Ethan's shoulder as Ethan's hands stroked up and down his back. "You always have me," Ethan breathed into the hair over his ear. "Always."

They slept in the next morning, Ethan holding on to Jack throughout the night and then into the morning, clinging to his waist and burying his face in Jack's back. When the sun rose, Jack rolled over and wedged into Ethan's arms, nuzzling his face against Ethan's neck.

When Ethan woke, he opened his eyes to Jack already awake, watching him sleep as he lay beside him on the bed. He smiled and reached for Jack's hip, pulling his warm body flush against him.

"Morning." He dropped a kiss to Jack's nose. "How long have you been awake?"

"About an hour."

"Could have woken me."

Jack shook his head. "I wanted to watch you sleep."

Ethan smiled but buried his face in his pillow as a crimson stain spread out along his cheekbones. He peeked one eye out of the pillow, the corners still crinkled.

"I love you," Jack breathed. "I love you, Ethan. I've only said that to two people in my life."

Shyness gone, Ethan rolled over, his eyes wider than they had been. He lay on his back, watching Jack.

"I love being in love with you. I love this. Waking up together. Seeing the sunlight on your face. Running my fingers through your hair." He did. "Touching your body." His leg slithered over Ethan's, sliding between them. "When you smile, my heart skips a beat."

Ethan smiled and took a shaky breath.

"I love what we have built. I only have to say I need you, and you have me. You have me, no questions asked. I trust you more than I trust myself, sometimes. I can look at you in the Situation Room and know what you're thinking, and take your hand when I need to." He took Ethan's hand and pressed a kiss to his palm. "Or when I want to." Another kiss. "Which I always do."

Ethan's lips parted, falling open in the face of Jack's declaration.

"I don't want to hide this anymore," Jack whispered. "I don't want to hide how much I love you."

"We're not hiding." Ethan frowned, but he kept his voice soft, keeping the dreamy, still mood that Jack had woven around them. "I'm living here with you. That's public."

"Not public enough. We still hide from the media. Refuse to talk about our lives and our love. We don't really seem proud about this, do we? About us together, or who we are?" The images from Evgeni Konnikov's funeral, the rainbow flags, and the marchers had stayed with him.

"I'm damn proud, Jack. Damn proud to be with you." He shifted, stroking one hand up Jack's leg. "And I'm proud of who I am. I've never hidden it. And I've done my share of marching in pride parades."

"I think I was hiding. Until yesterday. My first pride march was a funeral. I hate that." Jack closed his eyes and looked down.

Ethan slowly stroked Jack's thigh.

Eventually, the tightness in his chest loosened, his throat opened again, and Jack was able to speak. "I want," he began, clearing his throat when he croaked. "To show the world how much I love you. I don't want to hide. I don't want to let other people define this—define *us*—anymore. I want everyone to see that I am proud to be with you. Proud of who I am. That I'm not ashamed. Not hiding."

The hand stroking his thigh rose, sliding over his hip and up his ribs, until Ethan cupped his cheek and leaned in for a slow, tender kiss. Jack murmured into his lips, his eyes falling closed. Somewhere, deep in the center of his heart, a part of himself unfurled, and hanging within, Ethan's smile, the sound of his laugh, and the color of his eyes lingered. The feel of his soul when they kissed oh-so-slowly.

Ethan broke away first, peppering Jack's face with tiny kisses scattered over his cheeks, his nose, and one to the center of his forehead. "I'm with you all the way."

28

Paris

Adam moved slowly with Sergeants Coleman and Wright, creeping down the creaking, rat-infested hallway of Noah William's rundown flat in the 18th *arrondissement* of Paris. They had their handguns out, and so far they'd stayed out of sight of the others living in the squalid tenement building. Blaring French daytime television seeped into the hall alongside screams from children left alone and ignored.

Coleman froze outside one warped door, listening. He shook his head a moment later. Slowly, he moved into position and pushed it open, the barrel of his handgun going in first. The hinges squeaked, an earsplitting racket, and he froze.

Next to Adam, Wright froze as well, glancing up and down the tenement slum's hall.

Nothing. Coleman led Wright inside, out of the dingy, desperate hallway that stank of hot urine and day-old feces. Newspapers cluttered the ground, sticking to their boots.

After Moscow, Reichenbach had sent the bulk of Adam's men to Somalia to hunt Madigan down and Adam and a two-man insertion team to Europe, chasing the ghosts that had smuggled Madigan's bombers into Russia.

They had tracked Noah Williams across half of Europe, from closed-circuit TV cameras, border crossings, and satellite imagery until they spotted him entering and exiting the same run-down flat in Paris for three days in a row.

They'd moved in immediately.

Inside Noah's flat, a single bare bulb hung from the ceiling, droning, but barely lighting up the flat. A moldy mattress lay in the corner and a jacket bundled at the head doubled as a pillow. Next to the mattress, a rifle lay on the stained carpet, ready to be grabbed at a moment. One dingy window let in fractured light, and through the grime, the distant *Sacré Cœur* cathedral rose on its hill.

Wright and Coleman moved in silently, back to back, peering into the dark corners. "Clear," Coleman called.

"Clear," Wright answered, a moment after.

Adam followed, checking the hallway one last time before he slipped inside.

Lowering their weapons, they walked backward to the center of the tiny room, frowning. "What the fuck?" Coleman whispered.

Adam shook his head.

On the walls, maps of Russia had been tacked up haphazardly with colored pins pushed into cities and towns scattered across the country. Surveillance pictures of President Puchkov and of his cabinet covered the map's edges. There was a young Russian man, blond-haired and blue-eyed, at the president's side. These were pictures taken without their knowledge, and from too close a range.

Routes were highlighted over the map, lines of red and black crossing borders into Eastern Europe, and south through Georgia, Armenia, and Turkey.

A third map of the Arabian Gulf hung as well, with pictures of three speedboats. More pictures of a Russian destroyer, sitting dockside at an unknown port, and a tanker, listing slightly, with a beach in the background.

There were maps of the Arctic and pictures of oil derricks in the heavy ice.

Covering another wall, newspaper cutouts of President Spiers and Ethan Reichenbach. Photos of the two clipped from magazines and printed off the Internet.

The whole tableau seemed crazy, like a collection had turned into an obsession that didn't know when to quit.

"Get pictures of this shit." Adam jerked his chin to Coleman, and his sergeant pulled out his phone and snapped pictures of the walls and Noah's mad display. "What the hell are we looking at? Ratlines across Europe? Smuggling routes into Russia?"

A board creaked in a far corner, shrouded in darkness.

Wright whirled, his weapon raised.

A silver barrel rose in the darkness, a handgun rising. Fingers squeezed the trigger, the aim dead on Coleman's back.

"Guys!" Wright shouted. "Look out!"

Adam and Coleman ducked and whirled, but the shot slammed into Coleman's phone, shattering the device out of his hand. Wright opened fire, shots into the darkness.

A light flicked, and then a whoosh of flame rose, igniting on a soaked rag hanging from a glass bottle.

"Molotov!" Adam roared. He grabbed Coleman and ran for the hallway, Wright on their heels. They dove to the ground as the Molotov flew. Glass shattered and flames roared as the bottle crashed into the map and photo-strewn wall.

"We've got to get the intel!" Adam scrambled back toward the door, trying to crawl inside.

Gunshots chewed through the floorboards in front of his hands.

"Shit!"

Flames licked up the walls, spreading over the ceiling. Pictures curled and fell, and the map crashed to the ground, scattering to burning pieces. The mattress ignited, flames bursting to life. Heavy smoke clung to the air.

"L-T, we have to go!" Coleman coughed and kept low. Fire licked the ceiling above their heads and snaked out of the open apartment.

Wright had his eyes on the flames. His gaze darted to the end of the hallway and the stairs they'd climbed. "We've got to go, now!"

"We have to get him," Adam growled. He threw himself down, lying on his back in the open door, and fired toward the dark corner of the apartment. "We have to get something, damn it!"

A man cursed, and then Noah Williams rushed out of the darkness, heading for the grime-covered window. He covered his head with his arms and barreled through the glass, tumbling from three stories high. Adam hesitated when Noah ran. His shots missed. The bullets slammed into burning walls.

"L-T! We have to go!" Coleman shoved Adam toward Wright, already heading down the flame-engulfed hallway as he scrambled to his feet. Behind them, a section of the ceiling collapsed. Screams started, shouts in French above their heads.

Adam cursed and followed, thundering down the cramped stairs and exploding out onto the back alley behind the building. Above, black smoke billowed out of Noah's destroyed flat. Flames curled through the building, bursting out of open windows above and below Noah's flat.

Sirens sounded in the distance.

"Where the fuck is he?" Adam spun, searching the alley. There was no one down there. No body. No tracks. "Where did he go?"

"Dunno, but we have to move." Coleman shoved his pistol into his belt and pulled his jacket down, covering the grip. "The fire department will be here any minute. We have to go! Now!"

Wright was already at the corner of the building, keeping watch. He jerked his head back to them, signaling the way was clear. For now.

Adam glared at the smoking flat but followed Coleman as he sprinted to Wright. Together, they slipped out of the alley, just before the Parisian authorities screamed in.

29

White House

Pete was overjoyed when Jack came to his office, asking for a word in private and revealing that he and Ethan wanted to be more open about themselves and their lives. He clapped his hands together and shouted at the ceiling, calling, "hallelujah."

He also had someone, he said, that Jack needed to talk to. Someone who could help rehabilitate Jack's sagging approval numbers, revitalize his presidency in the eyes of the nation. Jack had been suspicious at first and dismissed the suggestion, but Pete pressed the issue, and Jack agreed to one meeting.

Later that week, Jack and Ethan headed to a private, off-the-record meeting in the Roosevelt Room with Pete's guy. Pete and Brandt joined in.

Gus Miramontes was late, but he came bursting into the room in a flurry of sound and movement, unwrapping his scarf and looping it around his arms, carrying his trench coat, and cursing up a storm. "It's the fucking weather, I swear. I can't stand this shit. I can't fucking stand spring. The Goddamn pollen—"

Pete gestured to the head of the table, and to Jack, trying to smother his smile.

"Fuck. Mr. President." Gus dropped his jacket, scarf, and briefcase on the chair closest to him and paraded to the end of the table, his hand outstretched. "Pleasure to meet you, Mr. President. Sorry. I hate the damn weather right now. Do you like spring?"

Jack stood and shook Gus's hand. When he stood, he saw how short Gus truly was; he only came to Jack's shoulder. "I'm not a fan of DC spring," Jack said, grinning.

"Good man." Gus winked and then pulled out a chair across from Ethan, next to Jack.

Brandt and Ethan shared wide-eyed looks.

"Shit, Pete, slide me my briefcase, will ya?"

From the end of the table, Pete shoved Gus's briefcase down the polished wood, the leather squeaking as it spun until Gus caught it two-handed and dragged it close.

Ethan's foot nudged Jack's beneath the table. Their eyes met.

"So, Mr. President," Gus began, pulling out a notepad and a stack of clipped newspapers all about Jack and his presidency. "Your poll numbers are rotting at thirty-six percent. Your party isn't taking your calls anymore. You're getting lambasted by that Senator for your business deal in Russia. You have a gigantic, sucking image problem."

"To put it simply."

"Which is fucking astounding, because over fifty percent of Americans support same-sex relationships. And, both of you are relatively young. In decent shape. Some would call you good-looking."

Jack pressed his lips together, desperately trying not to laugh. At his side, Ethan blinked, once, twice, three times.

"The media in this country is almost solidly liberal leaning and should automatically love everything you are. It's built-in support. So, how on God's green earth did you fuck this up?"

Silence.

"I'll tell you why." Gus slid the stack of newspapers across the table, patting them with his palm. "Because you haven't done jack shit for yourselves in the press."

"Thank you," Brandt singsonged beneath his breath.

Ethan shot him a mock glare. Pete tried to smother his own grin.

Gus gestured wildly, almost bouncing in his chair. "You've let jackasses like Senator Allen run the media for you. Putting out their own spin on your lives. Everyone *but* you has an opinion on you. It's time to join the game, ladies and gentleman. Well, gentleman and gentleman." He shrugged at his own slip.

"What do you suggest?"

"First, you gotta get in front of the media more. You gotta be more personable. The White House looks like a secret society right now, and everyone wonders what kind of crazy sex games are going on in there. I mean, your staff is crazy loyal. Freakin' insanely loyal. But that's also a mystery because you're not human to anyone in the public. You're this mysterious other thing, weird Ken dolls, and no one likes weird." Gus didn't hold his punches.

Brandt cleared his throat. "People should see you for how dedicated you are."

"You just have to be you. Both of you. Anyone who really knows you both loves you guys." Pete shrugged, pursed his lips, and played with his pen.

For a moment, there was silence as Jack squeezed Ethan's hand.

Gus rolled his eyes. "Look, has Pete told you what I do?" Gus pointed at himself as he leaned over the table, and his thick reading glasses slid down his nose. His hair, more gone on top than actually present, was combed over, the strands left trying valiantly to cover his shiny scalp.

"Not in a great deal of specificity," Jack demurred.

"I'm a fixer. I fix things. Mostly campaigns. I can turn a struggling campaign around and win an election, for anybody. I'm gold." His fingers tapped the table, punctuating his words. "And I am what you need to win."

"We're not in an election."

"No, but you do need to win back the American people in order to govern. To get anything done. You've lost them, somehow." Gus leaned back, his hands in the air as he boggled the ceiling. "And I can help you do that."

Jack looked to Ethan, his eyebrows raised. Ethan gave him a tiny smile and rubbed his ankle with his foot.

"How? What do you propose?"

"God, everything. A complete overhaul, from top to bottom. Rework your press, your media approach. Do interviews, get people to actually like you for a change. Woo the media, which should be eating out of your hands anyway. Pete told me you want to show your stripes a bit more. Be who you are with the first gentleman."

Jack was nodding along, agreeing in principle to Gus's points. "And yes, definitely that."

"Good, good. No more of this hiding crap. And," Gus added, "you've got to ditch the Republican Party."

Jack's jaw dropped. "What?" Beside him, Ethan stiffened, the lightness of the room suddenly vanished.

"What are you sticking around for?" Gus frowned at Jack. "Your party is in open revolt, they don't take your calls on the Hill, and they're actively duking it out to see who your successor is. Never in American politics have people so actively worked against the leader of their own party, the sitting president. Why the fuck do you stay?"

He fumbled for something to say. "I've been a conservative my whole life. There are parts of the platform I don't agree with, yes. But—"

Gus grinned. It wasn't pretty. "Those parts you don't agree with on that Republican platform? Those are the parts that *hate* your *guts*. Because of who you *are*, and because of who you *love*." He punctuated his words by pointing at Jack and then at Ethan.

Jack shifted in his chair. It was one thing to know it, in an abstract, polling numbers kind of way. He saw it in the headlines, of course, and heard the sound bites, but it was easier to push those seconds of hate aside.

It was a whole other kind of gut-clench to hear it said to his face.

"And no one likes the entirety of their party anyway." Gus went back to his notepad, oblivious to Jack's unease. Beneath the table, Ethan rested his hand on Jack's thigh, a warm, grounding presence.

Jack shook his head. "I have not been the staunchest conservative by any stretch. I've made a name for myself as a moderate. And yes, I don't have much loyalty to my party after everything that's happened. But I can't just switch parties overnight." He sighed and leaned back in his chair. "To be honest, there is no party that matches who I am and what I believe."

"Join the club. More Americans identify as Independent than either Republican or Democrat. And, over sixty-five percent of the nation hates the way the current political system looks," Gus snapped, still buried in his notes.

A moment later, he paused. He looked back at Jack, a curious sort of wonder in his gaze. "If ever there was a person," he said slowly, "it would be you."

"It would be me what?"

"To start your own political party. Branch off. Make the mythical third, inclusive party in American politics. Capture all those other disgruntled, unrepresented people in the world." Gus's hands rolled in the air, trying to capture the people he spoke of like capturing fireflies in a backyard. His eyes narrowed as he assessed Jack, his beady eyes seeming to lance right through him. "The only time in American history a new political party has succeeded was when it began from the top. The Federalists splitting and reforming under John Adams. Democrats under Andrew Jackson."

Sputtering, Jack laughed, a helpless sort of snort. "You've got to be joking. There's no way anyone would go for that! Not with me."

"Just you watch." Gus winked.

"What's up?"

Scott and Daniels waited a few steps down on the Residence stairs, hands in their suit pockets as they frowned at Ethan.

Ethan closed his eyes. He was crouched on the stairs, dressed down in jeans and a canvas jacket with a ball cap pulled low over his head. His hands were fisted in front of his mouth. One foot bounced up and down. "Jack in his meetings?"

Scott nodded. "Cabinet meeting for the next two hours. Then he's in with the national security team." He frowned. "What's going on?"

"I'd like your help." Ethan coughed, clearing his throat. "I'd like you to take me somewhere."

"Dude. What's up? Where do you want to go?" Daniels crossed his arms.

Ethan pulled out his cell phone and passed it over.

Scott took one look at the website he'd opened and whipped his head up so fast his neck cracked. His jaw dropped, and he stared at Ethan until Daniels grabbed the phone out of his hand with a soft curse.

"Ho-ly shit," Daniels said slowly. "Hey. Hey." He smacked Scott on the arm. "You need to answer your phone, man."

"The hell, Levi?" Scott glared, shaking him off. "What are you talking about? Why?"

Daniels punched the air, his shoulders rocking back and forth as he beamed. "Because I fucking called it!"

An hour later, they were parked outside one of DC's older jewelry shops, a family-owned store that had been in business for generations.

The idea had been bouncing around in Ethan's head, a desire that had grown from his soul and wouldn't quit. When he woke in the morning and held Jack close, he dreamed of it. When they drank coffee together and walked down from the Residence. When Jack glanced his way during meetings, a smile in his eyes. When he sent silly text messages and took crazy selfies with Ethan. When he laughed. When he brushed his teeth and stared at Ethan in the mirror, still with those smiling eyes, or wiped sweat from his face after a workout, or just did any of the thousand things that were all Jack.

He *wanted*, desperately. He wanted with an intensity that scared him, a thrumming, living desire that burned in his chest.

He wanted *forever* with Jack.

Sitting outside the jewelry store, he felt like he was going to fly right out of his skin. He wanted forever, but actually taking that step was almost too terrifying to imagine.

"Well?" Scott and Daniels turned together, staring at him with boisterous grins from the front seat. "We going in?"

"I think I'm going to be sick."

Daniels waved away Ethan's rising panic and hopped out of the car. "Get your butt out here."

They bracketed him with maniacal grins from the SUV to the store. Daniels went in first, scoping the place out as nonchalantly as he could, and Scott waited outside.

Scott couldn't stop smiling at him. "Really? You're really going to do this?"

"Not if you keep it up." Ethan glowered beneath his ball cap, arms crossed tight over his chest.

Daniels motioned them both in, and they wandered around the store like a pack of wide-eyed children. Scott pointed out the basics, stumbling as he tried to remember what he'd learned when he bought his engagement ring for his wife, all those years ago. Daniels told him to shut up and quit being wrong every other sentence.

When the only other shopper left, the owner, a short, older man, locked the front door and closed the blinds. Scott and Daniels moved in front of Ethan and reached for their weapons.

"I can recognize someone wishing for privacy." The old man's smile was soft. "How can I help you today?"

They looked at every ring, going over different metals and designs. Nothing felt right, felt perfect, until the old man brought out the custom designs and the options Ethan could put together.

Everything clicked into place when he picked out the right mix of metal and diamonds. His design spun on screen, winking at him, and even Scott and Daniels kept their smart comments quiet as he smiled, breathless. "That's it."

"And what is the president's ring size?"

Scott and Daniels turned sharp glares to the old man, who kept smiling serenely at Ethan.

Jesus. He swallowed hard. The reminder of what he was doing, of *who* he was thinking of asking, hit him like a bucket of ice. What the hell was he thinking? A year ago, he'd been a committed bachelor. And now he was thinking about asking the *president of the United States* to—

No. He was asking *Jack*.

The old man's patient smile helped him through the moment, and he grunted that Jack's old wedding band, which he kept in an envelope in the bottom of his valet, fit on Ethan's pinky. A few quick measurements and the jeweler said the rings would be ready in two weeks.

Ethan left the shop with a terrified smile, Scott's arm around his shoulders, and Daniels whistling away.

30

Taif, Saudi Arabia

Adam met the rest of his team at what had become their home away from home, Faisal's palace. They could have set up desert tents and kept a low profile, operating under the radar without anyone's knowledge. Eating MREs and shitting in a hole, brushing their teeth with bottled water, and not showering for two weeks at a time.

Faisal offered his palace, and Adam's hollow, aching heart was a poor reason to subject his men to shitty field conditions. Plus, Faisal and he shared intelligence again, and even Reichenbach agreed it was easier for them to just remain on location with Faisal while they figured out their next move against Madigan.

His men hadn't found much in Somalia. They'd waited too long. Had been too careful. By the time the bombs went off in Moscow, Madigan must have already been miles ahead of them.

When Adam's team scoured the Somalian wilderness, all they found were dead rebels, destroyed villages, and the smoking remains of Madigan's camped army. Scavengers had been picking through the burned earth, searching the rubble.

One starving Somali man caught scavenging had tried to run, but Adam's team had caught him. He'd pissed himself when they tried to interrogate him, working through the digital translator Doc had on his tablet.

All they had managed to get was that Madigan had vanished. The old man, skeletally frail, had pointed to the sea.

Doc gave him his canteen and all of his rations and sent him on his way.

Adam sent Coleman and Wright to shower, shit, and relax when they got back, and he spent too many hours trying to recite for Faisal the crazed menagerie of pictures and maps and landmarks and people that had been tacked up on Noah's walls. His palms itched as Faisal asked question after question, trying to put the puzzle together.

Faisal had always been the smarter one, had always been able to put things together better than Adam. He was white-knuckling it more often than not. Then, and especially now.

He escaped as soon as he could.

Beating Doc at basketball always took his mind off Faisal, at least for the game. He kicked Doc as he passed through Faisal's sunroom, knocking his feet off the ottoman and waking him from a nap. Doc cursed and chased him to the courtyard, where Adam stripped off his T-shirt and dribbled the ball between his legs. Doc charged as Adam made a layup, twisting out of Doc's reach.

"All right," Doc said, cracking his knuckles. "All right. If you want an ass-kicking, I'll be more than happy to give you one."

The Arabian sun slowly sank, dusk turning to night, and the courtyard's lights winked on. More of the team joined in until it was an all-out war, every man playing all-out.

Adam's gaze caught on Faisal, standing on the edge of the court and watching with hooded eyes. He froze, and the ball slammed into his chest. He fell to his ass with a grunt, rolling to his back as his team laughed.

Faisal appeared over him. "You all right?"

"Only hurt my pride." He scrunched up his nose and threw his arm over his eyes.

Faisal said nothing for a moment. "I have something I'd like you to look at." He held out his hand.

Adam let Faisal pull him to his feet with a groan. "Yes, Your Highness."

Snickers behind his back made him turn. Some of his men were looking away or staring up at the sky as they whistled. Others, like Doc, grinned and stared at him.

Adam scowled back at his men as a flood of terror circled down his spine. God, no. No one could know. Not ever.

He jogged after Faisal, already back inside the palace. One of the guys started to holler after him, but Coleman's deep timbre shouting at the Marine to *shut the fuck up* washed out whatever was about to be said.

Like a coward, Adam was grateful.

He followed Faisal up to his office. Well, now their office again. Faisal had rearranged everything and added in a desk and a dedicated computer just for Adam... just like old times.

It was those kinds of moments that made his deadened heart clench all that much more until it hurt to breathe every moment he was around Faisal.

"You did a great job remembering the intel." Faisal gestured to the monitors and the images he, Coleman, and Wright had tried to resurrect. Maps, ships, and pictures of President Spiers, Reichenbach, and the Russian government. "Is this a fair approximation?"

Adam pointed to one of the pictures, an oil tanker. "Yeah. That looks like the ship we saw."

"I wondered if you would recognize it. It's a coastal tanker. Two years ago, a Yemeni-flagged tanker was hijacked by Somalian pirates in the Gulf of Aden. The Yemenis refused to pay the ransom. The tanker was old and due to be scuttled. Everyone assumed the pirates torched the vessel like they always do when ransoms aren't paid. It has never been seen again."

"You think Noah had a picture of the Yemenis' missing tanker?"

"Madigan disappeared from Somalia into the sea, yes? He's not floating on the ocean on dinghies and dhows."

"And a ghost ship would be perfect for him." Adam groaned. "A mobile base of operations he can take anywhere." He headed for his computer, calling up a dump file of satellite images Reichenbach had sent their way to the large flat-screen on the wall. The images were everything taken over Somalia and her waters, and the greater Arabian Peninsula and Gulf.

Standing side by side, they watched the satellite images scroll by.

Adam's gaze kept drifting, though, sliding sideways to Faisal.

Faisal had ditched the long, loose robes and the keffiyeh, and he was back to his designer jeans and slim long-sleeve shirts, the ones that framed his shoulders perfectly and had first made Adam reach for him, years ago. His fingernails dug into his palms, the sting of half-moon bruises stilling him. He forced his eyes back to the satellite images.

Empty patches in the feed, grayed-out zones, filled more than half the screen.

Adam groaned. "How are we supposed to track a ship if we can't see the entire ocean?"

"It is a large planet, and even your United States doesn't scan every corner. Your general knows all of the holes inside your country's intelligence. He's planned around your weaknesses, every time."

"He can scoot right off the edges of the map," Adam grumbled. He made a loose fist and knocked on the flat-screen, over a gray patch of empty imagery. He leaned forward, resting his forehead on his fist. "He's vanished again."

Faisal reached for Adam, but lowered his hand, aborting the movement. He stepped closer instead, crossing his arms over his chest. "You're fighting against a man who knows all of the moves you will make. Who knows weaknesses you don't even know you have. It's like fighting your shadow."

"Like losing to your shadow. I hate this. Always being ten steps behind. All the unknowns. We need a win."

"You will prevail."

Faisal's soft voice tickled down Adam's neck, and all the hairs on his neck quivered.

"Don't you mean 'we'? 'We' will prevail? We are working together, right?" He eyeballed Faisal as he chewed on his inner lip.

Faisal's smile burned brighter than the Arabian sun and scorched his parched, aching soul. "We are, as long as you let us." Faisal shifted, peering at Adam, and reached out, one hand tucking a stray hair behind Adam's ear. He and his men had grown out their hair for their operations, some even growing beards, trying to look rugged and blend in.

Adam turned into Faisal's touch for just a moment. He pressed his cheek to Faisal's fingers, breathing over his wrist. Cardamom and peach filled his nose, and honey and orange dizzied his brain.

"Did you get my text while you were in Paris?"

Adam nodded. He'd saved it on their sat phone, even though that was so many different kinds of dangerous. Too many to count, in fact. But, he reread it six times a day, until his heart bled. *'As always, I will endlessly pray until I hear your voice again and I know you are safe. May Allah watch over you,* azizy.*'*

Azizy. My darling. He'd rubbed his thumb over the sat phone screen, as if the word weren't really there, as if he was just making it up in his desperate mind.

Faisal's gaze seared his soul. "*Samaya...*" Naked yearning poured from him. His lips trembled, seeming to beg for a kiss.

Adam shuddered. He couldn't take this, couldn't take Faisal's endearments. Couldn't take being called Faisal's bright sky, or his darling. He closed his eyes. He was fighting against himself, wanting to reach out, wanting to pull Faisal close, and struggling not to.

"We're going back to DC tomorrow," he blurted. "We leave at dawn."

Slowly, Faisal breathed out, somehow managing to capture the sound of a heart breaking in his soft sigh. He took a step back, moving away from Adam. "Travel well," he finally said. "As always, my home is open to you and your men when you return for your next mission." His eyes pinched. "*In shaa Allah*, you will catch your shadow, Lieutenant. You will prevail."

Faisal strode out of the office, walking away, and it was all Adam could do to choke down his own voice, his heart's desperate pleading. Instead of chasing Faisal, running to him and throwing himself to the ground at Faisal's feet, he turned back to the slowly cycling satellite feed. Empty holes stared back at him, mocking, like the empty spaces of his own heart.

Adam leaned forward, resting his forehead on the screen.

President Spiers Sits Down for First One-on-One Interview, Discusses Sexuality and Announces New Political Party

President Spiers sat down for a one-on-one interview with TNN's own Nancy Conners, during which he spoke candidly about his sexuality for the first time, stating unequivocally that he is bisexual, and proudly so. "I've been lucky enough to find love twice in my life," he said. "First with a woman, my wife, Captain Leslie Spiers, and then I discovered love again with a man, my best friend, Ethan Reichenbach. Finding love with Ethan was a process. A discovery of who I was, and who I was capable of loving. I couldn't be prouder, or happier, to be who I am and to be with the man I love."

The president also announced he was leaving the GOP and forming his own political party, the American Unity Party. A website describing their independent and inclusive platform with a video message from the president went live just before the interview aired. Over thirty million hits to the new party's website in the first twelve hours caused it to crash, and just under three million Americans have already opted into the party's platform online, asking to be counted as "Uniters." State voter registration offices have been flooded with calls since the announcement.

The president's actions come after his new engagement strategy with the press unfolded, a change in tone and tenor welcomed by many. President Spiers has taken over the Friday briefings at the White House, turning the afternoon brief into a lighthearted conversation. Nothing seems to be off the table, the president answering questions ranging from his controversial support of a Democratic piece of legislation to his weekend date plans with his partner.

Senator Stephen Allen, leading Republican challenger to the president, continues to hound Spiers, and recently called him a "traitor to his own party and toxic to the American people."

President Spiers's poll numbers have jumped ten points since the announcement.

31

Washington DC

Jack and Ethan met with Cooper and his men out of sight from the press at Andrews Air Force base after they landed. Cooper filled them both in on the Paris mission and their suspicions that Madigan was now in possession of the Yemeni freighter lost two years before, and had gone off the edges of the map.

"And two years ago he was still in the White House, even before I was. He would have been privy to the intelligence about that freighter. Would have known about it all along." Jack shook his head.

"You think he planned this, Mr. President? All of it? Everything?"

"I think," Jack said slowly, "that Madigan has about a dozen plans. And we need to stop all of them. He only needs one to succeed. And a few already have."

Cooper nodded, a scowl stretched across his face. "I've asked Prince Faisal to search for any sign of the missing tanker. Madigan would have repainted and reflagged it by now, I'm sure, but someone has to have seen something. Sailors everywhere have one thing in common—they all talk and they love to share stories. We'll find it."

"This man worked in the shadows for decades. He created modern black ops for this nation. No one, save for your friend, Prince Faisal, and his associate, has figured out Madigan's plans. He's a snake, and we have to be careful. Madigan is dedicated to his mission. And he's shockingly psychotic."

Cooper stared out over the runway.

"We have to acknowledge that we're fighting a man who has bested us for years. We've got his trail, and we just have to keep going." Smiling, Jack held out his hand for Cooper. "Well done, Lieutenant."

Cooper shook his hand, and then Jack shook the hands of the rest of his team, thanking them for their hard work. A C-38 readied for takeoff on the runway, and Ethan told the team he'd arranged for a night flight back to Tampa so they could sleep at home. Smiles and muted cheers rose, as the guys jogged to the plane. Jack and Ethan watched it take off, disappearing into the night sky.

They headed back to the White House, silent in the SUV, watching the city lights play over the blacktop. Daniels kept peeking at them in the rearview mirror, a soft frown on his face.

Jack took Ethan's hand as they climbed up to the Residence. He kissed Ethan in their bedroom, slowly.

"You all right?" Ethan's hands stroked up Jack's sides and down his back.

"A lot on my mind." Jack smiled. "I'm good now."

Ethan's hands slid up Jack's sides again, this time burying in his hair before he tugged Jack down for a long kiss.

"Mm." Jack hummed as he pulled back, smiling before he opened his eyes. "I'm going to hop in the shower. Wash the day off me."

"I'll be here." Ethan smiled and watched Jack go, holding his hand until their fingers slipped apart. He turned on his laptop and sat at their desk, frowning as he clicked through analyses and raw intelligence briefs. The shower started in the background, humming away. He lost track of time, buried in the reports, and didn't hear the shower turn off or Jack pad back into the bedroom.

"Ethan?"

Starting, he turned in his chair.

Jack kneeled on the bed, slowly stroking himself. His burning eyes locked on to Ethan's. "I want you to make love to me, Ethan."

Time stopped.

He couldn't breathe. All the air had vanished, sucked out of the world with Jack's words. His skin burst into flames, lines of fire tracing over his body and curling in his belly. He tried to swallow and couldn't. His heart was suddenly too big, taking up too much of his chest, ready to explode out of him with the slightest touch or movement.

"Jack," he breathed. "Are you sure?"

Jack smiled. "I'm sure," he whispered. "I want you to make love to me. I'm ready."

Everything else was forgotten: the intelligence, the reports, the briefs. He rose, walking toward Jack like a man swept up in a current, racing toward the inevitable plunge into the unknown. At his sides, his hands trembled, a lifetime's worth of practice suddenly vanishing as he forgot how to caress a lover. No, not just a lover. The love of his life, the man who meant everything to him.

He hesitated at the edge of the bed. How would they even begin? He'd imagined the moment too many times, dreamed of this day, but now, his plans, his seduction, fled. Jack was on his knees, watching him with hooded eyes, his body bathed in soft light and carved from the deepest of Ethan's temptations.

Jack reached out first, tugging on Ethan's pants. A flick of Jack's wrist, and he had Ethan's suit pants undone and falling to the floor. Ethan's cock rose, already achingly hard just from the moment, the anticipation of being with Jack. He shivered as Jack leaned in, his fingertips tickling over his thighs. Jack's hand closed around his shaft. He leaned close. "Ethan," he breathed, before sucking Ethan down, his lips flush against his skin, nose buried in his short fur. He sucked slowly, his tongue laving at the base of Ethan's cock before he pulled off and pressed his lips to Ethan's heavy balls.

Ethan pulled back, shivering. "Too much. If you want me inside you, that's too much right now."

Jack scooted back, a coy gleam to his eyes. Ethan pounced, tumbling Jack back to the bed, and stretched out over his body. Jack hummed, his arms and legs folding around Ethan, enveloping him in a perfect embrace. Ethan caressed Jack's face as they kissed, lips merging, tongues sliding against one another.

Ethan breathed in Jack's skin at his shoulder, at the curve of his neck, behind his ear. Tasted his lips again and again. His hands traced patterns over Jack's ribs, following tracks he knew by heart. He painted passion with his touch, breathed love with his lingering kisses, leaving Jack breathless and moaning.

Slowly, Ethan started down his body, trailing kisses over his collarbone. Down his chest. He followed Jack's light trail down past his quivering stomach, over his hipbones. Down, all the way to his legs, where he sucked a kiss bruise at the fold of Jack's thigh until Jack squirmed and sighed and ran his fingers through Ethan's hair.

Jack's cock quivered, rock-hard and swollen, but he only pressed a faint kiss to the tip and moved on, dropping down, past Jack's balls, until he had Jack's thighs spread wide and his puckered asshole tilted up.

Jack moaned, and his hands slid through Ethan's hair again, fingers scraping up the back of his neck.

He stayed down, opening Jack with his tongue, diving as deep as he could go as Jack moaned and arched his back. He nibbled and sucked on Jack's edges, hummed as he dove deep, and laved against him until Jack was wet with his spit. Jack trembled beneath him, his legs shaking, loosening as Ethan kept on.

He tried to hold back from humping the mattress, but he was already imagining being inside Jack.

"Ethan," Jack breathed, his fingers tangling in Ethan's short hair. "Ethan, please. Make love to me."

Fire and ice raced through him, disparate rushes consuming his soul at Jack's words. He lowered Jack's legs and crawled up his body, dropping kisses to his heaving belly, his ribs, and his flushed neck. Jack groaned into an open-mouthed kiss, and his eyes flew open as Ethan sucked his tongue into his own mouth.

Wrapping his arms around Jack's shoulders, Ethan rolled them over, until Jack was sprawled on top of Ethan's chest, his legs splayed on either side of Ethan's hips. Something cold touched his thigh, and he reached down. Their bottle of lube. Jack must have brought it to their bed before Ethan got there.

Jack pushed up, straddling Ethan's hips and bracing his palms against Ethan's chest. His fingers played in Ethan's chest hair, gently scratching down his skin.

Ethan poured too much lube onto his fingers, dribbling it onto the mattress. He held the bottle behind Jack's back, over Jack's round ass, and squeezed again, trailing a glistening river in between Jack's cheeks and down to his opening. Jack's head tilted back, a loud gasp falling from his lips.

Slowly, Ethan's fingers stroked up and down Jack's hole. He rubbed on the edges, pushing lube inside him, and then slipped a finger into his lover. They'd done this before, and Jack responded like he always did, pushing back on Ethan's finger, rocking his hips in time with Ethan's slow thrusts. He rested his forehead against Ethan's, his eyes closed, breathing soft pants over Ethan's cheeks.

One finger became more, and then more than Jack had ever taken. Lube was everywhere. On the sheets, on their skin. They were slick with it, slippery in it.

"I'm ready." Wide-eyed, Jack hovered over Ethan, breathing hard, his hands gripping Ethan's shoulders. His chest was flushed. Sweat glistened on his skin. His cock was hard, jutting out. "Ethan, I'm ready. I want you. Want this."

Ethan lined himself up, slotting his cockhead at Jack's virgin entrance. "Lower yourself down," he breathed. "Push against me. Go at your own pace."

At the first press, the first stretch, Jack hesitated, his ass cheeks clenching and pushing Ethan out. "Sorry," he breathed, eyes wide. "I'm—"

"'S'okay." Ethan stroked his lube-slick hands down Jack's lower back, over his ass, and between his cheeks. His fingers played at Jack's entrance, massaging his rim, dipping within him again. He stared into Jack's eyes the whole time, pressing long, open-mouthed kisses to his chest. Soft licks to his nipples. Gentle, slow bites around the curve of one pec.

Jack's hips rocked against Ethan's drenched fingers. He nodded down to Ethan. Another alignment, as Ethan slid himself between Jack's ass cheeks again and rubbed the head of his cock over Jack's hole. This time, his head slid in, stretching through Jack, and then kept going.

As Jack moved, his eyes rolled back, his jaw dropped, mouth frozen in a silent moan. Fractionally, incrementally, he sank down on Ethan, pausing to adjust, and his asshole clenched and squeezed over Ethan's cock. Ethan gripped Jack's hips, his fingers leaving bruises where he desperately held himself back.

Jack's body swallowed his cock, inch by inch.

And then, Jack was all the way down.

"Oh my God," Ethan breathed. "Oh my God, Jack..." There was nothing, nothing at all in the world that could compare to Jack and him in that moment, breathing each other's breath, gazing into each other's eyes. They were so close. Inseparable.

Jack lunged, cupping Ethan's face in both hands and kissing him deep, deep enough to chase away all the empty places in Ethan's soul, all the corners where his fears hid. Jack writhed and rocked forward, and then Ethan shuddered, the feel of Jack's body sliding around him too much. Too intense; he was going to burst apart. His hands slid around Jack's waist, wrapping around his back and pulling him close.

As they kissed, Ethan's hands stroked over Jack's back, fingers caressing the knobs of his spine, all the way down. Ethan thrust—long, unending strokes deep into Jack's body. Jack's breath came fast, and his hands flew to the mattress beside Ethan's head, fingers curling until he had the fabric bunched in his grip. One of Ethan's hands threaded through Jack's hair and held him close for a kiss as the other kneaded his ass.

Jack's body was burning Ethan, searing his soul.

"Ethan, I love you," Jack breathed, breaking their kiss to press their foreheads together. Little by little, Jack's hips rocked forward with each of Ethan's strokes, and he began to slide up and down Ethan's cock. Ethan kissed his collarbone, grunting, and Jack ground down on him again. And again, slowly building up a rhythm until he was riding Ethan.

Ethan laced their hands together and stared into Jack's eyes. Jack was riding him. Good God, Jack was riding his cock.

He met Jack's rolling hips, driving into Jack. Jack's mouth dropped open. His hands squeezed Ethan's. He moved faster, his hips grinding down until the wet sound of skin slapping against skin filled the room.

God, Ethan was going to come, but he didn't want to. Not yet. Gently, Ethan maneuvered Jack, guiding him until Jack was on his back. Eyes wide, Jack stared up at Ethan, panting.

Ethan waited, watching Jack.

Jack surged up, trying to chase Ethan's lips, his enormous eyes pleading with Ethan for more. He spread his legs wide, holding his thighs open as one hand cupped Ethan's cheek, dragging him back for another soul-searing kiss. "Ethan," Jack pleaded.

"I know; fuck, I know." Ethan's hand shook as he lined his cock up at Jack's ass. His eyes locked with Jack's as he slid within Jack's body again. Jack arched his back, a silent scream breathed in a faint whimper, but he didn't look away. Jack's heat fluttered around him, his body shuddering, and he clung to Ethan, his hands gripping his neck, the back of his head.

He was going to die, right here, right now, and it would be perfect. This was perfect, beyond everything he'd dreamed of, everything he'd imagined. Jack was supple and searing beneath his hands, his body sculpted from Ethan's dreams. And yet, this body he saw every day suddenly became new beneath him. Had Jack's eyes always been that blue, gazing up at Ethan with so much love? His mouth, so perfect and alluring, whispering Ethan's name endlessly, a babble of pleasure. Sweat clung to Jack's heaving chest, flushed crimson.

One of Jack's legs rose, desperately trying to rise to Ethan's shoulder. He grasped it, pressed kisses against Jack's shin, breathed in his scent. Watched Jack's toes curl as he made slow love to him, sliding in and out of his body.

Jack let out a breathy moan and tugged at Ethan, pulling him even closer. He went down, curling over Jack, his shoulder underneath Jack's knee. He drove deeper, long thrusts where he pulled almost all the way out before driving back in. Jack panted by his ear, a ceaseless whimpering groan mixed with his name as his fingers scraped up Ethan's back.

"Ethan. Ethan, Ethan—" His face scrunched up, his head tipped back, and his eyes opened, brilliant and blue, blazing as they stared up at Ethan, shock streaking from his gaze. His mouth formed a perfect O as all his muscles clenched. He jerked, shuddered, and then come exploded out of his cock, pooling on his belly. Jack's toes curled, his leg pressing against Ethan's hold, and he let out a wail, long and low, his body arching as he gripped Ethan with everything he had.

That was it for Ethan, seeing Jack come undone beneath him, because of him. All the air left him in a rush, torn from him in a ragged scream, ripped straight from his pounding heart. The world spun, and all he could hear was the roar of blood in his ears and Jack's shuddering whimpers, pleas, and his name, falling from Jack's hoarse throat. Jack rippled around Ethan, and Ethan's world whited out as he pressed into Jack's body and emptied what felt like his soul. He buried his face in Jack's hair and whispered into his ear, an endless litany of "I love you" and "Jack."

He collapsed around Jack, their bodies intertwined, clasped together, arms around each other, Jack's leg still held in Ethan's grasp by his shoulder. Sweat dripped from their hair and soaked the sheets, already sticky with lube. The bed was ruined, drenched through with their lovemaking, sheets pulled free from the corners. Lube was everywhere: the sheets, their skin, even their hair.

Jack nuzzled Ethan's face, his breath still too fast. He didn't say anything, just stared into Ethan's eyes.

Ethan tangled their lips together, murmuring, "I love you."

Hours later, the bed was still a sticky, wet mess, but they had curled on the edge in the only dry patch of sheets. They lay together, foreheads touching and arms wrapped around each other, legs twined, lazy kisses pressed against lips and warm skin until they finally drifted off.

Jack woke before Ethan.

Darkness hovered outside the windows. The sun hadn't risen yet.

They could push the day off some more, push back the world and stay wrapped up together. It was a not-so-secret dream of his; some days, he wanted to run from the White House, take Ethan by the hand and just run for the hills.

Shifting, his breath caught as he rolled his hips. They'd *done* it. *He'd* done it. He'd made love to Ethan, taken his lover inside his body. Crossed the final border, an invisible line he'd been chipping away at since he first kissed Ethan on Air Force One. He rolled his hips again. There was an emptiness deep inside, a place within him where Ethan now lived.

In the grand scheme of things, it shouldn't mean much. The night before was just another moment in their love life, another expression of their love. The whole world thought Jack had been taking it from Ethan since the beginning, and he'd never corrected anyone's assumptions. Now that he had taken Ethan inside of him, Jack had a new realization about just what that really meant. What it was to have the man you loved so deep within you that a part of him touched your soul.

He wanted more.

Carefully, Jack reached for their bottle of lube discarded in the loose sheets on the destroyed half of the bed. They were almost out. God, Ethan had used so much. His ass still felt wet, something slipping from within him. It was strange, and he clenched against the new feeling, reaching back. His cheeks burned a moment later. It was Ethan's come. Lube, yes, but also Ethan's come.

He poured fresh lube on his fingers and reached back again, circling his rim. He was still wet and sticky, but he pushed two fingers inside, biting back a groan. It was like nothing he'd ever felt before, fingering himself after making love to Ethan. His body seemed both foreign to him, remade in some fundamental way, and yet absolutely perfect at the same time. As though it was always meant to be like this. He was always meant to love Ethan, in this and every way.

He crawled over Ethan.

The rest of the lube went into his palm. He slicked up Ethan's rising cock, stiffening in his sleep.

Ethan's eyes fluttered, his head thrown back as he gripped the sheets. "Jack," he breathed, even before his eyes opened. Jack's heart skipped a beat.

"Hey, love," Jack whispered. His gaze wandered over Ethan's naked body, one hand rubbing up and down Ethan's thigh.

"You okay?" Valiantly, Ethan tried to focus through Jack's handjob. "How are you? After...?"

"Perfect." He straddled Ethan's hips in one move, rubbing Ethan's cock over his slick, loose entrance. "I actually want to do it again."

Ethan's hands flew to his thighs, short fingernails biting into his skin as he hissed. "Jack. Maybe you should wait—" His words died as Jack sank down on him, faster than the night before. There was burning, and stretching, but that need within him was instantly filled, warm and wonderful. He began to move, rising and falling as Ethan breathed fast and stared at Jack with wide eyes.

"You feel so good inside me," Jack whispered, smiling. "I should have known. Everything about you— *Oh.*" His head tipped back as he rocked, and he scraped his fingers down Ethan's chest, through his dark fur. "Everything about you, about us, has been so perfect. Why would this be any different?"

"Jack..." Ethan's jaw clenched, and his hands rose to Jack's hips, fingertips pressing into his skin hard enough to leave bruises.

The thought sent a hot spike down Jack's spine. He'd wear Ethan's handprints on his hips. He'd wear them with pride.

He sped up as Ethan grunted, his eyes squeezing closed until his legs trembled and sweat dripped down his chest. Faltering, he fell forward, collapsing on Ethan and pressing a sloppy kiss to his lips.

Ethan took over, planting his feet flat on the bed as he bent his knees and caressed Jack's face. He moved in Jack slowly, deep strokes almost all the way in and out. Jack felt every inch of him, a rake of searing pleasure that had him howling. His fingers dug into Ethan's shoulders, his teeth bit down on the sweaty skin at his collarbone. He reached for his almost-too-sensitive cock, leaking all over Ethan's stomach, and jerked it as he trembled.

In moments, he was convulsing and squeezing all over Ethan as he came again. Cursing, Ethan thrust deep, gasped, and then kept rocking, driving into Jack through his orgasm, his arms flying around Jack's back and holding him close, holding him tight.

Ethan kissed him breathless, cradling his face in both hands until the sun rose, scattering golden rays across their drenched and sticky bodies.

32

Tampa, FL
Outside MacDill Air Force Base

"Hey, asshole, come on. Wake up!" Doc banged on Fitz's door, rattling the cheap wood on its hinges. He and Fitz were both on Cooper's team, and they'd become friends through bullshit and bonding and shared cigarettes smoked on Prince Faisal's sun-drenched pool deck.

"Come on! You said we were going to go the bars. Pick up some chicks." Doc banged on the door again. They'd gotten back to Tampa late the night before and crashed, but now they were free, at least for the night. "Asshole!" He rattled the doorknob.

It turned beneath his hand.

"I'm coming in! Put your dick away!" Doc pushed open the unlocked door and headed in.

The doorknob crashed to the tile floor of Fitz's cheap apartment with a loud bang. It rolled away.

Doc frowned. Nothing moved in the silent apartment. "Fitz?"

Nothing.

Creeping forward, Doc peered into the dimly lit hall leading past Fitz's bachelor-messy living room, toward the apartment's single bedroom. On his right, a tiny kitchen.

The refrigerator was open. A milk carton lay on the floor, on its side.

"Fitz!" Doc jogged down the hallway, pushing open Fitz's ajar bedroom door. "Where the fuck are you?" He turned and shoved open the bathroom door.

The shower curtain was pulled down, the bar angled sideways and sticking up from the bathtub. Blood pooled on the tiled floor and had splattered on the walls and the mirror. A broken chunk of Fitz's porcelain sink lay shattered on the floor. And, wrapped in the shower curtain in the bathtub, Fitz's broken body lay. His neck jutted at a crazed angle, and his eyes were bulging, shock and terror frozen in his last gaze. Blood covered his naked body, from gashes across his arms, his chest, and one giant head wound above his eye.

Doc backed up, hitting the towel bar as he cursed. His hands shook, shock and rage racing through him. Eyes darted around the bathroom, searching for something, anything, any sign or clue or hint as to what had happened.

He froze, his breath choking off as he found the M circled in Fitz's blood on the cracked white tiles over Fitz's broken body.

He tore out of the apartment, bouncing off walls as he ran for the open door. He fumbled in his shorts, trying to pull out his cell and his keys at the same time. "Fuck!" he shouted, dropping his keys as he tried and failed to unlock his car door. Shaking fingers managed to swipe through his cell and pull up Cooper's number. He threw himself into his car, finally, as Cooper's phone rang in his ear.

"*What?*" Cooper answered, snappish and grumpy.

"Fitz is dead!" Doc roared. "There's a fucking M in his apartment!"

"*What?*"

"Fitz is fucking dead! He was fucking murdered!" Doc swerved across four lanes of traffic, speeding around a minivan and a sedan. He floored the accelerator, gunning his car up to sixty on the residential drag outside Fitz's neighborhood. "It was Madigan! His Goddamn sign was there!"

"*Where are you?*" Cooper was back to professional, his ice-cold mask falling into place as his voice chewed glass over the phone line. "*Get back to base, now.*"

"I just left his place. We were— Fuck!" Doc punched his steering wheel, his fist flying into the worn leather, over and over. "I'm on the way," he growled.

"*I'm calling the rest of the team.*" Cooper cut the line, and Doc threw his cell phone into the passenger seat. His hands gripped the steering wheel, hard enough that the whole column shook. He bellowed, screaming at the windshield.

Behind him, a pair of headlights merged into his lane.

A red light ahead forced him to stop. He slammed on the brakes, a squeal of tires and burning rubber barely helping him to stop in time. He cursed through the light, fury and frustration coursing through his body, making him shake, making him want to rip his car apart with his bare hands. How? Why? Fitz was one of the best on their team, quiet and professional. And young. One of the youngest. Just twenty-two.

How had Madigan found them? Why kill Fitz?

He froze, his breath still heaving as ice flooded through him. Just who *had* found Fitz? Madigan was somewhere in the Indian Ocean, floating on a stolen tanker, or so their best guesses said. Who was here in Tampa doing his dirty work?

The light changed, red to green, and Doc floored it, his tires wailing again.

The headlights behind him matched his speed, hanging on to his bumper.

His stomach clenched. Fingers slid down the steering wheel, knuckles going white. Ahead, a flyover bridge approached, rising over one of Tampa Bay's watery offshoots. The other cars had disappeared, and it was just him and the headlights behind, approaching the bridge.

The car behind him swerved, veering to the right and accelerating fast, drawing up alongside him.

The other car's window was down, and a black balaclava blocked out the lone driver's face.

Doc ducked as bullets smashed through his car, shattering his windows and thudding into the frame. Jerking the wheel, he tried to ram the other car, but the driver swerved away. He came back, firing again, and a bullet popped one of Doc's tires. His car jerked, pulling hard to the left, and he struggled against the momentum.

The bridge rose beneath them, taking their cars over the dark water. On his right, the black-clad driver lined up for another shot, balancing the barrel of his weapon on his forearm. He fired.

Doc's right tire blew, and something ground in his engine. He cursed as his car jerked again, sliding to the right and heading straight for the shooter.

The shooter gunned it, flying forward, and Doc barely scraped past his rear bumper, flying toward the bridge's guardrail.

"Fuck," Doc hissed. It had to be water. Fucking of course. He closed his eyes, gripped the edge of his seat, and threw himself back as his car crashed through the guardrail and sailed out over the tributary, heading for the inky water below.

The car hit the surface like it slammed into a brick wall. His airbag burst. He flew forward, bouncing off the hard canvas. Dizziness crashed over him, his ears roaring and his vision going triple as the lights of the bridge bounced above. Blood trickled from his throbbing nose and the taste of copper filled his mouth. Water poured in through his shattered windows and his broken windshield, flooding the compartment. Cold; the shock hit his system, and he managed to order his crazed thoughts again. *Escape. Get to safety. Report to the L-T.*

He fought out of the seatbelt as water rose to his neck, his car plunging to the depths. The impact had crumpled its frame, and the car door wouldn't budge. He couldn't kick out the windshield against the water, and instead took a deep breath and twisted through his shattered driver's window. Glass scraped over his skin, cutting into his sides and his legs, but he kicked free and rose to the surface.

Breathing hard, he floundered toward the shore. His eyes still swam, blacking out every third stroke. He fell beneath the surface, sputtering, coughing, hacking up dirty bay water and spitting blood.

When he made it to the shore, he crawled up the wet, sucking mud and collapsed, facedown.

His eyes slipped closed.

Taif, Saudi Arabia

Summer Palace of Prince Faisal

His bodyguards lay in the palace entrance, their throats slit.

Blood pooled beneath him, coating the marble tiles.

Faisal tried to put pressure on his wounds, but the blood kept coming. His hands were dripping, coated in his own blood, and he smeared messy palm prints across the tile as he dragged himself across the floor.

They'd trashed his office. Destroyed his computers. Cut his phone lines. Set fire to his palace. Flames curled up his walls, ate through his curtains. Destroyed centuries of art and hand-painted wooden panels, millennia old. A rafter came crashing down, splintering behind his feet.

He kept crawling, his bloody fingernails digging into the seams of his tiles. He gritted his teeth as he pulled himself forward, using his knees and his thighs and all of his waning strength. A trail snaked behind him, too much blood leaking from his wounds.

The attackers had destroyed his cell phone, but they hadn't found the sat phone, the one he used to communicate with Adam. The one he kept hidden, protected. His one link to Adam, and he kept that phone safer than he kept his office.

Faisal had to wipe the blood staining his palm on his Turkish carpet when he got to the safe in his bedroom. At first, the palm reader denied him entry, but after he rubbed the blood away, the lock chirped, the electronic bolt sliding back. Inside the safe, his mother's gold jewelry, her wedding gift, and a picture of his father lay next to the sat phone.

He grabbed it and rolled to his back, slumping against his bedroom wall. Smoke filled the air and his nose, acrid and poisonous. He coughed.

Blood dribbled down his chin. Ash floated, sticking to his skin and to his blood.

Shaking fingers turned the phone on. Dialed Adam's number.

"*Hello?*" Half a world away, Adam's voice crackled through the line, hard and cold, like the strongest steel. Still, Faisal smiled. His head fell back, hitting the wall.

"Adam," he breathed. Coughing stole his voice.

"*What's wrong?*" The steel in Adam's voice wavered. "*Fuck! Faisal, what's wrong? What's happening?*"

Fire licked over his ceiling, curling through the panels over his head. He watched the flames spread. "I love you, Adam," he said. "I never stopped loving you. Ever."

"*No!*" Adam shouted. "*No! Not you too!*" Panic had replaced Adam's normal steadiness, and his breaths came harsh and frantic over the line. "*Hold on, Faisal! Hold the fuck on!*"

"Want to hear your voice," he whispered. "Please. Please, say something to me."

"*Fuck!*" Adam shouted across the satellite line, his voice falling apart as he gasped. "*Faisal,*" he moaned. "*Faisal, Goddamn it. I love you too. I do. I love you so Goddamn much. I'm such an idiot. Such a fucking idiot—*"

"Adam," he breathed. "Adam—"

The flaming ceiling came crashing down, plaster and wood shattering and falling to the floor. Faisal ducked into a ball and dropped the phone, curling and trying to drag himself farther away from the all-consuming flames. In the distance, the wail of sirens rose, the long, two-tone beat of the Saudi emergency services. Maybe, if he held on.

His fingers stretched for the phone, but it was too far. Adam's voice bellowed from the speaker, shouting his name and begging him to say something, anything.

"I'm here, Adam," he whispered. "I love you."

Darkness closed in, wavering on the edges of his vision. He tried to breathe, but ash coated his bloody lips, and he coughed hard. His stomach pulsed, another gush of blood pumping from his slit abdomen. He laid his head down on the warm tile and stared at the sat phone, listening to Adam shout his name as the world blacked out.

Tampa, FL

Adam squealed to stop outside the Gator Bar, a dive bar and strip club on the industrial side of Tampa Bay. In one fist, he gripped his satellite phone so hard his hand ached. The call had long since cut off. Tears dried on his cheeks, salt tracks that he hadn't wiped away.

Against the shadowed side of the clap steel dive bar, a dark shape shifted, and then a man stood, stumbling toward Adam's truck. "C'mon!" Adam shouted when he threw open the door. Doc, mud-and-blood-covered, fell into the passenger seat.

Doc slumped sideways on the truck's bench seat as Adam took off, burning rubber as they roared out of the parking lot.

"Are you fucking hurt?" Adam's shifted the sat phone to his other hand, also holding the steering wheel, and grabbed at Doc's shoulders, his arms, and his chest. "Talk to me, Doc!"

"Concussion," Doc groaned. "Broken face. Broken ribs." He coughed, moaning as he squeezed his eyes closed.

"Do I need to take you to the hospital?" Adam's truck veered right and then left, swerving around cars as he floored it down the side streets. "'Cause I don't know if we can."

"No," Doc groaned. "I can handle it." He rolled, grimacing, and looked up at Adam. "What the fuck do we do now?"

"Ghost protocol. We vanish. I told the guys. Get cash and get the fuck out of here. Throw away their phones. Check in online in a week."

"So where the fuck are we going?" Doc groaned again, trying to stay still as Adam drove like a madman, a bat out of hell.

Adam's jaw clenched, and his fingers kneaded the steering wheel, over and over.

"L-T? Where the fuck are we going?"

"Where I should have fucking stayed."

BREAKING NEWS
Russian Destroyer Attacked and Sunk in Indian Ocean

A Russian destroyer, the Vinogradov, heading back to Russia after finishing her tour of duty in the Persian Gulf in support of antiterrorist operations in conjunction with the United States, was attacked and sunk in the Indian Ocean. Initial reports indicate terrorists, in possession of a hijacked tanker, attacked the destroyer by surprise, luring her in under a false distress signal and a request for assistance. Final transmissions from the Vinogradov show they had come alongside the tanker to render aid and assistance to what they believed was a vessel that had lost all power and was drifting off course.

Frantic messages received after indicate chaos and a fierce battle for the destroyer. Suicide bombers boarded, detonating and punching the first holes in the destroyer's hull. An invasion force swarmed the destroyer, killing most of the crew. Captain Anatoly Lukyanenko was executed by the terrorists on the bridge, shown in a brutal video released online.

The attack comes amid a season of unrest and violent upheaval in Russia. Multiple suicide bombers detonated at a state funeral President Puchkov held for a murdered homosexual victim of a targeted terrorist attack, an event for which he was roundly criticized. Hardline elements protesting against President Puchkov's government clashed with federal police in Moscow and St. Petersburg and turned violent at a gay pride parade in Moscow. Some in the federal police stood by, watching as riots erupted, and members of the LGBT pride parade were attacked. And, in two separate terror attacks, homemade bombs exploded at a shopping mall in downtown Moscow, and a shooter opened fire at a busy basketball game.

General Moroshkin, Commander of the Russian Armed Forces, has repeatedly blasted President Puchkov, saying that the president has made his country the target of terrorists with his reformist policies. Moroshkin has emerged as the number one challenger to President Puchkov, and some in the Russian government have called for Puchkov to step down. The Federal Duma in Moscow began discussions on calling for a vote of no confidence in Puchkov's government just last week.

33

White House

Phones buzzed and muted conversations flew through the Situation Room. Watch officers relayed up-to-the-minute intelligence. Video footage from ten different news stations played on monitors along one wall. Admiral McDonald spoke to the captain of the *San Jacinto*, steaming at full speed toward the site of the Russian destroyer's sinking. Old coffee and the stink of shock and sweat filled the room.

Jack scrubbed his hands over his face. The attack had come in the middle of the night, like all terrible news was bound to. Two nights before, it had been Cooper's terse voicemail to Ethan, his message that said he'd enacted ghost protocol and would check back after securing the situation. And a growled, bitten-off request to recover Fitz's body.

Too much was happening, too much swirling at high speed. Madigan was everywhere. In Tampa, in the Indian Ocean, in Russia, and even in the air Jack breathed inside the White House. They'd closed ranks, tightened their inner circle. He could count on one hand the number of people who knew the details about Cooper's team, his men, and his black ops mission.

And yet, they'd been targeted.

And the prince.

Jack lowered his head, rubbing at his temples.

The sinking of the destroyer was too much to contain. He'd kept Madigan's deadly attacks under wraps for months, kept his destruction of bases and breakouts of prisoners from making the news. He'd kept Ethan and Cooper's team buried, their mission so compartmentalized that only Irwin, Ethan, and Prince Faisal knew about their movements around the world. The release of the intel cables was the only publicly attributable action he'd labeled as Madigan's.

But now, it would all blow wide open. Everything Madigan had done, his destructive race around half the world. Their attempts to stop him, always a half step behind the man who had invented the game of modern black ops himself.

A man who had just murdered three hundred and fifty Russian sailors in the open ocean. The ship had sunk in the shark-infested waters off Arabia. If there had been survivors, there weren't likely to be any now.

The *San Jacinto* made fast time toward the coordinates on an ill-fated rescue mission while the world's media feasted on the political blood in the water.

Ethan, Irwin, and Director Rees had their heads together, scanning through intelligence reports as fast as they came in. Drone overflights from the US base in Bahrain showed a spreading oil slick and a floating debris field—life jackets, personal effects, and still, unmoving bodies.

"Mr. President, President Puchkov is on the line for you."

Jack grabbed the handset of the phone nearest him. He'd sent Sergey a text to call when he was able to. He could only imagine the nightmare unfolding in the Kremlin.

"Sergey, I'm so sorry," he said, still rubbing one hand over his forehead. "This is a terrible day for the world. You have my condolences."

"*It is even more terrible than you know, Jack,*" Sergey grumbled on his end of the line, snapping in Russian to someone nearby. "*The destroyer wasn't alone. She had a submarine escort. And we have lost contact with our sub.*"

"Was it destroyed?" Jack scribbled a note to Ethan and slid his notepad down the table. Ethan grabbed it, read the message, and then passed it to Irwin and Rees. All three stared back at Jack, grim, their mouths pressed in hard, straight lines.

"*No.*" Sergey swallowed. "*We believe it was captured. By Madigan.*"

Jack took over the press briefing from a harried, snappish Pete. He strode across the platform as the press pool exploded, standing and shouting questions over each other. Recorders hovered in the air as cameras flashed and pencils scratched across notepads. Pete sent Jack an exhausted look and stepped back.

"Ladies and gentleman," Jack began, "please, sit. I have an update, and then, yes, I will be taking your questions." He took a deep breath. "I have just met with my national security team and convened with President Puchkov regarding the sinking of the *Vinogradov*. First and foremost, I want to extend America's deepest condolences to the families and friends of the sailors lost in this terrible tragedy. We have reviewed all available intelligence, and we are confident in our assessment that the perpetrators of this attack are none other than the terrorists and criminals who have gravitated to Madigan's message of hate and treason." He swallowed, and his hands gripped the podium.

"Over the past several months, the criminal and traitor, former General Porter Madigan, has been engaged in terrorist operations against the United States and, increasingly, against our ally, the Russian Federation. The sinking of the *Vinogradov* is also the work of Madigan and his terrorist forces. He and his followers are engaged in a war against the United States, her allies, and the world's balance of power. Madigan's attacks reveal a sequence of coordinated, planned efforts designed to maximize his forces' attempt to destabilize the current order."

The pressroom hummed. Cameras flashed. Hushed whispers flew back and forth.

"Madigan remains a threat to the United States. However, we have extraordinary individuals dedicated to his destruction and that of his forces, and to protecting the United States. Our mission is to destroy Madigan, and to that end, we will be escalating our operations. I will be meeting with President Puchkov in the coming days, and together, we will forge a strategy that will achieve this joint objective. Let me be clear. Anyone who targets America or her allies will be hunted to the ends of the earth. There is nowhere you will be safe."

Jack swallowed. The walls in the briefing room seemed to close in, the White House collapsing around him. The lights were too bright, the sounds of the recorders and cameras and pencils and cell phone keys too loud. He closed his eyes, and his sweat-slick fingers smudged on the edge of the podium.

The pictures from Moscow, tucked into his duffel, were a near-ceaseless reminder that Madigan still had friends within the government. Cooper and his men, and their teammate Fitz, who was now lying on a slab in the CIA morgue, flown to Langley in secret. Noah Williams and his seeming resurrection. His death, a smokescreen for Madigan to operate his ghost army in the shadows for over a decade, it seemed.

Madigan hovered over his shoulder. He hung in the shadows everywhere Jack went. He saw his sly eyes in the faces of so many around him. Doubt, and the edges of paranoia had slipped into his soul, a terrible poison.

No. He had to fight back. There were some he could trust. Scott, Ethan's best friend, and Daniels, who practically lived at the White House now, refusing to leave their sides. Irwin. Cooper. Director Rees. Elizabeth. Pete. He wasn't alone.

And Ethan.

Jack looked dead into the camera, broadcasting his message to the world. "I *will* see Madigan destroyed and the world made safe again."

He looked down, shuffling his notes on the podium and then back up, to the crowd of silent, still reporters. "I'll take your questions now."

34

Tianjing, China

"We have some concerns."

Colonel Song crossed his legs and sipped his tea, watching the boats ferry passengers up and down the Haihe River. Overhead, the sun shone down on Tianjing, glinting off steel-and-glass skyscrapers. A pretty young waitress headed his way with a smile, but he waved her off.

He turned, pressing his cell to his other ear. "We don't feel that your organization is making any substantial progress. And, your recent activities have attracted significant attention."

Madigan's voice scratched over the connection. Wherever he was, he was buried, far on the edges of global connectivity. *"It was meant to."*

"We no longer are confident in the assurances you provided to us. We have not seen the potential that you promised. The world remains stubbornly normal, Mr. Madigan."

"*It's General,*" Madigan growled. "*And I'm surprised by you, Song. You Chinese should know better than most; it's the long game that counts. It's about getting inside your enemy's head. Unbalancing them. Destroying their equilibrium. Throwing their sense of safety, their sanity, into question. Ripping away everything they cherish. One. By. One.*"

"How does a Russian destroyer tear apart your American president's world?"

Madigan chuckled. "*Another thing you should understand. Distraction. Deception. A feint. The purpose of which will be clear to you shortly.*"

Song *hmm*ed, and he frowned behind his sunglasses. Was it just more talk?

"*Tell you what.*" Madigan's voice crackled through a burst of static. Water crashed in the background, like a wave breaking. "*You can call me back in two days and offer me your government's apology. Until then, I've got work to do.*"

The line cut out.

35

White House

"Hey." Daniels checked right and left, making sure the hallways were clear, before slipping into Ethan's office. He closed the door behind him.

"What is it?" Ethan rose from his desk and crossed the room, his body already primed for bad news. Adrenaline started flowing, his low-level panic a constant companion now.

Daniels pulled out a small square box from his suit pants pocket. "They came in." He held the box out to Ethan. "Picked 'em up on my way."

Ethan froze.

"I know it's not a good time. But they're here."

Ethan plucked the box from Daniels's palm and cradled it in his own hand. A simple black velvet box. It shouldn't terrify him so much. But, God, it did. It quaked the foundations of his soul. "When will there ever be a good time. This is stupid. This isn't a good idea." His fist closed, as if he could hide the very thought the box—and what lay inside—represented. Shove it away, like he'd never, ever imagined it.

"It's not stupid." Daniels crowded close, and he reached for Ethan's fist. He shook Ethan's hand until Ethan's fingers uncurled. "Nothing about this is stupid."

"I never thought—"

"Neither did I, brother." Daniels gripped his shoulder. "When you asked us to help you, I thought I was dreaming."

Ethan stayed stock-still.

"At least look at them. You designed these, man."

Slowly, he lifted the lid, the black velvet soft beneath his fingers. White satin folded over itself within, and in the center, two rings sat.

He stopped breathing. Blinked fast, as the world blurred.

They were thick rings of dark titanium, and in the center, a channel of diamonds ran all the way around. An eternity band, the jeweler had called the diamonds. Ethan knew, that moment, that was what he wanted for them both. Forever. Eternity.

"Damn. You did good," Daniels barely whispered, and his voice broke through the fragile haze that had descended over Ethan.

He snapped the box closed, gripped it tight in his fist, and shoved it in his suit pants pocket. Daniels stepped back.

"It's not the right time." He looked away. They were headed to Russia tomorrow to pay their respects and coordinate a massive joint attack on Madigan's forces. The time for subtlety had ended.

"But it will be again. Do you have a plan yet for how you're going to ask?"

He glared.

"Better start thinking about one." Daniels grinned again at Ethan and backed up, heading for the door. "It's going to be great. I promise. It's meant to be." Daniels ducked out, closing the door behind him.

Ethan stood in the center of his office, his eyes closed. The weight of the velvet box rested against his thigh, a quiet, terrifying presence that ignited a burn deep in his heart.

He *wanted*, oh so badly.

36

Riyadh, Saudi Arabia

Adam roared south down King Fahd highway, speeding out of Riyadh's airport and heading for the city center.

Riyadh looked like a neon wonderland after dark, the multicolored lights of the buildings playing off each other and the glow from the hundreds of headlights snaking through the city. The Kingdom Tower, the glittering jewel of Riyadh, rose from the sparkling downtown. It looked like a silver tower of Sauron, minus the great glowing eye, and Adam's stomach knotted again. He looked away, focusing on the crowded highway as he gripped the steering wheel of his rental car.

Doc glared at Adam, one hand pressed over his ribs. "Could you make this *more* uncomfortable? Please? I think there's probably another way you can jerk this car around. Go ahead. Try it. I believe in you."

Adam ignored him.

"Will you please tell me why the fuck we're back in Saudi Arabia?"

Swerving, Adam sped past a cargo truck and floored the accelerator. Doc swore and glared out the window.

The royal hospital in the center of the city was where Faisal had been taken. He'd called everyone, every person he'd ever known in Saudi Arabia, trying to find out anything. In the end, he'd had to pose as a reporter and call the royal palace and beg for any information, any statement for his fake paper. The office of the governor of Riyadh had finally broken, giving him the tiniest shred of information.

Prince Faisal is at the royal hospital in Riyadh, following an accident.

It was better than nothing.

He and Doc flew from Miami to London and then grabbed a flight to Riyadh. Doc wore Adam's workout clothes to board the flight, ditching his mud-and-blood-stained clothes in an airport trash can after they'd parked.

On the way to London, he'd done what he could for Doc, cleaning his cuts and wrapping his ribs in the airline's cramped bathroom. After, Doc struggled to stay awake, leaning on a bag of ice against the plane's window as he watched in-flight movie after in-flight movie. In London, Adam bought them both new suits at the airport and ignored Doc's dumbfounded bitching.

Seven hours later, they landed in Riyadh.

His phone chimed, signaling his exit, and he swerved off the highway. A few turns, and then he pulled to a stop at the valet entrance to the royal hospital. Doc stared at the hospital and then at him.

Adam pressed a hundred to the valet's palm and ran inside. Doc followed behind, cursing every step of the way. Adam spoke in fast Arabic, talking his way past nurses and hospital security, leaning on the little knowledge he had about Faisal's condition and the royal family, forcing his way through. The suits helped, an added touch of respect.

He made it as far as the entrance to the royal wing.

Security guards made of towering muscle stopped him, shoving him back.

He fought, punching one and kicking another before they picked him up by the throat and slammed him against the wall. Thick fingers closed around his neck, choking the air out of him. He grasped at the bouncer's wrists, legs kicking, as the second bruiser grunted into his wrist mic and pulled out his pistol.

"Hey!" Doc shouted as he caught up. "Hey, asshole!" Even though he was clutching his side and holding his ribs, Doc took off running, charging at the security guards as Adam wheezed.

The second bouncer raised his weapon, aiming for Doc.

Doc skittered to a halt, eyes wide.

"What is happening?"

An older Saudi man moved down the hall, loose, dark robes trimmed in gold flowing behind him. Beneath the white ghutra on his head, haggard lines etched deep furrows on his face, made worse by his glowering scowl. His gaze flicked from Doc, frozen, to the two bouncers pinning Adam against the wall.

"*You*," the older man breathed. "What are *you* doing here?"

Adam coughed, and his feet kicked weakly.

"*Yallah*," the older man grunted to his security guards.

The bruiser gripping his neck dropped him, letting him fall to the ground in a sprawl.

Doc took a step forward. The bruisers squared off against him. Doc froze.

"*You*, you pretended to be that journalist," the older Saudi hissed.

Slowly, Adam pushed to his feet. He coughed, rubbing his throat, but kept his eyes and his head lowered when he stood. He used the Saudi's full title, pouring all his respect into his words. "Your Royal Highness,

Governor of Riyadh, Prince Abdul al-Saud," he grunted. "I'm here to see your nephew."

"It is *forbidden*!" Prince Abdul, the crown prince of Saudi Arabia, heir apparent to the kingdom and next in line for the throne, hissed at Adam. "Faisal told me it was finished! That you had *left* him!"

Adam cringed. "It was. It *is*," he said quickly. "But he's hurt—"

"And you think you have some kind of right to see my nephew?" Prince Abdul's dark eyes blazed. "After what you did! *Wallah!* You will stay away from him!"

"I love him," Adam breathed, the tough exterior he was trying to cling to shattering. His face twisted, and he gasped again. A year's worth of anguish, of burying his feelings, of bullying his own heart into cold dejection, exploded and a sob strangled his voice. "I *love* him!"

Doc's eyes burned into Adam.

"That makes it *worse*!" Prince Abdul grabbed Adam's arm and hauled him down the hall, away from the hulking security guards. "Do you *not* understand? The *mutawwa'in* could kill him! He is not safe from their punishments just because he is royal. Not anymore!"

The *mutawwa'in*, Saudi's infamous religious police.

"We were careful—"

"This is *not* careful!" Prince Abdul shouted. "Storming into the hospital? How many saw you? How many will ask questions?" The prince closed his eyes and exhaled. He turned away from Adam, his hands clenching the gold braided edges of his robes. "When Faisal's father and mother died, I promised my brother's memory that I would raise his son and care for him. That he would be safe, and he would be loved. Faisal is my blood." He turned, a fierce glare burning straight through to Adam's soul. "My *blood*. My *family*."

"Please," Adam whispered. "*Please*... Can you tell me if he's all right?"

Prince Abdul was silent for a long moment, staring at Adam like he was looking at spoiled garbage. "His liver was punctured. Almost all of it has been removed. He'll need a new one cloned and another surgery. But... for now, he is resting. They say in time, he will recover completely."

A sob burst from Adam's chest, his heart finally unclenching after it had seized back in Tampa. Tears blurred his vision and he turned away as he buried his face in his hands. He'd thought, when he heard Faisal's voice, that it was the end. He'd thought he'd be too late.

Prince Abdul watched him weep into his palms, watched him try to collect himself, try to gather the bits and pieces of his shattered heart and scrape them together into a mound of splintered glass. He heaved one shaking breath after another and, finally, wiped his eyes and faced the prince again.

"I thought," Prince Abdul said slowly, "that he was merely exhausting his lust. It's not unheard of for young, virile men to seek out a willing body for their needs, provided they end up with a wife in the end."

Adam looked away. "It was so much more."

"And yet, you abandoned him."

Silence, as Adam's soul shriveled.

"It would have been easier if it was just lust," the prince growled. "Love makes it complicated." He shook his head and peered at Adam, his eyes narrowed. "Are you familiar with Abu Hurairah?"

His head ached, the pressure and fear over Faisal finally bleeding out of him, but he wracked his memories. "A bit. Faisal used to speak of him. He was a scribe of Mohammed?"

Prince Abdul muttered in Arabic, the words of blessing said after the prophet's name. "*'Alayhi as-salām*. Yes. There is a *hadith* that speaks of Abu Hurairah's torment as a young man. His lack of desire for women and marriage, namely. He went to the prophet, begging for advice. Four times he asked for the prophet's guidance, and on the fourth time, the prophet spoke. 'The pen is dried to what you are experiencing,' the prophet said." Prince Abdul paused. Held Adam's stare. "What is fixed is fixed," he elaborated. "A man's fate is sealed when the pen's ink over his life dries."

Prince Abdul rubbed his forehead, his fingers running along the creases furrowing his brow. "*Al-hamdu lillah,* my nephew's ink may be dried in this matter. Faisal has refused all talk of marriage. He's refused all of the brides I have arranged for him."

Adam's gut squeezed hard, like all his organs had been tossed in a blender set to grind. His teeth scraped together as his jaw clenched. Jealousy raced through him, a wave of frantic heat he felt all the way to the tips of his fingers. But why? He'd known it would end this way. Faisal was two steps removed from the Saudi crown. Of course he would marry, would marry multiple women, and father children with them. At best, he could have only ever hoped for being a scandalous side affair, and a forbidden one at that. They had no future, none. He closed his eyes.

"*In shaa Allah*, he says he is waiting for you," Prince Abdul said softly. "We have been talking at great length."

Adam's eyes snapped to the prince. He stopped breathing.

The prince scowled, and his lips curled back, a silent sneer. "He is my *blood*," he snapped. "My *family*. And I will do anything for my family." Another glare as he looked Adam up and down, as if he could see into

Adam's soul. "You will *never* bring him harm. He will never hurt, ever. Not from the body, and not from the heart."

"No." Adam licked his lips, his breaths coming fast, practically a frantic pant. "No, never. Never again," he said, his mind flashing back to Faisal's breathless good-bye, his tortured plea for Adam's love, the sound of flames crackling, and a thunderous crash before the endless silence. "Your Royal Highness..."

"This is *not* concluded. We have much to discuss, Faisal and I. I do not condone this, or you. Especially not *you*. What you have done. What you left behind." He sighed, like his soul was pained. "But... he is my nephew."

Adam nodded and bowed his head again. "I understand, Your Highness."

"Your friend." The prince nodded to Doc, still frozen behind the security guards, but staring fiercely at Adam and the prince. "He is injured."

"He was attacked at the same time Faisal was. Probably by the same people."

"My nephew has been helping the Americans with a sensitive operation. Is this connected?"

"That's me." Adam ducked his head when the prince's eyes narrowed. "Faisal has been helping me and my team. This is our medic. He's a friend of Faisal's too. Not that kind of friend," he added quickly.

"No. He speaks only ever of you. *Wallah*."

Adam pressed his lips together, trying to stop them from trembling. "Please, Your Highness. Can I see him?"

The prince closed his eyes. "You will find the men that did this to my nephew. You will make them suffer." He sighed, a single, slow exhale. "Faisal is down the hall. The recovery suite."

Adam took off, his new shoes racing over the polished marble of the hospital. His eyes flicked to the doors, searching for Faisal's room. The suites were palatial, grand retreats for royals who needed medical care, private and completely isolated. Priceless artwork and gold-glittering mosaics stretched along the walls. Quotes from the Qur'an, the statement of faith, scrolled in every room.

"You," Adam heard the prince call to Doc. "Come with me. We will see to your injuries."

Finally, he skittered to a stop, breathing hard before slipping into the recovery suite. Medical machines crowded within, beeping monitors and IV poles holding too many bags of fluids and antibiotics. Faisal lay still on the single, huge bed, propped up on pillows with a giant bandage wrapped around his abdomen. An IV went into one arm, and stuck on his chest, EKG pads monitored his heart. His arms were wrapped, and the smell of burn cream hung in the air.

Adam stopped at the foot of Faisal's bed, his hands clenching into shaking fists.

Faisal's dark eyes slowly opened. He blinked.

"I'm dreaming," Faisal whispered, his voice faint and rough. *"Ahlam beek*, Adam. *Qalby."*

Adam shook his head. He couldn't speak, not when Faisal was telling him he dreamed of him and called him his heart.

"I am dreaming," Faisal repeated. "The one I love wouldn't be here. He wouldn't come to me. He's too afraid of our love."

Damn it all. Four steps took him to the side of Faisal's bed. Faisal's bleary eyes tracked him and went wide when Adam dropped to his knees at Faisal's bedside and took his hand in both of his own. "I'm here. I'm here, Faisal. This isn't a dream."

His breath trembled as he whispered, *"When God designed your features and joined your brows/Paved my way, then trapped me with your gestures & bows/United the knots of my doing and of my budding heart/Fate convinced me to be enslaved to thee."*

As he finished reciting lines from Faisal's favorite Islamic poet, he pressed a kiss to Faisal's knuckles, letting his lips linger on his warm skin. Long ago, Faisal had breathed those words into his shoulder, into the back of his neck, as he moved deep within Adam.

Faisal's fingers curled around Adam's, and his other hand rose, reaching for Adam's hair. Adam leaned into his touch, sighing, and dropped the faintest kiss to the center of his bandaged belly, and then to his hip, hidden beneath the royal hospital robe he wore.

"Why?" Faisal whispered. "How?"

He answered both questions together, squeezing gently on Faisal's hand as he smiled. *"Ana bahibak,"* he breathed, and then repeated in English, kissing Faisal's knuckles again. "I love you."

There was still the world to answer to, Prince Abdul, Director Reichenbach, the Marine Corps, and everything else. Their mission, to put Madigan down for good. All the darkness. Their past. All the reasons why they shouldn't, couldn't be together. The world was still out there, still ready to tear them apart, but that was for later.

Now, Adam pressed another kiss to Faisal's hand and lay his cheek to his skin, sighing softly. *"Ana bahibak."*

Vinogradov Sinking: General Moroshkin demands President Puchkov's resignation

General Moroshkin today demanded President Puchkov's resignation after the terrorist attack and sinking of the Vinogradov led by former American General Porter Madigan. "President Puchkov has opened Russia up to senseless violence and despair," Moroshkin stated. "He is a disgrace to the motherland, and he must be removed from office immediately." Moroshkin went on to assert that Madigan's targeting of Russia most likely occurred because of President Puchkov's close friendship with President Spiers, the former target of Madigan's attempted coup in the United States last year.

37

Air Force One, en route to Sochi, Russia

Jack and Ethan worked during the entire flight to Sochi, spreading out in Air Force One's conference room alongside Irwin and Director Rees. Satellite images taken over the Indian Ocean searched for Madigan's tanker. There were hundreds of tankers in the water, transiting through the Persian Gulf and the straits, and more were docked in deep water harbors. Orders went out for a visual confirmation on each and every one. The Navy was on high alert, searching for the Russians' rogue sub with radar and sonar.

All options were on the table. Jack put the military on alert, up to DEFCON Four, with orders to be ready to initiate combat operations within forty-eight hours. Director Rees and Irwin briefed him on a laundry list of options, from surgical air strikes—once they found a target—to a surge of Special Forces soldiers. A blitzkrieg, or a silent kill mission. Ethan's dark eyes held Jack's gaze through the briefing.

When they landed in Russia, at Sochi, Sergey met them at the airport personally before they headed for the secured presidential retreat on the banks of the Black Sea. They'd dispensed with the press for the trip, and it was just Jack, Ethan, Irwin, and Director Rees, along with Scott, Daniels, Welby, and only the most trusted Secret Service agents, men who Scott had personally vetted and knew, without a doubt, were loyal.

Jack rested his head on Ethan's shoulder and closed his eyes for the short drive to the retreat, his fingers laced through Ethan's on his thigh. He grabbed a few moments of sleep on Ethan, his only respite in hours. Ethan stroked a hand through Jack's hair and pressed a kiss to his forehead.

In Ethan's pocket, the velvet box sat like lead, a presence he couldn't ignore or push away. The rings were all of his hopes, all of his fragile dreams, made manifest. Held, literally, in the palm of his hand. He couldn't leave them behind. Since Daniels had given the rings to him, he'd kept them close, tucked away, but always near.

It was the height of selfishness to think that he could ask this. Could ask a man as amazing and wondrous as Jack to join his life to Ethan's. And now, with the world on the brink, his desires seemed even more like an impossible dream. The world had shifted since the Russian destroyer sank, a new vibration to the air. Tension filled the air at the White House, on Air Force One, everywhere it seemed, so palpable and thick. Everyone moved with scowls on their faces, deep lines etched into their skin. Words were bitten off, people speaking in harsh, hushed voices. Russia hung by a thin thread. They were a breath away from catastrophe, pushed to the brink by a madman's plots, his ceaseless war against Jack and the world.

Limits were being pushed, and pushed hard.

He shook Jack awake as they pulled up to the retreat. For the first half hour, Scott and his team swarmed the place, checking the rooms set aside for their small delegation, and then they began the business of settling in: charging laptops and cell phones and changing out of wrinkled suits from the long flight.

Sergey, Ilya, Sasha, and General Kuznetsov, a Russian general loyal and sympathetic to Sergey, met with Jack, Ethan, Irwin, and Director Rees in the retreat's glass-walled dining room overlooking the Black Sea. Maps went up on the walls. Plans were sketched out on the glass in marker, only to be wiped away and reworked. Intelligence passed back and forth, satellite images, photo reconnaissance, reports from sources on the ground, bitten-off whispers and rumors shared among fishermen and villagers.

General Kuznetsov and Ilya excused themselves as the sun went down over the water. Director Rees and Irwin retired to their rooms above, each holding a tumbler of whiskey poured by Sergey.

As the Russian sun dipped into the Black Sea, Sergey slid open the glass patio door and motioned to the broad wooden deck and the lounge chairs outside. "Come, Jack, Ethan. Let's take a moment to ourselves." He held the door for Sasha with a smile and led Jack and Ethan to the end of the deck.

Jack sighed as he folded himself down onto the patio lounger. He held out his hand for Ethan to slip in beside him. Sasha looked out over the water, eyes squinted as he straddled his lounger, and Sergey threw his lanky body down onto his own, stretching his long limbs off the ends.

"To the crew of the *Vinogradov*," Sergey said, sitting up and raising his whiskey for a toast.

Silently, Jack and Ethan raised their glasses. Sasha clinked his with Sergey.

"Captain Lukyanenko was a friend of mine." Sergey stared into his glass. "He was a good man."

Sasha reached for Sergey, rubbing his hand over his president's shoulder. Sergey smiled sadly and leaned into the touch.

"I'm sorry, Sergey. We're going to get him. I promise."

"My country is on the brink, Jack." Sergey's eyes shone as the sun fell further, almost beneath the water line. Golden light played over the sea, and waves of red stained the sky. "I love my country. I love Mother Russia. I want her to be the best. This is a fantastic dream, bringing my motherland out of the darkness. But the darkness fights back. I dreamed I could rid us of corruption. Bring true freedom to our people. All people." He tried to smile at Sasha. "The world had other ideas, it seems."

Jack pressed his lips together. Ethan gripped his hand.

"Worries for another day." Sergey seemed to try to shove away the melancholy staining his soul. He clapped Sasha on the shoulder. "We must take care of one thing, and then another. What is right before us." Leaning back, he closed his eyes and poked at Sasha's thigh. "Tell them that story you told me of your first flight supersonic." He sipped at his whiskey, chuckling as Sasha blushed.

The stars winked through the darkening sky. Water lapped at the worn wood, gentle splashes burbling in the night. Sasha relayed one story after another, and the whiskey went down as the conversation and gentle laughter continued. Ethan's thumb stroked the back of Jack's hand as Jack rested his head on Ethan's shoulder, surrendering himself completely to Ethan's hold. Through the dim light cast from the patio lights behind them, Ethan saw Sasha's glittering eyes watching him and Jack, and then his sidelong stare at Sergey when Sergey wasn't looking.

In the midst of another of Sasha's flight stories, this time relaying the first time his fighter had brushed the edge of space, he cut off mid-word, frowning over the sea.

"What is it?" Sergey poked Sasha's thigh. "Aliens?"

Sasha grabbed his finger, stilling Sergey. "Hush."

Ethan sat up, staring into the darkness with Sasha. Jack's hands trailed down his back.

There. Just barely, but there. He could hear the soft whoosh of helicopter blades, of a near-silent attack aircraft buzzing low over the sea.

Sasha whirled, his eyes wide. "Yours?"

Ethan shook his head. "Everyone get inside!" he shouted. "Now!"

Splashes tore through the sea, geysers leaping from the surface as bullets spat from the stealth helicopter, aiming right for them. Short by a few feet, the gunner adjusted, and the bullets chewed up the end of the deck just shy of where they lay.

Wood splintered through the air.

Jack's glass of whiskey hit the deck, shattering.

Ethan pushed Jack up, throwing him toward the house and running behind to shield him. Sasha did the same for Sergey, curling over his back as they ran.

Men burst from within the retreat, Scott, Daniels, Welby, and more of their agents alongside bellowing Russian Presidential Security Services men, rushing toward Sergey and Sasha. Overhead, twin fighter jets screeched, roaring when they banked. A silent moment as Ethan spotted the silver silhouettes bearing down on them.

"Get down!" he hollered. "Get down now!"

He threw Jack to the ground and covered him. Another heavy weight landed on top of him, and he saw Daniels's face next to his own. Jack cursed, and to their left, Sergey shouted in furious Russian.

The patio lights shorted out, plunging the rear of the retreat into darkness.

Gunshots cracked, Scott and his men taking aim at the incoming fighters. The Russian security agents went full auto with their rifles, filling the sky with bullets.

Jack jerked beneath Ethan at the sound of the gunfire.

"Hang on, Jack," Ethan whispered. "Hang on."

The fighter jets fired back at the Russian agents, heavy guns tearing through the men, the patio, and the retreat. Glass shattered, exploding. Shards peppered the back of Ethan's neck, tiny cuts opening with bitter stings. Smoke and gunpowder hung in the air, and the burn of hot metal and jet fuel as the fighters pulled up into the sky, turning for another pass over the sea.

"Go, go!" Scott shouted, grabbing at Daniels and Ethan. "Go!"

They clambered to their feet and stepped over the shot-up bodies of the Russian security agents. Sergey moved with Sasha at his side, and they raced through the blood-covered patio and into the dark retreat. Gaping holes punctured the retreat's frame, wounds from the fighters' attack. Glass crunched underfoot. Plaster hung in the air, gritty on the tongue and between the teeth.

Flashlights bounced over the walls, men running. Shouted Russian and English flew, radio static bursting from handhelds as more agents from both Russia and the US moved together.

Welby ran to Scott, covering Irwin, bleeding from his forehead. "Rees is dead. His room was destroyed," he said, speaking just loud enough to be heard over the din. Ethan caught Scott's eyes, shining in the dark.

"Power's been cut." Scott pressed his back to the wall and quickly ducked around the corner and into the industrial kitchen. He cleared the room and motioned for Daniels to bring Ethan and Jack in, along with

Irwin. The rest of the agents formed a ring around them, a human wall, as Scott peered out at the destruction engulfing the retreat.

Ethan squeezed Jack's hand before slipping out of the ring of agents, sharing a long look with Agent Beech. Ethan headed for Scott, even though Scott sent him a furious look over his shoulder.

In the destroyed main room, Sasha hovered at Sergey's side. He'd picked up a rifle from one of the dead agents on the way in, and he held it up and ready to fire. The Russian agents who were still standing took positions at the destroyed windows, kicking aside shattered glass and kneeling behind what was left of the walls.

Shouting echoed from the front of the house. More gunshots. In the distance, sirens wailed.

"Baker team, come in," Scott hissed into his wrist mic. "Baker team, respond."

Ethan swallowed as Scott looked him in the eye and shook his head. Baker team had been in charge of covering the front of the retreat and the private drive up to their location, along with the presidential vehicles.

More agents down. More agents dead. His friends, once his family.

"Haunted House, Ghost Six," Scott said again, his voice edged with steel, this time to the Secret Service control unit holding at the airport with Air Force One. "We've got a situation."

"Ghost Six, so do we." Ethan and Scott shared a quick look.

"Status, Haunted House?"

"A whole shit ton of Russian military has descended on the airport. They closed the tower, and jeeps are moving in to block the runways. Russian media is broadcasting the same message, telling everyone to stay inside until the military operation is concluded. Looks like a platoon is lining up on our runway, setting up guns against us."

"Shit, is this a coup?" Scott's dark eyes fixed to Ethan's.

"Could be, sir."

"Keep our runway clear and get the engines started. We need assistance here, and we need to get out of this fucking country. Where's the backup plane?"

"An hour out, Ghost Six."

"Shit." Scott shoved Ethan back. "Get back to your place. This is fucking real, Ethan. You're *not* an agent anymore."

The front door blew open, a hard crash banging through the house. Hollered Russian burst through the retreat, followed by thundering boots as a Russian army officer ran in with his men, flashlights bobbing and weaving through the darkness, picking their way to the edge of the destruction, and to Sergey and Sasha.

Scott threw his arm across Ethan and held him back against the wall, covering him and keeping them both out of sight.

"Mr. President," the Russian soldier grunted. "Are you all right?"

Sergey ran his hands through his hair. "Yes, fuck, yes. What the hell is going on?"

"Where is the American president?" The Russian soldier nodded to his men behind him. They fanned out, slowly searching through the house.

Every hair on the back of Ethan's neck rose.

My country is on the brink, Jack.

His eyes flashed to Scott.

The darkness fights back.

"His men have him secured. What's our plan for getting out—"

Sergey never got to finish.

The Russian soldier lifted his rifle, aimed for the center of Sergey's chest, and pulled the trigger.

Sasha bellowed and shoved Sergey sideways, tackling him to the ground, and the soldier's bullets grazed over Sergey's shoulder and slammed into Sasha's arm.

Sweeping out with his feet, Sasha kicked the Russian soldier down and then leaped up, firing three rounds into his face. The soldier's body shook, trembling with the bullets' impact.

"Fuck!" Scott hissed. Beyond him, the soldiers who had backed up the now-dead Russian soldier shouted and opened fire, taking out Sergey's last security agents along the wall.

"Mr. President!" Scott laid down cover fire and motioned to Sergey. "Over here!"

Sergey scrambled for the kitchen, trailing blood from his shoulder. Sasha hovered at his back, one arm stained with blood, droplets falling from his fingers. Ethan ducked under Sasha and helped him stumble to the circle of agents protecting Jack and Irwin. The ring of Secret Service agents opened briefly, swallowing Sergey, Sasha, and Ethan. A moment later, the agents were shoulder to shoulder again, weapons raised, aiming into the shadows.

Scott stayed in the kitchen's doorway, firing at the soldiers until his gun clicked. Out of bullets. He pulled another clip from his belt.

"We've got to move!" Daniels bellowed. "We've got to get out of here!"

"I'm open to suggestions!" Scott shouted back.

Trapped in the middle of a coup. Ethan reached for Jack, running his hands over him quickly, making sure he was whole.

"I'm all right," Jack breathed. "I'm all right. Sergey's hurt. And Sasha." He hovered over them both, pressing his hands to their bloody wounds. Blood slicked down Jack's arms, stained his shirt and his pants. Cursing, he undid his button down and rolled it up, wrapping it around Sasha's arm over the wound. He tied it tight.

Sasha grimaced but said nothing.

Scott ducked back to the group as Welby took his place. "Looks like a coup is in the works." He glanced quickly at Sergey, then back to Jack and Ethan. "Our fighters launched from Incirlik a few minutes ago. They'll be here in ten minutes. The quick reaction force is locked down at the airport. We've got to get clear of here and survive until they can get us some cover and an evac."

"Is that all?" Sergey snapped. He took over from Jack, slapping Sasha's pale cheeks gently and holding his face, staring into his bloodshot eyes.

"Do you know another way out of here?" Scott ignored Sergey's snap.

Heavy footfalls echoed beyond the kitchen, at the front of the house, and gunfire snapped on the private drive. Sharp bellows in Russian, interspersed with the crack of gunfire from Welby, broke over the group. Through the destroyed back of the retreat, the roar of the fighter jets circling overhead drowned everything out for a moment.

Sergey frowned. "Down the shore. There's a boathouse within the grounds of the retreat. We can take the boats away from here." He helped Sasha stand until Sasha waved him off.

"They'd have it surrounded by now. We'd be walking straight into their forces."

Sergey snarled. "Would you like to die here, in this kitchen?" Bullets rang through the house. Heavy thumps shook the walls. "It is reinforced, but it will not hold for long."

"They will use grenades any minute to flush us from here," Sasha ground out.

Scott looked to Ethan.

What other options were there? Ethan reached again for Jack, keeping him close.

They had to get moving, get out of the killbox before they were completely surrounded. He nodded.

"We'll have to fight our way out of here. Through the back. Stay in the shadows, get to the tree line, and then take them out when they pursue. Agents, cover Vigilant, Vigor, and Potomac." Scott nodded to Irwin, using his codename, and then grabbed two agents and spun them around, shoving them in front of Sergey. "You two, cover him."

Sasha stayed glued to Sergey's side, gripping his rifle in blood-drenched hands. Ethan grabbed a kitchen knife from the counter as Scott and Welby led the group to the doorway, scanning left and right in the darkness.

Welby fired, and across the room, a Russian soldier dropped. Bullets flew again, slamming into the walls around them.

"Go!" Scott shouted over his shoulder. "We'll cover!"

A line of agents squeezed around him, firing with Scott and Welby and dragging Jack and Ethan with them. In front of Ethan, Daniels had Jack bent over, lying almost fully on top of him as they ran for the blown-out hole in the side of the retreat. Glass and shorn steel crunched under their feet, and splintered wood as they ran across the destroyed deck. Pine needles and the dewy carpet of the forest softened their footfalls as they reached the woods. Overhead, fighter jets screamed. Everyone hunkered down as they reached the cover of the tree line.

Ethan crouched beside Jack, peering back at the house. Scott and Welby were firing and running, dashing away from the retreat and toward the edge of the forest. Soldiers followed them.

"He's bringing them to us," Daniels called. He shoved Jack down, flat on the ground behind him. "Everyone get ready." Weapons rose.

Bouncing beams from the Russians' flashlights darted through thick tree trunks. Musty air and dust collected on the back of Ethan's tongue, mixing with the tang of adrenaline. In his ears, his heart thundered.

"Fire," Daniels breathed, once Scott was close enough to nod. He and Welby hit the ground. The agents kneeling in the trees opened up, gunfire slamming into the Russians chasing them.

The Russians fell, one by one, until the forest was silent again.

Daniels stayed with Jack as Ethan went to Scott. Dirt clung to Scott's rumpled suit and streaked across his face. Plaster coated his lips. Ethan helped his friend up, pulling him from the ground as Scott breathed hard.

Ethan turned away, heading back for Jack.

Scott went down to the ground again a second later.

A Russian soldier, not dead yet, had kicked out his feet and yanked Scott down, leaping on top of him. He straddled his hips and shoved the barrel of his rifle under Scott's chin, his finger half-clenching on the trigger.

Before anyone else could react, Ethan grabbed the Russian's hair and jerked him back, slamming his knife into the base of his skull in one fast move. He ripped the blade out and shoved it into the side of his neck, severing his artery. Blood arced, spraying over Scott and coating Ethan's hands.

The soldier jolted once and went limp, and Ethan tossed him to the side.

Scott's saucer-wide eyes and blood-spattered face stared up at him, and beyond, Jack watched, frozen in a crouch behind Daniels.

Ethan stared back. Blood dripped from his fingers. The world around him roared, his senses heightened to every sound, every sight. His heart and his soul fixed on Jack, one thought, one purpose echoing through him: *get Jack to safety. Get my love out of here.*

One of the agents ahead called out, signaling the path to the boathouse was clear.

Daniels crowded next to Jack, and Sasha to Sergey, and then they all took off, jogging into the darkness. Welby ran at the rear.

Ethan and Scott wound their way up to Jack's side, Ethan wiping his hands on his suit pants until they were just sticky, but not soaked. Crimson stained his skin.

Jack reached for him, though, when he fell in beside him; his hand gripped Ethan's, a rock-solid hold.

Scott's radio chirped and Ethan leaned in close, listening to the leading agent relay back to Scott as they all took a knee.

"We're at the boathouse. Six soldiers are inside, two on the dock."

"Friendlies?"

"Don't think so. They look too comfortable to be on our side."

Scott cursed. He glared at Ethan and then at Jack. "Stay the *fuck* here," he hissed. One more glare to Ethan, and then he slipped ahead, going to the front of the line of agents holding in the trees just outside the boathouse.

In the darkness, Ethan heard Jack's heavy pants. He reached for Jack, wrapping his arms around him, and Jack pressed his face to Ethan's neck. Dust clung to their skin, damp with sweat and the wet fog of the forest. "We'll get through this," he breathed into Jack's ear. "I swear, Jack."

Welby moved in close, bracketing Jack. "Get ready," he whispered. "They're about to go."

Ahead, Ethan watched Scott slide forward from the tree line. Another agent followed him, ducking in the other direction. Sasha went last, crawling on his belly until he was in position.

I should be with them. Ethan's heart leaped to his throat. *I should be with Scott. I can't leave Jack, not for anything, but damn it, I should be right there.*

In the dim light, Ethan saw Sasha nod, a bare hint of movement. Shots rang out around the boathouse, six loud cracks. Heavy thumps hit the ground, men gurgling and gasping as they bled out. Another two shots, almost instantly, and a splash sounded. One of the soldiers on the dock.

"*Clear,*" Scott called softly through the radio. "*That will have attracted attention. Let's go, let's go!*"

Welby ran with Ethan and Jack, following behind the other agents into the boathouse. They kneeled around the entrance, covering every angle.

In the boathouse, Sasha fell into place beside Sergey, and Ethan saw Sergey reach for him.

"You all right?" Sergey murmured.

"*Da.*" Sasha shook, though, his whole body trembling.

Bodies lay on the boathouse deck, blood pooling beneath them. Sergey rolled one and cursed. "These are soldiers loyal to General Moroshkin. Under his direct command."

"The one who has been challenging you, stirring up discontent?" Jack knelt next to Sergey and Ethan.

Sergey nodded. He dropped the soldier's body back to the deck. "Ilya was worried about this possibility. I thought it could not happen. The days of coups are behind us, I thought. We live in a more civilized time."

Splashes sounded from the dock. Scott and Welby, together, rolled the dead Russian soldiers into the water. Scott's voice leaked from Daniels's earpiece. "*We're clear here. Bring them to the boats.*"

Agents started to file out, moving fast and covering each other as they headed down. Scott and Welby knelt dockside, aiming for the woods with rifles lifted from the dead Russian soldiers.

Ethan grabbed a rifle from the nearest fallen Russian and took the soldier's earpiece and radio transmitter as well. A thin filament stretched from his ear, and a pressure switch activated the push to talk.

Jack watched him, and then reached for a rifle and radio earpiece on another Russian. Sergey did the same, as did Sasha and Daniels.

"Let's go," Daniels breathed. "Ethan, you take Vigilant. Sasha, you and President Puchkov. I've got the rear."

Ethan crept alongside Jack, holding his rifle tight. Jack moved silently, the rifle not quite at home in his hands as it was in Ethan's. Sasha stayed with Sergey, and Daniels moved behind them all.

"Haunted House, Ghost Six." Scott spoke softly into his radio as Ethan neared, guiding Jack to crouch behind him and Scott. "We're in position at the dock. Can't move until the air is secure. What's the status on those fighters?"

"*Ghost Six, fighters on station in one mike. Hold tight. They'll clear the skies for you.*"

Gunfire raked over the dock, wood splintering as bullets hammered through the boathouse. Shots slammed into the back of Agent Hawkins.

He fell forward, into one of the speedboats. His partner jumped in after him, and the others ducked low, firing back into the woods.

"We don't have a minute!" Scott hollered into his radio. "We're taking fire!"

"Skies are not clear, Ghost Six!"

"We don't have a choice! Get in the boats! Get in!"

Agents jumped into the four speedboats along the dock. Irwin slid in with the wounded Agent Hawkins, holding pressure on his back as his partner fired into the woods. Sasha and Sergey were supposed to go in Welby's boat, but gunfire blocked their path, and Sasha hauled Sergey into the back of Jack and Ethan's.

Scott cursed and jumped on board, still firing, as Russian soldiers ran for the dock. "Go! Go!"

Ethan moved to the speedboat's control console, pushing Jack down beside him, behind the controls and out of sight. Jack rested his rifle on the speedboat's rail, firing shots from behind Ethan.

Two of the boats took off, Irwin and the wounded Hawkins in the lead.

"All agents, be advised," Scott growled into his radio as Ethan gunned the engines and roared away. Daniels, in his boat, followed close behind on Ethan's six. "Skies are not clear. Repeat, skies are not clear." He dropped opposite Jack and took aim at the dock.

Overhead, the scream of fighter jets banking broke the sky. Sasha knelt next to Sergey in the speedboat's rear tray. "MiGs," he shouted. "And at least two choppers."

Bullets sliced into the waters around the speedboat. Water rose into the air like geysers. Ethan swerved, and Jack crashed into his knees. He reached down, steadying Jack one-handed as he spun the boat, trying to evade the fighters' gunfire.

"Where's our air support?" he hollered.

"Haunted House, we're taking heavy fire!" Scott shouted into the radio. "We need air support, now!"

"Ghost Six, it's turning into a shootout at the airport. They're locking down the runways. Bringing in tanks to block our takeoff and men in position to storm the plane. We've got guys on the ground holding them off for now."

"Don't let them close that runway. Take off, now!"

"What about you? What about Vigilant and Vigor?"

"Get in the air! And get us some Goddamn air support!"

As Scott spoke, the fighters peeled off, and the roaring whirr of an attack chopper moved in. Water sprayed, caught in the rotors' backwash, and nearly blinded Ethan. A spotlight winked on, illuminating the waters dead ahead, and backlighting the ugly, harsh outline of a Russian attack chopper staring them down.

Ethan turned the boat hard, Daniels still on his tail. Everyone opened fire on the chopper as one. Bullets plinked off the metal hull, a seemingly endless stream peppering the attack helicopter. The chopper turned, following Ethan's boat with its searchlight, and then veered away.

"Everyone all right?" Scott hollered. "Mr. President?"

Two shouts of "fine" rose from both ends of the boat, Jack and Sergey speaking together.

"Two fucking presidents. My fucking luck." Scott's voice shook. "Get ready!" he shouted as the roar of fighter jets closed in again. "They're coming back!"

Instead of the MiGs screaming overhead and raining fire on their boats, four American fighter jets flew low over the sea, buzzing Ethan and Daniels. They banked hard, one launching a missile.

A whoosh and then a hiss crackled above, and white steam trailed behind the launch. Seconds later, a fireball lit over the sea, the largest firework Ethan had ever seen.

One of the attack choppers split apart in the sky.

Scott whooped. Over the radio, Haunted House chimed in. *"Fighters on station, Ghost Six. We're preparing for takeoff now with an escort."*

"That other chopper is still out there." Scott leaned into Ethan. "We've got to get across this section to the east bank. Olympic Stadium is there. We designated it the emergency site in case of a disaster."

"I'd call this a disaster."

Another missile hissed over their heads. The roar of an aerial dogfight fought between the fastest fighter jets on the planet shook the skies. Heavy guns blazed and tracers streaked through the night. Jet fuel and gunpowder choked Ethan's throat. Salt spray clung to his skin, his clothes. He reached down, blind, for Jack.

Jack gripped the back of his leg.

He turned toward the south bank as Scott radioed the other agents, ordering them to head there and form up, protecting their boats and cargo. Daniels stayed close, right in Ethan's wake.

Fifty feet from the southern bank, rotors roared overhead.

Ethan ducked, cursing, as bullets slammed into the front of their boat. He swerved, and the gunfire missed the boat's tray but took out the engines. Black smoke belched, the engine dying with a hiss and a clank.

Scott fired at the Russian chopper closing in. The boat spun, adrift and moving on the inertia of Ethan's last turn.

The chopper's guns spat bullets into the water, a long, perfect path coming right for them.

"We've got to go!" Ethan grabbed Jack, slung his rifle over his shoulder, and leaped with Jack over the side of the boat. Next to him, Scott, Sasha, and Sergey leaped as well, Sergey held Sasha tight as they jumped together.

As they jumped, Daniels gunned forward, throwing his boat in the line of fire. Fiberglass shattered on impact, exploding, and Ethan saw Daniels jump free of his boat at the last moment and into the black, frigid waters of the sea.

Jack popped up, gasping for breath and treading water. He reached for Ethan, frantic. Above, the chopper's searchlight flicked through the wreckage of both boats, Daniels's and theirs, destroyed by the chopper's guns.

"Are you all right?" Ethan grabbed Jack's face in both of his hands. "Are you okay?"

Jack nodded. Wide eyes stared at Ethan, and he gripped Ethan's soaked shirt too tight.

Splashes sounded nearby. Sasha and Sergey surfaced, Sasha hauling Sergey close, and then Scott, shaking water from his eyes. Daniels swam to their loose group.

Damn it, where did their fighters go? Had the MiGs drawn them away? They needed them, *now*, or they were all going to die. In moments, the chopper would find them in the water, and they would be an easy turkey shoot.

"Swim for the bank!" Ethan hollered. "Go!" They still had to fight their way forward. He wouldn't give up, not ever, not with Jack's life on the line. He reached for Jack's waist, pushing him through the water as Jack began a furious free stroke.

Rotors whirred overhead. The searchlight zipped right and left, flicking through the wreckage. Moments, and it would be upon them. Ethan kicked forward, surging after Jack. He'd throw his body over Jack's, shield him to his last breath. Take the bullets in his own back.

Everything stilled as he reached for Jack, sliding alongside him in the dark sea. Jack's eyes darted to his, and he stopped swimming, just reached for Ethan, water cascading down his soaked face. Ethan cupped his cheeks, pulled him close, and turned his back to the chopper, blocking Jack's view.

A hiss, and a streak of fire above.

The chopper exploded, bursting into a million shattered pieces of steel and flame. The air quaked, a shock blast pummeling them under the choppy waters of the Black Sea. Debris fell, and burning fuel stayed lit on the surface as superheated shards of metal steamed on impact, and glass sprinkled like raindrops on their heads. An American fighter zoomed over the fireball, flying straight up, engines blazing like a Fourth of July firework.

Jack smiled, a frantic, relieved laugh bursting from him. He reached for Ethan as Ethan reached for him, and they pressed their foreheads together as a wave crashed over their heads. Flaming jet fuel crackled and burned on the water around them both, but impossibly, they were alive.

"Move!" Scott shouted. "Get going!"

They swam, and when they reached the shore, Ethan shoved Jack onto the muddy riverbank first before following behind, slipping in the mud. Jack collapsed face-first in the tall grass while Scott and Daniels crept up the bank. Sasha and Sergey hovered beside them, Sasha checking Sergey over as Sergey leaned on the younger man.

"Jack? Are you okay?" Ethan leaned low over his lover, running his hands over Jack's sides and back, checking for hidden wounds. "Talk to me."

Jack opened one eye, staring up at Ethan. "You getting frisky with me?" He winked.

Ethan grinned and slapped at Jack's soaked butt. "Only you could joke right now."

He unslung his soaked rifle and tried to shake as much water off as he could. Jack pulled himself to his knees and did the same.

"How far to Olympic Stadium?" Ethan called softly to Scott.

They kneeled on the edge of a dark, empty road. The Russian military must have closed everything down for the coup. No traffic moved through the area. All the electricity was off. Sochi was like a ghost town, and pitch black.

"Two miles." Scott nodded down the riverbank. "The other boats landed three hundred yards down. They're covering for us. Let's move."

Scott took the lead, keeping low, his rifle ready. Ethan followed, one hand reaching back and holding on to Jack. Sasha and Sergey moved together, Sergey's old FSB training seeming to rise to the occasion. Daniels brought up the rear, swiveling back and forth.

"Hello, Jack."

The whole team froze, ducking low and hunkering on the edge of the road.

"We can see you, you know. Your frantic scrambling, trying to hide, is adorable. And it tells me you can hear me. Thank you for that."

Jack whirled, staring at Ethan. Madigan's voice rang in their ears, coming from the stolen earpieces taken from the dead Russian soldiers.

Scott cursed at Madigan's words, and he motioned for everyone to hide back down on the riverbank.

Madigan chuckled. "*Agent Collard's dedication is admirable but irrelevant.*"

Saucer eyes met Ethan's. Jack's lips thinned. He gripped his rifle so hard his hands shook, his knuckles ghostly white, even in the darkness.

"*You didn't expect to hear my voice during this coup. Surprise, surprise. We're everywhere.*"

Down the line, Sergey cursed.

"*The time for men like you and your puppet President Puchkov has ended, Jack. There's a new sheriff in town. A new dawn is coming. You thought you could stop us once before. How wrong you were.*"

Jack reached for his earpiece, pressing the push to talk button before Ethan could stop him. "You sick son of a bitch," he hissed. "Your new world involves slaughtering millions."

"*Sheep are often led to slaughter. It's the wolves that own the world's true nature. And just like them, humanity has a hierarchy, Jack. Has sheep and has wolves. Hunters and prey.*"

"You're mad. Absolutely mad."

"*Take a look at your lover, Jack. Take a good, hard look at Ethan Reichenbach.*"

Jack stared into Ethan's eyes.

"*What do you see? Someone you love? Someone who loves you? Or do you see a killer? A hardened predator? A wolf, trying so hard to be a good little sheep for you.*"

Ethan's blood ran cold. He held Jack's stare as silence stretched over the line.

"*He's not that different from me when you get down to it.*"

"Fuck you. You don't know anything about him."

"*Oh, on the contrary, Jack.*" Madigan laughed again, slowly. "*He's the exact same as us. It must be you who's keeping him sane. I wonder, what will happen to him when you're gone?*"

Ethan's heart stopped.

"*It's not him I want to talk with you about, though. You see, I have something for you. It's waiting, right here at Olympic Stadium. Yes, I know where you're headed.*"

Scott cursed. He spoke low into his mic, calling for backup and an update on the agents down the road.

"*I have a gift for you. Something that's no longer useful to me, but I think will be very useful to you.*"

"Fuck you, Madigan." Snarling, Ethan pushed on his mic. He turned it off and threw it into the water as soon as he was done. Jack did the same.

Sirens bellowed down the road, beyond Olympic Stadium. Overhead, the fighters roared, zipping away from the sea.

"We have to move," Ethan grunted. "Now."

"There's a V-22 inbound. Headed for the stadium to pick us up." Scott listened to his Secret Service earpiece and then managed an exhausted, wan grin. "Sochi police forces are firing on the military blockades around the stadium. They're fighting back against the coup."

"My people would not give up their country easily," Sergey growled. "I must get to those men. I must help them."

"Be on the lookout," Ethan hefted his rifle up, propping it against his shoulder, his finger half clenched around the trigger. "Madigan is watching." Beside him, Jack hovered close, close enough that the warmth from his body bled into Ethan and he could feel the expansion of Jack's ribs as he breathed in and out.

Together they crept forward, moving fast on the riverbank and staying off the road. Mud slipped beneath their shoes, and river weeds caught on their soaked dress pants and the untucked ends of their button-downs. Dress shoes and business suits weren't the tactical gear for the moment, but it was what they had.

In minutes, they met up with the other team of agents. Irwin had Agent Hawkins's arm draped over his shoulder, helping him to walk. The others crept on either side of the road, guns at the ready.

Olympic Stadium loomed large, dark like a claw rising from the earth. Gunshots peppered the night, alongside flashing red and blue lights.

"Hold!" Scott raised his fist. Everyone dropped down on both sides of the road.

Standing in the middle of the street, facing them, a man stood in the shadows, his dark outline barely visible.

He had a hostage, gripping someone in a tight headlock with a heavy blade to their throat. The hostage had a black hood over their head and wore a bulky jumpsuit.

"American president!" the man shouted in a thickly accented voice. "I know you're out there! I—"

Rising from the riverbank, Ethan fired. His bullet flew slammed into the center of the man's forehead and cut off whatever he was about to say.

He fell backward, dead. His blade clattered to the ground.

His hostage collapsed, unmoving.

"Go," Scott ordered the team forward. Ethan held back with Jack, creeping ahead only when one of the agents kicked the blade far out of reach and patted down the hostage, ripping open the jumpsuit to check for explosives.

Scott ripped the hood off the hostage.

He froze. Whirled back to Ethan and Jack.

Jack peered at the crowd of agents, squinting, trying to see.

Agent Beech turned his flashlight down into the hostage's face for a better look. Beside him, other agents frowned, casting confused looks back toward Ethan and Jack.

Legs in dark suit pants blocked their view.

Finally, Ethan's gaze landed on the hostage's face.

His heart stopped.

Beneath Agent Beech's flashlight, Leslie Spiers winced and shied away from the light.

Jack took off with a strangled gasp, running at top speed toward her. Cursing, Ethan followed, shouting at him to wait.

Jack ignored him, sliding to a stop on his knees on the asphalt next to his long-dead wife, suddenly not dead, suddenly breathing fast and panicking and trying to fight off the agents patting her down and working to restrain her. She kicked, shrieking, and swung her fists.

"Les! Les!" Jack reached for her, grabbing her shoulders and turning her toward him. "Les, it's me. It's Jack."

Leslie froze. Beneath her matted hair, sticky with mud and dried blood, her gaze flicked up. A filthy face turned to Jack, trembling. Her hands—one curled and disfigured, burned and blackened—reached for him.

"Jack?" she breathed. Her eyes darted over Jack's face. "*Jack*? How— What—"

"Mr. President, we have to move!" Scott tugged on Jack's arm, trying to get him to stand.

Jack shook him off. His gaze was fixed on Leslie, his eyes filling with tears. "How are you alive?" he whispered. "I thought you were dead."

"*President*?" she gasped. "Jack?"

"Mr. President!" Scott snapped. "We have to go! *Now!*"

Overhead, a V-22 Osprey circled Olympic Stadium and started its descent on the street, yards away from their position. A floodlight lit up their huddle. The Osprey's gunner sprayed bullets at Russian soldiers taking shots at them. Farther down the road, a Russian jeep burst into flames.

Scott and the other agents ducked over Jack and Leslie, shielding them from the Osprey's rotors and its VSTOL jet engines. Road grit flew, peppering their faces. Ethan spat out asphalt and tried to shield his eyes.

"Go, now, now!" Scott waved his men forward as the Osprey touched down and the crew piled off, covering for the agents.

"Jack—" Ethan leaned in and tried to reach for Leslie.

"I've got her!" Jack snapped. "I've fucking got her!" He wrapped his arms under Leslie and stood, cradling her close to his chest. Scott ran Jack to the Osprey with Irwin, leaving Ethan behind.

Ethan stared.

He watched Jack gently carry Leslie over and hand her to the flight medic kneeling on board. Watched Jack brush the matted hair from her face. Watched him smile a wavering, watery smile at her and watched Leslie smile back at him.

Time slowed, stretched. He felt every beat of his heart.

Sergey and Sasha knelt at his side, silent.

"Time to go!" Daniels shouted over the roar of the Osprey. "We have to get out of here!"

Then Jack turned and jogged back to them, and Ethan could breathe again. His eyes tracked Jack, every step, every footfall.

Jack never looked his way.

He crouched in front of Sergey, instead. "We're headed for Turkey. We can take you, too. Give you political asylum."

"No." Sergey shook his head. "No, Jack, I have to stay. I have to fight for Russia." Nearby, police sirens wailed; the gunfight between the police and the Russian military was getting closer. "I have to help my people."

"Sergey, that's suicide—"

"Yes, Jack. Maybe. But I will die the right way." He reached for Jack's shoulders. "Go. Get out of here. Save yourself." He turned to Sasha. "Sasha, you should go, too. You should save yourself—"

"No." Sasha glared at Sergey. "I will stay with you."

Jack grasped Sergey's elbows. His face twisted, anguish and bitter fury warring for dominance. "I'll do *everything* I can for you. Everything."

Sergey nodded. he released Jack. Sasha at his side, he ran for the darkness on the side of the road and took cover from the Osprey and her imminent takeoff.

"Jack." Ethan reached for his lover.

Jack stepped back, out of Ethan's reach. "Let's go." Turning, Jack jogged back to the Osprey.

He never looked at Ethan.

Daniels ran with Ethan as the police sirens wailed, getting closer. Gunfire peppered the asphalt behind him, kicking up sprays of concrete and tar. He stumbled as the world moved in slow motion, sounds fading away, bleeding into a deafening, all-consuming roar. His vision narrowed, the world going dark aside from the pinpoint of perfect clarity that saw Jack climbing into the Osprey and reaching for Leslie, pulling her into his arms.

Reality snapped back as Scott hauled him into the Osprey, clasping his hand and hefting him up. "Here we go," Scott grunted, setting Ethan down on the opposite bulkhead from Jack. Scott kneeled in front of him, blocking his vision. "Are you with me? You with us?"

Daniels collapsed beside Welby and Hanier. Ethan blinked. The Osprey's VSTOL engines roared, pushing them in a vertical climb over the erupting gun battle in front of Olympic Stadium. Below, Sergey hunkered down with Sasha, firing at Moroshkin's forces, and then ran toward the line of police vehicles and their strobing lights.

Scott grabbed the handholds on either side of Ethan. Over Scott's shoulder, Ethan spotted Jack holding tight to Leslie, his face buried in the curve of her neck, his eyes clenched tight. Tears poured from the corners of Jack's eyes.

He still wouldn't look at Ethan.

Ethan grabbed his rifle and took up position at the open cargo door. He scanned the ground, scanned the skies, and tried to crush his wailing heart. Roaring drowned out the world, the engines mimicking the sound of his soul. His vision blurred, and each breath came harder than the last. Had he been shot? Or was this just his heart cracking in half? Was this what it felt like to die? Or just to wish he was dead?

No. It was going to be all right. This was shock, surprise, desperation. Adrenaline, and crazed emotions.

He and Jack loved each other.

But Jack had loved Leslie, too, and he'd never fallen out of love with her. She'd just been ripped away from him, and an unanswered question hovered in Jack's life: what if?

Holy God, what if?

Russian Parliament Leveled In Coup: Martial Law Declared

Russian General Moroshkin executed a successful coup over President Puchkov's government last night, while President Spiers was in Russia. The presidents were at the state retreat in Sochi, which was targeted during the attack before the Secret Service managed to rescue President Spiers from the unfolding coup.

Some districts in Russia have resisted Moroshkin's coup, including the Siberian and the Far Eastern federal districts. Southwestern Russia and the Krais around Sochi have also violently resisted the coup, and there are reports of an insurgency forming in the Caucasus. President Puchkov's last known whereabouts were in Sochi, but no details have emerged since. Presently, it is unknown whether deposed President Puchkov is alive or dead.

General Kuznetsov was found shot to death outside Sochi. The head of the FSB, Ilya Ivchenko, a close friend of President Puchkov, remains at large.

38

Air Force One

"Yes, I worked for Madigan."

On Air Force One, over the skies of Turkey, Leslie spoke softly as she lay on the gurney in the medical suite. Monitors beeped beside her, jagged lines in reds and blues set against black screens. An IV went into one nearly emaciated arm. The other was a disfigured, charred, and grotesque mess that she kept hidden beneath a thin sheet.

She was older than her pictures on the mantel. She'd aged, like they all had. Her wrinkles were a little deeper, her skin a little more wan. Sixteen years of deprivation and torture?

Jack perched on a wheeled stool, leaning forward, his hands steepled, covering his mouth like he was too shocked to speak. He'd been frozen like that since he sat down, his gaze locked on to Leslie. He was in sweats and a white undershirt, and mud still clung in clumps to his hair.

Irwin had changed and washed his face and had run a wet comb through his hair at some point. He still looked like career DC, his gray fluffy hair combed to the side, wearing a pair of khakis—wrinkled—and a pullover. He leaned against the medical suite's counter, arms crossed.

And Ethan stood in the back, watching Jack watch Leslie as his mind stuttered to a halt and refused to work. Refused to process anything beyond the sheer devastation bleeding from Jack. His lover was in agony, and Ethan could feel it, could feel his anguish choking him, even from across the room.

It was the first time they were in the same place since the evacuation.

Jack had carried Leslie off the Osprey, refusing the medics who met them on the flight line at Incirlik. Air Force One waited across the tarmac, fueled and ready to scream back to the United States as the world fell apart around them.

Jack took Leslie to the medical suite onboard, but was pushed out by the doctor and her nurses.

Ethan sat in the conference room in a soaked, muddy daze, and Daniels and Scott stayed at his side.

Later, they were all called back to see her.

"I worked for him in Iraq." She sent Jack a thin smile. "I was recruited through Jeff to work with him, after my unit was attached to his for interrogations. It was deep black. I couldn't say anything to you."

Back then, Jack was a small-time attorney practicing in Austin, and he'd never once thought of becoming the president. Ethan knew Jack's history almost better than he knew his own.

He watched the memories crash through Jack, his shoulders trembling beneath his stretched-tight T-shirt.

And to top it all off, Leslie had been recruited through Jeff Gottschalk, Jack's once-friend and deepest betrayal.

"I didn't know what I was really getting into," she said softly. Her thin fingers picked at the white cotton sheet, tugging on a frayed string. "And then, my unit was attacked." Her gaze rose. Her eyes met Jack's.

A heavy tear hovered at the corner of Jack's eye. He blinked, and it cascaded down his cheek.

Ethan looked down. Stared at the dark corrugated decking.

"I don't remember much of the beginning. They say I was in a coma for the first six years." She shrugged.

By then, Jack was a Senator in Texas's legislature and was already making a name for himself. Ethan swallowed hard.

"When I woke up, Major—I mean, General Madigan—came. He told me how they'd taken me and used the most advanced medical care in the world on me. That I was lucky to be alive. I was so grateful." She smiled, and a tear fell down her thin, pale cheeks. "I thought I was going home. That I was about to see you again."

Jack closed his eyes.

"And then," she croaked, "he told me how much time had passed. How everyone thought I was dead. How I couldn't ever go back."

"Why?" Irwin frowned. "Why did he keep you captive?"

"You never worked for him. You can't understand." Leslie shook her head. "Madigan makes the whole world revolve around him. He is his own god. When you work for him, you're just thankful for the opportunity to breathe the same air as him. I was *alive* because of him. But I couldn't walk. I was a corpse on a bed and he had my life in his hands. How could I ask for more than what he was giving me?"

Jack's eyes fluttered open. More tears spilled over his cheeks.

Irwin's frown deepened.

Leslie took a deep, steadying breath. "I still had some of my skills. Was still fluent in a couple of Arabic dialects. Still knew more than was probably reasonable about interrogations. I was useful to him, and I was happy to be useful. I was so happy." She looked away, into the middle distance. "For years, I provided translations of secret records. Bitten-off conversations. Things obtained without any legal grounding. I learned to walk again. Watched interrogations at black sites on video. Started offering advice on how to do better. How to break terrorists and jihadis faster." She shrugged. "I'm not a hero. But it was how I survived."

Tears rained down Jack's cheeks, tiny drops that crashed to the deck.

"When I realized that some of his plans were targeting Americans..." She trailed off. "I had my suspicions. I tried to investigate. And what I found—" She shook her head. "I tried to fight back. Tried to argue. I was punished." She almost smiled, but it fractured and she bit her lip. "He was done with me. I thought I was dead. I thought I was being taken out to be killed. I'd seen it before."

She smiled, a happy, dazzling smile, as she gazed at Jack. Her teeth were aged and one was cracked, but joy radiated from her, illuminating her. "I couldn't believe it when I saw you," she whispered. "I still can't. And," she laughed breathlessly, her eyes wide. "The *president*? Jack..." Pride shone bright from her gaze. "I knew you were made for greatness."

Jack heaved a ragged breath between his steepled fingers as he squeezed his eyes shut again. Tears raced down his eyelashes, pooled at the corners of his eyes, and dripped from his fingers.

"You didn't know he was the president?" Irwin's frown had turned into a scowl.

"I was kept insulated from any media. I lived in tin cans, isolated with others. We were our own world. And, I was okay with that." She shrugged. "I couldn't ever rejoin the world, so I didn't want to know what I was missing."

"Others?" Irwin stood, his gaze flicking to Ethan. "There were others like you?"

"Yes. He had others he saved from the grave. Others he kept around for his dirty work."

Ethan closed his eyes. Noah Williams and the others they'd tried to track across Europe and into Russia. They truly were ghosts, echoes of a twisted path born from Madigan's deranged mind.

The silence lingered in the air, heavy and rancid.

"Mr. President." Irwin reached out and gently touched Jack's shoulder. "We need to speak privately."

Jack didn't move. Ethan watched him inhale, exhale, and inhale again, his shoulders shuddering. Mud clung to his elbow, to the curve of his bicep, flaking to dust with every tiny shake of his body. He stared at Leslie.

Stared at his wife.

Ethan's stomach curdled. He looked down, looked away. He didn't want to watch this. Didn't want to see their eyes lock and hold, didn't want to see the brutalized agony lancing through Jack. Didn't want to see the hero worship bleeding from Leslie, awestruck as she watched her husband, the president of the United States.

Slowly, Jack stood, his bones seeming to creak and break at the joints as he unfolded from his perch on the stool. He stared at Leslie. "I'll be back," he whispered. "I promise."

"I'll be here," she said, grinning lopsidedly before her smile vanished and a shadow of fear fell over her bright eyes again. Her arms crossed, her deformed limb still hidden under the sheet, and she sucked a chapped, cracked lip into her mouth.

He couldn't watch this. Couldn't be there for this. Ethan pushed out of the medical suite first, holding his breath until he hit the hallway. His lungs heaved, gasping the recycled, dry air of the plane. The medical suite smelled like death and dust, like history and anguish and aching regret.

Two agents stood guard outside the suite. Ethan could feel their eyes boring holes into his back, curiosity mixed with horror. The sick fascination of watching a disaster unfold before them.

What now? hung in the air.

Ethan headed for Jack's office without waiting for him. He heard Irwin's low voice and two pairs of tired feet shuffling down the hallway, but he stayed out of sight, slipping into the office and sitting on the edge of the couch opposite Jack's desk.

The couch where they had made out so many times. He'd cradled Jack close, kissed his neck above his collar. Pushed him down and pressed their bodies together. Stared at Jack's laughing face in wonder, basking in his love.

The door slid open. Jack shuffled in. He headed straight for his desk, his red-rimmed eyes downcast. His nose was rubbed raw on the edges and a line of wetness on his arm betrayed the snot he'd wiped away.

Irwin glanced at Ethan and sighed. He stood in front of Jack as Jack collapsed in his desk chair.

They were like points of a terrible triangle, opposing values in lines that would take them all apart. The gulf between him and Jack suddenly felt chasms wide, far wider than the five feet that truly separated them. He wanted to stand, wanted to go to Jack. Run his hands through Jack's hair, wrap his arms around his waist, bury his face in the back of Jack's neck, and just know—*know*—that everything was going to be all right.

He didn't know, though. Uncertainty tasted like terror.

He gripped his hands into fists. His nails bit into his skin. He stayed right where he was.

Silence stretched through the office, thick like the cloying pall of a funeral. Something was dying, and Ethan didn't want to look too closely at what. He could sense it, though. Smell it, even. The stink of despair and terror hitting the back of his throat.

Irwin broke first, speaking with a roughened voice. "Mr. President… we have so much to discuss."

Jack blinked and stared at the surface of his desk.

"General Moroshkin has taken Russia. He parked tanks outside the federal legislature in Moscow and leveled the parliament building. Forces loyal to him have secured military sites around the country. His coup has been successful. There are pockets of resistance forming, but…" He trailed off.

Sergey was out there somewhere, trying to fight back. Him and Sasha, left with what remained of the Sochi police forces, vastly outnumbered. Ethan's head dipped. *I'll never see them again.*

"Director Rees is gone." Irwin swallowed. "He was killed in the first strike on the retreat. Six Secret Service agents were killed as well. We're trying to figure out how to repatriate their remains and bring them home."

Ethan's jaw clenched so hard he swore he felt his bones break. Those men were his friends, his family. Men he'd laughed and drank with. Men he'd trusted and who had trusted him in return. And now they were gone. So many agents, gone.

Fury sizzled against his soul.

"Deputy Director Olivia Mori at the CIA is being briefed now. She'll meet us when we land in Washington."

Jack nodded slowly, his lips pressed into a hard, thin line.

"We need to discuss our options, Mr. President. General Moroshkin and Madigan now have under their control the full arsenal of Russia's nuclear weapons, and their conventional stockpiles as well. Control over their military forces. Madigan just went from a stateless terrorist to a major player within the world's largest nuclear power." Irwin's eyes narrowed as Jack stayed silent. "Mr. President. We *need* you. Now."

Jack's gaze flicked to Irwin. Fury burst from him, cold in the depths of his eyes. "What do you need from me, Lawrence?" he growled. "Someone to say yes? Someone to nod? I'm not very good at anything else. I don't come up with any grand plans as president. I haven't done anything meaningful except fuck up the world! Fuck up everything I ever touch! My *grand* legacy!" His hands flew wide as he jumped to his feet. "I'm not very good at being what anyone *needs*," he hissed. "My wife *needed* me. And look what I did!"

A thousand blades sliced through Ethan's back, burying in the center of his heart. His lungs seized, not a single whisper of air moving through him.

"I wasn't there for her!" Jack hissed again, his voice trembling. "Sixteen years…"

Irwin looked Jack dead in the eyes. "Mr. President, we have to be objective about Mrs. Spiers's return."

Jack's jaw dropped.

"She spoke of others. Other people Madigan kept alive while the world thought they were dead. We've run into several of these individuals throughout our mission against Madigan. At every turn, they were working *against* us. Working *for* Madigan." Irwin squared his shoulders and raised his chin. "We have to consider the possibility that Mrs. Spiers's loyalties are *not* what they appear. Who knows what Madigan has done to her? What kind of psychological experiences he subjected her to. Sixteen years is a long time."

Ruby rage flooded Jack's skin, colored his cheeks bloody. Veins bulged from his neck, pounding fast and furious. "Lawrence—" he growled.

"Mr. President, you are not objective—"

"Damn it!" Jack shouted, slamming his palm flat on his desk. "Leave my wife to me!"

"Jack! You're *too* close to this!"

"I'm *not* abandoning her again!" Jack roared, leaning across his desk and bellowing into Irwin's face. "I will *never* abandon her! I failed her already! I won't again! Not after—" His voice broke, and he clamped his mouth shut, his jaw trembling.

Irwin's gaze slid sideways, again, to Ethan.

Ethan closed his eyes.

Jack leaned forward, his hands flat on his desk, and hung his head between his shoulders. "Lawrence," he choked out. "I can't *do* this. Not right now. I need *you* to do what you do best. Bring me options. Options I can say yes to."

Irwin's soft exhale seemed overloud in the silent office. "Yes, Mr. President." This time, he didn't look at Ethan. "Excuse me. I'm sure you two have much to discuss."

Turning, Irwin slipped out. He closed the door behind him, a soft *snik* almost shattering the world.

Ethan's hands slicked with sweat. Frantic, panicked sweat, like a caged animal leaking terrified stink every which way. His heart was beating too fast, far too fast, and he was dangerously close to hyperventilating through his nose. He tried to calm down, tried to breathe slower, but the walls were closing in, the same beige bulkheads of Air Force One he'd leaned against with Jack, watching the sunrise over—

Squeezing his eyes shut didn't stop the memories. There was a hollow emptiness to it, though, the memory tinged with the taste of fear.

Would he ever have those moments again?

His heart ached, burning like a fresh-picked scab with nothing new underneath.

"Jack," he tried. His voice was steady, at least. He'd learned how to hide that much. "Jack…" He licked his lips. "What—"

What happens now? What happened back there? What are you thinking? What do you want? What do we do?

What are we now?

"What can I do?" he said instead, turning and looking at Jack. He held his heart in the palm of his hands, an offering to his love. "What can I do for you?"

Jack closed his eyes. He shook his head slowly, back and forth. "Turn back time? Make it so I never abandoned her?"

If you went back in time and stayed with her, we would never be together.

Ice flooded through his veins, collecting and building at all the junctures of his soul, the places where he'd nurtured dreams of him and Jack. His lungs seized again, like he'd jumped into a frozen lake too suddenly, but it wasn't his body that was turning to ice. It was his soul. Clawing panic rose within him, the desperation of survival.

"You didn't abandon her—"

"She's alive, and I'm—" Jack bit off his words with a harsh swallow.

"You thought she was dead. Everyone did. You buried her, Jack—"

"I never got a body," Jack breathed. His eyes were still closed; he was facing the door, angled away from Ethan. Ethan couldn't see his whole face, couldn't even see all of him. Jack wouldn't turn his way. "I should have pushed harder. Should have… demanded an inquiry. It was so strange, how she died. The report I got. The building she was in, it blew, they said. Vaporized everyone and everything. But there weren't any other details. No mission report, no copies of orders she'd received. The nameless battle of an exploding building. God, the dates on the death certificate didn't even match the DOD letter." A helpless, panicked laugh turned into a sob, and Jack ground his teeth together, struggling through his words. "I thought it was just standard Army bureaucratic mistakes."

"I would have thought the same thing." Should he stand? Should he go to Jack? Try to hold him? Could he survive if Jack rebuffed him? "No one ever would imagine that this had happened. It's not even in the realm of possibility."

"But it did happen!" Jack snapped. His furious eyes flashed once to Ethan and then away. "It *did* happen, and I didn't even try to help her." A sob caught in Jack's chest. He breathed deep, half caught in a mourner's wail. "I didn't help my wife."

That word again, grating over Ethan's soul.

Another choked moan, a restrained wail, and Jack's shoulders trembled as his hands gripped his desk edge.

Fuck it all. Ethan stood, and his aching heart led him to Jack with open arms.

"Jack."

He got as far as the desk. Jack shied away from him, jerking away, his eyes squeezed shut.

Ethan's soul shrieked, that frantic panic back full force. He was losing this conversation, losing Jack, losing everything. It all just kept slipping through his fingers, and he had no idea how to grab hold. Like trying to grasp water in a fist and hold on forever. Instead, he was drowning, sinking beneath the glaciers forming over his heart.

"What do we do?" he whispered. "Jack? What do we do?"

Without opening his eyes, Jack turned away, hiding his face. Silence hung in the air, the sting of it like a serrated blade slicing across Ethan's heart.

There was no *we* anymore.

He took a step back, and then another.

Slowly, Jack unclenched, no longer holding himself back from Ethan, on guard against him.

Never, ever, had Jack shied away from him. Tried to escape from him.

It felt like a slap to his soul.

"I, uhh—" Jack swallowed, and he edged around his desk, not looking at Ethan. "I need to be with my wife." He swallowed a tiny whimper. "I'm sorry," he whispered. "But I need to help her. She's my *wife*. And I abandoned her once already. I can't—"

A weight pressed against Ethan's thigh, hanging in his pocket. A small box, and within it, a fragile hope. He'd dreamed that one day Jack would call him his, that he would be Jack's "my husband."

The glaciers moving over his soul slipped into his heart, covering all the spaces where Jack had lived, where he'd breathed life and love and bright laughter into Ethan. His heart closed, a block of solid ice clenched tight in his chest.

It felt worse than death. Like dying would be an improvement.

"I understand. I won't interfere," he whispered. "I won't cause any problems."

"I'm so sorry. I'm so, so sorry." Jack's voice shook, but he still wouldn't look at Ethan. He headed for the door, his eyes fixed to the blue carpet.

Jack was going to leave, going to walk out that door and not look back, and that would be it. That would be the end. There wasn't anything he could say; no magic words would fix this, would undo the impact of Jack's wife coming back from the dead.

He couldn't watch. Ethan turned away, and through the roar of blood screaming through his veins, through the wails of his frozen heart, he heard the slide of Jack's door open and then shut again.

The next moments passed in a blur. One breath, and he was in their cabin, pulling his ratty duffel out from the valet. Tugging free his dress shirts from the hangers the stewards had arranged for him. Grabbing his toothbrush, his razor, his deodorant. Piling everything on top of each other, a mess of wrinkled clothes and smeared soap. In moments, it looked like he'd never been there, had never been a part of Jack's life.

The slide of the cabin door as he left was too loud. The lights in the hallway too bright.

He made it to the Secret Service compartment in the forward cabin, lured by Scott's baritone and the voices of the other agents speaking softly about the attack and their fallen comrades.

He shouldn't intrude. He shouldn't be there, shouldn't be interrupting. He hung back and squeezed the strap of his duffel in his fist.

"Clear the room," Scott said. "Everyone go get some rest. Charlie team, you're lead when we land." Nods and murmurs rose, and the agents filed out, heading for the sleepers with worn and weary faces.

Scott was in front of him, suddenly, his face haggard and wan. Crow's feet lined with dried mud and hair that stuck up every which way. "Ethan?"

He shook his head, slow jerks back and forth that built until his body was shaking, and he couldn't hold Scott's gaze any longer. "It's over," he grunted, staring down at Scott's ruined dress shoes and his mud-splattered suit pants. "We're over."

Scott exhaled, and strong hands guided him into Scott's—once Ethan's—onboard office. It wasn't fancy, but there was a simple desk with

Scott's open laptop and two chairs sitting before it. Scott guided him toward one, a hand on his elbow.

And then it all came out, Ethan's legs buckling like he didn't have bones, and he crashed to the deck on his knees. His hands rose, covering his face as he pitched forward, a soundless scream caught in the hollows of his chest. Scott went to the deck with him and pulled Ethan against his filthy shirt. His arms wrapped around Ethan's shoulders, holding him tight as Ethan screamed into Scott's chest, wailed into his friend's body. A nuke had gone off in his chest, in the center of his heart, and he was dying. He knew he was dying.

He kept his face hidden, clinging to Scott. His world had just upended and his soul felt like it was peeling away and all he wanted was to disappear. Fade away into nothing, silence the screaming in his mind.

If he let go of Scott, maybe he would. Maybe he'd collapse into pieces, shatter apart, like his life had just collapsed.

Scott held on to him for the entire flight.

Ethan stayed with Scott on Air Force One until the plane touched down at Andrews, and Charlie team got the president, Leslie, and the staff into the convoy and back to the White House.

Daniels wandered back to Scott's office when the plane was empty. "Everyone's gone. I've got a car outside."

Dried salt tracks cracked on Ethan's cheeks when he sat up. Scott groaned as he stood, but he kept hold of Ethan, one hand on his elbow. They made their way off the plane, Daniels and Scott bracketing Ethan all the way to the waiting SUV at the base of the stairs. Daniels took the driver's seat, and Scott and Ethan slid into the back.

Numb, Ethan collapsed against the black leather. Scott wordlessly buckled him in, reaching around and pulling the seatbelt over his shoulder.

He closed his eyes, fighting against the rising agony. Damn it, he didn't want to cry again. He'd cried more than he ever had before, until it felt like his soul had come undone.

And Scott had stayed through every tear. Was still there, right beside him.

Tears still leaked from his clenched eyes and slid down his cheeks, dripping from his jaw.

Scott mumbled something to Daniels, giving directions, and then leaned back again with a heavy sigh. His body pressed against Ethan from shoulder to knee, a solid wall of support.

Except, his thigh pressed on the velvet box Ethan still had in his pocket. Ethan pulled it out, turning it over and over in his hands. The velvet was muddy and one corner was torn and frayed. Salt lines had dried over the dark fabric, the Black Sea leaving its mark.

Scott hissed as he saw what Ethan was playing with. "Jesus, Ethan."

Ethan flicked open the lid.

Dirty water stained the white silk and the neat folds were rumpled and pulled out of place. But, still tucked in the center, still gleaming, were the two rings Ethan had designed. Rings he'd dreamed would one day rest on both his and Jack's left hands.

"Jack," he whispered to the hum of the car. "Would you have married me?"

Scott reached over and pressed the lid closed, tangling his fingers around Ethan's and holding their hands in a tight fist around the box. Ethan let the car's rumbling push and pull his limp body.

His mind played over all the different ways he'd imagined asking Jack to marry him. Each was a stake through the heart, but he kept going, examining everything he'd dreamed, everything he'd imagined.

He had to remember. He had to keep everything real, hold on like it was something that had existed. Something that meant everything to him, instead of the nothing he'd been left with, the emptiness that had flooded his heart.

He felt lost in a surreal painting, as if the sparkling sunshine and spring colors were bleeding around him, melting from the world like the slide of his soul, descending into numbness and nothing. The car accelerated and an oak smeared to gray, leaving a puddle of green blood on the concrete. Flowers wept and the black asphalt beneath their tires seemed to wail, a constant shriek as they rolled ever onward.

Maybe he was just losing it. Maybe heartbreak was what would kill him in the end, wreck his world until he just couldn't take it any longer.

They pulled into Scott's driveway almost an hour later. Scott whispered to Daniels, and then Daniels drove off while Ethan followed Scott into his house.

"Liz and Stacy aren't home. Stacy took Liz to her mother's house for… a while." Scott rubbed his eyes. "Thought you should have some peace and quiet until—"

Ethan blocked out Scott's last words. He couldn't go there, not yet. "Liz graduates this year, right?" Once, Ethan had been like an uncle to Liz, going over almost every other week. Now he wondered if she was graduating high school this year or next.

"Yeah." Scott sighed. "She's refusing to go to college though." Scowling, he jerked his head to a pair of double doors to the left of the front door. "In there."

Scott's study, done in oak hardwood and dark brown leather, greeted them. Ethan tossed his duffel down at the foot of the leather couch and collapsed in the center.

"I couldn't take you to your place." Scott headed to the back wall, opening cupboards. "It's locked up, and the media will be camping at your condo after this anyway. Hopefully they stay the hell away from here." He trudged back with two tumblers and a bottle of whiskey and set them down on the low table in front of the couch. He popped the seal and poured four fingers in each glass, sliding one to Ethan before he sat beside him with a groan.

"You told me it would end like this," Ethan said softly. He cradled the tumbler in his hands, rolling the glass back and forth in his palms.

"No. I said he wouldn't want to take the chance. But then he did, and it was good. Goddamn, you guys were real good. I liked seeing you happy." His mouth pursed as he shook his head. "Whoever could have thought *this* bullshit would happen?" Scott gulped down the whiskey.

"I was always afraid he'd leave me for a woman one day. My biggest fucking fear."

"He wouldn't have left you for *any* woman." Scott smiled sadly, agonizingly. "Except for this one."

Ethan pressed his lips together, his chin resting on his chest as he felt the shape of Scott's words, felt their impact shatter within his frozen heart. Only this one woman. Only this one, who had been buried and mourned for and was out of Jack's life.

And now not.

"*This.*" He pointed to nothing, squinting. "This is why I never, ever wanted a relationship. I never wanted to fall in love." He threw the glass back, swallowing everything in one gulp. "It's the being ripped out of love that will kill you."

Scott slid the bottle of whiskey toward him and downed the rest of his tumbler as well.

A couple of hours later, Daniels walked through the front door loaded down with shopping bags. Scott was passed out cold on the couch, his cheek on Ethan's shoulder.

Ethan stared at the two rings in the palm of his hand, silent tears cascading rivers of salt down his cheeks.

39

Moscow
The Kremlin

Madigan toasted Moroshkin, crystal tumblers of the finest Russian vodka clinking against one another beneath a gold-gilt chandelier in the president's suite.

"General." Madigan dipped his head, smiling at Moroshkin. "Welcome home."

Moroshkin beamed. His mustache gave a happy twitch as he settled back. "We did it. Russia is mine."

"And now it's time for *my* plans to unfold." Madigan held Moroshkin's gaze as he slowly drained his vodka, never blinking. "In return for my help in getting you here."

Moroshkin's eyes narrowed. "Will you finally tell me what it is you're planning? What you want with my sub and ships?"

"For now, we wait. Once we receive the signal, then it will be time to act." Leaning back, Madigan threw both his arms out along former President Puchkov's sofa. "Enjoy your victory, General," he purred. "You have earned this."

Captain Leslie Spiers Recovered Alive in Russia. President Spiers And White House Keeping Quiet About Ethan Reichenbach

Stunning news emerged from the White House after President Spiers's return from Russia following the coup that ousted his friend and ally, President Sergey Puchkov. Captain Leslie Spiers, President Spiers's deceased wife, was found alive in Russia in the midst of the coup.

The White House hasn't released any details about how or where she was recovered, only saying that she is in fair condition, suffering from the effects of neglect and suspected torture, and is recovering at the White House. Captain Leslie Spiers was reported killed in action sixteen years ago during the Iraq War.

There has been no statement so far on the status of the first gentleman, Ethan Reichenbach, but White House observers state that he did not accompany the president or Mrs. Spiers back to the White House following their return from Russia.

40

Jeddah, Saudi Arabia

Prince Abdul insisted that his nephew go to his seaside villa in Jeddah to rest and recuperate when he was allowed to leave the hospital, and that Adam had to accompany him.

Adam stood stiffly at Faisal's bedside, trying to pour respect into the width of his stance, the spread of his shoulders, and the way he consciously unclenched his hands. That the crown prince would even allow him to speak with Faisal, much less begrudgingly allow them to be together, was almost too much.

Once, Prince Abdul's bodyguards had burst in on them, and they had thrown Adam through the plate glass windows of Faisal's Persian Gulf bedroom. He'd landed in a naked skid on the scorched sand outside of Dammam.

Sending them to Jeddah—the Kingdom's loosest city, though that wasn't saying much—meant so much more than his gruff words conveyed.

"You will assist him in his recovery and in his healing." Prince Abdul fixed Adam with a hard glare. "You will be at his side for anything he desires. He will want for nothing. You will care for him as if he is your blood. As if you are family."

Adam bowed his head. "Yes, Your Royal Highness. The prince is more dear to me than my family."

A gruff hum was his only response.

On the far side of the room, Doc leaned against the wall, watching silently. He'd stayed clear of Adam as Adam camped in Faisal's room. He'd sat through rounds of bone growth stimulation treatments, knitting his ribs together with the Saudi royals' equipment.

They left in a convoy of armored SUVs that sped them to the airport and boarded Prince Abdul's glittering executive jet. Two hours later, they touched down in Jeddah, where a fresh SUV was waiting for them. Adam, Faisal, and Doc piled into the back of the vehicle, two stony and silent bodyguards up front.

Silence reigned as Adam held Faisal close and Doc stared out the window. Eventually, they pulled into the private drive leading to Faisal's beachfront villa, perched on stilts over a boulder-strewn section of the beach and extending over the gently-lapping Red Sea. Waves burbled beneath the stilts and under the wide deck wrapping around the house and stretching into the turquoise waters. For over a mile on either side of the villa, empty sand bled away, pristine.

When they entered, Doc whistled as he walked in a circle around the villa's bright open layout, white walls and white furniture everywhere. He stared out the wall of two-story glass windows overlooking the water and the deck.

Adam walked slower with Faisal, holding his lover close and helping him through the villa to the master suite that stretched over the water, walls of windows refracting the waves into the bedroom. "There are more rooms upstairs. Go pick one out for yourself."

"Been here before, then?"

Adam nodded and looked away.

He hovered over Faisal as his lover slid back into bed. Their trip had been long, and almost too much for his still-early recovery. Faisal plucked at one of his laptops while Adam grabbed a bottle of water and a cool washcloth and fluffed the pillows behind his lover's back while Faisal watched him with a smile.

His smile disappeared, though, as he stared at his laptop. "Adam." Spinning it around, he showed Adam the breaking news headline scrolling across the screen. *Russian Military Coup Successful. General Moroshkin and Hardline Supporters in Control of Russian Government. President Puchkov's Whereabouts Unknown.*

Adam leaned in, scrolling through the report. "President Spiers was there when it happened," he breathed. "Jesus…"

"He was targeted with Puchkov."

Adam reached for his phone, a throwaway he'd asked one of the bodyguards to buy for him at the hospital. Should he call Reichenbach? The comms blackout was still in effect, but this was a coup, and with everything else—

"Adam." Faisal's low voice broke his thoughts. He followed Faisal's finger to the next blaring headline: *President Spiers's Long-Dead Wife Found Alive in Russia, Held Prisoner for Years.*

Holy shit.

Details on her rescue were vague. Who had been holding her, even vaguer.

Nothing added up.

But, he definitely wasn't calling Reichenbach. Not now. Not with that. He slid his phone into his pocket and went back to hovering over Faisal's shoulder as Faisal read through the news and reset his intel scrapes to download to his current laptop. His old computer had been destroyed in the attack, but his server had backed everything up and could redirect to any of his other systems.

Faisal set his laptop aside and patted the massive bed. "*Habibi.* What would make me feel better is if you were sitting with me."

Adam folded down into the bed, his arms wrapping around Faisal like they'd never left him. Faisal sighed into his hold, tucking his forehead against Adam's neck, and watched the sea until his eyes slid closed.

Adam's thoughts raced, from Russia to Reichenbach to the president's wife and back. It would be Madigan's style to upend everything. Keep everyone off balance.

Later, Adam extricated himself and laid his lover down gently. He went to Faisal's closet and pulled out shirts and jeans, some of the thousands of pieces of clothing that Faisal owned. Faisal and Doc were about the same size, both on the slender side, and Doc was still wearing the same suit he'd bought him in London, rumpled and worn-looking. He slipped out of the bedroom and stilled, catching sight of Doc sitting on the edge of the deck, his toes grazing the azure waters.

He brought cold beer as a peace offering, holding it out to Doc when he sat beside him. Doc nodded his thanks and took a long pull.

Doc said nothing. He just kept staring out over the waters, his eyes squinting behind a pair of sunglasses he'd picked up somewhere.

Adam picked at the label on his bottle. It was one of the Carakale beers, from the time he and Faisal had spent a long weekend in Jordan, and he'd introduced Faisal to beer at Jordan's sole microbrewery. It had been his first drink—

He cut his wandering thoughts short with a sigh.

"Just say it. Say something." It had been a few days since Adam's breakdown and confession in the hospital hallway under Doc's frozen stare.

Doc exhaled, his cheeks puffing out, and took another gulp of his beer. "The nephew of the crown prince of the Kingdom of Saudi Arabia?" Squinting one eye almost all the way closed, he turned to Adam, his head cocked to one side.

"I know."

"Jesus Christ. I knew you were fucking insane, but this…" He shook his head.

"He wasn't the nephew of the crown prince when I met him. He was just Faisal."

"Oh, so that little fact snuck up on you? You missed it between the palaces and the armored cars and the royal bodyguards?"

"It wasn't like that." Adam rolled his bottle in his hands. "He was... undercover, I guess. Not living like a royal. Working in the Saudi Intelligence Directorate, instead of overseeing it."

"How long?"

"Two years. But I ended it almost a year ago."

"Doesn't seem like it's over."

Adam stayed silent.

"Who knows?"

Adam shifted, and his toes flicked at the surface of the sea. Warm water rolled over the top of his foot, arching away in fat droplets. "You. Prince Abdul."

Doc tipped his head back. "Jesus Christ, L-T. You are an *absolute* shitshow."

"Don't think I'm going to be an officer much longer." He kicked the water again, harder, an angry splash breaking the clear surface.

"You think?" Doc's tone wasn't kind. "This has international incident written all over it. Not to mention the serious 'foreign influence' violations with your security clearance. You're fucked, man. They could throw you in jail for this."

"You don't know the half of it," he whispered.

"I don't fucking want to." Doc drowned the rest of his beer, setting the glass bottle down with a hard clink. "We joked, you know. They guys. About you and him. There was this intensity between you two. Like raw fucking lightning. We joked about it, but we're always joking. I never actually thought you two were..." He shook his head. "'Cause that would be crazy. Insane. Totally whacked out." He sighed. Turned and squinted at Adam for a long moment. "So. What now, L-T?"

Adam shook his head. "Team checks in in three days. I'll reach out to Reichenbach and see where we are. I suspect we'll be on the move again. Probably Russia."

Doc was quiet, and he turned back to the sea and the lapping waves. "Don't you want to spend all the time with your lover boy that you can, then?" He squinted at Adam.

Adam swallowed down the hard lump that choked his throat. He bumped shoulders with Doc, his lips twisting into a relieved grin. "In a minute. Right here is good too."

41

White House

"Mr. President?"

Swallowing, Jack snapped his eyes up to General Bradford, his chairman of the joint chiefs. Heads around the Situation Room were pointed toward him, dozens of eyes staring at him. No one spoke.

They were all waiting for him.

His mind was a million miles away.

No. It was three floors up, stuck in the Residence. And stuck back in Sochi, on a bullet-riddled street.

Jack gripped his pen in both hands and leaned forward. "Could you, ah, repeat the question?"

On his left, Irwin sighed, glaring at the tabletop. To his right, where Ethan used to sit, Elizabeth's gaze pierced the side of his face.

When they'd all filed into the Situation Room, everyone left the seat to Jack's right open out of habit. It was Ethan's seat, and everyone had gotten used to his presence and him and Jack bouncing ideas off each other.

It stayed empty until one of the Secret Service agents yanked it away, tugging it out of sight.

He couldn't think about Ethan's absence. Couldn't think about their last moments together on Air Force One. Everything about Ethan was boxed up tight, an impenetrable fortress of memories in his mind. Ruthlessly, he squashed any veering yearnings wandering toward the aching hole inside him, a hole in the shape of Ethan's smile.

If he thought about Ethan, for even a moment, he would shatter.

Instead, his mind circled frantically over Leslie. Despite Irwin's protestations, he'd ordered the White House Medical Unit to move her into the Residence, setting her up with a private care team.

He and Irwin had argued since Turkey, bitterly so, over Leslie.

"We need to be cautious," Irwin had urged, over and over. "She can recover at Bethesda Naval Hospital. We can have her under complete surveillance. Guarded, for her safety and for yours. We don't know what we're dealing with."

"She's my *wife*." How could he leave her again? How could he ever betray her again? "The safest place in the world is the White House."

"Sir—"

In the end, Jack pulled rank, and the Navy doctor grudgingly agreed that Leslie wasn't in any immediate medical danger. She needed rest, recuperation, and a healthy diet. "She will get all of that at home," Jack growled. "I'll make sure of it."

Irwin had glared and then walked away when the doctor leaned in and asked softly what bedroom Leslie's hospital bed should be set up in. "Would you like her to be set up in the master bedroom, Mr. President? Or another bedroom?"

God, Ethan. He'd almost lost it then, but he clamped down hard on his heart. He couldn't bring her into the spaces he shared with Ethan, the life he'd lovingly built within Ethan's arms. They were two black holes in his heart. What would ever happen if their worlds touched? He would be obliterated; he knew that much for sure.

He told the doctor to put Leslie in the Queen's bedroom, where Sergey had stayed.

She was resting there now. He'd left her—had been dragged away from her by an impatient Irwin—as she was settling in, talking with the doctor. Irwin had taken him to the Situation Room and to the emergency meeting with his entire team.

"Could you, ah, repeat the question?" He squinted at General Bradford, his pen flexing between his hands.

General Bradford smothered his sigh and gestured again to the screens at the head of the table. "Mr. President, we need to decide *now* how to deal with the Russian coup. General Moroshkin has taken most urban centers and the Northern Fleet in Murmansk. He controls Russia's nuclear weapons and nearly all of the military. Russia's Pacific Fleet has scattered. Most of the Pacific Fleet were on deployment to the Gulf, and the ones that weren't on deployment have vanished from Vladivostok. Pockets of resistance have cropped up. Police forces. Some of the rural districts. Some military units. The biggest is in the area around Sochi, and we believe that President Puchkov might be involved in their success. Moroshkin has put out through the media that all resistance will be crushed and destroyed and enemies of the state executed. The country is locked in full-scale conflict."

Jack swallowed. "Any news on Sergey?"

"Nothing confirmed, Mr. President. Neither side is saying anything. Which means he's dead and no one knows, he's dead and no one is saying, or he is keeping quiet and hunkered down somewhere."

Sergey… Please take care of yourself. "How is Europe responding?"

"Massive troop movements across NATO. Our allies are positioning their forces along all borders connected to Russia, and their air and naval forces are on high alert. Germany, France, Sweden, and the UK are flying joint air patrols over the continent and the North Sea. Sweden and the UK are patrolling the waters of the North and Baltic Seas."

What had Leslie's last troop movements been? She'd mobilized for an operation, a light strike force, and then—

What had it been like, being in the building as it blew, covered with debris, blood-strewn and listening to the screams of her fellow soldiers? The roar of gunfire?

Had she thought of him, in those last moments? And then, waking up years later, in Madigan's clutches, a ghost to the world. Had she wondered why? Why her husband would abandon her, leave her behind and move on in the world? Why he hadn't done something, anything, to help her?

"Mr. President?"

He coughed, blinking hard. Damn it, he had to focus. He turned to his right, to steady himself with Ethan's presence. God, he needed—

Elizabeth stared back at him, her expression hard, but her eyes soft and worried.

"What are our options?" Jack turned away from Elizabeth. He pressed his palms flat to the table, watching the surface condense around his fingers. His soul was a kite in a hurricane, and he was hanging on by one, tiny thread.

"We've already put our forces in Europe on high alert, sir. From the UK to Turkey, our forces are ready to go. NATO is asking for our assistance in overflight operations. Turkey has quietly indicated they would allow us to use their country and airspace as a corridor to launch into Russia."

"You want to go to war?"

"We either deal with this directly, *now*, or we're looking at years of instability within Russia and a move back to the hardline repression and warmongering from the Putin years."

"And, Mr. President," Olivia Mori, Director Rees's replacement in the CIA said, "we have the Madigan element to consider. General Madigan is a part of this coup. He's a part of this new Russia, and that represents a grave threat to the United States."

His fingers curled, his nails scratching the surface of the table. "*Former* general."

Silence, for a moment. "Sir, we have models for this type of incident. In the event of…"

General Bradford's voice faded away, lost in the haze of Jack's mind. He tried to focus, tried to listen to the words coming from Bradford's mouth. Tried to focus on the map and the options of troop movements, insertions into Russia, different types of attacks.

There was an ache inside him, an emptiness. Memories flashed through his mind, like photos exploding into the air and falling to the floor. Leslie's emaciated body, nearly weightless as he'd carried her to the Osprey. Her smile, wondrous, when she'd recognized him, lying on the pavement in Sochi. Her beaming smile from twenty years ago, laughing in the sunlight in her wedding dress. The shy grin she'd graced him with when he'd worked up the nerve to say hello to her, decades ago in college. His palms had been sweating and his heart racing, but that smile had been like the first ray of sunlight after a thunderstorm.

He squeezed his eyes shut.

Ethan's smile, soft and warm, stared back at him. Ethan, peeking out from where he'd buried his face in his pillow, embarrassed at Jack's compliment. His laugh, so big and bold his head tipped back when he truly laughed out loud. The smile in his eyes, when just his gaze said it all. Waking up and seeing Ethan, already awake, watching Jack sleep with a gentle smile that made his whole world turn.

Two smiles, two lives. One heart, ripped in two. One soul, broken.

"Mr. President?"

Again, all eyes were on him. Waiting.

Damn it, he couldn't do this. The whole world was waiting for him and he was lost between memories and the black holes in his heart.

"Elizabeth, Lawrence, can I see you outside?" he mumbled, sliding out of his chair and heading for the door.

In the hallway, he braced himself against the wall, leaning with his arms over his head as he tried to breathe. Elizabeth and Irwin bracketed him on either side.

"What do you recommend?" he asked softly. "What do we do?"

They shared a long look through him before Elizabeth spoke. "I think airstrikes are the way to go for now, Mr. President. We can launch from the Fifth and Sixth Fleets. Back up the resistance and hopefully give them room to grow. We can't penetrate deep into Russia, but we can work in from the borders. Also, work with our NATO allies. Get birds in the air."

Irwin nodded. "I have some ideas for getting intel from on the ground. We need to know more about what's going on."

Jack nodded. "All right. Sounds good." He closed his eyes again and then snapped them open when Ethan's wide smile blazed in the darkness behind his eyelids.

"Jack?" Elizabeth leaned in, trying to catch his gaze. "Are you okay?"

"No. I'm very, very far from okay."

He canceled his appointments for the rest of the week and hid in the Oval Office after the disastrous briefing in the Situation Room. Irwin and Elizabeth promised to stay on top of the operations in Russia and bring him regular updates. He tried to text Sergey, but the message bounced back, undeliverable. Cell service was barely functional in Russia, disabled by Moroshkin. They needed to get cell towers to Sergey's insurgency, get their service up again.

He was supposed to be working, supposed to be figuring out how to save the world, save his friends, protect America, but instead he sat slumped at his desk, his head buried in his palms.

Knocking at the office door, finally, made him stir. "Come in."

Pete and Gus poked their heads in, hard looks on their faces.

God, he did not want to do this. "What's up?"

"Mr. President, we have to talk about the current situation." Pete's expression shifted, his jaw clenching as he strode toward Jack's desk.

He inhaled deeply. "Which situation, Pete?"

"Your *wife*, Mr. President." Gus squinted at Jack. "The press is going crazy. You guys have released exactly *jack shit* about what happened with her rescue, and rumors are flying. And people have noticed that someone is missing at the White House. Where's Reichenbach?"

Pete looked down at his feet.

Where's Reichenbach? echoed in Jack's chest, bouncing off his ribs and sinking to his curdled stomach. "The White House doesn't comment on the personal lives—"

"No, no, no!" Gus interrupted Jack. "We don't *do* that shit anymore, remember? We changed our tone and we can't go back now."

"What do you want me to say? What the hell do you want me to say about this, when I don't even know what the fuck is going on?"

"You want my advice?" Gus's voice rose with Jack's until they were both shouting. "Dump Reichenbach for good! Stick with your wife! Play up the rescuer angle and how devoted you are to her. The public loves hero stories, and you'll poll a hell of a lot better with your hero wife back from being held captive, and probably tortured for years, on your arm instead of her being tossed aside for a piece of dick."

Jack's jaw dropped. He stopped breathing.

"You are going to be forgotten as 'that gay president' if you don't ditch Reichenbach, *right now*."

"How *dare* you..."

Gus ignored him. "Your legacy—"

"I have done important things in this office!" Jack's teeth clenched and his voice shook, rage underlying his words. "I've dedicated my *heart* and *soul* to this presidency. To the world!"

"No one cares! No one cares about the details. The public wants someone they can like. Nixon opened China; does anyone give a *fuck* about his legacy? Anyone say he's their favorite president? What he *did* for the people, for the world, doesn't matter! How he's remembered *is!*"

Silence.

"The choices you make *right now* will define you, Mr. President. Be remembered forever for being a white knight. Or fade away as the public chews you up and spits you out. Another forgotten, meaningless president."

He was shaking, trembling, and he couldn't stop. White-hot rage raced through him, searing his bones. "*I. Matter*," Jack hissed. "I *matter*, and who I'm with doesn't change that."

"Grow up! Who you choose to fuck *does* matter. You made a big Goddamn deal out of being bisexual, Mr. President. Time to prove it. Stick with your *wife*. Dump this gay thing. End it. Now!"

He thought about murder for a moment. About launching across the desk, grabbing Gus by the neck and squeezing his hands around his throat. Squeezing so tight, until Gus was down on his knees, gasping for breath, begging for forgiveness.

Exhaling hard, Jack turned away.

Pictures of him and Ethan were scattered on the table behind his desk. Smiling in the Rose Garden. A selfie on the couch. The Christmas ball. His heart stuttered, wailing, and his lungs refused to work.

"Gus," Pete growled through gritted teeth. "Get the fuck out of the White House. Don't come back."

Gus threw his hands up in the air and stormed out of the Oval Office. He slammed the door behind him, rattling George Washington's portrait over the fireplace.

Jack's mind was just a blank hum, a buzz of static. Gus's words popped in and out. *Dump Reichenbach. Stick with your wife. Prove it.*

Prove it.

He closed his eyes.

And there was Ethan, lying beside him in bed and reaching for him, tucking a stray lock of hair off his forehead.

His eyes snapped open.

Pete stared.

"Pete, I won't make this political. I can't play politics with this. God, not this."

"I know you won't, sir." Pete rolled his jaw as his hands went into his pockets. "You're too good a man to do that. But... what do I say to the press? It's a deluge out there." Pete leaned in. "I don't want to misspeak. I don't want to be wrong. Not with this. What do I do? How do I help you?"

"I have *no* idea," he whispered. Ethan was gone, but actually saying the words, confirming to the world that they were over... He couldn't do that. Not yet. "I have no idea what to do."

He bailed from the West Wing and headed back to the Residence.

Never had the stairs up to the Residence seemed so ominous. Or taken so long to climb. Each step added a sorrow's worth of weight to his soul.

Secret Service agents were inside the Residence, standing post along the main hallway and outside Leslie's room. He recognized their faces. Remembered laughing with them on Air Force One and around the White House. Remembered getting to know them over Christmas, and taking pictures with them in front of the tree. Remembered feeling like he had, if not friends, friendly faces around him.

No one met his gaze. Their steely eyes stared ahead, jaws locked, muscles clenched.

Soft voices floated down the hall. He headed toward Leslie's room, even though his stomach lurched, rancid shame burning a hole through his guts.

Flickering light from the TV on the wall flashed over Leslie's stunned face. Her cracked lips were parted in surprise, and her wide eyes stared at the screen. Sixteen years of history to catch up on, and she'd turned on the news.

Images of him and Ethan together, his happiest moments, flashed across the screen—them arm in arm at Sergey's state dinner, dancing at the Correspondents' Ball in early spring, and at the Christmas ball before that, and then the world-shaking kiss they'd shared in the back of an ambulance on the North Lawn after they'd emerged, bloody, from retaking the White House—overlaying a news anchor spouting unnamed sources within the White House who claimed Ethan was *gone*. That Jack had kicked him out. Or that Ethan had fled.

That Leslie had taken his place.

Vomit rose in his throat. He swallowed hard, trying to push it away. Agent Caldwell glanced sideways at him but said nothing.

"Hey," he called out to Leslie, leaning against her doorframe. Shoulders hunched, hands in his pockets. He could barely stand straight with the weight of shame bending his spine.

She whipped around, stared at him, and grabbed the remote, turning the TV off one-handed after fumbling with the controls.

Silence. He looked down at the gray carpet.

Leslie took a deep breath. "Ethan?" she finally breathed. Her eyebrows arched sky-high, nearly climbing off her forehead.

Jack reached for the open door and pushed it gently closed, blocking out the agents on duty. He faced the white wood for a moment, his back to Leslie.

"Are you..." Leslie hesitated. "Gay?"

He heard the questions she didn't ask wrapped up within the one she did. *Were you lying this whole time? Were you faking? Was our marriage real? Did you even want me? Did you ever really love me? What kind of man are you?*

As if everything that had come before loving Ethan was suddenly cast in doubt, suddenly fraudulent. How could he truly have loved them both? One must be a lie.

"I'm bi," he said, turning to her. He shuffled closer, but not too close. "I didn't know, though, until—" He swallowed down Ethan's name. He hadn't known the love he was capable of before Ethan, the way his heart could expand, could fill so perfectly, so fully with another.

Leslie frowned down at her lap, and the fingers of her good hand picked over her blanket. Her blackened, disfigured hand and arm had been bandaged and put in a sling, even though it was clear nothing would save them and the damage had long been done. Maybe they could amputate and clone a replacement, sometime later, but that was just another thing for Jack to excoriate himself over.

"I used to fantasize, you know," she said softly. "That one day, I'd escape. One day I'd fly home to you. Find you practicing law in Austin. You'd have your own firm." She smiled up at him. "I figured, of course, that you would have moved on. Married again. Had kids." She sucked her top lip into her mouth, her chipped teeth chewing on her skin. "I never, *ever* thought you'd end up sleeping with a *man*."

Her eyes were filled with questions, and beneath those, all of the accusations, all of the wonderings, even some of the derision that had been flung his way in the aftermath of his falling in love with Ethan. Gus's voice blared in his mind, his words pounding into his skull over and over again.

He looked away. Stared at the baseboards on the far side of the room. Blinked fast and tried, desperately, not to feel like less than half a man, made small by the world who derided him and Ethan, and their love—

No. That wasn't who he was. He'd fought for his and Ethan's love, had bled for it. He'd stood up to the world, refusing to compromise either his love or his presidency. *Look at everything I've done*, a part of him screamed. *I became the president! I forged peace where there was none. Don't discard me—my achievements, my identity, my masculinity—so quickly! Don't discard my love! I am* worth *something!*

But the world was in shambles, just like his life, and the more he examined his own actions, his own choices, the more he wanted to shrivel up and disappear. Sergey was missing, possibly dead. The peace he'd built had been destroyed, his identity and the narrative of his life, upended.

Ethan… gone. Their love…

Hard knocking at the door made him jump, and he whirled as the door shot open. Welby strode in, his face a mask of stone.

"Mr. President. We require this door to be kept open at *all* times." Welby lifted his chin and stared Jack down. Gone was the slight—very slight—curl to his lip. The way his eyes had smiled when Jack had asked him to buy his first box of condoms and lube for him and Ethan. The way his voice had warmed when Jack asked if he would help them slip off to Walter Reed and pay respects to the wounded.

These men weren't Jack's men, though. They were Ethan's. They were his friends—his family—before they were anything to Jack, and now he and Ethan were—

Jack gave Welby a tight smile. "I was just leaving," he said quickly, heading to the door. Welby stepped aside, watching him like a hawk.

"Jack." Leslie leaned forward on her bed, her lips moving, searching for something to say. "I'll see you tomorrow," she finally said, her voice rising, almost like a question.

Nodding, he fled, striding down the hall as the hot stares of the Secret Service agents burned through his suit, into his skin. His eyes closed and then snapped open again, and his breaths quickened, fast, shallow pants that left him dizzy. Fingers clenched and unclenched, his tongue thickened, his mouth suddenly dry. Diving sideways, he pushed open the door to his bedroom, raced inside, and slammed the door shut.

He pressed back against the dark wood and his heart thundered in his chest, so hard it ached. His head tipped back as he tried to breathe, tried to hold on to the air in his lungs.

Ethan's Secret Service sweatshirt, lying on the foot of their bed, caught his eye.

Ethan's suit jacket, draped over the back of his desk chair.

Ethan's running shoes, toed off and kicked under the bed.

Ethan's Christmas gift to him, the Secret Service teddy bear he'd made, sitting on Jack's dresser.

Their gigantic pump bottle of lube, a monstrosity, one he'd laughed at—and then loved—sitting on Ethan's bedside table, next to a pack of wet wipes. A basket of clean towels, rolled up, on the bedside table's lower shelf.

The detritus of their love, and their life together.

A sob choked his throat, and his mouth gaped wide as he tried to breathe. Instead he screamed, a raw, guttural bellow, and slid down the door, collapsing to his ass, boneless and breathless.

Pitching forward, Jack let loose the sobs that wracked his body and soul.

His bones were made of shame, his veins filled with sorrows and regret. His heart had turned to a void, an empty ache, a sucking black hole of misery and anguish. What kind of a person, what kind of a man, was he? Everything he'd done in his whole life had come undone. His peace with Russia, destroyed, and his friend Sergey gone. His presidency in tatters amid a country ripping apart. A madman loose in the world, toppling governments.

His dead wife, alive. The man he loved to the *depths* of his *soul*, gone.

Everything he touched turned to disaster, to ruin. Everything and everyone.

Shame burned hot within him, a hatred of himself so searingly intense that he buckled over against the sting, curling down and pressing his forehead to the carpet.

He was worthless as a man. Utterly, absolutely, worthless.

42

Jeddah, Saudi Arabia

"Adam. I've got something."

Faisal's fingers danced over his laptop keyboard. The flat-screen hanging on the wall in the living room winked on. A flick of his fingers, and a file snapped from his laptop to the screen.

Adam leaned forward on the couch, frowning. A freeze frame from a border crossing, a man in sunglasses and a low ball cap turning his face away from the cameras. Trying to hide.

"Noah Williams," Faisal said. "He used a fake passport, but my programs scraped his facial recognition off the Israeli-Jordanian border patrol checkpoint."

"When?"

"A day and a half ago."

Doc wandered back in from Faisal's space-age kitchen, tossing and catching an apple in one hand. He threw a water bottle and a bottle of pills to Adam. "For lover boy."

Faisal sent Doc a flat glare over the edge of his laptop. But, he plucked the water from Adam's hands and nodded to Doc. "*Sahtein.*"

Doc froze. Wide-eyed, he glanced at Adam.

"Now you say *ala'albeck*." Adam gestured from Doc to Faisal.

Doc fumbled through the delivery, flustered, and then glared at the screen. "So what's he coming south for?"

Adam folded his arms and crossed the room, peering at the image of his long-ago friend. "Paris to Jordan is a long way overland. Whatever it is, he worked hard to get there."

Faisal tucked the water bottle into the couch. "Madigan's base was in Somalia for some time. They took that Yemeni freighter, and after sinking of the Russian destroyer, they disappeared again. It's possible his base is still in the region."

"Can you find him in Jordan? His car, that license plate? Can you track it through their surveillance systems? Find his voice print on the telecom network? Use CCTV cams for facial recognition?"

Faisal grinned, already typing fast on his laptop. "I am way ahead of you... lover boy." He winked at Doc.

"Oh. Oh, hell no." Doc shook his head, grimacing. "He's so not the lover boy. Have you seen him?" He shuddered, looking Adam up and down. "He's so... broody and cavemanish. So dour and dejected." His fingers waggled, waving Adam away. "He's no lover boy."

"You do not know *habibi* as I do." Faisal kept typing, folders and files and online bridges opening up in cascading windows on the flat-screen. "He is an amazing 'lover boy'." A final series of keystrokes, an execution string, and his scrape ran through the Jordanian networks. "Hearing him sigh as I stroke up his—"

"Whoa! Hey!" Adam whirled. "Could you not?"

"I'm totally up for hearing more." Doc wagged his eyebrows at Adam, not even trying to smother his salacious smirk.

"Go to hell," Adam grunted.

A ping from the computer and a flashing window on the screen drew their attention.

A fresh image capture of Noah appeared, out of the ball cap and in a ghutra and dressed for the desert in khakis and a sun shirt. He was sitting at a café, drinking coffee, and watching the street. Waiting.

"I've got him. Ma'an, Jordan." A few more keystrokes. "An hour ago."

"We need to grab him. We need to grab him and bring him back here. Put some more pieces of this puzzle together. What's he doing, and why. What does he know about the coup? His flat was brimming with intel on Russia. What's next?"

"A snatch and grab op?" Doc leaned over the back of the white leather couch. "The three of us?"

"Two of us." Adam nodded to Faisal. "He's staying here."

"L-T," Doc huffed. "I'm a doc, not a super-secret operative. Sure, I tag along with you to buy camels and get the shit beat out of us, but I'm not one of the big spooks."

"Then you can drive the getaway car." He snorted at Doc's elaborate eye-roll and sat next to Faisal, already back to his keyboard. "Can you get us in there?"

"There is a Jordanian military airport outside of Ma'an. Rarely used anymore. Skeleton staff. I've just received clearance for a Saudi royal jet on official business." Faisal smiled.

Adam hesitated. "I don't want to leave you. Your uncle's bodyguards should come up here. Stay in the main house until we're back."

"*Habibi*, I will be all right. It won't happen again."

"You can't know that."

"I will be fine. You will be back soon. Yes?"

"I never want to leave you." He cupped Faisal's face in both hands and leaned in, pressing a long kiss to his lips. *"Ana bahibak."*

Faisal hummed and tried to chase Adam when he pulled back. His hands curved down Adam's neck. "I will be waiting, *qalby*. But, *habibi*, you need to be safe, too." He kissed Adam, gently. "And you should take the Lear. It's faster."

"You know, I'm starting to understand the appeal."

Reclining on a leather lounger in Faisal's Learjet, Doc looked ridiculous. He'd found the closet filled with luxury silk pajamas, down feather slippers, a cooling satin sleep mask, and one of the most expensive—and ridiculous—ergonomic pillows on the planet. He'd stripped immediately, leaving his boots and clothes in a pile, and donned the pajamas, slippers, and sleep mask, and then stretched out on the couch, poised like some *femme fatale* in a fifties film. In the jet's overhead compartment, he'd found a cashmere Burberry throw, and that now lay stretched across his lap, his hand stroking over the ultrasoft material.

Adam stared at him, one eyebrow raised. Far more sensible, he was sitting at the window, tablet in hand, waiting for any updates from Faisal to ping through. So far, Noah seemed to be holding steady drinking coffee.

Adam was also trying not to go out of his mind, fighting the urge to turn around and go right back to Faisal's side. Leaving him, walking away, felt too much like the biggest mistake he'd ever made, when he'd tried to walk away for good.

"This kind of luxury is sweet." Doc grinned. He had the mask over his eyes, even though he wasn't trying to sleep, and only a satiny slip of white stared back at Adam.

Adam shook his head.

"So, I guess I can see why you'd go for this kind of thing."

He snorted. "This stuff just gets in the way. It wasn't like this at all when we met."

Lifting a corner of the sleep mask, Doc stared.

"Early on, we had this... rat hole of an apartment in Kuwait. I worked intel, so I could get away a lot. We had a mattress on the floor, dark, heavy wood everywhere, shutters nailed closed. You know." He glanced at Doc.

Doc clearly had no idea. He stared back blankly.

"We drank coffee at dusty Internet cafes and wandered the slums. No bodyguards, no royalty, no Marine Corps..." He trailed off. "He'd recite poetry by candlelight. We didn't have any electricity. He drew sketches of us on the walls with charcoal from our fires."

"The fuck did you do for him? Teach him how to badly use a compass?" Doc sat up on one elbow and pushed the white satin sleep mask up to his forehead, ruffling his hair.

Adam glared. "We practiced Arabic together. All the dialects we could."

"I'll bet you practiced Arabic together." Doc's eyebrows waggled. "*Habibi*."

"Don't say that. And I don't know why I bothered saying anything."

Doc lay back, rearranging his sleep mask and unfolding the Burberry blanket over himself. He sighed, blissful.

A moment later, Doc piped up again. "You're happy around him. It's easy to see. He makes you happy. And," he shifted on the couch, "you're basically a miserable, dickish asshole most of the time, so anything that makes you happy is a damn good thing."

The flight took just over two hours, and the pilot called back to Adam in Arabic when they were on approach. The Jordanian military airfield was barely anything at all, two dusty runways and a squat tower surrounded by a rusted chain-link fence. Someone had scared up an ancient gold Mercedes sedan and parked it next to their runway. Bored Jordanian military guards watched them through binoculars.

Doc groaned and changed out of his silk and satin and back into his borrowed jeans and long-sleeve shirt. They were going in plainclothes, trying to blend in as much as they could until they reached Noah. There was nothing they could do about Noah being able to recognize Adam on sight, but that was part of the plan. Turn it around and use it to their advantage.

Faisal texted Adam's phone, saying that Noah was still at the café, across the street from the central mosque in Ma'an.

Adam drove, despite joking with Doc about driving the getaway car, and Doc slid into the passenger seat, navigating them from the airfield and across the desert to the village. They wound through the sandy streets, past stalls selling oranges and dates and almonds, and past cafés where men and women drank coffee and smoked shisha. Ahead, towering minarets pierced the hazy orange sky: Ma'an's central mosque.

"Take this alley, and then make a right. The café will be ahead on the left." Doc alternated between watching the road and the tablet in his lap. "Lover boy says he's still there."

At Faisal's nickname, Adam glared before he turned onto the street. He slid in behind a Land Rover, parked just down the block from the café but with a clear line of sight to the people sitting outside.

There, off to the side and alone, was Noah Williams.

"What now?"

Adam watched Noah. His old friend was fidgeting, drinking his coffee too fast, as if he didn't know what to do with his hands. He checked his watch every two minutes. Looked up and down the street.

"He's waiting. And he's nervous."

"For someone? Or some*thing*?"

"We'll find out." Adam settled into the driver's seat, his gaze glued to Noah.

Doc huffed, blowing air through his smacking lips. "Great. I hate stakeouts." He thunked his head against the passenger window, but kept his eyes on the café.

An hour later, Noah finally stood. He dropped a handful of coins to the table and downed the rest of his coffee before striding across the dusty street and into the white walled courtyard of Ma'an's mosque.

"Shit. Now what?"

"I'm following him." Adam unbuckled his seat belt and slid out of the car. He tucked his small pistol into the back of his waistband, covering it with a sport coat of his that Faisal had kept for two years.

"What should *I* do?" Doc crawled over the center console and plopped into the driver's seat. His whiny emphasis on the *I* grated over Adam's ears.

"Stay here. Keep a lookout. I'll call if I need you."

"*When* you need me."

Adam took off, heading for the mosque. Above, the piercing *adhan,* the call to prayer, cracked the sky. Speakers in the minarets blasted the *muezzin's* cry out over the city, cajoling all to come and worship. That mournful wail, the curling stutter-stop and ground-out vowels had been etched into his eardrums, carved into his bones. He knew the ritual, knew the rhythms of Islam. Memories tried to pull him back, hearing the *adhan* in a hundred different places, a hundred different ways, but never so sweet as from Faisal's lips.

Inside, the prayers would be starting. First the lingering *takbir*, and then the *shahada* sounded. Only minutes until the *iqama* began.

He buttoned his sport coat, trying to feign the hurried impatience of a businessman who had lost track of time and was late for evening prayer. His eyes scanned the crowd of men flooding into the mosque, passing through the courtyard and slipping out of their shoes.

There, just inside. Noah Williams was standing before the imam, hands folded over his heart, reciting the first of the *salah* prayers.

He toed off his shoes and followed the mass of men into the mosque. Threadbare carpets stretched from wall to wall. Honeycomb lattices rose overhead, dark wood casting a dim pall over the interior. Bare bulbs hung from the ceiling, covered in sand and dust. Low voices murmured the lines of the prayers as everyone lined up, shoulder to shoulder. Adam squeezed past two Jordanians and ended up just down the line from Noah.

The *iqama* began, a low, droning hum of recitation and repetition, followed by the louder call of "*Allahu Akbar.*" Adam joined in. It had been over a year since he'd prayed, longer since he'd been in a mosque, but the rhythm of the service came back to him as his eyes slipped sideways, watching Noah.

Arabic flowed over the crowd, the men's voices like tumbling rocks down a mountainside. They bowed, kneeled, pressed their foreheads to the floor, and then sat back, softly reciting words of prayer under their breath. Adam kept his gaze fixed on Noah.

His contact isn't here. And he's nervous.

At the end, when the worshipers kneeled and turned their heads over their shoulders, looking to one side and then the other—

His eyes caught Noah's.

He watched the color drain from Noah's face, watched his eyes widen.

And then Noah shot up, running through the lines of kneeling men and vaulting over bowing worshippers as he tore out of the mosque. Adam followed, shoving his way through and leaping over men in prostration as shouts rose, angry Arabic coming from every direction.

Noah pushed his way through the courtyard, taking off down the street barefoot. Gritting his teeth, Adam followed, the sand and the road grit slicing the soles of his feet. He heard an engine roar nearby and then tires squeal. A glance over his shoulder, and he saw a gold Mercedes following them down the block.

The road dead-ended at a souk. Noah dove into the dark maze. Fruits and vegetables lay limp in the afternoon heat, sheltered above by corrugated steel laid haphazardly over the endless array of stalls. Sunlight poked through drilled holes, narrow shafts of light barely penetrating the gloom.

Shouts and snarls ahead led him toward Noah. He pushed on, chasing the man past angry old women clutching vegetables and men shouting, machetes raised over their heads and carcasses of butchered goat hanging from hooks. Wet dust and fruit squished beneath his feet.

Brakes squealed at the entrance to the souk. He heard the roar of the Mercedes engine as Doc circled around the outside.

Noah ended up trapped between a butcher and a coconut vendor and between the two shouting men wielding machetes. A panicked glance behind him, to Adam gaining, and he shoved the coconut vendor and leaped over his stall, knocking stacks of coconuts into the beam holding up that section of the rusty corrugated steel roof. The roof clattered down, falling into the butcher's stall. Screams rose, women clinging to their hijabs as they fled.

The crash helped Adam, and he skirted the commotion and lunged, tackling Noah around the shoulders as Noah tried to spin and make a break for it past a stand selling bruised tomatoes. They toppled sideways and landed in a heap of squished fruit and dust.

Adam rolled on top of Noah, shoving him down face-first. "The hell is wrong with you?" he shouted. "What the hell are you doing?"

Sirens blared. Angry Arabic shouted, voices directing the police to them.

"Shit." Hauling Noah to his feet, Adam shoved him forward, one hand wrapped around his neck, the other bending back an arm, holding it behind him. "Get moving!"

They jogged together, Adam pushing him left and right through the souk, winding into the darkness and heading for the far side. Noah seemed just as interested in avoiding the police as Adam was, and he used that. Still, he held tight to Noah's neck, his fingers digging into the soft flesh.

When they burst from the souk, into the sunshine on a dusty side street, Adam hauled Noah into a rancid alley and threw him against the mud brick wall before slugging him across the face. "What the fuck is going on, Noah?"

Noah spat blood to the dust. His eyes stayed low, fixed on the ground.

"What the fuck are you doing working for Madigan? That's not you! You're the guy who tattled on the senior prank in high school because you thought it was disrespectful!"

Noah's gaze darted around the alley, frantic. Adam crowded closer, shoving him against the crumbling wall. "I looked up to you, damn it."

Stilling, Noah's eyes flicked to Adam. He squinted, holding his stare, before he burst into a whirlwind.

His leg kicked sideways, catching Adam's ankle. His arms spun, breaking Adam's hold. He kneed Adam in the stomach and dropped him in the dust.

Adam rolled to his feet. He grabbed Noah from behind and dragged him down, punching him hard in both kidneys.

Grunting, Noah tried to roll Adam off, but Adam clung on, holding him from behind in a headlock with his legs wrapped around Noah's waist.

Noah slammed his head back, once, twice, three time. Dazed, Adam didn't see the elbow flying toward his face. He fell back, and Noah scrambled to his feet.

Instead of running, he turned back, hands held in loose fists.

Adam rose and reached for the gun tucked into his waistband. "What the fuck? Talk to me. Tell me why. What the fuck is worth sixteen years as a ghost?"

Snarling, Noah charged. He ran right for Adam, his fists flying.

Adam aimed low, firing twice into Noah's knees. Blood flew, staining the dust and mud brick as Noah stumbled but kept coming. Lunging, he wrapped his arms around Adam and tackled him.

Their hands scrabbled for Adam's gun.

Adam's finger snapped as Noah ripped the gun sideways. Adam howled, his finger broken and tangled in the trigger guard.

Noah straddled him, his heavy weight pinning Adam to the dust.

Adam shoved at him, his face, his neck, his palm sliding on sweat and grit.

Noah pressed on his arm, his hand holding the gun, and started to turn it toward Adam.

"Fuck..." Thrashing, Adam tried to buck Noah, tried to get free. Noah punched him once, slamming his fist into Adam's temple, and leaned, pressing his forearm into Adam's throat and cutting off his breath.

Gasping, Adam tried to shove him off. Tried to pinwheel his legs.

It was like trying to move a mountain.

His broken finger pulled. He grit his teeth, his arm, his hand shaking as he tried to fight Noah, fight the gun turning toward his face. Still, the barrel kept moving, almost aiming for straight for his head.

Noah watched him, taking in everything—Adam's gasps for breath, his bloody hands, split knuckles, his wide eyes, his raw panic. Noah stared, unblinking, as if waiting.

He leaned down, pressed his own temple against the barrel, his cheek resting right on top of Adam's, and forced his finger on top of Adam's broken one.

The trigger squeezed.

Adam heard a roar, a crack, and then his hearing shattered, like a giant gong breaking in two. He felt the reverberation, felt a rush of hot liquid flood the side of his face. Felt a burning flash burst over his skin. Tasted gunpowder in the air, wet copper. Pressed his lips together and rubbed thick blood between them.

Noah collapsed on top of him, a heavy, dead weight.

Doc appeared over Noah's shoulder, eyes wide and lips moving fast. He was saying something, but Adam could only hear the roar of clanging bells, so loud his head wanted to split in two.

Frantic, Doc rolled Noah's limp body off Adam. He grabbed Adam's face, rubbing through the splattered blood, his hands pressing into Adam's temple and his fingers searching through his blood-soaked hair. Adam tried to shake his head, tried to wave him away, but the bells roared louder. He squeezed his eyes shut.

Doc tugged at him, shaking his shoulders until he opened his eyes. Doc was still shouting something, his eyes wide enough to show a ring of white all the way around. He pointed to Noah and then to the car idling at the opening of the alley, driver's door thrown open.

Adam's gaze wandered over Noah's facedown body. Bits of bone and brain had blown out from the side of his head, splattered in the dust. His hand clung limply to the gun.

He'd shot himself. Why had he shot himself?

Doc shook him again, his thumb jerking to the car. He tried to pull Adam to his feet.

"We have to take him!" Adam thought he said it normally, but Doc ducked down, his eyes wild, and waved his hands in the hair, as if Adam had shouted. "We can't leave him," he tried again, softer.

Rolling his eyes, Doc grabbed one of Noah's arms and then snapped at Adam, his soundless lips moving. "Help me!" Adam managed to lip read. "We gotta move!"

He stumbled to Noah's side, grabbing his other arm, and ran with Doc to the Mercedes. They shoved Noah in the back seat. Doc ran to the driver's side, and Adam collapsed into the passenger seat. Doc took off in a cloud of dust, tires kicking back and stuttering. He fishtailed down a side street and then slowed as he hit the main drag. A few more turns, and then it was the straight desert road to the airport.

Adam's hearing came back in a high whine, the bells' roar turning into a smear of static and nails on a chalkboard. Groaning, he mopped at the side of his face with his coat sleeve, wiping away Noah's blood and a trickle coming from his ear. Through the electric whine, he managed to piece together Doc's diatribe. "...the *fuck* happened? I thought you wanted to interrogate him, not kill him?"

"He shot himself." His jacket sleeve was drenched, and in the car's mirror, his cheek was a mess of blood, his hair matted with it. "He leaned into the gun. He killed himself."

"What the *fuck*?"

"I don't fucking know."

"And where the fuck are your shoes?"

They blew through the airport's dilapidated chain-link fence and drove right to Faisal's waiting Learjet. The pilot had wisely lined up on the departure runway, ready and awaiting their return. Doc drove straight to the jet's stairs, screaming to a rubber-screeching stop.

Adam shucked his jacket and threw it over Noah's head. He and Doc manhandled Noah's body out of the car and up the jet's stairs. One of Noah's arms dropped. Doc lunged, flipping it up onto his chest, hopefully before the bored Jordanian military police caught it.

Faisal's pilot paled when they dropped Noah's body on the Berber carpet in the center of the Learjet. Blood smeared on the lambskin leather seats.

"Let's go. Now!" Adam kneeled by Noah and shooed the pilot back to the cockpit. A moment later, the engines turned over and the plane began to taxi.

Panting, Doc glared over Noah's body at Adam. He gestured to the mess, to their failed mission. "So, he recites poetry to you by candlelight and you fuck up his jet and bring him dead bodies?"

Adam laid back, exhausted, on the jet's ruined carpet as the plane took off, the weight of the lift pushing him against the deck.

Why hadn't Noah said anything? He hadn't even tried to explain himself. Why had he run? Who was he waiting for?

Why kill himself?

43

White House

Jack knew, without a single doubt, that he had to spend the rest of his life in penance.

He could never fix what had become of his life. What had become of the world around him. Of the people around him.

He couldn't undo what had been done to Leslie. The long years she'd spent in solitude, in captivity. Years of her life gone, lost to a madman. Years of her life spent in agony, wondering about the life she'd lost. About Jack. About his life.

About how he'd left her, and how he'd moved on.

She was back now, and he had to do something, anything, for her. To try—even though it was oh-so-futile—to attempt to make up for those long years she'd wasted away while he'd been living his life.

While he had found love and joy again.

No. He couldn't think of Ethan. He *couldn't*. Delirious panic hung on the edge of his mind, threading through his memories of Ethan. Clung to the thought of his smile, the sound of his voice. There wasn't a single part of his heart that didn't ache, that didn't yearn, for Ethan, and for their life. He could never repair that hole, the rend in his soul shaped like Ethan's smile.

Now, Ethan was gone and Jack was a broken, worthless, wreck of a man, and the only thing he could do, for the rest of his life, was try to put the pieces of Leslie's life back together. Give her something to counterbalance the darkness.

He'd tried, damn it, to do the right thing. He'd tried to put his life back together after losing her. Tried to focus his efforts on honoring her memory. One cause led to another, and then he was running for office, and suddenly he was running for president. His life had been made out of honoring a wife who wasn't even dead, who was silently suffering, and everything he'd done, everything he was, seemed to crumble and fall in the face of that truth. In the face of Leslie's battered, emaciated body.

Except for Ethan. His love for Ethan—

Panic fluttered under his skin, and the ache slammed into him, straight into his heart.

He *had* to *stop*.

He gripped the kitchen counter as the world tilted and his stomach rolled over. He tried to breathe, in and out.

Ethan's smile hung in the darkness behind his eyelids.

Jack forced it away.

He went back to his work, blinking away the bright spots in his vision and the dark edges around his gaze. Methodically, he picked up the kitchen knife again, slicing the steak before him into long strips, and then dropping them into the glass dish to marinate. He tried to force his mind to blankness as he set up the stove, pulling out a frying pan—

Ethan would make the salad while I prepared the steak.

He sliced strawberries and tossed them with spinach and a blueberry vinaigrette. Rice simmered next to the pan, just hot enough as he dropped a bead of water to the metal. He laid out two plates—

Damn it, Ethan always made the rice better. His was never mushy.

The marinated steak slices sizzled as they hit the pan, a few quick seconds flash frying, and then he pulled everything off the burner. Rice on the plates, steak on the rice, salad piled around—

I remember the first time we had this. Ethan made me wait at the table, no peeking, and he brought over the plates with a flourish and such a shy smile.

Jack closed his eyes and grasped the counter again.

He had to get a grip. He *had* to.

He ignored the frigid stares of the Secret Service agents as he made the long walk from the kitchen to the Queen's bedroom on the opposite end of the Residence. Silence hung, impenetrable, and his footfalls on the plush carpet broke the air like cracking glass. He couldn't meet their gazes, and he shouldered past the agents standing guard outside Leslie's door with his eyes downcast, shame curling his spine.

Leslie looked up as he crept in, a warm smile breaking over her gaunt face. She had a newspaper spread out over her lap, and to her side, a TV tray left over from lunch.

Jack plastered a smile on his face and walked to her bed, sitting on the end. He set the plates on the tray and put it between them.

"What's this?" Leslie smiled down at the food, then at Jack.

"I made you dinner." He coughed, trying to get his voice to stop sounding so strangled. "The doctor says you need to build your strength up. Get your health back. *Voilà*."

Leslie laughed, soft and musical. She speared a piece of steak and sniffed it, arching her eyebrow, before she took her first bite. A moment later, her eyes closed, and a blissful expression took over her face.

"Good?"

"Do you remember the first meal you made me?" She shoveled rice and steak onto her fork, taking bite after bite, eating fast like she might not have time to finish.

Jack froze.

"The chicken?" Leslie laughed again, wiping her mouth. "I came home from training, and you had burned it so badly, but you wanted to surprise me."

"The whole apartment smelled like smoke…" he whispered.

"You had a can of baked beans—barely warm—and some grocery store potato salad, and this black hunk of chicken." She shook her head, alternating talking and eating as she smiled at Jack.

The memory hit him like drowning in the ocean, a wave descending over him and pulling him under. They were so young, just out of college, newlyweds, and she'd been in the field, training for ten days. He'd desperately wanted to do something for her, but he was so painfully inexperienced in the kitchen. Dining halls in college and fast food had turned him into a terrible cook. He'd tried—and failed—to make her a welcome home dinner.

"I loved you so much that I ate it," Leslie breathed. "And I loved it, even though it was terrible." She laughed again. "But it was something you did for me."

God, the memories were pouring in, everywhere, all around him. Leslie, laughing just like this, at the burned chicken. Eating at the table in her Army uniform pants and her tucked-in undershirt, showing off her strong muscles, her corded arms. Her hair in a tight, professional bun. Her eyes, twinkling as she ate burned chicken and cold beans and held Jack's hand through it all.

His stomach rolled again, clenching, and he slid the second plate to Leslie as she scraped her first clean. He pressed his lips together. Blinked fast.

"You got good at cooking." She winked at him. "Where did you learn this?"

Ethan. Ethan made it for me, and it became my favorite the moment I tried it, the moment he fed me the first piece of steak, feeding me while I played footsie with him under the table, and we'd had half a bottle of wine on empty stomachs—

He wanted to vomit.

"Ethan," he said softly. "He made it for me. I learned a lot from him."

Leslie stilled. Her gaze flicked from her second half-empty plate to Jack. She slowly finished chewing, her fork picking through the remnants of salad and rice and turning over strips of steak.

She set the fork down. Swallowed. Pushed the plate aside.

"Are we going to talk about this?" She chewed on her lower lip. Pushed a strand of limp hair behind her ear. "Are we going to talk about him?"

"No." Jack shook his head. "No."

"Jack." She leaned forward, almost leaning into his space. He forced himself not to jerk away. "We're going to have to. We need to figure out what to do. What's going to happen now—"

"I'm going to take care of you." He couldn't meet her gaze. "You'll never want for anything. I'll make sure you have everything. The best doctors. The best therapists. The best of anything you want—"

"What about a husband?" She reached for his hand. "What about having my husband back?"

Her touch burned, a sizzle on his bones that stabbed the center of his heart. He jerked away.

Silence.

Her hand hovered over where she'd barely touched the back of his. "Oh," she breathed.

"Damn it, Leslie." Curling forward, Jack braced himself on his knees. "I'm hanging on by a thread."

"I'm your wife, Jack. We loved each other, so deeply. We can find that love again... if you give us a chance."

He squeezed his eyes closed.

"Can we try to get to know each other? Maybe... see what happens?" Her chin wavered, but she held her head high. "I never stopped loving you. Never. Could you... maybe just try? Can we at least see if our marriage is still there?"

He bolted to his feet. The walls were closing in; the floor was rising up. His stomach was rolling again, too fast, too hard, and he was going to vomit. Cold sweat prickled along his skin, clinging to the back of his neck. "I need time," he grunted. "I need—"

Ethan.

Quick steps took him to the open door and out into the hallway. The agents stared at him again, hot gazes burning his skin. He ran, down the hallway and back to his bedroom. Shoved open the door.

He barely made it to the toilet before he collapsed to his knees and heaved, green bile and empty nothingness spilling from him.

He sat back, leaning against the bathroom wall.
What was he going to do?

Anti-Moroshkin Insurgency Gains Strength in Southern Russia; US Launches Airstrikes in Support

An insurgency mounted against General Moroshkin's coup is gaining strength, based out of southwestern Russia in the Caucasus, from Sochi all the way to Kazakhstan and beginning to stretch into the Volga valley. Former federal and local police have flocked to the insurgent movement, reportedly led by the deposed President Puchkov.

The United States led a series of NATO air strikes against Moroshkin's forces in the region, hoping to give the insurgents some cover and protection against the general's forces.

44

Silver Springs, Maryland

Scott and Daniels went back to the White House the next morning, leaving Ethan alone in Scott's empty house.

"There's food in the kitchen. And we got you some clothes." Scott kicked the bags Daniels had brought in. "Thought you might need something, until—"

Until he figured out what to do next.

Where do you go from here, Ethan? Where do you go when your life shatters and everything you planned for evaporates? You're forty-one, and you changed everything for this man. Your job, your home, your whole world. What's left for you now?

He ended up flat on his back on Scott's couch, slowing working his way through Scott's bottle of whiskey. He'd drift off, lapsing into unconsciousness masquerading as sleep. Dreams evaded him, his mind, instead, replaying memory after memory. They were so real, so vivid, that he'd wake up reaching for Jack, or laughing at his ridiculous jokes.

And then his eyes would open, and he'd see Scott's ceiling, he'd taste the whiskey and bile in the back of his throat, and it would all come crashing back. He'd grab the whiskey again and take another swig straight from the bottle.

He'd given up the tumbler a long time ago.

One day of whiskey and wallowing, and then he'd figure out what to do.

But for now, he lay back and let the darkness claim him again.

Jack's flushed face and kiss-red lips hovered over him, his hips grinding over Ethan's cock as he worked himself down. His face was half in shadow, but his eyes were burning, staring down at Ethan like his soul was the sun. Ethan's hands slid up his sides, over his shoulders, and his fingers carded through his hair. He tried to pull him closer, tried to kiss him. "Ethan," his dream Jack breathed.

The voice was all wrong. Ethan frowned, staring at Jack as he kept grinding. "Ethan. *Ethan!*"

A hard shove on his shoulder jerked him awake. He flailed, his arms pinwheeling as he struggled to sit up. He managed to grab a leather couch cushion in one hand and get one foot down on the carpet, but nothing else. Bleary, he blinked and let his head fall back, his eyes closing. It was probably Scott, about to ream him for drinking his whiskey.

"It's a law, I think. That you're allowed to fall completely apart when it feels like your world has ended. When you've lost the one you love."

Eyes wide open, Ethan scrambled up, hauling himself to his ass on the couch and glaring across the study.

Lawrence Irwin stood beside the coffee table, staring at him with his eyebrows arched and the half-empty bottle of whiskey in his hands. "You planning on drinking until the pain stops?"

His head screamed, the blinding roar of a whiskey hangover. "Something like that."

"Doesn't work. I tried it, too." Irwin set the bottle down on Scott's desk. "My wife passed away thirteen years ago. Cancer. I thought the same thing, for a little while."

Jesus Christ. If he never, ever heard the word "wife" again, it would be too soon. Ethan rubbed his eyelids, pressing on his eyeballs.

Irwin kept going. "I get what the president is going through. If Kathy walked through the door right now, you had better believe I'd be right at her side."

Ethan glared up at Irwin. "This pep talk supposed to be helping?"

"Jack's not seeing clearly right now."

Ethan snorted and buried his face in his hands. "He's still made his choice, and as you said, you understand him."

"But what if something else is going on?" Irwin sat on the edge of the coffee table. "We don't really know where Mrs. Spiers has been for all these years. We have no way to corroborate her story. No way to figure out if what she's saying is true. But the president insists that he wants her close to him—"

Irwin seemed to ignore Ethan's clenched fists, his trembling arms.

"—and we're looking down the barrel of a massive security risk. We're doing what we can, but it's still a waking nightmare. And he can't see it, not right now."

"Why are you telling me this?" Ethan shook his head, still staring at the carpet.

"Because I know you pretty well, Ethan. We've worked closely together now for months, and before that, we were both in the White House for years, even before Jack was president. I've seen you in action. I know how you think, how you operate. And I believe I can help you right now."

The only thing that would help him was Jack. Jack, asking him to come home. Jack, kissing him again. Jack, telling him he was sorry, that it was him, he chose him—

Ethan shook his head again. "How?"

"We need to get someone on the ground and retrace Mrs. Spiers's steps. Confirm her story. Dig into Madigan and his operation and see if she really was held captive, or if something else is going on."

"Something else? You think she chose to stay with Madigan?"

"I think she's one of several ghosts we've discovered around Madigan. These ghosts have been operational, smuggling people and weapons into Russia. We think they, specifically Noah Williams, smuggled the terrorists responsible for setting off bombs in Russia. For shooting up the basketball game. Those terrorists came from the prison breaks Madigan engineered. Does any of that sound like the behavior of a hostage to you?"

"What about since she's been back? In the White House? I assume you have eyes on?"

"Hidden cameras were installed before they set up her med suite. And there are agents posted at her door around the clock. She spends her days in silence until the president arrives. She doesn't seem to be trying to do anything. Her blood work is clear, aside from the sedative we found in her system in Sochi. Physically, she's been neglected, recently beaten, and there's some evidence of torture." Irwin shrugged. "Right now, she sleeps a lot."

"Maybe she is just recovering." Ethan sighed. "Maybe she's different from the others. Maybe she really did fight back, and she really is a hero." He leaned back, throwing himself against the cushions. "She's Jack's wife. She's got to be a good person. He doesn't… put up with bad people."

"Maybe. And I do hope that's the case. I really do. But we've been wrong before. Gottschalk blindsided all of us."

Ethan looked away.

"I don't like constantly planning for worst-case scenarios, but I do it because we always have to be prepared. We have to be sure. We have to be totally certain. Jack's life may depend on it."

"What are you asking me to do?"

"We're already investigating Madigan. Already chasing him. But he shook us off after Fitz's murder, and now this? And Russia? We've got to pick up the pieces on the search. Get going again. The world is focused on Russia and how they're tearing themselves apart. Madigan's in there right now, but he's left a trail somewhere, too. If Mrs. Spiers was held captive, there's got to be a holding facility somewhere. A base. A bunker. Maybe

Enemy Of My Enemy

something mobile. Somewhere where she was held. We have to find that. Find his base."

"Cooper's team flushed Somalia. Madigan burned his way to the sea. And he was only there for a few months—" His voice choked off. "The tanker."

Irwin nodded. "A mobile base. Completely off the grid. Before that, maybe it was something else." His gaze pierced Ethan. "We *have* to find that tanker."

"Any luck on your end?" Irwin's end was the complicated series of intel agencies, satellites, and sources he had access to.

Irwin shook his head. "Everything's going toward Russia right now. We're on the brink with air strikes against the military facilities we can reach, and the Russians are looking like they're getting ready to strike back. Everyone is holding their breath."

Ethan frowned. "And you think now is the time to go figuring out if her story is legit?"

"We track down her story, we track down Madigan's trail. We get his trail, we might find intel on what's coming next. What his plans are. And." Irwin tried to smile, but it didn't reach his eyes. "You need something to do. Something that will give you meaning. What has ever been more meaningful to you than making sure Jack is one hundred percent safe?"

Fuck. Ethan glared at Irwin. Even if it wasn't him at Jack's side, Goddamn it, he did have to make sure Jack was all right. The need burned through him, singeing his heart. Why hadn't he thought of this before? If Jack wasn't safe, he had to do something. It was a primal need, something built into his soul. Protect the ones he loved.

Even if they didn't love him back.

"I guess you do know me pretty fucking well."

"Here." Irwin pulled out a manila envelope from his suit jacket and passed it to Ethan.

Ethan unrolled it; a US passport, with Ethan's picture and a fake name, a thick stack of hundred dollar bills, and a sat phone fell into his palm.

"Burner passport to get you out of the country, disposable phone, and cash to get you going. I've also got a jet fueled up at Andrews. Ready to take you wherever."

"So sure I'd say yes?"

"For Jack? Absolutely."

Fucking Irwin. Ethan glared down at the phone. Slowly, his brain started to churn, working back to before Russia, to before everything had collapsed. Cooper and his team had been compromised. They'd scattered, going ghost. Thoughts of Cooper led him to thoughts of the prince—

wounded, but alive—and to their one, almost improbable ally. His thumb hovered over the keypad.

"All right. I'll do it."

Irwin nodded and stood. "I'm leaving a car behind to take you to Andrews. Get moving fast. And—" He frowned. "—be careful who you trust, Ethan. We don't have the full picture. We're playing chess without a full view of the board. Things are not what they seem."

Jeddah, Saudi Arabia

Faisal's cell phone rang as he heard Adam's SUV roll up to the front of the house, tires crunching on the drive. Doors slammed, and low voices murmured from outside.

"*As-salamu alaykum*," he said into the phone, watching the front door.

"*Prince Faisal?*"

"Who is this?"

"*Ethan Reichenbach. We met last year, and we've been working together through Lieutenant Cooper. I'm sorry to hear you were injured recently. Especially because of our investigation.*"

Faisal froze. The front door banged open, and Adam walked backward through it, carrying something. Doc followed, cursing loudly.

"Mr. Reichenbach. *Shukran,* and I am recovering very well, *in shaa Allah*. How can I help you?"

"*Your Highness, I need to ask for your help.*"

"My help?" Faisal's gaze followed Adam and Doc through his foyer and into the villa's utility room. The door slammed behind them, muffling Doc's cursing.

"*With everything going on in the world, we can't let up in the search for Madigan. Most everyone's focus is on Russia right now. But we think that if we can backtrace Madigan's trail, we can get new insight into his future plans.*"

Something heavy dropped in the utility room. Doc shouted. Adam snapped, and Doc shut up quickly.

Faisal frowned. "Of course, Mr. Reichenbach. I agree. How can I be of help?"

"*Lieutenant Cooper and his team are sequestered for their protection, following an incident. We're dealing with a couple internal threats over here.*"

Doc darted out, carrying a black plastic trash bag. He headed for the kitchen, and the icemaker churned on. The sound of ice cubes sliding against plastic went on and on.

Reichenbach continued. "*Uh, it may seem strange, but right now, you're one of the most solid and trustworthy sources I can call on. I'd like to come to you. Join forces. Search for Madigan's trail together.*"

Faisal's eyebrows shot up. Reichenbach, here? With Adam? Reichenbach clearly didn't even know Adam was with him. His gaze flicked between the kitchen and the closed utility room. Aside from the ice falling, everything had grown suspiciously quiet.

What could he say? Deny Reichenbach access when they were all working on the same side? It had been too good to last, his and Adam's newfound freedom. Kissing Adam in front of Doc had been exhilarating, thrilling, but that would have to be tucked away. They still had to hide from the world, for so many, many reasons.

Would Adam revert all the way back to the crippling fear that had broken them apart?

What could he do, though? Ignore the world, save his love? Risk his love, save the world?

"I'd be delighted to see you again, Mr. Reichenbach. Please, fly to Jeddah. I will have one of my men pick you up at the airport."

"*Thanks. And—*" Reichenbach paused. "*—I'd like this to stay off the grid. No need to involve your government. This isn't an official state visit. I'm not—*" His voice choked, for a moment. "*I'm not a member of the first family anymore.*"

Faisal frowned. "Not to worry, Mr. Reichenbach. We will be circumspect."

"*I'll text you when I'm on approach.*"

"I'll have someone waiting for you. *Allah yusallmak*, Mr. Reichenbach. May Allah protect you on your travels."

"*Thank you, Your Highness.*"

The phone clicked off.

In the kitchen, the ice machine stopped. He frowned and slowly stood, heading for the workroom.

"Whoa!" Doc veered by him, standing in front of the door, holding the handle closed. In one hand, he dragged the black plastic bag, full of ice, across the marble floor. "You don't wanna go in there, lover boy."

Faisal arched one eyebrow. "I may enter any room of my house that I wish."

"Yeah, sure, you *can*," Doc said, emphasizing his words. "But you really don't *want* to."

"Doc! Anytime!" Adam shouted.

Faisal gently pushed Doc aside. He exhaled and sighed and guffawed all in one, an undignified kind of huffing squawk. Faisal turned the handle and pushed his head into the workroom.

"Hurry up with the ice! Oh—" Adam froze, wide eyes staring at Faisal.

Across the room, Adam had a bloody body laid out on a tarp in front of his air conditioner, near the chilling unit. The corpse's skin had gone pale, except for the side of his face, turning a mottled plum and green.

"What is *this*?" He stepped in, staring at the body, arms thrown wide, jaw dropping. "What did you *do*?"

"He shot himself!"

"And you brought him back *here*?"

"Doc, the ice! Now!" Adam looked away, grabbing the bag of ice when Doc hefted it around Faisal. He traded with Doc, throwing another plastic bag his way, and Doc disappeared back to the kitchen. The ice machine started up again. "We couldn't leave him on the street in Ma'an. Someone—the Jordanians, Madigan, hell, anyone—could have found him, and we'd be in serious trouble. And there's something weird about this whole thing, Faisal. I *had* him. I was trying to talk to him. And he shot himself."

"What did he say?"

"Nothing." Adam packed the ice around Noah's body, under his arms and over his heart and around his head. "Not a damn thing."

"And your solution was to bring a *corpse* into my *home*?"

Adam sighed, hanging his head. "What else could I do, Faisal?"

What else could he do, indeed? Shaking his head, Faisal crossed his arms. "Why keep the body, *habibi*?" He jerked his chin to the ice, and to Doc, filling another bag in the kitchen. "Why pack him with ice and preserve him?"

"Just a feeling I have."

"You think he'll pop back to life like a zombie?"

Adam sent him a dry glare and hollered for Doc again.

"And where are your shoes?"

Doc came back, hauling another bag of ice. Adam packed more around the body until it was completely covered. He wrapped the tarp tight and duct-taped it closed.

He didn't look at Faisal. "I was tracking him in a mosque."

Faisal's eyebrows arched high as his lips pursed. "For *this*, you'd go to a mosque? *Wallah*..."

Adam cringed. Finally looked up. "*Your* Islam I like," he breathed. "What *you* believe. But I can't listen to people saying they hate us."

Faisal finally spotted the blood splattering Adam's clothes and smeared across his skin. "Is that yours?" His throat clenched.

"Some of it. Not most, though." He rubbed at his ear. "Hey, who called? Did the rest of the team check in?"

Faisal sighed. Adam was trying to change the topic, veer away from something they'd needed to speak about for years. Not in front of Doc, though. "Your men checked in online while you were gone. Everyone is safe. And..." Faisal paused. "Mr. Reichenbach is on his way."

Adam paled, his skin going bone white.

"He said he wanted to join forces. Hunt Madigan together." Faisal arched one eyebrow. "Said you were sequestered for your safety. He has no idea where you are."

Mute, Adam shook his head.

"He's on his way," Faisal repeated. "And I told him someone would pick him up at the airport when he arrives."

Doc whistled from the doorway. "Wow. You are *so* fucked."

"Thank you." Adam sent him a withering glare. "Thank you for that."

"I'm just stating the obvious, L-T."

Sighing, Adam tipped his head back. Faisal's heart squeezed, and his gaze raked over Adam. *Please, do not lose faith again. Believe in us. This is meant to be,* habibi.

"I'll go pick him up," Adam grunted. "I'll do it."

"Annnd... What will you say about lover boy?" Doc jerked his thumb toward Faisal.

Adam glared. He said nothing.

Ethan tried to nurse away his hangover on the long flight to Jeddah. He pounded ginger ales and Alka-Seltzers, but when the plane landed and the sunlight pierced his skull, his headache came throbbing back. Not even his sunglasses were enough to block the punishing Arabian sun.

He trudged down the jet's stairs, duffel slung over one shoulder as he scanned the tarmac. The prince would be able to get a car onto the runway. He shouldn't have to head through the terminal.

A revving engine caught his eye, and then the smooth, cherry-red plating of a Lamborghini roaring across the airport. It swerved, tires squealing, and made a beeline for the jet. The Lamborghini skidded to a stop.

Really, he should have been even mildly excited about the car, should have had some kind of interest. A vague sort of curiosity pierced his malaise, a tiny curl of intrigue at the back of his heavy mind. At the least, this was not the soft-spoken, gentle prince Ethan remembered from a year ago. Though, he'd only known him briefly.

Scissor doors on the driver and passenger sides rose as one, arching forward from the angular car like wings.

Lieutenant Adam Cooper rose from the driver's side. He stared at Ethan, barely holding back a grimace, and clenched the keys in both of his hands.

Ethan's jaw dropped. "Lieutenant?"

"Director."

What the hell was Adam doing in the prince's Lamborghini? He'd gone ghost protocol, going to ground, disappearing from the grid. He was supposed to be tucked away somewhere in North America, safe and secure. What the fuck was he doing halfway around the world?

Unease coiled along his spine. He froze outside the car.

You're playing chess but can't see the whole board.

Be careful who you trust.

Rage tunneled his vision, turned everything raw and aching. He lunged, his blood burning, and grabbed Adam's jacket in both hands, pinning him to the sleek Lamborghini's frame. "What the fuck are you doing here? Huh? You working for Madigan? You and the prince? This some kind of sick fucking setup?"

Adam struggled against Ethan's hold, against Ethan's forearm pressing down on his neck. "The *fuck* did you just say to me?"

"Why are you here, Lieutenant?"

Adam finally got leverage, and he shoved Ethan back. "Because when Madigan attacked my men, he also attacked Faisal, and I owed it to him to be there when he woke up! I owe him *everything*! I'm the asshole who dragged him into the whole fucking mess, so yes, I came here when we went ghost." Adam puffed up, fuming. "Madigan killed one of *my guys*, and he almost killed Faisal! Don't ever fucking accuse me of working with him." He slammed his sunglasses back on his face. "Get the fuck in."

Silence strained the sunlight between them as Ethan debated. After a long, long moment, Ethan slid into the Lamborghini. The doors closed, and Adam took off at breakneck speed, rubber burning behind them as he tore out of the airport.

"Faisal called on the way. Says he has something for you."

Ethan said nothing.

Adam didn't wait for Ethan when they arrived, pulling into a gated seaside villa on the coast of the Red Sea. He ducked out of the car before the doors were all the way up, jogging around the front and heading to the house. Ethan followed.

Faisal stood in the front entrance, waiting. Gone were the long Saudi robes, the keffiyeh. He wore designer jeans and a T-shirt, and Adam was striding toward him. Faisal's gaze wasn't on Ethan; it was on Adam, fixed to the lieutenant's face.

Beyond the two, another of Adam's team hovered in the background, leaning against the wall with his arms crossed. He tried to place the face and then remembered: Doc, the corpsman. He'd stitched Ethan back together, and he'd been none too gentle with the needle, or with his acerbic tongue.

His gaze snapped back as Adam stopped in front of Faisal, trembling. His whole body shook, and his shoulders were stretched taut, the lines of his dark suit pulled tight. Faisal stared into Adam's eyes, not moving.

Adam leaned forward. His forehead pressed against Faisal's, and his eyes slipped closed.

Oh. *Oh.*

The pieces slid together, a puzzle falling into place in his mind.

Faisal turned to Ethan. He said nothing, not until Adam stepped sideways, still looking down, but close enough for Faisal to reach out to and wrap his hand around Adam's waist. "Mr. Reichenbach. *Al-hamdu lillah.* We're delighted you're here."

A soft snort from Doc.

"I..."

Adam's gaze pierced his. Fear, so much fear, and an underlying current of desperate, frantic hope. Adam still clenched the Lamborghini keys in his hands, almost flexing the metal up and down.

Jesus, he'd been like that, once. He'd looked at the world like that while standing beside the man he loved, and he'd dared to dream.

How wrong he'd been.

Could it be different for Adam and Faisal? A Marine and a Saudi prince? If there was ever a pair more unlikely than him and Jack, this would be it.

"I guess this explains some things," he said softly. "How long has this been going on?" Did something happen while they were searching for Madigan and using Faisal's palace as a base? Or back in Ethiopia, when they seemed to know each other a bit more than colleagues?

Doc snorted again. "*That's* a long story."

"Off and on for three years. We kept it secret. Until last week." Adam looked at Faisal, his lips pressed hard in a thin line. "No more hiding," he whispered.

Faisal smiled, soft and sweet, and kissed the back of Adam's hand.

In the back, Doc's gaze burned into Ethan, watching him with the predatory intensity of a falcon.

He looked down as his heart bled down the inside of his ribs. Their love, seeing their hope, scraped down his spine. *I had that once! I had a man who would choose our love over the world, and I was happy. I was so happy.*

But no more.

Clearing his throat, Ethan hitched his duffel on his shoulder. "Lieutenant, you said Faisal had something for us?"

"Yes. This way."

Faisal led them back to his open living room overlooking a wide deck and the Red Sea. The room was ultra modern and whitewashed, and Faisal settled in the middle of a white, wraparound leather couch. He grabbed his laptop as Adam hovered behind him, gripping the cushions on either side of his shoulders, and Doc threw himself into the white chaise. On a flat-screen mounted opposite the couch, Faisal called up a series of maps of the Arabian Peninsula, markers placed in the Arabian Sea and the Gulf of Aden.

"I've been reaching out to my sources on the ground. Village elders. Bedouin. A few smugglers. I heard the same thing over and over. People have started avoiding this area," he said, zooming in on a section of Saudi Arabia north of Jeddah, still on the Red Sea, between Umluj and Al Wajh. "They say it's haunted by *djinn*. That anyone who goes there doesn't return."

Ethan peered at the map. "Are those reefs? Right off the coast?" A series of sandbars and shallow turquoise waters poked at the empty coastline, a wasteland of rocks and cliffs on Saudi's western frontier.

"Shark-infested cays and a barrier reef at the vertical drop. Fishermen occasionally dare the waters, or go specifically to try to catch a large shark to sell. Most people avoid it."

"What else is out there?"

"Nothing. Just desert and Highway Five. Goes all the way to Haql and the Jordanian border."

Adam turned to Ethan. "Shark-infested waters that fishermen avoid and rumors of *djinn* to scare people away even further? Sounds like a great place to hide."

"Could a tanker park outside those reefs?"

"Madigan's Yemeni tanker could." Faisal leaned back on the couch, looking upside down at Adam. "Could this be where Noah was headed? Back to base?"

Adam's eyebrows rose. "Possibly."

"Noah Williams?" Ethan frowned. "He's one of Madigan's ghosts." He kept his mouth shut about Leslie, and about how she'd been in hiding with Madigan for years.

"We lost him after Paris, but Faisal picked him up in Jordan. We, uh. We went and got him." Adam looked away.

"Have you questioned him yet? What has he said?" Finally, a break in the search. Finally, someone he would get his hands into, question until he got answers.

Adam, Faisal, and Doc all looked at each other. "He's here," Doc finally said. "He's chilling."

"Doc." Adam glared. "We went to get him and bring him back for questioning. But he blew his brains out when we closed in. Didn't say anything either."

"Fuck." Ethan dropped his duffel to the white marble floor. Back to square one.

"I have a forensic pathologist coming tomorrow to autopsy the body. Maybe there's something we can find." Faisal shrugged. "It's a long shot, but…"

"Then the only other lead we have is this." Ethan nodded to the screen. "How long a drive is that?"

"Five hours." Adam glowered at the floor. "I can't go with you, Director. I'm staying with Faisal. I need to keep him safe, especially after Ma'an."

"And I'm staying with him." Doc jerked his chin toward Adam.

Ethan sighed. "You got a vehicle I can borrow?"

Faisal nodded.

"I'll drive out first thing in the morning. Check it out. See if something is even there." He scrubbed his hand over his face, pressing on his aching eyeballs. "Is there somewhere I can crash till then?"

Adam was in nothing but his briefs, leaning against the cool marble of the kitchen counters and slowly batting a beer back and forth between his palms when he heard Ethan stir in the middle of the night. Moonlight flooded the villa, bathing the living room in a silver glow.

He waited, counting the steps as Ethan crept down the stairs.

"Hey."

Ethan scrubbed his hand through his messy hair and headed his way. He wore sweatpants, new enough to still have creases, and no shirt. His muscular chest and stomach were covered with short hair, dark, save for one or two silver strands that caught the moonlight. Adam's gaze lingered, comparing Ethan's larger body to Faisal's sleekness, Faisal's smooth chest and golden skin, his lean muscles and angular features. Ethan's jaw was square where Faisal's was pointed, his lips pouted like a cupid's bow. Faisal's deep, dark eyes held gold in their depths, glittering whenever he gazed at Adam.

Faisal had captured his heart from day one. Ethan was attractive, for an older guy, but he was nothing compared to his love.

"Got another?" Ethan slumped against the counter.

Adam grabbed him a fresh bottle from the fridge and slid it down. "So."

Ethan took a long drag from his beer and stared at Adam.

"You and the president…" He trailed off as Ethan looked away. "It seemed like you were really in love," Adam mumbled.

"I was." Ethan frowned. He exhaled, his shoulders sagging. "I still am. I always will love him. No matter what."

"I, uh… I know the feeling." The beer turned sour in his stomach, memories of sleepless nights and endless days where he forced himself to stay away from Faisal, from his voice on the phone, his words over text, and even the memory of him.

"In some crazy way, I even kind of understand. Her memory was always there, always a part of him. I knew he loved her like crazy. I knew she was his first love. They didn't break up. She was ripped away from him. How could I ever compete with her resurrection?" Ethan leaned forward, resting his forehead on the marble counter with a sigh. A loud, metallic *plink* sounded, something heavy hitting the surface.

When Ethan pulled back, Adam's eyes went wide. He hadn't seen the chain around Ethan's neck, or the two rings nestled against his chest. Dark, with tiny diamonds glittering around both rings. The shine had dulled, but they were unmistakable.

"Holy shit. You—" He swallowed. He didn't know what to say.

Ethan reached up, rubbing the rings between his fingers. "Funny how fast things change, huh? Never even got a chance to ask." He cleared his throat. "Get your team back together. We might need them. Get everyone over here. Operate out of Faisal's place as long as you can. We can't trust anything or anyone back home right now."

Adam's jaw clenched. "Yes, sir."

Ethan lifted his empty beer bottle, a kind of salute, and set it down. He headed back for the stairs, but stopped. He didn't turn around.

"If you love Faisal. Really love him. Don't let anything stop you two. Don't let anything get in the way. You never know how much time you have together."

Adam finished his beer and went back to his and Faisal's bedroom. Faisal was stretched out on their bed, blinking as he stared at the moon-drenched sea beyond the windows.

"Hey. I didn't mean to wake you."

Faisal pressed his lips together. "I was afraid you had left again, and everything that happened was just a dream."

Fuck everything and everyone. I will stay with you until the end of everything. Adam slid into bed, wrapping Faisal up in his arms and pulling his warm body tight. Faisal grabbed him in return, stroking his hands everywhere, and then they were kissing, fast, hard kisses against lips and skin. Faisal pushed Adam flat on his back and trailed wet kisses down his body until he buried his face in Adam's crotch.

Desire slammed through Adam, going off like a gunshot. He arched back, breathless as Faisal slid his briefs down and swallowed his cock, sucking him deep. He spread his legs wide, clutching his knees to his chest as Faisal grabbed a bottle of lube from the bedside drawer.

Two fingers pressed against his asshole, and Adam squeezed his eyes shut.

Faisal licked him open, going from his cock to his asshole and back, over and over, until he was a slick mess, until he was shamelessly begging for Faisal to fuck him. His hands gripped the sheets, the pillows, the headboard.

Faisal grabbed his ankles and spread his legs, tilting Adam up just so, until his cock lined up with Adam's hole. He slicked his cock and pressed into Adam.

It had been a long time since Ethiopia.

Adam's back arched as Faisal slid within him, all the way in, in one move. All the air punched out of his lungs, and his spine turned to molten gold. He gasped, his open mouth moving soundlessly as his hands fluttered over the mattress, fingers scratching at the sheets. He cried out when Faisal's balls nestled against his ass, and the softest kiss pressed against his ankle.

Faisal knew Adam's body better than Adam knew himself. He knew what Adam needed, always. Adam sighed as Faisal's palms stroked down the back of his legs, soothed over his quivering muscles.

Faisal's warm breath ghosted over Adam's shin. He rolled his hips deep into Adam, not pulling back. Adam whimpered.

Faisal pitched forward, dragging Adam's legs over his shoulders, until he had Adam bent in half. Adam's hands flew, one hand landing on the surgical seal glued shut on Faisal's side, the other grasping Faisal's face, cradling his cheek. He stared up at his lover, panting, impaled, and desperate for more. "Please. Please, fuck me."

"No." Faisal leaned in, pressing a kiss to Adam's lips. "No. I will make love to you, *habib albi*."

Adam moaned. How long had it been since Faisal called him the love of his heart? Too, too long.

Faisal slowly thrust, gentle rolls in and out of Adam's body. "'*My eyes drown in tears, yet thirst for but one chance'*."

"Faisal, *please*. I can't—" Tears pricked at Adam's eyes as Faisal began reciting the words of an Islamic poet writing love songs to his male lover.

"'*I'll give away my whole life for my beloved'*." Faisal kissed his tears, his hips pressing deep as Adam groaned. "*Ya hayati*."

My love. My life.

Adam pulled Faisal down for another long kiss. In the moonlight, Faisal made love to him for hours, worshipping his body, until his heart and soul overflowed and his breathless moans mingled with Faisal's poetry, whispered onto every inch of his skin.

45

White House

One day rolled into two, and then into three.

Jack moved in a daze, a haze of shame that clung to him like a shroud of tangled, wet silk. The burn of guilt, of self-contempt, haunted his footsteps, a shadow he couldn't shake.

He barely functioned as a human being, much less as the president. Elizabeth stayed with him, sitting at his side through briefings and emergency calls to the Situation Room. He quietly deferred almost everything to her, decisions on where to strike inside Russia and how to deal with the rogue General Moroshkin coming from her through him. He caught Brandt and Pete whispering in the hallway, eyes wide and heads leaning in together, but they shut up as soon as they saw him.

Stares followed him around the West Wing, chasing him from meeting to meeting. It was so much worse, *so* much more so, than when he'd outed himself and Ethan. He'd grieved Ethan's loss then, but he hadn't been crushed with so much caustic contempt, so much self-hatred.

It ate away at him, an ache that grew larger every hour.

He could barely sleep, tortured with dreams of him and Ethan.

The bed he shared with Ethan was a no-go zone. It sat like a tomb in their bedroom, untouched, and he folded himself onto the couch, clutching a pillow to his chest like it was Ethan he held.

He tried, he really did, to imagine it was Leslie.

But he *couldn't*. He couldn't replace Ethan with Leslie, couldn't conjure up the love he'd once cherished for her. Couldn't close his eyes and imagine running his fingers through her hair, like he could with Ethan. Couldn't imagine their bodies oh-so-close, sharing breath as they rocked together.

He couldn't imagine a future with her. Not anymore

His shame, his utter shame, bloomed like a corpse going rotten, the stench of self-disgust clinging to him, sinking into his bones.

His wife was alive, rescued from years of neglect, of manipulation and torture at the hands of a madman, and all he could do was yearn for his missing lover.

He forced himself to try. He made breakfast and dinner every day, carrying eggs and pancakes and waffles down the hall, and then steak, chicken, and pizza. Leslie smiled at him, laughed when they talked, and asked so many questions, trying to catch up on a world that had moved on without her. They watched a movie together, one of the hundreds she'd missed, and she rested her head on his shoulder and reached for his hand with her good one.

Tears rolled down his cheeks as he held her and felt nothing.

He kissed her hair and tucked her in when it was time to sleep, even though her eyes asked him to stay.

There were some things he couldn't do. His body felt alien to him, like Ethan had the keys and had taken them with him. He was a stranger in his own skin, a puzzle with pieces out of place. A house of cards about to collapse.

Sleep evaded him again, and he watched the rise and fall of the moon through the window. Memories played through his mind, a film reel gone crazy, out of order and racing at high speed. Snapshots in time, isolated moments of love and laughter. He closed his eyes, trying to block them out, and pressed his face to the couch cushion.

When he opened them again, his gaze strayed to the mantel and to Leslie's folded flag cased in a triangular frame. He barely remembered her funeral, except for the gun salute punching him in the gut and the warm brass shells tucked in the folds of her flag, burning his palm even through the thick fabric. He'd felt the same at Ethan's funeral and had searched for the shells, tucked inside from the gun salute when a stern-faced soldier had presented the flag to him while "Taps" mournfully echoed over Arlington.

Rising, he dropped his pillow and went to the mantel, pulling down her flag and case.

He'd given back Ethan's when Ethan appeared alive again. What should he do with Leslie's?

Crinkling paper broke the silence of his bedroom as his fingers strayed over the back of the frame.

He pulled out a worn envelope, yellowing with age. The creases were frayed from being opened and closed too many times.

It was the last letter she'd written him. Her goodbye letter, only to be sent if she'd died.

He remembered reading it in the Texas sunshine outside their apartment mailbox, still numb from the official notice of her death days before. And then, her letter in the mail, like a voice from the grave. He'd read it over and over, his last link to her. Ancient tearstains warped the paper, had smeared the ink long ago. He'd slept with it, even, holding the envelope in his hand all through the night.

When he framed her flag, he'd tucked her letter in the back of the frame and left it there.

He untucked the flap and pulled out the worn, crinkled sheets.

"I decided to come to you this morning." Leslie smiled at Jack, leaning in the kitchen doorway and wrapped in a bathrobe. "I'm supposed to get up and get moving. Take walks." She shrugged. "Thought I'd come here for breakfast today."

Jack froze, hovering over the stove, spatula in hand. Scrambled eggs sizzled and toast popped from the toaster.

"Hey. Have a seat. I'm almost done." He loaded up a plate for her and brought it to the table with a glass of orange juice.

Her gaze froze on the sweatshirt he wore. Her lips thinned.

Jack lowered himself into the chair next to her. Ethan's Secret Service sweatshirt hung loosely from his shoulders, looser than it had before. He'd lost weight, and he had to push the sleeves up his forearms over and over.

Silence built like dominoes as Leslie ate her eggs and nibbled at her toast. Jack chewed his lips, watching the tabletop.

When she was finished, she leaned back, watching him.

He reached for an envelope, tucked beneath an untouched cup of cold coffee. "Les," he breathed. "Do you remember writing this for me?"

She stared at the old, worn paper, her eyes wide.

"You said—" He closed his eyes, swallowing hard. "You said you wanted me to be happy, even after you died. That you wanted me to go on living. Find someone to fall in love with again."

She looked down.

"I didn't. Not for years. I didn't feel anything for anybody."

"Until him." Leslie finally met his gaze. "Until Ethan."

He nodded, trying desperately to hold it together. Trying to not fall entirely to pieces. He squeezed his eyes shut, breathed hard, tried to stop his trembling chin. "Until Ethan," he whispered. His eyes opened, blurry.

She bit her lip.

"I love him, Les. I do, and I can't turn that off. I can't just *stop* loving him." He was losing the battle against his control, his eyes blurring as he dragged in a ragged breath. "I didn't know you were alive. I didn't know, and God, I'm *so* sorry. I'm so, *so* sorry that I didn't know. But I can't change what's happened." The edge of his control vanished, and the tears cascaded from his eyes. "I can't change that I fell in love with him. Or how happy he makes me."

Her eyes glistened, a wet shine building. "I do want you to be happy, Jack. Once, it was with me."

"Oh God." His heart burst, and his breath ripped from his lungs. He buried his face in his palms. Tears leaked through his fingers, falling to the floor, and in the devastated silence, he swore he could hear them falling like rain. "I'm sorry. I tried, Leslie. I did. But…" It was easier to speak to the darkness of his hands. "When I think of the future, I imagine it with him. I think of growing old with him. And I miss him *so* damn much."

Leslie sniffed and turned away, covering her mouth with her good hand. She nodded, fast jerks of her head, over and over. "I always thought you had moved on," she said after a long moment. "But I *never* thought it would be with a *man*."

Jack pulled his hands down, away from his eyes, until he had them pressed together in front of his face like he was praying, his lips resting on the edges of his fingers. "Does it matter that it is a man?"

Her face twisted, raw agony finally cracking through. "Did you ever really love me at all, Jack?"

He reached for her, resting a hand on her knee. "I *did*, Les. I did, so much. I still do, in a way."

"Then—" Sobbing, she lunged for him, holding his hand. "Then, Jack, we can—"

He shook his head, and her words died, swallowed up as she snapped her mouth closed.

"It wouldn't be fair to you if I forced this. You would never have all of me, and I'm afraid I'd grow to resent you." He bit on his upper lip, dragging it between his teeth. "It wouldn't be fair to Ethan, either. We love each other."

She looked down, her shoulders shaking.

"I will always be here for you, Leslie. *Always*. I will take care of you, give you the best of everything. Everything I can give you, you will have." He tried to smile, but it felt like a grimace. "But as a *friend*," he whispered. "As a friend only."

She finally nodded, staring at the floor. "Okay." Tears dripped down her cheeks, but she fought through. "Okay."

"I'm so sorry." His eyes squeezed closed, but the tears kept coming. He let them fall, wiping them with the sleeve of Ethan's sweatshirt as Leslie turned away, staring into the middle distance, her own tears making salt trails down her cheeks.

He could feel his presidency shattering, feel his reputation and his legacy drop like a sandcastle beaten down by the sea. He'd lose it all, with this.

But he'd be with Ethan, and that outweighed everything else.

It was a Saturday, and even though the White House was mostly empty, Jack headed to the West Wing after walking Leslie back to her bedroom and leaving her tucked in her bed. Her eyes were wet and red, but she tried to be strong. He heard her sobs, though, as he walked away.

He kept walking, going down the stairs and past the Oval Office, and then went down one more floor, stopping at the secured doors outside Horsepower, the Secret Service's White House headquarters.

He took a deep breath and knocked.

They knew he was there, waiting outside. His movements were tracked around the White House, a little red blip on their monitors moving over their giant map, tracking him everywhere, all the time. If he thought too much about it, he ended up wanting to climb out of his skin and run from the White House, and never, ever come back.

Slowly, the door opened. Scott poked his weary head out. Deep lines furrowed into his forehead and his cheeks, and dark bags hung beneath his eyes. Cold fury flowed off him. "Mr. President. If you have a request, you should make it through official channels."

"Scott..." His skin buzzed, crawling, and he just wanted to jump and scream and shout until his voice went hoarse. "Scott, can I speak with you? In private?"

Scott stared at him, and if possible, his expression grew fiercer, angrier, the lines around his eyes tightening, his lips thinning. "Mr. President. One moment."

He said something to the agents behind him and then ducked out. He folded his arms, spread his legs, and stood like a linebacker in the hallway, squaring off against Jack like he was about to deliver some kind of raw high school locker room justice.

Well. He had hurt Ethan, Scott's best friend. He deserved Scott's wrath, and so much more.

"Where's Ethan?"

Scott looked away.

"*Please*, Scott. Where is he? I've been trying to call him, but he's not answering."

Scott glared at the wall. "Why do you want to call him? Just to tell him it's over? Give yourself closure? Trust me, he knows. He doesn't need you to twist the knife any deeper."

"God, no!" Jack ran his fingers through his hair, gripped the back of his skull. "That's not it at all! Scott—"

"Why are you wearing his sweatshirt?"

"Because it's the closest I can get to him right now. I'm falling apart, and I need him—"

"You can't just use him like that, call him whenever you feel like you need him—"

"Damn it, Scott!" Jack shouted, his hands fisted in his hair. He spun, gasping, and glared. "Damn it, I'm not trying to use him! I'm trying to bring him *home*! I just told Leslie that I couldn't be with her because I'm in *love* with Ethan! And, because he's *it*! He's the one for me! I want to grow old with him. Spend forever with him. I want *everything* with Ethan!"

Scott stared, his jaw hanging open. He squeezed his eyes closed. "Goddamn it, Mr. President."

"*Please*," Jack pleaded. "Where is he?"

"I don't know." Scott slumped against the White House basement wall. "He was staying at my place. I came home and he was gone."

"Gone?" Panic clawed at Jack's heart.

"Gone. Left his cell and his wallet." Scott's eyes narrowed. "Irwin wanted to know where he was that day. I think he went to see him."

"Irwin." Exhaling, Jack pushed back his frantic nerves. "Lawrence. Okay. So… he's probably on a mission, then. Black bag. Compartmentalized." He squinted at Scott. "Right?"

"I guessed the same."

"Okay." Jack paced in front of Scott. "I'll talk to Irwin. See what's going on. I don't want to interrupt if… if it's something dangerous." His heart leaped into his throat, nearly strangling him, and he felt the color drain from his face. *God, be safe, Ethan. Be safe. Come home to me. Please.*

"Here." Scott dug in his suit pants and pulled out Ethan's cell phone. "I've been holding on to this. In case he calls or something. I don't know."

Jack took the phone, turning on the screen. A background picture of him and Ethan, smiling for the camera on a sunny day in the Rose Garden came up, and a moment later, his thumbprint registered, unlocking the phone. The same picture smiled back at him, behind Ethan's icons. Seventeen missed calls—all from him—and five unread text messages—

again, his—blinked. "At least he's not deliberately ignoring me." He tried to smile.

Scott didn't smile back. He stared at Jack. "Are you certain?" he growled. "Ethan loves you more than you know, and this is tearing him apart. If you're not *absolutely* certain, dead sure, about this, it will break him. He's like a brother to me. I don't want to see him like this again."

"I'm one hundred percent certain. It's him. Forever."

"When he gets back," Scott growled. "Don't fuck this up, Mr. President."

46

Jeddah, Saudi Arabia

"We don't cook. Like, at all. So this will be fine." Doc shrugged, crossed his arms, and grinned at the gobsmacked Saudi pathologist.

Adam and Doc had draped tarps over Faisal's kitchen, across the countertops, and over the floors, and laid out Noah's body along the tarp-covered marble surface. Ice lay packed around his pale, ghostly skin, and on top of his clothes, soaking wet with the ice melt. His head was near the large sink.

"I think that's how it's done on TV," Doc had said.

Faisal watched from the doorway, staying well clear of the corpse.

"What… is it you want me to do?" The doctor glanced at Faisal, incredulity straining his features. He wore a tailored suit and a ghutra, the checkered pattern hanging off his face and down his back. "The cause of death is clear." He gestured to Noah's skull. On one side of his head, a small entrance wound, and on the other side, a blown out depression, skull and brain gone, like an ice-cream scoop had dug in and taken a portion of his head away.

"Is there anything medically… off about his body?" Adam spoke when Faisal arched his eyebrows toward him. "Any evidence of drugs? Or torture? Anything odd in his system at all? Or, hell, do his vocal cords even work? Were they cut through? Anything weird about him in any way?"

The doctor's cheeks ballooned, and he stared down at Noah's corpse with wide eyes.

Across the island, Doc snapped on a pair of latex gloves. "I'm ready to assist."

Adam and Faisal rolled their eyes.

Ethan finished another water bottle and chucked the empty plastic into the back seat of the Land Rover. Saudi Highway Five rolled on beneath his tires, an endless stretch of two-lane blacktop heading north through the sun-scorched rocks of Western Saudi.

He'd left before dawn, taking one of Faisal's three Land Rovers, a set of binos, a case of water, and a collapsed inflatable boat in the back seat. It had a two-stroke engine, and he'd be able to get through the cays and reefs with ease.

If there was anything out there.

Adam had given him a compact M4 with a mounted flashlight, a bulletproof vest, and a tactical pack, lifted from Faisal's security team. Faisal had banished the security team to their separate house down the private road by the gate, but they still had a cache of weapons at Faisal's main villa. He wore the vest and the attached tac pack, and the rifle lay in the front seat, beside a bag of figs, a map, the binos, and three bottles of water.

Finally, his GPS pinged after he passed Umluj and the turnoff to Kuff in the Saudi foothills, and forty-five miles before the village of Al Wajh. He slowed and turned off the highway, his tires crunching over baked dust and chipped red rock. Uneven ground rocked his Land Rover until it gave way to smooth, golden sand, stretching endlessly along the coast.

He parked near the shoreline above the waves and pulled out the inflatable. A quick break of the seal, and the boat started filling up while he filled the engine with gas. His rifle went over his head and shoulder, tucked on the side of his body, and he tossed water bottles into the bottom of the boat as he scoped out the reefs through the binos.

Just on the edge of the horizon, he could make out the rough outline of a tanker, shivering in heat waves. It was easy to miss, buried amongst the cays and reefs and in the distance. Whoever had parked it there had used the curvature of the earth to their advantage.

It would take time, winding his way through the reefs and cays. He plotted out a route, sketching it on his map, folded to just the reefs. A few hours to get there, winding in and out of the tangled sand barriers and low waters. Faster, if he stayed south and went over open waters. But he wouldn't have cover, then, and anyone onboard would spot him coming from miles away.

Engine in one hand and boat in the other, he headed for the water, shoving off in the shallows and paddling out until he could attach the engine and get it going. Perfectly clear waters lapped at the edges of the boat. Rainbow-colored fish darted to and fro, and at the nearest cay, a line of orange and purple coral winked at him under the surface.

Jack would love this. We could have gotten married on a beach.

He shoved his heartache down and pointed the boat toward the tanker.

Ethan stopped at the last cay, a long, narrow stretch of empty white sand, and peered at the tanker through the binos.

No movement. Nothing on deck. A limp line hung over the side, seemingly abandoned. A rope ladder dangled toward the waterline, drifting in the light breeze.

No signs of life anywhere.

He crawled back to the boat, pushed off the sandbar, and started up the engine again, heading for the rope ladder. Up close, the tanker was huge, towering overhead. At the bow, the tanker's name had been scratched off, and dents marred her steel sides. Bullet holes pierced the hull, some huge, others smaller. A deep gouge dented half her beam. The battle with the Russians had left its mark, when Madigan had sunk the *Vinogradov*.

He tied the boat to the bottom rung of the rope ladder, pulled his rifle across his chest, and started climbing.

As he reached the top, he gripped his rifle, holding it one-handed. The barrel went over the tanker's edge first, and then his eyes, scanning the deck, right and left, clearing his line of sight.

Again, nothing.

Ambling up, he came over the side and landed on the deck in a crouch, moving forward slowly, his head on a swivel. The mottled deck of the tanker was a mess: toppled barrels, cut lines, pieces of scrap metal and shorn steel piled in heaps. Tangled electrical cords lay across the deck, zig-zagging into piles before snaking off toward the bow. At midships, one cargo manifold was open to the sky, one of the wide iron doors thrusting upward, and whatever had once been in the cargo hold was long gone.

An open door banged at the tanker's house, the boxy protrusion rising from the aft of the vessel.

Whirling, he aimed for the house, but loose hinges on the swinging door creaked, rocking on the waves, and it banged again, flapping with the current only.

No one was there.

He headed down the deck, toward the ship's aft. The house used to be white, but blown sand had chipped the paint and rust had taken over the lower half.

A torrent of blood stained the deck iron-red and had splashed against the house's exterior walls.

The swinging door whined when he pushed it open. He scanned the hallways, eyes darting right and then left. Old blood dried on the walls, on the floor. The tanker's former crew, perhaps. He crept up one hallway and down the other, his rifle up, finger half-squeezed on the trigger.

An empty mess hall. Chairs tipped over.

A destroyed bunkhouse, where a crew had once slept, bloody mattresses scattered on the floor.

On the bridge, someone had taken a gun to the consoles, destroying the equipment. Shattered glass covered the tile floor, crunching beneath his boots. Spiderwebbed lines cracked through the bridge's windows, bullets still lodged in the thick glass. Nothing worked. Everything was dead. Charts lay in a heap in a wastebin, burned to ash, the edges of a map of the Persian Gulf and the Arabian Sea sticking out.

He headed back down to the main deck, frowning. This had definitely been Madigan's ship. It had been his base. The damage, the bullet holes, the bloody detritus left behind. He'd been here. Where was he now?

His gaze landed on the open cargo manifold.

Ethan silently moved down the ship, keeping to the shadows and darting from structure to structure. Pylons and giant pipes snaked across the deck, and he crouched low, running down the side of a chipped pipe heading toward the bow and right past the cargo manifold.

Every hair on the back of his neck stood straight. A light breeze skittered over the ship, tickling his skin and whispering through the ghostly vessel. He wanted to believe it was just the wind and the sun, and the eerie otherness of the broken tanker, but something kept prickling at his senses. A sense of wrongness.

A sense that he wasn't alone. That he was being watched. He could almost feel the slick, hot slide of someone's eyeballs against his skin.

He scanned fore and aft, crouched low at the manifold. Still, nothing moved. Beneath him, the dark mouth leading to the belly of the vessel yawned wide, an almost impenetrable darkness. From where he crouched to the water line, the ship was almost thirty feet tall, and most of that height was swallowed within the black hole below his feet. A rickety metal stair ladder descended into the pit. He could barely make out the first landing, a catwalk ringing the hold, fifteen feet down.

Electrical cords dangled into the darkness across from him.

Ethan flicked on the flashlight mounted on top of his M4 and swept the interior of the hold. His beam couldn't penetrate the bottom. He pulled out a glow stick from his tac pack, snapped it, and tossed it down.

A clang echoed upward, the plastic hitting the metal bottom. A soft yellow glow surrounded the stick. He waited, rifle up and ready, aiming into the black.

Nothing.

Slowly, he slipped into the hold, down the first steps of the stair ladder. The stench of the cargo hold hit him like a gut-punch. Sulfur, rotten eggs, and the rancid tang of tar, decades of crude oil sloshing in the hold and searing the stench into the iron and steel. He gagged and his eyes watered.

Still, he moved on, creeping down the ladder to the landing. He kept going, all the way down.

Past the first landing, his flashlight beam caught on something at the bottom of the hold. What looked like tables set up, and monitors arrayed along the sides. Chairs, facing the monitors. The skeletal outlines of flood lamps.

Heart pounding, he quickened his pace, descending into the belly of the vessel, the bottom of the hold. Scanning left and right, he kept his rifle up, finger curled over the trigger, as he crept forward. Electrical cords dangled in his face, and he used the barrel of the rifle to push them aside.

His flashlight beam landed on a control panel and one softly illuminated power button. The cords all connected there, and to a huge rack of computer servers and a single display, and then veered out again, connecting the rest of the hold's tech.

Shadows loomed around him, long lines of the shapes in the hold throwing odd angles into the darkness. He leaned forward, pressing the power button on the control panel, and stepped back fast.

Whirring hums echoed through the hold, the servers roaring to life. Flood lights winked on, some cracking to brilliant illumination, others blinking before droning to life. Monitors buzzed, pixels and video streams slowly turning on, paused mid-motion. Next to the monitors, rolling whiteboards and glass boards covered the wide deck of the hold, pictures tacked haphazardly and what looked like flow charts, battle plans, and targets. Chairs sat in a circle, facing the monitors, their backs to each other, each with a dedicated bank of monitors and boards and pictures arrayed before them.

Restraints were fixed to the chairs, at the wrists and ankles, and a crude piece of wood had been fixed to the backs. A strap on the boards had held someone's head immobile. On a tray next to each chair, a terrifying set of glasses with spikes facing toward the eyes lay, dried blood coating the pinpoint ends.

Ethan's stomach clenched. He'd seen those before, long ago. A way to force someone's eyes to remain open. A prisoner, or someone under enhanced interrogation.

He crept closer to one of the whiteboards before a chair, pictures of the sunk Russian destroyer and the ship's captain tacked together. Maps of Europe and highlighted routes heading into Russia. Pictures of Sergey and the closest members of his government. Sasha, walking next to Sergey, caught in a sidelong glance toward Sergey. Ethan could see the devotion in Sasha's eyes as Sergey smiled at someone out of the frame.

His heart stopped when his gaze fell on another board. Pictures of Jack. Pictures of him. Pictures of the two of them in the White House. Sitting on the steps of the Residence, watching the Marines practice for Sergey's state dinner. The two of them laughing in the Rose Garden, side by side. Sharing a secret kiss in the shadows of the West Wing. Holding hands as they walked up the stairs to the Residence.

Photos only someone deep within the White House could have taken.

There were more infiltrators. More of Madigan's men still right beside Jack.

Behind him, a deep voice rumbled.

He whirled, rifle raised, his blood rushing through him, freezing as he half squeezed the trigger.

He stilled, though, when his eyes landed on a monitor, and the video that had started to play.

Jeddah, Saudi Arabia

"Hmm."

"Hmm?" Doc poked his head up from where he was washing Noah's stomach and running the gut, flushing his intestines into a pan balanced over the sink. "Hmm, what?" He stared at the Saudi pathologist, eyebrows arched high over his medical mask.

On the tarp on the counter, Noah's naked body was cut open from neck to groin, a Y-incision at his collarbone spreading his skin wide. His rib cage had been sawed in half, the top part removed, and his internal organs taken out one by one. Doc whistled Disney songs softly and washed each organ in the kitchen sink.

Adam leaned back against the fridge, close enough to see everything—and smell everything—but far enough back to be out of the way. His fingers drummed over his crossed arms, one foot bouncing against the marble floor.

Faisal hovered far away at the door, pale.

"His teeth are so strange." The pathologist was knuckles-deep in Noah's mouth, headlamp shining into his throat. "What was his diet? Did he consume liquids his whole life?"

"He was a red-blooded American. Steak, burgers, and fries."

"Then his teeth should show more signs of wear, especially along the molars. For a man in his late thirties, I would expect to see much more wear and use. These are the teeth of an adult with the wear pattern of a toddler."

"He's supposed to have a tattoo as well." Adam barely kept his voice from shaking, barely held back the fury coursing through him. "He's supposed to have a big tattoo, right there." He pointed to Noah's bicep, unadorned and skin smooth. "He showed it off when he came back home. I remember it. Perfectly."

The pathologist frowned.

Doc stared at Adam. Even he didn't have anything smart to say.

"He didn't say anything. I thought—" Adam shook his head. "Now I'm wondering if he even knew who I was at all." He glared at the doctor. "Are there any war injuries? Bullet wounds? Shrapnel? Any scars at all? I know he was fucked-up over there." Adam braced himself against the counter and stared down at Noah's cut-open body.

The pathologist shook his head. The autopsy had begun with a full body examination. Other than the bullet hole in his head and two shots to his knees, there was nothing wrong with his body. No scars of any kind. No tattoos.

"L-T?" Doc cocked his head to one side. "Is this the guy you knew? Is this even Noah Williams?"

Saudi Arabian Coast

"*State your name.*"

"*Leslie. Christina. Spiers.*" Leslie spoke slowly, deliberately. Ethan recognized the touch of sedatives in her voice. He crept closer to the screen, watching as a man on the video, his back to the camera, talked to Leslie, seated and restrained in one of the chairs.

"*State your age.*"

"*Forty-five years old.*"

"*Who is your husband?*"

"*Jack. Jack Spiers.*"

God, he didn't want to watch this. He didn't want to watch Jack's wife be tortured onscreen. No matter how he felt about her reappearance, he didn't want to see this. Moving quickly, he headed for the laptop balanced near the monitors, trying to end the video. He'd take the laptop with him, bring it back to Irwin. They could analyze the footage, figure out what had happened. He didn't need to see this.

More video files were queued up. Dozens of them. He held his breath, and despite himself, clicked on the next link.

She was fighting back in the next video, shrieking and twisting in the chair, thrashing against the restraints. What came out of her mouth wasn't human, howls that scraped down his bones. Men rushed through the frame, stabbing her with needles as she wailed. Eventually, she slumped in the chair, breathing hard, and the same man walked into the frame.

"*State your name.*"

She stared back at him, a thin line of drool falling from her bottom lip.

"*She needs more cognitive structuring. Set up the implantation protocols again. We'll start with—*"

He clicked another file, further down the line.

Something older popped up, an interview with Jack from years and years ago, back when he was a new Senator from Texas. *Honoring Fallen Heroes* blazed across the screen, and then there was Jack, painfully younger, sitting on a couch in his office on Capitol Hill, smiling for the camera.

"Tell us more about your wife, Senator. What was she like?"

Jack smiled on screen. "*She had the biggest heart, especially for her goofball husband. Let me tell you this story. We'd been married maybe a year. She was gone for over a week on field training, and I, wanting to welcome her home the right way, tried to cook her a great chicken dinner.*" Jack laughed, shaking his head. "*I burned it all. I mean, charcoal for chicken breasts. I forgot about the sides entirely, I was panicking so much. She came in, the apartment was full of smoke, and I had this black hunk of chicken on the table.*"

Jack and the interviewer laughed together. "*So what did she do?*"

"*She ate it. Bless her heart, that woman ate my horrible attempt at cooking. I microwaved a can of beans and slapped some store-bought potato salad on the table, and she just laughed and ate it all.*" His smile turned wistful onscreen, and then his lips pressed together, and he looked off to the side, away from the camera.

Ethan paused the video.

A chill tap-danced down his spine, frigid fear that coiled around his guts. He scrolled down, through the files.

There were hundreds of files. Videos, photos, saved posts from social media. Clicking furiously, he opened file after file, the videos starting automatically, playing on top of each other on different screens. Photos of Leslie in training, at her wedding, candid shots of her and Jack flashing across the hold. Social media posts captured from the Internet came next, paragraph after paragraph, tweet after post after picture after video, each a moment of her life.

A part of her story.

A part of her identity.

He scrolled back to the top, to the first video, and pulled it up again.

Playback resumed where he'd left off.

"*Who is your husband?*"

"*Jack. Jack Spiers.*"

"*Who is your target?*"

Leslie's voice turned cold, hard as steel. "*President Jack Spiers. First Gentleman Ethan Reichenbach. General Bradford. Lawrence Irwin. Director Rees. Vice President Elizabeth Wall.*" The names continued, a list of Jack's key staff, the national security strength of the nation.

"*State your attack plan.*"

She spoke with no inflection. No emotion. A hardened operative, reciting her battle plan. "*I will ingratiate myself into the White House as Jack's wife. Return to President Spiers's side. Remind him of our history together. Reconnect through shared experiences and recitation of deep emotional memories. I will build trust through emotional bonding and gain access to key staff and personnel. When a critical mass of personnel has been reached, I will execute on American soil in a location selected for mass terror infliction.*"

"*Excellent,*" the man purred. His back stayed to the camera, his voice just a dark, low purr. "*You've come so far.*"

What the hell was this? Had Leslie been brainwashed? She seemed like a robot, like an automaton, and nothing at all like the emotional, heart-wrenching woman they'd carted off the streets of Sochi and treated on Air Force One. Was it all an act? But which one? The killer, trying to navigate out of her torture? Or the loving, devoted wife, living in the White House at Jack's side?

Sweat beaded on his forehead. His breath came fast, his heartbeat even faster. Shaking fingers scrolled through the files, all the way to the beginning. There had to be something in there, something that would show what she had been put through. "Cognitive structuring," the man had said. "Implantation protocols."

A single video file sat at the bottom of the file, time stamped from months ago. His fingers trembled, hovering over the mousepad, before he clicked.

He held his breath.

The camera hung over a tank, filled with what looked like gel. Stamped on the bottom of the frame were the words "SAMPLE THIRTEEN" and a time-elapsed series of hours and days. The video sped up, and slowly, shapes took form in the gel. What looked like a tadpole, and then a chimera. An alien, almost, with a gigantic skull and translucent bones and a long skeleton. Legs formed, and then arms, and the flutter in the chest turned into a heart. Frames jumped forward, and the shape turned into a human baby, unconscious in the ooze. Then a child. Then a teenager.

At fifty days from timestamp zero, the video stopped.

Ethan couldn't breathe.

His mind was screaming, an endless wail, shrieking at him. *Get out of there! Get out of there now! Get Jack! He's not safe!*

He was frozen, though, his feet fixed to the deck, his fingers numb, trembling over the laptop's keyboard. Dread poured through him, filling his lungs, flooding his veins, dragging him down until his vision darkened, and all he could see was the image onscreen.

A perfect, genetic duplicate of Leslie Spiers, aged forty-five, lay in the gel.

Next to his ear, a rubber band snap shattered the air. The laptop screen exploded. Warm wetness oozed down the side of his face as his ear burned.

He dove to the side, huddling behind Leslie's interrogation chair.

No. Not interrogation. *Programming.* That thing wasn't Leslie Spiers. *Wasn't* Jack's wife.

"I didn't expect it to be you." A voice, the same deep rumbling voice from the video, called out of the darkness above Ethan. "I thought it would be Lieutenant Cooper. He's done a nice job of putting the pieces together." Ethan could hear the slick smile in the man's voice. "Lining up the colors on that Rubik's cube."

"Who are you?" Ethan bellowed. His hands clenched on his rifle, trying to hold it steady. He blinked fast. Tried to breathe through shuddering lungs.

"I guess I shouldn't be surprised it is you, though. After all, you're running Lieutenant Cooper's little operation. And," the deep voice laughed aloud, "you're certainly not living in the White House anymore."

Ethan's blood chilled. "You're brave in the dark, aren't you?" he hollered. "Come out and face me!"

Another rubber band snap, a fizz through the air, and a bullet slammed into the armrest next to Ethan's head. He spun away, scrambling beneath the table in front of a cluttered whiteboard.

"Have you figured it out yet?" Footsteps clanged above, the voice walking along the catwalk. "Or are you as dumb as the media makes you out to be?"

"You cloned her!" Ethan listened for the footfalls, closing his eyes after he shouted. The footsteps stopped. "You cloned her, and you dropped her in Jack's lap like a fucking Christmas present!" He raised his rifle, aiming in the black for where he'd last heard the footfalls. "Did you clone the others too? Noah Williams?"

He squeezed his trigger.

Bullets pinged against the steel catwalk, the iron frame of the cargo hold. A grunt, and then a curse from the voice above, and Ethan scrambled behind the server rack just before bullets chewed through the table he'd been covering under.

"You're not as dumb as they make you look. But you have no idea what's really going on."

"Why don't you tell me?"

"You and Jack, fighting the good fight against Black Fox. Determined to take General Madigan down." The man laughed. "You haven't got a clue."

There was a whizzing sound, something he knew but couldn't place, and then heavy boots slammed into the bottom of the cargo hold.

Ethan cursed. The man had just roped down from the catwalk. He was down there with him, in the shadows in the belly of the freighter. Footsteps echoed. "Black Fox was one of the hundreds of different incarnations of us, Ethan. Just one. We've been here for years, and there's nothing you can do to stop us."

"What the hell is it you people want?" Ethan pressed back against the chairs.

"A world of our own," he snapped. "A place where we can be what we were always meant for. This isn't how we're supposed to be." He sighed, and joints cracked. "But it's all right. Our new world is almost here. A new dawn is coming. A new sky awaits us all." He paused. "You *know*, Ethan. You know what I mean."

"You're fucking crazy."

"How many times have you wanted to just get away from the world? Press pause on everyone's stupidity? Bring an end to all of the bullshit," the man groaned. "Do you know how disgusting it is to watch the world spin on? Endless piles of crap. Worthless people doing worthless things. The political garbage. Mindless politicians. Empty promises. It's so monotonous. So trivial. So utterly boring. Do you remember when it was simpler? When there was black and white and the choices were clear? Remember how good that felt?"

"You want to bring the world back to war?"

"Conflict and war are the truths to human life. Combat is the ultimate test of a human's worth. There's too many idiots, Ethan. It's time for a purge, and the right kind of people need to rise up and claim what's up for grabs. Power. Back in the hands of the powerful. You could join us. You're a natural, Ethan. You were born for killing."

"I'll never join you," Ethan spat. "You and your sick delusions can go fuck yourselves."

"Mmmm." The man sighed. "I feel sorry for you. I really do. You have no idea how deep this goes. How far we've gotten. How many people are with us. How your whole world is about to change." He laughed. "We're everywhere, Ethan. Everywhere."

Those pictures. Taken of him and Jack in their home. His blood burned. "Then why are you rotting on this piece of shit tanker? Huh? Can't find a real base to call home?"

"I'm just closing up shop." More footsteps, and then the man's shadow fell across the bottom of the hold, almost reaching Ethan. He peeked around the chair, trying to catch a glimpse, but the man stood in the lights and all he could see was a slim silhouette.

"Come on out, Ethan," the man purred. "I want to see you again." His rifle chambered, and a round dropped to the floor, plinking as it bounced and rolled away. "I won't even shoot you."

Ethan closed his eyes. They needed intel. He needed to bring this man in alive, no matter how much he wanted to turn around and empty his magazine into his chest, spray him full of bullets until he was nothing but ground meat and a smear against the cargo hold. They needed him alive. They needed to know what he knew.

He spun out from the servers, standing and holding his rifle high.

He came face-to-face with Captain Ryan Cook.

Cook's face had weathered some since his last official Army photo. Deep lines etched into his pockmarked face, and his wiry hair was cut short, almost shaved. He wore black combat pants and a black T-shirt tucked in tight, and a rifle hung off his shoulder. His hands were crossed over his belt.

Cook smiled. "My, you grew up big." His smile turned into a leer. "Don't you remember me?"

"Shut the fuck up," Ethan growled. "I never met you."

Cook *tsked*, wagging one finger toward Ethan. "Now that's just impolite. Tikrit. Eighteen years ago. Just after that big offensive.

Remember blowing me in the showers? That first shower we'd had in three weeks? Us Special Forces guys got the shaft." Slowly, Cook grinned.

Memories played fast, sounds and shapes and colors zipping through Ethan's mind. Tikrit, Iraq. He'd been young, painfully young. Early twenties. New in the unit. They'd been attached to Special Operations Command, and there'd been a young captain who had caught his eye. He'd looked one time too many. The captain had cornered him in the showers after they had survived a battle Ethan had known he'd die in at least six different times.

Instead of him getting a black eye, he'd blown the captain under the hot spray, the rest of their unit just outside the stall. The captain, in turn, had pressed his hand over his mouth—until he couldn't breathe— and fingered his ass as he'd jerked himself hard, spraying the walls in moments.

"Fuck you!" His finger half squeezed the trigger, but the barrel of his rifle trembled. He blinked hard. Grit his teeth. "Fuck you, asshole!"

Cook laughed. He sauntered to the side, pointing to another laptop. "May I?"

"Fucking freeze!" Ethan squeezed, and three bullets spat from his rifle, slamming into the boards over Cook's shoulder. Cook ducked, rolling smoothly into the darkness, and disappeared.

Ethan dropped behind the circle of chairs, cursing himself. Cook was an expert in reading people, in interrogation, in breaking a man down to nothing. A minute in front of him, and Ethan's soul had wavered.

"Oh, you know how it is," Cook purred. "In war, men will turn to each other for relief. It just makes it so much easier when there are guys like you around. So easy," he singsonged.

Ethan exhaled, shaking.

"You worked your way up, though. Bigger and better after the Army. Tell me," Cook said, a grin in his words. "How's that presidential ass?" A pause in the darkness. "Think some of my guys should try a piece of it?"

Ethan bit his lip until he tasted blood. Damn it, he had to get back under control. Rage nearly blinded him, nearly made him jump up and empty his rifle into the darkness. He held his M4 close, listening, trying to find Cook.

Take control back. Make this conversation yours. He licked his lips. "You cloned them all, didn't you? Noah. Leslie. All of them."

"I was one of the first to receive a fancy cloned body part all those years ago. Fucking amazing." Cook had made it to one of the laptops and called up new images on the scattered boards. Pictures of Leslie's clone, her eyes forced open, watching Leslie's life and identity play by, every scrap of her that Madigan and Cook had found online. "Have you ever heard of

Aralsk-7?" A pause. "No? Old Soviet bioresearch station. A true house of horrors. A thing of beauty. It got shut down when the Soviet Union fell, but a plucky band of generals restarted it, up by Lake Baikal. You remember the Wild West days of Iraq? Back when the killing and the looting was good? Well, I had a shiny new organ and all my medical records, and the Russians wanted to buy. A few drinks in Bahrain, and I made a decent twenty million. And they, my cocksucking friend, perfected the magic of human cloning."

"Where'd you get the raw material? You couldn't make a clone without her DNA."

"That was easy," Cook deadpanned. "You do know she was my protégé? I trained her, in the sandbox. She was so brilliant." His voice turned almost wistful. "Taught her everything I knew about interrogations. And, when she died, when she was blown to bits, Jeff and I helped pack up all her little bone fragments and shattered teeth and pieces of skin into a tiny little box to send back to the States. Not enough for a casket and a funeral, but enough to store in the vault at Dover. They log that, you know. Keep track of all our DNA." Keystrokes pounded on the laptop. "Hell, I could have cloned you if I'd stolen your DNA samples."

"Why didn't you?" Ethan crept around the side of the chairs. Cast in the shadows from the floodlights, he could just make out Cook's form, silhouetted behind the boards, typing away. "Why didn't you clone me? Seems like that would have been easier. Replace me. Instant access to the White House."

"Because," Cook snorted. "Look at all this *crap*." Around the hold, videos of Leslie played, social media posts and videos and images and tweets scrolling by at breakneck speed. Interviews Jack had given, telling stories about her. Home videos. Snippets from campaign speeches. Interviews with her parents, even. A perfect preservation of a hero, forever immortalized in cyberspace. "Clones come out blank. You can't clone memories. Can't clone life experience. But, through the careful application of stimuli, you can implant anything you want. Including a life they never lived. God, America loved her sob story, didn't they?" Cook whistled. "And isn't it just so sweet how America has really rallied behind Jack and Leslie? Hoping for them both? Sorry, Ethan. You're on the outs." He chuckled softly, his deep voice raw, his laugh just on the wrong side of unhinged. "I really hope Jack is enjoying all the special skills I taught that clone. She couldn't go back to him a virgin now, could she? Not with all the married sex they'd had. I had to break her in. Make sure she could properly seduce her husband."

His heart screamed, his vision turning crimson with furious rage. He tried to breathe, but his lungs seized, and for a moment, he imagined rising up, roaring, and ending Cook in a hail of firepower.

He dragged in a ragged breath, tasting sulfur and wet copper at the back of his throat. He bit down on his lip again, and blood oozed into his mouth. The pain grounded him, brought him back from his crazed high.

"You're predictable, Ethan. You have a blind spot anyone can see from space."

"You did this with all of them? All the clones?" He edged his way toward the boards, toward the stair ladder. But— Fuck. Cook had placed himself squarely between Ethan and the stair ladder leading up and out.

"Fuck no." Cook laughed. "It takes forever. Leslie almost wasn't ready in time. For the others, we just programmed targets and missions into their blank little minds. Williams blew his brains out when he was captured, right?"

Ethan stayed silent.

"Excellent. Just like his programming. He had his eccentricities. We cut him loose after he fulfilled his purpose. He was heading back here in a blind panic, and we were hoping to lure Lieutenant Cooper." More keystrokes on the laptop. Screens shut down, and a file transfer began, files disappearing faster than Ethan could catch. "But you'll do."

"Why Cooper? What did you want with him?"

"Oh, I could flip him. I could get him to turn. Be one of us."

"You're out of your mind. He'd never turn."

"I know *exactly* what it is that he wants. And I know how to use that against a man. To break them."

Ethan eyed the stair ladder, Cook, and the spaces in between. It was past time to go. He needed to get the hell out of there. Ideally, put a bullet in Cook's brain on his way. Fuck bringing him in.

"You're too dumb to know what it is I want?" Ethan snorted. "You're not so smart."

"I know exactly what you want, Ethan." Cook chambered his rifle, the heavy bolt sliding back into place. "And I'm going to give it to you." An instant later, Cook raised his rifle and fired, spraying Ethan's cover with bullet after bullet.

Ethan ran, sprinting across the hold, trying to outrun Cook's shots. He knocked down two floodlights and shot out a third, wildly firing behind him, trying to hit Cook. Boards fractured and a server hissed, the drives whirring as bullets slammed into their casing.

"Time to die!" Cook crowed. Gunfire blazed. Bullets pinged and ricocheted, sparks snapping in the blackness. One zinged too close, opening a line of fire across the small of his back, just beneath his bulletproof vest. Ethan spun, firing as he ran deeper into the darkness, into the cargo hold, and then dropped low, going still.

Cook's fire stopped.

Silence filled the hold, save for Ethan's breathless pants.

Fuck, fuck, fuck. He was trapped in the corner, backed into the darkness. The stair ladder was twenty feet away, and beyond that, Cook waited.

What now?

He reached out, his fingers resting on the rough iron of the hold. It was just enough, just porous enough, to get a grip. If he found a girder, he could shimmy up the beam in the darkness, maybe.

It was worth a shot.

Cook's footfalls echoed across the hull and up the stair ladder, all the way to the top landing. Ethan watched his silhouette against the azure sky getting smaller as he climbed and climbed.

"Good-bye, Ethan!" Cook shouted into the blackness. He reached down, hefting something onto his shoulder.

Fuck. It was an RPG. The tanker was old enough to be a single-hulled freighter, and the RPG would rip right through her. Ethan scrambled, jogging for the stair ladder as fast as he could.

Cook aimed low. "When you see Jack in hell, and you will, soon, tell him I said hello." He fired.

A burst of flame roared through the hold, illuminating the darkness for the moment that it sailed through, straight for the waterline. Ethan froze, three steps up on the stair ladder, and watched in horror as the rocket slammed into the ship's hull.

Iron and steel cracked, wrenched apart in the blast. Water rushed in, a furious bellow of the ocean pouring into the hold, sweeping away everything in its path. Computers shorted out and boards fractured in two, tossed apart on the cresting wave. The water crashed, folding back on itself, and then rose again, raging.

Ethan ran, taking the stair ladder two steps at a time and hauling himself up, but the water was too fast. It slammed into him, throwing him from the steps. Waves crashed over his head, and he had just enough time to gasp a sulfurous breath of soaked air before the water sucked him down and pulled him under.

47

Saudi Arabian Coast

Gasping, he struggled to stay above the surface. Waves sucked him deep as the water formed a tight whirlpool. He thrashed, desperately trying to claw his way out.

He fought for every inch against the swirling water. Waves beat him, tried to drown him, until his fingers closed around cold steel. He tried to rest, for a moment, but the water rose too quickly, swallowing him down, and he nearly lost his hold.

Hauling himself up the ladder nearly broke him in half. He heaved, puking water he'd swallowed as he forced himself to climb, outrace the rising tide swallowing the hold and pulling the tanker down.

When he made it to the opening, the tanker had already tilted on her side, and the ladder met the ship's deck at an oblique angle. He had to crawl upside down, hanging over the swirling maelstrom, and drag his exhausted body over the lip of the cargo manifold.

Weak arms shook as he collapsed face-first to the tilted deck. He heaved again, coughing out seawater as he forced himself up, clinging to pipes and railings as he dragged his feet beneath him. Blood rained down the side of his face, a cut on his forehead pulsing warm and wet.

Panting, he scanned the deck. No sign of Cook.

He'd lost his rifle in the water, and the sat phone Irwin had given him was ruined. He cursed, bending over at the waist, and tried to drag air into his lungs.

He had to get Jack to safety. Jack was in danger. God, what if something had already happened? Irwin. How would he contact Irwin?

He had to get back to the car. Faisal had a satellite phone. He could call from there.

Jogging faster than his battered body wanted, Ethan headed for the side of the ship and the ladder he'd climbed up. The deck kept tilting, and he ran at an angle, stumbling.

At the railing, frayed ends of a sliced rope greeted him. Below, his inflatable boat drifted, deflated, just a mess of bullet-riddled red rubber floating with the remnants of the rope ladder.

"Fuck!" He kicked the deck, grasping the railing in both hands as he growled. The tanker was tilting even farther, and soon she'd be on her side against the reef. He squinted down at the water line. They'd gone down maybe ten feet? Lower than before, that was certain.

Only one way off the tanker now. Ethan clambered over the railing. Beneath him, the water turned from turquoise to almost black, the drop of the Red Sea shelf giving way to a mile deep of open waters. Blood dripped between his eyelashes, down over his lips.

Into the sea, with the sharks, and bleeding. It was almost fifteen miles back to shore, a mix of reefs and sand bars.

He closed his eyes before he let go. *I'll get back. I'll get Jack to safety. I swear it.*

Ethan hit the water like a torpedo, sliding feet-first into the depths. At least he remembered to hold his nose. The salt water stung his eyes, burned in his cut, but he fought his way to the surface. Gasping, he swam hard from the tanker, toward the nearest sandbar.

It took hours, swimming from sandbar to sandbar and then dragging himself across the barren, scorched cays. The sun set, but the temperature didn't drop. Around him, the reef came to life in the moonlight, fish splashing and sea turtles paddling curiously near him. He swam away. Sea turtles meant sharks, and it was already night, well into their hunting hours.

Halfway to the shore, he collapsed facedown in the middle of another seemingly endless sandbar. His parched, chapped lips cracked, and sand stuck to his oozing head wound.

Get up. Get moving. Jack needs you. One arm dragged him forward, and then a knee. *Jack. Jack needs you. Move. Move!*

He pushed to his feet. Stumbled forward. When he entered the water, again, he tripped, falling beneath the surface. Spluttering, he barely managed to pull his above the waterline.

A dark shape swimming in the shallows on his right made him freeze.

A black triangle, rising above the water, cast a long shadow in the glow of the full moon.

Terror fueled him as he swam hard, shouting, forcing his muscles to work, forcing his body to go faster.

The fin stalked him, staying on his right.

He broke bits of coral off with his bare hands, hurling it at the fin, bellowing as he smacked at the water. One of his throws landed, and the fin dipped underwater, vanishing.

He moved quickly, scrambling across the sandbars and back into the water, swimming for the next cay while the shark was gone. His eyes stayed open, scanning the water.

Only three more cays and stretches of ocean, a couple miles, and then he'd be there. Ethan dropped to his knees, counting out a thirty-second break as he pictured Jack's face.

In the end, he crawled out of the water and dragged himself to his parked Land Rover, gasping for breath. He barely summoned the strength to break the window. Ethan clung to the door as he wrenched it open and collapsed inside, reaching for the glove compartment with trembling hands.

Finally, he had the satellite phone. Shaking fingers dialed Irwin's number. The moon had dropped low in the sky, and Ethan stared at the dull glow through the windshield as he lay across the front seats.

"*Lawrence Irwin.*" Irwin's gruff voice answered after the third ring. He sounded tired, like he'd just woken up.

"Where's Jack? Is he all right? Is he okay?"

"*Ethan? Jack's at the White House. He's asleep by now.*"

God, not next to her. Please, not next to her! "Get there. Get him out. Get him to safety."

"*What did you find?*"

"You're right. It's a trap. Madigan. Cloned her." He spoke between deep breaths, and he reached for a water bottle, unscrewing the cap with his teeth and upending it in his mouth. "She's not the real Leslie. Leslie is—" His throat closed, and he remembered the look on Jack's face, the devastated, anguished, hopeful look when he gazed at what he thought was his wife. "The real Leslie Spiers is dead. All the ghosts are dead. These are clones. She's got all of Leslie's memories scrapped from the Internet inside her brain. Some kind of programming." He tried to sit up, but a wave of dizziness crashed through him and he fell back against the seats with a curse.

"*Jesus fucking Christ.*" Irwin was scrambling on his end. Ethan heard doors opening and slamming, the sounds of clothes being thrown on as Irwin grunted. "*Are you all right? You sound awful.*"

"Found the tanker. Ran into Cook. He sank the ship with me inside it."

"*Did you kill him?*"

Ethan closed his eyes. "He got away."

Cook's voice slammed into him, running through his memories. *You have no idea how deep this goes. How many of us there are.*

"Irwin, be careful. Cook said some things. Everything, this whole thing… It's bigger than we know. Be careful."

"*You too, Ethan. I'm going to the White House. Get to safety. Take care of yourself. I'll call you soon.*"

"Tell him—" Ethan's throat clenched. He sighed. "Just keep Jack safe for me."

"*I will.*"

48

White House

"Mr. President!"

Wood splintered, Jack's bedroom door breaking open. Flashlights bobbed, their beams cutting through the black of the bedroom. Welby marched in, flanked by Caldwell, their weapons raised and ready to fire.

Jack stared at the agents, eyes wide, frozen in place on the bed. His fingers clenched the bedspread beneath him, digging into the blue fabric. He'd lain down on the bed for the first time that night, on Ethan's side, clutching Ethan's pillow to his chest. He was still dressed, still in his suit pants and Ethan's sweatshirt. "What's going on?"

"You need to come with us, Mr. President. *Right now.*" Welby beckoned him to the door, his weapon drawn and up.

Screaming sounded down the hall, Leslie's voice rising and shouting.

"What the hell—" Jack was on his feet in a moment, heading for the door.

Welby stopped him, a hand hard on his chest. "Mr. President. This is for your protection. Irwin is waiting for you downstairs."

Leslie's screams rose again. "Jack! Jack! Help me!"

"What's happening?" Jack pushed past Welby. "My protection? What are you talking about?"

Down the hall, Leslie was being dragged out of her bedroom. Two agents had her by the arms. Others flanked them with their weapons drawn.

"Jack!" Leslie saw him, and she jerked, trying to break free. "Jack! Help me! Please!"

Welby grabbed his arm, holding him back. "Mr. President, she's a threat."

He stared at Welby, Leslie's screams bouncing off the walls of the White House. "Wha— How—" He couldn't think, couldn't process what he was seeing.

"Irwin needs to see you. *Now.* Let's go, Mr. President."

Jack found his anger on the way down to the parking garage. He pulled away from Welby's gentle handling, fury crowding his mind.

Agents were waiting at his SUV, the door already open for him. Inside, Irwin was talking on the phone and barking out orders. "Get her into containment as soon as she arrives. I want an interrogator in there within the hour. Yes, into the tank. Get Flynn. He's the best we have stateside." Irwin glanced at Jack, his eyes dark. "The president just arrived. We're leaving now."

The SUV door slammed. "What the fuck is going on, Lawrence?"

Irwin rested his cell on his knee, twisting it just so until the edges were parallel to his leg. He pressed lips together, exhaling through his nose. "Jack..." He blinked, long and slow. "Jack, I'm sorry, and I didn't want to be right. But I was." A moment, as the SUV peeled out of the White House underground garage.

Irwin took a deep breath. "She's *not* your wife, Jack. She's a plant. Your wife died sixteen years ago, and she was a hero. Whatever this is, whoever she is, this is *not* your wife. She's been sent by Madigan."

He stared at Irwin, static filling his mind, blocking out everything else. His vision tunneled, darkening until all he saw was Irwin's face, watching him with too much sympathy. "What?"

"She's not your wife," Irwin repeated. "She's been sent here by Madigan. And we need to find out why."

"Her blood tests came back. She's Leslie." Hysteria clung to Jack, colored his words. "She's *Leslie*! She knows everything Leslie knows! We've talked about the past, about our marriage, for Christ's sake!"

"She's a clone."

Jack laughed, helpless and hysterical. "A clone?" He glanced out the window, watching as Washington whipped by. Wherever they were going, they were going fast. "A *clone*? Are you kidding me?"

"We, and the other signatories to the treaty banning human cloning, use cloning procedures only for medical purposes. Cloned organs. Replacement body parts. We can grow tissues and save lives. Cure diseases that killed so many not that long ago. It's a modern miracle. But, not everyone signed the treaty, Jack. Human cloning has been sought after as a weapon for years. DARPA did threat analyses on *exactly* this scenario six years ago. Ordered by guess who?"

Jack's mind screamed, the world tilting off its axis. "So, what, did they put her together like a puzzle? Clone all her organs and taped her together?

She's not a paper doll, Lawrence!" Jack laughed again, hysterical, losing his grip on reality. "Are you telling me her memories are cloned, too?"

"The memories were implanted. Cognitive implantation. A form of brainwashing, but in this case, the original mind is a blank." He sighed. "For her, they used anything they could scrape from public sources. Think about it. How much of her life, her memory, is out there online? Interviews you've done? Retrospectives? The deceased wife of the president was a hot topic during your campaign."

Jack's eyes slid closed. Doubt crept in, lingering in the shadows. *I told that story about the burned chicken at least a hundred times over the years.* He chewed on his top lip. "A clone?" He shook his head. "How do you know? How did you find out?"

"I sent Ethan to track down anything he could about her story. Make sure what she said was true. He and I both share a desire to see you safe and protected, Mr. President."

"Ethan?" Jack leaned forward. "*Ethan* found this out?"

"Ethan almost died bringing this back to us."

His heart clenched. "Is he—"

"He got out of there. Called it in. The first words out of his mouth were asking if you were all right."

Jack stared down at the floorboards, his hands clenching until his fingernails pierced his skin. *Ethan.* His heart was too bruised, too broken to do anything more than ache. If all this was true, then what did that mean? That Madigan had dropped the *one* person into his life who could destroy everything he'd built, professionally and personally? Shatter his relationship with Ethan, right when he needed him the most? When he needed to fight back, try and right the world, but the only way he could *do* that was with Ethan by his side?

Had this been the plan all along? Separate him and Ethan? Divide them? Break them?

He'd played *right* into Madigan's plan. Walked right into crippling shame and endless guilt. Split from Ethan and cast himself adrift. Was on the verge of giving Leslie everything he could.

But he couldn't just *stop* loving Ethan, and he'd chosen Ethan and their love over what he'd thought was his wife. That choice had been the first *right* thing he'd done in days, then and now. Even if this was his Leslie, he still wouldn't give up Ethan. That was something true, all the way down to his bones.

She w*asn't* his Leslie, though. She was a plant, and he'd played right into Madigan's schemes. *Right* into them. *God, Ethan...*

"Where are we going?"

"Langley. We're going to interrogate her. Immediately."

Ice-cold rage flashed through Jack's veins. His head whipped up, and he stared at Irwin across the dark SUV. "I need to be there. I need to know what this sick son of a bitch planned."

CIA Headquarters
Langley, Virginia

"We will begin in a moment, Mr. President," Irwin said softly at Jack's shoulder.

Jack said nothing. He stared into the sublevel interrogation room through a two-way mirror, his gaze fixed on the woman he'd thought was his wife.

Leslie sat in the dim tank beneath a bare bulb. A chain hung between two cuffs, clipped to a thick leather prisoner's belt around her waist. Her ankles were shackled together. Her sling and bandage had been removed and the cuff on her blackened arm had been tightened around the damage, almost to the bone. Her disfigured arm sat curled on the table, motionless.

Had that injury been done to eke out his sympathy? To make him feel worse about seeing his dead wife come back to life? Jack ground his teeth, his gaze fixed to her rotted arm.

The door within the interrogation room opened. Flynn, Irwin's handpicked interrogator, strode in. He wore cargo pants and an untucked shirt and sported an unruly mop of dark hair. He didn't look at her, just pulled out his chair, metal legs scraping over bare concrete. He sat, his face impassive as he stared her down.

Leslie's breaths stuttered. She fidgeted, tugging with her good arm on the handcuffs. She kept glancing at the two-way mirror.

If she really had all of Leslie's memories, like Irwin said she did, then she knew he'd be on the other side. She knew he wouldn't walk away.

Flynn kept staring at her, not saying a word. Leslie jerked her good wrist, yanking on the chain, and she whipped around, staring at the mirror. "Jack," she pleaded, her voice wavering. "Jack, *please*. Help me."

Jack stared back, not blinking as he crossed his arms and his fingers clenched in the bunched fabric of Ethan's sweatshirt.

Flynn cocked his head, just so, staring Leslie down.

"Where's Jack?" Leslie breathed. She bit her lip, shrinking in her seat as she seemed to collapse in on herself. "Where's my husband?"

Jack's veins singed, raw fury roaring through him.

"If I could just talk to Jack," she begged. "Something's misunderstood. Something's wrong. If I could just *talk* to him. See him. Please?"

"We know who you work for. We know you work for Madigan. We know you've been sent here on a mission."

"I *used* to work for Madigan. I fought back! When I figured out what kind of monster he was!"

"We know you were sent here on a mission," Flynn repeated. "If you tell us how the attack is going to happen, we'll be able to help you." He paused, steepling his fingers together. "Where and when are you supposed to attack?"

Panic seemed to settle in around Leslie. Her breaths came fast, and she stared at Flynn, her fingernails scratching on the surface of the bare metal table. "What attack? What are you talking abou—"

"Where and when are you supposed to attack?"

"I-I-I don't know what you're talking about—"

"For the last time, before I have to be impolite. Where and when are you supposed to attack?"

"I'm not part of any attack!" She slammed her good hand on the table. "I'm not attacking you! You've got the wrong person!" Tears glistened at the edges of her eyes. "Please, *please* let me speak to my husband…"

Flynn looked down. Pursed his lips as he spun his thumbs. "How do you communicate with Madigan?"

"What?" A tear slipped down her cheek.

"Where is Madigan's current operational location?"

"I don't know what you're—"

Flynn cut her off. "Where and when are you supposed to attack?"

"I'm not attacking you!"

"What is your name?"

"Leslie. Christina. Spiers," she ground out. "My husband is Jack Sp—"

Flynn kept going, rapid-fire questions on full blast, never letting Leslie have a moment to think, to maneuver.

"How many others are in your operation? Who else is a part of this mission?"

"There is no mission—"

"Where is Madigan's current operational location?"

"I don't kn—"

"How do you communicate with Madigan?"

She leaned forward, snarling. "Fuck yo—"

"What is your name?"

Her hand slammed down on the table, metal jumping. "Leslie! Christina! Spiers!" she bellowed. "Leslie! Christina! Spiers!"

Next to Jack, Irwin let out a shaky breath.

"Jesus," Director Mori mumbled, sharing a long, uncertain look with Director Campbell of the FBI.

Jack glared into the interrogation room. She was good. He had to give her that. She had Leslie's behaviors down, her mannerisms, all the tiny little things she did that made her her. All her imperfections, all her quirks. Her frustration, the quick snap to anger. The tightening of her eyes, the way her fingernails scraped over the skin around her nails. How she bit her lip until her skin frayed.

But she wasn't Leslie. She wasn't his wife. No matter how closely she acted, how perfect her behaviors were, she was something else. Something that was trying to steal Leslie's memory, remake her and use her in some sick, twisted way. He clung to that with both hands.

He kept watching, even as Campbell turned away.

"Where and when are you supposed to attack?" Flynn repeated.

"I'm not a murderer," Leslie hissed through clenched teeth. "But maybe I'll make an exception for you."

"You believe you're her," Flynn said, leaning back and crossing his legs. "You really do."

Leslie froze, her eyes going saucer wide as her jaw dropped. She even stopped breathing. Jack counted the seconds until her shoulders rose again. "What?"

"Where and when are you supposed to attack?"

"My name is Leslie. Christina. Spiers," she repeated.

"Where and when are you supposed to attack?"

"I am forty-five years old—"

"Where and when are you supposed to attack?"

"My husband is Jack Spiers—"

Flynn burst to his feet, flipping the table and sending it flying across the room in one motion. It slammed into the concrete wall with a clang. Leslie jumped, her good hand grasping the arm of her chair as her dead arm flopped uselessly to the side. Flynn caught her, pressing hard on her wrist, grinding it into the metal frame of the chair until she screamed.

"Captain Leslie Spiers died sixteen years ago in Iraq! She died a national hero! You are *nothing* compared to her memory!" Flynn shouted in Leslie's face. The two-way mirror vibrated.

Leslie squirmed, pain contorting her features. "I *am* Leslie," she finally growled. "You're making a mistake!"

Flynn shoved her chair backward, metal legs scraping until he slammed her into the far wall. Her head hit the concrete, but she glared up at him, fury in her eyes. He shoved his face into hers. "We know what you are! We know you're here on a mission! You've been caught! It's all over! Where and when are you supposed to attack?"

Leslie spat in his face.

Flynn stepped back. He wiped her spit with the back of his arm and shook his head.

"What do you think will happen after this? Hmm? Think Madigan will take you back? Welcome you home?" He scrunched his nose. Shook his head again. "You're a failure. He won't want anything to do with you. You want anything, any kind of life at all after this? You're going to have to play ball with *us*."

She glared at him, her head held high, and said nothing.

Flynn dropped down in front of her, resting one hand gently over hers, the one he'd ground into the metal moments before. His voice softened and he leaned in close, like he was sharing a secret. "You know, Madigan will kill you for failing. We can help you start a new life. You don't have to do what he's ordered you to do. You could have a real life of your own." Flynn paused. "You say you fought back. Prove that now. Answer our questions."

Silence, save for her fast pants, and the panicked look she shot toward the two-way mirror.

Flynn waited.

He shook his head again. "You've made a big mistake."

"Jack!" She hollered. "Jack! This is *wrong*! You're all *wrong*!" Her voice cracked, breaking apart, and then she was sobbing, huge, aching sobs that shook her thin frame.

Flynn stepped back, folded his arms, and spread his legs. "How many others are in your operation? Who else is a part of this mission?"

She glared, red-rimmed eyes raining tears down her splotchy cheeks.

"Where is Madigan's current operational location?"

"I'm Leslie—"

"How do you communicate with Madigan?"

"Please," she sobbed. "You're making a mistake."

"What is your name?"

"Leslie Christina Spiers," she chanted. "Leslie Christina Spiers. Leslie Christina Spiers…"

"Mr. President." Director Mori frowned. "Are we *absolutely* certain about this intelligence?"

"Do we have anything concrete to review? Anything other than a verbal statement? Any independent verification?" Campbell said as Julian Aviles, secretary of homeland security, looked away. Irwin glanced sideways at Jack.

"Keep it going," Jack said.

"Jesus Christ, Mr. President!" Aviles shook his head. "That's your wife in there!"

"You are not Leslie."

"My name is Leslie Christina Spiers—"

"You are *not* Army Captain Leslie Spiers, an American hero and patriot of this country." Flynn's voice rose.

"My name is Leslie Christina Spiers—" She spoke louder, trying to drown him out.

"You are a science experiment—"

"Leslie Christina Spiers!"

"—and a failed mission!" Flynn's shout shook the concrete walls.

"You're wrong!" Leslie shrieked. "You're wrong! You're wrong!"

Flynn flew at her again, grasping the arms of her chair. He hissed, right into her face. "Where and when are you planning to attack?"

She stared into his eyes and didn't say a word.

A buzz sounded. Flynn pulled back. He turned without a word, shutting the door behind him with a faint *snik*.

Leslie collapsed forward, sobs shaking her shoulders and leaking over the audio feed, weak moans as she whimpered and cried out for Jack.

Flynn wouldn't look at Jack when he walked into the observation room, rubbing at his eyes with one hand.

Director Mori, Director Campbell, and Secretary Aviles stood together. Irwin had his arms crossed, his forehead resting in one of his hands.

Jack watched Leslie through the glass. *It's not her. That's not her.*

"Are we fucking sure about this?" Flynn grabbed a paper cup of coffee he'd left behind before the interrogation began, downing the cold brew in two swallows. "She's not showing any signs of deception and she's sticking to her story." He wadded up the paper cup and chucked it in the trash. "I mean, this whole thing is pretty fucking nuts to begin with. Are we sure about this intel?"

All eyes shifted to Jack.

"I trust the source of this intelligence one hundred percent."

"What's this amazing source? What's so certain?"

"Someone I trust with everything." He held Flynn's incredulous stare, ignored his arched eyebrows. "*Absolutely* everything."

"What the…" Leaning close to the two-way mirror, Campbell peered into the interrogation room. "What the hell is she doing?"

They turned together.

Gone was the sobbing, panicked, frightened, stubborn woman. Gone was the slouching, the practiced art form of vulnerability. Gone was the trembling, the show of fear.

Leslie had turned her chair, facing the mirror head on. She stared into the center, as if she was staring straight into Jack's gaze.

"Fuck me." Flynn took off, tearing out of the observation room and back to the interrogation.

"I have a message," she started. "All of this, every single thing we've done, was all for Jack," the not-Leslie clone purred. "You got in our way, Jack. You and Ethan. But you won't be in our way any longer." She grinned. "General Madigan sends his regards."

Flynn burst through the door as Leslie grabbed her mangled, disfigured hand and slammed it down on the metal arm of her chair, just above the wrist. Bones snapped, two audible cracks, and she tipped her head back as she started to laugh.

"Mr. President!" Irwin lunged for Jack, throwing himself on top of Jack and hurling them both to the ground, right before shattered concrete and roaring flame ripped through the lower level of Langley.

Jack's entire world went white.

BREAKING NEWS
Massive Blast Tears through Langley CIA Headquarters' Underground Complex; Terror Attack Suspected

A massive explosion tore through the CIA's headquarters in Langley, Virginia, in the early morning hours. Sources say the blast originated inside one of the underground interrogation centers, and that it may have been a suicide detonation with explosives concealed within the attacker's body. Part of the complex has collapsed. The estimated death toll is not yet known.

The president and Leslie Spiers were whisked away from the White House last night and taken to an undisclosed location. Whether this was in response to the terror threat or unrelated, the White House isn't saying. However, the blast site at Langley has been fully locked down, and the no-fly zone over Washington and Langley has been extended. Military helicopters are hovering over the site, and multiple rescue agencies have responded.

The whereabouts of former first gentleman Ethan Reichenbach remain unknown. No statement from the White House has yet been made.

49

Jack's world existed in snatches, bursts of sound and fury blanking to white, all jumbled together with smears of static and an ever-present whine ringing in his ears.

Shouts. Men and women screaming. Orders yelled, but he couldn't hear right, like he was inside a bell after it had been rung and the world was still vibrating. It was dark, too dark, and nothing changed when he tried to blink. Something heavy lay on his back, pinning him flat, choking the air out of him as he struggled to breathe. Concrete dust filled the air, coated his tongue. Something wet and sticky covered the side of his face.

He licked his lips. Tried to speak.

Tasted blood on his tongue, burnt copper and flame.

"Here! Over here!" Hands moved something above him. The pressure eased, and he gasped, one hand weakly reaching out, fingers sliding through shattered concrete and broken glass.

Someone grabbed his hand. "I've got you, Mr. President." The voice sounded familiar, but he couldn't place it, not with the world flying apart. "He's alive! He's alive!" the voice bellowed. "Over here!"

"Irwin's dead." Something else rolled off his back, a wet weight that had lain heavy on top of him. "Took the brunt of the blast."

"Saved his life." Hands ran over his body, patting him down. "Jesus, look at all that blood. Where's it all coming from?"

"Horsepower, Welby. Vigilant has been located, but he's down. Looks fucking terrible. We need a chopper, *now*—"

His eyes closed, and then they opened again.

He was being carried, bridal style, over a destroyed and devastated landscape. Shattered blocks of concrete lay at sharp angles. Fires burned to his right and left, black smoke thick in the air, burning his eyes. He rolled his head, blinking bleary eyes at his rescuer.

Welby, his shirt and face bloodstained, carried him forward, clenching his teeth as he climbed over another shattered concrete block.

Suddenly, there were more hands on him, hands everywhere, patting him down, and the world veered from too slow to too fast. He gasped, trying to arch away from the touches.

"—just got here. Bringing a chopper down into the west parking lot! They're taking us to Bethesda!"

He knew the voice. Jack blinked, reaching out, and grabbed hold of a black suit jacket.

Scott's face—wrecked gaze, deep lines, and frantic expression—loomed over him. "Mr. President?" One hand slapped his cheek. "Damn it, Mr. President, come on!"

Then they were running, Welby grunting with every step, Scott leading the way. Above, heavy whooshing burned out all other sounds, the whirr and roar of rotors descending. His eyes tried to find the chopper. God, it sounded so close—

His eyes closed, and then they opened again.

He was lying down, staring up at a white hallway, flashes of fluorescent lights flying by every other second. He was on a white bed, silver rails on the sides, a plastic mask over his face. Scott and Welby ran at his side.

Where was Ethan? He had to find Ethan. His eyes darted every which way, and his breaths came too fast. He couldn't breathe; God, he couldn't breathe. Where was Ethan? He had to find him!

He grasped the rails and tugged, sitting up just enough to make everyone scream and alarms wail over his head. Scott reached for him, pushing him back down with wide eyes. "Lie down!" he shouted. "Lie down, Mr. President!"

He tried to tug on the plastic mask. "Ethan…" He coughed, struggling against Scott's hold. "Ethan? Where— *Ethan*!"

Scott grimaced, but he pasted on a tight smile. "He's on his way," he choked out. "Just lie back, Mr. President."

"Ethan!" He tried to sit up again, reaching—

His eyes closed, and then they opened again.

Doctors hovered over him, green scrubs and face masks crowding his vision. He jerked back, trying to push through the mattress. Pain, so much pain, and he wailed, screaming until his chest caved in and he couldn't breathe. Machines beeped as the sting of a needle slid into his veins. He tried to gasp, but gloved hands grabbed his cheeks, pulled his head straight.

Everyone shouted as an alarm wailed a high pitch, a steady tone that kept going on and on and on.

His eyes closed.

50

Saudi Arabian Coast

Ethan still felt wrecked, his muscles torn apart. Even his bones ached. The headache he'd nursed through his swim back to shore had turned into a blinding migraine, made worse by the punishing Arabian sunlight.

When he'd hung up with Irwin, it was all he could do to roll into the back seat and pass out, lying in the open vehicle in the stifling desert until the sun had finally cracked over the horizon. The heat followed the sunrise. He clambered to the front and drove off, squinting at the road as he downed water bottles, one after another. He made it twenty miles to Kuff, a dusty village, and pulled off outside of town to sleep under a scraggly Ghaf tree.

A wet camel nose poking into his broken window woke him hours later. An older Saudi man berated him in fast Arabic, too fast for Ethan to catch anything. He grumbled, waved, and started back down the highway.

He kept the radio off. His migraine raged, and he propped an elbow on the windowsill and rested his head in his hand for the long hours of the drive back south.

As the miles rolled on, his tires slapping on the burning asphalt, sand whipping through the broken window and stinging his face, every one of his thoughts fixed on Jack. *Irwin's got him. Irwin will keep Jack safe. He's going to be all right. He will be.* Still, his fingers squeezed down on the steering wheel until it shook beneath his grasp and the leather whined.

He got back to Jeddah late and ended up stranded in the city's traffic, breathing exhaust fumes and biting down on sand grit between his teeth.

Finally, he made it through the city, winding south along the coast until the turnoff to Faisal's private drive. Hulking security men let him through, glowering at the damage to the Land Rover. He flashed them a peace sign and parked in the circular drive.

Exhausted, heavy footsteps took him to the door. He almost fell over when he entered and the cool air slammed into him.

Shoes slapped against marble. Someone running for him. He waited.

Adam skittered to a stop in the foyer, his suit jacket swishing around his hips. He stared at Ethan, his face bone white. He clenched his phone in one hand, and his mouth tried to form words as he stared at Ethan.

"Clones—" Ethan started.

"We know." Adam tried to speak again, but his expression fractured.

"What?" Ethan's heart plunged. *No. No, no, no.* "What?" he snarled, exhaustion forgotten as he charged Adam. "Tell me now!"

"I've been calling you!" Adam hissed. "Why didn't you pick up?"

Ethan shoved Adam back, pushing him against the white foyer walls, "Tell me what's going on!" He tried to clamp down on his raging heart. "Jack—" His voice stopped, choked off.

He couldn't ask. Couldn't say the words.

"L-T!" Doc shouted from Faisal's living room. "It's starting! She's on!"

Ethan's eyes searched Adam's. Pain, so much pain, and a crushing wave of guilt crashing in on all sides. "No—"

"I'm sorry," Adam grunted. He grabbed Ethan's arms. "I'm so fucking sorry."

The drone of the TV filtered through Ethan's static-filled mind, a haze that had descended over him as Adam spoke. He heard the words, felt their impact like gunshots to his chest.

"...we'll listen now to the just-confirmed president of the United States, Elizabeth Wall."

He headed for the TV.

Elizabeth appeared, striding toward the podium, a hard look hanging on her exhausted features. The White House seal screamed in technicolor behind her, and off to her side, Pete stood like a ghost, ashen and staring at nothing. His jaw worked, biting the inside of his cheek.

"*I will not be taking any questions at this time,*" she started. "*My fellow Americans,*" pausing, she pressed her lips together before continuing. "*Today, our nation came under attack, targeting the very heart of our government and intelligence operations. An explosion at CIA Headquarters, in Langley, Virginia, has devastated the CIA and this government.*" She breathed in, carefully.

"*The explosion at Langley took many from us—friends, family, and neighbors—and, in particular, this attack has taken a great man and a great president.*"

No. He stopped breathing, every single one of his hopes clinging to the seconds she took, the hitch in her breathing, desperately wishing she'd say he was just in surgery, just down, but not out.

She looked dead into the camera, as if she was looking straight into Ethan's soul. "*President Jack Spiers was observing a top-level interrogation of a high-value target at Langley at the time of the blast. He was gravely injured in the explosion and is currently being kept alive only with life support at Bethesda Naval Hospital."*

Gasps rose around the room, and in the background, Pete squeezed his eyes shut.

"His status will not improve," she continued.

Tremors settled over Ethan's hands, his arms, his whole body. His legs gave out, and he gripped the back of the couch before he fell to the floor.

The high-value target. It must have been Leslie's clone.

"Moments ago, by the governance of the twenty-fifth amendment of the United States constitution, I was sworn in as president of the United States." Elizabeth's eyes slid closed. *"It was, and always will be, the saddest moment in my life."*

Ethan's blood burned, and he grit his teeth as his fingers ripped through the leather. He swayed, barely able to stand. Somewhere, he heard some kind of noise, a low, keening wail, but he couldn't place it.

"We also lost Lawrence Irwin, President Spiers's chief of staff and former director of the CIA. Other senior officials were seriously wounded in the blast." Elizabeth squared her shoulders and looked straight into the camera. *"The FBI and CIA are working diligently to uncover the full details of what transpired this morning. We will continue to brief the American public as more information comes to life. Until then, please join me in praying for our president, a man we all had too short a time with, and a man who will forever be one of my closest and dearest friends. I plan on continuing his important work and his legacy, and I am proud to call myself a Uniter."* She stilled, closing her eyes briefly. *"For everyone who is grieving, everyone who is wounded, and everyone who is lost, I give you this promise. We will purge this world of the terrible forces of darkness and hatred. We will find the people responsible for this act, and we will bring them to justice."*

Behind Elizabeth, Pete's shoulders shook as he stared at the carpet. The camera cut away, showing the faces of the press pool for a moment. Shock, grief, tears. Hushed whispers. Half-bitten lips and furious scowls.

She said no more, merely nodded to the camera and strode off the podium. Pete followed in her wake, and then the screen cut and held on a silent picture—a close-up of Jack, bright-eyed and laughing as he sat at his desk in the Oval Office.

His smile hit Ethan like a shotgun blast to the heart.

He stumbled backward, away from the couch like he could escape the message, the moment, run from the terrible truth. Red-hot fury roared, swirling around blinding grief, the shattering of his heart. Both choked him, forcing rancid vomit up his throat until he could taste his own failure on the back of his tongue.

He hadn't been there. He hadn't been able to save Jack.

Madigan's plan had succeeded.

Whirling, his arms swung out, clearing the top of one of Faisal's decorative tables. A vase shattered, followed by a statue and a decorative plate, Arabic etched in gold letters swirling across the surface. Everything clattered to the marble as he fell to his knees.

That keen, that mournful, warbling wail was back, louder and louder, surrounding him until his bones vibrated with it. He realized it was him, his own body—his own soul—making that dreadful noise.

Nausea crashed through him. He fell forward, vomiting on Faisal's white floor. He gasped, but couldn't breathe, couldn't do anything but drag in ragged half breaths that left him lightheaded. Vomit clung to him, a thin dribble hanging from his lips.

Hands grabbed his shoulders, spun him slowly. Adam's face floated in front of him, watery on the edges, and then Faisal, kneeling beside Adam. They both had a hold on him, as if he were about to explode or burst into a hundred different pieces or vanish into thin air.

Adam moved first, grasping the back of his neck and pulling him forward until he fell against Adam's chest, the side of his face buried in Adam's button-down. Tears and snot and leaking spit drenched his shirt, but Adam held on tight, wrapping him up in both arms.

They sat on the cold marble floor as Ethan's heart and soul bled out of his body.

51

Bethesda Naval Hospital
Two Hours Earlier

Steady beeping pulled Jack awake.

He tried to focus. Hazy shapes floating in his vision. Something dark was beside him, a lump of black against a sea of muddy tan. He reached for the darkness, and a needle pinched on the back of his hand, the sting of an IV line tugging when he moved.

A grunt, and then the shape moved, sitting up.

"Mr. President?" It loomed closer, and Jack's vision finally focused in on Scott.

Exhausted didn't even begin to describe how he looked. Devastated would be closer. Something that had gone through a meat grinder. A man who had lost against his demons. "Scott?" His voice cracked He coughed.

"You had us terrified, Mr. President." Scott helped him sit up and passed him a cup of water. "When we dug you out, we all thought you were dead."

"What happened?"

Scott sighed. He rubbed both hands over his face, rubbed his fingers against his eyelids. "What do you remember?"

Sights and sounds played back out of sequence. Leslie in the interrogation room, screaming. Welby kicking down his door. Irwin in the back of a dark SUV. Leslie breaking her arm, and then Irwin diving on top of him. Heat, so much heat, and the world seeming to collapse.

"Her arm." He coughed again. "She broke her bones."

"Her disfigurement was a ruse. We think, based on the video, that her radius and ulna had been hollowed out and explosive compounds packed inside. None of the doctors picked it up. The bone hid the explosives. And, when she broke her arm, they met." Scott looked down. "A quarter of Langley is gone."

"How many?"

"Don't know yet. It was late—or early—so the numbers were down." He squinted. "Lawrence Irwin is dead. Director Campbell and Secretary

Aviles were injured, but they'll be all right. Director Mori is still in surgery."

He didn't need to ask about Flynn. Nothing made it out of that room. Not with that kind of blast. "You said there was a video?"

"Acting President Elizabeth Wall confiscated it. Only three people have seen it. Her, myself, and Welby."

Acting President. His heart stuttered. "How long have I been out?"

"Hours. Morning news has been going insane. Someone leaked a photo of you being carried out of the rubble. It's… not a good picture." He chewed on his lip, his heels bouncing on the hospital's squeaky linoleum floor. "Your heart stopped on us. You have twenty stitches across your ribs. You have damaged organs. You nearly fractured your pelvis and half your body is black and blue. You're damn lucky, Mr. President."

"I'm not lucky. Lawrence saved my life. He took everything."

"We haven't said anything about your condition yet."

Jack's mind raced, thoughts moving too fast to cling to. "Good. Keep it quiet for a little while longer."

"I have to call Acting President Wall. She wants to talk to you in person."

"I need to talk to her, too."

Scott rose, pulling his cell phone out with a sigh. He stood in the corner, talking softly, and Jack's head rolled to the side, his cheek resting on the cool pillow.

Irwin, gone. Ethan, gone. What was it not-Leslie had said? This had all been for him? Him and Ethan? They'd gotten in the way.

But now they were separated, driven apart by Madigan's schemes, schemes he'd played right into. Ethan was God-knows-where, and the only person who had known about Ethan's mission was dead.

What now, Mr. President, when you've been played so perfectly? So completely, utterly perfectly. Everything Madigan had done, everything, had been a game. A game designed to agonize. Dig deep into his heart and wrench it apart, split it in half with broken memories and a rusty crowbar.

What now? How did he even *begin* to pick up the pieces from this?

There was only one place to start.

He *had* to find Ethan. Had to stand side by side with him and face the world. Had to hold tight to Ethan for the rest of their days.

Madigan wanted them apart. Damn that madman; Jack would find Ethan, and he would never, ever let him go again.

Together, they'd stop Madigan. They'd end his reign of terror, obliterate him from the planet.

Deep within him, something shifted, some kind of sea change moving parts of his soul across a line in the sand he'd naïvely drawn so many, many years ago. A conviction to play by the rules, to be an upright man in a sea of shady politics. To commit to good deeds and good actions, and believing that the world was made of fundamentally good people doing decent things.

Oh, how his lines had been blurred.

And now, evaporated. Gone.

His hands shook, and the beeps on the monitor at his bedside sped up, louder, faster. He could feel his heart in his chest burning. Raging. Wailing.

Sixteen years ago, Leslie had died on a mission he didn't know much about, but the one thing he did know, with utter certainty, was that Madigan had been involved.

She'd been the first thing he'd ever taken from him.

And now, he'd taken Ethan. His presidency. Damn near his life and his sanity.

And had remade him, through everything, into a man willing to do anything—*anything*—to stop him. By any means necessary.

By the time Elizabeth arrived, he had the IV out and had limped up and down the hospital corridor a dozen times in borrowed blue scrubs. The entire floor had been cleared, and Scott had posted agents at all entrances, locking down everyone except for the one doctor and one nurse keeping watch on Jack.

Elizabeth came in with Daniels at her side. She had her hair pulled back in a simple ponytail, and her smart suit was rumpled. She'd probably been yanked out of bed by frantic Secret Service agents before dawn, and she'd been going a mile a minute since.

"Jack." Her smile wavered as she fought back tears, holding her arms open.

He wrapped his arms around her, shaking. A moment, and then he leaned into her, the weight of the past week ripping out his spine and pulverizing his heart. He didn't even try to hold back his sobs.

She held him through it as Daniels went to Scott's side, checking in with him with gruff words and a tight shoulder squeeze.

"We're deep off the edges of the map on this one." Elizabeth pulled back. "What the hell do we do now?"

He took a deep breath. "You're going to stay president."

Scott and Daniels's heads whipped around.

Her jaw dropped. "What?"

"Everything that's happened, everything he's planned, has been because we've reacted exactly as he expects us to. He's been playing us from the beginning. He knows everything, knows our operations better than we do. We have to change the game. Have to do something different."

"What are you saying?"

"I'm saying that he came after *me*. He's targeting *me*. And Ethan. And people are dying because of it. If I live through this, then he'll just come at us again. How many more people are going to die because of his madness?"

"If you live through this…" Elizabeth frowned, and Scott and Daniels were at his side, instantly. "Jack, what are you planning?"

"I need to go off the grid. I need to get far away from here. I need to find Ethan." He tried to smile, but his fractured heart wailed at Ethan's name. "And we need to hunt this man down and put an end to him. For good."

"How?" Incredulity strained Elizabeth's voice, pulled at her tired face. "Jack, you're the *president*, not a soldier."

"First, I find Ethan. He's been running a black kill squad, hunting Madigan. They went ghost, but we can put them back together, someplace safe. We can try to connect with Sergey. His insurgency is making inroads against Moroshkin, and we know Madigan is working with Moroshkin. Together, we can find him. We have to approach this differently. We have to come at Madigan in ways he won't expect."

"The world needs you here, Jack—"

"No, the world needs a leader who isn't compromised, Elizabeth. And let's face it. I've been a disaster since we got back from Sochi. You've been doing *everything*. The world would be rotting in flames if it weren't for you."

She said nothing.

"I'm just a man." His whole body shook, barely holding together. "Just a man pushed beyond all of my limits. Pushed over the edge. And I can't *do* this anymore. I can't be the president. Not right now. Not like this." *Not without my other half.*

"So you want to be *dead*?" Daniels spoke when everyone else stayed silent. "That's not something you can come back from. Not something a 'Whoops, our mistake' press release can take care of."

"Maybe not dead." Elizabeth still looked like she wanted to puke, but her eyes told Jack she'd accepted what he was saying. "The wounded are here, a few floors down. I'm getting briefed on the half hour on everyone's status. There's a man, one of the janitors at Langley." She chewed on her lip. "He's brain dead. The doctors say he'll never wake up."

"Are you saying we should pretend the president is brain dead?" Scott threw his hands in the air. "Mr. President!"

"I'm not the president anymore. She is. And this is happening, Scott, with or without you."

"This is a military hospital. You're being treated by military officials. We can control this. I'm scheduled to make an announcement later today about your medical status. I can let everyone know then." She paused. "But, if we do this, and you get killed somewhere hunting down Ethan, or Sergey, or Madigan, and they hang your body from a streetlight, there *will* be questions."

"Call it a fake. Most people won't believe the pictures, and the ones who do will believe anything anyway."

"Wait. Just fucking wait." Scott got between them, glaring. "Are you seriously considering this? Actually seriously considering this? Goddamn it! What would Ethan say?"

"He'd probably try to talk me out of. But, Scott, if he were here, none of this would have *ever* happened. He'd have saved us. Hell, he *did* save me. Who knows where or when she was going to blow?" Jack took a slow breath, his hands on his hips. "The world *needs* him. *I* need him. I *love* him." Three simple statements, but they were bedrock truths to the foundations of his soul, the cornerstone of what his life had become. A life he'd made with Ethan. A life he loved and wanted back.

Desperation clawed at him, frantic for action, for the need to run and act and do and fix everything that had gone wrong. There was one road opening before him, one path he needed to tread if he was ever going to be able to live with himself again.

The road back to Ethan.

"Scott, he's everything to me. I'm better with him, and maybe we're past where that matters as a president, but it matters to me as a *man*. And we still need to take out Madigan. So I need to go find him. Find him and never let go. He's worth everything to me."

Scott was turning purple and working up to something, some kind of protest, but Jack spoke first. "I love him and I'm going, Scott. I'm going to find him, before it's too late. Before Madigan finds him first. I buried him once. I won't do that again. Not if I can do *something*."

Turning away, Scott cursed and kicked the hospital room's garbage can. Black plastic flew, smashing into the wall, and paper towels fluttered to the linoleum. "You're not fucking going alone," he snapped. "If you are actually going through with this batshit insane idea, then you're not going alone. Ethan would fucking kill me."

He scowled at Elizabeth. "Madam President. Permission to accompany this Goddamn idiot?"

"Absolutely. And." A tiny smile curled the corner of her lip. "I can make this whole thing a secret National Security Presidential Directive. Which means you have a new assignment, Agent Collard. Starting immediately."

"Guess you're the new chief, Daniels." Scott grimaced. "God, it's going to be a shitshow."

"You just go find Ethan. I'll be waiting here for you guys." Daniels eyeballed Jack. "All three of you, back in one piece."

"We need to get out of here." At the foot of his bed, the nurse had hung a plastic bag with Jack's clothes. They were still drenched in blood. He couldn't walk out like that. "We need to sneak out before the media descends. Find a place to lay low while we make our next move."

Scott closed his eyes. "I've got somewhere."

"Elizabeth, I need Lawrence's information. His phone, his briefcase. Notes he kept in his office—" Jack's legs buckled, and he swayed against the wall, almost collapsing before Scott and Daniels got their hands under his arms, steadying him.

Scott cursed, scathing fury on his tongue. "You can't even stand! How are you going to—"

"I will be fine. And, damn it, Scott—"

"Jack." Elizabeth squeezed his hand, interrupting. "Get a little more rest. You need it. I'll have Lawrence's things copied and brought to you, and then you can go. I'll hold off on the announcement as long as I can. Congress and the Cabinet are both convening now in emergency sessions, so I don't know how much more time I can buy you. But I'll give you as much head start as I can."

Jack eased back into the hospital bed. He ignored the pain shooting through him, the stitches he could feel pulling over his ribs. A near-blinding headache building behind his drooping eyes, and the exhaustion tugging on his soul. "Only an hour more. And then we're out of here."

52

Jeddah, Saudi Arabia

"The hell you think you're going?" Adam bellowed at the top of his lungs, chasing after Ethan.

Ethan grabbed a shotgun and a mandolin of shells. He said nothing.

"You just going to take off? *Where*? Where will you go where any of this will matter?" Adam's hands flew wide, gesturing to the pile of weapons Ethan had plucked from the armory. "He's *dead*, Ethan! But we still—"

Ethan flew at him, slamming him back against the wall. A picture rattled and fell to the marble floor, glass shattering. "Shut your mouth," Ethan hissed. "Shut your Goddamn mouth."

"You're trying to ride off into the sunset and die." Adam shoved Ethan back. "Just going to give up? Kill yourself by rushing the enemy?"

Ethan slid two shells into the shotgun and locked the barrel.

"Stay here!" Adam shouted. "Stay here with us! My team is on the way! We can fight together! Actually *do* something instead of just throwing your life away."

Ethan still said nothing, and Adam reached for him, grabbing his bicep.

Whirling, Ethan decked Adam, a hard punch slamming across his jaw.

"You don't want me anywhere near your guys," Ethan growled. His voice shook, his words trembling like a roaring volcano right before eruption. "I'm not your leader. I'm not your savior. I'm going to go find the bastards who took Jack. I'm going to kill them. And I'm going to kill anyone in my way." His eyes gleamed, a black, crazed ferocity. "I won't take anyone else with me. Not into that. This is *my* fight," he hissed. "*Mine*."

"You're going to die."

"Then I'll be with Jack."

"We *need* you, Ethan—"

"You don't need me. I've done nothing but fuck *everything* up." He shook his head. "Get your guys. Base them here. Stay with Faisal forever, if you can. Cut yourself off from the US." His jaw clenched, and the pictures taken of him and Jack flashed behind his eyes. "This goes deeper than what we know. You can't trust *anyone*. No one at all, except your own people. Your team. Got it?"

"And what the fuck are we supposed to do?"

Ethan grabbed his bag and stormed away. "Do what you can to protect your team." He kicked open the front door. Jeddah's evening sun had crept over the horizon. "Keep the people you care about in the world safe." He threw his bags into the Land Rover, tossing the shotgun and a rifle into the front seat. "And don't ever, ever let go of the man you love." He wouldn't look at Adam as he climbed into the driver's seat. "Forget trying to be a hero. Trying to change the world. You just lose everything, and it's not worth it. It's not fucking worth it to be in the world without them."

Adam grasped the driver's door, broken glass shards biting into his palms. "Ethan—"

"Stay away from Cook, Adam." Ethan stared straight ahead, out through the windshield. "Stay the *fuck* away from him." Finally, Ethan looked Adam's way. "I mean it."

Ethan gunned the accelerator, and burning rubber spat smoke against Faisal's drive. Adam leaped back as Ethan peeled out.

Something flew out the broken driver's window, smashing against the pavement.

He jogged ahead, picking up the pieces.

Adam sighed, closing his eyes, and then hurled the shattered plastic and broken wires against Faisal's stone wall.

Ethan had chucked the satellite phone out the window.

He was gone.

Flowers, Flags, and Candles Blanket the White House Fence, Honoring and Remembering Jack Spiers

Americans have come out by the thousands, laying flowers and lighting candles outside the White House to honor and remember President Jack Spiers. American flags and pride flags cover the sidewalk, sticking out of flowers and standing next to pictures of the president and his partner, Ethan Reichenbach. Pins and bumper stickers from the president's new political party, the Unity Party, dot the tableau.

Speaking to TNN, Senator Stephen Allen said, "It's always a sad day when an American life is lost. President Spiers lived a controversial life, and I am certain that we will come to find his death came about because of the causes he chose to support."

53

Moscow
The Kremlin

"We got the signal." Madigan grinned. It was a madman's smile, and it made Moroshkin's skin crawl.

"The bombing?"

Madigan nodded.

Moroshkin's eyes narrowed. How had Madigan penetrated the heart of the American military-intelligence machine? "What have you done, General?"

"Exactly what I promised you I would. I sowed terror. Ripped apart our enemies. Tore their souls to shreds until they collapsed in on themselves."

Moroshkin stayed silent. His fingers tapped, nervous, against the leather sofa. "And this is the next move?"

"This is the fourth move, but they won't know that." He leaned back, smug satisfaction leaching from his bones. "General, begin preliminary maneuvers for our operation. When everything is set, launch your invasion force."

"Where are you going?" Moroshkin frowned. "You're not a part of the invasion. Why not? I thought this was what you wanted."

"My own plans are sending me elsewhere, General, for now. But don't worry. It will all be over soon. Our new dawn is coming. A new sky awaits us all."

54

Silver Springs, Maryland

Jack tried his best not to limp as he shadowed Scott up his driveway, keeping his head down and his borrowed hoodie pulled forward. Scott had his belongings wrapped up in a paper bag, and Jack wore stolen hospital scrubs under the hoodie and thick sunglasses over his eyes. His facial hair had grown out, two days of not shaving, and silver patches mingled in his blond scruff. It was a passable disguise, along with the heavy bruising and the black eye.

The key turned in the lock and Scott hauled him inside. He leaned back against the door, pulling off his shades.

A scream tore through the house. He froze.

"Dad!"

Scott paled but ran for the kitchen. A teenage girl wearing a baggy plaid pullover, her long brown hair loosely braided down her back, raced down the hall, crashing into Scott at the foot of a dark staircase. "Dad!" she cried again. Scott grabbed her, pulling her into a massive hug. His face disappeared into her braid.

A middle-aged woman, her hair cut into a short bob, appeared next, tears streaming down her cheeks as she watched Scott and his daughter. Scott reached for her with one hand, pulling her close, and the three ended up in a three-way hug as Scott kissed both their heads.

Jack stayed frozen at the front door, watching.

"I thought you were at your mother's house?" Scott pulled back, just slightly, just enough to talk to his wife and keep his arms around his daughter. His daughter clung to him, her face tucked into his filthy shirt and his chest. "Why did you come back?"

"After last night? Of course we came back. We've been calling and calling. Why didn't you pick up?"

"Phone died. I'm sorry. And—" Scott glanced back, over his shoulder.

His wife and daughter spotted Jack. They stared, speechless. Scott spoke first. "Mr. President. This is my wife, Stacy, and my daughter, Liz."

"Mr. President? I thought you were—" Stacy looked from Jack to Scott and back again. "We saw the press conference, from President Wall—"

"We've got to talk," Scott said softly, reaching for her hand.

Jack's legs jiggled. He wanted to pace, but his aching body kept him frozen on the couch in Scott's study. Scott had plopped him down, given him an unreadable look, and vanished with his family to the kitchen.

Loud voices bounced down the hallway minutes later, Stacy's frustrated anger rising and falling in time with Scott's muted words.

He pulled a white pillow at the end of the couch into his arms, breathing deeply Ethan's lingering scent. Just days ago, Ethan had been right there.

Copies of Irwin's things he'd gotten from Elizabeth lay scattered over the coffee table before him. It wasn't everything, but it was a start. Buried in Irwin's notes, he found Prince Faisal's cell number. For a moment, it felt like he'd struck gold.

He'd given his phone to Elizabeth and charged up Ethan's, pulling it from his blood-soaked clothes before they left the hospital. The screen was cracked, but it still worked. Elizabeth had given him a secured cell encrypter, and he plugged the boxy device into the phone's battery port before dialing the prince's number.

The buzz of an international ringtone whined in his ear, once, twice, three times. He chewed his lip. If anyone knew where Ethan had gone, other than Irwin, his money was on the prince. Cooper had spent so much of his time there, and Ethan had spent long hours talking through intel with Cooper and the prince for months. He'd fled to the prince before when he'd been dead and in hiding. It was a good place to start.

"*As-salamu alaykum.*"

"Prince Faisal?"

A long pause. "*Who is this?*"

He took a shaky breath. He'd talked to the prince exactly once, thanking him in private for his help and the assistance he'd given to Cooper and Ethan after Ethiopia. He didn't know how this would go over. "Jack Spiers," he said softly. He dropped the "president."

Silence. "*Whoever this is,*" Faisal said, his voice frigid, "*this is not humorous.*"

"It's not a joke, Your Highness. I called you last year. Thanked you. You told me no matter what, your family remained strong friends with the United States. That even if something came out in the media, our two countries' friendship wouldn't waver. And that we could call on you for anything."

More silence. "*Mr. President?*" Faisal finally breathed. "*How?*"

"I needed to disappear. Needed to get off the grid. But now I need to find Ethan. Do you have *any* idea where he is? Has he reached out to you, or to Lieutenant Cooper?"

"*Ibn al-kalb,*" he spat, cursing. "*Adam! Yallah!*"

Shuffling, muffled voices, and then a string of curses and pounding feet running on marble. The phone clattered to the ground. Someone picked it up.

"*Mr. President?*" Cooper's breathless voice strained over the phone line. "*What the fuck?*"

Well, he wasn't the president anymore. He let Cooper's curse slide. "Do you know where Ethan is?"

"*Yeah, he was fucking here!*" Cooper cursed again. "*He was here with us, but he fucking left.*"

"Left?" Jack's heart plunged. "Where?"

"*I don't know, he wouldn't say. He fucking fell apart after that press conference. After President Wall told the world you were basically dead. We got him down, but he went crazy after. Worse than Ethiopia. He's fucking gone. Ready to die.*"

Ethan gone. Ready to die. His heart plunged, his stomach turned inside out. "She spoke too soon. Congress pushed her to do it. I wasn't ready. God, I should have called sooner. Damn it, where did he go? Do you have any idea?"

"*He said he was going to find the men who killed you. That's it.*"

Vanished, on the warpath, and seeking revenge. Madigan's threat from Sochi came back. *He's the exact same as us. It must be you who's keeping him sane. I wonder, what will happen to him when you're gone?*

Fucking Madigan. Jack knew Ethan, knew him better than that monster did.

Where would his lover go? What would he do, if he thought the worst?

"I have an idea. Call me on this number if you learn anything. And… don't tell a soul about this. About me."

He hung up before Cooper could say anything. The next number he dialed, he knew by heart. Elizabeth had air-dropped cell sites into the region, and supposedly everything worked there again.

Another international buzz. He waited, the phone pressed to his skull as he counted the seconds.

After six rings, a gruff voice answered. "*Da?*"

He knew that voice. He smiled, his first real smile in ten days. "Sasha?"

A beat. "*Who is this?*"

"It's Jack."

"*Jack Spiers is dead. Who is this?*" No inflection. Nothing but a cold, hard fact.

"It's Jack, Sasha. I know you. I know you're in love with Sergey. I can see it in the way you look at him. And I know he didn't bring that statue of one of your heroes of the Soviet Air Force out of storage for nothing."

Long, long silence, save for Sasha's harsh breaths. In the background, distant gunshots fired, isolated bursts followed by shouts in Russian.

"I need to talk to Sergey, Sasha. Please. Is he there?" He'd called Sergey's personal phone.

"*Da.*" More sounds of shuffling, someone moving, and grunted Russian.

Then, Sergey's rough voice, too much emotion choking his words. "*Jack?*" he breathed. "*Sasha says it is you, but this is impossible. I heard the news. You are dead!*"

"Not yet, Sergey. I needed to get off the grid. Madigan will just keep coming after me until he believes I'm dead. I'm giving him what he wants, for now. Until I kill him."

Sergey cursed in Russian, a long, unending string of growls. "*I toasted you already! I shed tears for you!*"

"We'll drink again together, Sergey. Right now I need to beg you for your help."

"*My help? Jack, I am running an insurgency against the bastards in Moscow. I am living out of a rat hole and a convoy of trucks. I do not know how I am still alive, save for your country's airstrikes. How can I possibly help you?*"

"I need to find Ethan." His voice wavered, and he dug his thumb into one of the bruises on his thigh. "I think he's headed for Russia, overland from Saudi Arabia. I think—" He swallowed. "I think he's trying to take out as many of Madigan's men as he can, before—"

"*He has no idea, does he?*"

Jack closed his eyes. "I couldn't find him in time," he breathed. "Elizabeth announced early. She was pressured. Please. I need to find him. And I need to go to him." His voice changed, turning from pleading to a harsh growl, his hatred come alive. "And after that, I need to kill Madigan, Sergey. I need to wipe him from the face of the planet."

Sergey *hmmed*. "*If Ethan is smart, he will go through Kurdistan and then into the Caucasus. My people control the western mountains. The east, it has gone to the rebels, and they have declared for the Caliphate.*

Chechnya, Dagestan..." He sighed. "*He should stay away from those areas if he knows what is good for him.*"

"I don't think he cares about that right now," Jack whispered.

"*If he comes to me, we will be able to save him, yes. We control our territory.*"

"Your insurgency is going well, Sergey."

"*Airstrikes help,*" he deadpanned. "*I will put out the word to all my forces to search for him. One American as crazed as he is right now should be easy to find.*"

"Thank you." Jack exhaled, rubbing his eyes.

"*Jack,*" Sergey breathed. "*Come* join *us. Come here. Come* fight *with us. We are fighting for the same thing, you and I. Madigan's death. Moroshkin's death. We will find Ethan together. And then go on the* hunt." His voice shook with rage and fire.

Jack's heart pounded in his chest. *Yes*, his soul screamed. *Yes, go! This is what you need to do*! But—

"How, Sergey? How do I get there?"

"*Get to the Russian embassy in DC. The ambassador is my friend. He has been feeding me information from Moscow. I will call him. He will smuggle you to me. Talk to him. Only him!*"

Put his life and his trust entirely in the hands of the Russians. A desperate plan, a desperate hope.

Not just any Russian. Sergey. His closest friend, other than Ethan.

It was madness. Utter insane madness.

"I'll do it," he breathed.

"*Get to the embassy at midnight tonight. He will be ready.*"

"Thank you, Sergey. I can't—"

"*We will drink when you get here, Jack. And we will talk then.*" Sergey cut the line.

He closed his eyes and pressed his forehead to Ethan's phone. *Ethan, wherever you are, stay alive. I'm coming for you. Like you came for me. I'm coming for you.*

What was it Ethan had said to him once? *I will tear through the whole world to get to your side. Always.*

"Ethan," he whispered. "I'm with you all the way."

All the way to disappearing off the grid. To the Russians. To the Caucasus and to the ends of the world. To the end of them, together.

Shouts rose from Scott's kitchen, muffled faintly through the closed study doors. Guilt clawed at him. He was taking Scott from his family, from his home, his wife and daughter, and disappearing to a war zone on the other side of the world. But, no, Scott had volunteered. Had insisted on coming. Maybe he should put his foot down. Insist Scott stay behind. This was Jack's mission, and he had nothing to lose and everything to gain. Scott had too much to lose.

He padded out of the study, heading down the hall toward the kitchen. Soft sniffles stopped him at the foot of the dim stairs.

Looking up, he saw Liz squatting in the stairway, hunched over and picking at the sleeves of her plaid pullover. Tear tracks stained her cheeks, and she'd rubbed enough snot into her forearm to leave a wet spot.

"Hey," he whispered.

She sniffed. "Hey."

He didn't know what to say. Scott and Stacy continued to argue, just beyond the kitchen's closed French doors.

"I know what I signed up for when we got married, but this is insane. *You've already made the huge sacrifice. I buried you once already! Can't the president ask someone else?"*

"He didn't ask. I volunteered."

"Unvolunteer then! You can't go, Scott! Do you have any idea what this will do to our daughter?"

"Stacy—"

"Do you know why she doesn't want to go to college next year? Because she's too terrified to leave! She's absolutely petrified that you're going to die one day, and she won't be here! She can't stand the thought of losing you, so much so that she doesn't want to spend a moment away from you!"

Silence.

"I love my family, Stacy. I love Liz." Scott's voice was rubbed raw. *"But Ethan is my* brother. *We've been at each other's side for more than half our lives!"*

"And we're just *your family."*

"I can't leave him!"

"You can leave us?"

"I would do the same for either of you. Drop everything and go do what I could. Everything I could. He's part of my family. Part of this *family, Stacy! He was the first call I made when Liz was born. I cried on the phone with him telling him we had a baby girl."*

"And your baby girl is going to have a corpse *for a father!"*

Jack's eyes slid closed. Liz sniffed again.

"He's going to go with you," Liz said softly. "He and Uncle Ethan are best friends. They'll do anything for each other."

"Uncle Ethan?" He sat one step down from her, leaning against the stairwell. Somehow he hadn't learned about this side of Ethan.

Liz nodded. "He's always been the best. He and Dad are best friends, and he and Mom are pretty cool too. It's always fun when we're together. Sometimes we'd all go camping when I was little. Baseball games when I got older. He'd babysit when they wanted to go out. He'd show me movies Mom and Dad said I couldn't watch." Her voice died, and she looked down.

The argument kept circling, Stacy's tears added to the mix.

"You and Uncle Ethan... Are you guys still together?"

I hope so. "I love him very, very much."

"He's needed someone to love him." Liz picked at her frayed jeans. "I think we were all he really had."

He reached for her, taking her hand in his. "I love him more than I can say," he choked out. "He's the one for me. The love of my life."

She squeezed his hand hard. Hard enough to hurt. "Bring him back, okay? Bring my dad back, too."

"I promise." He held on to her hand, and she turned, leaning against the wall with him as she rested her head on his shoulder. He stroked her hair, listening to the end of Scott and Stacy's argument.

Stacy was sobbing, the sounds muffled as if she was crying into Scott's chest. *"I don't want to lose you again,"* she said, her voice warbling.

"I have to do this." Scott didn't sound any better. *"I have to go. But I will be back. I swear. For you, and for Liz. I swear to God I will be."*

Silence descended over the house.

Hours later, Scott emerged, looking like he'd lost it all. Stacy silently took Jack's bloody clothes into the laundry room, and Scott brought down a pair of cargo pants that were a little too large. Jack explained the plan, and Scott nodded, though his lips were pressed in a thin line and all the blood had fled from his face.

When it was time, he pulled Ethan's clean sweatshirt back on and then an old canvas jacket on top of that, borrowed from Scott. Scott wore the same cargo pants, a long-sleeve black shirt, and an old camo jacket. He shoved as many weapons and as much ammunition as he could into a duffel. Jack packed up Irwin's information, tucking it into the inside pocket of his jacket, along with Ethan's phone.

Scott and Stacy hugged for a long, long time.

When it was Liz's turn, she started to cry, but Scott held her through it. He wiped the tears from her eyelashes and whispered into her hair, telling her how smart she was, how beautiful she was, and how he was coming back. "I have to walk my little girl down the aisle at her wedding," he said, pressing a kiss to her forehead. "I've been dreaming of that moment since you were born."

Her watery smile wavered, but she wrapped him up in a hug.

A moment later, she hugged Jack. She whispered in his ear, "Give Uncle Ethan a hug for me when you find him."

"I will."

Stacy didn't look at him.

They piled into Scott's personal car, leaving behind the Secret Service SUV. Stacy and Liz watched from the windows until Stacy turned away.

En route to the Russian embassy, Jack had one last call to make. Even though it was close to midnight, he had a funny feeling someone would still answer.

It came with the job.

Elizabeth picked up on the first ring. *"Good news never comes after the sun goes down."*

Jack tried to smile. "You're a natural, Elizabeth. And this isn't bad news. Well..." He ignored the harsh glare Scott sent his way. "I guess it depends on your perspective."

"Jack..."

"We've got a plan. Or, the beginnings of a plan. We'll be meeting up with a good friend of mine. Great conversationalist for you, too. Your pillory of pop culture over dinner was a sight to behold. Our friend has an idea on where to find Ethan. I'm going to stick with him while we search."

"Jesus Christ," Elizabeth breathed. *"From the frying pan and into the firefight. You're telling me this so that I'll know where to expect news reports of your body being dragged through the streets?"*

"It won't come to that. You'll know where we are and what we're doing. And, for when you send us intel on Madigan." His voice hardened. "We're going to get him, Elizabeth."

She was quiet. *"I'll be waiting to give you back this desk when you get back."*

It was his turn to say nothing.

He'd most likely never step foot in the Oval Office again.

"I sent Secret Service agents to your parents' house in Texas. Agent Daniels handpicked them. We set up a secured video call, and I talked with them both this evening. They understand what's going on. What they need to do."

Jack exhaled, his cheeks puffing out.

"*I do have something else to ask you,*" Elizabeth said, clearing her throat. "*The identity of the bomber at Langley. What do we say?*"

What do they say to the world about Leslie? Jack let his head fall back against the headrest. "My wife died sixteen years ago. I loved her, Elizabeth. I did. And she will always be my hero. She will always be an American hero. She needs to be remembered that way. Honored for the life she truly lived. The amazing, incredible woman she really was. Not this. Not whatever Madigan tried to do."

"*You want to go public with what that thing was? What she did?*"

The world would reel, but then again, wasn't it already reeling? Was there some kind of terminal velocity of terrible things, a finite limit the world could take? Or was that just the human soul?

"Yeah. Yes, go public with everything. What she was. How we were duped. How a... covert intelligence operation discovered the truth and warned us just in time."

"*The world thinks you're gone, Jack. It wasn't just in time.*"

"Just in time so that it was only thirty-one who died, not hundreds, or thousands. Who knows where she would have detonated if given the chance? I wasn't the only target. She could have detonated anytime if it was just me."

Elizabeth's quiet exhale echoed over the line. "*I'll make the announcement tomorrow. This is going to be awful.*"

A grim smile tugged at his lips. "You know, it wasn't long into my presidency that I realized I didn't want to be president anymore."

Elizabeth snorted. "*Good luck,*" she whispered.

"You too."

55

Ethan drove for hours, never stopping.

He took the road north to Medina, and then northwest across the barren Arabian desert. Across the Iraqi border and then north, all the way through Baghdad, Kirkuk, and Erbil.

He'd been there before. Seen it all before. One dilapidated truck of masked fighters thought about running him off the road, but he fired a burst of gunfire into their engine and tires. They snaked off the highway, into the sand, and he floored it another hundred miles.

He'd filled up jerry cans with fuel on his way out of Jeddah. More than enough to get him where he needed to be.

Outside Erbil, he jerked the Land Rover off the road and stumbled out on shaking legs. His boots kicked at the packed sand, kicking up dust. Baking rubber, oil, and melting asphalt burned his nose. Overhead, the sun scorched his skin. Sweat dripped down his neck.

He knelt down, his stomach heaving, and waited for the vomit to rise. It did, and he hurled the bottle of water and half a fig he'd struggled to get down. Spitting, he laced his hands behind his head and stayed in a crouch.

Maybe if he closed his eyes, everything would change. Maybe this was all some kind of nightmare and he just needed to wake up. Maybe if he stayed down, he'd never have to rise again.

Eventually, he ran the back of his hand over his mouth, his skin scraping over the half-beard that had grown in. He looked like a man on the run, a man on the very edge.

He got back in the vehicle and kept going.

From Erbil, he greased the palm of a Turkish border guard, and he went north through the eastern wilderness of Turkey. He paid crossing into Georgia and then again leaving Georgia.

The border to Russia was closed, they said. No entry.

A stack of American hundreds changed that.

He wound through the narrow mountain roads, through the primeval forests that clung to the Caucasus. Spruce and fir loomed above him, and farther still, ice and snow clung to the peaks. His road twisted and turned, switchbacks with a steep ravine dropping off to nothing on one side.

Six miles into Russia, buried in the impenetrable black forest blanketing the Caucasus, the first roadblock appeared outside a mountain town. Six men stood at a barricade of armored trucks, all wearing Russian military uniforms and holding heavy rifles.

Moroshkin's men.

Sergey's rebels—policemen and everyday Russians—wouldn't be in uniforms, and they wouldn't be riding Russian military jeeps. Sergey's forces were a ragtag slice of Russia's people, and these weren't them.

Finally, something to do with all of his anger, all of his furious rage. Rage at Madigan, rage at the world, and rage even at Jack. Jack was *gone*, and what was Ethan supposed to do now? How was he supposed to go on without him?

There was no place for his fury, no place for it to go except poured into raw brutality. His hands trembled, yearning to fight. To hurt. To cut into someone as deeply as he'd been cut into. To make it agonizing.

Moroshkin's men—Madigan's men—were just what he needed.

He slowed, just enough to ready the shotgun he'd plucked from Faisal's house. As the first soldier waved him down, ordering him to stop, he slid the barrel against the window frame of the Land Rover and pulled the trigger.

All hell broke loose.

Bullets flew, pinging into his vehicle. He slammed on the accelerator, gunning it for the center of the barricade. The tires popped and his SUV swerved hard toward the ravine's edge. He yanked on the steering wheel, overcorrecting, and plowed through two of the Russians. They dropped beneath his car, but he kept sliding, right into the side of a Russian jeep.

He still had too much momentum. The bullets were still flying, shattering glass and pinging off the steel frame of both the Land Rover and the jeep, impaled together and careening toward the ravine's edge. Trees spun, tilting like a carnival ride as his Land Rover fishtailed wildly and arced out of control.

He saw the back end of the jeep tumble over the side of the ravine, and then he saw nothing, a pitch blackness that seemed to swallow the world. The Land Rover's tires left the ground, and for a moment, he was floating.

Ethan closed his eyes, gripped the steering wheel, and prepared to drive into Hell. His world blacked out, vanishing.

He didn't quite make it to Hell.

It could have been an hour or a day, but the next thing Ethan knew, the door of his crumpled vehicle was ripped off and the barrel of a rifle was shoved into his face. Russians shouted at him, bellowing. He was dragged out and thrown to the ground. The rifle ended up on the back of his neck.

Cook was right.

Clinging to the dirt, his fingers digging into pine needles and black earth and patches of snow on the side of the mountain, Ethan had an epiphany. *Cook was right about what I wanted most.*

He closed his eyes. *Jack.*

One of the Russians kicked him in the ribs. Pain flared, agony roaring through him like he'd been kicked in half. Searing heat spiraled through his body. He heaved, struggling to breathe, his face pressed into the cold, damp dirt. He didn't try to move.

"Get up!" One of the Russians shouted in heavily accented English. "Get the fuck up!"

Two soldiers hauled him to his feet. The world spun. He nearly vomited.

"You are American?" The Russian in charge advanced, pulling out his handgun and pressing it to Ethan's forehead. "You are American spy?"

Ethan didn't blink. He stared into the Russian's eyes as blood dripped down his forehead.

The Russian hissed, shoving the barrel of his handgun harder against Ethan's forehead. "Why you are here? An attack is coming? You are scouting targets for air strikes, yes?"

Ethan spat into his face, hocking a thick wad of blood-specked spit into his eyes.

Barks in Russian all around him. The leader snarled, murder in his spit-soaked gaze.

Dead is dead. Here or there, dead is gone. Ethan closed his eyes.

Something heavy hit him on the side of the head. He slumped to the ground. Rainbows burst in his mind behind his eyelids, and then white noise, and finally, a freeze-frame image of Jack, smiling as he sat at his desk in the Oval Office.

56

Washington DC
Russian Embassy

"In here. Make no noise. Others here work for Moroshkin. If they find out you are in the basement, we will all die." The Russian ambassador glared at them both before slamming shut the van's heavy door.

Jack and Scott had been shoved into the back of an anonymous white van in the Russian embassy's underground parking garage, tucked between classified packages and parcels addressed to Moscow. They lay down, huddled close together, and a tarp went over their bodies.

The van drove through Washington, and Jack felt Scott's heartbeat race, felt his blood pressure skyrocket as they lay silently side by side.

The Russian ambassador himself pulled them from the van at the airport, helping them stand inside a private hangar next to an executive jet. He nodded to Jack and handed him an envelope. "For Sergey. Now go. This plane will take you to him."

He and Scott jogged up the stairs, settling in behind two stern-faced Russian pilots.

Scott fell asleep right after takeoff. Jack glared at him for hours, envious. Every time he closed his eyes, thoughts of Ethan filled his mind. Was Ethan all right? Where was he? Had Sergey found him yet? Was he in danger?

What would he do if Ethan was gone?

He couldn't think of that. Instead, he stared out the window, watching the impenetrable midnight sky and puffs of impossibly soft clouds float by.

Hours later, after he'd finally nodded off, a wailing alarm jerked him awake.

Scott grabbed him, holding him back in his seat as the plane bucked, bouncing in the air.

"Get your seat belts on," the pilot barked over his shoulder.

"What's going on? What's happening?" Jack shared a wide-eyed look with Scott.

"You think flying into rebel territory is easy?" The copilot laughed. "We have to land in the dark in Crimea, and then you will transfer to where the rebels are. But we must land with nothing. Nothing that can tie us back." He flipped another switch off, and more electronics shut down. "Hold on."

Jack's nails dug into the plane's seat as the jet almost glided with no power onto a fog-soaked blackened runway in Crimea. Only the faintest light showed the patchy outline of a runway, and for a moment, he was certain they were dead. Dead and lost in a plane crash off the ends of the map.

The plane's rubber tires slapped and skipped down the wet runway, squealing, and the jet shuddered as he and Scott grasped each other's hands in the pitch-black cabin.

When the plane came to a halt, shouts echoed outside. Clangs sounded as the hold was opened. Someone banged on the door, and the pilot got up to let them in. Scott edged his shoulder in front of Jack, as if anything he could do would help at that point.

The barrel of a rifle entered the cabin first, pointed at the pilot before sweeping around to Jack and Scott. The pilot pointed to Jack, shouting in Russian, and backed away.

Men in balaclavas dragged Jack and Scott from the plane, throwing them to the wet asphalt in front of another group of masked men. Scott fought the whole way, thrashing and kicking and taking out three Russians before he was pummeled to the ground. Jack stayed silent, glaring at the men with his hands behind his head.

A black hood over his head. There was pressure against his nose and mouth. He inhaled, gasping, as something sickly-sweet hit the back of his throat. Next to him, Scott shouted.

The world went dark.

He woke slowly, bouncing in darkness, blinking. The darkness didn't change, but the scratch of heavy canvas against his cheek clued him into the hood still pulled over his head. He tried to stretch, tried to move, but his hands and feet were bound and he was pressed into a tiny space, barely big enough for his body.

It felt like a coffin.

Panic tried to latch on to his mind, to the endless darkness, his claustrophobic restraints, and the braying Russians laughing and barking nearby. He bounced again, jerking his head against the end of wherever he was.

Driving. They were driving somewhere.

He was being *taken* somewhere.

The lingering dullness of the chloroform slowed his mind. His tongue was heavy, dry like cotton, and he rasped, desperate for something to drink.

"Scott?"

Nothing.

There was nothing he could do but wait.

They jerked to a halt hours later, his head banging against the hard end of his captive space again. Grunting, he tried to roll himself over, tried to get into position to maybe see what was going on. Russian sounded all around him, the men in the car reporting to someone else, it seemed. Doors slammed.

The car door next to his head opened and he realized he'd been crashing into the base of a door the whole time. Something lifted, and a beam of light rained down on him. Even through the black hood, he winced.

Angry Russian barked. His hood was ripped off.

Squinting, he blinked fast and tried to take stock of where he was.

He was lying inside the hollowed-out back seat of a rusty car. The seat had been lifted, and a fat Russian was peering down at him. They were parked in a foggy clearing, surrounded by maple, ash, and birch trees. Black dirt covered the ground, and messy tire tracks cut deep grooves in the loose earth.

Another man shouldered the fat one out of the way, wielding an angry-looking knife as he leaned over Jack.

He pushed back, trying to wiggle away, but the man grabbed his hands and sliced through the tape binding him. "Be still," he said softly. "I will not hurt you."

He *knew* that voice. Jack sagged, boneless, into the smuggler's hold inside the ratty car. "Sasha?"

"*Da.*" Finally, the light changed, and Jack could just make out Sasha's barely there smile. "I am here to buy you from these smugglers and take you back to our base."

"Scott. Scott was with me. Where is he?"

Shouts rose from a car nearby, bitter cursing in muffled English and Russian. The car door flew back as Scott erupted from the smuggler's hold, stumbling and struggling against the bound arms and legs. A strip of duct tape was over his mouth, fury in his eyes.

Sasha sighed. "The smugglers want an extra ten thousand because of him." He helped Jack out of the car, letting Jack lean on him when his legs almost gave out.

Scott saw Jack leaning on Sasha and shouted. He turned to the nearest smuggler and hollered through the tape. Even muffled, Jack could make out his words. "Get this off me, you fucker!"

The smuggler waved a knife in Scott's face.

Sasha snapped something in Russian and the smuggler stopped immediately, shoving Scott around until he could cut through the tape at his wrists and ankles. As soon as Scott was free, he whirled on the smuggler and punched him in the face, sending him sprawling to the ground.

Scott jogged to Jack's side as Sasha tossed a wad of cash at the smuggler rolling in the dirt.

"You all right?" Scott took over for Sasha, holding Jack up.

"I'm good. Legs just fell asleep."

Scott nodded, but his gaze took in everything, his head moving on a swivel. "Looks like we made it to Russia. I can't believe we're still alive."

Sasha slapped on the hood of his jeep, idling on the side of the clearing. "Time to go!"

Barricades and roadblocks slowed their drive, but Sasha was waved through at each checkpoint. Gunfire echoed in the distance, and Jack couldn't tell if it was just around the corner or three mountains away.

Camps of civilians littered the mountains. Russians, rebels, and separatists, ethnic minorities who had been fighting in the forest for decades, all camped together under the thick canopy.

"Moroshkin has bombed much of the region hunting us," Sasha said, catching Jack's eye in the rearview mirror. "We have over a hundred thousand refugees in this forest alone."

Bullet-riddled police cars sat beside minivans outfitted with machine guns. The sights of a civilian insurgency run by an exiled president fighting against a totalitarian coup.

"Where is Sergey?" Jack leaned forward, his head between the front seats. Sasha had a radio and two rifles propped up in his passenger seat. Crackling static and low Russian faded in and out.

"Near the front. We are pushing north. But." He glanced at Jack. "We have something to do first."

They drove on, up and through the mountains until the air grew colder and fog formed in front of their faces. The sun set, and the forest dropped into darkness. Sasha kept the jeep's lights off, driving slow by flashlight through the impenetrable blackness. He spoke quietly into the radio and listened for whispered Russian in return.

All around Jack, the darkness of the forest played on his mind. Banked coals were the only light for the people huddling in the thick woods, and dimly lit faces seemed to appear and then fade into the black. There were no sounds other than the crunch of the forest floor beneath Sasha's tires—crackling leaves, skittering rocks—and soft, staticky Russian and a radio whine. His heartbeat seemed to fill the empty spaces in the world, his breaths as loud as gunshots. The chill air pressed in on him, as did Scott, and the jeep seemed too small, too tiny an oasis in this crazed world of hidden armies fighting against madmen. What was he doing? Entering a warzone? Trying to find Ethan? What could one man do, set against the impossible vastness of the world's evil?

He was going after the love of his life. That was the goal. That was the mission. Ethan. Always, always Ethan.

His stuttering heart slowed somewhat, and he focused on the smell of the forest, the clean dirt and snow-slick air. He let his hope unfurl, hope he'd clenched tight to. Hope that he'd find Ethan. Hope that he'd feel his arms again.

The forest was the way to Ethan: through the darkness, back to his lover.

Finally, Sasha's dim flashlight bounced off something other than a thick tree trunk. A concrete bunker, weathered and dilapidated, stood in the middle of the forest. Sasha whispered into the radio and parked the jeep.

"Old Soviet monitoring station," he said. "We took it over."

Jack and Scott piled out of the jeep and followed Sasha through the darkness, down the concrete stairs, and into the dark bunker. Over the door, an ancient red light flickered. Sasha shrugged before he pushed open the bunker's door.

A bare concrete hallway stretched into darkness. Flickering bulbs hung down, most more dead than working. The bunker seemed to be empty, but at the end of the hallway, footsteps rang out, someone jogging their way.

Jack glanced at Sasha, trying to read him. Sasha's faint smile told him everything.

"Sergey?"

"Jack!" Sergey appeared in the ring of light beneath a flickering bulb. His gaunt face beamed, and he held his arms wide as he jogged the last distance toward Jack and Scott. "You made it."

Scott grumbled. "Thought we weren't going to, once or twelve times."

"You are fine now." Sergey waved away Scott's glower. Jack smiled as he pulled out of Sergey's long hug.

"Jack." Sergey's eyes gleamed in the low light. "Jack, we found him. We found Ethan."

57

Russian Caucasus
The Forest

"Five more klicks."

Beside Jack, Scott checked his rifle again, sighting down the scope. Sasha drove and Sergey sat in the passenger seat. Behind and in front of their jeep, five more vehicles full of Sergey's insurgents crept through the early morning fog toward their target.

Jack's elation had been muted when he'd realized Sergey didn't have Ethan there at the bunker but knew where he was being held. He'd been captured, Sergey had said, by Moroshkin forces working against them from the east. They'd intercepted communications back to Moscow talking about an American they'd captured, a wild man on a seemingly suicide mission.

Sergey had laid out their plan to recapture Ethan and Scott had pitched in while Sasha rallied the forces for the predawn raid.

Jack had started to pace.

He'd never been a religious man. Had never quite believed, after losing too much and seeing too many prayers go unanswered. Couldn't reconcile the world as it was with the hope of faith. But for a moment, pacing beneath a flickering bulb burning in a bunker in the Russian wilderness, he'd thought about it. Thought about tipping his head back and begging God, begging for Ethan to be all right. For them to get through this without losing another person.

He'd kept pacing, one foot in front of the other.

Jack bounced in the back of the jeep beside Scott, waiting.

Scott forbade Jack from joining the raiding party, but Jack refused to be left behind. Sergey intervened before the shouting got too outrageous, plopping a medical kit in Jack's hands and telling him to wait in the jeep for when they brought Ethan out.

He clutched the medical bag, his muscles burning.

Finally, the jeeps pulled to a stop on a rise overlooking a tiny mountain outpost. It was long abandoned, an old mining dump, but Moroshkin's forces used it as a drone base and a communications center. Sergey sent short orders through the radio, dispatching one team to knock out the comms tower and another to detonate the drone base. He, Sasha, and Scott would storm the small main building in the center.

"Ethan is in there," he said, leaning close to Jack. "We'll be back with him. I promise."

Sergey, Sasha, and Scott set off, creeping away and leaving Jack alone with the radio, a medical kit, and the silent forest.

Scott moved with Sasha and Sergey down through the trees, keeping his eyes locked on the sentries manning their posts. At Sergey's signal, the snipers he'd placed above would take the sentries out. They would rush the main entrance.

Sasha stacked in front of Sergey, despite Sergey's glare, and Scott stayed out of that snapping Russian argument.

Three claps shook snow from the fir branches above. The sentries dropped.

They moved together, racing forward. At the same time, the comms and drone teams would be moving in, packing explosives around the communications tower, generator, and drone hangars. They had three minutes from the snipers' shots to get in and get out.

Sasha fired into the door lock and kicked it down, rushing inside and sweeping right and left. Sergey came in behind him, taking the left side while Sasha pressed right, clearing the hallway. Scott went down the center, his rifle ready to fire.

Shapes appeared down the hall. He squeezed the trigger. Three rounds spat out, and the soldiers ahead dropped.

More shapes huddled around the corner, shouting in Russian. Scott flattened himself against the wall, shouting to Sergey and Sasha just before shots rang out, pinging off the concrete next to their heads.

Unfazed, Sasha dropped to one knee and pulled two grenades from his belt. He looked to Sergey first, and when Sergey nodded, he ripped the pins from the grenades and hurled them down the hallway.

Their impact echoed, steel against concrete. The Russian soldiers shouted, frantic hollering as they spotted the grenades.

Booming shook the corridor, concrete dust and plaster raining from above. Screams sounded, shrill. Then silence.

Scott waited, counting down. Nothing.

They crept forward, picking their way through the dead. It had been a small team, just a skeleton crew holding down the main building. Granted, it was a tiny base, but there should have been more men.

Not everyone was home.

"We've gotta move fast," he grunted.

The building was a T-shape, the first corridor where they entered intersecting with the cross hallway. Offices and locked doors stretched on either side. Sasha turned to the right. Sergey padded silently down the left. In the smoke of the grenade, his tall, lanky frame seemed to vanish. He moved like a predator, and Scott's stomach clenched. Sergey, for all his friendship with Jack, was still a dangerous man. He'd been a spy and a soldier all his life before becoming a politician.

And this was the man Jack had thrown his lot in with.

Swallowing, he set off after Sergey.

Sergey blew locks off doors, searching empty office after empty office. He dropped to one knee and patted through the dead, pulling out papers and CDs and flash drives as he moved. They reached the end of the hall.

No Ethan.

Was he even there?

"The other end. Go."

Echoes of shots from Sasha blowing off locks bounced through the corridor. They jogged to catch up with him.

Scott slowed, though, his gaze catching on a glinting bit of metal shining beneath the neck of a dead Russian soldier. Sergey ran on, but Scott stayed back, reaching for the dangling chain falling free from the soldier's jacket.

Two dark rings, each with a channel of tiny diamonds buried in their middle. A chain that looked suspiciously like the one he was missing.

Ethan was *here*.

Scott's fist closed around the two rings. He yanked, snapping the chain's release, and the dead man's neck jerked. He wanted to throttle him, empty his rifle into his face. Whoever he was, he'd taken the rings from Ethan, and if there was one thing Scott knew, *knew*, it was that Ethan wouldn't let go of those rings without—

"Scott!" Sergey's bellow sounded from the end of the hall! "Scott! Down here!"

Scott pocketed Ethan's rings, glaring down at the dead Russian, and took off.

He skittered to a stop outside the farthest door. A dead Russian lay on the ground, fresh blood still oozing out of him.

Sasha was inside, kneeling in a pool of blood. In his arms, he cradled Ethan's bone-white and unmoving body.

Jack was a bundle of blown nerves and clenched teeth when the drone hangar exploded, followed by the comms tower. Metal shrieked, shattering, and steel blew through the air. Flames roared to the sky, trees nearby alighting. Snow hissed as drone parts rained down around Jack, dull thumps crashing into the earth. He waited, trying not to panic, next to their jeep.

Shouting in Russian, and then feet running back toward the convoy. His heart seized, but started again when he recognized Sergey's men. Doors slammed, engines roared. Jeeps around him started up.

Where were the others? Where were Sergey, Sasha, and Scott?

And Ethan. Where was Ethan?

Three figures emerged from the smoke, running toward Jack. One of them had a body thrown over his shoulder.

Time slowed, the burning steel, the raining destruction, the roaring of the jeeps and bellowing Russian all fading away as he stared at the three men running toward him. The next moment could break him, break him entirely. Could shatter him like the base had exploded. Could scatter his heart in burning fragments.

Sasha hopped into the driver's seat, shouting into the radio in harsh Russian. Scott raced past Jack, Ethan over his shoulder, a river of Ethan's blood running down his side.

"Move, move!" Sergey rushed Scott, pulling Scott back after he threw Ethan into the back seat. "Get up front!"

Whirling, Sergey reached for Jack. "Jack! Get in and hold his head! We have moments! They tried to kill him when we stormed the base!"

He leaped, throwing the medical kit at Sergey and clambering over Ethan's battered, bloody body as Sergey crowded in on top of Ethan's legs.

Sasha peeled out, dirt and snow kicking up behind his tires. He spun the wheel as Jack cradled Ethan's head in his lap.

Sergey ripped Ethan's shirt in half, exposing an angry, ragged tear in his side, weeping blood all over the jeep. "Press!" he shouted. "Press down!"

Jack balled his jacket up and leaned down on Ethan's wound, right over his ribs. He still had on Ethan's Secret Service sweatshirt underneath his jacket.

He stared into Ethan's pale face. Traced his blue lips with his eyes.

Sergey unzipped the medical bag, grabbing the suture kit. "Scott! Under the front seat!" he barked. "Now!"

Scott ducked down, rummaging.

"Hurry!"

"This?" Scott popped back up with a plastic bottle of vodka, the label scraped off.

"Yes!" Sergey snatched the vodka and unscrewed the top with his teeth. He pulled out a pre-threaded hooked needle from the suture kit and sat on Ethan's thighs, pinning him down. He spat out the vodka cap.

"Jack, when I say, pull back the jacket and hold him down. *Hold him down*, and do not let him move." Sergey's eyes blazed, burning as he stared at Jack. "Understand?"

"What are you doing? Sergey—"

"I am FSB, Jack! I know what I am doing! I can save him, but only if you shut up!"

Jack's lips clamped closed as Scott grabbed one of Ethan's wrists.

"Now," Sergey breathed.

Jack flew back, dropping the jacket and leaning down, pressing everything he had into Ethan's thick shoulders. He pushed his face into Ethan's, staring at him upside down, practically nose to nose. *Ethan, come back to me. Come back to me, please, Goddamn it. Don't do this. Don't die, not now. Please, Ethan.*

Sergey doused Ethan's ragged wound in vodka, soaking the torn edges of his skin and washing away the blood.

Ethan's eyes popped open. He roared, blindly trying to fight against the surge of pain. He bucked, but Sergey stayed on him. Wild, Ethan tried to punch, thrashing against his restrainer.

"Ethan!" Jack shouted. "Ethan, stop! It's us! It's me! It's Jack!"

Ethan froze, his wild gaze darting left and right before he zeroed in on Jack. Jack watched it, saw his lover go from some kind of wild animal to slow, defeated recognition. Saw the terror creep into his eyes, and then the agony.

"Jack," Ethan whispered. His voice was a fragile, broken thing. "Jack. I'm sorry. I'm so sorry you're dead."

"I'm not dead." He tried to smile, even as Sergey readied the needle. He wiped away the blood, trying to see Ethan's wound, but more kept pushing through.

Keep him calm. Keep him steady.

Jack plastered another smile to his face, even though his heart was about to burst. "Ethan, I'm *here*. I'm alive because you saved me. You told

Irwin what happened and he got me out in time. And then I left it all behind. I left *everything* to come find you. To be *with* you."

Ethan's face contorted, anguish and rage fighting for dominance. "No. No, this is just a dream. This is just my dream. I'm dead, I'm dead—"

Sergey stabbed him with the needle, digging in deep, and pulled the dark thread through his skin quickly.

Ethan screamed, his eyes widening. He went rigid beneath Jack's hold.

"It's not a dream!" Jack's hands rose over Ethan's neck and his bruised face. He stroked his cheeks, his eyebrows, threaded his fingers through Ethan's hair as Sergey stitched up his side and Sasha spun the jeep through the forest, sliding and careening on the black dirt and patches of snow. "Scott's here too. He's got your hand."

Scott gripped Ethan's hand.

Ethan clenched down, his knuckles going white.

Sergey's fingers slipped over Ethan's skin, slick with vodka and blood. Ethan's teeth ground together. He groaned, but he never let go of Jack's gaze.

He blinked, over and over. His eyes darted down to Jack's sweatshirt—Ethan's Secret Service sweatshirt. "*Jack?*"

Jack couldn't speak. He fought the swelling of his heart, the panic he'd held just at bay since everything had fallen apart, and stared into Ethan's eyes. "I'm here," he whispered. "I had to come find you. I *love* you. I couldn't let you go. I won't leave you. Not ever."

Ethan's voice was wrecked, his expression wrenched apart. "Your presidency—"

"How many times have I told you that you're more important?" Wet drops appeared on Ethan's cheeks, salt splashes raining from Jack's eyes. "I meant it every single time."

Ethan's free hand rose, grasping Jack behind the neck. He tugged, pulling Jack down until their foreheads were pressed together. Jack's tears flowed over Ethan's pale skin, and even though Ethan roared through the agony of Sergey's rough stitches and Sasha's wild driving, he kept his gaze fixed on Jack as Jack whispered that he loved him over and over again.

58

Ethan was burning up by the time they got back to the bunker and fading in and out of consciousness. Scott carried him inside, jogging behind Sergey. Sasha ran with Jack, guiding him to the storage room they had turned into a clinic.

Jack lingered on the side as Sergey tossed two prefilled syringes to Sasha and Scott laid Ethan down on a ratty cot. Sasha pulled down Ethan's pants, stripping him to his underwear, and then stabbed him in the upper thigh with both syringes, one after the other. Scott watched, glaring, and grabbed a blanket to cover Ethan, wrapping him up tight as Sergey primed Ethan's vein for an IV bag of fluids.

"What'd you give him?" Jack slowly stepped forward.

"Antibiotics and a pain reliever. He will need both. And rest. He lost a lot of blood." Sasha wet a rag from a water bottle and rubbed at dried blood snaking over Sergey's cheek and down his neck.

"He will be out for a while. You should stay, Jack. Be here when he wakes up." Sergey sighed, but he rolled into Sasha's touch. "We need to go over some things." He eyed Scott. "Would you like to join us?"

For a moment, Scott seemed torn. Stay with Jack, a man he'd been professionally—and now personally—sworn to protect. Or, go with Sergey and get firsthand information on just what they were doing out here.

Jack nodded to Scott. "Go," he said softly. "Please."

Scott followed Sasha and Sergey out of the dim corner of the clinic, the private space they'd tried to give Jack and Ethan.

Slowly, Jack settled down on the concrete beside Ethan's cot. Ethan had always seemed larger than life, a fierce fighter, sleek and powerful on the outside and hiding quiet depths and a sun-bright core within. Now, lying on the cot, he seemed small, almost boyish, and his battered face made Jack's stomach curl. He reached for Ethan, cupping his cheek. "I love you," he breathed. "Know that. No matter what. I love you. And I'll do anything for this love, Ethan. Anything."

His thumb stroked over Ethan's black-and-blue cheek, the edges mottled with yellow and green. His skin was hot and damp, sweaty with fever.

Every piece and part of Jack ached, worn through with his own bruises and his own injuries, and the weary turmoil his heart had been put through. He was forty-six, not a young man anymore, and even his bones were exhausted. He wanted to rest. Not just lie down and sleep, but truly rest. Take Ethan and vanish, disappear to some corner of the world where they weren't locked in a pitched battle with a madman, weren't dead men living off the grid, weren't trying to find a way to live their lives, and the only guide stone they had was the anchor of their love.

That wasn't for them, though.

He pitched forward, resting his cheek on Ethan's stomach and his palm on Ethan's jaw. The slow rise and fall of Ethan's breathing calmed him, centered him, and eventually, lulled him to sleep.

Buzzing woke him, a clatter vibrating against his chest.

Dazed, Jack fumbled in his pockets for Ethan's phone. The battery was low. The screen was too bright. He squinted, but his blurry eyes managed to make out the number dialing in.

"I'm alive," he grunted. "We're all alive."

"*That's great,*" Elizabeth said quickly. She was all business. "*But I'm calling about something else.*"

His eyes slid closed. It was always something else, something more. "What is it?"

"*Moroshkin's forces have initiated a polar invasion of Canada. Russian naval forces have breached Canadian waters and missiles are landing as far south as Toronto and Vancouver. Russian soldiers are on deck, sweeping south through the Northwest Territories. Towns are falling like maple leaves. They're attacking Yellowknife as we speak. Capital of the Northwest Territories.*"

Jack stopped breathing.

"*Russian helos and fighter jets are in the air. Canada's military is scrambling to respond and they've asked for our support. I'm granting it. We're about to be in an all-out war with Moroshkin's Russia in Canada.*"

"Why?" His mind raced, trying to put the pieces together. "Why invade Canada?"

"*It's the land route down to us? Step one of their invasion?*" Elizabeth sighed. "*Unfortunately, that's not all. We lost two polar satellites and Thule Air Station just before the invasion.*" Thule, at the top of Greenland in the Arctic Circle, was one of the Air Force's first strike Arctic bases. It made sense to take the base out, from a tactical perspective. But something niggled at Jack, a conviction he'd learned the hard way.

"He didn't just destroy those satellites and Thule to cover his invasion force. Madigan is up to something."

"*My thoughts exactly. There's a Swedish weather satellite up there, pretty ancient, but it's been taking air density photos for the past decade. The Swedes just sent us a few.*"

Jack waited, his dread rising.

"*Something up there in the Kara Sea, in the Russian ice, is causing methane hydrate to leak into the atmosphere. There's a lot of it in the ice caps, and it looks like something or someone is breaking it loose. It's leaking out. The Swedes' density photos show enough methane hydrate has entered the atmosphere to penetrate the jet stream. It's starting to snake around the world.*" She paused. "*Some of the science guys here are saying that this could turn into an E.L.E.*"

Another one of every president's nightmares, an Extinction Level Event. "How?"

"*If enough methane hydrate saturates the atmosphere and something lights it all? It could set off a thermobaric explosion that would burn through the atmosphere of the planet. Incinerate the sky.*" She swallowed. "*That's what our people are saying.*"

He could imagine it. Could see his advisors panicked with wide eyes and pale skin, could see the Situation Room up in arms, furious and frantic.

And here he was, sitting in the dark with stiff knees beside Ethan's cot, buried in the Russian wilderness.

In the Russian wilderness.

"Elizabeth. I'm *here*. With our friend. We're already planning to work north. We can *go* to Madigan. We can get eyes on, get intel on what's happening up there. He has no idea we're here. We can *finally* get the upper hand on him."

She was silent for a moment. Static hummed on the line. A muffled voice in the background murmured, asking her when she'd step back into the Situation Room. "*If you could figure out what the bastard's up to, I could send subs from Pearl. Send them to you and your friend, along with a few surprises. Get you guys under the ice up there. Throw a wrench in whatever he's doing.*"

"Do it. We'll get going on recon on our end. We'll find out what he's up to. Take the fight to him. Finally be one step ahead of this asshole."

She breathed out, long and slow. "*All right, I've got to get back in there. Talk to your friend. I'll get things in motion on my end.*" She cut the line.

As Jack pulled the phone away from his ear, he spotted Ethan blinking up at him, bleary-eyed and frowning.

He leaned in close, scooping up Ethan's hand, dropping the phone and cupping his cheek. "Hey," he breathed. "Hey, how are you, love?"

Ethan frowned again. "Is that my phone?"

"I'm borrowing it. I left mine in DC. Didn't want anyone tracking me."

Ethan hummed, and he pressed his bruised cheek against Jack's palm. "I don't think this is real. I don't think you're really here."

Jack pressed a kiss to Ethan's cracked lips. "I'm here with you, love. I'm never going to leave your side. Not ever again."

"Jack…" Ethan rolled his head away, frowning at the dark corner. "A lot happened—"

"I know." Jack stroked Ethan's hair, pushing strands off his sweaty forehead. "I know. I have so much to make up for, if I even can." Jack's shoulders slumped. "But first, we have to try to save the world again."

"I know where we have to go. Here." Scowling, Sergey pointed at the faded and worn map of Russia—actually, the Soviet Union—tacked up on the wall in the bunker's main conference room. Dominating the opposite concrete wall, a chipped mural of Comrade Lenin saluting his brothers, and the hammer and sickle of the Soviet Union, played out in bright colors.

Ethan leaned on Jack, squinting at the map. "You pointed at the Pacific Ocean."

"No. Simushir Island, in the Kurils. In the Okhotsk Sea, north of Japan."

Jack blinked. "Could you pick someplace farther, perhaps? That's on the other side of Russia. The other side of the continent, Sergey."

"*How* small is this island?" Scott stepped close to the map, trying to find the speck of land.

"It is there!" Sergey snapped. "Kraternyy naval base. It is an abandoned submarine base. The island is a string of four volcanos. The northernmost one, it blew, long time ago, and left behind a flooded caldera. A perfect deep water cove inside the island. Very protected. Soviet engineers blasted an opening, turned it into a submarine base to spy on you Americans." He wagged his finger. "See? You had no idea!"

That shut Jack up. Scott grumbled under his breath.

"We go there. We can base there. Your subs can dock. We head north for the Arctic. The only way to the Arctic is through the Pacific now.

Moroshkin has the North Sea, and the GIUK Gap. We cannot go that way. But here, we can regroup, gather our forces on the island, and then strike."

"What's out there now?" Jack had called for their impromptu meeting after Elizabeth's call. He'd gotten Sergey, Sasha, and Scott together, and Ethan had insisted on joining. He bitched his way out of the cot, grumbled his way through a fresh bag of IV fluids and antibiotics, and shadowed Jack all the way down the hall, trying to hide his limp. He carried his IV bag over his shoulder, scowling.

When he saw Scott, he glowered and said nothing, standing apart from his best friend.

"Nothing. Empty land. Nothing is out there. No one goes, no one." Sergey cut his hands through the air. "Even getting there is difficult. Kamchatka Peninsula," he said, tracing the finger of land stretching south from the farthest reach of Russia, "is practically wild. Little infrastructure. One navy base, but no one has heard anything from it since the coup. There are bad roads, or," he said, bobbing his head. "No roads. Only boats can go, but the weather is terrible."

"This is sounding better and better," Scott grumbled. "How do we get there?"

"We take this route." Sergey traced a thin, spidery web of lines from their current position west of Kazakhstan, north across Siberia and into the Russian Far East. "With Moroshkin and Madigan invading Canada, and something happening in the Arctic, they will not be watching all of the roads. These are rural. Difficult to traverse with military vehicles."

Difficult for them to traverse as well. Jack felt Ethan stiffen, standing just inches away from him. Ethan's hand pressed over his own side, his fingers ghosting over Sergey's fast stitches.

"Siberia has rejected Moroshkin's government. The Far East has rejected him as well. The police forces there have blocked most roads. Set up armed checkpoints. We will be safe once we cross the borders." He shrugged. "Safer."

"Great. Safer." Scott shook his head.

Sergey squabbled with Scott, the both of them bantering back and forth over the route to take from the Caucasus to the Far East.

Jack's gaze turned to Sasha, standing silently off to the side, fingering a different portion of the map.

"Go talk to him," Ethan murmured. "Something's up. I need to sit down for a minute." He eased himself down into one of the rickety metal chairs scattered in front of a leaning table.

Jack waited until he was down before he caught Sasha's eye.

Sasha stole a quick glance toward Sergey. He motioned Jack out to the hallway. Jack followed.

"What's going on, Sasha?" Jack said, folding his arms. "Is there something you know about this place? This island? Some extra information we don't?"

"No, no. Nothing like that. I would not keep information from Sergey." He looked away, squinting down the corridor.

"Then what's going on?"

"Near here, maybe forty miles, there is an air base. MiGs flew out of there. Your country bombed it, but it may be possible to find a jet still working. Get it ready for flight. Use a road for a runway."

"You want to fly everyone to Simushir Island in a MiG?"

"No." Sasha's eyes were bright, gleaming as he turned back to Jack. "I want to overfly the Kara Sea in one. See what it is Madigan is doing."

Holy shit. Jack whistled. Eyes-on intelligence, actually getting to within a few steps of Madigan's plans. Get enough intel to get into position to finally end the man, this monster. He opened his mouth.

Sergey's rough snarl beat him to it. He'd followed them silently into the hall, listening to Sasha's half-formed idea. "Out of the question! Are you *insane*?"

Sasha's eyes flashed, Russian-red fury striking like a match. "It is good plan! We need to know what is happening! I am only qualified pilot who can make the flight."

"You haven't flown in months! And you were injured! How can you fly with no spleen?"

"You do not need a spleen to fly! I can do—"

"*Nyet!*" Storm clouds darkened Sergey's hawkish face. "No, you cannot do this!"

Jack cut in. "Sergey, it's a good plan—"

"Why do you say this, Jack? It is terrible plan! It is a suicide mission!" Sergey whirled on Jack. "I will not allow it!"

"We must have intel! It is the right thing to do!" Sasha snarled, hurt flickering through his eyes for a half moment. "You think I cannot do this, *da*? That I cannot fly this mission?"

"Of course you could fly this. You are not incapable. But we cannot *lose* you, Sasha." Sergey threw his arms wide. "You cannot throw your life away! Everyone here needs you!"

It was the wrong thing to say, and Jack knew it. Sasha's eyes narrowed, and the hurt that had been lingering on the edges flared and then vanished, extinguished in raw anger. "I would help everyone more by finding out what Madigan is doing up there. I would happily give my life as a hero to Russia. I would die for my country, for Mother Russia, and for *you*!"

Purple rage built in Sergey's expression, his thin-pressed lips trembling. His dark eyes were fixed on Sasha's, holding like a falcon on the hunt.

"I will not allow you to die," Sergey growled. "I will not allow it!"

Sasha snapped something in Russian. Jack made his retreat.

Inside the map room, Sergey's chase after Jack and Sasha left Scott and Ethan alone together at last. Scott fiddled with a broken pencil from the table, flicking it against his palm as he pursed his lips. He finally looked up, catching Ethan's glare.

Ethan sat stock-still, a furious scowl etched on his face.

Scott tossed the pencil on the table and spread his hands wide. "What do you want from me, Ethan? He was bound and determined to come after you. He was going to chase you around the globe. Did you want me to let him go alone?"

"How about you talk some sense into him? He's thrown everything he ever worked for away! Everything he had!"

"You don't think I tried?"

"Lock him in the White House, then!"

Scott rolled his eyes. "Do you remember how you were after Ethiopia? How crazed and single-minded you were? That's him, right now." Scott held out two fingers. "He's got his mind focused on two things and only two things: finding you and killing Madigan."

"He's not a soldier!" Ethan cried. His side pulled, and he winced, his hand flying to cover his stitches. "This isn't where he's supposed to be!"

"But he *is* right about one thing, Ethan. Madigan targeted *him* and targeted *you*. *Personally*. He's coming after the both of you, and as long as you both are off the grid, Madigan's attention is elsewhere."

"So put him in a bunker, or a safe house, or something! But send him to *Russia*? To a *war zone*?"

"I don't want to admit it, but… Jack is right. This is the one thing Madigan won't ever see coming. We have to think more like him. Act more like him. And this is the first step."

Fury still crackled in Ethan's veins. It was too dangerous, far too dangerous, and no matter how much he wanted Jack by his side again, this was not the way he'd imagined it.

"He held his own in Sochi and he did good getting over here." Scott was trying to placate him. "You did good with him at Rowley. He's a good shot."

Ethan scowled.

"Kept a cool head, too. Let me tell you about the human smugglers who duct-taped him and shoved him in a box."

Ethan's palm hit the table, slapping the surface. The sound cut through the air.

"You know, maybe if you hadn't run off half-cocked on a suicide mission, he wouldn't have had to chase you."

Ethan looked away. "I lost everything, Scott. Everything. Twice in one week." He coughed, wincing again at the pain flaring from his stitches. "Honestly? I'm not even sure this is all real. Maybe I *am* dead and this is my fucked-up version of hell."

Scott frowned.

"Is this my punishment? I get him back, but I just get to see him die out here? Feel like this over and over and over?" The grinding, endless grief, the void that used to hold his heart. Endless, endless rage.

Scott stared at him like he'd lost his mind. He scooted his rickety metal chair toward Ethan, the legs scraping over the concrete bunker floor. He dug in his jacket pocket. "You're fucking alive, Ethan. And it's a good Goddamn thing, too, 'cause he would have lost it if we were too late. Look, you didn't see him lose his fucking mind over you. He's been an absolute shell of himself until we found you here. You *have* to know, Ethan: back in DC, when he still thought that thing was his wife? He chose *you*. He chose *you* over her. No, no, don't do that." Scott slapped Ethan's cheek.

Ethan's eyes blazed. He wanted to snarl, but his throat had closed and his heart was trying to decide what to do. Ache, or finally start beating again? Before he'd opened his eyes and saw Jack above him as his side was stitched closed, he'd last seen Jack walking out on him. Choosing Leslie over him. Choosing his undead wife, in a moment, over what they had built together.

It was a hurt that had festered, a wound that went soul-deep.

Jack appearing in the Russian wilderness, confessing his love and cradling Ethan close was a nice dream, but it came after the exposure of what Leslie actually was.

The sting of second choice left a sour taste in his mouth. He wanted to be Jack's everything, like Jack was for him. Not Jack's settlement.

Scott's words, though, plucked at his wounded heart. He squinted, a question in his eyes.

"Yeah. He picked you, even before he knew what she was. He was out of his mind all week long, walking around like a damn zombie. He couldn't function. Like someone had pulled the plug on his sanity. We all were freaking. Welby took over in the Residence keeping eyes on him 'cause I couldn't be near the man. Not after what he did to you." Scott sighed, hard. "We watched her, but we also watched him. I thought he might put a bullet in his brain. I went and took back the gun I gave you."

Ethan's head whipped up.

"Look, he told her about you from day one. He never tried to hide you. And, he defended you guys and your relationship, even though it seemed like everyone and their mother wanted him to jump right back in with her."

Ethan swallowed. "Did they—" He couldn't say it. Couldn't ask. Jealousy was an ugly, sour thing, but it lapped at his blood, burned at the base of his spine.

"No. Didn't even sleep in the same room."

He didn't know what to do with that. Didn't know how to feel, how to process the bitter relief.

Scott kept going, barreling through Ethan's wildly swinging emotions. "He ended up outside Horsepower begging me to track you down. After you went on your little mission, by the way." Scott glared. "Thanks for that."

"What did he say?" Ethan braced himself, staring at the ground as he picked dirt from beneath his nails.

"He said he had told her he loved you and only you and that you were the one for him. Forever. Told her he couldn't be with her because he was in love with you. He said he wanted to grow old with you. Not her."

His eyes slammed shut. His jaw wavered, trembling. He'd long believed he loved Jack more than Jack loved him, but to walk away from the resurrection of a woman he thought was his wife? Jack had loved her to the depths of his heart, he truly had. Ethan had always known that, and in some paradoxical way, that truth had made Jack's walking out on him both easier and harder to understand and accept. How could he compete with the first love of Jack's life?

But Jack chose *him*.

Ethan reached for his neck, for the chain that hung there. He'd turned the rings over countless times on the drive from Jeddah to Russia, believing Jack was dead and gone and they were all he had left, twin monuments to what they had discovered together.

His hands found nothing. "Fuck."

Metal clanged, something heavy hitting the table in front of Scott. He opened his eyes.

Scott had his hand palm-down on the table, covering something.

He lifted his hand away, revealing Ethan's matching rings. "You said he's thrown everything away. I bet if you ask him, he'll say that coming here and finding you alive means he's found everything he truly cares about."

Ethan cradled them both in the palm of his hand. A war zone at the end of the world was hardly the time or place for any kind of dreaming about the future, but for a moment, he let his heart go.

He imagined the look on Jack's face as Ethan dropped to one knee. How he'd wrap him up, swing him around and kiss him breathless after sliding the ring on. What would their wedding look like? Some kind of state affair? A billion journalists vying for the best photo? Or something private? Just the two of them hidden on a quiet beach somewhere?

An ache weighed down his dreams.

He could still imagine it, though. Still see the two of them together forever. Could imagine Jack old and gray and holding his hand, still with that smile in his eyes.

Would they ever get there? With Madigan ripping apart their lives over and over again?

Damn it, how had it all gone so wrong? How had everything ended up this way? He could imagine a future with Jack, dream of their wedding, but a madman loomed on top of the world and they were buried in a desolate war zone, wounded, struggling to survive, and planning an attack to try to save the world.

Again.

He didn't want to be a hero. He didn't want to have the world hanging on his decisions. He just wanted to love Jack.

And, his heart still throbbed, wounded deep in the cracks and crevices. Lingering anguish, a canyon in his soul, painted in memories of Jack walking out. The way his heart had gone cold, freezing over, when Jack had pulled away.

He closed his fist around the rings and the broken chain and shoved them in his pocket.

59

Russia
Volga Air Base

Sergey had lost the battle over Sasha taking the flight up to the Arctic. There was too much to gain, too much intel potential, and with the world on the line, the choice was already made.

At the Volga Air Base, one MiG still functioned. Their small recon team pulled it from the blackened wreckage of its hangar. The base had been obliterated, but the one fighter remained, and even better, one of the runways had only minimal damage. Getting the MiG out of the hangar and rolled to a smooth section of tarmac had nearly killed them all.

Sergey remained bitterly opposed to the mission, almost petulant in his fury. He hovered behind Sasha, pouncing on every problem.

The MiG wasn't fueled up. The runway was damaged. There was no tower, no air traffic controls. No secure radio to communicate back and forth.

Sasha found fuel and directed everyone to clear the runway, sweeping the surface clear of any debris that could catch on the tires. He plotted his own course, calculated the winds and navigation based on charts and his memory.

He stared at Sergey, silent, when Sergey complained about the radio.

Scott, Jack, and Ethan stayed back, waiting for the keg to blow.

"I found these." Sasha dumped two satellite phones on the burned table they were using in the wreckage of the hangar. One side of the table had snapped off, but Jack had rolled over a few giant jet rims to stack and use as table legs. It was tilted, but it worked.

Sergey glared at the phones and then at Sasha, his face scrunched up like he was looking at something repugnant.

"No radio. We cannot use the Russian frequencies. But we can use sat phones."

"Flying and talking?" Sergey arched an eyebrow. "This sounds terrible. Sounds even worse than driving and talking!"

"For reporting back what I find."

Sergey fingered the plastic casing. "You will be blown out of the sky as soon as you take off. Moroshkin will track your plane. You will be dead in minutes."

Reaching into the pocket of his flight suit, Sasha pulled free the MiG's GPS beacon and tossed it in front of Sergey. Black soot puffed up from the table.

"How will you navigate?"

"The old-fashioned way. With maps and a compass." Sasha scowled. "I know what I am doing. Despite your lack of confidence in me." He glared, and when the angry knot in his chest tightened, he turned and left, heading back for his MiG, parked just past the destroyed and blackened asphalt.

Sasha tilted his head back, staring up at the slate-gray sky. He'd found a flight suit in the destroyed ready room and he'd rolled down the top, tying the arms around his waist. It wasn't warm, but the day's hard labor had wrecked him. He'd ditched his shirt hours ago. His pale chest heaved, the dog tags he could never bring himself to get rid of resting in the hollow between his pecs.

If final flight checks went well, he'd be taking off in just under an hour. A strange mixture of relief and regret flowed through him, an itch under his skin that desperately wanted to be scratched. Should he say something? Should he confess—

No. It was better this way. This was his purpose. He could finally be useful, die for his motherland. Maybe Sergey would say beautiful things at his funeral. He kicked at a bit of torn rubber tire.

Footfalls pounded the ground behind him.

Sergey's snarling voice broke his reverie. "I am not a fool. You think I have not figured it out?"

Sasha's heart clenched. No, no pretty words, nothing beautiful would be said for him. After everything, after watching Sergey unconditionally accept everyone else, this was how it would come out between them?

Fine. It would all be over soon anyway.

He walked away from Sergey, focused on his jet. His gaze traveled over her lines, cataloging her features, searching for dents and dings, tears in the metal, shorn or loose bolts. Anything at all. He tried to block out Sergey.

"Sasha! I am speaking to you!" Sergey stormed after him, following under the MiG's wings and toward the jets.

Sasha's shaking fingers danced over the cool metal. *It is nothing. I will get through this moment like I have gotten through everything else.*

"You think this is some kind of joke? You can fool everyone else, but you cannot fool me!"

The knot in his chest pulled tighter, constricting his heart. *You knew it would never happen. There was never a future to this, never.* Sasha ducked beneath the jet's tail and trailed forward, tracing the edge of one wing.

Sergey slapped the side of the MiG, bellowing at the back of Sasha's head. "You are *not* a man! Not a Russian! You are a *coward*!"

Sasha whirled, fury roaring through him, so much so that he was suddenly shaking with raw, scathing rage. If there was one thing—and only one thing—that he was not, it was a coward. He'd done everything in his life with his chest open and his shoulders back, lived through everything his life had thrown at him. Lived through his shame, his brokenness, and made something of himself. Fine, Sergey could hate him. He could berate him and throw him away. But he could *not* call him a coward.

He was on fire, burning from his soul. "I am *not* a coward!" Sergey took a half step back, his eyes widening.

A second later, Sergey shoved Sasha's folded flight map in his face. He saw his route, sketched out in pencil, and his fuel calculations, obscured and outright faked at the end. "I know what you are doing," Sergey hissed. "Even with this jet fully fueled, you only have enough to get there. You do not have enough fuel to get *back*!" Anguish laced his words, underpinned his voice.

Sasha's rage fell away. Emptiness slammed into him, punching him in his stomach.

He turned back to the wing, tracing the smooth metal with his palms. He had to move, had to do something, or he'd fly out of his skin. Or do something that couldn't be undone. "It does not matter. We need this. And, it would not matter if everyone knew or not. They would still ask me to fly this mission. This way, their conscience is clear."

"Why are you so determined to do this?" Sergey ducked under the wing, popping up right in Sasha's face. Hurt split Sergey's expression.

"Let my life mean something!" Sasha's hands made tight fists, his nails biting into his palms. "I was thrown out of the Air Force in disgrace! Let this be my legacy! Let me *do* something!"

"Your legacy is already stunning! Your life means everything! *You* are everything to our fight! Our troops look up to you. They love you! They *need* you! I cannot *do* this without you!"

Pretty words, but not the ones he wanted to hear. Sergey wanted him for the mission, for the fight. For everyone else.

He headed for the nose of the jet.

"Sasha..." Sergey growled, chasing him. He reached for Sasha's arm, tugging him around. "This is not good. Do not do this," he breathed. "*Please.*"

"We need to know." Sasha stared at Sergey's hand, still lingering on his elbow.

"Send someone else! Send *anyone* else. Not you."

"Send another to their death?" Sasha shook his head. "No."

"Damn it, Sasha!" Sergey squeezed down on his elbow, almost bruisingly tight.

It was too much, Sergey chasing him around the jet and begging him not to go. His pleading eyes and his body pressing too close. He'd thought Sergey was going to hate him, belittle him for his affections, for his gratitude that had morphed into hero worship and morphed, yet again, into something deeper, something intractable that lived in the center of his heart. Instead, Sergey was almost begging him to stay at his side, and that yanked away the last of Sasha's crumbling restraint.

He shook Sergey's hand off and grabbed his shoulders, shoving him against the cockpit ladder. "Damn you, Sergey. Damn you."

He captured Sergey's lips with his own, pouring everything he felt, every urge, every yearning, every hopeless desire, into his kiss. He swiped his tongue over Sergey's lower lip, sucked it into his mouth. Nibbled down, and when Sergey gasped, he snaked his tongue between Sergey's shocked lips. Moaned into the kiss.

He crowded close, pressing his body against Sergey's and trapping him on the ladder. Sergey was taller, leaner. Sasha trailed his hands down Sergey's body, over the dirty long-sleeve shirt covering his thin chest, his loose combat fatigues hanging on his sharp hips. back up, curling his hands around Sergey's neck. "So beautiful," he murmured, kissing him again. "*Sergey.*"

Sergey hadn't moved. He stared at Sasha, frozen, mouth open in shock, as Sasha slowly pulled back.

Dread, and the certainty that he'd made a mistake, roared in on all sides. Suddenly, the world felt *exactly* like it had the moment he'd seen those hockey sticks in the hands of his so-called friends.

Sergey stared. "You—"

You knew there was never a future to this, to this hopeless love. You promised yourself you wouldn't dream—

Sasha stepped back, pulling away and dropping his hands, freeing Sergey. "It is nothing. Do not worry yourself."

Sergey said nothing. Did nothing.

There was a hollowed-out void in his heart, filled with dark shadows and nightmares from his past. Sergey's biting sarcasm and quick smile had filled his life, wrapped up the void in an acceptance of who he was that he'd fiercely cherished. Sergey had been the very first to *know* him, to accept him for exactly who and what he was. The first who had ever encouraged him to be both opposing sides of himself at once: a proud Russian and a gay man drowning in shame and self-hate.

Sergey had helped him chip away at his own self-hate, piece by piece, with his smiles and his sarcasm and his unending confidence in Sasha.

After that, Sasha had to make room for his silent yearning, for the way his heart had opened to Sergey. How could all of him not crave all of Sergey? How could he not fall entirely in love with the man? With the best man he'd ever met?

Falling for his country's leader, and Russia's best hope for her future, was the best and stupidest thing he'd ever done.

But he'd made peace with his hopeless desire. Accepted what he could have, and tried not to dream of what he could not. He lived in the yearning, in the way he could quietly love Sergey from his side. He could bask in his love like it was a warm summer day, let Sergey—all of what he was—permeate his soul.

And he'd just thrown *everything* away.

"Final preflight brief in thirty minutes." Sasha headed back for the hangar, leaving Sergey and his own broken heart frozen at the base of the MiG's ladder.

I will get through this moment like I have gotten through everything else.

And, by the end of the day, the hurt, the silent scream, wouldn't matter anymore.

"My flight will take me through the Urals and north by northeast to the Kara Sea. I will stay beneath the radar deck, out of sight of the air defenses. The peaks of the Urals will cover my flight from the North Fleet, based here, in the Barents Sea and around Murmansk."

"Much of the North Fleet went to Moroshkin," Sergey grumbled.

"They are likely scattered, with the invasion over the pole into Canada and whatever they are doing in the Arctic ice." Sasha fingered the map, tracing the target zone he'd circled in red. To the west, the long, finger-like Severny Island stretched into the Arctic. He tapped the ice-covered island. "This is my western boundary. I will fly over Novaya Zemlya—" He pointed to the archipelago of scattered ice islands in the Russian arctic. "—and into the Kara Sea. After, I will call my report in on the sat phone."

Sergey clenched Sasha's paired sat phone in one hand. His arms were crossed and he glowered over the table, ignoring Jack's questioning looks.

"I will begin my return flight then."

Silence. Sasha waited for Sergey's protest.

He said nothing. He turned his head and stared at Sasha's jet.

"They're going to fight back when they see you overflying." Scott stood at Ethan's side, wearing Sasha's radio and carrying his old rifle. He'd fallen back into his former days as a soldier with seeming ease, and surprisingly, Sasha had discovered he liked the older man's dry observations and even dryer humor, once they spent time on the same side. He'd given command of his patrol team to Scott, and his people were around the airfield, keeping watch while they prepped for his flight. Sasha had heard a few comments about the burly American, but for the most part, his people listened to Scott's commands.

"I am expecting a few moments of confusion. After that, yes. They will open fire."

Sergey growled.

"Our training makes us fight each other. Air Force against Navy, Army against Army. I am used to their tactics. I know what to do."

Jack and Ethan shared a long look, unreadable to Sasha. He chanced a glance at Sergey, hoping, stupidly, for a special look of his own.

Instead, Sergey scowled and stormed out of the hangar.

They all followed, and then it was time. Sasha slipped into his G-suit and shook Jack and Ethan's hands. Ethan held on for longer, and Sasha tried to smile at him. Ethan had been kind when he didn't have to be. Memories danced, but bitterness sat on the back of his tongue. Ethan had gotten his desire.

Sasha never would.

Scott nodded his good-byes.

Sasha searched for Sergey.

He'd moved far away, standing apart from the group and down the runway. Far away from Sasha.

Fine. Sasha nodded once to Sergey and headed for his jet.

There weren't any ground crew to guide him out of his lane or send him into the lineup for takeoff. Everything was on him as he fired up the engines and lowered the glass canopy over the cockpit. He propped up his folded map and compass, tucked the sat phone into his chest pocket, and started the crawl down their cobbled runway. Spray paint warned him away from cracks and potholes.

As he passed Sergey, he glanced out the cockpit window. One last look.

Devastation clung to Sergey, rage and fury and desperate anguish twisting his features.

Agony lanced through Sasha's heart.

Slowly, Sergey lifted one hand in a sharp salute.

Sasha saluted in return, staring at Sergey until he nearly passed him.

At the last moment, he dropped the salute, pressing his gloved hand to the canopy and reaching for Sergey as grief tore through Sergey's expression.

His engines rumbled, vibrating beneath him. He faced forward, white knuckling the stick as he stared down the short runway and the nose of his fighter. *Full burn. Short lift. Soar high.*

The engines roared, throwing him back against the seat.

Do svidaniya.

After Sasha's jet hurtled into the sky, Sergey stormed down the tarmac, his furious gaze fixed on Jack. "*You,*" he bellowed. "This is all *your* fault!"

Ethan limped in front of Jack, and Scott stepped in front of both, blocking Jack from Sergey. Jack pushed them both aside gently. "What are you talking about?"

"They say it is not contagious! But who knows?" Sergey shouted. Spit flew from his lips. "Everything was *fine* until you!"

Ethan was slowly turning purple, his hands clenching into fists, and Scott watched Sergey like he was a rabid tiger. Jack frowned. "What the hell is wrong with you? What's not contagious? What did I do?"

"You changed the *world*, Jack! You changed the whole world, and *my* world, and now—" He stopped talking, abruptly swallowing his words. Shuddering, he tried again. "Sasha—"

Jack's eyes found Ethan's. So he finally knew.

"He loves you."

Sergey shuddered again, curling in on himself and then flying apart, his hands raking through his thin blond hair. "*Why?*" he hissed. "I've never been with a man! Only women!" His gaze narrowed, and he turned on Jack. "Do you remember women, Jack? Big, beautiful breasts bouncing in your face? Soft curves? Their heat, *God*, swallowing you?"

"That's *enough*." Scott shouldered Sergey, bumping him off his laser-focused course toward Jack.

Ethan hovered at Jack's shoulder.

"Yes, I do remember. But I'm not in love with a woman, Sergey. I'm in love with Ethan. And it's *his* body that I desire. *His* shoulders. *His* legs. I can't get enough of his thighs. His rock solid chest. And yes, his chest hair. And his big, fat cock," Jack finished, staring Sergey down. "*He's* the one I love, and he's who I want."

Sergey's face twisted, and for a moment, Jack was certain he was going to puke. "Why did he not *say* anything? He said *nothing*! This whole time!"

Silence.

Until Scott's radio crackled, and broken English and a whole lot of Russian came through.

"Contact," Scott said. "Someone's coming to check out the launch."

"We have to leave. Now." Sergey scrubbed his hands over his face.

"Sasha's return flight—"

"Sasha is not coming back," Sergey snapped, whirling on Jack. "He is not coming back," he repeated, softer, his voice trembling.

"Sergey—"

"We move out. Now." Sergey headed for the hangar, sweeping their maps and charts, everything they'd put together for Sasha's flight, to the ground. He kicked it all into a pile and pulled out a lighter. In moments, the heap was burning to black ash, destroying all traces of what they'd done.

Jack, Ethan, and Scott followed Sergey to the jeep. No one said a word.

Sasha zoomed over the foothills of the Urals before snaking into the high elevations, keeping close to the mountains to hide his signature from any prying radar. As long as he stayed under the radar deck, he'd be in the clear. Snow-covered craggy peaks and carpets of evergreen blanketed the ground zipping by underneath him, Russia's spine guiding his way north.

Being behind the stick again felt amazing. His heart soared, and he tried to look everywhere all at once, take everything in. He was back in the skies, soaring over his homeland, his blood singing as he sped faster than the speed of sound.

It was perfection. It was everything he'd imagined kissing Sergey would be like. Coursing adrenaline, clinging to the edge of control, and a breathless exultation screaming through his bones.

Their actual kiss hadn't gone that well. Still, it had happened. Sergey *knew*, and in the end, there was some comfort in that. He had no more secrets. No more dreams. Just a vague numbness in the center of his heart where Sergey lived.

The mountains turned harsher, rugged, and then turned to taiga and untouched wilderness. Herds of reindeer ran across the permafrost, the muted gray and green landscape stretching in every direction. Finally, he reached the frigid waters of the Kara Sea, the Russian waters just south of the North Pole, and the Arctic ice sheet covering the top of the world.

Arctic ice plunged deep into Russian waters, and the endless stretch of white snow almost blinded him, almost sent him careening off course. Sasha turned back to his map, meticulously plotting his route through the white and gray smear the world had become.

And then, he spotted it.

A submarine, the sail poking up through a gigantic ice sheet covering so much of the sea. Oil derricks dotted the ice around the sub, some destroyed, their metal bones scattered across the blinding landscape.

Sasha zoomed closer, trying for a better look. Around the oil derricks, something shimmered out of the ice and the boreholes, rising into the sky. Ice caps for miles had been bored through, dozens of destroyed derricks, dozens of exploratory dig holes. And under the ice, Sasha saw blasts lighting up the sea, underground demolitions sending lightning streaking through the dark waters.

They are doing it on purpose. They are releasing the methane hydrate on purpose.

He banked over the ice sheets, aiming low for the deck. The sub had spotted him, as had a ship standing guard with the sub. Gun batteries were set up on the ice, and soldiers ran toward them, sighting in on Sasha's jet.

He hadn't been able to load the MiG with any weapons at the air base. He was flying with nothing, and if he didn't get out of there, he'd be just another smoking hole in the ice.

Still, he needed to see more. Sasha banked again, flying low enough to blast the soldiers on the ice with his jet wash. He craned his neck, trying to see just what it was they were doing under the ice, but a flash of light on his right made him yank back on the stick. He went straight vertical, spinning as his flares popped.

A missile launched from the sub's protector ship slammed into his flares and burst apart, raining hot steel on the soldiers below.

He banked hard, his fighter riding a tight arc like it was sliding down a greased track, and then dove to the deck again, just missing a burst of bullets fired from the gun batteries below. He dropped fast and buzzed the length of the sub right over the sail. Bullets pinged off the black metal, the men manning the gun batteries overenthusiastic with their cyclic rate of fire.

Wait. Those people, on the ice...

Sasha had seen plenty of Russian soldiers and sailors in his time. He knew how they moved, how they acted, what they did under attack.

Those were *not* Russians.

They were Madigan's men, his ragtag, prison-break army, using Russian ships and Russian technology.

Another burst of light as a missile launched. Sasha cursed, yanking on the stick again. He climbed, but the missile had been fired closer this time, and it was gaining on him.

Time to go. Flattening out, he pushed his engines hard, eyeballing the low fuel warning light steadily blinking on the console. His alarm wailed, a constant tone screaming at him about the missile gaining on his jet wash.

He had seconds, seconds until the fuel ran out and seconds until the missile reached him. No barrel rolls, break turns, or wingovers would save him now. He was out of fuel and out of time.

One-handed, he grabbed the sat phone out of his flight suit and punched the speed dial, ripping his oxygen mask away from his helmet.

He couldn't hear, but he could see on the display when Sergey answered.

"Coordinates located!" He read off the coordinates on his map, right where he'd found the sub. "Madigan is purposely drilling into the Arctic ice!" he hollered. "He is in the oil fields. He is releasing it all on purpose. One main sub engaged in underwater operations. Multiple explosions underwater. One ship on escort and protection. Entrenched defensive positions on the ice around the sub. Hostiles are not Russians. Repeat, not Russians. Fuel low. One of the ships launched a missile and they have tone lock!"

His eyes watched the missile closing in on his jet. Closer. Closer.

Was there anything else he needed to say? He'd done it, he'd found Madigan, and he'd seen what he was planning. Sergey would figure it out. He'd put it all together, find out what Madigan was doing, and he'd stop him. He'd save everyone. He'd save the world, and Russia.

Was there anything more he wanted to say?

"Sergey, I—"

The missile closed, his computer wailed, and a roaring fireball burst around his jet, swallowing him whole. He flew forward, dropping the phone, and slammed against the restraints.

Metal screamed, like the jet was being torn in half. His body was pinned, but his fingers automatically reached for the ejection handle, curving around the bright metal at the base of his seat.

He yanked, pulling with all of his strength as he bellowed. The cockpit canopy blew off.

He roared into the gray sky as his jet exploded, a blazing fireball against the snowy landscape reflecting off the black sunshield on his helmet.

His body stayed pinned to the seat, even as the roaring Siberian winds slammed into him full force, punching the breath from his lungs.

The drogue chute popped first. He jerked, seesawing back and forth as the ejection seat spun wildly through the air. He fumbled against the wind, trying to grab the seat release. Finally, the ejection seat fell away, ripping his personal chute open, and the soft folds of silk pillowed against the sky, slowing his wild descent.

He gripped his harness and watched the craggy landscape come closer.

How far had he traveled, speeding away from the Arctic? He'd headed southeast, into deep Siberia. Permafrost and desolation lay beneath him. Patches of trees careened toward the sky, trying to scrape him from his fall. He'd be dead in moments if he plunged into the branches, breaking all his bones or ending up stranded hundreds of feet above the ground. He'd starve to death, his eyeballs and his liver plucked out by birds for a hundred days.

No. He kicked, jerking, and forced his chute away from the trees.

The ground came at him, hard and fast. He tucked, curling into a ball, but he hit hard, scraping over his left side. His helmet bounced on the frozen rocks. He kept sliding, dragged across the rugged landscape by his ballooning parachute. It took him a second—too long—to remember to strip free of his chute.

Another jerk, his body sliding over the sharp ground, his full chute tugging him across Siberia's wasteland. His hands shook, but he got the clips loose and the chute finally billowed free, flying into the air.

He lay back on the frozen ground, arms and legs spread wide. He pushed off his helmet. It rolled away, clattering over ice and stone.

He was alive. Somehow, he was alive. Groaning, he closed his eyes, thunking his head on the frozen rock beneath him.

Sergey's face flashed behind his eyelids. The first time he'd seen him, caught hovering in the doorway, eyes wide as a frightened deer. Sergey had held him that night when he'd fallen to pieces, comforting a complete stranger. He'd fallen in love a little bit right then, exposed and vulnerable and baring his soul. He'd expected harshness, and had instead received affection. Acceptance. And then, he'd watched Sergey deliver his address and saw his president stand up for him against the world.

He hadn't known what to do or where to go after his life had been beaten to a pulp, but Sergey had helped him rebuild and had given him a place and a purpose at his side.

So where did he go now that he was alive, still breathing on the other side of a one-way mission?

Sergey. He had to get back to Sergey.

The need was a magnet, a pull on his soul that had to be fulfilled.

Slowly, his mind started to work again, pieces of panic and rationalization rubbing against each other. Of course he had to get back to Sergey. He had to tell them what he'd seen. What if Sergey hadn't been able to hear him? What if they still didn't know what was happening?

Madigan was flooding the atmosphere on purpose. That couldn't be good.

He hauled himself to his feet, his entire body screaming, begging him to just rest, just lie down and stop. Stop everything.

He pushed his hand flat into the snow, palm down, fingers extended, like he had pressed his hand to the canopy right before he'd lost sight of Sergey.

He had to get back. There was no future to his love, but maybe Sergey would let him stay around. Wouldn't throw him out. Would let him quietly serve from afar and keep his love buried, deep down out of sight. He would never ask for anything. Never hope for what he could never have.

A survival pack had ejected with his seat, the twenty-pound package buried in a patch of snow a short distance away. He stumbled to it, grabbing the rations, water packs, medical kit, compass, and map. An automatic beacon had turned on as soon as he ejected, announcing his location to every Russian military computer on the planet.

He grabbed the pistol, also in the survival kit, and emptied one clip into the radio. It sputtered and died. Still, in minutes, Moroshkin's forces would be searching for him, zeroing in on the signal and hunting him down.

Grabbing the rest of the clips, Sasha piled everything into the survival backpack and checked his map and compass. For the moment, he'd head east, until he found cover. Found time to make a plan.

And then, he'd head for Simushir Island.

And Sergey.

60

Russian Caucasus
The Forest

Ethan watched the blood drain from Sergey's face as the satellite connection broke, ending in a roar of flame and screaming steel and Sasha's last words. Sergey stayed still, not moving aside from the slow closing of his eyes and the thinning of his lips.

Jack went to him, but Sergey shook his head and walked away, still clenching the sat phone as he covered his mouth with one hand.

"I can't believe Sergey had no idea," Jack breathed, heading back to Ethan's side. They sat on the hood of Sasha's jeep, alone at the rear of the command bunker and watched the gray sky through thick pine boughs.

"You had no idea about me. I rocked your world pretty hard when I kissed you."

Jack stayed quiet.

Until he spoke again, whispering into the silent forest. "Ethan... What do I do? What do I do to make this right?"

Ethan frowned at him. "Gotta stop Madigan—"

"No." Jack's hand slid into his own, their fingers carding together.

It was the first time they'd touched—really touched—since Ethan had gotten out of the cot, had shaken off the painkillers, and realized what the fuck was going on. Reality hadn't sunk in yet. Or it had sunk in too much, hitting him face-first like crashing into a brick wall. He was still dazed, still just trying to put the pieces together and get through it all.

"I'm so sorry," Jack breathed. "Ethan, I'm so, *so* sorry. I wish I could take it all back. Everything. I wish..." He bit his lip. "I wish I'd grabbed onto you on Air Force One and we'd faced this together. I wish I had never let you go. If anything had happened to you—" He shook his head. "I'm such an idiot."

Ethan stayed quiet. He stared at their hands, at their joined fingers. One thumb brushed over Jack's watch. He'd given it to Jack at Christmas. The face was cracked and water had seeped inside. It didn't work.

"Sochi. But I couldn't take it off. You gave this to me."

Ethan's eyes closed.

"It was always you," Jack whispered. "Always. I could never get you out of my mind. Every moment was agonizing because all I wanted was to run back to you. I *missed* you so *much*. And I felt so *guilty*, for everything—" Jack shook his head. "I told her you were the one for me. That I wanted to grow old with you. That I loved you and I wanted you back."

Swallowing felt like he was swallowing sand and stone, his throat dry and clenched too tight.

"What do I do?" Jack's burning eyes piercing Ethan's soul. "I want to make us whole again." He brought Ethan's hand to his lips, pressing a long kiss to his knuckles. "I love you. You are my *whole world*, Ethan."

Jack had given everything up, *everything*, to sit on the hood of a dilapidated jeep in the Russian forest and tell Ethan he loved him. Everything. His career, his presidency, the most powerful position in the world. He wasn't a soldier, but he'd risked his life just to find Ethan and hold his hand again.

Ethan had no idea what he was feeling, not anymore. He'd never been so hurt, never been so furiously wounded and achingly alone. Had never loved someone so much, soul deep, in a way that remade his entire world.

Whatever lingering anguish he'd had vanished, a singe against his soul that left him aching, desperately wanting to pull Jack close and hold him forever. Jack was here at his side, holding his hand and telling Ethan he loved him. That was what he wanted, what he would have given anything for. He would have lassoed the sun and pulled down the moon to prove his love to Jack, and now Jack was here, doing the same thing.

They were meant to be together. Wasn't that what everyone who knew them said? It was a truth he knew, something fundamental that had remade his life when he and Jack had first committed to each other. Jack completed him, fit into his soul in a primal, perfect way. The world—as insane, as crazy, as horrible as it was—made sense with Jack. It spun right. All his edges were smoother, his dark spaces calmer.

Two rings rubbed together in his jacket pocket. He was wearing clothes taken from Sasha's things, combat fatigues and a long-sleeve Russian military pullover. He'd scrounged a jacket, and the rings lived in the inner pocket, right over his heart.

He reached into his jacket. Closed his fingers over the warm metal. "Jack..."

Jack stared at him, and the muted gray light filtered through the forest above, catching on the angles and shadows of his face. God, he was breathtakingly beautiful. Hair mussed, dirt smudged on his bruised cheekbone, blond and gray stubble grown long and prickly over his cheeks and chin. The edges of a bruise fading on his temple, green and mottled yellow.

He wanted a life with Jack forever, wanted his love for the rest of their days.

But, Ethan bit his lip and let go of the rings.

It wasn't the right moment. Wasn't the right time. When he asked Jack, he wanted perfection. He wanted joy and love, and Jack saying "Yes" because he wanted Ethan for forever, and not because he was apologizing and trying to make their hearts whole again.

There were things he couldn't say, couldn't put into words, not now, but he could pour his love into his hands and into his touch, reach for Jack and caress his soul into Jack's skin.

He cupped Jack's cheek, ran his hand through Jack's hair and down the side of his neck. He kissed him, leaning into Jack until they were pressed back against the jeep's windshield. His stitches tugged, but he ignored the dull ache, stroking Jack's face and pressing kiss after kiss to his chapped lips. Jack beamed, but Ethan tasted salt beneath his gentle kisses.

He pressed his forehead to Jack's. "I've been afraid," Jack murmured. "So afraid I'd lost you for good."

"No," Ethan whispered, kissing the tears at the corners of Jack's eyes away. "I'm with you all the way."

Jack smiled. He caressed Ethan's face, his thumb tracing Ethan's lips. "All the way. Forever."

Sergey found them later, his eyes red-rimmed. He spat out Sasha's frantic last message.

"Purposely drilling?" Ethan frowned. "Purposely releasing the methane hydrate? Why?"

The reason slammed into Jack, cymbals crashing in his brain. "This is the real attack. Canada is just a diversion. Goddamn it, he doesn't even want Canada or the US."

"What *does* he want?" Sergey scowled

What was it Elizabeth had said? If enough methane hydrate entered the atmosphere, it could ignite? "He's trying to burn it all down. Flood the atmosphere and light everything on fire. It's already in the jet stream. When he ignites it all, it will burn through the world. Incinerate millions. Billions."

Scott's jaw dropped. Ethan stared at him, not blinking. Sergey grumbled under his breath, long curses in bitter Russian.

"He doesn't want to take over," Jack said, a dark laugh falling from his lips as he finally, finally figured it all out. "He wants to watch the world burn and sit on top of the ashes. Inherit the wasteland at the end and call it his kingdom. Anarchy and the apocalypse, all by his own hand."

Ethan paled at Jack's words. "It's exactly what Cook said. They want a world of their own. Endless war. 'A new dawn is coming. A new sky awaits us all.' I thought he was just being an asshole. I didn't think he was being literal."

"They mean it," Sergey growled. "They mean to burn this world and take what is left for themselves."

"A new dawn. A new sky. Code words for the ignition?" Jack frowned.

"This is all fucked-up." Scott shook his head. He glared at the sky. "What are we waiting for? Let's go get the bastard. I've got a family to protect."

They moved quickly after that, Jack calling Elizabeth and giving her the intel while Sergey, Ethan, and Scott packed up the bunker. Sergey spoke to the men and women he had placed in command of his insurgency, and they spread the word through the ranks. They were moving out, heading into the desolate Far East, and waiting for their allies.

Elizabeth promised subs from Hawaii in one week.

"We need to be careful, Jack," Ethan breathed into his ear, his words for Jack alone. "We never did find the person who put the pictures in your duffel. And there were pictures of us, pictures *only* someone in our inner circle could have taken, in that tanker. Someone in the White House is on Madigan's side."

Jack's face turned to stone. "Should we call Cooper? You trust him, right?" Jack helped Ethan pack their jeep. It had been Sasha's, but Sergey had been carefully avoiding it like a black hole. "Do you think he could help?"

Ethan frowned. "He's a good man. He's got a good team. And yes, I do trust him. I'll make the call." Ethan took his scrambled cell and dropped a kiss to Jack's cheek, trotting off into the forest.

61

Jeddah, Saudi Arabia

Cooper's whole team had descended on Faisal's villa. They'd arrived in ones and twos, and Cooper ferried them all from Jeddah's airport to the compound. Doc took over, giving them a grand tour and assigning bedrooms and beds.

When everyone was settled in, Cooper called them all down to the main room for a briefing.

Cooper stumbled, though, before he spoke, and his eyes fixed on the prince.

All eyes turned to Faisal. Faisal looked away.

Tension grew, everyone eyeballing each other left and right.

Before they could speak, Faisal's phone rang. He and Cooper shared a long look and headed for the kitchen together to speak privately with the caller.

Minutes passed. People started fucking around.

No one was watching him. Perfect.

He slipped outside to the massive deck overlooking the Red Sea.

It was gorgeous. Utterly breathtaking.

He pulled out his own cell phone. Dialed.

Cook's voice answered on the second ring. *"Is everyone there?"*

"We are. The entire team is in the prince's villa."

"Excellent. Exactly where we want you."

"What are my orders?"

"Hold tight for now. The president and his lover are gone. Our decoy is making inroads in Canada. We'll send you something soon." Cook paused. *"You did well in Tampa. Good kill. And your intel on the Arab was spot on. Attacking him was the key to breaking it all open."*

"Thank you, sir." He smiled, trying to smother it beneath his palm. "We're close, sir? Not much longer?"

"Not much longer. I know you can feel it. We all can. Our new dawn is rising. Our new sky awaits us all."

The door behind him slid open, and one of his teammates poked his head out. "Hey, you need to get in here. Serious intel coming in. We're on the move, like, yesterday."

He slid the phone down, out of sight, and ended the call. "What the hell are we waiting for? Let's move."

62

Russian Caucasus
The Forest

Finally, the convoy was packed and ready to leave the forest. Simushir Island lay ahead, and beyond that, everything after.

Where they'd make their stand. Take the fight straight to Madigan. Save the world from his madness.

Sergey finalized the route. Every jeep had a highlighted map taped to the dash. Shooters rode shotgun with the drivers. Gear was stowed, equipment packed away. Sergey drove in the lead, Scott—unbelievably—as his side shooter. Behind them were Ethan and Jack, Jack holding a shotgun propped against the windowsill with a rifle between his legs.

Ethan held out his hand over the center console and over their packed magazines and spare ammunition. Jack grasped his hand in return, and Ethan smiled down at their joined fingers.

Two rings burned over his heart.

The world was still crazy, still dangerous and deadly, and they had to do something about that. But after, when they'd put Madigan down and righted the world, there'd be a perfect moment when he could drop down to one knee, take Jack's hand in his, and breathe his question.

But right now, Jack was riding shotgun at his side and they were about to head east, gearing up for the fight to save the world again.

Together.

"Ready?" He smiled at Jack, squeezing his hand once.

Jack grinned. "I'm with you all the way."

Bonus Content

The following are samples of *Bauer's Bytes*, short stories I post weekly on my website. *Bauer's Bytes* are worlds between the words, expanded content beyond the boundaries of the *Executive Office* series novels.

Please enjoy the following *Bauer's Bytes*, exploring moments from *Enemy of My Enemy*.

IN A MOMENT, SHAME
JACK'S POV OF SOCHI

It can't be.
No. It's impossible.
But, right there, struggling against too many hands grabbing at her and holding her down, was Leslie.

His wife. His *dead* wife.

No. Not dead.

Alive.

He took off, running full speed across the cracked asphalt and heading for her. Overhead, the Osprey was coming in, lowering itself down as her two giant arms rotated up, turning the plane into a heavy helicopter. Road grit blew, peppering his cheeks and chin and eyes with sharp slices that he should have felt. The roar of the rotors should have quaked his bones, sent shockwaves through his eardrums.

Instead, it was like he was underwater, plunged beneath the sea, everything distorted and out of focus. Hazy black shapes, the agents beside Leslie, moving too fast and too slow all at once. Blocking his path, no matter where they were.

Cotton-stuffed ears, the drone of a trans-Atlantic flight and the dullness right before falling to sleep. Nothing came through; he couldn't hear beyond the molasses-slow haze that had descended over him. Had the world fallen to pieces? Was this the calm before the blast? In a moment, would it all be gone?

No.

That moment had already happened. The blast had already hit.

It had slammed square into his chest, into his heart, with Scott's flick of his wrist, the removal of the hostage's hood.

"Jack! Wait!"

Ethan. Ethan, Ethan. Where did Ethan fit into this suddenly new world, a place where Leslie was alive? His brain wouldn't process Ethan's words or Ethan's voice, instead translating the sound into ravaging slashes against his heart and bullet wounds digging into the muscles between his shoulder blades.

A few more steps, running through the thickened soup that seemed to separate him from her. As if the properties of the world had changed in a moment. What once was air, matter made light with buoyancy, was suddenly a viscous fluid, fighting against him with every step he took.

Had the world stopped spinning? Had the earth stopped moving beneath his feet? Without the planet's spin, could he even take another step?

He slid the last foot, dropping to his knees on the loose asphalt. His pants tore and grit dug into his skin, burning and stabbing all at once. Leslie kicked, screaming. Her arms flailed. She was a wild thing desperate for freedom. Fighting for her life, fighting against strange men who tried to hold her down. God, how many strangers had tried to hold her down? What had turned his wife, the strongest woman he'd ever known, an Amazon warrior goddess, his own Wonder Woman, into this shrieking, flailing thing?

Sixteen years. How much freedom had she lost? How could the months, the day, the hours be quantified into moments? Into a life lost?

How many times had she struggled?

"Les! Les!" No more. She wouldn't struggle again. Never again. He'd keep her safe, like he had sworn to do. Like he should have been doing for sixteen years. "Les, it's me. It's Jack."

She froze, as if she'd dropped dead. Had her heart given out? He wouldn't blame her. His was about to burst, tear itself to pieces, rend itself to shreds, bleed out inside his chest. How did the heart handle the reappearance of someone long given up as dead, as gone?

He got his first look at her and wanted to vomit. Gone was his vibrant wife. Thick, dark hair, so long he could wrap her ponytail around his hand and make his palm and fingers disappear. He'd brushed her hair every night she was home until the dark lengths had shone and she'd lean back against him, smiling that warm, honey-smile. A round face, her cheekbones made for hearts to fall from, and lips that could smile and tease and bark orders that made men's spines stiffen from one moment to the next. Her strength, with muscles that seemed more impressive than his, so powerful on her frame, set against his softer lawyer's body. She had been ferocity and suppleness, power and love, all wrapped in one body. She'd been his Venus, his Aphrodite. How could one body hold everything that she was, he'd often wondered. How did her bones and muscles contain all of her magic?

They no longer did. Lank hair, stringy with oil and tangled with mud and dried blood, hung limp around her skeletally thin face. Sunken hollows lived beneath her cheekbones and canyons had formed beneath her eyes. Years of scabbed and swollen lips had turned her mouth into a bruise, flaking with dried blood and peeling skin.

What had happened to her?

What had he abandoned her to?

"Jack," she breathed. Her eyes, her beautiful eyes, that used to convey so much to him with just a single glance, darted over his face. That telepathy that couples had, where they could read each other in a moment, a single flick of the eyes, a breathless sound. He'd built that connection with Ethan; he couldn't read her anymore. "Jack? How— What—"

"Mr. President." Scott tugged on his arm. "We have to move, *now*!"

No, he couldn't move past this moment. *Things* were going to happen when he stood again, and he couldn't face those things. Not yet.

Dammit, his heart already knew, though. Anguish crawled up his throat, clenching it shut. Fingers of grief, of rage, of agony clawed at his neck, and tears swam before his eyes, obscuring her terrible face.

Not yet. Not yet. He didn't want to face this new world yet. He shook Scott off.

"How are you alive?" he whispered. "I thought you were dead."

"*President*?" she gasped, ignoring him. "Jack?"

"Mr. President!" Scott snapped at him and tugged on his arm, not kindly. "We have to go! *Now*!"

The Osprey circled and started its descent, only yards away. Bullets spattered against her massive metal frame. In response, the door gunner sent a never-ending volley back toward the shooters, bracing on a ridge overlooking the street. The hum of the bullets droned in Jack's ears, like a mosquito buzzing too close. The heavy *whomp* of the rotors spun too slowly in his mind. Like some terrible drum beat, the musical accompaniment to a heartrending scene of a movie. The sounds filled him, slithered through his veins all the way to his heart, where the thrumming tried to split apart the muscles and fibers, tried to dislodge his blood and shatter his soul.

"Go, now, now!" Scott, shouting for the crew to cover Jack. Preparing for his evac. Always a helicopter, always pulling him away.

It was all so unreal, so suddenly. This wasn't right. This was a dream. A terrible dream. He'd wake up in a moment and grab Ethan and hold him tight. Ethan would wash his nightmare away with his hands, and then with his lips, and everything would be back to the way it was supposed to be. Not this. Not this terrible thing.

"Jack—"

Ethan. Leaning in. Brushing against Jack, his warm weight pressed against his side. Jack's knees ground into the asphalt, twisting in his own blood, and streaks of pain shot up through his thighs, grounding him.

Not a dream. Not a nightmare. He couldn't wake, not from this.

Ethan's hands reached for Leslie.

"I've got her!" he snapped, almost manic. "I've fucking got her!" Ethan couldn't touch Leslie. They shouldn't be together, shouldn't even be near. Could the universe survive the meeting of the two, or would some cosmic hole open up, a rend in the universe that would swallow Jack whole? The Mobius strip of his life would come undone, torn down the center of his soul.

Ethan stared at him, his jaw hanging open.

Don't look. God, don't look.

He gathered her close, her painfully light frame nearly weightless in his arms. Scott came alongside him, wrapped one hand around Jack's waist, and hauled him to the Osprey. As they ran, her hand clenched around his arms, her thin fingers digging into the soaked fabric of his torn shirt. Her face turned into his chest, burying in the valley between his pecs.

His stomach twisted, and then twisted gain. That spot wasn't hers. It wasn't her place any longer. His body had been given to Ethan, had become a temple for Ethan's worship, and it was Ethan's place to nuzzle at the side of his pec, press his lips to Jack's skin and breathe out, making Jack shiver. It wasn't right having another in the places that were Ethan's.

But before his body was Ethan's, it had been Leslie's.

The Osprey saved his sanity and his heart from going any further. He set her on the flight deck, passing her to the hands of the flight medic. Her eyes went wide—another pair of unknown hands grabbing at her body—and she reached back for him, terror blazing through her.

This close, the roar of the rotors was too loud for any words to be spoken. He did what he could. Brushed her hair, flapping in the wash of the Osprey, off her face and behind her ears. Smiled at her. Squeezed her hand, like he had on their wedding day, a promise in every inch of his skin.

He had to turn away from her, but he didn't want to. He had to face what was behind him, but he wasn't strong enough for that.

She squeezed his hand back and smiled.

His heart cracked, a dark fault line splitting him in two.

He strode back to where Sergey and Sasha were kneeling on the asphalt, still holding a defensive line that had crumbled away, the agents disappearing into the Osprey one by one. All save Daniels, still standing sentinel at Ethan's side.

Don't look. God, don't look at Ethan.

He dropped in front of Sergey. "We're headed for Turkey. We can take you, too. Give you political asylum." Police sirens wailed, mixing with the *rata-tat-tat* of bullets and explosions blooming into the night, only blocks away. Screeching tires, shouts in Russian and English. The sounds of the world ending.

"No." Sergey shook his head. "No, Jack. I have to stay. I have to fight for Russia. I have to help my people."

No, not Sergey too. He couldn't lose everything in so few minutes. It couldn't be possible. "Sergey, that's suicide—"

"Yes, Jack. Maybe. But I will die the right way." Sergey grabbed him, holding his shoulders, and for a moment, Jack thought he'd shatter beneath his friend's grasp. Break into a billion pieces and collapse to the Russian street. Blow away in the wind. Part of him yearned for the release. "Go. Get out of here. Save yourself." Sergey kept speaking, even as Jack swayed beneath his hands. "Sasha, you should go. You should save your—"

"No." Sasha scowled at Sergey. "I will say with you."

Vomit choked his throat. Sasha's steadfast love, his eternal devotion to Sergey, even in the midst of the world falling apart around them. *I had that love*, he thought, wailing from the corners of his soul. *I had that love.* Beside him, Ethan's presence was like a whirlpool, pulling at every atom of his being. *I had that love,* he whimpered again, as the remains of his heart shivered and shriveled, drawing up like a wounded, anguished thing.

He reached for Sergey, his one friend through everything, one half of a friendship that had redefined the world, and remade his own world. Was this goodbye? It was too much, too fast. Too many goodbyes, too many closed doors. Too much change happening between one breath and the next. He couldn't keep up. How was everyone else keeping up? How were any of them still standing?

"I will do *everything* I can for you. *Everything.*"

Sergey nodded once and then moved off to the darkness at the side of the road. Sasha, ever faithful, shadowed his movements. Jack watched them disappear into the darkness. *Do svidanya.*

"Jack."

Ethan. Ethan's voice. God, if he turned, Ethan would be right there, ready to hold him, pull him into his arms, and shield him from this upside down world. He ached, *God,* he ached for that. *Yearned.* Ethan could make this right. Ethan was his shelter, his rock, his home. He'd carved a life between Ethan's arms, laid his cornerstone beneath the shield of Ethan's heart. They could get through this together.

No.

They couldn't.

How could he reconcile loving Ethan when his wife was suddenly alive? He'd mourned her, sobbed for her, cried himself to sleep for a year, and had used every wish he'd been granted for five straight years on begging for her return. Every fortune cookie, wishbone, and birthday candle spent on this very wish. That she was truly alive, hidden somewhere, and would come home. Would come back to him.

He'd lost faith after the years had passed. Accepted what was written fact, etched on a piece of parchment and a marble headstone in Arlington. His wife was dead.

He'd never asked for Ethan's love, never sought it out. Never went seeking a new life, or a love that had remade everything about himself. His soul had been purified with Ethan's love. His body, remade down to his veins with Ethan's kisses, the caress of his hands, the stroke of their bodies together. He was a man reborn, like a phoenix rising from the ashes of his former life, his soul more radiant than he'd ever been before.

God, he *loved* Ethan. Loved him in a gut-punch purity, a fire that circled his heart. Loved him to his marrow, and beyond.

But how could it go on? How could they go forward with this?

He'd vowed to love Leslie until death did they part. She wasn't dead. He'd made that mistake already. How many years had she been tortured? How many times? How many nights had she cried out for him? Whispered his name in the darkness, like he had hers in the early years? How much hope had she spent, and had she ever given up on him?

Like he'd given up on her? How could he ever make this right?

Penance. Eternal, everlasting penance. He had to make up for the years, the months, the days, hours, and minutes that he wasn't there for her.

How could he ever be happy again, knowing what he'd left her to? Knowing what he'd given up on?

She, half-dead, forgotten, anguished and alone, and him, in love, glorious, soul-on-fire love, and happy.

There was no way for those two realities to coexist. No way for him to keep Ethan, keep his love, and serve at her feet, whispering apology after apology to the ground she trod on.

He could never be happy again.

Don't look.

Don't look at Ethan. Never again.

You don't deserve happiness. You don't deserve him. You, vile creature that found love and laughter while Leslie was tortured.

Don't you dare look at Ethan.

He was weak, oh-so-weak, and he'd fall into Ethan's arms if he looked into the burnished bronze pools of his eyes. If he felt the warmth of his skin, the gentleness of his hold. He'd fall, as hard as he'd fallen in love, but that path wasn't open to him any longer.

The world had stopped spinning. His world had stopped, and it would never start again. Ethan would have to spin on without him.

And his own heart, whatever was left of it after the cold concrete of Sochi, would spin on, tangled with Ethan's memory for the rest of his days.

He jogged back to the Osprey, his eyes picking out Leslie's emaciated face in the hold. She was biting her lip, desperately searching for him through the mass of Secret Service agents and military uniforms. Her shoulders were drawn, tense in a way that he hadn't ever seen before. Like a caged animal, wounded prey searching for safety. That wasn't his wife. God, what had happened to her? What had turned her into this? What had he abandoned her to?

He hauled himself up into the hold, ignoring the agents and soldiers all trying to help him. His hands, bloody, slipped on the metal grips, and he stumbled, then crawled toward Leslie. Pain flared in the ground meat of the skin over his knees, squelching blood with every forward crawl. She kept her eyes fixed to him, hope and terror mixing in equal parts. He could never make her whole again, bring back the vibrant woman that she once had been.

Instead, he had to make do with his failure, his complete failure as a man, and as a husband. He would scrape together the pieces that remained, help her reassemble the fragile shards of her life, build her back up into a beautiful mosaic. He'd give her everything, everything that he'd taken for himself while she'd been hidden away from the world, beaten and brutalized. He would lay the world at her feet, completely devoted to healing her soul.

Tears overflowed his eyes as he crawled to her and reached out with both his arms. A strangled sob caught in her throat as she poured herself into his arms, curling against his chest and burrowing her face in the hollow beneath his neck.

He shivered, his skin not used to a body that wasn't Ethan's. Ethan's, that space on his body was Ethan's. He was meant to hold Ethan in this way. Was meant to be held by Ethan in this way.

Behind him, Scott's gruff murmur slipped through the shouts of the crewmen, the rotors, the bullets, and the Osprey's creaking frame lifting off from Russian soil.

"Are you with me?" Scott grunted. "You with us?"

Ethan.

Don't look. Don't ever look. You don't deserve to look.

He squeezed his eyes shut, but tears flowed from the corners, cascading down his cheeks in dirty waterfalls. Leslie clung to him, but in his mind, he held Ethan, and spoke to him as he whispered into her hair. "I'm so sorry. I'm so Goddamn sorry. How could this happen? How?"

There were no answers for him. There was nothing but the grasp of her frail fingers against his arms and the sounds of Ethan chambering a round in his rifle and taking up position against the hold's open door.

His wife was alive, and his love, his life with Ethan, was at an end. It could not be his any longer. There was no more happiness for him, not in this world of his broken assumptions, failed promises, and a guilt that swallowed his soul. He tasted ash and fire on his tongue, the ruins of his life; no, the ruins of three lives. Three lives destroyed, because of him.

He was nothing. Less than nothing. Worthless. Beyond worthless.

As light as love had made him, guilt, followed by the ravaging snarls of shame, suffocating, clenching shame, dragged him down deep within himself, until all that he was lived in the dry and dusty canyons of his once-full heart.

THE CUT-OUT HEART
HOW DOES SASHA BECOME SERGEY'S RIGHT-HAND MAN?

Sasha placed one foot in front of the other, taking careful steps across the cold tile floor of his hospital room. One hand rested on the stitches above his belly button. The other made a loose fist, trembling at his side. The hem of his baggy hospital scrub pants brushed across the floor, and his white undershirt clung to his sweat-damp skin. Spring sunbeams faded across the square tiles, fingers of cold light that poked at his bare toes.

Finally, he reached the far end of his recovery room. Resting one hand against the white wall, he turned, readying himself to begin his trek again.

A figure slouching in the doorway made him jerk back. He smothered a curse on his lips as fast as it rose, straightened and squared his shoulders. Dropped his hand from beneath his shirt, pressing over his belly. "Mr. President."

President Puchkov smiled. "How goes the march?" He flicked a finger back and forth across the room, following Sasha's pacing.

"Slow."

"The doctor tells me you have been at this all day. You have likely marched from Moscow to St. Petersburg and back."

Sasha glared at the blank wall. He said nothing.

"It has only been three days." Puchkov padded into the room and dropped his bunched-up suit jacket on the end of Sasha's bed. "Give yourself some time."

Sasha stepped off the wall, petulantly placing one foot in front of the other as he began his trek again. The bruised and swollen skin over one eye started to throb.

It was Puchkov's turn to sigh and say nothing. He shook his head, but a small smile played over his lips. He watched Sasha's careful footfalls until he reached the opposite wall.

Sasha leaned back, resting, his hand rising over his stitches once again.

"We have made some inquiries," Puchkov began. He cleared his throat and looked down, pursing his lips. "At Andreapol Air Base."

Tension thrummed through Sasha's body, stiffening his muscles and hardening his gut. His free hand fisted again, and his teeth ground together as his jaw clenched.

"The base commander insists that you have abandoned your post. That your squadmates saw you leave the base and not return."

A bitter curse burst from his lips before he could stop it. "That is not true! I went back! I was there early for my duty! My car is *there*," Sasha growled. "It is outside my hangar!"

"Your car is not at the base," Puchkov gently corrected.

Sasha's head whipped away. He blinked fast as he stared into the corner.

"My good friend is head of the FSB. Ilya Ivchenko. Do you know him?"

"I recognize the name."

"I asked Ilya to look into this situation as a personal favor to me."

"The FSB—" Shocked, Sasha's head spun back around. He stared at his president, his jaw dropping open. If the FSB were involved, there was no telling what way an investigation would go. What if they sided with his old commander? Or with his squadmates who had tried to kill him? What if the FSB believed he had gone rogue? Would he be punished, for his choked and sobbing admission to President Puchkov? Damn it, he'd been so weak!

But, after falling apart in Puchkov's arms and not being turned away in disgust, he'd thought Puchkov was a good man, a man and a president he could believe in, perhaps even trust.

Would he turn him over to the FSB?

"The FSB is very different now than when my predecessor was in power. I trust Ilya with my life, and with things even greater and larger than that. I knew he would get to the truth of this matter, and quickly. There is no one I have trusted more."

Sasha swallowed. He'd started to tremble at some point, and he couldn't stop.

"Ilya sent his best men to turn this situation upside down." Puchkov hesitated, and a frail, apologetic smile tugged at the corners of his thin lips. "They found your car crashed in a snowbank seventy kilometers away from the base. It looks as though a drunk driver had crashed it and then stumbled off into the snow."

"That is not what happened!" He tried to take a step forward, toward Puchkov, but his trembling robbed him of his balance and his strength. He fell against the wall and cursed again.

"I know, Sasha. I believe you." Puchkov's voice rumbled across the room. "We both believe you. It was badly staged."

Sasha met Puchkov's gaze. Fractional hope, almost choked to death with his crushing fear, punched him in the belly.

Puchkov sat at the foot of Sasha's rumpled hospital bed. "But I do not know what to do now. The FSB of old would make this problem disappear. They would make the base commander, and all who attacked you, vanish. It would be a lesson to anyone who thinks they can do the same and get away with it. We would make an example out of them. All of them."

Sasha's breath faltered.

"But…" Puchkov shook his head. "That is not the man that I am. That is not the country I want to live in. So it falls to you. Do you wish to press charges? Do we take this to the courts? Let the legal system work this out?" Puchkov shrugged. "Or *try* to work this out?"

His teeth brushed over the scab crusting his lower lip. Two days ago, he'd made the mistake of chewing on his still-healing lip, and blood had gushed from the reopened wound, down his front and into his mouth. Like a switch had flipped, he'd been transported back to the moment at Andreapol, his mind reliving the memories of the hockey sticks and kicks slamming into him over and over again.

The men who had attacked him had been men he'd trained with. Had flown with. Had visited in their homes. He'd honestly thought they had been friends. One day, he'd dreamed that with them, he might be able to admit to what he was. If he could ever admit it to himself. Say the word out loud to his own reflection in the mirror.

How had they found out what he was? How had they discovered his deepest secret?

Did he want to see any of them again? Reopen the memories, like gnawing off his scab, and put his trust in the fitful Russian criminal justice system? What were the odds that one of his former squadmates—or the base commander, even—had connections with the *Bratva*, the mafia known as the Brotherhood? Could they pay off the investigators or the judges? Would the entire thing be twisted and contorted until it was him rotting in a jail cell, or taken out into the wilderness again and left to die?

He'd seen it happen before.

President Puchkov kept silent, watching him think.

When would Puchkov's support run out? When would Sasha be on his own again? He had to plan for that. As considerate and compassionate as Puchkov had been, that all had to have an end date. How could he pick up the pieces? How could he go forward with his life, in the wake of its total destruction?

What was the right choice?

"No charges," he mumbled, shaking his head. "No. Not that."

"Sasha—"

"I do not want to," he snapped, cutting Puchkov off. "I just want to live. *Quietly*. I do not want to be a martyr, or a figurehead, or a puppet. Or a *cause*. I won't look over my shoulder every day."

Silence.

Finally, Puchkov nodded. "I understand," he sighed, and then gave a tiny quirk of a smile. "I am doing quite a bit of over-the-shoulder looking myself these days."

Sasha frowned. He took a breath, held it, and then took another. His shudders were ebbing, finally slowing, and he pushed himself off the wall, taking careful baby steps until he stood in front of Puchkov. "The media says there have been threats against your life."

Puchkov tried to grin up at him. "Quite a few, in fact. I expected as much. I am surprised I am still alive even now, to be truthful. To have lived to accomplish this purge of corruption. And, to still be alive three days later." He grinned again, but it was tinged with weariness.

"You cannot die."

"I am doing my best," Puchkov said softly. His smile grew warmer before he slapped his knee and rose. He held out one arm, as he were offering it for Sasha to loop his own through. "Now, is this marching of yours strong enough to accompany me to dinner in my apartments, or should I have something brought here for us?"

Sasha gaped as Puchkov took his hand and looped it through his arm.

The bruises had faded and the scabs had fallen off, and his stitches didn't sting anymore. The ache was mostly gone in his belly, and he could manage through most of the day before becoming exhausted. He still needed an IV of fluids and antibiotics every night, and he was still living out of the sterile recovery room. Each night, Dr. Voronov asked him about his day while he slid the IV needle into his arm. Sasha regaled him with his very boring stories of pacing the halls of the Kremlin, and, once, trying to jog in the inner courtyard.

And, every night, President Puchkov came to his hospital room to visit. He sat with Sasha through the IV and even stayed after, bringing dinner or asking Sasha up to his presidential apartments to dine informally with him. Upstairs, they ate at Puchkov's long state dining table alongside stacks of reports and binders stuffed with papers and briefings, and maps unfurled and held down at the corners with small marble statues and crystal candleholders.

It was nothing like what he expected the president—the office, the institution, and the legacy—to be. But it was *exactly* what Puchkov was like, as he was slowly coming to understand.

He'd started to look forward to the visits. *Danger*, his mind shouted. *The president is not your friend. You have no friends. Not anymore.*

But he still welcomed Puchkov with a tiny grin and laughed at his dry sarcasm. He hung on his every word when Puchkov spoke about the changes rocking their country. Russian oligarchs that hadn't been swept up in the corruption purge were holding court in Europe, wailing about Puchkov and his government from Paris to London. Workers who found themselves unemployed overnight and their workplaces seized by the government had hit the street, protesting everything, it seemed. The closure of their workplace. The corruption. Their money running out, and a creeping sense of terror and dread that their pain was only the beginning. Food rationing had already begun in St Petersburg. Riots had erupted in Volgograd.

"I am heading to the US in ten days," Puchkov said one night, stretching out his long limbs and crossing his arms behind his head as he sat in the single bedside chair, the recovery room's only furnishing. They were eating takeout Chinese and sharing cartons back and forth. Puchkov had finished, and given the rest to Sasha to polish off.

Sasha hesitated, his chopsticks holding a piece of crispy beef over the paper carton.

"A state visit. Jack's first state dinner, in fact. And then we will announce the American investment plan. It is…" Puchkov sighed, and his hands scrubbed over his face. "My advisors are complaining. But this is what the people need. It will get them back on their feet and working again faster than anything else. We need to make sure our people are taken care of."

"Traveling right now. That is too big a risk, no?" Sasha dropped his chopsticks into the carton and set it aside. The IV line tugged, but he ignored it.

Puchkov hadn't left the Kremlin once since the corruption purge. He was kept insulated, and his security services were scrambling to keep on top of every threat. Even their Chinese food—ostensibly ordered for a low-level businessman not even in the Kremlin—had been tested for poison before they ate.

"Now you sound like Ilya." Puchkov smiled ruefully. "But it has to happen. For now, I will put my trust in the people closest to me."

Sasha stayed silent.

"You are one of those people, you know." Puchkov held Sasha's gaze. His eyes twinkled.

Sasha scoffed. He jerked his chin toward their takeout carton and waved one hand around the recovery room. "That is because you cannot get rid of me. I am stuck here. I have nowhere to go." His lips clamped shut after he spoke. Reminding Puchkov of his uselessness would only get him kicked out faster. And, if he was honest with himself... Sasha was just beginning to allow himself to enjoy being around there. Being around President Puchkov.

"Would you choose to stay?"

Sasha glared at the IV in his arm and at the thin hospital sheet bunched beneath his knees. He couldn't look at Puchkov.

"What if," Puchkov finally asked, his voice soft. "There was a position here for you?"

He frowned, and his heart hammered out a pounding beat in his chest, a heavy rhythm that ached. What would Puchkov want him for? A symbol? As a project? A cause? Exactly what he never wanted to be?

"Ilya is stretched too thin. He's running ragged with his people spread across the country and around the world. He needs help."

Sasha's jaw dropped. "Ilya Ivchenko? The head of the FSB?"

"My very good friend Ilya." Puchkov braced his elbows on his knees and rubbed his hands together. "I have told him I want to appoint a presidential aide dedicated to him and me. Another person to help us try and make sense of the world. If that is even possible."

"What purpose could I have in all of this?" If Puchkov was going where Sasha thought he was, he was a crazy man. He couldn't possibly want Sasha for that. Puchkov and Ilya had been comrades for their entire life. Sasha had known him for a week. It would be an honor to serve at that level, to support Puchkov in the best way he could, but the thought was an impossible one.

"I think you would be a great man for that position. And I would like you to stay. To *choose* to stay," he corrected. "Everything I know about you—from your records, from spending time with you, from..." Puchkov vaguely waved his hand through the air. "Everything I have learned about you makes me confident that you *are* the right person for this." He smiled again, almost sweetly, and then ruined it with a wicked wink. "And I am FSB, too. Reading people, and knowing them, is what I do.

"So, will you stay? Will you accept?"

From Andreapol to the Kremlin. From the bloody fists of his former friends to the enigma that was President Puchkov. And Puchkov's compassion. His care. The seemingly all-encompassing way he'd thrown himself into a friendship with Sasha. At first, Sasha had thought it was all due to some vague sense of duty. After all, President Puchkov had made supporting gay rights a pillar of his office, especially after the American president and he had become such firm allies. But…

For all of Puchkov's friendly overtures and his gregariousness, some part of Sasha had still thought it was all an act. That Puchkov, somewhere inside, was like all powerful men who believed people were there to be used. He hadn't quite figured out how he was useful to Puchkov, unless it was as some kind of budding charity chase. Or a publicity campaign. He'd been bracing himself for both possibilities.

But Puchkov had listened when he said he didn't want to press charges against his attackers, and he'd accepted Sasha's request for privacy. There was nothing about him or his attack in the papers, even though it could have bolstered Puchkov's campaign for equal rights and his new center for GLBT protection in Moscow.

But Puchkov spoke like he wanted Sasha for something more than just a political play. Or as a pawn to be moved around and then exchanged for a better move down the line. Unbelievably, Puchkov seemed to actually want *him*.

And Puchkov knew almost everything there was to know about him. Even his proclivities. Puchkov had held him when he'd fallen apart, when everything he'd tried to shore up within him had tumbled down so spectacularly and his soul had been rubbed raw against the edges of his complete and utter shame. So much loss, and so much agony, on the loneliest night of his life, sitting in an empty, bleak hospital room.

Puchkov had held him—a complete stranger—through it.

He'd be an absolute fool not to accept this offer.

But where would it lead? Where would this new path in life take him? Dangerous terrain lay ahead. He could practically hear the warning klaxons. Already, he was looking forward too much to Puchkov's presence. Already, he was enjoying their stolen time together a bit too much. The first man to truly know him, know his shame and everything else, and he'd accepted Sasha. Unconditionally accepted Sasha and all the mismatched parts and pieces of his life and his soul. It was unprecedented, completely so. Puchkov showed him kindness, showed him compassion, and Sasha turned to that like a tree growing out of the Siberian ice and greening into the sunlight.

He *wanted* to stay. But would it be wise?

Everything he'd worked for had been ripped away from him, though. And this was more than a dream come true. It was a chance to start anew. Build a new life, a good life, where he could be useful. Still serve, and serve someone he looked up to with no small amount of hero worship.

So he'd grab on with both hands and make it work. No matter what. No matter if he had to cut out his own heart one day. He would do it. He would offer it up on a platter for Puchkov. For this man, his president, he would do anything. Whatever Puchkov asked, whatever he needed. He could feel the conviction settling into him like a vow, deep into his bones and into his blood.

"On one condition," he said, his voice low.

Puchkov's eyebrows arched high.

"I will go with you to the US," Sasha began.

Puchkov's mouth opened, a protest forming as he scowled.

"And I will never leave your side," Sasha finished quickly. "I will stay with you for your protection."

Puchkov's protest turned into a soft smile. "A condition of my own. You will call me Sergey now, as all my friends do."

Sergey arranged for a private apartment in the Kremlin for him, not in the palace itself, but on the grounds and within the red walls. They were, for want of a better word, neighbors.

He met with Ilya—fast-talking, hawk-eyed Ilya, a cigarette seemingly perpetually dangling from his lips, bouncing up and down as he moved from topic to topic in rapid-fire sequence. He sat in on the briefings Ilya gave Sergey—a riotous cloud of smoke and arguments. He started reading through the mountains of intelligence that Ilya and the FSB managed, the never-ending stream of analysis and collections. So much of it was focused internally on the reactions to the anti-corruption sweep. Watching and worrying over civil unrest. The rise of hardcore nationalists within Russia, and their belief that President Puchkov was poisoning Russia from within. That Sergey was a pawn of the Americans. That he was a degenerate homosexual and trying to destroy Russia with the vileness of the West.

He and Sergey still ate dinner together. Ilya often joined them, and he invited himself to Sergey's liquor cabinet afterward. That became a routine for them: Sergey, Ilya, and Sasha sharing drinks and slowly moving from discussing matters of state and the sometimes-blistering intelligence reports to more personal matters.

Sasha learned Ilya was divorced once and Sergey twice. Ilya was an outrageous flirt, and was currently working on a voluptuous bartender at one of Moscow's premier lounges, but had never made a move on her, something Sergey teased him about endlessly. Sergey and Ilya wheedled stories about flying out of him. The first time he'd gone supersonic, and how he'd been convinced his jet was broken. The first time he'd seen the blackness of space and the curvature of the earth. He'd known, that day, that he wanted to go higher. To fly above the earth and among the stars.

He admitted his favorite hockey team was the *Ugra* Mammoths, and that he—embarrassingly—didn't like basketball at all. Sergey liked the plucky, Far Eastern *Amur Khabarovsk* hockey team, preferred whiskey over vodka, books over films, and wanted to get away to the Russian Far East once things had calmed down. Ilya wanted to go to Copacabana.

One day, a golden bust of Aleksandr Pokryshkin appeared, casually sitting on the end table next to the sofa where Sasha always sat. It gleamed, shining with fresh polish.

Sasha had stared, jaw agape.

"You know this man?" Sergey had gestured to the bust, his eyes glinting.

"Of course," Sasha breathed. "He is three-time hero of Soviet Union. The father of the modern Soviet Air Force. History says he won World War II." He stared at the figure, at the man's severe gaze and harsh, metal lines. "I learned about him in flight school. We all did."

Ilya had chuckled around a cigarette. Sergey had beamed. "It was gathering dust somewhere. Now it has a better home." Winking, Sergey had nudged Sasha's knee with his own and asked for another story of his days in flight school, when he was much younger and had been all feet and hands and fumbling more often than not. His call sign had been *Likho*, Bad Luck, for the string of calamities that had followed him around in training.

The days and nights rolled on, as did the stories. Unbelievably, Sasha realized he was, for the first time in a long while, on the way to being truly happy. Content. Wholly accepted, at very least. And he didn't even have to pretend to be something he wasn't. When Sergey looked at him, he saw *him*. All his broken parts and pieces.

And he, in turn liked spending time with Sergey and Ilya. He liked their jokes, their playful sarcasm, and how they'd bicker until inevitably Sergey would turn to Sasha and beckon him into their arguments, egging Sasha into agreeing with his side of whatever they were fussing about. He sat next to Pokryshkin's golden bust every time he visited.

Finally, they went to America for President Spiers's state visit.

Sergey kept his word and Sasha stayed at his side. They only separated to sleep in different bedrooms, set apart by a small sitting area. Ilya remained in Moscow, but Sasha and he stayed in close contact throughout the trip. Other than Ethan Reichenbach figuring out that the way he looked at Sergey had more to do with his timid, tiny heart and less to do with hawkish personal security protections, the trip had gone smoothly.

And then, Evgeni Konnikov's body was dumped in Moscow's Red Square.

When he saw the breaking news alert on his phone, waiting outside the Situation Room in the bowels of the White House, he'd been transported again, back to the cold concrete floor of the locker room at Andreapol. To the sneers and hatred of his squadmates and his commander hovering above him, fist clenched and spitting in his face. "Disgusting," he'd growled. And then the beating, the kicks and the hits and the broken bones, over and over again. Until blood was smeared on the ground beneath him, flowing from his nose and his mouth and his torn skin.

Why hadn't they killed him? They'd done all but by dumping him on the side of the highway in the snow, but why hadn't they finished the job by their own hands? Was he supposed to slowly suffer and see which would kill him first? The ruptured spleen and internal bleeding, or freezing in the snow?

Miraculously, he'd survived.

But another man like him had not.

Sergey appeared sometime later, his face ashen and haggard. "I'm so sorry," he'd muttered, speaking in low Russian before pulling him away from the White House staff and telling him everything. About the murderer, his connection to Madigan, and the rogue general's vendetta against President Spiers.

It seemed the hatred was shifting, attaching itself on to President Puchkov and to the things he believed in. Supported. Cared deeply about.

Guilt by association was something Sasha was well familiar with.

He shoved his heart away in the lead up to Evgeni Konnikov's state funeral. He couldn't think about it. Couldn't dwell on the horrific murder, or on Sergey's state honors for Evgeni Konnikov. Both thoughts took him to two extremes, to places in his mind and his soul that he couldn't go. He shoved his heart down, as deep as it could go.

Until Sergey spoke to the nation about how great a man and a Russian Evgeni Konnikov was. Never, ever before had he heard someone publicly call someone like him—a gay man—a great man. A great Russian. Sergey had said it once to him, in between his wrecked sobs as he fell apart, but he'd dismissed it as mindless comforts. Sergey didn't actually believe that, did he?

For Evgeni Konnikov, he did.

Perhaps, Sergey could believe the same for him?

No. This was wrong. He knew it was wrong, and he'd warned himself against it. *No.* He wouldn't let Sergey's compassion, his kindness, his unconditional acceptance, unmake his heart and soul. Unmake his entire world. He'd sworn to himself that he'd guard against this. The warmth building in his chest, the way a part of him, a fractional, tiny part of him, desired Sergey, were dangerous signs, light towers warning of high terrain and deadly mountains ahead.

He tried to shove it all away. The burning hope, the screaming, wailing, desperate desire for Sergey to see him as a *man*, as someone he could be proud of… even, perhaps, maybe, *want*. Buried it, fast and furious, under the rubble of his own broken heart. *There is no future to this. There is no future to this desire. It is hopeless. Utterly, completely hopeless.*

But his heart still thundered whenever he looked at Sergey, opening like a blooming flower with a silent yearning that scratched at his raw insides.

When the bombs went off in Moscow after the funeral, during the procession, he'd grabbed Sergey and thrown himself on top of him, taking on the role of one of Sergey's security agents. He'd thought, for a moment, that bullets were flying, heading their way, and he'd prepared for their heavy bite and hot sting into his back. It wasn't his job to take a bullet for Sergey, but he would. He'd do it faster, better than the security agents, because none of them cared for Sergey the way he did.

Instead, Sergey had grabbed him in return, holding tight as they sped through the streets and into the Kremlin, and even hours later, when they were all trying to make sense of what had happened. Sergey still stood too close. Hovered. Reached for him, for his arm or his knee, and touched him, as if he was reassuring himself that Sasha was still there at his side.

Of course he was there. He would never leave Sergey's side. Not when he'd fallen so entirely in love with the man. He would rather cut out his heart.

Enemy Of My Enemy

BEGINNINGS
ADAM & FAISAL MEET

Why hadn't he gone the traditional route?

Everyone said, back at Officer Candidate School, that he shouldn't talk to those creeps from the Defense Intelligence Agency. They talked a good game, but all they did was sell empty promises and broken careers. Anyone who knew what they were doing would tell the DIA recruiters to fuck off.

Well. First, it had been a simple conversation over coffee. Then lunch off base. Dinner in DC. Meeting the head of the Clandestine Program. He was smart enough to know when he was being wooed.

Going from being smoked at OCS, having to do push-ups until his arms gave out, run until he puked, stay up for three days straight on a training exercise, to being told how valuable, intelligent, and unique he was by the DIA recruiter, was an almost intoxicating pull. Like a seduction, he followed the recruiters exactly where they wanted him to go.

You speak Arabic? Multiple dialects? We have so much need for you. You'll be perfect. Rocket through our agency. Make a real difference in the world.

Eighteen months later, he was sweating his balls off in divided Iraq, tired of smelling shit and chicken guts in the sewers, tired all the Goddamn time, and frustrated up to his eyeballs. All his days were spent chasing leads, chasing sources, chasing people who would rather see him fail than share the slightest bit of helpful intelligence. Iraq was a nation divided on fault lines. He could cross a street and go from a war zone to a suburb. Gangs of Caliphate members roamed, striking like fundamentalist ninjas. The people he needed to get intelligence from distrusted him on sight. One of the oppressors, a spy for pick-your-own-bogeyman, someone too dangerous to associate with for fear of reprisal by the Other.

The best information he got was from kids. The younger the better, but too young, and they thought it was a game.

His patience was not long enough to play 'guess the intel' with a five-year-old standing ankle-deep in shit and trash on the side of her mud-road.

What did you see? What men came by? Did they dress like this? Did you hear them talking about anything? Did the mention places? Buildings? Markets? Have you seen any weapons? How many?

A month ago, a seven-year-old contact of his bragged about hearing their neighbors talking about the market off Falestin Street. Two days later, security forces stopped a car bomber heading for the center of the market.

He got an *'atta boy* back slap via text and a reminder that his expense justification report was due.

Two thousand dollars on sweets and candy, payment to his sources. A comic book or five. Crayons. Tools of liberation, surely.

He was a regular James Bond.

Fuck it all. He needed a break. His career was spiralling, sinking into the desert like a lost city, about to be covered by endless piles of sand. Great wins did not come from the mouths of children. He wouldn't be stopping the next big terrorist with lollipops. Wouldn't be changing the world. He wanted to save lives, make a real difference. Change the course of everything. Put an end to the endless circle of death and slaughter.

Lofty goals. The goals of a young man.

Two years in, and he was already turning dejected. A dead-end life and a dead-end career would do that, though.

Adam leaned his head back on the silk sofa and exhaled. Music wailed around him, drums and tambourines and a pounding rhythm that offset the scratchy minor chords the Arabs loved so much. At first, the music had been like nails scratching down his bones, or a rake scraping over concrete. Now, he thought in the minor key, and American rap seemed too slow.

Vibrant silk and cotton twirled in the breeze, strung between poles in loops and swirls. Torches as tall as a man leaned out of brass holders staked in the ground. Lanterns sat at angles on mounds of sand, their candles flickering within punched bronze cylinders and orbs of colored glass. Bonfires burned along the mile, the riverfront promenade where Ramadan *Iftar* celebrations abounded, lasting through the night.

Long tables stretched along the riverfront, low on the sand and scrub grass. Everyone sat on cushions with piles and piles of food stacked on the table beside pitchers of juice in every color of the rainbow. Men and women had already broken their fast, taking bites of dates and sipping yogurt as they cheered and clapped. The more devout rose to pray after their first three dates.

Food and drinks flowed. Roasted chicken on red rice with a shaved boiled egg, slivered almonds, and raisins. Lamb stew and *kubbat halab*, rice dough stuffed with goat and chicken. Diamond flatbreads, *sammoun*, and sweet juice to drink: tamarind sherbert, apricot, mango, grape, and sweetened yogurt. *Baklava* and *zlabya*, desserts that made the molars ache.

As everyone broke their fast and celebrated, the din and rise of conversation flowed over the party. People came and went, rising from the tables to wander along the riverfront, or sit on the sofas and chaises spread outside. Ramadan was the biggest party of the Islamic year. Everyone wanted to be together, connected with joy, celebrating with fires lit in their hearts. You could feel it, the pulse in the air, the thrum of happiness, of gratitude, and, for the moment, peace. Simple pleasures—connection, family, friends, safety—and delight. Gratitude. Calls of praise to Allah rose, louder and more heartfelt as the celebrations wore on. Smiles grew. Laughter bloomed. Dancing began. Men and men and women and women dancing, simple movements that spun each other in circles at arm's length.

Adam had never felt more alone.

Ramadan was a prickly time to work intelligence. Some fighters called a cease-fire for the holy month. Others, struck like lightning by the intensity of their beliefs, lashed out with vicious force, devastating celebrations like this one.

Why was he even there? He wasn't a Muslim. There was no intel that something was going to happen, that night or on the riverfront. There was absolutely zero reason for him to have joined in this celebration, plopping onto a couch someone dragged to the park and watching everyone else experience their joy.

Children ran by him, waving candles and singing loudly, off-key. An Arabic rhythm, a Ramadan version of trick or treating. One little boy, maybe six, waved to him with sticky fingers.

He tried to smile. Waved a few fingers back. That kid could be a spy for him in another neighborhood. In a different part of the city, or the country. If he were wearing torn clothes and mismatched shoes, instead of pleated pants and a pressed sweater.

His thoughts turned on him, growing barbs and biting his soul.

He needed to leave. Now.

Taking a breath, Adam pulled himself up, moving like a doll with broken limbs. He was tired, so fucking tired. Tired of it all. He just—

A man, standing by the river, caught his gaze.

A circle of lanterns rested by his feet, tilted panes of red, yellow, and green glass throwing a rainbow glow over his burnished skin. Dark hair, cut neat. A slim figure, but tall. Designer jeans, the kind that came from Dubai or Damman or Bahrain. A long-sleeve shirt, light and fitted to his frame. Honey eyes that stared right back at Adam. A gentle smile curved the man's lips, and a flicker from one of the candles below spread blue light over his cheek. The angle of his jaw could cut diamonds. The sun could set beneath the arch of his cheek.

Adam's breath faltered. His jaw dropped, just a bit, as he stared.

A couple twirled between them, a man holding a woman's hands gently as he spun her toward the river. A tambourine rattled as the drums beat on. Adam blinked. He clamped his mouth shut.

The man was gone.

Good. He couldn't do that here. Couldn't do any of it. Couldn't even look at men. Couldn't think about what he wanted, what he yearned for. Not just because of where he was; strictly speaking, it wasn't illegal in the Marines any longer, but openly parading your personal life—any personal life—was suicide. The Marines issued your life. It did not come with any desire for another person, male or female. Putting anything else before the Corps was the first death knell.

But, lusting after an Arab, inside Iraq? He'd only be more stupid if he tried to pick up a Saudi. Religious police were unforgiving, and especially intolerant of his tastes.

Time to go. His thoughts were jumbled, mixed-up as a curl of desire bloomed in his belly. Fuck, he hadn't been turned on in months. Had it almost been a year, even? Porn had lost its charm long ago. His hands weren't interested, and he wasn't interested in his hands, either. Had it gotten so bad that one smile, one striking man by candlelight, was all it took?

He scrubbed his hands over his face. This had been a bad idea, the whole thing, and now he was paying for it. He stood—

"Hello."

He froze.

Behind him, a gentle, warm voice chuckled and spoke again. "I hope I'm not interrupting. I saw you just now, and I wanted to come over here and say hello."

Adam turned slowly, like a screw fighting its last spin. The man, the man in the candlelight, stood behind him. Torchlight and lamps from the tables, from the river walk, from the streetlights, lit him perfectly. God, he was even more breathtaking than before.

His brain spun on opposite tracks. One side, cataloging his accent, his diction. The man spoke carefully with a slight British accent. UK-educated, which meant money. His jeans weren't cheap. His coloring wasn't quite Iraqi. Somewhere farther south. Gulf countries. And, he had the confidence to seek Adam out, approach him. Why?

The other side of Adam's brain dribbled out his ears. His jaw fell open again. Cardamom and coriander filled his nose, followed by cinnamon and orange, a hint of peach. Honey. He breathed in, trying to drag the scent closer. His heart hammered in time with the drums, a fast, crazed beat that never stopped.

"Hi," he finally grunted. "Um—"

"Faisal." Smiling again, Faisal held out his hand.

"Adam." Shit. Greeting anyone in the Arab world was a trigonometry problem. Would this be a handshake, like America? His whiteness put others off, often excluded him from the cultural greetings that surrounded him. Would Faisal pull him close for a kiss on the cheek? How many kisses? They'd just met, surely it was going to be a hand hold.

Adam took Faisal's hand, squeezing and starting to shake. Faisal drew him close with a smile. He pressed their cheeks together and kissed the air beside Adam's ear twice, pulled back, and did the same to his other cheek.

Two kisses. All right. Basic Arab greetings 101. Faisal was being polite.

Faisal pulled him back, pressing a third kiss to his cheek. This time, he turned in, ghosting his lips over Adam's sideburn, his cheekbone. "*Marhaban*," he breathed.

That was definitely not a normal hello. Adam's breath quickened, and he tried to catch Faisal's gaze as Faisal pulled back. Why—What— He swallowed hard.

Faisal smiled. "May I join you?"

Thoughts of leaving vanished. He sat back down. "Sure."

What the hell was he doing? *Run! Get away! You have no idea who he is or what he wants. It could be a trap!*

Faisal leaned back, reclining on the couch with effortless ease and style. Adam rubbed his palms together. Sweat made them sticky.

"You don't know anyone here, do you?" Faisal kept smiling at him, a soft curve of his lips that teased Adam's blood.

He flushed and grinned, spreading his hands. "You caught me."

Faisal captured one of his hands before he brought it back to his lap. He laced their fingers together and rested their joined hands between them on the couch. "Now you know me."

Oh, shit, he shouldn't be rocketing off from a simple touch. Faisal was only doing what was normal. Holding hands, a sign of friendship in the Middle East, especially among men. Nothing more. *Don't stroke the back of his hand with your thumb. Don't!*

He felt his palm slick with cold sweat. Faisal would feel that. God, what an idiot he was. "*Shukraan.*"

"What are you doing in Iraq?" Faisal seemed content to sit back and hold his hand, chat the night away. And why not? It was Ramadan, the time of connection.

"I'm a reporter." His lie tumbled from his lips, his cover story. "Following the country's continued civil war, the fight against the Caliphate." He shrugged. "Same stuff, different decade."

Faisal nodded. "Wouldn't it be nice if this could be every night here?" He gestured to the celebrations. The people, the happiness, the peace.

"It would." Adam bit his lip. "*In shaa Allah*, it will someday."

Faisal's eyes brightened. "You are Muslim?"

"No."

"Respectful, then." Faisal's smile turned, from polite to something else. Something that slithered down Adam's belly and sent jolts through his legs. "Something unusual in western men."

"You spend a lot of time with western men?" Jesus, someone should ban him from talking. He clamped his lips shut and looked away. "Sorry, that was rude."

"I do not," Faisal said, ignoring his apology. "Most want nothing to do with me. And thus, I want nothing to do with them."

"Their loss."

Faisal's eyes locked onto his. Something simmered in the amber depths, something he didn't want to stare too hard at.

Slowly, Faisal's thumb stroked over the back of his hand. "Has anyone shown you around the city? The best place to have a coffee? Eat *halawat sha'riyya*? Watch the sunrise?"

He couldn't speak. He shook his head.

"Would you like to watch the sunrise with me?" Faisal's head tilted, a coy little grin on his lips.

"Would we stay here?" His voice had dropped, low and gravelly. He squeezed Faisal's hand. Was this for real? Was Faisal actually picking him up? Or was he reading too much into Arab friendliness and congeniality? Was he only seeing what he wanted to see?

Or, worse. Was this a trap? Iraq wasn't Saudi, but there were still gangs of religious police. Caliphate infiltrators that loved to 'expose' hedonism and infidel corruption as proof that they were essential, a needed force for their firebrand, medieval Islam.

The smart thing to do would be to walk away. Politely thank him for the conversation and beg off, back to his apartment and go to sleep. He'd jerk off for sure to this tonight, and probably for the next month or four, remembering Faisal's smile, his eyes, the warmth of his skin.

"We could stay, if you want." Faisal's thumb brushed his hand again. "I would prefer to show you something other than this river, though. But only if you would like."

Jesus. He flushed all over, heat racing through him from head to toe. No mistaking what it was now. A blatant invitation. But was it honest? Was it true? Was he about to be the star of his very own YouTube video and end up a sad, tragic headline, the American who couldn't control his lust? Couldn't keep it in his pants?

He wanted it to be true. God, he did. What would Faisal be like? Would he smile that way throughout the night? Keep it light and fun, playful even? He seemed the type. But, there were depths there, in his eyes, in the way he held Adam's hand. Pursued Adam. How long had it been since someone had wanted him, picked him out of a crowd and wanted to fuck him? Take him home?

He stared into Faisal's eyes. His confusion, his lust, his uncertainty had to be plain as day. What he wanted, he shouldn't, couldn't have.

"Come with me, Adam," Faisal breathed. His eyes burned, searing Adam's skin as they raked over his body, from his feet to the tips of his hair and back to his lips, his eyes. "Keep me company all night long. Tell me stories about you. I will show you the sunrise in the morning."

How the hell was he going to walk out of here with a half-hard cock? *Don't be an idiot, Adam! This could ruin the rest of your life!*

He squirmed. Licked his lips. Looked away.

And then looked back, deep into Faisal's eyes. He squeezed his hand. "Okay."

CHIPPING AT WALLS
SASHA FINDS SERGEY AFTER THE LANGLEY BLAST

Sasha trudged up the last slope, heading for their bunker at the top of the ridge. Loose black dirt and lingering remnants of trampled, muddy snow squelched beneath his boots. Finally, winter was dissipating in the mountains. It was only just freezing most days.

Living in the forest, deep in the Caucasus on the run from General Moroshkin, was not glamorous. It reminded Sasha of being back in training exercises from his Air Force days, when they were dropped in the Russian North with absolutely nothing and told to get back to base. Driving snow, ice storms, pounding rain. Bears and wolves. Sucking mud that was practically frozen coating his boots. The rub of hunger in his belly, an ache that wanted to be filled. And the stench. God, the stench.

As bad as those days were, this was worse. Those exercises had had an end. He could look forward to sleeping in his bed again, a warm shower, and a hot meal, if he only endured.

What would be waiting for them all after this? Would there even be an 'after'? How did a country put itself back together after two sides of the population tried their hardest to kill each other? History didn't prophesy well. In the Caucasus, in the very mountains and the forest they were sheltering in, the endless, bloody Chechen wars had raged. There was no happy ending to those wars, no settlement over a handshake and a brandy while people got on with their lives and learned to live in harmony.

When Sergey was back in Moscow, back in the Kremlin—he refused to think that anything else was possible other than Sergey's return to power—how would he deal with Moroshkin? With the nearly half of the military that had joined his coup? Or the others who had simply melted away, vanishing from their oaths and posts into nothing?

The questions were too big for Sasha. He wasn't a politician. He wasn't in charge of a country, nor was he the man upon whose shoulders lay decisions that could shape the world, their nation, and millions and millions of lives. He could only do what he could do: fight. Fight, every single day, for Sergey. Give everything he had to Sergey.

Breathing hard, Sasha frowned as he reached the flat, empty patch of dirt they used as a parking area outside the bunker. It was empty.

"He went out."

Leaning against the cold concrete wall of the bunker, Anton Aliyev casually smoked a cigarette, his cheeks hollowing as he sucked it down, the embers burning bright in the dim shadows.

"Where?"

Anton jerked his head to the side. "Down the back track. He did not say much when he left." Smoke slipped from his lips with every word.

Sasha headed for the rear of the bunker.

He found the jeep, the one he and Sergey shared, halfway down the rear track, just as Anton had said. It was parked in the middle of the dirt path, thick branches scraping the sides and roof. The track was just wide enough to drive through, if the scrapes and scratches of the branches on the windows and the metal frame didn't shred your eardrums.

Why had Sergey just stopped? Was there something in the road? A fallen log, or a boulder dislodged from above, rolling into the track? Why was he just sitting there?

Picking his way through the branches, Sasha tugged open the passenger door and climbed inside.

And froze.

Sergey sat in the driver's seat, hands clenched so hard around the steering wheel his knuckles were white and the wheel was shaking. His jaw was tight, his muscles straining, and he sat ramrod straight, like he was struggling to hold himself that way.

Half hovering over the passenger seat, Sasha's jaw dropped. Guilt swept through him, flooding his body with heat. Of course. What had he been thinking? The news of Jack's condition after the explosion at CIA headquarters had come through that morning.

Jack was gone. Sergey's friend was gone.

"Sorry," Sasha grunted. He backed away, all hands and feet and uncoordinated, stepping on the doorframe instead of opening it, before his fingers even fumbled with the latch.

"Stay?"

Freezing again, Sasha glanced at Sergey. Sergey had turned his way, staring at him with eyes that glimmered, red-rimmed and lost. Desperation leaked from his gaze, and something else. Anguish.

Sasha's heart lurched. He ached to go to Sergey, offer himself up to ease the hurt. Open his arms and welcome Sergey into his hold. Kiss away the tears that threatened to fall, rub his hands down his back when he cried, stroke his shaking muscles. Soothe his pain, his grief. Remind him that he was not alone, no, he was never alone.

He sat. Shut the door. Exhaled. "I am sorry," he breathed. "Jack…"

What could he say? He hadn't known Jack like Sergey had. The connection Sergey and Jack had was strong enough to shake the world.

They'd leaned into each other and built an alliance, a friendship, even. Made jokes in the press about the scandal of their closeness. Sergey had even risked the disgust of his nation to dance with Jack at his state dinner. Friendships like that didn't happen between world leaders, not anymore.

A sniffle, and then a shaky breath. Sergey gripped the steering wheel again, kneading the worn leather, and groaned. He sniffed again, exhaled hard. Tried to level out his breathing. Every breath quivered.

"Sergey…" Sasha laid his hand on Sergey's trembling shoulder. What could he say? What could he do? His tongue sat heavy in his mouth, weighted down with uselessness.

And then Sergey cracked, fracturing down the center of his being. Curling forward, the first sob came, physically wrenched from his chest. And then another, an anguished moan. Tears followed, flowing down his cheeks as he shook, as he screamed through clenched teeth and shook the steering wheel like it was the cause of his agony.

Utter helplessness speared Sasha. Sergey's pain was devastating, the grief of losing his friend and his country seeming to come out in one gut-tearing sob. It was awful, seeing a man come apart, consumed by soul-wracking pain.

Another night came back to Sasha, from months ago. Another night of grief and mourning, and a soul-shattering emptiness that had made him want to claw his own bones out. Escape his very skeleton. Be anyone, anywhere, other than who he was. Not have to face what had become of his life.

Sergey had held him through it. They were strangers then; he only knew of Sergey through the headlines and video clips he saw. Sergey knew of him only through his military record and Dr. Voronov's retelling of his incident. But Sergey had cared for him, man to man, giving comfort freely when he saw Sasha's aching emptiness.

His hand snaked up, rising from Sergey's shoulder to grip the back of his neck. Tugging, he turned Sergey toward him, gently pulling and prodding until Sergey faced him on the bench seat.

Tears cascaded down Sergey's cheeks, falling from his jaw like tiny diamonds. They splattered the leather between them, little splashes that Sasha swore he heard.

Sergey wouldn't look at him. He kept his gaze downcast, his eyes closed.

Sasha wrapped both hands behind Sergey's neck. "Look at me," he whispered.

Sergey sniffed. He didn't look up.

"Sergey. Look at me."

Slowly, Sergey's eyes opened, and from beneath his lashes, his eyes met Sasha's.

Pain. So much terrible pain. Despair that stole Sasha's breath away. Loneliness. Fear. Doubt.

He moved his hands, cupping Sergey's wet cheeks, and held his face in a gentle hold. As if he was going to kiss Sergey. "I am here with you," he breathed. "Always." *You're not alone. You're never alone.*

Another sob wrenched free from Sergey. He pitched forward, burying his face in Sasha's chest. His tears fell into the scratchy wool of Sasha's sweater, enough to soak through and dampen Sasha's skin.

Tentatively, he wrapped his arms around Sergey, around his bony shoulders and his thin back. A part of him rejoiced—he was holding Sergey, cradling him close. Could feel the warmth of his skin, his breath. It was almost like in his dreams.

Except not, because Sergey was sobbing, heartbroken and lost, and devastation was the only thing they had to look forward to.

He shouldn't be happy about having Sergey in his arms, not when the price was this many tears. This kind of hurt.

Sergey's blond hair was mussed and dirty—they were all dirty—but Sasha laid his cheek on top of Sergey's head. His hands stroked over Sergey's trembling back, mapping out his thin muscles. Counted the bones of his ribs, the knobs of his spine. Slowly, Sergey's sobs subsided, quieting, until he was just sniffling against Sasha's collarbone, one hand fisted in the loose fabric of Sasha's jacket.

"M'sorry," Sergey mumbled. His hot breath ghosted over Sasha's skin.

Goose bumps erupted down Sasha's arms, his legs, behind his knees. He fought not to shiver. Instead, he squeezed Sergey, wrapped his arms tighter around him. Drew him closer. "No sorrys. None of that. You cared for me once. I will do the same for you."

Exhaling, Sergey lifted and dropped his fist against Sasha's chest, once.

A moment later, Sergey tried to pull away. "We should—"

Sasha held tight, not letting him go. His arms encircled Sergey, keeping him pressed against his chest. "Not yet. Sergey, not yet." He held his breath and closed his eyes. Had he just given himself away? Was he taking advantage? Where did him wanting to comfort Sergey end and his shameful desire begin?

He just didn't want to let go yet. Not when Sergey's back still trembled and his eyes were still drenched and hollow. Looking down, he brushed one thumb over Sergey's cheek, wiping away a tear that had slipped free from Sergey's soaked eyelashes.

Their gazes met.

He fought for something to say, his lips fumbling through half-broken words as he tried to explain away what he knew was in his eyes. *Never, ever,* he hissed in his mind. *You swore! Nothing can ever happen. Never, ever!*

Sergey's eyes closed. His forehead rested against Sasha's chin and his body went boneless as he slumped into Sasha's hold. "Maybe this is just a dream," Sergey murmured. "Some terrible nightmare. Maybe I can wake up from this."

Sasha's terrible delight, and Sergey's dark pain, all in one moment. A moment Sergey wished he could be rid of, wake from. Sasha's lips twisted as he fought against himself, trying to hold back his own sudden grief. "Maybe," he grunted. "You can try. Sleep, Sergey. Try to wake from this." He kept his arms around Sergey, hoping his message was clear. Sergey could sleep in his arms, in his hold.

Sergey didn't move. Didn't say a word.

Finally, Sergey's breathing leveled out. His jaw went slack and his head turned into a heavy, limp weight on Sasha's shoulder. Since the coup, Sasha hadn't seen him sleep more than a few hours at a time. Dark circles had grown beneath his eyes, paunchy bags that started growing their own bags.

This was his chance. Sergey was asleep in his arms, resting finally in his care. He could press his lips to Sergey's skin, drop a kiss to his hair. Whisper everything he wanted to confess into Sergey's palm before placing a kiss in the center. He could say, finally, what had grown in his heart. Paint his love all over Sergey's skin with confessions and declarations, promises he'd swear to the stars.

No. He could not.

Leaning back, Sasha tried to get comfortable. The doorframe dug into his back, the handle gouged his spine, and the glass was cold enough to chill his blood. He didn't move though. Didn't readjust. Didn't do anything that could wake Sergey.

As the hours crept on, Sasha stayed awake, stroking Sergey's back as he held him close, sheltering him in his sleep. This was his terrible dream now: being, for a moment, the man who could love Sergey and could care for him. Be someone who could love him when his heart was broken.

When Sergey woke, his dream would end.

But, this moment, the closeness they shared. The comfort given and received. The warmth of skin on skin, and his promise to Sergey: *I am here with you. For you.*

The memory of that, at least, would remain.

HOW TO (NOT) SAY GOODBYE
ADAM DISCOVERS FAISAL'S SECRET

Scorched sand spread in every direction, as far as Adam could see from the plane's cramped window. Riyadh glittered in the distance, south of King Khalid Airport, shimmering in heat waves rising from Saudi Arabia's central plateau, the Najd. Farther south, he could pick out the rolling sands of the Rub' al-Khali, the Empty Quarter. Endless waves of empty, burning sand, and the classic images of Saudi Arabia. Nothing could survive in that endless desert.

His blood quickened, thrumming through his veins. He gripped the curved seat handles, his sweat-slick fingers slipping on the plastic as the flight attendant called for all seatbacks to be put forward and seatback trays to be returned to their upright positions.

This was it. His first visit to Saudi Arabia… for him. *Exclusively* for him. For Faisal.

Eight months. It had been eight months since he'd first met Faisal, had first followed him back to his Baghdad flat and writhed beneath his hands, his lips, his touch, for hours. Never, not in a million years, not in his wildest, most crazed thoughts, had he ever thought he'd find a lover in Baghdad. Much less a *Saudi* lover.

Faisal's nationality wasn't the most scandalous aspect of their… relationship? Was it a relationship? What were eight months of intense, almost constant lovemaking called? Sneaking away every chance they got? Making love in Baghdad and Kuwait City, where Faisal had another flat. Whispering Arabic to each other all night long by the light of a dozen flickering candles.

Sharing intelligence. Adam, quietly passing along the names of his targets, individuals he was tracking. Faisal, sliding him information the Kingdom had on America's targets and pointing him in new directions, toward the quieter, insidious threats. The hand that wagged the dog.

Realizing Faisal was, like him, an intelligence officer. *Conspiracy*, his mind whispered. *Espionage. Revealing secrets.*

But what they'd shared had been beneficial for both of them and their governments so far. At least, that's how he rationalized it. Adam had been applauded for his intelligence efforts, his wins in identifying deep Caliphate assets that had eluded the US for so long. Faisal's efforts were focused half on the Caliphate and half on Iran, and Adam slipped him a signals intercept on Iran that Faisal had hand-carried back to Riyadh.

What they were doing was wrong on so many, many levels. He was violating the Espionage Act. He was sleeping with a foreign national and not disclosing it. He was engaging in homosexual activity with a Muslim in a Muslim country. In *multiple* Muslim countries. He was violating laws and agency regulations right and left.

And now, flying to Riyadh to meet with Faisal.

Faisal had texted the day before, saying that his people in Riyadh were beyond pleased with the signals intercept and that he had some time to spend in the Kingdom before flying back to Kuwait and then Baghdad.

Would Adam like to come down? They could steal a day away. No one would ever know.

He paid cash for his ticket, flying out of Baghdad before dawn.

Finally, the jet's tires squealed and skipped down the runway at King Khalid Airport and then taxied to the gate. *Alhamdulliah as salaama* echoed around the cabin, the passengers thanking God for the safe flight, as custom. The Saudi morning sun burned down on the terminal, scattering gleaming silver light in every direction. Bodies shuffled out of the plane, men in long white thobes and ghutras, a few women in hijabs, and a scattered businessman or three. He caught eyes sliding sidelong to him. Not in a suit, and not in a thobe. What was he doing in the Kingdom, the capital of conservatism in the world?

Inside, the airport glittered, white and cream marble seeming to stretch forever. Arches interlaced overhead, like the cornices of the Great Mosque of Cordoba in Spain. Ferns crowded around fountains and indoor lagoons, and ivy crawled up the marble in carefully orchestrated patterns. Whisper-soft footfalls and hushed conversation made the airport seem larger than it was, colossal as opposed to cavernous. He hurried as fast as he could without standing out, slipping through slow-moving crowds of Saudi men holding hands and groups sharing coffee and tea.

And then, finally, he was outside. Heat slapped him in the face as he stepped from the ice-cold air conditioning of the airport to the sun-scorched heat of Riyadh. Cars and taxis cluttered the curb, dark-skinned Bengalis and Pakistanis loading the luggage of aloof Saudis into the back of their cabs.

He swallowed. Where was Faisal? He fumbled for his cell in his pocket. It buzzed as he pulled it out.

To your left.

Frowning, he turned.

A cherry-red Lamborghini convertible waited at the curb, all alone, set apart from the bustle of the main terminal. A man rose in the front seat, holding onto the windscreen as he stood in the foot well. He wore a cream linen suit, setting off his golden skin, and a deep blue button-down, the buttons around his neck open and showing off the hollow of his throat. He smiled at Adam and titled his head. Even though he wore mirrored sunglasses, Adam could imagine the sparks burning in his amber eyes.

He headed for the Lamborghini with a grin, as if pulled by a magnet. Torn, his gaze wandered over the car's slick lines, the compact power of the sports car, and then flicked up to his lover, still standing in the driver's foot well. Faisal held just as much unrestrained power as the Lamborghini, just as much thrust and passion. His sleek muscles, his lithe body, always made Adam think of a jaguar, always on the prowl, always ready to strike.

"*Ahlan wa sahlan,*" Faisal called, grinning.

"*Marhaban.*" Adam whistled as he stood by the Lamborghini's passenger door. To anyone watching, he might be gazing at the sports car.

But his eyes were fixed on Faisal's, and, slowly, he dragged his gaze down Faisal's body, from his taut shoulders encased in cream linen to his narrow waist, and then farther down.

"Hurry up and get in," Faisal breathed. "We have a long drive."

"In this?" He hopped over the passenger door and dropped into the bucket seat, throwing his small bag behind him. "How could any drive last long in this car?"

"I am taking you to the Gulf."

"The Gulf?" Three hours away, at least. But, the beaches were phenomenal, and, across the bridge in Bahrain, the nightlife was some of the best in the world. He wasn't here for the nightlife, though, and he wasn't here for the beaches. What he wanted was sitting right beside him.

"I have a place there. We won't be disturbed." Faisal threw him a sly smile and stepped on the accelerator. They jumped smoothly into the traffic lane winding away from the terminal and out of the airport.

"You have lots of places."

Faisal said nothing. He shifted into second. Wind flicked through his dark hair, ruffling the cropped strands.

When they hit the highway, the 80M, the open, empty stretch of sunbaked asphalt leading from Riyadh to the Gulf coast, Adam leaned over in his seat, ducking down out of sight and lying across the central dash. He palmed Faisal's crotch as he reached for his fly.

"*Wallah*, Adam..." Faisal stepped down hard on the accelerator as Adam slowly undid his zipper.

"I'll bet you can get us there in half the time." He winked up at Faisal as he buried his head in his crotch.

"*Maa shaa Allah…*" Faisal groaned. The Lamborghini zoomed forward, the speedometer needle rising and rising as the engine roared, covering Faisal's soft moans and gasps.

Neither man noticed the blacked-out SUV trailing behind them, hiding in the shimmering heatwaves a mile behind.

Christ, he loved this. Maybe he was compromised, and maybe he was completely guilty of sharing intelligence secrets. But conspiracy tasted so sweet, so delicious. Like all victims trapped in honeypot plots throughout the decades, he supposed, he believed this was special. He believed this was different.

Faisal had worshipped his body, stripping him slowly, tasting every inch of his skin. Kisses pressed everywhere, to his shoulder blades, the curve of his spine. The backs of his knees, where Faisal's soft breath made his leg hair shiver and his body tremble. He was a strung-out bundle of nerves, lit on fire from within, every muscle quivering, every piece and part of him tingling with anticipation. Every time he reached for Faisal, Faisal batted his hands away, smiling coyly as he kept up his seduction, his quest to melt Adam's bones.

Finally, Faisal rolled him over and spread his legs, and then buried his face in Adam's ass. He'd groaned, long and loud, and he felt Faisal's grin against his ass cheeks.

What felt like hours later, after his spine had liquefied and every one of his muscles had gone taut, struck with lightning bursting from the center of his body, from the places Faisal's hands and fingers touched and stroked, Faisal finally kissed his way up his back and nuzzled his hair. "Ride me," he breathed. "Ride me, Adam."

He mumbled something, some string of consonants and vowels, and managed to push himself up on shaking arms, enough for Faisal to slide beneath him and between his legs. Their hands laced together, Faisal helping support him as he sat back, as he scooted until he found what he needed.

Adam held Faisal's gaze as he sank down, as the burning need Faisal had ignited inside him was satiated. Faisal stopped breathing as he moved, his mouth falling open, his eyes wide, staring at Adam like Adam was the most beautiful thing he'd ever seen. They rocked together, hands clasped.

In Faisal's Gulf bedroom, one wall was made up entirely of glass, overlooking the rolling sand, and in the distance, the azure waves of the Gulf waters, gently lapping at a private beach.

Whoever Faisal was, he was loaded. Most Saudis were, but not to this level. A brand-new Lamborghini and a house on the Gulf with a private beach? He must be a top-performing intelligence officer, richly rewarded by the Kingdom. Of course he was a great intel officer. Adam was in his bed, wasn't he? Adam was passing over American information to him, wasn't he?

Faisal rolled deep into him, sighing. *"When I sink my eye into yours,"* he breathed. *"I catch a glimpse of a deep dawn and I see ancient yesterday."*

"What?" Frowning, Adam squeezed Faisal's hands, pressed his thumb into his palms. He could barely think. All he knew, all he could feel, was Faisal pressing in at the root of his spine, like a beacon shining into his soul. Christ, he was *so* hard. Faisal unlocked some kind of new pleasure within him, some kind of brand-new feeling, sensations he didn't know he was capable of feeling.

"It's a poem," Faisal whispered. "By Gibran to his love." Groaning, Faisal's eyelids fluttered closed. "When I am with you, these poems make sense to me at last."

What could he possibly say to that? What they had together... he'd purposely not thought about it, hadn't tried to put it in a box or slap a label on it. If Adam sat down with himself in the middle of the night and squared himself with reality, then yes, he'd admit to the skeletons that rattled deep in his closet that he was far too close to Faisal. On every level. And... that he wanted to be closer. Much, *much* closer.

Close enough that Faisal whispering an Arabic love poem to him while they made love was almost enough to send him over the edge.

Faisal kept whispering, holding Adam's gaze. *"I see what I do not know, and I feel the universe flowing between my eye and yours."*

Shuddering, Adam tipped forward, capturing Faisal's lips in a deep kiss. Faisal's hands left his and traced up his sides, his ribs, over his shoulders, and buried in his hair. Came forward, and cupped his cheeks. "Adam, *wallah*," Faisal breathed around their kiss. "I—"

Splintering wood broke through Faisal's bedroom, the sound like a canon blast. Shards sliced Adam's back, splinters bouncing off his bare skin.

He reared back, still on Faisal's lap, twisting around as Faisal jolted upright, wrapping one hand around Adam's waist and holding him close as if he could protect him.

Six men poured into the room, hulking men in dark suits with muscles straining beneath their jackets and deep scowls etched on their brutish faces. And, behind them, an older Saudi man with a gray beard, wearing a white thobe and a white ghutra and with a gold-braided dark cloak over his clothes.

Adam recognized the man immediately: Abdul al-Saud, the Crown Prince of Saudi Arabia.

Faisal spoke first, panic lacing through his voice. "Uncle—"

Adam whipped around, staring down at Faisal. *Uncle?*

Fury crackled over Prince Abdul, twisting his expression, darkening his skin to a raging, wrathful deep maroon. "*Ajlabh,*" he growled. *Get him.*

The six men stormed the bed, reaching for Adam. He thrashed, kicking out, trying to punch. Faisal shouted, ordering them to stop, screaming for his uncle to order them to stop, but it was no use.

Hands grabbed Adam and ripped him from Faisal, tearing their bodies apart. Three men held his arms, another two his legs.

He felt the heft, the swing, and then he was flying, soaring across the bedroom. He heard Faisal's scream, his bellow.

And then, he slammed into the wall of glass, shattering the bay window as he soared through it. Cuts opened on his shoulder, along his back, on one cheek. Glass peppered him, struck every inch of his bare skin. He curled, trying to protect himself, rounding into a ball as heat and noise slammed into him, the desert sun and the roar of the shattered glass, and the slap of waves against the coastline.

Adam landed in a skid, in a puff of loose, burning sand, facedown. He didn't move.

Later, he sat in Faisal's sitting room, wrapped in a bloodstained sheet, and listened to Prince Abdul holler at Faisal.

Holler at his *nephew*. At *Prince Faisal al-Saud*, a member of the Saudi Royal Family.

How could he have been so stupid? How did he not know? Christ, one of the heads of the Saudi Royal Family had just caught him having *sex* with one of their own. The punishment for a non-Muslim engaging in homosexual sex with a Muslim in Saudi Arabia was death by stoning. And he'd slept with a member of the Royal Family? God, they'd probably fast-track his death sentence. He'd be dead before dusk.

The six bodyguards hovered menacingly nearby. They hadn't cared about his cuts. He bled all over the sheet one of them threw at his face after he was dragged off the sand and dropped back in Faisal's house.

Prince Abdul was already shouting, already shaking the walls. He could hear his bellows vibrate off his bones, even from the other room.

"*How could you let an American turn you,* ya *Faisal? How could you let an American breach Kingdom security?*"

Silence, from Faisal.

"*He is* working *you! Do you not understand? He is stealing secrets from you! He has* compromised *you! You have given up the Kingdom for this?*"

Christ, Faisal didn't deserve this. If anything, the reverse was true. He gave far more to Faisal than Faisal gave to him. Faisal wasn't turned. He wasn't working for the Americans. He wasn't working for Adam.

"*You have failed,* ya *Faisal. You have failed in your duties. How ashamed I am of you! The king, have you any idea what he will say? How he will handle this failure? You will be cut out! You will be forgotten! Alhamdulliah, you will be lucky to be banished!*"

Adam bowed his head. He'd known they both risked so much, pursuing this, this white-hot connection, this fire in their souls. But to risk his family, his Kingdom?

"*Speak,* ya *Faisal! Do you have nothing to say for yourself?*"

Faisal murmured something, but Adam couldn't parse it out.

"*You believed you were—? Rahimullah, you were seduced and made a* fool *of,* ya *Faisal. That is not love—*"

Fuck, he couldn't just listen to this. Couldn't just let Faisal be destroyed. Had Faisal truly loved him? What had he been about to say, cradling Adam's face as they kissed, after he breathed poetry between their bodies? Adam's heart lurched, twisting, wringing his own tender, fragile feelings of love out in droplets that bled down his ribs. He'd wanted, *God*, he'd wanted. He'd dreamed of one day, perhaps beyond all the intelligence games, all the subterfuge, to whisper the confession to Faisal's lips.

Adam waited for the bodyguards to look away before he leaped. He hauled the sheet around his waist, trying not to trip, and ran for the bedroom.

Six pairs of feet thundered after him, an elephant stampeded, but he made the door and burst within.

Faisal sat slumped on the edge of his bed—the bed they'd made love in, just an hour ago—wrapped in a satin robe, his head in both hands. Prince Abdul paced before him, wearing a tread in the marble floor with his sandals.

"I wasn't running Faisal," he blurted out, right as the six bodyguards burst in behind him. Three grabbed his arms and one grabbed his head in an armlock, almost tackling him to the ground.

Faisal jumped up, reaching for him, but Prince Abdul barked something guttural, and Faisal stilled.

Everyone froze. The bodyguards' hold loosened. They didn't let go, though.

"Faisal ran *me*." Adam swallowed, and his gaze flicked to Faisal's. Honeyed sorrow poured from Faisal's eyes, like a candle melting in the desert. Loss, aching loss. "Faisal was running *me*. *I've* turned. *I'm* compromised. *I* gave him intelligence. Information. Those Iranian intercepts? *I* gave them to him. I give him *everything*."

Prince Abdul's mouth dropped open. He peered at Adam, his eyes narrowing. Slowly, he turned back to Faisal. "*Bismillah*, is this true, *ya* Faisal?"

Adam held Faisal's gaze. *Say yes. Say yes.* He'd compromise himself even further with this, but Faisal, at least, would be protected in his family. It might save his life. His freedom.

Faisal's watery eyes closed. He lifted his chin. "Yes, Uncle. I turned him. He works for me."

Silence, save for the wind whispering through the broken window and glass shards tinkling across the marble floor.

Adam sat slumped in the back seat of Prince Abdul's SUV, behind two massive bodyguards. The SUV hummed up Route 95, screaming at one hundred and forty miles an hour toward the Kuwait border. Prince Abdul had ordered his banishment.

Better than his death.

He never got to say goodbye to Faisal.

What had their relationship been, in truth, though? Faisal had lied to him about his identity. Granted, if he'd known Faisal was royalty, he'd have run screaming in the opposite direction. In fact, if he'd woken up after that first night and realized he'd just slept with a prince of the Saudi Royal Family, he probably would have booked the next flight back to America. He'd have shoveled as much shit as needed to get his duty assignment changed. Anything to get him out of the Middle East.

And he'd never have shared what they had created between themselves. Experienced what Faisal gave him. What he made Adam feel.

Would never have fallen, even the littlest bit, in love.

Better to have loved and lost, as the old poets said. But that was crap. The emptiness, the blank way his emotions had smeared and gone flat, the hollowness in his heart. He'd rather have anything else than the aching desolation he felt deep within. This was the kind of feeling that called for tequila, and lots and lots of it. Enough to drown out the barren spaces, make sloshing waves in the hollows of his broken heart.

His cell buzzed, vibrating in his pocket.

Eyeing the bodyguards, Adam slid it out carefully. He'd been ignored so far, but he hadn't moved once, other than to throw his head back and try and fight the snarl that wanted to rise, the fight that his blood begged for.

He swiped the screen on.

When love beckons to you, follow him,
Though his ways are hard and steep.
And when his wings enfold you yield to him,
Though the sword hidden among his pinions may wound you.
And when he speaks to you believe in him,
Though his voice may shatter your dreams.
All these things shall love do unto you, that you may know the secrets of your heart.

Christ, Faisal. His eyes blurred, and his thumb hovered over the screen. How did he respond? What the hell did he say? They should just *walk away*, forget about each other, forget about *ever* knowing each other at all. He could bury this, salvage his career. Faisal could repair his reputation with his family.

Though, his uncle hadn't seemed shocked by Adam being a man. Just that he was an American. Did he know—

His phone buzzed again.

It was never about the intel for me.

Adam swallowed. *[me either]*

I just wanted to keep seeing you.

How could he feel worse than he had before, when Prince Abdul had torn them apart? Was this it? Was this goodbye? Faisal, in his way, telling him he loved him and telling him goodbye? Over text, no less? Christ, he was a shit show, in every single way.

He pulled up the Internet, plugging in the lines of Faisal's poem. The full poem's text loaded on his screen. His eyes blurred again as he read, the poem a treatise on the aching cost of love, the tribulations of falling headfirst into the uncontrolled eddies of the heart.

There was one line he could send back.

[Think not you can direct the course of love, for love, if it finds you worthy, directs your course.]

Adam... yaghfir Allah, I want to keep seeing you.

Adam's eyes slipped closed. He clenched his phone, hard enough that the case creaked, groaning in his hand. *Allah forgive me*, Faisal said.

He should say no. He should walk away. He shouldn't let this become larger than it was already, a bigger mess, a bigger problem. The wise choice, the right choice, was to say no. No, they were through. He'd made a mistake, and he had to clean it up, and that started with deleting Faisal's number. Ignoring his texts. Walking away, far away, and never looking back.

Instead, he typed back with shaking fingers *[me too]*.

About the Author

Tal Bauer is an award-winning and best-selling author of LGBT romantic thrillers, bringing together a career in law enforcement and international humanitarian aid to create dynamic characters, intriguing plots, and exotic locations. He is happily married and lives with his husband and their Basset Hound in Texas. Tal is a member of the Romance Writers of America and the Mystery Writers of America.

Other Books By Tal Bauer

Please visit your favorite ebook retailer to discover my other books

The Executive Office Series
Enemies of the State
Interlude
Enemy of My Enemy
Enemy Within

Hush

Connect With Tal Bauer

Visit my website: www.talbauerwrites.com
Email me: tal@talbauerwrites.com
Friend me on Facebook: https://www.facebook.com/talbauerauthor
Follow me on Twitter: @TalBauerWrites

Printed in Great Britain
by Amazon